THE JANUSITE TRILOGY

OTHER BOOKS BY ANNA DURAND

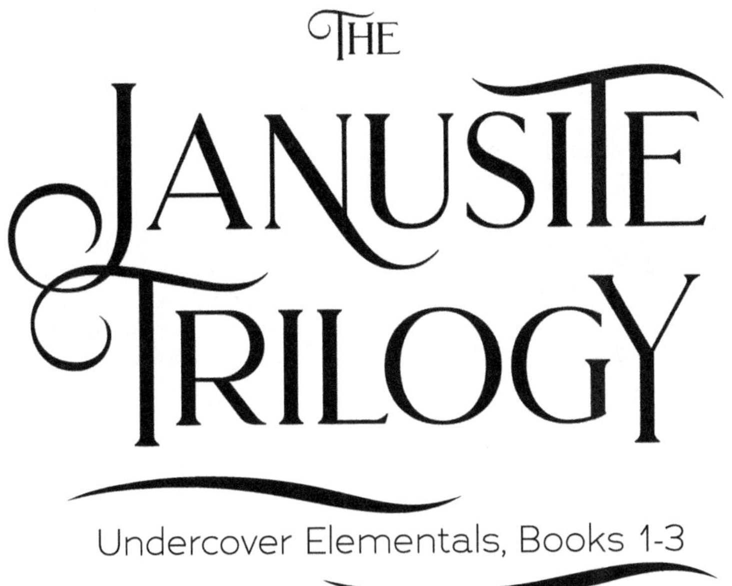

THE JANUSITE TRILOGY

Undercover Elementals, Books 1-3

ANNA DURAND

JACOBSVILLE BOOKS · MARIETTA, OHIO

THE JANUSITE TRILOGY

Copyright © 2019 by Lisa A. Shiel
All rights reserved.

The characters and events in this book are fictional. No portion of this book may be copied, reproduced, or transmitted in any form or by any means, electronic or otherwise, including recording, photocopying, or inclusion in any information storage and retrieval system, without the express written permission of the publisher and author, except for brief excerpts quoted in published reviews.

ISBN: 978-1-949406-08-5 (paperback)
ISBN: 978-1-949406-09-2 (ebook)
ISBN: 978-1-949406-10-8 (audiobook)
Library of Congress Control Number: 2017936798

Manufactured in the United States.

Jacobsville Books
www.JacobsvilleBooks.com

Publisher's Cataloging-in-Publication Data
provided by Five Rainbows Cataloging Services

Names: Durand, Anna.
Title: The mortal falls / Anna Durand.
Description: Marietta, OH : Jacobsville Books, 2019. | Series: Undercover elementals, bk. 1-3.
Identifiers: LCCN 2019940077 | ISBN 978-1-949406-08-5 (pbk.) | ISBN 978-1-949406-09-2 (ebook) | ISBN 978-1-949406-10-8
Subjects: LCSH: Magic--Fiction. | Spirits--Fiction. | Fairies--Fiction. | Shapeshifting--Fiction. | Time travel--Fiction. | Paranormal romance stories. | Romance fiction. | BISAC: FICTION / Romance / Paranormal / General. | FICTION / Romance / Paranormal / Shifters. | FICTION / Romance / Fantasy. | FICTION / Romance / Collections & Anthologies. | GSAFD: Love stories. | Occult fiction. | Fantasy fiction.
Classification: LCC PS3604.U724 J36 2019 (print) | LCC PS3604.U724 (ebook) | DDC 813/.6--dc23.

CONTENTS

CONTENTS

Book 3: *The Mortal Tempest*

THE MORTAL FALLS

Undercover Elementals, Book One

CHAPTER ONE

I TROTTED OUT THE DOORWAY OF THE ROCK SHOP AND HURRIED AROUND the corner of the barn-red metal building, past the rock garden with its whimsical statues frolicking among the boulders and flowers. My boots clomped as I hustled down the path through the woods, straight into the area marked by a big wooden sign. White-painted letters declared "HEALING VORTEX." Three boulders, shaped like benches, hunkered in a semicircle around the empty space that was the so-called vortex of mystical energy. I stopped in the middle of the space. No spiritual effects lightened my psyche, or whatever the thing was supposed to do.

Maybe the vortex shunned me because I'd stopped believing in the supernatural. I liked the charming idea of an invisible energy field that healed what ailed you, but ridicule from school kids had squelched my fascination with the paranormal. I'd long since given up on caring what others thought of me, yet I couldn't quite get back to those beliefs.

Glancing around, I realized no one was here. My customers must've left already, or meandered down the trail to the waterfall. If I returned to the shop without speaking to the customers, or at least verifying they'd left the premises, my boss would chew me out good. "Go act like a tour guide," Stan Lagorio had commanded, and I obeyed. A thirty-two-year-old woman should not have to schlep rocks and chase down tourists for minimum wage. Still, with my lackluster work history, I was grateful to have any job.

Sultry air stuck to my skin as I trudged down the trail. I swiped a bead of sweat from my temple. Summer on the Keweenaw Peninsula—the way-way north of Michigan's Upper Peninsula—shouldn't scorch. I mopped more perspiration from my brow, plodding onward. Up ahead, out of sight, the waterfall drummed a dull rhythm. Something else moaned beneath the rumbling, something like…

The throaty bellow of a human in agony.

I slid to a stop. My heart raced. Adrenaline electrified my every nerve as I struggled to peer through the trees, but the foliage blocked my view. The urge to flee blasted through me, but someone needed to check this out. If I galloped back to the store for help, the injured party might bleed to death or stumble into the water and drown. I inched forward.

A strangled cry reverberated through the woods.

I slipped my right hand under my blouse to close my fingers around the grip of the Bond Arms derringer holstered on the inside of my waistband—legally, thanks to my concealed carry permit and the permission of my employer. The pistol's grip felt warm in my cold hand, heated by my body temperature. The two .357 rounds, one in each barrel, could stop a bad guy or at least slow him down. *Never a victim again.*

A chill seeped into me, penetrating to the very depths of my being. The air crackled with invisible energy that skittered across my skin. The trees towered above me as before, the sun still blazed overhead, and the waterfall still thundered further down the trail. But the atmosphere had shifted, like a shadow snaking across my soul.

Baloney. Energy didn't crackle. No shadows infected me. I'd let my imagination mushroom into paranoia.

I pulled out my derringer and tiptoed two steps. Hesitated. Took another step. Listened.

The falls rumbled. Jagged breaths hissed from my lips. The weight of another gaze squirmed down my spine, but I saw nothing except aspen and maple trees, and wildflowers sagging under the weight of morning dew. I would've accepted I was alone and had confused the cry of a fox or bear for a human scream, if not for the worm of doubt burrowing into me.

A raven swooped down out of the high trees.

The bird squawked as it passed within inches of me. I ducked down. When I raised up again, the raven was gone. Had it been aiming for me? Christ, I was losing my mind.

I jogged down the trail and broke through the screen of trees into the clearing surrounding the falls. The water gushed over the twenty-foot-high red sandstone cliff into the small pool below, where it disgorged into a stream. No one stood on the wooden bridge that arched over the stream. I dragged in a breath, inhaling the clean scents of water and grass, but a sharper smell, almost metallic, lurked beneath the woodland aroma. The trail angled left, away from the falls and into the deeper woods. I sprinted around the curve, into the trees.

And tripped over the man sprawled across the trail.

My derringer popped out of my grasp as I stumbled sideways. Blood dripped from the man's forehead onto the ground. The fluid stained his red hair and congealed as a dark puddle in the dirt. One arm lay twisted under his body. His eyes stared at nothing. His mouth gaped open, caught in the final scream.

I crouched beside the man, extending a trembling hand to check his pulse, but I sensed the truth before my fingertip dug into his flesh.

The man was dead.

Chapter Two

A FORCE AS POWERFUL AS A BLACK HOLE HAULED MY ATTENTION TO the body. The man. Christ, he was still a human being, not a slab of meat. I collapsed to my knees, unable to tear my gaze away from the lifeless body of the man whom—less than an hour ago—I'd caught shoplifting a pair of copper ore bookends, stuffing them into his backpack. Baffled at why a grown man would risk jail time for slabs of polished rock, I'd seized his arm and demanded he give up the items.

He'd bared his teeth and hissed, "Go to hell, bitch."

Now the shoplifter lay dead at my feet. The police would probably think I'd argued with the guy, chased him through the woods, and murdered him in cold blood. The sheriff already thought I was a psycho. He'd dream up some kind of motive, just like last time.

I swallowed hard. The dead man's eyes. They stared into nothingness. Into eternity. I jiggled the body. He didn't rouse. I shook him hard and shouted, "Wake up!"

The head lolled at an unnatural angle. I yanked my hands away. What had I expected? The man was stone dead.

A shiver coiled down my spine. *You have to call the cops.* I jammed a hand in my jeans pocket, yanking out my cell phone, and punched the 9 key. The inescapable pull of the dead man tugged my gaze back to the body at my feet, to the blood pooled around his head and the vacancy in his eyes. My fingers twisted around a clump of grass, clenching it until the blades crumpled. Dew seeped over my fingers. *Rein it in, Lindsey.* I drew in a long breath and let it out slowly.

My other hand gripped the phone so tight my fingers ached. *The phone.* I lifted my damp fingers to the keys.

A crunch pierced the silence.

I whipped my head around. The noise originated behind me, in the woods. Goose bumps erupted up and down my arms and I snatched up my gun, scrambling to my feet. The stench of blood suffocated me. Straight ahead, a three-foot-wide pine tree loomed.

Rustling. Behind the tree.

I bit my lip. "Who's there?"

A figure leaped out. The naked man loped down the path away from me, toward the falls. His footfalls thwapped. He craned his head around, shot a grin at me, and sprinted faster.

Maybe he killed my shoplifter. By the time the cops arrived, the stranger would've escaped into the wilderness. I bolted after him.

It was like a crazed spirit had possessed me, propelling me into a reckless pursuit. *Chase a naked man through the woods. Brilliant plan.* I'd mutated into the dumb chick from a B horror movie, but I could not stop. Something in my soul drove me onward, legs pumping, blood rushing. My veins burned with adrenaline. My breaths huffed so hard and fast my head started to spin, but I drove my body on and on. I closed the distance between us just as the man touched down on the main trail. The stranger swerved right and vaulted over the wooden railing meant to deter people from jumping into the water. He sailed through the air, powerful, graceful, beautiful. His feet whomped down on the rock ledge at the cliff's base and he trotted toward the falls.

I hollered through cupped hands. "Stop right there!"

The man dived straight into the torrent.

At the railing, I stopped so fast I almost toppled over headfirst. The waterfall pummeled the pool, churning up foam that dissipated as it oozed across the surface. Drops spattered my face and I blinked at the sting in my eyes. The rumbling of the falls, though far from deafening, drowned out my thoughts and obliterated my intentions. Why had I run here?

The man. He'd fled the scene of a crime, or at least a possible crime. My shoplifter died from a severe head wound and the naked man I'd chased must've either been a witness or the killer. The sheriff would never believe I'd seen a naked man unless I delivered him on a silver platter with the recipe for roasting him pinned to his chest. I must track him down.

Where? He'd vanished into the waterfall.

"Hello again."

I yelped, scrambled sideways, tripped over a rock. My arms flailed. I caught a peripheral glimpse of the stranger as I staggered backward. My heel dropped into a hole. My feet flipped out from under me and I sailed toward the ground.

The man snagged me around the waist. He hoisted me up, hugging me to him. My derringer thumped onto the ground beside his feet, but his only reaction was a quick glance at it and a faint lift of one brow.

Panting, I gaped at my savior. The murder suspect. Or witness. Or... something. His arms, roped with taut sinews, pressed me to his muscular body. Despite his jump through the falls, he wasn't wet. *Impossible.*

I wriggled against his grip. "Let me go."

He released me, stepping back. "You should exercise more care, darlin', or you'll crack that lovely head of yours."

"What?"

He nodded toward the ground. I followed his gaze down to a fist-size rock situated right where my head would've struck. *Ouch.* I gulped.

The man watched me, his brows furrowed.

Not a man. A murder suspect. I scuffled away from him, drawing out a distance of several yards. My gaze flicked to the gun, but I couldn't retrieve it without approaching him. "Why did you run away?"

"So you would follow."

His Irish brogue tickled my senses like a feather grazing my skin. I gave myself a mental shake, but the sensation lingered. "Excuse me?"

My suspect sighed, as if I were the dumbest human on the planet. Maybe I was. Right at this moment, I wouldn't have bet money on my intelligence. Still, I had my pride.

I crossed my arms over my chest. "Why did you run?"

The man hooked a thumb over his shoulder, toward the trail. "To draw you away from the body. It seemed to upset you."

When I leaned to the left, I glimpsed the trail but not the dead man. The stranger blocked my view, which made me wonder if he'd positioned himself there on purpose. Him. The strange man who'd leaped into the falls only to pop up behind me a split second later. *Impossible.*

He glided one step closer, into a shaft of sunshine that painted his face in hues of gold. The shadow from his elegant nose kissed the corner of his mouth. The sun's rays ignited his amber eyes, gracing them with a vividness beyond the normal. I roved my gaze up and down his golden body, soaking in the alien beauty of him. He wasn't actually naked. A tan loincloth clung to his flesh, but since the scrap of fabric covered his buttocks and groin and not much else, the impression of nudity wasn't entirely unfounded. The loincloth's color blended into his complexion. The way it hugged his body accentuated his male physique, the way it clung to his lean hips and the upper swathe of his powerful, tanned thighs.

My gaze fell across a long scar on his chiseled torso, right over his heart. I wrestled against the bizarre urge to lunge toward him and run my hands over that glorious chest. Heat swept through me, the suddenness of it shortening my breaths.

Get a grip. I was suffering from shock. Nothing else explained this. I should not be ogling a murder suspect twenty feet away from the victim's corpse. I wasn't like this, not ever, especially not since—I severed the memory before it swallowed me whole. Nothing supernatural was going on here. I had a half-naked murder suspect to question. Once I knew the answers, I'd subdue this guy—somehow—and call the cops. Only then might the sheriff believe me.

Okay. Time to grill the suspect.

Straightening, I lifted my chin. "Did you kill that man?"

The stranger shook his head. The light glimmered on his shadow-dark hair. The breeze tousled his wavy locks around his face, brushing them across the tops of his ears. His lips, thick and luscious, cinched together. Strands of glossy hair fanned across his eyes, but he seemed not to notice. "You ask the wrong question."

"Did you see what happened to the dead man?"

The stranger shrugged. His broad shoulders undulated. "Not really, darlin'. But I wasn't on the lookout...for a man."

"What are you talking about? Who are you? And what are you doing out here dressed like—" I flapped a hand toward him. The loincloth, and what it concealed, snagged my attention and warmth rushed through me anew. I clamped my upper lip between my teeth. Zeroing in on his face, I said, "Nobody dresses like that in the woods."

"Is that so." A statement, not a question.

"Yes. It's not proper." Cripes. I had more urgent matters to worry about, like the corpse rotting in the woods behind this crazy man. Since the moment I found the body, nothing made sense. It all seemed...paranormal.

My gaze fell on my derringer, where it lay in the grass near the stranger, so close yet so far beyond my reach. I needed the hard metal in my hand, an anchor to reality.

I cleared my throat. "What do you know about the dead body? Who are you? Where did you come from?"

"Again with the questions."

"I'd quit asking if you'd answer."

His mouth slid into a wide grin and he strode toward me. One step closer. Two steps. Three. I stumbled backward as ice frosted over my skin, leeching into my flesh. His long legs spanned the distance faster than my feet could travel. My spine smacked into a tree. His body blockaded my view, a wall of muscle and bronzed flesh. Pinned there, I clutched at the trunk. Bits of bark crumbled under my nails, fluttering to the ground. I flattened against the tree. Breaths gusted out of me in sharp huffs. *Brilliant, Lindsey, get yourself trapped between a tree and a weirdo.*

He slanted his head down to whisper in my ear. "Take it easy, darlin'. I won't harm ye."

Did I fear him? No. The realization shivered through me. I should fear him. I ought to hurl him away and flee back to the shop. But I didn't. Call it intuition or a sixth sense, but I understood he meant me no harm, even before he spoke the words.

Wait. I didn't believe in intuition. I'd gone insane. Snapped, at last.

He fingered a lock of my hair, studying it as if he'd never seen such a thing before. "Lovely. Like chestnuts powdered with gold dust." He switched his gaze to my eyes. "And your irises are pale as glacial ice, but with substance behind them. Fire. Spirit." He squinted, angling his head side to side. "Something else too. Can't quite place it. An energy bubbling up from a hidden well."

"Cut the poetics, pal." Wow, I'd actually sounded forceful. I tried to glare at him, but chewing the inside of my cheek probably ruined the effect. My ears rang and I suddenly realized I'd forgotten to breathe. "What on earth are you?"

He clapped his palms on the tree, straddling my shoulders. His body radiated heat. It poured over me like liquid sunshine. I sucked in a breath. The scent of him devoured my senses—an earthy tang, underlaid with exotic spice and a sharp sweetness that evoked thunderstorms. His breath whispered over my lips. "What are *you*?"

"Uh…" I squirmed. "I'm a woman, a human being, like you."

He chuckled. "We are nothing alike."

His laughter twanged a nerve inside me, breaking the spell. I blinked three times and hauled in a deep breath, letting it out slowly, overcome by the need to clear my senses. I stared at his chest, desperate to banish all thoughts of the supernatural. I needed to get back to the interrogation. "A man is dead. You must've seen something. Don't you care about that, or anything?"

"Another question."

"Which you aren't answering. Again."

"I regret I'm unable to become involved in mortal affairs."

"Mortal affairs?" I shook my head, dumbfounded. "How can you be so heartless?"

A strange expression flickered across his features and he bowed his head. "Because I am. You would do well to stay away from me and my kind."

His kind? That implied he was—No. Oh-no-no, I would not go there. I cleared my throat. "*You* approached *me*."

He looked up, but his shoulders slumped. "Alas, I don't always do as I should."

"Don't you feel anything?"

"This has nothing to do with emotions." He rubbed my hair between his thumb and forefinger, his attention riveted to the lock. "But to answer your question, I do feel. More than I should, in fact."

I craned my neck to scrutinize him across the six-inch gap in our heights. A tightening around his eyes, coupled with a falter in his smile, led me to believe—or maybe hope—he did feel. He bent his head to peer at me. Those eyes. They smoldered from within. Shades of gold, bronze, and silver swirled inside the irises. No one's eyes swirled. But heaven almighty, his did.

He dropped my hair. "Have ye lost the power of speech, love?"

"N-no. Why?"

His tone rife with amusement, he asked, "Don't ye ever speak a declarative sentence?"

I snapped my spine straight, glared into his supernatural eyes, and said, "You're an obnoxious twit. How's that for declarative?"

"You astound me with your charm and slay me with your wit."

Slay. The word plucked me out of this bizarre conversation and back to the reality of why I'd pursued this man in the first place. Someone was dead. My damn intuition, or whatever it was, refused to let me believe he had killed the shoplifter, but I must get an answer from him. A concrete, rational answer. "Did you kill him?"

The arrogance flooded out of the stranger's expression. His lips angled downward in a slight frown. "Kill him? Oh, you mean the poor fellow out there."

He tipped his head back and to the side, indicating the trail through the woods.

"Yeah," I said. "I mean the guy with his head bashed in. The one lying dead at the scene you fled from—which is a crime, by the way."

At least I thought it was. I didn't know for sure, but the statement sounded good.

"I'm not bound by your rules."

"They aren't my rules. It's the law."

"Not my law." He jerked his head, glancing past me, past the tree. I listened, but my ears detected nothing except the soft rumble of the falls and the thudding of my own heart. His gaze shifted to the water. "I wish I could assist you, but I'm afraid I must go."

"You can't. We have to call the police."

He pushed away from the tree. "Sorry, darlin'. Can't help ye with that."

"You must've seen something."

He shrugged, his shoulders flexing. "I saw what you saw, nothing more."

"You have to stick around and tell the police your story."

Humor glinted in his eyes and his lips twitched into a half-repressed smirk. "My presence would do nothing to help the situation. Take my word on that."

Well, he did have a point. A half-naked man with freaky eyes corroborating my story probably wouldn't console the sheriff. Oh hell, given my relationship with the sheriff, he'd slap cuffs on me for being in the vicinity of trees, never mind my stumbling onto a corpse.

The stranger swung his head to the left, diving his face into my hair, and inhaled deeply. Sniffing my hair? What the hell? I slapped my palms on his chest and shoved. He didn't budge. I pushed harder, but I might as well have wrestled with a giant redwood.

He lifted his head, eyes clouding with confusion. "How odd. I thought it was your hair, but it isn't. You smell of—I must've imagined it."

"I don't understand a word you've said."

He fingered my hair, then withdrew his hand. "At least I succeeded in distracting you from the poor dead fellow."

The stranger pulled back and opened one palm. A flower appeared there, as if by magic. A daylily, its white petals blushed with pink. His other hand spread open, revealing my gun balanced on his palm. He pressed the derringer into my hand and curled my fingers around it. "Thought ye might like to have this."

I stared at him. "Uh…yeah."

He tucked the flower behind my ear, planted a kiss on my forehead, hopped back a step, and vanished.

A gasp burst out of me. He hadn't scampered away, or even flown up into the sky. He had vanished. Poof. Gone before I could blink. A dream? A hallucination?

Great. I *was* insane.

I tossed the flower on the ground and blazed down the trail, back toward the shop. Where the path forked, heading off into the woods, I halted. A chill sprouted in my chest. It branched out until the tendrils invaded every cell in in body. I swiveled my head—and gasped again.

The dead man had vanished.

CHAPTER THREE

A COPPERY ODOR BLUSTERED OVER ME ON THE WIND AS I CROUCHED over the blood stain. I gagged and coughed, one hand flying up to cover my nose and mouth. My brain refused to process anything I'd experienced since leaving the shop. I squeezed my eyes shut, took long breaths until my ears stopped ringing, and stared at the stain again. The blood proved a corpse had rested here. I hadn't imagined it.

Well, it proved *something* bled here.

I'd touched the body. Now it had vanished, or been moved. Without a witness to corroborate my story, no one would buy it. I had to report it anyway. *Suck it up, Lindsey.*

Holstering the derringer inside my waistband, I spotted my phone on the ground where I'd dropped it and snatched it up.

Sirens wailed, muted as if far away. I knew the woods could swallow sounds, tricking the ear into believing the source lay distant. The cops might've been coming for me, or they might be rushing somewhere else, called out on another matter. I punched 9-1-1 into my phone.

The crack of a twig snapping reverberated off the trees. Someone was coming.

My went dry. I pulled in a breath, counting to ten as I released it. A tourist, that's who approached from down the trail. A goofball intent on visiting the vortex.

The breeze kissed my face. A familiar scent teased my senses. Earth and thunderstorms—and blood.

I bit down hard on my lower lip. A salty, metallic flavor seeped onto my tongue and I ran my finger across my lip. Blood slicked my fingertip. Great. I really would have blood on my hands when the sheriff arrived. I licked it off, wiped my hands on my jeans, and flipped my phone open.

Darkness draped over me. I hesitated, my finger hovering over the keys.

"What the blazes are you doing?"

The gruff voice arrowed straight into my chest. I jerked my head up, yet even before my eyes met his, I knew whose face I'd see. My heart pounded against my ribs, the air froze in my lungs, and every muscle in my body turned rigid. I clapped the phone shut.

Sheriff Travis Blackwell towered over me from several feet away, the apex of his shadow engulfing me. The sunlight imbued his dirty blond hair with a harsh glint, like tarnished gold. When he planted his hands on his hips, the dark brown shirt of his uniform stretched taut over his broad shoulders and chest. His tan pants mirrored the color of the dry earth. In one sinewy hand, he held a black box by its handle.

"Were you planning on calling me?" His Texas drawl reshaped the words.

I stretched my neck back to meet his gaze. He squinted his slate-gray eyes at me, head listing to the side, lips compressed. Sunlight glanced off his badge, spearing my eyes. My brain struggled to form coherent thoughts, but my words emerged in disjointed clumps. "Yes. I was. Going to report. Uh, what happened."

"Somebody beat you to it."

One of his deputies raced up behind him. Kal Ruoho was breathing hard, his face red.

"Get back to the shop," Travis told him, setting his black box on the ground. "Interview the staff."

The staff consisted of me, Stan, and Stan's brittle wife who filled in on my days off. Travis knew this, yet he made it sound like his deputy would have a passel of employees to question.

Kal trotted back toward the shop.

Travis settled a hand on the gun strapped to his belt. "Who'd you kill this time, Lindsey?"

Anger seared through me, evaporating my anxiety. Travis must've had magical powers, the way he always turned up at the worst moments in my life. But how in the fires of damnation did he hear about the body?

I heaved myself to my feet and, hands on hips, drummed my fingers. "What are you doing here?"

His mouth twitched downward. His Texas twang thickened a little when he said, "My oh my, ain't this the highlight of my day. Seeing the sweetheart of Mandan County."

Though I didn't overlook the sarcasm in his tone, I did let it go this time. After all, I'd torn him away from the rampant crime in the tiny village of Lutin Falls, the county seat ten miles from here, where right now someone was probably stepping on an endangered wildflower. "Why are you here?"

He slanted his head and rolled his eyes toward the ground. The blood stain. Right. "I assume that's the alleged crime scene."

"It's not alleged. I saw the body." How he knew about it mystified me. "Who called you?"

"Anonymous tip. The caller said you killed a man. That true?"

"Of course not."

"Not like it'd be the first time."

He locked his burly arms over his chest, tilting forward just enough to project menace. I stiffened. Tried not to, but this man had a way of triggering my fight-or-flight instinct. My stomach churned and the sourness of bile rose into my mouth. *Dammit.* I'd sworn Travis would never intimidate me again.

Yeah. How many times had I vowed that? Ten, twenty, a million?

"The better question," he said, "is why didn't you call it in?"

He shifted his weight. The .40-caliber Sig Sauer strapped to his hip bounced. I scratched my arm and stared at the white bark peeling away from a birch tree, but my gaze drifted back to the sheriff.

Travis cleared his throat, scowling. "Well? What's your excuse this time, Porter?"

I ground my teeth. Travis had used my last name, like he was interrogating a damn suspect. I cranked my face into a glower of my own. "I don't need an excuse. As usual, I've done nothing wrong." I jabbed a finger toward the blood stain. "I found a dead body there."

He quirked an eyebrow. "An invisible dead body?"

"No. Someone took it."

"Who? The corpse fairy?" His lips contorted, as if he struggled not to laugh. "How much cash you get for tucking a dead body under your pillow?"

Jackass. I choked down the word and said, "I left for a minute and when I came back, it was gone."

"Where in tarnation did you go?"

Aw hell. I ransacked my brain for an explanation, because no way could I tell him the truth. I hugged myself and fixated on the birch tree again.

"Spit it out," he said.

"Um, I…" *Took off after a half-naked man I thought might've been the murderer, but he vanished, and then he came back and sniffed my hair. You understand, right?* Sure, I'd say that. A straitjacket might flatter my figure. "I thought I saw someone fleeing the scene."

Good. That almost made sense.

He scrutinized me, squinting again. "Hmmm."

I dropped my arms and huffed a breath out my nose. "What do you mean *hmmm*?"

"Your story sounds like a load of horse shit." He narrowed his eyes. "Ain't like this is the first time I found you standing over a blood stain yammering about a disappearing victim."

My nerves bristled, as if he'd scraped a stiff brush up my spine. "There was a body, goddammit."

His expression blanked. His eyes widened, though only for a second. My glacial tone had shocked me too. Though he tried to frown, his eyes crinkled with a repressed smile. "The ice princess returns. Or maybe she never left, huh?"

The wind rustled the trees and the aspen leaves sizzled with a phantom fire. My hair feathered across my face, tickling my nose. I sneezed.

"Gesundheit," Travis said.

"Thanks." Why on earth was he being polite, I wondered, but discarded the thought. "Can I go, please? I have a job, you know."

He lodged one hand on his cocked hip. "I see a dark patch over there that might be trace evidence. I got a tip there was a murder committed and I find you admiring the crime scene."

A viscous chill oozed over my skin. *I can't go through this again, please no.*

"Listen up, Porter. Things'll go a lot easier on you if you tell me what you did with the body."

"You really think I could drag a body off by myself?"

He shrugged one shoulder. "Maybe you got an accomplice. Or maybe you planted some fake blood here and called in the tip yourself, just to rile me up. The caller had a funny voice that coulda been a man or a woman."

"Don't be ridiculous. There was a body."

"Nobody but you saw the alleged victim."

I clenched my teeth so hard pangs jolted through my jaw. "The body was real. I can't help that no one else noticed the man bleeding to death on the trail."

Travis blew out a breath, his cheeks swelling and deflating. "That's all you got for me?"

"Yes."

"All right then." He whipped a pair of handcuffs from his belt. "I'm taking you in for questioning."

I shuffled backward two steps, checking left and right for an escape route. The trail led to the falls or back to the shop, and tearing off into the woods without a map or GPS terrified me more than a jail cell.

"I got no choice," Travis said, and sounded almost sorry about it. "See, I know you're not telling me everything. There's been a report of a death, so I gotta take some action."

The handcuffs glittered in the sunlight.

I flicked a finger toward them. "Are the cuffs necessary?"

"No, but it's more fun for me this way."

"You're a bastard."

His scowl slackened into a blank expression, his lips parting. His gaze zeroed in on a sight beyond my shoulder.

"Perhaps I can be of assistance," a cheerful Irish voice said.

My heart skipped. Anticipation chased across my skin. *Him.*

The stranger who'd sniffed my hair traipsed out of the woods behind me to halt at my side. His hand brushed against my wrist. A tingle coursed up my arm and outward into my body, suffusing me with his warmth. The scent of him enveloped me and every hair on my body prickled with awareness. I resisted the urge to glance at him. My strange, bronzed god.

Not that he was mine. We weren't...anything to each other. I didn't even like the guy, really. But I itched to peek at him, and so I risked a sideways glimpse. I choked on a breath. Instead of a loincloth, jeans and a cotton dress shirt cloaked his chiseled frame. The sun glistened on his dark hair, swept back into a conservative style. He winked at me.

Was I still hallucinating? Part of me prayed I was, since that would make the dead body a figment of my mind too.

The stranger slipped his right arm around my waist. His hand bumped my gun and he ran his middle finger around the outline. His touch teased my skin through the fabric of my shirt. He drew me close, tucking me into the crook of his shoulder. Though I tried to wriggle free, but he kept his arm around me in a hold more supportive than threatening, as if we were intimately familiar with each other.

I flitted my gaze from the stranger to Travis. Wait a minute. Travis saw the other man. My Tarzan fantasy was real? Relief sluiced through me, but panic swept in behind it. There was, after all, the minor matter of the wayward corpse.

His fingers moved over my hip in a light circles. *Real.* I wasn't totally insane, at least.

Travis eyed my new friend with his best policeman glare. "Who are you?"

"Nevan. And you?"

"Sheriff Travis Blackwell. You got a last name, buddy?"

"I demand to know why you are threatening Lindsey."

Nevan knew my name? Duh, he must've overheard Travis using it. I poked Nevan with my elbow and muttered under my breath, "Shut up and let me go. I can handle this."

He ignored me and spoke to Travis. "While you've been harassing my Lindsey, I've been searching for the body."

Travis's gaze bored into me for a few seconds, then he squinted at Nevan. "You saw the alleged victim?"

"Indeed," Nevan said. "I saw the poor dead fellow. Lindsey's telling the truth about that."

Travis swung his attention back to me. "Is she now."

"Absolutely," Nevan said.

"Did you see an individual fleeing the scene?"

"I did."

Travis rammed his tongue into his cheek. His gaze never vacillated from me, though he aimed his words at Nevan. "Can you describe the suspect?"

"Not really. We saw the back of him, nothing more."

"Uh-huh. And what happened to the body?"

"Not a clue," Nevan said, his expression overflowing with innocence.

Travis glowered at him with such ferocity I expected flames to shoot out of the sheriff's eyes. Nevan matched Travis's eye contact with unwavering intensity, yet managed to hold onto his look of utter innocence.

I waved my hand between the men's faces. When Travis rotated his eyes toward me, I asked, "Are we done here?"

"Hardly," Travis said. "You're still a suspect."

"I didn't do anything."

"Gotta take you in for questioning. None of this adds up and I want some frigging answers. From both of you."

My mystery man bounced on his heels, jostling me against his firm torso. My stomach fluttered, but I coerced a calm demeanor from my traitorous body. His voice took on a decisive edge, though somehow he imbued his words with politeness. "Lindsey has answered enough of your questions."

Travis curled his lip at Nevan.

I jabbed a finger in Nevan's side. He either didn't notice or didn't care. I poked him again and hissed out the side of my mouth, "Cut it out. You're not helping."

He ignored me. Again.

Travis crouched beside the blood stain. He cracked open the black box he'd brought, which held plastic bags and other equipment.

I rose onto tiptoes for a better angle. "What are you doing?"

"Collecting evidence." He donned a pair of latex gloves and set about his work. When he'd finished gathering a sample of the blood-soaked dirt, he closed up his kit and rose. "No tire tracks or drag marks, no footprints other than yours."

No footprints? But Nevan had run past the body. *Impossible.*

Travis sighed. "You're coming with me, Lindsey."

"But—"

Kal jogged up the trail, halting at the edge of the clearing. Travis held up one finger to me. "Wait here." His lip curled once more as he told Nevan, "That means you too."

Travis retreated to the clearing's edge to chat with Kal, their backs to us, their voices too indistinct to make out.

I murmured to Nevan, "Thank you."

"Are you expressing gratitude to me?" Surprise tinged his voice.

"Yes. Thank you for sticking up for me with Travis."

"You're most welcome." He hesitated, and when he spoke again, I swore I detected a note of anxiety in his voice. "But in the future, take care when thanking me. It may have unforeseen consequences."

"Such as?"

Another pause. "Take my word for it, that's all I ask."

His clothes dissolved. No other way to describe it. They simply evaporated into nothing—save for the loincloth, which coalesced around his hips. His skin burned hot against mine as his arm shifted up to my shoulders and one fingertip traced a circular path on my upper arm, carving a trail of sensation in its wake. It felt so good I wanted to snuggle into him, lost to the tingle his touch ignited.

No. I did *not* want to.

I could not be attracted to a man I'd just met who had swirling eyes and the ability to poof in and out of view, who was arrogant and annoyed me. Then again, he had lured me away from the dead man because I seemed upset. And he distracted me from the problem until I calmed down. And he saved me from cracking my skull on a huge rock. He stood up for me with Travis too. Maybe I did know a little bit about him.

But not nearly enough.

I disentangled myself from his hold, scurried a few steps away, and spun to confront him. "Why did you do it?"

He sauntered to the nearest tree, a couple yards away, and leaned his long body against the trunk. "You'll have to be a bit more specific, love, if you want me to answer."

"Are you saying you will answer my questions?"

"Possibly." He raked a hand through his hair and his biceps bulged from the movement. His voice dropped to a husky whisper. "If you're nice to me."

"Nice?" I stomped closer. "What the hell do you mean?"

"If you'd quit swearing at me, that'd be a start."

I clenched my hands into tight fists. My nails dug into my palms and pain shot through my knuckles. "I'm so sorry if my language offends you. I'd think a guy who can poof in and out of sight would have a thicker skin."

"My, but you are fetching when you're vexed."

I scrunched my lips, fuming with an anger rooted in more than this man's sarcastic, blasé attitude. Yet I had seen glimmers of deeper emotions under the surface, which made me wonder if his nonchalance was a cover. For what, though?

He arched an eyebrow. "Are ye all right?"

"Fine." I forced my hands to unclench. "What are you?"

"A man. Has it been so long since ye had one that you're unsure?"

"I—wh—" My thoughts disintegrated, but I gathered the bits and pieced them back together. My brain ached from the effort. "My personal life is none of your business."

He pushed away from the tree. Strode toward me. Stared into my eyes. The molten metal of his irises feathered a tingle down my spine.

I floundered backward. "What do you want from me?"

"To understand," he said in a sultry tone, as his eyes towed me down into their depths. "You intrigue me and I must deduce why."

"Huh?"

His gaze stroked over me from head to toe. "Shall we play, darlin'?"

"This isn't a game."

"It could be. If you'd loosen up a bit."

"Loosen up?" The spell shattered, I shot my best glare at him. "Forgive me if I have trouble relaxing around a complete stranger."

"It was a suggestion, not a command. Though I cannot comprehend how a person could be so tense and not snap like a twig underfoot."

I had the most ridiculous urge to explain myself, but I bit it back. "This conversation is over. Thanks for the assist, but I hope I never see you again."

His face pinched and he glanced away. When he turned back to me, the nonchalance swept in again. "I suppose you'll be returning to the shop then?"

"Not that it's any of your business, but I plan to scarf down an insanely fattening lunch, gain five pounds in the process, and then go back to work and pretend none of this ever happened."

"Your friend the sheriff seems intent on detaining you."

"He's not m—Ugh, forget it. Maybe I can talk him out of arresting me." Riiiight. And then I'd take my pet unicorn for a stroll.

Amusement tugged at one corner of Nevan's mouth. "Good luck with that, darlin'."

I whirled on my heels and stomped toward Travis. I felt Nevan's gaze tracking me, like a warm breeze tickling the back of my neck. *Don't look back, just keep walking.*

A raven squawked overhead.

I shielded my eyes to spy the bird swooping in front of the sun. Its head angled in my direction, those coal-dark eyes sharp on me. I had the strange sensation the bird was sizing me up.

The raven flew out of sight.

I tapped Travis on the shoulder. He started, half turning toward me. How he missed the weirdness unfolding right behind him baffled me, but I didn't have time to worry about that. I held out my hands, wrists together. Right now, a jail cell sounded like a haven from the insanity around me. The supernatural around me. "Arrest me or let me go, please."

Travis's brows shot up. He nodded to Kal, who set off down the trail toward the shop. Travis hooked the cuffs around my wrists, each locking shut with a metallic *snick*. My stomach twisted. My fingers grew cold, despite the sweltering day.

"You ain't under arrest—yet." Travis placed a hand on my shoulder to guide me down the path in front of him. "But I am taking you in."

A pang tightened the back of my throat.

Travis's brow furrowed, his gaze scanning the woods behind us. "Where'd your friend go?"

Good question. Nevan was gone, again. "He had to leave. Urgent personal business."

"How the hell'd he get past me and—Never mind." He cursed under his breath. "I'll track him down if I have to comb the whole county to do it."

I bowed my head. A bead of sweat rolled down my temple to splat onto my chest.

Travis gave me a little shove, urging me to move faster. "You won't see the sun again, Porter, till I get answers to every damn one of my questions."

***

"COULDN'T FIND A BODY, IF THERE EVER WAS ONE," TRAVIS SNARLED. HE slammed the driver's door of the vehicle. A sticky breeze surged in through the open windows. I slumped into the backseat, a sour taste infiltrating my mouth. He'd left me here for an hour—inside his Ford Expedition marked with the sheriff's logo, branding me a suspicious character by association—while he, Kal, and Stan searched for the missing corpse.

They found nothing. No body, no tracks, no evidence aside from the blood stain. For a moment, I feared I'd imagined the whole incident. But Travis had met Nevan, which meant I wasn't crazy. Probably. Hormone-addled, yes. Crazy, not so much.

Revving the engine, Travis rolled up the windows as the air conditioner rushed cool air through the car. "I'm sending the blood sample off to the state lab for analysis. If it comes back as porcupine, you're in big trouble for wasting police time."

"There was a body." My attention wandered to the rear of the rock shop and the woods beyond it. I pitched sideways, straining for a better view. "Nevan corroborated my story, remember?"

He twisted around to nail those cool, gray eyes on me. "Yeah, I'm sure your boyfriend wouldn't lie for you or anything."

"Nevan is not—" I'd almost blurted out he wasn't my boyfriend. *Don't tell him the truth, dummy, it'll blow your alibi.* Yeah, because I had such an ironclad one. "Nevan's not a liar."

But I was. Nevan hadn't exactly lied to me. He refused to tell me much of anything.

Travis's lips flattened into a thin line. He let out an exasperated sigh. "I don't get it. Why'd you hook up with a sleaze like Nivea?"

I clamped my lips between my teeth for a second to avoid laughing. "His name is Nevan. And it's none of your business who I hook up with."

Jeez. For the first time in my life, I'd uttered the phrase "hook up." Not that I'd done any such thing.

"Guess you're right," Travis said. "And I reckon I should worry more about what you'll do to him than what he'll do to you."

"You have no clue what really happened with Calder."

"Enlighten me."

I ground my teeth, which only made my jaw ache.

He draped one wrist over the steering wheel, his fingers coiled into his palm. "No body, no crime. If you won't talk, I can't help."

I fidgeted, the cuffs biting into my wrists. "I didn't ask for your help."

"But ya sure as hellfire need it."

Maybe I did need help, but I positively did not want *his* assistance. So I changed the subject. "Why did you follow me here?"

"Somebody called in a tip, Porter."

"No. Why did you follow me to Michigan?" I'd moved here to get away from the Blackwell clan and everything I'd suffered in Texas. Six months after I came here, Travis showed up and wouldn't explain why or how he'd found me. "How'd you even track me down?"

He scratched his neck, eyes averted. "I'm a cop, Lindsey, and you ain't exactly an experienced criminal. Tracking you down wasn't that complicated."

"Why bother? You hate me." I'd avoided asking him for three years, because I avoided contact with him as much as possible and I avoided conversation with him at all costs. He might think he wanted the truth about his brother, but he'd never believe me if I told him what Calder had done.

Travis stared into space for several seconds, while I squirmed in an attempt to scratch an itch on my back by rubbing it against the seat. At last, he looked at me over his shoulder. "I gotta protect the good citizens of Mandan County from the likes of you."

He steered the vehicle out of the parking lot onto the highway, taking me back to his office for an interrogation. I glanced behind the car, into the woods. My life had changed irrevocably and I still had no idea how or why.

I wrinkled my nose at a strange odor wafting over me, something like cat urine but not quite. Did Travis never clean this car?

A sensation of pressure slithered down my neck, almost like fingertips closing around my throat. Tighter. Tighter. I fought for breath but couldn't budge a muscle. My pulse thundered in my ears. In the rearview mirror, Travis's eyes stayed focused on the road ahead. The pressure choked my throat and a voice growled in my ear.

"Mine forever, sweet thing, or no one's."

Dark splotches encroached on my vision. I struggled to shout for help, but it came out as a strangled hiccup.

The phantom fingers sprang free of my neck. I sucked in a wheezing breath.

"You okay back there?" Travis asked, studying me in the rearview mirror.

I coughed, rubbed my eyes with the back of my hand, and drew in a slow breath. "Just got a little overheated, I think."

He cranked up the AC and cool air flooded into the backseat. The blessed relief of it calmed my nerves, but a lingering doubt niggled at me. Maybe I'd had a panic attack due to the stress of the day, or my mind snapped under the strain of paranormal shenanigans. I might've believed that, except the words I'd heard a moment ago were familiar. Calder Blackwell issued the same threat on the night that destroyed my life.

I tucked my hands between my thighs, my fingers suddenly chilled. He wasn't here. He couldn't be.

Calder had been dead for three years.

CHAPTER FOUR

THE SHADE OF A TALL ASPEN TREE BLANKETED ME, SHIELDING MY SKIN from the sun's heat. With the late-afternoon air temperature in the high eighties, though, and the humidity almost as high, sweat oozed out of my pores to dampen my flesh and hair. I rested against the tree trunk, an uneaten turkey sandwich in my hand and an unopened bag of baked potato chips on my thigh.

Travis had relented on his promise I wouldn't see the sun again. After three hours of interrogation, he'd let me go. I honestly couldn't provide the answers he wanted, because I had no clue what was going on. The memory of those hours replayed in my mind, still fresh. Travis had ordered me to sit in a chair beside his desk, which abutted the wall, and then he dragged a folding chair in front of me, flipped it around, and settled his large body onto it with his forearms resting on the back. His knees grazed mine.

Once he uncuffed my wrists, Travis started in on me. "Come on, Lindsey. Fess up."

"To what? I didn't even know the guy."

His fingers moved as he spoke, punctuating his words. "I'm not buying any of this. You were first on the scene and all you can tell me is some *person* fled the scene."

"Nevan told you. He saw the suspect."

"Right." Travis elongated the syllable into a sarcastic insinuation. "Nevan. There's a high-quality witness. He skedaddled and left you high and dry."

He kind of had. But as Nevan had warned me, his presence did nothing to alleviate my predicament. Instead, he chafed the sheriff even more. There in his office, Travis's questions had run in circles, a tornado of accusations and demands for answers I either didn't know or didn't dare give.

"Who's the suspect you claim fled the scene?"

"Are you sure the alleged victim was dead?"

"Where did the body go?"

"How come you didn't call nine-one-one?"

"If somebody fled, why aren't there any footprints besides yours?"

He'd insisted on verifying I had a permit to carry a handgun, though he damn well knew I did, adding more time to the ordeal.

The grumble of car engines roused me from the memories. The noise originated just over a little rise that hid the shop building from my view. Customers rarely visited this part of the woods, because the only trail leading to it was a narrow track worn down by deer. This was my little sanctuary. Every day, I tromped out here on my lunch break to escape the stress of work—and the incessant watchfulness of Stan Lagorio. Today, Stan had given me honest-to-God permission to take a late lunch, even though I'd been gone for hours in the middle of my shift. He knew the sheriff had taken me in for questioning and I swore he was…sympathetic.

The world really had flipped upside down and inside out.

For the umpteenth time, I lifted the sandwich to my mouth. Although my stomach growled at the prospect of food, I stared at the layers of meat and cheese with a growing sensation of nausea. I dropped my hand to my lap.

"Your meal doesn't look particularly fattening."

The sandwich popped out of my grasp as I jumped at the masculine voice emanating from behind me. The sandwich flew apart. The bread landed on the grass while the meat and cheese plopped onto my jeans.

Nevan ambled from behind the tree and halted near my feet. "Not that I have much experience with mortal food, but from what I've seen, that sort of meal is considered healthy."

"Could you please quit scaring the daylights out of me?"

"I do apologize. I had no intention of frightening you."

"Hmph." I plucked the tatters of my sandwich off the ground and tried to reassemble it. "What do you want this time?"

"I see your gratitude has waned."

Flicking bits of grass from the sandwich, I raised it for a bite. The scent of turkey and swiss cheese wafted into my nostrils and my gorge rose in my throat. I stuffed the sandwich back into its plastic bag. "I was grateful, yes, but that's done and gone. You split before Travis could interrogate you and he took his frustration out on me."

"I'm deeply sorry for abandoning you."

"Yeah, whatever." I played with the zipper seal on my sandwich bag. "Why are you here?"

"To be quite honest, I'm not certain."

I glanced up at him. Big mistake.

From this angle, his loincloth provided me with a glimpse of what lay beneath it. Just a glimpse. A hint of flesh. But I recognized the shape of the flesh and my cheeks flamed at the realization. I'd caught a peek at his manly parts.

Squeezing my eyes shut, I clamped my lips between my teeth. The spark of pain did nothing to free me from the knowledge of what I'd seen. Almost seen. Sort of seen. Oh jeez. Why me? Why did I have to stumble over a teleporting corpse? And out of all the billions of women on earth, why did I have to acquire a supernatural stalker who pranced around in next to nothing?

Burying my face in my hands, I groaned. The heat of my blush warmed my fingers.

"Are ye not well, darlin'?" His voice sounded too close.

I peeked out between my fingers. He was crouching so near me I could've extended one finger to poke his nose. His face hovered inches from my hands, his expression concerned. He laid a hand on my upper arm, the touch light and casual, but it stirred something inside me. A want I'd suppressed for too long. The sensation wasn't sexual, not entirely. I longed for more than a kiss or a sensual caress. I longed for connection, belonging, for someone to need me. But a stranger could not need me.

"Lindsey."

"Everything's fine." My hands muffled my voice.

"Why, then, are you hiding in this manner?"

"Um…" *Blast it all.* I was acting like a teenager who'd sneaked into her first R-rated movie with nudity and sexual content. I lowered my hands, the fire in my cheeks somewhat abated. "Really, I'm fine. Thank you for your concern."

His eyes widened a hair, enough to remind me of what he'd said earlier about thanking him. The statement had made no sense. Gratitude exacted no consequences, at least none so dire it justified his fear. Then again, I was talking to a half-naked man who popped into and out of sight whenever he felt like it.

I drew my knees to my chest, erecting a barrier between us. "Sorry. I know you hate it when I say thank you."

He sat back on his heels. "On the contrary, I enjoy your gratitude."

A hint of sensuality warmed his tone. I hugged my knees. "But you said I shouldn't be grateful. It would have unforeseen consequences."

"I said you should take care when expressing gratitude to me. Feel as grateful as you wish, but refrain from voicing it. You'd likely come to regret it."

"That makes no sense. If I'm grateful, I say it and I don't backpedal later."

"You misunderstand." He edged closer, his firm chest bumping my knees. "I'm not suggesting you'll regret thanking me. I'm saying you'll regret letting me know you're appreciative."

I cracked my mouth open, tapping my tongue on the bottoms of my front teeth. "I don't get it. What is the big deal about being polite?"

His voice grew wistful. "Alas, you may never understand the rules of my world. I'm not at all sure I'd want you to."

I had the weirdest urge to slide my fingers through the dark, sleek curls tumbling over his ears. "You keep saying your world, like we live on different planets."

He tilted his head up, his eyes seeking mine. "Not different planets. Separate realms of reality."

"You've got to be joking."

"Ah, but you know I'm not." He released my arms, but tension lingered in his body. "I should have said nothing. Don't know what I was thinking."

"Hmm."

He canted his head, regarding me with curiosity. "Afraid I don't understand your noises, love."

"Sounded an awful lot like you were apologizing for telling me the truth."

"Yes, I was. I should never have told you anything."

I snorted. "That's rich. You apologize for honesty, but not for evasion."

His body shifted as he settled onto his buttocks, one leg outstretched and the other bent to support his arm. The pose also shifted his loincloth, but I resisted the temptation to look. The last thing I needed was my cheeks on fire again.

Nevan balanced his wrist on his knee. His fingers rose and fell like swells on the ocean. "What would you have me do then?"

Another snort ripped out of me. I really couldn't control it. How could any man be so dense? I stretched my legs out alongside him, clasping my hands on my lap. "If you want me to be nicer to you, then try being a little more cooperative with me."

"I can't."

A half-strangled roar of frustration erupted out of me and I threw my hands in the air. "You follow me around but won't explain anything. Do you have any idea how infuriating that is?"

He tilted his head, eyes alight. "I'm beginning to see."

A shorter roar broke out of me and incited a closed-mouth smile from him. I seized my bag of chips and tore it open. Crispy potato slices sprayed up, pattering down on my jeans and the grass.

Nevan chuckled. Little stars glittered in the whorls of his eyes.

I crushed the now-empty bag in my fist and tossed it aside. The foil unraveled with a crinkling noise. "Why do you keep showing up?"

He shrugged. "You intrigue me."

"I'm not that interesting."

He stretched his foot out to nudge my calf. His bare sole was dirty, but then he did apparently live in the woods. "I disagree. You are the most unusual mortal I've ever encountered."

Unusual? Intriguing? Baloney. I was the most boring person on the planet, a hermit nobody liked. Except my family. And this…man, or whatever he was.

Another term he'd used circled back around to the front of my thoughts. "You called me a mortal, and earlier you said something about mortal affairs. But everybody's a mor—" The words died on my tongue, annihilated by an insane revelation. "You can't mean that you…"

"At last you're beginning to see."

"No. It's not possible." I clung to my preconceptions for one second longer, then I flung them out into the universe. "You're immortal."

Nevan's smile was mischievous. "I am immortal, yes."

My thoughts floundered. I opened and closed my mouth, shook my head, and gaped some more at the creature seated across from me. No. Not a creature. I had to think of him as a man, albeit one with incredible powers, because the alternative was terrifying.

I resorted to my comfort zone—asking annoying questions. "Are you really Irish?"

"Well now, I was born on the island currently known as Ireland. But I'm more of an ancestor to the humans living there today."

"Ancestor?" The earth wobbled under me. I clutched at the grass, my nails cutting into the blades, bleeding moisture from them. "How old—"

"Tell me about yourself. Where do you hail from? This place?" He made a sweeping gesture with his arm.

"I'm from nowhere. My family moved around a lot for my dad's work."

"Tell me more. I'm enthralled."

I rolled my eyes. "You are so full of it."

"At times, I'll admit. But not now." He settled a hand on my knee and squeezed lightly. The warmth of his flesh penetrated my jeans. "Do you see your family often?"

"No." An ache pulsed in my chest. "I haven't seen them in over three years."

His hand slid a couple inches down my thigh, braced by his wrist on my knee. The action seemed unconscious, so I pushed aside the notion it meant anything. He tapped my thigh with one finger. "You miss them."

"Yeah." Why was I confessing all to him? I couldn't explain it, but talking to him eased some of the weight in my chest. "Every summer, they travel the country in a big RV. They keep wanting to visit me, but I put them off."

"Why is that?" He watched me with deep interest.

The paranoid part of me, admittedly sizable, wondered why he was asking these questions. "Enough about me. What does being immortal mean? You can't ever die?"

"I can." He wiggled his fingers, eliciting a tickle that spread up my thigh. "But if you're investigating ways to get rid of me, I'm afraid I'm rather difficult to kill."

His fingers. They teased.

"Please stop that." I reached for his hand, to shove it off, but he withdrew it before I could touch him. His intense scrutiny made my skin itch. I picked at the hem of my shirt. "Can anything hurt you?"

"I'm immortal, not invincible. Many things can injure me, but I heal rather swiftly." He hesitated, rubbing his chin. "To destroy me requires extraordinary power. An endued sword, a magically enhanced poison, things of that nature."

"Endued?" I asked.

"Invested with power."

I straightened my posture, which pressed my gun into my belly. I must've winced, because he surged toward me. In the space of a second, maybe less, he went from lounging at my feet to kneeling before me—too close, just like before.

His hand settled on my shoulder. "What causes you pain?"

"Nothing." I shrugged away from his hand. "And please quit touching me."

His lips twisted into a half frown.

I tried to look stern. "You're sure you don't know anything about the dead man."

"My, you are a suspicious one."

"You've got that backwards. You're the one acting sus—"

My phone warbled. I wrestled it out of my pocket. Nevan's gaze held mine as I muttered a greeting.

"Porter, where the hell are you?" Stan's voice bellowed through the speaker, rattling my whole ear, inside and out. "Your lunch break ended six minutes ago."

Checking the time on my phone, I saw he was right. "Be there in a minute."

I disconnected the call before he could scream at me anymore. My brain couldn't handle another shock. I hauled my body off the ground, brushing chips and bread crumbs off my jeans. Nevan rose too, his expression unreadable.

Shoulders hunched, I snatched up my lunch. "I have to go."

He executed a little flourish with his hand, the fingers curved toward the palm. Then he opened his hand to reveal a perfect peach seated in the center. He offered the fruit to me. "Do eat a little something before you go."

"Not hungry."

"Humor me."

I grumbled, but accepted the peach.

He nodded and vanished.

I didn't know which bothered me more—that he could disappear in an instant, or that I was getting used to it. My fingers rubbed across the peach's fuzzy surface. I lifted the fruit to my mouth. The fairy tale about Snow White sprang to mind, the poison apple glimmering in my inner vision. Poison peach? Maybe Nevan intended to drug me and abduct me to his "separate realm." Whatever that meant. Deciding I didn't care to find out, I tossed the peach into the grass.

Once again, Nevan had evaded my questions. He told me next to nothing, except how to kill him. I couldn't figure out why he divulged that info. Of course, it wasn't like I could visit MagicalDeathWeapons.com and order an endued sword.

As I topped the rise, headed down to the parking lot, a shadow swept across the ground in front of me. I looked up to see a raven swoop low overhead. Its wings pumped up and down, whooshing with each down stroke. For a second, I swore the bird locked eyes with me, its gaze probing, before it soared out of sight.

Twice today, I'd been convinced ravens were spying on me. The idea sounded ludicrous, but then so did vanishing corpses and men with swirling eyes.

I shivered, and trotted back to the store.

"THE HEALING VORTEX IS AROUND BACK. HEAD OUT THE BACK DOOR, through the rock garden, and follow the signs." Over the past two hours, I'd given the same directions to a dozen tourists and smiled at each and every one of them. My dimples hurt. I longed to rub my temples, to stop the seed of a headache from sprouting, but Stan was surveilling me from the other side of the shop. I pasted on my professional smile for the young couple standing across the counter from me. "When you're done there, please stop back in to check out our wide selection of native rocks and semiprecious gemstones."

The brunet man nodded. "Thanks, ma'am. We'll do that."

I opened my mouth respond but a visceral recognition of an alien presence shivered across the back of my neck and swept over my entire body, freezing my voice. My pulse pounded in my ears, drowning out the hum of the industrial fans and the chattering of my customers. The sensation unleashed a repressed memory. Calder Blackwell on top of me. Eyes wild. Teeth scraping down my throat.

"You okay, ma'am?"

I jolted back to reality. The brunet man gazed at me with concern in his topaz eyes. Heart still racing, I cranked up my smile again. "I'm fine. May I help you with anything else?"

What was wrong with me? Why did I keep feeling Calder's presence, to the point it hurled me back into the memories I'd locked away in the deepest vault of my mind? I scratched the back of my neck, but the icy tingle endured.

The man's blonde companion batted her mascara-laden eyelashes at him. Seriously, she batted them. And then she focused her denim-blue eyes on me. "Does, like, the vortex spin you? I get seasick."

I tilted my head. "Spin? Uh, not as far as I know. It's invisible."

A man sauntered into the shop through the front doors. The sun shimmered on his glossy, platinum-blond hair, a startling contrast to his olive skin. He scanned the shop, head swiveling, until his gaze landed on me. His lips skewed upward, but the expression failed to reach his eyes. The man rolled his broad shoulders back.

My scalp prickled. Though I tried to convince myself I was overreacting, I sneaked a hand to my waist to pat my gun through my shirt.

"But you can feel it, right?"

At the blonde girl's voice, I jumped. "What?"

"The vortex. You can feel what it does to you, right?"

"Uh-huh." I caught sight of Stan peripherally, his squinted eyes trained on me with the precision of a sniper sighting his target. No more sympathy for me, my duty called. I squared my shoulders and cleared my throat. "The healing energies wash over you like a cool breeze, infusing your body with ancient wisdom."

The brunet guy tucked an arm around the blonde. "Awesome."

Her gaze drifted past my head. Pencil-thin brows crinkled as she struggled to mouth the words emblazoned on the wall—Rock the Keweenaw, the Copper Country's Geology Superstore.

"What's a Kay-wee-now?" the girl asked.

I smiled again, for real this time. "It's pronounced Kee-win-aw. Don't worry, nobody gets it right the first time."

The girl's mouth hung ajar, like an oven door cracked open to release the hot air. Her brain must've overheated. "I thought we were in Michigan."

Oh jeez. Stan owed me more than minimum wage for this. "It's kind of confusing. The Keweenaw is part of Michigan's Upper Peninsula, but it's also a peninsula of its own." I pulled a map out of a drawer, unfolded it, and flipped it around to face the girl. I tapped a sliver of land protruding from the U.P.'s northwest corner. "Right here. It's attached to the U.P."

"Cool."

"Yeah, it is. And it's a beautiful place to be." Not to mention a great place to hide—until your past caught up with you and got himself elected sheriff. An image of the missing dead body ruptured my thoughts. Maybe this wasn't such a great hideout after all. I should've left the second Travis turned up in Lutin Falls, but something about this place kept me rooted to it, as if I belonged here. *Now you're believing in fate? So much for logical Lindsey.*

Vanishing corpses. Half-naked men who blipped in and out of sight. The fingers of Calder Blackwell, my dead fiancé, gripping my throat...Logic flew to Tahiti a while ago.

The brunet tugged his companion's arm. "Better get moving if we wanna see the vortex today."

The couple thanked me and walked out the back door. I ducked my head, rubbing my neck.

A shadow distended across the counter to engulf me.

I popped my head up. The man I'd seen in the doorway loomed before me, his smile duller now. His polo shirt and khaki pants barely contained his marble-hard muscles. His dark eyes, fixated on mine, glimmered with hints of metallic hues.

My feet tried to take a step back, propelled by the thumping of my heart, but I restrained the impulse. I was probably being paranoid. Nevan's eyes were metallic, but they swirled with vivid ribbons of color. And I never feared him. This man…

He bent his head left and right, scrutinizing me. "Are you all right?"

"Fine." I aimed to lay my hands on the counter but missed. My knuckles banged into the counter's edge. A little "ah" hissed out of me.

"You don't seem well."

His eyes, they curled out invisible tendrils that collared my neck, choking me. *For Christ's sake, rein it in.* I coughed, massaged my neck, and mustered a cheerful voice. "May I help you, sir?"

"Yes, you may." He leaned forward, his body a hulking mass. "Might I share a meal with you?"

"I don't date anymore."

"What a pity." Lips pinched, he tipped his head to stare down at me. He was huge, taller than Nevan. His focus migrated to my breasts, hidden beneath my blouse. "You are a tolerable specimen, worth bedding once, or perhaps twice."

"Excuse me?"

The metallic sparks in his eyes erupted into seething torrents of green and orange. "My watcher sees all. The guardian is bound to me, mortal. Remember that."

He winked out of existence, right there in front of me.

I swung my head left and right, desperate to spot him dashing out one of the doors. The huge fans blustering air through the shop seemed to roar like jet engines, jarring my eardrums. I stared numbly at the doorway, certain of nothing anymore. The man, or whatever he was, had vanished just like Nevan did.

Plunking my elbows onto the counter, I cradled my forehead in both hands. A guardian. A watcher. And one creepy son of a bitch who apparently wanted to "bed" me. This day kept getting better and better. The headache seed behind my eyes shot roots out to burrow into my brain. I shuffled out from behind the counter and headed toward the nearest aisle. The heat sweltered around me in an unwelcome embrace.

Movement flashed in the corner of my eye.

Across the store, an elderly gentleman observed me. Sunshine streamed in the open back door to bathe him in a golden, almost ethereal glow. The door swung shut behind him, severing the light. Cloaked in shadows, he scuffled forward, supported by a metal cane. His attention stayed fastened on me.

Though Stan had returned to his office, I recalled his command from earlier today that I get out to the vortex and inform our customers of its healing wonders. My feet heavy, I headed toward the back door. The old man's gaze transfixed me and goose bumps pricked my arms. I walked closer. And closer. He held his position, his face a mask of serenity. Closer. My shoes scraped on the rough concrete floor. The old man winked, a faint smile on his lips.

I bumbled into the corner of a display table, lost my footing, and flailed forward. My hands grasped the table's edge just in time, sparing me from smacking into the concrete face-first.

The old man took a step toward me, clutching his cane harder. "Are you all right, miss?"

He spoke without an accent, yet something in his voice twanged a memory inside me, though I couldn't latch onto it. With a clumsy effort, I righted myself. "Fine. I'm a klutz, that's all."

He moved forward another step. The sunlight from the front door struck his eyes.

My hand flew to my chest. *His eyes.* They burned a golden amber, as if lit from within. He stared at me with such intensity my breath caught in my throat. Shades of gold, bronze, and silver twirled in his irises. No. It couldn't be. But those eyes. They drilled into me, down to my very core. Into my heart, my soul.

Nevan. Somehow, he was the old man.

Footsteps clapped behind me. I whipped my head in that direction, in time to see the blonde girl I'd helped earlier, the one who wondered if the vortex spun you. She flapped a manicured hand at the old man. "Are you coming? I thought you wanted me to show you the vortex."

"I do," the old man replied. "Thank you, child."

The old man wandered past me, leaning on his cane with each step. He glanced at me as he shambled past. I stood immobile, my gaze trailing him out the door. It couldn't be Nevan. The man I'd met was young and virile, not elderly and frail. But it *was* Nevan.

I dashed out the door. My shoes cracked on the gravel. I didn't stop until I'd cleared the corner into the parking lot. At the far side of the building, the blonde tugged the old man's sleeve. He followed her down the path through the rock garden, and soon, the pines and blackberry bushes swallowed them.

Wind gusted over me. My hair fell into my eyes and I blew it aside.

Nevan had the power to alter his appearance. I shuddered. What else could he do? And what was he doing with the girl? If he hurt her...

Never trust a man.

I sprinted after them.

CHAPTER FIVE

A CARAMEL SCENT RUSHED OVER ME AS I PASSED A GROUP OF BLACK-berry bushes at the other side of the rock garden. Up ahead, through the bushes and trees, I glimpsed a blonde head.

Nevan would not hurt the girl. I wouldn't allow it. My hand instinctively went to my gun. Maybe I couldn't kill him, but I could damn sure injure him.

My pulse thundered. I pumped my legs faster, despite the pains in my thighs. *Got to catch up. Stop him, help her.* A small branch thwacked me in the face. The sting made me wince, but I forged onward. This girl wasn't me. Nevan wasn't Calder. I knew these facts, but none of it mattered. I had to stop him from—doing whatever the hell he was planning to do to her. I sped past the vortex and its stone benches. Feminine laughter echoed through the woods from ahead of me.

An instinct impelled me to glance at the spot where I'd found the dead man. My throat tightened, but I had no time to spare on those thoughts. I stopped at the railing beside the falls. Foam sprayed up to tick on my skin and clothes. Where were they?

Laughter. It bubbled out of the woods to the left of the falls. A narrow game trail wended through the trees there. I rocketed down it. Weeds lashed my legs and I raised my arms to block branches from hitting me. Partway down the trail, I halted. If I wanted to discover Nevan's true intentions, I ought to sneak up on him—conduct a little surveillance, catch him in the act. I might intervene before he...did whatever.

My heart pounded so hard I could barely breathe. I tiptoed down the trail. Voices murmured, too far away for me to make out words. Soon though, I spotted a clearing straight ahead and slowed my pace even more. I took care with each step, so I wouldn't snap a twig or smack a branch in my face again. At the clearing's edge, I ducked behind a thick aspen, peeking around its bulk.

Weeds, tall and fragile, quivered in the breeze. High above, a squirrel chattered a warning call. The blonde knelt on the soft grass on the opposite side of the clearing, her back to me. The "old man" leaned on his cane a few feet from her, near a fir tree.

The image of the old man crumbled away, revealing Nevan.

Holy heaven. What was he?

Nevan posed with one arm extended, his palm braced on the tree and one ankle crossed over the other. A shaft of sunlight blazed across his muscled chest.

He reclined his head, impassive. "Don't be afraid, Sandy. I mean ye no harm."

The gentleness of his tone didn't match his assumed posture. I studied him, noting the way his free hand clenched and loosened repeatedly. His shoulders were stiff and he avoided Sandy's gaze, his own darting here and there.

Sandy's features had slackened, her lips parted. She pitched forward, eyes large. Her full lips split into a dazed grin. "Whoa." She drew out the syllable into a long, breathless word. "What are you?"

"Ah…" He dragged a hand over his cheek. "We'll have time for that later."

Her grin mellowed. She undulated a little, like a cobra enthralled by a snake charmer.

Nevan coughed and scratched his head. I watched his chest inflate with a deep breath, which he let out little by little. I'd expected him to be confident and easygoing, as he had been with me. The man across the clearing from me behaved the way someone would if he were…ashamed.

No. I had to be misreading him.

With a quick nod, as if he'd reached a decision, Nevan closed the distance to Sandy. He cupped the girl's chin in his hand. "I need to ask you a question. Consider it carefully. Can ye do that?"

"Sure."

His long body descended as he knelt before her. Sandy's head blocked most of my view, so all I could glimpse was the top of his head. I must see his face. The reason baffled me, but the need clawed at my chest. I lowered into a crouch and crept around the clearing's edge, behind the trees and bushes, until I found a good vantage point. My skulking brought me closer to the duo, alongside them at slight angle that granted me a better view of her face than his. Sandy's pupils had dilated into black disks, nearly consuming her irises. Her hand rose to her throat and her fingers lightly caressed her flawless skin.

One corner of Nevan's mouth crimped downward.

Sandy, oblivious, puckered her face. "What's the question?"

His shoulders buckled forward. He ducked his head and his fingers dug into his thighs. I had the weirdest urge to hug him.

Dammit. I refused to empathize with him. This man—creature, thing, whatever—was manipulating Sandy. I didn't know how or why, but I was witnessing the effects.

Nevan lifted his head and squared his shoulders, his face now a mask of polite detachment. Yet when he spoke, sensuality infused every word. "I want to take you somewhere you've never been before. A special place. You belong there." He took hold of her hands. "Will you come with me?"

She blinked a few times in slow motion. Her tongue sneaked out to moisten her lower lip. "Can my boyfriend come with us?"

Nevan's gaze was nailed to hers, but a muscle in his jaw twitched. His voice stayed sultry, if a bit forced. "No, child, you will return to your lover afterward. This is for you alone."

"What's your name?"

He huffed out a breath, his gaze switching to the trees on my side of the clearing. His gaze homed in on mine and my heart thudded. He saw me.

Sandy, lost in her own realm of reality, said, "Don't you have a name?"

Nevan shut his eyes briefly, then swiveled his focus to me for a heartbeat before he turned back to Sandy.

I hugged the tree, desperate to see but dreading what I learn.

Grasping Sandy's shoulders, Nevan tugged her closer. She tilted her head back, her lips open, eyes unfocused. He bent his head and pressed his mouth to hers.

He was *kissing* her? I ground my teeth. I shouldn't care. I didn't care. Only one thing mattered—protecting an innocent girl from a predator.

I stormed into the clearing, yanked the derringer out of its holster, and whipped it out from under my shirt. I flipped the safety off, leveling the muzzle at Nevan. "Get the hell away from her."

My shout ricocheted off the trees.

One half of his mouth cinched up into a smirk.

With my right hand clamped around the Colt, I braced it from underneath with my left. "I mean it. Move or I'll shoot."

My gun was a few inches from his head. I poised my finger over the trigger, tensed, ready to take hold and squeeze if necessary.

Nevan touched one fingertip to the derringer's muzzle. "Your little weapon will do no good. But you know that, don't you?"

"A couple slugs in your skull might slow you down."

"I've caused no harm to the girl."

I planted my feet wide. "Let Sandy go."

He spread his hands, palms up. "She came here freely and she may leave whenever she wishes."

The girl still rocked in place, hands on her thighs. She licked her recently kissed lips, as if anxious for another taste of Nevan.

"Bastard," I muttered under my breath.

"Lay down your weapon and let me explain."

I indicated Sandy with a jerk of my elbow. "She's hypnotized or enthralled or whatever. Release her."

"The enchantment will wear off in a moment."

My gaze boomeranged from Nevan to Sandy and back again. His arms fell limp at his sides. He looked away and gave a half-hearted shrug.

I sank to my knees beside Sandy. Setting my pistol on the ground, I grasped her shoulders and shook. Her pupils had returned to normal, but she kept mooning at Nevan.

"Wake up!" I jostled her again. "Snap out of it, Sandy."

Her eyelids fluttered. Her slack expression solidified. She touched a finger to her lips, surveying the surroundings, then rubbed her forehead. "Where am I?"

Nevan flinched when I glared at him. "Would you care to tell her how she got here?"

He slid back into a sitting position, his legs bent before him, and fiddled with a weed.

My face tightened, a sure sign I was frowning. "Will she remember any of this later?"

"No." He ripped the weed out of the earth, tossing it aside. "The enchantment ensures no memories of me remain in the mind of the…uh…"

"Victim?"

He murdered another weed, but crushed this one in his palm. "If you give her instructions, she will follow them with no recollection of any of this later."

"How convenient for you." At least I could spare Sandy the memory of being used, for whatever Nevan wanted from her. I snapped my fingers to get Sandy's attention. "Listen. You went for a walk and got lost, but found your way back to the main trail. Go back to your boyfriend and forget this ever happened."

Sandy nodded, chewing her lip. She pushed up onto her feet, shuffled around, and hiked back down the game trail. I grabbed my gun and started after her.

Nevan sprang up to seize my arm. "Where are you going?"

"To make sure Sandy gets back okay." I grated the words out between my grinding teeth. "Not that you give a damn."

"You've got the wrong impression of me." His fingers relented a bit. "Please, Lindsey, allow me to explain. This is my duty—"

"Screwing with a woman's head and kissing her while she's half-conscious? That's your job?" My skin crawled at the thought of what he might've done if I hadn't intervened. I threw my arms up to shed his hands. "When you have a crappy job, you quit."

"Have you resigned from yours?"

"I have no choice. I need the money." I backed away several steps. "Besides, I don't abuse vulnerable women for a living."

"Believe me, I have no choice either."

My hand ached. I realized I'd been gripping the gun tighter. Loosening my fingers, I stomped closer to Nevan, until I had to crane my neck back to glare at him. "My job may suck, but I don't do anything morally reprehensible."

He wiped my spittle from his chin. "I am bound to my duty, by magic. Skeiron, my king, forced me into a bargain from which there is no escape. He throttled back my powers to prevent me from disobeying him."

"What a fabulous excuse." I raised the derringer, muzzle aimed at the sky. "Stay away from Sandy—and me."

I spun away from him and stalked off down the trail. In what seemed like seconds but must've been a few minutes, at least, I broke out of the woods into the rock garden. Once in the parking lot, I paused to collect myself.

Good luck with that. Nevan's voice echoed in my mind, his words from earlier even more relevant. My dignity and self-control shredded the instant I found him with Sandy. Maybe he lured women to clearings all the time to hypnotize them into making out with him. Afterward, he probably lugged them off to a cave and shackled them to the wall so he could debase them in private. Whatever his motives, I refused to engage in his machinations anymore.

Across the parking lot, Sandy's boyfriend was helping her into the passenger seat of a Jeep Cherokee.

Nevan had *kissed* her.

I stomped to my car, a cherry-red Chevy Malibu parked at the periphery of the woods, just inside the gravel parking lot. I moved to unlock the door, only then realizing I didn't have my keys or purse. I'd left them in the shop, because my shift wasn't over yet.

A creature squawked.

My every muscle went rigid at the familiar cry. I scanned the sky for the source. Where in blazes had the noise come from? The hairs on the back of my neck lifted. I swung my head to the right, to a pine tree at the forest's edge. A raven perched on a low branch, its weight dragging the limb down to within feet of the ground. The fading sunlight glinted off the bird's black eyes. Its gaze bored into me, ripping a shiver through my body.

I tried to pry my attention from the raven, but I couldn't. Its eyes pinned me in place, freezing my will. The raven squawked again.

"Shoo," I said, unable to move my eyes, much less wave a hand at the beast.

The bird swooped down onto the roof of my car. It waddled toward me, its talons ticking on the roof. The bird approached so close it could've snapped my nose off with its beak if it wanted. Instead, the raven pitched its head left and right. Its beak popped open.

The creature screamed.

My ears rang. I stumbled backward, tripped, and plummeted onto my ass. I struck the ground hard and I choked back a cry.

Red flames exploded in the depths of the bird's eyes. It leaped onto my chest. Talons sank into my breasts. They would've punctured my flesh, if not for the barrier of my shirt and bra. I dug my fingers into the gravel, but my body ignored my commands to move. Gravelly sounds emerged from the raven's open mouth. My mind insisted they were words, scrambling to comprehend them. The noises coalesced into clipped syllables.

"Guardian—not—yours." Its talons penetrated deeper, pulling a gasp out of me. "Stay—away."

The bird launched off me with a thrust that forced the breath out of my lungs. The beast swooped low over me. Its wings scraped the crown of my head.

The raven blasted off into the sky, out of sight.

CHAPTER SIX

I STAGGERED BACK INTO THE ROCK SHOP A FEW MINUTES LATER, MY thoughts whirling, adrenaline heightening my senses and sharpening my paranoia. A bird assaulted me? Really? Pinpricks burned on my breasts where the raven scratched me. Today sucked like a vacuum-powered toilet.

The raven had spoken to me. Actual words. I had no clue what they meant, but I was certain the bird uttered them. A few years ago, I'd watched a documentary about ravens that explained how they could mimic human speech. The attack bird must've been mimicking…someone. Maybe the sinister guy in the shop. He talked about a guardian and issued a similar warning I didn't understand.

The guardian wasn't mine. Okay, whatever.

I dragged my feet, heading back behind the counter. The soles of my tennies scraped across the concrete. In my absence, the store had emptied. The huge fans stood silent, their blades motionless. The air hung stagnant and humid around me, redolent with the odor of human bodies on a hot day. I pushed a lock of damp hair away from my eyes, lodging it behind my ear.

An odd sensation wisped through me. Fiery, but with a frosty undercurrent and a low-voltage bite. *He's watching.*

I gnawed the inside of my cheek as I scanned the shop. Nevan was not observing me. Oh hell, maybe he was. A being who vanished at will might also possess the ability to go invisible. Then again, my stalker might be my favorite customer—Mr. Tall, Blond, and Menacing. He had delivered a vague threat. I slipped a hand under my shirt to fondle the derringer's grip.

"Porter!" Stan shouted from his office doorway. "Time to close up. Get a move on."

His gaze flicked down to my shirt, and his brow scrunched the tiniest bit. I'd retrieved my emergency scarf from the car, strategically positioning

it over the blood stains my raven pal caused. The bright floral print was a bit gaudy for my taste, but it distracted the eye from any stains peeking out from under the fabric.

Stan flapped a hand at the cash register. "Count 'er out."

Next time I changed careers, maybe I could choose a duty like Nevan's and kiss attractive men every day as my job. Switching from paralegal to rock peddler, via a string of temp jobs, wasn't a lateral career move. If I'd never moved to Texas, if I'd gone to grad school instead and stayed with my parents and brother then—No, I couldn't get lost in regrets and what-ifs.

By the time Stan and I finished closing the shop, and I settled into the driver's seat of my car, the odd sensation of being watched had dwindled. Sunset plunged the day into a deep twilight. I revved the engine, flooring the accelerator as I guided the car onto the highway. Two cars whizzed past in the other direction, but soon the night closed in around the car, severing me from the rest of humanity. I usually enjoyed the freedom of feeling like the last human on the planet. Tonight, the notion scraped my nerves.

The AC blasted crisp, dry air over me. The twilit sky descended into blackness sprinkled with stars. The headlights pierced the night to lay bare the road ahead as trees zipped past. The yellow line blurred.

Unseen currents of energy pulsated through the air, stirring the hairs on my arms. The scent of damp, virgin earth tantalized my senses. I clenched the steering wheel and fought against the excitement fluttering through me.

A shape materialized in the passenger seat.

I should've yelped or jumped, but I wasn't the least surprised. The disturbing realization prickled my nerves. I didn't bother looking at my newly arrived passenger. "I told you to stay away from me."

Nevan draped an arm across the back of my seat. I risked a quick sideways glance to spy his bronzed body a few feet away, then I nailed my gaze to the road. His fingertips trailed over the nape of my neck. My belly tightened, arcing delicious tension down between my legs. *Get a grip.* Though I tried to obey my own command, the itch deep under my skin begged to be scratched.

"You anticipated my arrival." He sounded far too certain of himself.

I considered lying, but it offered no advantage. "I felt something. Don't pretend to understand what."

"You felt me, naturally."

The words danced over my skin like fingertips. I cleared my throat. "What do you want?"

He leaned closer, his face inches from my cheek. "I want you, of course."

Numbness tingled over my scalp, down through my face, to paralyze my mouth. Oxygen, I needed oxygen. I swallowed. Bit my lip. My lungs refused to work, but I mentally yelled at the bastards until they drew in air spiced with his essence. When I'd regained mastery of my lips, I said, "Tell me why you're here. I told you to stay away."

In my peripheral vision, I couldn't help but notice his every move. His head slanted left and right, his gaze hot on my skin. A squadron of butterflies took flight in my stomach and fanned out into my chest.

"Have you eaten?" he asked. "You look a bit peaked."

I hadn't eaten since breakfast, but for darn sure I wouldn't tell him that. My stomach growled. *Traitor.* "I repeat, what do you want?"

"We need to talk, love."

"No." My hands tightened on the wheel. "We don't, *love.*"

A twinge of guilt pinched me at the sarcasm dripping from my voice on the last word. But dammit, if he called me "love" or "darling" one more time, after what he did to Sandy...

His tongue flitted over his bottom lip.

I fidgeted in my seat, unable to get enough clearance from him. The far side of the moon wouldn't have been enough. I threw a sideways glance at him. "I saw what you did."

"I don't understand what you're implying."

"You know damn well what I'm implying." I blustered a breath out my nose. "Sandy. She could barely speak, she was so out of it. You claimed you enchanted her, whatever that means. For all I know, you drugged her."

He pulled away, withdrawing his arm. "I've no need of drugging anyone. I may have whatever woman I choose, whenever I choose."

I bristled. "Great. Go pester one of those hordes of women who throw themselves at your feet. I'm not one of them."

"No, you are not."

The silken tone of his words slid over me like velvet on bare skin. "I am positively not interested in cavorting with a woodland lothario. Poof out of here immediately."

"Poof?" He lifted one eyebrow.

"Yeah." I slowed the Malibu for a curve before speeding up on the straightaway. Silhouettes of trees whizzed past, the headlights flashing over them. "Poof. As in disappear."

"Ahhh, I see." He adjusted his position with a sideways rock of his hips. I successfully resisted the urge to glance at his crotch. *Score one for me, ten thousand for him.* He sighed. "I will gladly poof away once we discuss what you witnessed earlier."

"I keep asking and you keep deflecting."

His gaze settled on me with physical weight. Crazy, but true. The intensity of his stare aroused certain parts of me and chilled others. I longed to look at him, to drown in those alien eyes, but I feared what I might find there.

Instead, I concentrated on the highway and locked my hands around the steering wheel. The headlights glanced off a road sign up ahead. Black let-

ters on the rounded, triangular sign declared this highway U.S. 41. The sign marked one mile from the rock shop. One mile closer to home. If a cheap little apartment with peeling wallpaper counted as home.

The Malibu raced toward the highway sign.

Nevan bolted upright. "Stop the car."

"Excuse me? Why on earth would I—"

"Stop the car!"

"I will not."

Nevan seized the steering wheel and yanked it to the right. The car fishtailed. It straightened out, veering straight toward the roadside ditch. I rammed my foot on the brake. The tires screamed, the car skidded and slammed to a stop. The force thrust me forward, my seatbelt tore into me, pain ricocheted through my shoulder and stomach. The car's bumper just missed the highway sign.

Nevan released the wheel. He grabbed my face in his hands, turning me toward him. My breaths huffed hard and fast, my mouth was agape. He ran one hand up my face to my forehead and back down again. "Are you hurt?"

"No." I shook free of his grasp. "What the hell were you thinking?"

"I…" Unidentifiable emotions, dark and intense, flickered across his features. He bowed his head, exhaled a long breath, and lifted his face. The tension eased out of his shoulders. His features relaxed into the familiar expression of serene confidence. He eased his arm across my seat's back. I folded my hands on my lap and his big, warm palm enveloped them. "I don't wish to talk while you're driving."

"Gah!" I threw my head back, bumping the headrest. "Are you kidding me? You nearly got us both killed. Brilliant plan, Romeo."

Lines creased his forehead. "Romeo?"

"You know, like Romeo and Juliet. The play. Shakespeare wrote it."

"I understand the cultural reference. I have visited playhouses." A hint of annoyance colored his tone, but it dispersed into the ether as he threaded his fingers between mine. "I'm asking why you called me Romeo. It didn't strike me as complimentary."

"I meant to call you Casanova."

"Unflattering as well, I gather. As is the term lothario, yes?"

I wrestled my hands out of his. The cool air erased the heat of his touch. "Do you always lurk in the woods hunting for women to seduce?"

"No, I lurk in the shop." He flattened two fingers over my lips to silence my objection. "And I had no intention of seducing the girl."

I batted his fingers away. "Why were you enchanting her? Assuming I believe in any of this nonsense."

"You do." He captured a lock of my hair and twirled it around his forefinger. A shadow seemed to enshroud him, weighing down his shoulders. "My duty requires me to seek out mortal women who possess a touch of the Unseen realm. I sensed the energy within her. The next step is a test, to determine if she is the one I'm tasked to find."

"I don't get it."

He combed his fingers through my hair over and over, clearly fascinated with the task. "One hundred years ago, a prophecy was issued. It told of a human female who would become the gatekeeper of the realms. This mortal is known as the Janusite."

"Janusite? Sounds like a disease."

His fingers skimmed up my neck and began to massage my nape. The headache stabbing pangs into my skull fled at his ministrations. It felt so good I almost moaned, but choked it back just in time. Score another one for me. *What exactly are you competing for, huh?*

I peeled my lids apart and shrugged his hands off. "Thank you, but I'm okay."

"You dislike accepting help of any kind, don't you?"

"None of your concern." I propped my elbow on the window frame and rested my head on my fist, my face aimed toward Nevan. "What is a Janusite?"

"The one I seek." His teasing smile elicited a tickle in my chest. "Janus was, in your world, the Roman god of doorways and transitions, beginnings and endings. Have you ever seen a Janus coin?"

"A picture of one, yes." I scratched behind my ear. I could at least get rid of this tickle, if not the strange one behind my ribs. "On the coins, Janus is shown with two faces looking in opposite directions. Sometimes, though, he was depicted with four faces, pointing to the four corners of the world—the cardinal directions. North, south, east, west. This represented his dominion over the whole world."

His hand on my nape went still. "Are you a scholar?"

"I'm a minimum-wage slave."

He looped a lock of my hair around his finger, lifted it to his face, and inhaled deeply. His eyelids drifted half shut.

I coughed—loudly.

His eyes sprang open and he released my hair. The lock unwound, falling to brush my neck. "Few mortals, aside from scholars, know so much about Janus."

"I like mythology." I yawned, shielding my open mouth with one hand. "You mentioned a test."

He spread his thumb and forefinger wide over his forehead. "Yes, the test. Once I detect a touch of the Unseen realm, I must determine if the energy I sense in the candidate is strong enough to warrant taking her to Skeiron."

"What is the Unseen realm?"

"The place I come from. A world of magic."

"The separate realm you mentioned earlier."

He nodded.

"And what does this test involve?" I worked my fingers under my shirt collar to pull it away from my skin. The air in the car seemed to have gotten warmer, though the AC still blasted away.

Nevan traced the glowing numbers on the dashboard clock with one finger. "The test is a kiss, which you already knew. Why does it bother you so?"

"Doesn't bother me. You can suck face with anyone you please." Heartburn simmered in my chest and I had the sudden urge to punch something. "When we first met, you claimed you sensed energy in me. But you didn't kiss me."

His head swiveled toward me. Those eyes flared hot. His lips curved into a slow smile. "Would ye like me to?"

"Would I like you to what?" I could be evasive too. *So there.*

Nevan edged closer. His hip brushed mine. He sneaked his arm over the back of my seat, the hollow of his shoulder too near my body. His voice smoldered like his eyes. "Would ye like me to kiss ye?"

"No." A part of me said yes, but I shut that slutty girl up quick.

"Don't be jealous, darlin'."

"I am *not* jealous." Was I? No, absolutely not.

His hand slid down the seat. His fingers lighted on my shoulder. "You are a feisty one. I can't for the life of me deduce why the sheriff called you an ice princess. Unless you're of royal blood and hail from a cold climate."

"I'm far from royal and I hail from nowhere."

Ice princess. Travis's words lashed my mind. I'd battled long and hard to earn that insult and my practiced restraint had rescued me more than once. Yet Nevan stripped it all away with two words—*hello there.* The ease with which he'd unraveled me made my stomach churn. Me off balance was exactly what he wanted. Therefore, I would not give it to him.

Not often, anyway.

I ratcheted my spine straight. "Why did you help me with Travis? The sheriff, I mean."

Nevan's smile crumbled. He gave a tiny shake of his head. "I don't know."

"What are you? I demand you explain yourself."

His face pinched. "Love to, but I can't."

"You already told me about the Janusite and your duty."

"That I did." He groaned, his gaze distant. "I oughtn't be here at all."

"Drop the cryptic bullshit." I nodded toward the highway sign. "Or I'm driving past that sign. You don't want me to do that, do you? It's why you freaked out when you saw it."

"Can't tell ye that either."

I shoved his arm off my seat. "I want answers. Pronto."

He stared at me for several seconds. His attention shivered powerful currents through me. Cool as fall air. Crisp as green grass. Strong as hurricane winds. I flattened my back against the door and hugged my shoulders.

His expression morphed into stone. "I must go."

"Wait. You have to tell me—"
I was speaking to empty air.

———

I TRUDGED INTO MY APARTMENT AND SLUNG MY PURSE OVER A COAT hook. The door clicked shut. The faint scent of burned toast wafted over me, a remnant of my scorched breakfast. The only thing I'd eaten today. Toast flambé, drowned in cinnamon and sugar.

The lights outside my door cast a wan glow through the windows. I flicked a switch on the wall to power on the floor lamp by the sofa. Its pinkish-white light soothed my nerves. I flopped onto the sofa, tossed my phone onto the table, and sank into its overstuffed cushions. A sigh whispered out of me as the padding cradled my throbbing head. I removed the holster and gun from inside my waistband, setting both on the table.

Finding, then losing, a dead body could really damage a girl's brain. Mine hurt like somebody stabbed a trio of red-hot pokers into the base of my skull. I shut my eyes and succumbed to the weariness. I should've dragged my butt into the bedroom before passing out, but my muscles vetoed that idea. I let my body go limp, my thoughts draining away into the oblivion of sleep.

The phone rang.

With a groan, I flailed a hand out to grab my cell phone from the table. My fingers knocked it off and the phone clattered to the floor. It rang again. *Ugh.* Without getting up, I bent over to fumble for the phone until my closed around it. Two more rings assaulted my tired ears before I lifted the phone and grumbled, "Hello."

"Lindsey, honey."

My mom's voice blared through the receiver, her cheer twanging every nerve in my head. I rubbed my eyes, yawning. "Hey, Mom."

"You sound tired. Have you eaten anything?"

Why did everyone keep asking me that? I must look, and sound, worse than I thought. The mere idea of hauling myself into the kitchen to reheat some leftovers made my limbs ache. "I'm okay. How are you guys?"

"We're fine. Your dad's meditating and Ash is reading his comics, but he wants to say hi. I need to talk to you first, though." Her voice got muffled as she, no doubt, held her hand over the phone while shooing my brother away. "Ash says he'll text you. Lindsey, I've got wonderful news."

"Mmm?" My eyelids drifted shut, beckoned by the allure of sleep, wonderful sleep.

"We're coming for a visit, sweetie. We'll be there Friday."

I bolted upright, punching my fingers into the cushion so deep my nails almost punctured the fabric. "The day after tomorrow? Oh, uh, it's not a good time for me."

"Why?" Mom's voice took on a suspicious, mother-knows-all tone. "Is something going on? You don't sound like yourself."

I found a dead body that poofed out of existence and met a Tarzan wannabe who poofed into my car and nearly crashed us both into a tree. Other than that, I'm peachy.

My mind flashed back to this morning, in the woods, when Nevan cornered me against a tree, his vortex eyes blazing. I envisioned his sculpted chest, his broad shoulders, the loincloth draped around his hips, and those luscious lips tantalizingly close to mine. Tarzan wannabe? No, not him. He was my UFO—an unidentified flirtatious object.

"Lindsey? Are you still there?"

Mom's voice shattered my fantasy. "Yeah, I'm here. I've got to work Friday, all day and way late into the evening. Maybe you guys could stop by another time."

"Your aura is practically screaming at me through the phone. Something is not right, honey. We're coming Friday and that's that."

"How does an aura scream?"

"Don't get smart with me."

I gave myself a mental slap and rubbed my temples again, but I couldn't ward off the headache drumming through my brain. "I'm sorry, I didn't mean to be testy. It's just that this week's really, really not a good time."

"Eat a good dinner, get plenty of rest, and we'll see you soon."

"But Mom—"

"Good night, Lindsey."

What was the use? Parents did what they wanted. "Good night, Mom. Say hi to Dad and Ash for me."

We hung up and I tossed the phone onto the table. It skidded, thunking into the lamp's base. I leaned my head back, closed my eyes, and sighed. Just what I needed, a visit from the gurus of all things metaphysical. I'd never told them the truth about Calder, too ashamed to broach the subject, which was the reason I'd kept them at a distance—literally—for three years.

Static electricity sizzled over my skin, from toes to scalp.

I jerked my head up, glancing left and right. Goose bumps flared up on my arms. The sensation skittered up my spine, chilly at first, then warming into a curtain that enveloped me like a large, muscular body. Oh hell no, it couldn't be. I did not sense—

An electrical charge jolted me. I recognized this feeling. Inexplicable, undeniable, and unique. I sat forward. "Nevan?"

Silence answered me. Maybe I was insane after all.

Three crisp knocks rattled the front door.

I sprang to my feet but stared at the door, my feet glued to the frayed carpeting. Seconds elapsed, with nothing but my heartbeat to break the quiet.

Three more knocks, quick and precise, resounded through the door.

I sucked on my upper lip, then freed it with a smacking sound. My intuition—a faculty I'd long ignored, and worse, scoffed at—told me the identity of the person on the other side of the door. But it couldn't be. I mean, he'd zipped off to who-knew-where to escape my questions.

Another surge of electricity zinged through me. Hell with it. I marched to the door and yanked it open.

Nevan smiled that sensual smile, the one my body lapped up like an alcoholic swigging booze. He wore nothing but the loincloth. The interplay of shadow and light accentuated every hard line of his body. My breaths grew shallower, the air thicker, and my breasts heaved up with each intake of air. He caught sight of them and wet his lips. I fought my every impulse, because I'd learned the hard way impulses led to bad, bad things. At last, I peeled my gaze away from his body.

That's when I noticed the wooden tray he balanced on one palm, waiter style. The tray held a plate and two small bowls, each shielded by a half-dome lid. He gestured at the tray. "May I come in? I've brought you sustenance."

He offered me food, but his tone promised so much more. My mouth watered. "Not hungry."

Somewhere between lashing out at him after witnessing his encounter with Sandy and experiencing the inexplicable rush of anticipating his arrival, my anger had reduced to a simmer. I kept flashing back to his shamed expression when he enchanted Sandy and his defeated tone when he explained his duty. Looking at him now, I couldn't stop the simmer from fading away. Maybe he was his king's pawn.

"You're pale." He brushed the backs of his fingers across my cheek. "You must eat. But if nothing else, please accept this food as recompense for my poor behavior in your car."

"Are you apologizing?"

His eyes burned into mine, suffusing me with a liquid heat. "In this world, I might express gratitude. But alas, I'm simply stating a fact. I frightened you and nearly caused you harm." He reached for my hand, but when his grazed mine, he pulled his hand away. "I've no wish to ever harm you."

A door slammed further down the concrete walkway. I leaned out the door to peer down the length of the second-floor walkway hemmed in by metal railing. A gray-haired woman toddled toward us, heading for the stairwell beside my apartment. Oh great. Mrs. Kantola, a busybody of the first order, was about to see me conversing with a half-naked man.

A flicker of movement made me glance at the parking lot below. I didn't see anything, though, and returned my attention to the problem at hand.

"Lindsey, dear, is that you?" My neighbor flapped a hand at me.

I waved back. "Have a good night, Mrs. Kantola."

Teeth gritted, I snagged Nevan's arm and towed him inside. The door clapped shut.

He raised one eyebrow. "Pleased to see me, are ye?"

"You can't walk around dressed like that." I pointed at the door. "If my neighbor had seen you, I'd be the subject of town gossip for days, maybe weeks."

"Why do you care what others think?"

"I don't." I ran a hand over my forehead, back and forth. "Maybe I do."

"Relax, love." He cupped my elbow and guided me to the sofa. "You're far too tense. Sit and eat. I created this meal just for you and I'm certain you'll feel much better once you've gotten some food into your belly." He patted my behind. "Sit."

I made a half-hearted attempt at a scowl, then gave in and collapsed onto the sofa. He set the tray on my lap. I pushed up out of my slouch, tipping forward to examine what he'd brought me.

Nevan plucked the lids off the plate and bowls. Steam curled up from the food, flooding my senses with heavenly aromas—spicy and sweet, with a hint of berries. My mouth watered again, for a very different reason this time. The plate seemed to hold a meat dish, though I didn't recognize it. One bowl contained leafy stuff reminiscent of spinach, though with an unusual golden tinge. In the second bowl, what resembled fruit overflowed from a flaky, pastry-like shell.

Head down, I peeked up at Nevan. "You cooked this?"

"I did."

"For me."

"Yes."

He lowered his body onto the sofa beside me, the cushion compressing under his weight. My cushion tilted slightly toward him. My cheek skirted his mouth. I bounced backward and the dishes slid across the tray.

He tapped my chin. "Eat, before your meal gets cold."

"You sound like my mother."

His finger glided up my jaw, his touch feather-light on my skin. His fingertip traced soft circles under my ear, teasing the lobe. Every inch of my flesh awakened to the sensations around me. The soft, but uneven, texture of the sofa cushions. The weight of the food tray. The heat of his skin.

Slanting toward me, he splayed his fingers over my cheek, the heel of his hand rough against the corner of my mouth.

I struggled to keep from turning my face into his palm. "What do you want from me?"

"*From* you? Nothing." The exhalations from his husky murmur stirred the gossamer hairs on my cheek. "*With* you...I'm uncertain."

"Why do you keep coming back? I said awful things and told you to stay away."

"I deserved your words."

"But why come back?"

"Can't explain it." He dragged his hand down my face. His fingers trailed over my skin, falling away one by one. "I sensed an energy in you, but it's nothing like the touch I seek out as part of my duty." He lingered close to me, a gap of inches between us. "That's why I neglected to kiss you. I've wanted to, believe me, but I can tell you aren't quite ready for me."

I stammered, but couldn't form coherent words. My breaths quickened. I moistened my lips, as if I might taste his withheld kiss.

His gaze roved over me. "There is an unusual power in you, buried deep. Have you not felt it?"

"All I feel is you." I slapped a hand over my mouth. My fingers muffled my voice. "Forget I said that."

His lips parted, then closed. He canted his head. "Do you mean you've sensed my approach, as you did in the car?"

My limbs refused to budge.

Nevan pried my fingers away from my mouth. "Lindsey—"

"Yes, okay, yes." I locked my hands over my midsection. "Happy now?"

His chuckle rippled through me with physical pleasure. He patted my knee. "Happier, yes. But I won't be fully satisfied until you eat."

"Only if you promise to explain a few things while I stuff my face."

He drew a cross over his heart with one finger. The lines bisected the scar. He raised his hand, palm out. "I swear it on my very existence."

A brilliant smile enlivened his features, lighting him up from the inside. A matching glow ignited inside me. In spite of myself, I relaxed into the sofa and dug into the meal he'd prepared specially for me. I discovered a fork and knife hidden under the plate's lip. The meat dish melted on my tongue, rife with exotic spices, and I moaned my appreciation.

Nevan tensed, his eyes narrowed on me.

"What?" I asked with food in my mouth. Good thing Mom wasn't here.

He swallowed visibly. "Your noises confound me."

"*Mmm-mm* means I like it." I forked a hunk of meat glistening with savory sauce.

"I see."

The faint growl in his voice made me glance up at him. A hint of white teeth gleamed behind his parted lips. I froze with the fork halfway to my mouth. "Stop looking at me that way."

"What way might that be?"

"Like you want to...uh..."

"Kiss you?" The pink tip of his tongue danced behind his teeth. "As I said, I won't do it until you're ready."

"I suppose you're going to decide when I'm ready."

His gaze tracked down to my throat and he pulled in a heavy breath. "Perhaps you are ready."

"There you go, making assumptions about me again."

"No assumptions." He nodded at my chest and his Adam's apple bobbed. "The way you're touching yourself speaks to the truth."

"Excuse me?" I glanced down—and froze. My right hand hovered over my breast, concealed by my blouse and scarf. My fingers feathered over my breast, stroking along the inner slope. The slight tickle of my own caress hadn't registered in my brain, overwhelmed by the tingles coursing up and down my body, triggered by Nevan's proximity. I jerked my hand, clamping it tight, but my wrist chafed my nipple.

"Take it easy, darlin'. I won't kiss ye." He bent closer still, his skin a hair's breadth from mine. "Not tonight."

My chest pumped out quick, shallow breaths and my body hummed with a need I refused to acknowledge. "Keep your lips away from mine, please."

"As you wish."

He ducked his head to mine, his lips a millimeter from my cheek, and blew a steamy current across my skin. He moved his mouth down my face, never making contact but eliciting hard shivers with every whisper of his breath across my flesh. A tiny noise burst out of me, a cross between a gasp and a moan, so soft I prayed he hadn't noticed. His muscles tightened, his shoulders bulged. As his lips approached the corner of my mouth, he exhaled a soft, erotic breath that unleashed a crushing need within me.

I tried to speak with authority, but it came out breathless. "What are you doing?"

"Keeping my lips away from yours." His breaths fanned across my cheek to my ear. I heard nothing except his exhalations and my own pulse throbbing in my ears. He brushed his mouth across my lobe. "Is this far enough?"

He nibbled my earlobe.

A memory blasted through my mind. Teeth biting down, tearing, nails scraping down my neck, fingers grasping my throat, a voice snarling in my ear. *You're mine forever, even beyond death.*

I slapped my palms on Nevan's chest and shoved him away. I shook my head with such violence my hair flapped around my face.

Eyes wide, face blanched, Nevan searched my gaze with his own. "What in the name of the stars is wrong?"

"I—" Words clogged my throat, trapped there. I squeezed my eyes shut to banish the memory to the recesses of my brain, where it belonged, before I looked at Nevan again.

He rubbed his hands on his thighs. His smile was bitter. "I pushed too far too soon. You may have noted my tendency toward taking liberties."

I was too shaken to appreciate his attempt at humor. Other men I'd known would've gotten angry if I physically ejected them from my personal space. Nevan seemed to understand.

Right. After knowing him for less than a day, he understood me. Juiced up by hormones, I willed my voice to stay calm. "It's not you. I have…bad memories."

He nodded slowly. "I'm beginning to appreciate that."

I cleared my throat. "You should go. I'm seriously damaged, which means you're wasting your moves on me."

"Nothing is wasted on you."

Slumping into the sofa, I closed my eyes. "You seem nice enough, in a strange way, but I met you this morning. I have no idea who or what you are."

"I'm Nevan." He tipped his chin up, pride evident in his voice. "And I'm a sylph."

I whipped my head sideways to stare at him. "A what?"

"Sylph. I believe your kind describes us as elemental spirits of the air."

I poked his chest. His firm flesh resisted the pressure of my finger. "You seem pretty solid to me, not at all airy."

"I am not made of air. I was forged from the earth and the air, but I'm as corporeal as you."

"Sure, that makes perfect sense."

His lips twisted in a half smile. "After everything you've seen today, how can you not believe in the Unseen realm? I am an elemental being from another world parallel to yours. A land of magic."

"Uh-huh." Maybe I just wasn't smart enough to get it. I felt dense as a steel brick right now.

"You've seen some of what I can do."

"Yeah." I closed my fist around the knot in my scarf. "You can change your appearance. How do I know this is the real you?"

"Because it is. You have to trust me, but I've come to realize you have trouble with such things. Since you first began working at the shop, I've seen you every day while I carry out my duties. I would never approach you in glamour. Never."

"You've been stalking me for three months?"

"No." He rubbed the back of his neck. "I saw you, in the course of my duties."

From what he'd said about his duty, and what I'd seen of it, I believed him. "Okay, you're not a stalker. But what's glamour?"

"An incantation to disguise my appearance." He touched a fingertip to my jaw. "I've never hidden myself from you."

"Yes you did. When I saw you with Sandy, you were an old man."

"Ah. That." He scratched his cheek. "Our encounter then was an accident. Besides, you recognized me. I would never intentionally deceive you."

I wanted to believe him. Though the reason why eluded me, the compulsion was strong.

His finger fell away from my face, his gaze diverted to the floor.

I took in the lines of his profile, then my attention drifted lower, sweeping down to the waist of his loincloth. I jerked my gaze up to his face. "Earlier today, a creepy guy turned up in the shop and he sort of threatened me. He had weird eyes a lot like yours. Do you know anything about him?"

Nevan snapped bolt upright. He grasped my shoulders. "This man, how did he threaten you?"

"Well, first he called me a tolerable specimen worth bedding once or twice." I wound the end of my scarf around my fingers. "Then he said the guardian is bound to him and I should remember that."

Nevan's fingers clamped harder around my arms. "What else?"

"I'm pretty sure he poofed away."

"He said nothing else?"

"Nope."

He let go and sagged against the sofa.

"You know this guy?" I asked.

"Skeiron."

A cold serpent wriggled down my spine. "Your king Skeiron?"

"Correct."

"I've never met him. He has no reason to bother me."

"Protecting the sanctity of the Unseen realm is reason enough for him."

I closed my eyes, my head drooping. Sylphs. Kings. Magic. My brain spun its wheels, unable to find traction in this new reality. I cracked my lids apart.

Nevan leaned forward, elbows on his thighs. "Interfering in the mortal world is forbidden. You are forbidden."

He infused the word forbidden with both bleakness and sensuality. I was forbidden. Until today, nobody ever cared enough to label me off limits. I rested my chin in my cupped hand, my fingers partly covering my mouth. "I don't understand any of this."

Nevan shoved a hand through his hair. "I cannot explain further, I'm sorry, wish I could. The risk is too grave now that Skeiron has discovered my interest in you."

I squinted at him and let my hands fall. "What do you mean the risk is too grave?"

"The danger to me, not you." He grazed a thumb across my lips. "Please forgive me. I should never have revealed myself, but when I saw you weeping over the death of a man you'd never known, I had to intervene." He rose to his feet with the fluid grace of water flowing over a boulder. "I must go."

"You haven't finished explaining."

He pecked a kiss on my forehead. "Sorry, love. I have duties to fulfill."

"More women to kiss, you mean." Why did I sound grumpy?

"Don't worry," Nevan said, eyes sparkling. "I'll be testing no more women."

"Won't you get in trouble for shirking your duty?"

"Perhaps." He nuzzled the top of my head. "But not immediately."

He stepped back and I sensed he was about to disappear. "Wait. I have more questions. What about the missing body—"

Nevan vanished.

I was left to cuddle up with my confusion.

CHAPTER SEVEN

THE SUN STABBED INTO MY EYES THROUGH MY LIDS. A HEADACHE raged behind my eyes and cold sweat chilled my chest. The remnants of a gut-wrenching nightmare receded, leaving behind impressions of blood and anguish and terror. I pulled in breath after breath until my heart slowed its rapid thumping.

Rubbing the sleep from my eyes, I dragged myself out of the bed. My raven-attack wounds burned when I moved and the satiny fabric of my nightie brushed across the deep scrapes and punctures. I chose my softest cotton bra, but it still chafed. After dressing, I got a bowl of cereal and sat cross-legged on the sofa munching on the whole wheat biscuits. The glaze of frosting didn't fool my taste buds. They longed for more of Nevan's sinfully succulent offerings.

Oh crap. I stopped mid chew. I'd eaten his food, without balking, without thinking. *Calm down, if it was poisoned, you'd be dead.* Sure, but what if the food was cursed or enchanted or whatever? I might be magically bound to do his bidding.

If that were true, why had he left last night? He would've stuck around to play with his new toy. Maybe…the food was just food. Which implied he cared about my well-being. Why else bring me dinner and insist I eat it? He kept saying he shouldn't have been here with me, he shouldn't have told me anything, and yet he came back.

Even supernatural men had a knack for confusing me.

I finished my breakfast and drove to the shop. This was Thursday, my day off, but I needed to check out the crime scene again. If Travis found out about this, he'd laugh at me and tell me there was no crime scene, then handcuff me for the hell of it. Big mystery why I couldn't stand him.

A man had died. I witnessed the result of the foul play. If the sheriff wouldn't investigate, I would.

Stan's Toyota was tucked behind the shop, in his private parking area. I stowed my Malibu in the far corner of the gravel lot, under a sprawling pine with sagging branches that shielded my car. Nobody liked to park there, so I wouldn't be taking up a space a tourist might want. The morning was relatively cool, considering the heatwave, but humidity made the air sticky on my skin.

As I slunk across the parking lot and through the rock garden, I heard the hollow metallic rattling of Stan opening up the big front doors. Upping my pace, I hurried down the trail through the woods. Sweat dribbled down my chest to sear my wounds. I stopped at the healing vortex and perched on one of the stone benches. I might've been delaying because the thought of the blood stain, and what it signified, shivered dread through me. When had I become a coward?

I dug a wadded-up tissue from my jeans pocket. Lifting the neck of my T-shirt with my thumb and forefinger, I dabbed at the sweat on my chest, careful to avoid my wounds. The antibiotic ointment I'd applied to them last night didn't seem to do much.

Warmth suffused my breasts where the raven had punctured me, spiraling out into the rest of my body. I gulped air and the warmth infused my lungs. I slapped my palms on the rock beneath me, overcome by a sudden wave of dizziness. The woods twirled around me, yet the sensation sweeping through my body soothed me. The dizziness abated with a suddenness that left me slumped on the bench, breathless.

My wounds no longer stung. I palpated my breasts but no pain ensued. I snagged the hem of my shirt and whipped the fabric up to expose my chest. An iron fist hardened in my gut, heavy and cold.

The wounds were gone. Healed, as if they'd never existed.

I sat motionless for a moment, staring into space. The healing vortex was real. Why that revelation hit me so hard, after everything I'd experienced in the past twenty-four hours, mystified me. I just couldn't acclimate to this new world, or rather, this new version of the same old world.

Wake up, you're on a mission, remember? Right. My investigative mission. With a cleansing exhalation, I pushed up off the bench and headed for the crime scene.

The blood stain came into view. My throat tightened and my step faltered, but I kept my footsteps on a trajectory for the crime scene. My brain superimposed a vision of the body over the vacant dirt plot punctuated by the dark stain. I knelt beside the blood. The dried puddle seemed smaller than yesterday, or else my memory inflated its original size.

Christ. A man had died here.

Scanning the area, I spotted no signs of a struggle. Yeah, like I was a forensics expert. I had to try. I tiptoed over to the railing along the pool at the base of the falls. Though I searched the ground for any clues, nothing popped out. None of the rocks near the railing bore any blood stains and the railing itself was intact. If the man had fallen and hit his head on the railing or the rocks, surely a sign would remain. There was nothing.

I returned to the site marked by dried blood. Here he'd lain—and here he'd vanished.

A strange, yet familiar, sensation fluttered through me. I shut my eyes, struggling to decide if I wanted him to appear or hoped he'd give up and go away.

"What are ye doing?"

Every single hair on my body rose at his deep voice, and my skin tingled as warmth flowed over my skin, soaking in down to my bones. I took a breath, let it out, and faced Nevan.

He stood several feet away, arms folded over his chest, broad shoulders relaxed, a faint smile on his lips. Water dripped from his powerful body, spattering the ground. His hair was dripping too, the wavy locks drenched but springing back with amazing virility. He shook his head, drops sprayed out, and in an instant every speck of water evaporated from his toned flesh and skimpy loincloth. Waves of silky hair, now dry, settled around his face.

Nevan drank in my appearance with a long, slow appraisal. His lips curved up at the corners and he stroked his tongue over them in a languid lick. The memory of his mouth on my earlobe careened through my thoughts. Last night, I'd freaked out at the contact, but today my skin flushed at the prospect of his slick tongue and soft lips teasing my skin.

I clasped the back of my neck with one hand, fingers knotting in my hair. "Hi."

"Hello, darlin'." He strode one pace toward me, consuming half the distance between us. "What are you doing here? I thought this was your day of rest."

"Yeah, this is my day off."

"Why are you here then?" His arms fell to his sides, slack, yet he inched ever nearer.

I scuffled backward. "Checking out the crime scene. If Travis won't investigate, I will."

"I shall aid you." He glanced at the blood stain and pursed his lips. "Don't expect we'll uncover meaningful evidence. Whatever stole the body clearly had the power to cover its tracks."

"How come you say 'whatever' and 'its'? This must be a person."

"You persist in assuming the universe is home to humans alone."

"And you."

"I am not the only sylph, or immortal being, populating the realms." He slanted his torso toward me, his body suddenly too close. My feet refused to budge, though I wanted to move away. I did want to, didn't I?

He captured a lock of my hair, threading it between his fingers. "This is your day of rest, a time for fun. Why waste it on a fruitless search for answers you'll reject?"

"This could be a mundane crime, no immortals involved." My brain did a U-turn back to his two comments about my day of rest. I pointed a finger at him. "How do you know this is my day off?"

"Well now, I—"

"Oh right. You've watched me for three months, but not in a creepy stalker way."

He managed to seem offended and amused at the same time.

"Porter!" Travis's bellow bounced off the trees and the sandstone cliff, rattling my eardrums. He'd skulked up behind me while I had my back turned to the trail, my attention trained on Nevan. Travis, in his sheriff uniform, stomped up to us. His lip curled when he glared at Nevan. "Thought my mind was playing tricks on me last night, but no. You actually prance around in that getup."

Last night? Fury rose hot in my chest and I slugged Travis's chest. "That was you last night. In the parking lot outside my apartment. You've been spying on me."

He grunted. "You're a suspect in a crime, Porter. It's called surveillance."

I planted my hands on my hips. "Yesterday you said there's no body, so there's no crime."

"Not talking about the alleged body you claim to have found." He rocked on his heels. His forefinger tapped the grip of the Sig Sauer holstered on his hip. "Told ya, I gotta protect the populace from the likes of you. George of the Jungle here better watch out." His gaze swiveled to Nevan. "She's a man-killer."

Though I tried to speak, my voice abandoned me.

"I'm watching you, Porter."

Travis stalked back down the trail toward the shop.

Nevan rotated his head sideways to monitor Travis's departing silhouette. When Travis disappeared around a bend in the trail, Nevan harrumphed. "Why does the sheriff persist in maligning you with such lies?"

Okay. Time for full disclosure. I shoved my hands in my jeans pockets. "It's not a lie. I am a man-killer."

Nevan's gaze snapped to mine. "Impossible."

"You don't know me." I wouldn't look away, no matter how much I longed to break the connection. I must make him understand. "I killed my fiancé, Calder. Travis's brother."

"No."

I stepped up to him, so close my breasts nudged his bare chest. Standing tall, I tilted my head back to zero in on his eyes. "I shot Calder six times in the chest and once between the eyes."

His head whipped back. His eyes widened, the colors flared and whorled. He shook his head.

"I did it, Nevan. I emptied a full clip into the man I thought I loved and I don't regret it." I flattened my palm on his chest, feeling his heart hammer beneath it. "Listen to Travis. I am no sweet, innocent girl. I'm a woman who killed an unarmed man, and in the same circumstances, I'd do it again without hesitation."

He gave a weak shake of his head.

"Believe it, Nevan. I'm a man-killer."

I turned my back on him and marched down the trail.

Stalking around the bend, I caught sight of the rock garden twenty feet ahead. A tear rolled down my cheek, hot on my skin. I wiped it away, my breaths hitching, and stared at the ground as my feet pounded out a hard rhythm on the earth. What was wrong with me? So what if I told Nevan about my past—a part of it anyway. That gave me no reason to feel...exposed. Raw. Humiliated.

I tripped over my own toes, flailing forward in an uncontrolled zigzag. With a little hop and a grunted curse, I regained my balance.

"Best take it easy, love."

My stomach fluttered. I halted and swung my head up, a breath caught in my throat.

Nevan lounged upright against a tree, ankles crossed. One arm hung slack, while the other rested on his thigh. He studied me with an intensity that belied his casual demeanor. "I'd prefer ye don't make a habit of tripping and falling."

"I didn't fall."

He pushed away from the tree and strode closer, consuming the distance between us, stopping an arm's length away. A repressed smile tugged at his lips. "Congratulations. Ye managed not to crack your lovely skull, and without any assistance from me."

I grasped my shoulder with the opposite hand, my arm a diagonal bar across my torso, as if that might deter him from coming closer. "Did you not hear me before? I'm a man-killer."

He moved in, his breaths ghosting over my face, teasing me with enticing scents I couldn't identify. "Fortunately for us both, I am not a man."

"Would six shots to the head kill you?"

"No." His fingertips trailed down my arm. I sucked my lips between my teeth, overwhelmed by the pleasure of his caress as he danced his fingers back up my skin. "Bullets in my brain might slow me down a bit, but I would heal."

"Good to know."

He drew lazy circles on my skin, with his fingertips barely touching me. "Are ye plotting to murder me?"

"If I said yes, would you leave me alone?"

"Do ye truly wish me to?"

His husky tone, and the delicate stimulation of his fingertips, drove out rational thought. Slick heat pooled between my thighs and I felt light, as if I might float away—yet rooted to the ground, helpless to move. "Why are you here? I'm a killer and I'm annoying. You've said you shouldn't be with me anyway, so go. Save yourself a lot of trouble."

"You are neither trouble nor annoying. If you killed a man, I'm certain it was self-defense." His hand glided up, over my shoulder to my throat, and higher, to cup my cheek in his smooth palm. "You are intelligent, brave, beautiful, highly sensual, and thoroughly bewitching."

"Oh. Is that all."

I angled my face away, but he hooked a finger under my chin to coax me into meeting his gaze. He stroked his thumb over my bottom lip, back and forth, back and forth. My legs got wobbly and I locked them for stability, though my inability to break eye contact ensured my legs wouldn't firm up anytime soon. God, those eyes. They cast some kind of spell over me, twirling my thoughts until they scattered out into infinity. Even spellbound, I couldn't manage to keep my big mouth shut.

"Have you fulfilled your duty for the day?" I asked, with no desire at all to know. The image of Nevan's lips on Sandy's plagued me and I didn't need more unwanted visions. Especially since they made my gut twist and my chest ache and my fingers curl in preparation for clenching into fists.

Christ. Maybe I *was* jealous.

Nevan gave a small shake of his head. "I cannot."

"I thought you were magically bound to hunt down special women and shove your tongue down their throats."

He flinched. "They are not special. You are."

A bizarre little thrill shivered through me. I was special. Shouldn't care. *Didn't* care. But right then a memory exploded in my mind of Nevan pressing his lips to Sandy's, and I gritted my teeth hard enough to cause pain. *Rats*. I did care, more than I wanted to, more than reason permitted.

"The bargain with Skeiron," he said, "requires me to search for the Janusite. It does not require me to unleash my ethereal senses every time I encounter a mortal woman."

"I don't understand. If you hate your job, why did you agree to the bargain? And why do you stick to it, instead of saying 'to hell with this stupid agreement'?"

He slipped his hand into mine, twining our fingers. It felt so good I let my fingers wrap around his hand, and his sealed around mine in response. "Magic is new to you, love. You've no conception of the power a bargain wields."

My gaze became glued to his mouth, those luxurious lips, my mind fixated on the notion of what it would feel like to crush my mouth to his and take the flavor of him into me.

"Your lips are awfully close to mine," he purred, his eyes hooded and glowing with unfurling tongues of flame.

I blinked. Holy crap. My mouth was millimeters from his, my lips were parted, and—oh God. I was licking my lips with slow strokes. Somewhere in the middle of my fevered imaginings, I'd leaned toward him, risen onto my tiptoes, and gotten into position to smack one on him.

Hopping back a step, I shoved my hands in my jeans pockets, shoulders hunched. "Sorry about that." I bristled at his half smirk and hastened to add, "Not like I was about to kiss you or anything."

"Why do your desires frighten you?"

No, I wouldn't answer that question, so I chewed the inside of my cheek. "Have you done something to me? Like what you did to Sandy?"

"If you believe I would do such a thing to you, why are you still here?"

"Keep telling you to go away."

"And yet, you could walk down this trail and leave me behind."

Oh. Yeah, I probably could do that. "Won't you just pop up in front of me again?"

"Not this time." He lifted my hand and rubbed his thumb across my knuckles. "You were upset before, when you ordered me to leave you. This time, if you tell me to go, I will. Do you wish me to leave?"

I stared at his bowed head. His shoulders had sagged, his hold on my hand had weakened. *Aw hell.* "No. I don't want you to go."

His head came up. A faint smile lifted the corners of his mouth. His expression was almost…grateful.

With my hand still in his, I cleared my throat. "You, uh, could walk me back to the shop. If you want."

The smile brightened and he straightened. "I will accompany you."

He led me down the path at a leisurely pace, our hands linked. As we strolled toward the rock garden, he spoke, hesitantly at first. "Perhaps in your world it's possible to walk away from an agreement such as mine with Skeiron. But in the Unseen realm, a bargain is sealed by magic. If I fail to fulfill my portion of the bargain, Skeiron may mete out whatever punishment he sees fit, even destroy me."

"Destroy? You mean kill?"

"Worse. To destroy an immortal means to tear him apart at the most basic level—what I believe mortals call molecules—and scatter his essence and powers to the Four Winds. That is what the other gods did to Janus, because they feared his ever-growing power. It took all their combined magics to eradicate him."

I strengthened my grip on his hand. "In my world, we have a saying about a fate worse than death. Sounds like you immortals made it literal."

"We have."

At the edge of the rock garden, he stopped and turned toward me, blocking my view of the garden and the shop beyond. The sun lit him from behind with a halo effect, his body outlined in a golden glow. Though numerous birds twittered in the trees, a dove's voice rose above the rest, its mournful call tugging at my soul.

"Nevan, why would you make this awful bargain? What did Skeiron promise you in return for doing his bidding?"

The breeze tousled his hair, but he ignored the strands blown into his face. "The king agreed to spare his daughter's life."

"What's that got to do with you?"

Though his arms hung at his sides, his shoulders were tensed and his fingers worked as if untying invisible knots. His gaze drifted far away from me, from this place, this time. "I engaged in a dalliance with Skeiron's daughter."

"Oh." I stuffed my hands in my jeans pockets, refusing to think about him cavorting with yet another female.

When he shuffled around, angled sideways to me with his profile illuminated by soft sunshine, the pain in his eyes evaporated my jealousy. He scrubbed a hand across his mouth. "It was…a rather long dalliance involving numerous liaisons. When Skeiron found out, he commanded us to marry but she refused. Skeiron grew quite angry and threatened her life."

"He threatened to kill his own daughter? What a sweetheart." My dad was a good man who worked long hours to make sure we had everything we needed. I couldn't envision any circumstance in which he'd murder me. Nevan's world really was another realm of existence, alien in every way.

Alien in almost every way. He seemed more human than an awful lot of the people from my world.

"It was his right," Nevan said. "Though I did not love his daughter and had no more wish to marry her than she did me, I could never allow harm to come to her. I pleaded with Skeiron to spare her, vowed to accept any bargain in exchange for her life. He'd learned I've indulged in many amorous encounters with other females, even during my acquaintance with his daughter."

"Ouch. That must've seriously ticked him off."

"I was a cad in those days, had been for thousands of years. I deserved to be punished, but his daughter did not." Nevan's chin dropped to his chest, his hair flopping down in a curtain to shield his eyes. "Skeiron agreed to a bargain, but his price for her life was my enslavement. My rank as a general in his army was stripped and I became guardian of the falls, bound to this precise location, never to wander free again."

For a roving Casanova to be tied down in a near-literal sense must've been like, well…castration, I supposed. *Double ouch.* "And you were coerced into hunting for the Janusite."

"Yes." He absently touched the scar on his chest. "To seal the bargain, he imprecated my heart."

"Imprecate?"

"Cursed it. Cursed me to have no heart, no feelings, nothing but a yawning abyss in my soul." Nevan picked at the scar, but his gaze had retreated into the past. "To complete the imprecation, he cut my flesh."

"But you do feel."

"Only since I saw you." His fingers on the scar stilled. "Perhaps the energy I sensed in you diluted the curse."

What could I say to that? I couldn't have anything to do with it. Maybe Skeiron lied about cursing him, but I doubted he'd accept the suggestion. Thanks to his guilt over Skeiron's daughter, he'd become too invested in believing he couldn't feel.

"How long ago did you strike this ass-backwards bargain?" I couldn't help the disgust in my voice. Forcing a man to enchant and kiss innocent women, day after day, was repellent—even for a man who'd thoroughly enjoyed the company of women before the bargain.

Though I despised the deal he'd been forced into, I did not despise Nevan, in spite of his past and his current—er, occupation. I loathed Skeiron. Kill his own daughter? Enslave and curse Nevan? If I ever crossed paths with the king of the sylphs again, I'd empty my derringer's clip into the bastard's head and see how long it took for him to heal. Then I'd do it all over again.

A question popped to mind, one I was fairly certain I didn't want answered. But sometimes a girl has to ask anyway. "What will Skeiron do the Janusite if you find her?"

"I take the Janusite to him. My duty ends there and I am not privy to the remainder of his plan."

Rustling erupted overhead. A raven cackled and cawed.

I zeroed in on the frenetic motion partway up the trunk of an aspen tree. Leaves tumbled down from the branches. The raven flapped its wings in a tight arc, its glistening eyes trained on me.

Nevan shoved me behind him. His every muscle was tight, his body poised for battle. Head thrown back, he shouted at the bird in an alien language.

The raven laughed. Swear to God, it did.

With a final cackle, the bird launched into the heavens. Branches flapped and leaves showered down on us.

Nevan spun around to grasp my upper arms. The intensity of his expression, rife with fury and anguish, made my chest constrict as if he'd clamped iron bars around my ribs. He gave me a gentle shake. "Have you seen a raven before?"

I folded my arms over my belly. "Yeah. So what?"

He shut his eyes for a heartbeat. "Has the raven threatened you in any way?"

"I guess. If you call slamming me to the ground and digging his talons into me a threat. He told me the guardian isn't mine, the same thing Skeiron said." Comprehension blew the breath out of my lungs. "The bird meant you."

Nevan nodded.

"You are the guardian of the falls." I shook my head. "Why does Skeiron's pet raven—and I'm guessing it's more than a nasty bird—why does it care if I hang out with you?"

"I've no time to explain. I must go, if I'm to catch him."

"Him? Do you mean the b—"

Nevan vanished.

With no idea what else to do, I went home and scoured the Internet for information about sylphs and magical bargains, staring at my computer screen until my eyes burned and head ached. Cyberspace gave up nothing more intriguing than myths and legends, interspersed with New Age-y theories. None of it enlightened me. None of it clued me in on the motivations of a real-life sylph king. Or the motivations of a one sexy, mysterious male in a loincloth.

At sunset, I carted my trash bags down to the dumpster in the parking lot. The shadow of a skyborne object flashed across the pavement. I bent my head back to study the heavens, where a bald eagle sailed off into the distance. Not my raven friend after all. The sun sank lower every minute, though, heralding the darkness and dangers of the night. Of course, it wasn't like I could see my enemies coming in the daytime either.

I rubbed my arms in a futile effort to ward off a chill originating from deep inside. Kings and bargains and angry ravens. All those things would haunt my nightmares tonight.

CHAPTER EIGHT

THE NEXT MORNING, TRAVIS WAS WAITING FOR ME WHEN I ARRIVED at the shop. Ambushing me when I climbed out of my car, he penned me between his body and the open driver's door.

I hugged my purse to my belly. "What do you want?"

"Answers."

"You have no evidence I've done anything. This is verging on harassment."

Travis, his eyes flinty, slapped a hand on the roof of my car. "Dammit, Lindsey, I've got reasons to be suspicious of you. Not only did I catch you fooling around with some weirdo, but I also couldn't verify your report of a dead body."

Strange that his first thought had been about Nevan, aka "some weirdo." Why did Travis give a hoot about my relationship with Nevan? Not that I had a relationship with him. Hell, I didn't know what Nevan and I were to each other.

"You don't get to clam up on me, Porter." Travis grabbed my arm. "I gotta explain this crap to the state police."

My scalp prickled with a cold realization. "Something happened."

"A downstater is missing."

"So?"

"The last time his friends saw him, he was walking into this shop. He wanted to see the vortex, but his pals thought it was hokum. They dropped him off here and went over to the museum to check out the big honking steam hoist. Their words, not mine. Anyhow, they haven't seen him since. They reported his disappearance to the state police." He let go of my arm, backing up a couple paces. "Guess they don't trust us yokels. Point is, the fella they're looking for matches your description of the alleged corpse."

"I told you there was a dead guy."

"Yeah, I know." His gaze snapped to the surveillance camera behind me, mounted on the shop's exterior wall. "Stan emailed me the footage from the security camera. I know you had an altercation with the alleged victim."

"The creep was shoplifting."

"Your altercation looked pretty hostile."

I slammed the car door. "What are you hinting at?"

He lodged his hands on his hips, adjusting his belt and the gun holstered on it. "I have to search your car."

"What? Why?""

"Got an anonymous tip." He glanced away, working his shoulders up and down. "You're a person of interest in the case. And I got a warrant."

He plucked a folded sheet of paper from his shirt pocket and thrust it at me. I snatched up the paper. A sick feeling in my stomach, I unfolded the sheet and skimmed the text. Yep, a search warrant.

"It's a routine search," he said, his tone conciliatory. "You've got nothing to worry about, unless you're hiding a body in your trunk."

A cloud scudded in front of the sun. The heat of the sun abandoned me, supplanted by a frigid foreboding. Wind blustered over us, lashing my hair into my face. Behind the rushing of air, I swore I heard a faint cackling, strangely reminiscent of the cry of a jungle creature. Probably a barred owl. They made weird, monkey-like noises.

"Let's check your car," Travis said, "and go from there."

The empathy in his voice disturbed me more than I would've expected. This man despised me, had for years, a fact he'd proved two days ago with his hostile interrogation.

His search began with the car's interior, which he pawed through without expression or comment. "Pop the trunk for me. Please."

I reached through the open window and punched a button. The trunk clicked and floated open a few inches. Travis shoved it up the rest of the way.

His expression blanked. His eyes widened for a second, until his cop demeanor regained its hold.

I took a halting step toward him. "What is it?"

He backed away from the trunk, his gaze glued to whatever lurked inside it.

I couldn't breathe. Every instinct warned me not to look, but I had to know. Trotting forward, I whirled toward the trunk. *No, no, no.*

There, swaddled in a blanket from my bedroom, lay a human body.

Red hair. Pale skin. Green eyes gaping. The dead man from the woods. In my trunk.

Travis pulled out his handcuffs and moved toward me.

I bolted for the woods, blasting through the rock garden, careening around concrete statuary. Gravel crunched under my feet. The thorns of wild rose bushes nicked my arms and hands, but I ignored the stinging, intent on one goal. Stay out of jail. But how?

Nevan.

Only he could help me. Despite the quivery sensation in my gut at the idea of trusting a man—any man—with my safety, I recognized I needed him right now. Travis would arrest me. He'd have no choice. Who would believe my story? Nobody. I was the ice princess, a liar, the ruthless and crazy girl who fabricated stories.

I crashed through a hydrangea. White petals sprayed up around me. A faint perfume teased my senses, but it was whisked away on the wind kicked up by my flight. I punched through more bushes, leaping onto the dirt trail that led to the falls.

"Lindsey, stop!"

Travis shouted from far behind me. The crack of his footfalls on the gravel of the rock garden told me he'd catch up soon. Too soon.

I pumped my legs faster. I'd told the truth, always, yet none of it mattered. After what happened with Calder, no one would trust a word I said. Except Nevan.

A raven squawked overhead, the sound registering dimly in my panicked brain.

The raven swooped low in front of me. Its wings thwap-thwap-thwapped. Feathers scraped my face an instant before the bird rocketed up, out of sight.

I veered toward the sound of the thundering falls. My thighs burned, my chest ached, grit stuck in my eyes, water splattered my face. I tried to stop, skidded, and toppled over backward. My butt hit the ground with a splat. I gasped as pain shot through my tailbone.

Behind me, twigs snapped. Boots clomped. Voices hollered.

They'd catch me. I had nowhere to run.

Scrambling to my feet, I whirled in a circle. "Nevan!"

What kind of witless damsel in distress had I turned into? Screaming his name again and again, praying for him to appear and rescue me.

Boots clomping. Branches snapping. Water rumbling.

No Nevan. No escape.

I fell to my knees on the grass, my head sagging forward. Scents tantalized me. Sweat, grass, damp earth—and the sweet, sharp aroma of an approaching thunderstorm.

My head sprang up. Earth. Thunderstorms.

Foliage rustled. Footfalls pounded. Travis and his cohorts were seconds away.

A familiar sensation rippled through me. *He's coming.*

Relief and joy tumbled through me like a landslide. I leaped up and spun toward the falls.

A raven slammed into my chest. The full weight of its body, propelled by the kinetic energy of its flight, combined to flip me off my feet. I smacked into the ground flat on my back, my feet in the air. Lights exploded in my vision as pain ricocheted through my body.

The bird squatted on my chest and thrashed its head, its razor-sharp beak slicing my cheek, igniting searing streaks of pain. The raven's talons sank into my shoulders.

A figure reared up behind the bird, casting a shadow over me and my avian attacker.

Nevan latched onto the raven with one hand and pitched it aside. A thump resounded somewhere to the left. The raven must've hit a tree.

My savior knelt beside me, his face pinched, body stiff, eyes scanning up and down my body as he assessed my condition. He slid his hands into my hair to probe my scalp with unexpected gentleness, then bent close to peer into my eyes. His body relaxed on a long sigh and he raked a hand through his hair, but his expression remained tense.

Nevan slipped an arm under my back to raise me into a sitting position. Pain pulsed in my skull and I groaned. Nevan braced me against his body, cradling my face in one palm. "Are ye hurt, love?"

"No." I slurred the syllable a bit, but after a brief pause, I managed a steadier tone. "I saw stars for a minute, but I'm okay."

A flapping noise pulled my attention to the area past my feet.

The raven squatted there, its beak ajar, wings elevated and spread. The creature's black eyes darted up and down, left and right, as if measuring me up.

I huddled closer to Nevan. He folded an arm around my shoulders.

The bird's body glimmered and blurred, liquefying into an oily mass that hovered in the air. Ribbons of prismatic blue unfurled and writhed within the mass, as it swelled and lengthened into an elongated blob taller than Nevan at his full height. With a snap of electricity and a burst of sparks, the roiling mass coalesced into a humanlike being with male attributes.

The thing rolled his shoulders back, tightening his pitch-dark flesh and flexing his gargantuan shoulders. Thick sinews corded his torso and arms. Nevan boasted an impressive physique, but this man—or bird-man, or whatever—dominated my view with his mountain of muscles, devoid of any cellulite. His skin, from his bald head down to his bare feet, glistened with an iridescent blue sheen. His biceps were thicker than my head.

Nevan rose, though he stuck close to me. His voice seethed when he said, "Brennus."

The raven-man smiled. His lips peeled away from white teeth, each tapered to a blunt point. No amusement emanated from him, but rather his smile conveyed a menace that chilled me down to the deepest atoms of my being.

"Guardian," Brennus said, his voice as deep and dark as his fathomless eyes. "You act against your duty, and Skeiron will know of this. Inciting his wrath is unwise."

Nevan stalked toward Brennus. Hands balled into hard fists, his jaw tight enough to pulverize steel, he incinerated the raven-man with a glare so hot I swore it singed my skin. "If I rip your head from your body, you filthy shapeshifter, you won't have the chance to tell Skeiron."

Brennus laughed. Without mirth. Without pity. He sniggered like a demigod certain of his supremacy over all foes.

It was the most terrifying sound I'd ever heard.

Nevan clamped a hand around Brennus's throat and hurled him across the clearing. The monstrous raven-man whacked into a birch tree. The trunk shivered. A wide fissure splintered the trunk from the ground straight up to the lowest branch.

Brennus surged to his feet and took a single step toward me.

I dug my fingers into the damp earth, as if I might anchor myself there against the shapeshifter's assault.

The raven-man extended his arms to the sides and tipped his head left and right. The shivering branches of the birch tree cast undulating speckles of sunlight on Brennus's skin, sparking on the blue streaks in his flesh. "My master also wants your mortal whore and I am forced to obey his will. As you must obey your king."

Nevan stood a dozen feet from the raven-man, his stance wide. "I perform my duty. That is all Skeiron need know."

I stomped past Nevan to halt between the two supernatural beings. "Jesus, even immortal men have pissing contests. Since this conversation clearly involves me, how about including me in it?"

Brennus speared me with his jet-black gaze, and for a frozen second I wished I could reel my words back into my mouth. Until he spoke again.

"Guardian," he snarled, "silence your female before I do."

I stamped my foot. "Talk to the female, asshole. I'm not deaf."

Nevan grasped my shoulders from behind and whispered, "Allow me to handle this."

Brennus stretched out his fingers. The sunlight glanced off his wickedly sharp nails.

I gulped. Nodded. Sidled around Nevan so his body shielded me. Even I understood when to retreat.

Brennus let his arms fall to his side. "Beware, guardian. Protecting the female may bring about your own destruction. She will be his in either case."

Every muscle in Nevan's body had gone taut, sculpting him into a bronzed statue more beautiful than Michelangelo's David and more imposing than any Greek god. He squared his shoulders and met Brennus's cold gaze head-on.

Despite eclipsing him by more than two feet, Brennus paled next to the sylph. Even the raven-man's Himalayan Mountains of muscle could not compete with the awe-inspiring presence and raw sensuality of Nevan in his full glory.

And God, was he magnificent. Anger molded him into a spectacle straight out of ancient legends.

"Leave," Nevan said. "If any harm comes to this female, I will unleash my wrath upon you. Do you recall the power of my wrath, Brennus?"

The raven-man shuffled backward.

Hell, I would've too if Nevan had aimed his threat in my direction. Everything about him, from his stance to the seething undertone of his voice, screamed danger. Somehow, though, his anger didn't frighten me half as much as Calder's had, when he'd morphed from nice guy to demon incarnate.

Brennus turned his hands palm up, raising them to shoulder height. "These are not my commands, guardian. Heed them or do not, it makes no difference to me."

Nevan peeled his lips away from his clenched teeth. "Leave."

The raven-man shimmered and dissolved, his mass shrinking into a blob the size of a raven. Within a heartbeat, the figure solidified into a bird. Brennus took off into the sky.

Nevan turned to me, and the second our eyes met, his fiery tension was doused. His expression, once forged from wrought-iron, softened. I softened too, overcome with a need to throw my arms around him and kiss him until we were both mindless. I'd dived headfirst into romance with a deadly man once before, though, and I couldn't do it again.

"Can you explain to me," I asked, "what that insane conversation was all about?"

"I believe Brennus was threatening you as a means to control me. He is Skeiron's assassin and spy. Why he would claim Skeiron wants you, or for what reason that might be true, I cannot say."

"I see." Didn't really, but with the confrontation over, the electrical surge of adrenaline that had bolstered me snuffed out. I let my head fall onto his chest.

He smoothed my hair away from my face. "It's all right."

"No." I tilted my head up to stare at him. "It's not all right. A scary bird-man called me a whore and threatened to hand me over to an even scarier guy. All right is a distant planet and I don't have a rocket to take me there."

"Since I am from another world, you may consider me your distant planet." He splayed his fingers over my shoulder, gliding them down to my elbow. "And you have already touched down."

Oh, the idea sounded so good I wanted to melt into him. As badly as I longed to seek solace in him, I couldn't. "This is really bad, isn't it?"

"Yes."

I moved away from him. "I'm glad you don't feel the need to sugarcoat things. It's awfully comforting."

He narrowed his eyes. "What would you have me do, lie?"

"Of course not." I kicked the dirt with my toe and watched a little clod fly up. "Don't know what I want. Supernatural threats make me irrational. You'd think I'd be used to it by now, but no."

He took hold of my chin with a warm, strong hand, compelling me to look up at him. "Lindsey, has someone else threatened you? Someone besides Brennus or Skeiron?"

"Not lately."

His face went as taciturn and implacable as stone, though a muscle in his jaw ticked. "Tell me when. And who."

A command, not a request.

His hand still gripped my chin. I shied away from his touch, backing up another pace. "I don't want to talk about it."

Fingers twitching, he blew a breath out his nose.

The memory of Brennus's attack reeled through me. His beak piercing my cheek. His talons knifing into my shoulders. I yanked up my T-shirt to check for wounds, exposing the low-cut bra that shielded my breasts. The raven's talons hadn't broken the skin.

Nevan averted his eyes and winced.

"You're embarrassed? Seriously?" I rolled my eyes. "Nibbling my ear is okay, but one glimpse of my bra and you're humiliated."

He cleared his throat. "I am not humiliated. I'm simply trying to…respect your privacy."

"Whatever you say." I dropped my shirt and it fluttered down to cover me again. I glanced around the clearing, where the evidence of the Brennus tumult marked the ground and trees. The pounding of approaching men had silenced. "Wait a minute. The cops were coming for me and they were almost here."

"I made them believe you'd run the other way."

"You—How?"

"Magic, naturally." He strode toward me. "However, my illusions rarely last long. The fae from whom I acquired the spell refused to give it endurance."

"Oh. Sure. I get it." In a warped reality where magic made perfect sense, I would've gotten it. Confined to my world, I suffered from a pressure headache triggered by thinking about this insanity for too long.

"We must go." Nevan proffered a hand. "Well, darlin'? I haven't got all day. Even a sylph has work to do."

"Porter!"

Travis's voice bellowed through the woods. He burst out of the trees and stopped twenty feet away, breathing hard, his face red from exertion. "Why the hell'd you run?"

"You were going to arrest me. I can't go through that again. I won't."

Between huffing breaths, Travis said, "I wouldn't do that."

"You took out your handcuffs."

"Force of habit. I wouldn't arrest you."

"But you'll haul me in for questioning."

"Had to, and I kinda thought—" He shifted his weight from one foot to the other and back again, while his fingers plucked at the strap on his gun holster. "Never mind. I'm sorry."

I fumbled for a response but came up empty.

A shuffling noise jerked me out of my confusion. Nevan traipsed around me, planting himself between me and Travis, who leaned sideways to keep an eye on me. Every couple seconds, he'd shoot a dagger glare at Nevan, but the sylph ignored it.

Nevan, shoulders back and head held high, gazed down on us mere mortals with austere confidence. I was struck once again by the power he exuded, his aura of otherness, beautiful and yet so far beyond my reach.

Realizing with a start Travis had spoken again, I blinked rapidly and tried to focus on him. "Huh?"

The sheriff stared at me for a few seconds, then his gaze tracked to the loincloth-clad elemental being stationed between us. His hand on his holster, he tapped one finger on the Sig berthed inside it. "What's this freak doing to you? Drugs? Hypnosis?"

Travis stalked toward me, veering around my self-appointed protector.

Nevan thrust out an arm, blocking him.

"Outta my way," Travis snapped.

Nevan regarded Travis with remote interest, like a scientist observing a microbe—and preparing to squash it.

A minute ago, I'd reveled in his incredible power. What had I been high on? The last thing I needed was Nevan pummeling the county sheriff. I'd get blamed for it, for sure. "Nevan, cut it out."

He ignored me, though a single, dark brow ticked upward.

I shot for a reasonable tone, despite my hammering heart and the sweat dribbling down my temples. "Please let Travis go by. He won't hurt me. Will you, Travis?"

"Course not." Travis raised a fist at Nevan. "But if this freak don't get outta my way, I will pump six rounds of hollow-point ammo smack into his brain."

Great. That would defuse the situation for sure.

"Let's all calm down." I directed a serene smile first at Travis, then at the sylph. "Please, Nevan."

He stepped aside, but kept his steely gaze on the sheriff.

Travis rushed toward me, seizing my shoulders. "Wake up, Lindsey, shake it off. Let me help you."

Nevan's mouth angled into a cool smile. "Perhaps she doesn't trust you."

Travis slung a sidelong glare at Nevan. "Stay outta this."

"Afraid I can't, son."

Travis tore his hands away from me to stab a finger in Nevan's direction. "I am not your son. For one thing, you aren't old enough to be my dad, and believe me, I'm real grateful for that." His hands fisted so tightly the muscles in his arms bulged. "Back off. This is between me and Lindsey. I don't know who the hell you are, but I guarantee I will find out."

"Highly doubtful." A derisive smile tautened Nevan's mouth. "But go on and try, son. It'll be amusing."

Travis shook his fists in the air, his face flushing bright red. "You son of a bitch—"

"Gah!" I shouted. "Enough. You two are acting like cavemen."

Both men swung their gazes to me. Expectant. Questioning. Irritated.

I huffed. "Don't give me that look, either of you. I do what I want, re-member? It's called free will."

Nevan looked suitably chagrined, but Travis stared at me like I'd grown three extra heads—tiny gargoyle heads that were making rude faces at him.

Travis scrubbed a hand over his face, straightened, and held out a hand to me. "Listen, I know we ain't exactly been friends, but I never lied to you. Come back with me."

Something flickered across Nevan's features, something reminiscent of disappointment, but it dissipated too fast for me to be sure. He slackened his shoulders, cocking one hip. "Do what you want."

Despite his aloof pose, he fixed his gaze directly on mine. The metallic hues in his irises blended and twirled, diverging and joining, hypnotizing me for a second too long. I neglected to notice he'd moved closer, edging up beside me, until I realized—thanks to a muscle spasm at the base of my skull—I'd craned my neck back to maintain eye contact.

"Lindsey," Travis said, in his most commanding cop voice.

I ripped my gaze from Nevan, returning my attention to Travis.

The sheriff held his arms stiff at his sides, fingers coiled into his palms. "I know you don't trust me. Why would you? I shoulda believed you about Calder, shoulda supported you, but I couldn't accept my brother had turned into some kinda…monster." He tugged at his shirt collar, rolling his shoulders in jerky movements. "I shouldn't have arrested you three years ago. I won't do it to-day. You gotta believe me."

"Am I supposed to be grateful?"

Travis shuffled up to my other side, scowling at Nevan, his anger easing up as he snaked his hand around mine. His skin was cool, his hold awk-ward. "We can fix this together. Just stay."

Though Nevan said nothing, his lips had flattened and his nostrils flared the tiniest bit. When he curved one corner of his mouth into a faint attempt at a grin, the expression stopped short of his eyes.

I glanced back and forth between the two cavemen before me. How could I turn away from Travis, a man I'd known for five years, in favor of someone I met yesterday? Travis had always despised me—or so I'd thought. As for Nevan, I had no clue what he felt.

Standing rigid beside me, Nevan spoke in a low voice. "You know I am the only one who can protect you."

Travis had turned his back on me three years ago, when I needed a friend the most. In the past two days alone, Nevan had aided me more than anyone else in my whole life. Anyone except my family.

I slipped my hand into Nevan's. He squeezed gently. A genuine, if muted, smile relaxed his lips.

"No," Travis said, shaking his head vigorously. "You can't be serious. *Stay here.*"

I moved closer to Nevan, my shoulder bumping his chest. "I can't stay. Nevan's right. He can help me a lot more than you can."

"Are you kidding me? You can't run off with Kevin the jungle fairy."

Nevan shot ramrod straight, his gaze narrowing on Travis. "I am not a fairy."

Travis ground his teeth. "I ain't letting you take her."

What drug was he on? Travis had treated me like a criminal until abruptly deciding to help. "I'm going with Nevan."

Travis bolted his hand around my arm and I flinched at his steel grip. "I won't let you go, Porter. You're a suspect in a murder."

"You're giving me vertigo with your constant one-eighties. Make up your mind, Travis. Hate me, help me, you have to pick one."

Spittle spraying from his lips, he snarled, "I'll do whatever it takes to keep you away from—" He punched a finger in the air toward Nevan without looking at the other man. "Away from that *thing.*"

Confronted with Travis's vehemence, I sidled closer to Nevan. Travis's behavior had grown so erratic I had no clue what he might resort to next.

He wrested the cuffs from his belt. "This is for your own good, Lindsey."

Nevan flicked his wrist.

Travis's feet flipped out from under him and he sailed backward through the air. His body thwacked down at the far side of the clearing. Prone on the ground, Travis jacked his head up, grimacing, his eyes dull and his hair mussed.

I wrested my hand free of Nevan's. "What are you doing? You could've killed him."

"The sheriff is unharmed." Nevan grazed his knuckles across my cheek. "He threatened you."

"Now who's jealous."

"I said I'd protect you and I keep my promises." He dragged one fingertip down my jaw, a faint smile on his lips. "I seem to recall a certain mortal screaming my name, begging for my help."

Crap. I had. Worse, I didn't regret it. But still...

I studied Travis. He'd pushed up into a sitting position and was fingering the back of his head.

Nevan hauled me into his arms, pressing me into his body, suffusing me with his primal heat. He had hidden layers to his personality and I didn't know if I could or should accept his darker side. In this moment, though, he represented my best hope.

He spanned the small of my back with his large hands, tethering me to him. "Ready?"

"For what?"

"To cross the veil."

Sheesh, his world had screwy terminology. "To what the what?"

"You'll see."

The world evaporated into a roiling mist, the ground fell away beneath us, and we plunged into blackness.

CHAPTER NINE

ICE CLAWED AT MY FLESH. I CLUNG TO NEVAN WITH BOTH ARMS around his neck. His biceps flexed and tautened around me as he adjusted and strengthened his hold. I tried to speak, to ask where he was taking me, but couldn't. If my body still existed, my mind must've detached from it. I rocketed through an abyss, numb except for the pinching, slashing ice.

Whump. My feet touched down with a gentleness incongruous with the noise I'd heard. Or sensed. Or something. Sunlight swaddled me in its delicate warmth. A forest encircled us and I understood, on a visceral level, we had teleported to another spot in the same woods, in the vicinity of the falls. I strained to hear the rumbling of the water, but detected nothing more than birds twittering.

Nevan's embrace crushed me. No wonder I couldn't catch my breath. With my face mashed against his chest, I croaked, "You're squishing me."

He loosened his hold. "Sorry, love, I don't often travel with a passenger. And I assumed ye wouldn't appreciate it if I dropped ye."

"Absolutely not."

"I will never let you go." He combed his fingers through my hair. "Are ye all right?"

"Yeah." I propped my chin on his chest. "Glad to be back on the ground."

A relieved smile accompanied his sigh. "As am I."

I hesitated for a moment, entranced by the odd safety of being in his arms, before I pushed away. "Travis found the dead guy. In the trunk of my car."

A vein throbbed in his forehead. "Did he now."

"Could Skeiron have put it there?"

"I've no idea. Can't imagine why he'd bother mucking about with a corpse." His brows cinched together. "Someone else must've killed the poor fellow and waited for the right moment to plant the body, to place the blame squarely on you."

"Great." I rubbed my arms, scratching my elbow. "I have at least two mortal enemies. I love being popular."

"Your enemies aren't mortal. I'm quite certain, given the body thief's actions, he or she is no more mortal than Skeiron is."

"Thanks for the awesome pep talk."

His forehead wrinkled. "Pep talk?"

"Forget it." I surveyed the vicinity, arms belted around me like a strait-jacket. "I shouldn't have run. It was stupid, I know. I should've trusted the law to straighten out this mess. That's what normal people do."

Nevan harrumphed. "The innocent often suffer at the whim of any legal system."

"Do elemental beings have a legal system?"

"Of course." He canted his head, lips parted slightly. "When you men-tioned the law, were you referring to the sheriff?"

"Not sure. Travis did seem halfway sincere when he offered to help."

With a *hmt* noise, Nevan began to scrape his finger across his thumb in repetitive jerks.

It was my turn to smirk. "Jealous much?"

"Of a human? Bah." He waved a dismissive hand.

If he wanted to swim in denial, fine. "You said you can help me. How?"

"Hmm," he said, with a teasing glint in his eyes. "Let me think."

"You don't have a plan?" I was in no mood for jokes. Panic amped up my volume and elevated my pitch to a higher octave. "You swept me away, promising to fix things, and you don't even have a—"

Nevan snared me in his arms. I sucked in a sharp breath. He cradled my face in one hand, his thumb caressing the corner of my mouth, eliciting wave of heat that bloomed out into my whole body. "Hush, darlin'. I have a plan."

The intimacy of our position had me squirming against him. "You do?"

"Resurrect the dead fellow."

"You can—I mean, you seriously could—bring someone back from the dead?"

"I cannot do it personally, mind you, but I can access the magic." He pulled me hard against him, both arms folded around me. "We've got a journey ahead of us."

"A trip? Where to?"

"Through the veil. Into the Unseen realm."

"I thought we already crossed the veil thingy."

"Not quite. I brought us a short ways from the scene of the crime, as it were. We have yet to pierce the veil—the barrier between your world and mine."

My head throbbed, most likely from information overload. More than my head throbbed, thanks to the disconcerting way he'd bound our bodies together. The way Nevan exposed my deepest needs, inflaming them beyond reason, scared me more than being framed for murder.

"Are ye ready?" he asked.

Too many discomfiting layers to that question. I ignored all but the most obvious. "Take me there."

Nevan studied me for a moment, apparently uncertain whether I meant what I'd said or if I comprehended the gravity of my decision. Maybe I didn't. He'd explained and presented me with the option. I'd granted my permission. More than that, despite vowing never to do it again, I'd made the decision to trust a man.

A breeze fanned over us, feathering my hair across my shoulders and my chest. A stray lock flew across my lips and spilled down again to tickle my collarbone and stray over Nevan's hand, where it still rested there on my bare skin.

His gaze skipped down to my breasts, then blazed straight into my eyes. His chest heaved once. The swelling length of his erection strained against his loincloth but somehow stayed contained beneath it.

A bolt of searing need tore through me. Images rolled past my mind's eye, vivid to the point of making my skin tingle and my sex throb. I hungered for him to see me exposed before him and lay those big hands on my naked body. I craved the rasp of his tongue on my—

Noooo, I would not finish that thought. Passions of all kinds, sexual and emotional, must be restrained or bad things would follow.

His tongue rolled over his lower lip. "Tell me one thing first. Why does the sheriff call you ice princess?"

"You have to know now?"

"I would like to know, that's all."

I knotted a lock of my hair around my finger. Why not tell him? Maybe the truth would squelch his desire and I'd be safe again. *Do you want to be safe?* I wound the lock tighter, until it strangled my finger, then shook it off. "After I shot Calder, I told Travis everything that happened. Everything. Even the incredibly personal stuff, because I thought he needed to know in order to help me. Back then, I still believed he would help."

Nevan turned his hand over, skating the back of it down my breastbone until it encountered my T-shirt's neckline. He hovered his hand there, a millimeter from my skin. "He arrested you."

"Yeah." I linked my hands over my belly, only to let them drop away. "Weird thing is, he didn't yell at me about murdering his brother. He started calling me ice princess instead."

Nevan withdrew his hand. "Why?"

"Because I...well..." *Spit it out, you coward.* "When I told Travis what Calder had done to me, I also told him what I am. For some reason, it enraged him."

"And what precisely are you?"

My stomach churned, but I took a deep breath and told him what I'd never told anyone else except Travis and Calder. "I'm a virgin."

Nevan's mouth fell open and quickly clapped shut. His brows arched before knitting together. As the lines smoothed out of his forehead, he gave a slow nod. "That explains quite a few things."

"Really. Such as?"

"Why you forbade me to kiss you, for one. And why you're uncomfortable with my lack of clothing."

The ache in my head spread to my neck. Once again, he'd bared my secrets without the slightest effort. It made me feel as transparent as glass.

He rubbed his chin. "But your virginity hardly makes you cold and remote, as the term ice princess implies."

I stuffed my hands in my jeans pockets. "According to Travis, I string men along with tacit promises of sex, only to shut them down when they make a move." I cast my gaze to the ground as the old knot cinched tight in my gut. "He said I like to torture men and that's how I drove Calder over the edge. I deserved what happened, he said. I'm a rotten tease."

Was that my voice, so small and pathetic? I'd thought I could bury the past, but it kept rising up like a zombie to terrorize me.

Because I let it. Because keeping it alive gave me a fantastic excuse to hide inside myself. *Never a victim again.*

"Lindsey—"

"Forget it." I lifted my gaze to Nevan's and swung my hands at my sides. "I told you I'd cross the veil with you. Take me already."

His lips twitched with suppressed humor. "Well now, I thought it'd take far longer for ye to beg me to take ye."

My rebuttal turned into a choked grunt. After a few seconds, I managed to speak. "I didn't mean it like that. And I was not begging."

"I heard a note of..." He gave a soft chuckle, his mouth forming a slight smile. "Desperation."

"What you heard was frustration."

His smile broadened into a grin that set off glittering sparks in his eyes. "I'd be more than happy to assist ye with your *frustration.*"

Cripes, I'd done it again. I had to start thinking before I spoke. Maybe I ought to write the words down and read them three times first. "Let's get this veil-crossing thing over with."

With one fingertip, he charted a path down my breastbone until my shirt's neckline interrupted the journey. "The next time you beg me to take you, best make certain of your meaning, because I will take you at your word."

The sight of his penis peeking out from under the loincloth ripped away any response I might've formulated. I gave myself an actual shake, like a dog shedding water, but the discomfort lingered. "Take me to the damn Unseen realm."

Nevan surveyed the tree branches as if hunting for something, but then gave up the search. "Before I can take you there, I must make certain you have the touch. If you don't, the veil will not open for you."

"I don't understand."

"You must have a touch of the Unseen realm in you."

"And how do you figure out if I have it?"

"With a test." He twisted his mouth into a grimace. "You may not like what's involved."

"Just tell me."

"I must enchant you."

"Enchant?" My throat tightened, my jaw too. "That's what you did to Sandy."

His grimace dug in deeper. "Yes."

The blonde girl's face, dazed and befuddled, flashed in my mind. My muscles seemed to calcify, freezing me in place. "How is it any different from what you've been doing to me all along?"

"I've done nothing—to you." He slanted forward, his face hovering above mine, his breaths slow and deliberate. "I have never enchanted you, I swear it."

His fevered gaze bounced from my eyes to my lips and back again.

I laid a hand on my chest, but the tickle behind my ribs refused to quit.

"Not once," he said, "have I used magic on you. I wouldn't, unless I sensed the touch in you. And I haven't sensed it—yet." He closed his hands around my upper arms. "I do not wish to do this, but it's the only way. You must believe me."

Though the silent *please* in his tone had my lips straining to smile, I clamped them between my teeth. He was all but begging me to believe him, and if I wanted to fix the mess I'd stumbled into, I had no choice except to trust him. To let him enchant me. And kiss me.

My lips tingled. I became acutely aware of my hand on my chest—the warmth of it on my bare skin, the way my wrist brushed against my breast—and the feel of his hands on my arms. God, I wanted him to kiss me, like I'd never wanted anything.

He let his hands fall away from my arms and shifted his weight to one hip. "If you still wish to cross over into the Unseen realm, we should do this quickly. The sheriff, that persistent beggar, will soon find us."

Boy, my two cavemen totally despised each other. I couldn't understand the depth of their dislike, because it struck me as jealousy, which made no sense. Nevan being jealous, I could see. But Travis?

No time to worry about it. I had to fix my life, and a single viable option was available to me.

"Okay," I said. "If enchantment's what we have to do, I give you permission to go ahead with it."

He marveled at me as if I were a goddess incarnate, descended straight from the heavens, shimmering with remnants of stardust.

A rock settled in my gut. He'd called me intriguing and unusual, but then he also said he didn't want to enchant me. Maybe he didn't want to do it because I wasn't Sandy. I lacked the va-va-voom all men seemed to crave. Then again, he had gaped at my breasts.

He gripped the nape of his neck in one hand, his head lowered. "There is more."

"You can tell me."

His fingers, woven with mine, tensed. He expelled a ragged breath and wrapped his other hand around our joined fingers. "The test requires intimate contact."

"We are not having sex right here in the woods."

"Not that intimate." He started to chuckle, but stifled it. He watched me with uncertainty in his eyes. "You know of what I speak."

I let out the breath I hadn't realized I was holding. "A kiss."

"Yes. But I promised to keep my lips away from yours."

My mouth watered as my body began to ache in places I wished it wouldn't. "You have my permission. One kiss."

He took one large step backward. Though the gap between us measured less than an arm's length, the withdrawal of his body seemed to strip the oxygen from the air. His eyes burned with twirling flames of every color, spinning faster the longer he beheld me. My gaze traveled down to his lips, full and ripe and parted for a deep kiss. He swiped his tongue across his lower lip, leaving it glistening and slick.

"What are you doing?" I breathed.

"Unleashing my ethereal senses."

The erotic undertone in his voice brushed warmth across my skin, stirring the hairs on my arms and the nape of my neck to rise. With his hands on my shoulders, he drew me to him. My head fell back as my gaze sought his. My whole body seemed to lighten and lift off the ground, though my feet stayed glued to the earth. I battled to resist the allure of total surrender, but the part of me that yearned for it swelled larger and stronger every second.

"Can ye hear me, love?" he purred.

"Yes." A dreaminess infused my tone, matching the floaty sensation in my body. Dimly, I realized I should probably worry about my altered state, but the notion flitted away from my consciousness. "Am I enchanted?"

"Not yet." He ran a hand through my hair, trailing his fingers down to my neck, across my jawline, to curl under my chin. "I want to take you to a special place few mortals have ever seen. Will ye come with me?"

Someplace special. A thread of anxiety wound tight around my heart. "You told Sandy the same thing."

He bent his head nearer to mine, his voice barely a whisper. "That was my duty. This is my choice."

"In that case…Yes, I will go with you."

"Are you certain?"

Although my brain might've still been a bit muzzy, I understood what I'd agreed to and what he'd meant when he said this was his choice, not his duty. He'd asked for my trust again and reminded me, in his own way, he'd chosen me—against his duty, against the decree of his king.

I slanted forward until only a whisper of air separated our lips. "I'm sure."

His pupils flared wide, the metallic irises shrinking to a narrow ring.

"When's the enchantment start?" I felt warm and fuzzy, but nothing like what I'd witnessed in Sandy. She'd seemed…mesmerized. "I'm not really feeling—"

"Quiet." He exerted a light pressure, urging my chin up. "Look into my eyes."

"Already am."

He growled out a sigh. "Look harder."

I rolled my eyes. "What exactly am I supposed to be looking for?"

"Nothing. Just *focus*."

"On what?" I tried to shake my head free, but his thumb and forefinger locked my chin in place. "If you don't want to do this, tell me. I realize I'm not as hot as Sandy, or probably any of the other hordes of women you've—"

He thrust his thumb up, sealing my lips. "There are no hordes of women. I've told you that before and you claimed you believe me. Perhaps you're the one having doubts about this."

"No." It came out muffled and squashed, thanks to his thumb over my mouth.

"All right then. Look in my eyes, and relax."

I looked. And relaxed. Well, as much as I could under the circumstances.

Sparks ignited in his eyes, white hot against the warm, liquid shades of his irises. His heat enveloped me, soft and searing at the same time. A breeze tousled his hair and transported his scent to me, tantalizing my senses. His thumb traced circles on my lips, the brush of skin like satin, arousing me with a slow-building desire, until my skin felt tight, my breasts swollen, my lips engorged and aching for his kiss.

I flicked my tongue out to steal a taste of him. Salty. Earthy. With a spicy undertone. Hunger shivered through me. Seconds ticked by. *Tick, tick, tick,* went the clock in my head. I dared to lave the pad of his thumb.

He went stone still, the roiling currents in his eyes the only motion within him.

Tick, tick, tick.

A mosquito lighted on my nose. I tried to blow it off, but his damn thumb blocked my breath. I swatted the bug away.

He released my chin, withdrawing his hand.

I scratched my nose. "Did you start it yet?"

"Did I start?" His brow furrowed on a slight frown. "Of course I started, minutes ago. Yet you don't seem enchanted. How do you feel?"

"Peachy. What's supposed to happen?"

"You should experience a mild euphoria and…" He looked down at his feet. "An overpowering desire to be near me and to please me."

Laughter exploded out of me on a snort. I held up a hand, struggling to recover from the inappropriate outburst. "I'm sorry. Please don't take this the wrong way, but if that's how I'm supposed to feel then I don't think you're it right."

"Of course I'm doing it right," he all but snarled. "This has been my duty for a century. I know how to enchant a woman."

I shrugged. "Guess it just doesn't work on me."

His mouth flattened into a line as his eyes tightened into a squint. He nostrils flared on an explosive exhalation. "Enchantment never fails."

I raised my hands in supplication. "Hey, it's not my fault you've lost your mojo. Maybe I don't have any magical energy in me."

"Even if you don't, I should be able to enchant you. But clearly, I cannot." He locked his hands behind his back, rocking onto his heels. "My magic does not fail."

I patted his shoulder. "I'm sure it happens to every sylph at least once in his life."

"Bloody hell." He jammed a hand into his hair, scratching furiously. "You must be blocking it."

"Typical. Blame it on the girl."

"I sensed an energy within you when first we met. It must be the touch, but you've repressed it. It is unprecedented." He rubbed his eyes with the heels of his hands. When he lowered his hands, he stared at me blankly for a few seconds before shaking his head as a look of sheer wonder overtook his features. "You, love, are a unique human."

"Thanks. You're pretty unique yourself."

He cleared his throat. "Remember what I told you about thanking me. Gratitude can be dangerous, and you would do well to beware of expressing it. Please heed me on this, Lindsey."

"Fine, whatever. Now shut up, will you?" I slanted my body nearer to his, tipping my head back. "Try the kiss thing. Maybe that'll do the trick."

I shut my eyes. No longer able to see him, I felt the wisp of air displacement as he bent his head toward mine. The breath caught in my throat. I burned to fan my fingers across his chest, to slide up and down that silken skin.

He cupped his hands around my elbows, gliding them up my arms. His lips skimmed across mine, warm and soft and oh so tempting. I melted into him as he enfolded me in his arms, the embrace tender at first, intensifying little by little, his arms pressing me firmly against him. Plastered to him, aware of every hard line of muscle and his rigid shaft crushed against my belly, I trembled with a desperate hunger that eclipsed anything I'd known before, an all-consuming lust for his touch, his kiss, his body, his—

My knees threatened to buckle. I clung to him, rocked by the realization of what I burned for most. Him. Inside me.

His mouth coasted over mine one last time, then retreated.

I moaned, clutching at his biceps, reveling in the sensation of his sinews tautening under my fingers. His chest rose and fell erratically and he seemed as incapable of catching his breath as I was. I let my head fall back, my lips parting on another moan, guttural and wanton.

Crushing me to him, his hands fisting in my shirt, he scraped his mouth over mine once, twice, and with a rough, drawn-out groan he possessed my lips with his. I opened to my mouth to him, pleading for more, surrendering my will and my body without reservation.

"Lindsey," he breathed into my mouth, his lips still on mine. The vibrations from his mouth—from the uttering of that single, reverent word—reverberated through my entire body.

"Nevan," I murmured, moving his lips with mine. "Please."

He sealed his mouth over mine, thrusting his tongue inside, our lips molded together as our tongues tangled, as we devoured and tormented and inflamed each other with ever slick glide of flesh over flesh. Famished for the taste of him, I plunged deeper inside his mouth, loving the way he opened more for me and growled low in his throat.

Slow down, a muffled voice in my head urged. *Shut this down before it goes too far.*

But God, I couldn't.

Nevan's hands dropped to my ass, kneading with ravenous strokes, and I was lost. I flung my arms around his neck, holding on like I'd disintegrate without his arms to bind me together. He raked a hand up my back to spread his palm over my spine, between my shoulder blades, while his other hand clutched my ass, tugging my hips forward, angling them up and into him perilously close to his raging erection.

"Mm." I tunneled my fingers into his hair, pulling his head lower, opening wider for the kiss. Currents crackled around us, inside me, alive and electric, fueling an irresistible fervor. My head swam. We barreled toward an inescapable destination, about to blast away my barriers—and my virginity—and Christ, I wanted to go there. Right now. With him. With a man who wasn't even a man.

He wrenched away from me, staggering backward. The loss of his heat, his scent, his flavor, cast me out into an emptiness so vast my thoughts echoed back to me.

Mouth agape, eyes wild and fiery, he bored his gaze into me.

A chill frosted over my skin. "What's wrong?"

He staggered backward another step. The flaming hues in his eyes quieted to a faint glimmer, though he stared at me without blinking.

Shoving my hands in my pockets, shoulders bunched. "Kissing me was that bad, huh?"

Whatever panic had gripped him sluiced out in the space of a breath. He folded me in his arms, cradling my head to his chest. I closed my eyes, relishing the *thump-thump* of his heart beneath my ear. He did care for me, in some way, even if our kiss hadn't left him thunderstruck, the way it had me.

He nuzzled my hair and caressed my back. "You misunderstand my reaction."

My heartbeat accelerated, revved by a dangerous hope—and a hint of fear.

"Kissing you," he said, pressing his lips to my forehead, "transcended anything I've experienced in my entire existence. It was perfection."

Elation swelled in my chest and I curled my fingers against his chest. "Nobody's ever kissed me like that."

"Then every man who's touched you has been a bloody idiot." He threaded his fingers through my hair, the tips dancing across my scalp. All the remaining shreds of my anxiety fled and I snuggled into him. He sighed, as if the greatest pleasure of all was holding me. "Your bravery and intelligence impressed me, but your passion…You astound me."

What he'd said a moment ago resurfaced in my mind and I had to ask. "If kissing me was the highlight of your existence—" A knot hardened in my gut, but I lifted my head and finished the question. "How old are you?"

"I'm immortal, remember?"

"You must've been born, or created, or something."

The tips of his fingers found my nape and rubbed with a slow, sensual rhythm. "How old are *you*?"

"Thirty-two. Now it's your turn."

He fidgeted and coughed.

I rested my chin on his chest. "Please tell me."

He nodded and drew in a long breath. "Well now, I lost count after five thousand."

Chapter Ten

I STOPPED BREATHING, CERTAIN MY HEART HAD CEASED BEATING TOO. I COULD do nothing but gawk at him—with my mouth open, I suspected, given the draft coming in between my lips. Five thousand years old? Five *thousand*? More, even, since he claimed he'd lost count. This man was older than Stonehenge or the pyramids of Egypt. I had just made out with an ancient being.

Damn if that wasn't the hottest thing ever.

And sort of ooky at the same time.

"There's more," he said. "I sensed none of the Unseen realm in you."

My heart sank to the ground and I swore I heard it splatting at my feet like the limp, clammy rag into which it seemed to have morphed. "I'll go to prison for the rest of my life if we don't do this."

"I wasn't finished." He tickled my earlobe with his finger, an amused smile on his lips. "There is an energy deep within you, hidden even from your own perception. I've tasted it."

The idea of him tasting energy that lurked inside me shot an erotic thrill straight into my core. I licked my lower lip, the velvety feel of my own tongue triggering a sense memory of his mouth, his tongue, ravishing me with wild abandon.

His fingertip teased the skin behind my ear, summoning a little shiver of delight.

"This energy of yours," he said, "I don't know if it's the right kind to get you into the Unseen realm. It's like nothing I've ever felt before, but we could try."

"How?"

"I shall take you to the doorway. If it opens for you, we'll know."

"Okay, I'm ready. Take me."

Oh damn. I'd done it again. *Stupid mouth, stupid brain.*

His lips eased into a languid grin. "Since ye granted me one kiss only, I can't take ye in the manner I'd most like."

I opened my mouth to speak, but couldn't muster words.

His grin closed into a smirk. He knew damn well what kind of effect he had on me and he enjoyed pushing that button. If I were honest, I'd admit I liked it too. I tapped my toe on the grass, creating a faint swishing sound. "You know what I meant."

"Ah yes, I do." He slid his hands down my back to rest on my hips.

"Has your test ever not worked before?"

"Never." A darkness scudded over him, like a gray cloud obscuring the sun. "Everything about you is unprecedented."

"Do I get a gold medal or something? For being the most difficult human on earth?" After what we'd shared a moment ago, I shouldn't have let him put his hands on me. I ought to pull away right now. If I planned on keeping my wits, I had to maintain a distance from him. But the contact felt soooo good.

"If you attempt this," he said, "and you don't have the requisite trace of elemental energy, you will die."

I pushed away from him. "I have to risk it."

He folded his arms around me.

I squeezed my eyes shut. Padlocked my arms around him. Held my breath. And prayed.

The ground dropped away. The silence of a vacuum engulfed us as we spun round and round, up and up. Icy needles pricked at my skin. I gripped Nevan so hard my arms trembled from the effort. Whirling. Soaring. Shattering and reforming.

My feet plunked down on solid ground. Nevan's embrace loosened, though his hands lingered on my hips. The solidity of his touch grounded me, more than the actual earth beneath my boots.

The throaty roar of a waterfall pelted my eardrums. Light glowed on the other side of my lids. I peeled them apart.

And yelped.

We perched on the rock ledge alongside the falls. My right toe caught in a depression and I stumbled sideways, flailing my arms to regain my balance. My boot slipped off the edge, skewing my center of gravity. I lurched toward the precipice.

Nevan seized me around the waist, hoisting me up and over to plunk me down on the ledge. He braced my body with his, both arms snug around me, his hands fastened over my belly.

Terrible visions assailed my mind, of my body plummeting and crashing into the water, of bones fracturing, of water choking my lungs.

Nevan gave me a gentle shake and hollered to be heard above the thundering cascade. "Are ye damaged, love?"

"No." I mashed myself into him, my toes frighteningly close to the edge. "Terrified, but not damaged."

"It's a six-foot drop. Far from life threatening."

I peered at the pool below, at its water churning and foaming. "I don't like water."

"Then we have a problem." He nodded toward the gushing cataract behind us. "To reach the Unseen, we must first breach the falls."

"I don't like deep bodies of water, like ponds and lakes. A waterfall is doable."

He squinted at me, searching my face, a question poised on his tongue and evident in his eyes—but then he nodded, seeming satisfied. Nudging me away, he grasped my shoulders and rotated me to face the waterfall. "Jump."

The hairs at my nape bristled and my skin went clammy, not entirely from the water droplets peppering my arms and face. Jump into the falls? What if I blundered off the edge? Or smacked head-on into a rock wall?

"I've taken many mortals through the water," he said, his body blockading me from behind, leaving me no escape route. "This is not the dangerous part."

Great. That eased my mind. *Not.*

"I'll show you." Nevan hopped around me. His feet slapped onto the ledge in front of me. Water sprayed over his bronzed flesh, glazing it with a faint sheen. I stretched out my fingers to skate them over his damp skin, but just as I touched him, he spun away from me.

And leaped into the falls.

"Hey, wait!" I lifted my hands, as if I might hold back the raging waters or maybe part them like Moses. No such luck. I inched closer and my boots skidded on the wet rock. I flung a hand out to the solid sandstone cliff beside me, thwarting my fall, sparing my skull from a bone-splitting impact.

I took a fortifying breath. Straightening, my hand firmly on the stone wall, I edged toward the cascade. Drops spattered my face, raining particles of a chill on my skin as the liquid evaporated. The clean scent of water mingled with the dankness of wet dirt and the racket of water pummeling rock pulsated through my skull with deafening force.

What on earth was I doing? I worked in a rock shop, serving tourists who thought agate was the name of a teen pop singer. I did not allow strange, half-naked men to lure me into waterfalls.

Except today, apparently, I did.

From my position mere inches from the falls, I noticed the ledge extended behind the curtain of water, where I could just make out a yawning darkness indicative of an empty area beyond. Nevan hadn't thrown himself into the cliff of sheer stone behind the water. He'd leaped through the falls, into whatever space lay behind it.

Okay. I could do this. Saving myself from prison required a literal leap of faith, with Nevan on the other side to catch me. I tensed, bracing for the impact of hard, cold water. Clenched my fists. Shut my eyes.

"Porter!" Travis and his deputies rampaged toward the railing. The sheriff's voice echoed off the trees. "Porter, get the hell offa there! What in blue blazes are ya doing? Trying to break your fool neck?"

My attention diverged, like a TV displaying two feeds in a split-screen effect. My nails scraped at the rock, but my left foot skidded sideways. My fingers grasped at depressions in the stone, steadying my balance. I pushed away from the wall and confronted the curtain of water.

"Lindsey, no!" A note of panic quavered in Travis's voice.

I jumped.

The water swallowed me. Cold. Sharp. Tiny nails driven into my flesh. I cleared the falls and my boots struck solid rock.

Panting, but with both feet flat on the ground, I struggled to orient myself in my new environment. The frigid water left me shivering, my teeth chattering. My hair and clothes clung to me, sodden and heavy. I stood within a small cavern, from the outside hidden by the falls but now revealed before me. To my left and right, rock walls rose up to meet the ceiling, where it arched across the space at least five feet above. Water-filled depressions pockmarked the sandstone floor.

The thundering of the water had faded into a dull rumble. I glanced backward, but the cascade still blocked the entrance. I couldn't explain the dulling of its roar, though the effect reminded me of wearing foam earplugs.

To my left, a few feet away, Nevan braced his body with one hand on the wall.

"Why is the noise quieter in here?" I asked.

"Magic."

I supposed that was all the explanation I'd get, so I returned to surveying the cavern. The floor was level, if pockmarked, and strands of green copper ore weaved through the arching ceiling. In front of me loomed an unnatural darkness. It shimmered and swirled, in a striking echo of Nevan's eyes. In contrast to the bright metallic hues of his irises, this whirlpool gyrated with a fathomless blackness, as if it were made of crude oil sprinkled with starlight, a wall of glittering emptiness stretching into eternity.

The closer I approached to the shimmering void, the more colors I detected inside it. Thin ribbons of iridescent blue, green, and purple twirled within the black. I lifted a hand to touch it but felt nothing, as if I'd tried to caress the air. My fingertips disappeared into the opalescent shadows. Goose bumps materialized on my arms, heralding a tingling chill.

Get out of here.

My subconscious had a point. I ought to run. Right this instant.

I couldn't. I had to know.

Nevan's fingers wound around mine. He sidled past me, partway into the shimmering abyss. One side of his body vanished.

I stood paralyzed before the portal to another world.

He tugged my hand in quiet invitation.

My gut clenched. *Ohhhh, this is a really bad idea.*

I did it anyway. I marched straight into the blackness.

Light blinded me. Radiant warmth chased away the chill of the cavern, calming my shivers. I squinted into the brightness, which emanated from above like the sun. As my eyes adjusted to the change, I noted the source of the light. It was the sun.

Which made no sense. I'd walked into darkness. Yet here I stood, bathed in sunshine with a tepid breeze tickling my face.

Nevan strode past me, freeing my hand.

I turned in a circle, awed by my surroundings. Behind me, where the cavern and waterfall should've been, a six-foot-tall boulder hunkered. Water burbled up out of the boulder's top, spilling down its sloping sides and onto the ground, where the water collected in a pool about ten feet in diameter. Tiny waves lapped at the pool's edge, inches from my feet.

Everywhere around me, thick trees hulked at least a hundred feet overhead. In place of leaves, stringy stuff reminiscent of moss dangled from the branches. The sky shone an ethereal blue, as dark and lustrous as a sapphire. The sun blazed within the blue, a flaming diamond embedded in the sky. Unseen birds chirped and twittered, their songs like nothing on earth. Indescribable scents wafted on the breeze, tantalizing and mysterious, delicious and dangerous. Everything here struck me as beautiful but *wrong.*

Nevan leaned his hip against a tree trunk on the other side of the pool, his arms folded over his chest. Our trip through the waterfall had drenched him too, molding the loincloth to his flesh and slicking his hair back. My gaze tracked the lines of his muscles down his body, over his hips, along those powerful thighs. His skin had become a glistening tapestry, dappled with beads of water, kissed by the unearthly gleam of the sun.

My hand rose to my throat of its own volition, my fingers stroked my skin.

God, he was as beautiful and strange as the surroundings. The memory of our scorching kiss rocketed through me, my body reliving the bliss of his hands groping and his tongue milking every ounce of passion from me.

"Come back to me," Nevan murmured, suddenly right in front of me.

I blinked rapidly, but couldn't shake the lightheaded awe—of him, of this place, of the surreal dream my life had become. "Imposs—wha—"

His lips curved in a closed-mouth smile and lines of amusement crinkled around his eyes. "You'll need to finish a sentence, or at least a word, if you're wanting me to respond."

Rationality burst back into me with a jolt. I'd have to wait until later to process everything I'd seen and experienced. As for the lust-inducing memory of Nevan's mouth...Best not think of that at all.

Nevan studied me with his glowing, amber eyes. His tongue slipped out to wet his lips.

I repressed the urge to squirm under his scrutiny. "I gather this whole 'touch of the Unseen world' stuff is designed to keep pesky mortals out of your precious realm of magic and creepiness."

"Naturally." He brushed a lock of hair from my shoulder, his fingers teasing my skin. "If it were easy to enter the Unseen, marauding droves of your kind would overrun our world."

I stifled a laugh, sort of. It broke out as a wet snort. "Come on, we lowly humans aren't that bad."

"*You* aren't bad at all." He ran his finger along the top of my ear, tucking my hair behind it. "Allowing the teeming hordes free entrance would rather negate the *unseen* aspect of this realm."

"I see your point." But another thought occurred to me, and I scrunched up my lips. "But you guys have free entrance to our world. That's not fair at all."

"Not free entrance." He twined a lock of my hair around his finger, winding it loosely, letting it fall, and winding it again, his gaze trained on the task. "There is a boundary which limits our egress."

"Your egress?" My derisive grunt turned breathless as he trailed his fingertips down my throat. *Not fair at all.* "Nobody talks like that. Besides, I haven't seen any walls or fences blocking your way."

"It is a magical boundary," he said on a sigh, as if I'd questioned the existence of gravity. "We cannot travel more than one mile from any of the gateways between the worlds."

"The waterfall. It's a gateway."

"All bodies of water serve as doorways."

"Hmm." I thought back to our encounter in my car, when he'd freaked out at the sight of a mile marker up ahead. "That's why you nearly got us into a car crash. We were approaching one mile from the falls."

"Ah…yes."

"Jesus, why didn't you just say so?" I rolled my gaze up to the heavens, shaking my head. "Could've saved us both a lot of grief if you'd told me the truth right then."

"Perhaps." He winked, grinning. "But where's the fun in that?"

"Do you honestly think it's fun to almost get me killed?"

His grin crumbled. "I would never harm you, if I could prevent it. What happened in your vehicle was an accident, one for which I have apologized."

"Yeah, I know." I paused, then said, "But you've been in my apartment. It's outside the boundary."

"Outside one boundary, but inside another. There is a small, secluded waterfall nearby."

"Guess I'll take your word for that. What happens if you try to cross one of these invisible lines?"

"Annihilation."

"Of the world?" I squeaked the question, my heart surging into my throat.

"No, love." He patted my cheek. "Annihilation of the immortal being who tries to violate the boundary."

"Oh." I yanked my hands out of my pockets to rub my arms. "Guess I can understand why you flipped out in the car."

"I did not flip either out or in." Nevan backed away, tripped over a rock, and staggered forward, about to collide with me. Sputtering a curse, he righted himself with a little hop. "I requested you stop the car."

"Requested?" I laughed. "Oh, come off it. You totally flipped your lid."

He frowned, brushing himself off. "We'd best track down the bloody leprechaun, if we're to have any hope of resurrecting your deceased friend."

"Shoplifter."

"Pardon?"

"The dead guy. He was a shoplifter, not my friend. I didn't know him and I damn sure didn't like him."

"I appreciate the clarification." In one swift movement, he planted a firm kiss on my cheek, stepped away, and tugged my hand to urge me into motion. "But I wasn't concerned about your relationship with a corpse."

As we headed across the clearing, I bumped my shoulder against his arm. "And what about when he's not dead? Will your green beast rear its head again?"

He froze, forcing me to stop with him. "You think of me as a beast?"

"No, it was a joke." I'd nicked a nerve, but why? An instinct warned me not to pursue the topic further, at least until I'd learned a little more about my would-be savior. Pasting on a smile, the one I wore so often it hurt, I said, "Let's find this leprechaun, okay? I'd really prefer not to go to prison."

"Leprechauns are terribly unpleasant."

Enunciating each word with exaggerated lip movements, I said, "Take me to the leprechaun."

"As you wish."

Nevan shepherded me into the shadows of the forest, down a dirt path veiled in shadows. The further we traveled, the more his smile faded and his body stiffened. I struggled to keep up with his brisk pace. Underneath his flippant disguise, he must've been annoyed at the prospect of visiting a leprechaun. Pardon me, a *bloody* leprechaun.

Jeez, I hoped he hadn't meant that literally.

The path dead-ended at a small clearing. Nevan stopped at the edge of the trees, his body blocking my view. He turned sideways, his expression no longer amused but tight with tension. Whoa. He must've really disliked leprechauns.

"There," Nevan said, jerking a thumb toward the clearing. "You'll need to do the talking because the leprechaun won't speak to me."

"What did you, sleep with his sister?"

Nevan flinched. "Indeed I did."

"Oh." I'd been joking, but his confession spurred a stab of jealousy. I didn't want to know, not really, but my mouth seemed to have a mind of its own. "Of course you did. How many women have you screwed?"

He rubbed his forehead with his thumb and forefinger. "I have lived for thousands of years, and for most of that time, I recklessly indulged my baser instincts."

"In other words," I said, "you've boinked thousands, maybe millions, of women. Lovely."

He dropped his hand from his forehead, clenching it into a fist. "I make no excuses for my behavior, but never once have I forced a female into my bed. They came to me willingly. Tris's sister pursued me, in fact."

I tore my hand out of his and stomped toward the clearing, ducking under a low-hanging branch. Tendrils of mossy stuff drooped down from it. A clump of the gunk lodged in my hair and I batted it away. "I was right, wasn't I? You are a woodland lothario."

He growled in frustration, punched his fist into a tree, and shook his hand as if the motion could quell his temper. He breathed in and out, in and out, until the dark tension in him ebbed. "All you need know is that for the past century I have been celibate."

"A century?" I looked straight into his eyes, one part of me unable to accept his statement, another part wishing it were true. He hadn't lied to me so far—that I knew of—and I couldn't believe he would lie about this. Being a thirty-two-year-old virgin didn't sound so bad compared to a century of celibacy.

Nevan gave a curt nod.

"Okay then." I swung my arms at my sides, slapping my palms together each time they met in front of me. "I have no idea what to say to that."

"Say nothing. For once." He moved closer, taking my hands in his, and fixed an earnest gaze on me. "Listen to me, Lindsey. On this side of the falls, you cannot trust anyone."

"I trust you." No clue why, but I did.

"Don't." He leaned in, his voice infused with a quiet intensity. "Anyone you meet may try to trick you into a bargain. Do not speak the words 'please' or 'thank you' in this realm and never—*never*—agree to anything. Do you understand?"

"Not really." My throat constricted at the pain in his eyes. "But I'll do what you want. I prom—Is it okay to say 'promise'?"

"I'd prefer you didn't risk it." He freed my hands. "I know you will do as you say. There's no need for promises."

"How about if I pinky swear?"

Nevan's lips twitched. "Also not necessary, but not dangerous either."

He gestured for me to head for the clearing and walked alongside me as we entered the open area. Nevan slowed his pace, lagging by a couple paces. When I halted, he stayed behind me.

In the clearing's center, seated atop a flat boulder about two feet tall, hunched a rangy teenager. His brown hair, clipped into a buzz cut, matched the freckles dotting his peaches-and-cream skin. The clomping of my footsteps stirred him from his contemplation of a rock he gripped in one hand. His bright green eyes locked onto me briefly, but then his attention zipped straight past my shoulder. His lips contorted in annoyance.

"Go away," the kid said, his accent reminiscent of Chicago or the Bronx. "I ain't interested in the sylph's latest bimbo. I'm busy."

"I am not a bimbo." How many girls had Nevan brought here? *Thousands of years, remember?* "I don't appreciate the sexist jibe, you pubescent rat."

His brows shot up. "I been called lotsa things, but never that. Least Nev brought a sassy one this time."

The kid wiped his free hand on his ripped and faded blue jeans. He lifted the rock to inspect it. I recognized the chunk of green-tinged stone as copper ore, much like the chunks we sold in the shop. Two of the rock's edges had been sanded to a smooth surface and polished to a glassy shine.

My jaw fell open. No, not *like* the ore we sold in the shop. The rock had come from the shop. The kid was holding one of the float copper bookends my now-deceased shoplifter had tried to swipe. He must've sneaked back into the shop to finish his heist. But how did the leprechaun get the bookend?

The top edge of the stone, once curved and smooth, now looked ragged and raw.

My new friend raised the copper bookend to his mouth and bit into it. *Crunch.* Bits of copper ore peppered his green flannel shirt.

"Lindsey," Nevan said, nodding toward the boy, "meet Tris."

"He doesn't look like a leprechaun."

"If you were expecting a stout little fellow wearing a green outfit and a big smile, I'm afraid you've come to the wrong place. Tris doesn't do colorful or cheerful."

Tris threw a hot glare at Nevan before zeroing in on me. "We do not wear lame hats or dole out luck. Got it?"

"Yeah, I get it." Thinking I'd better ingratiate myself if I hoped to resurrect the dead man, I added, careful to avoid any dangerous niceties, "I didn't mean to offend you."

His glower softened, though only a smidgen. "I blame the sylph. If I could, I'd sue him for libel and I'd win." He bit off another mouthful of copper, munching it with great relish. "What do you want, lady? You're busting in on my lunch."

I decided to take the high road and assume rudeness was a defense against the weird magic rules. "Do you know what happened to the dead man?"

Tris gulped down the last of his copper ore. "Look, I don't got a clue what you're yammering about. Go away."

He flapped a dismissive hand in my direction.

To hell with ingratiating myself. If this kid was guilty, I wanted to know.

I marched three steps toward him, narrowing the gap between us to a few feet. His eyes, though glowing like Nevan's, lacked any motion or fire in the irises, imbuing them with a coldness. Yet behind the flat green light something sputtered, faint and well hidden, visible only from the right angle. He might not be as cold as he wanted me to think. "The man you stole that copper from is dead. Somebody bashed him in the head. I'm guessing it was you."

Tris made a thumbs-down gesture. "You guess wrong."

He hefted the bookend for another bite.

I snatched it from his hand.

Tris let out a loud hiss. "That's mine, sister. Give it back."

He thrust out a hand, waggling his fingers in the universal gesture for *gimme-gimme*.

I clutched the bookend to my chest. It was oddly warm, probably from the leprechaun's hands around the stone. "You stole it."

From another thief, but that was immaterial.

The kid shook his head, not as if denying what I'd said, but as if he knew I wouldn't leave him alone until he told the truth. Good. Let him stew.

Nevan bounded up behind me. "Tell her what happened, Tris. This one is willful. Ignoring her won't do you one bit of good."

Tris refused to glance at Nevan or acknowledge the man had spoken. Instead, he slumped forward to rest his elbows on his knees. "All right, all right. But I didn't kill nobody. He was dead when I found him. Seeing as how he didn't need the copper anymore, I sorta claimed it. As abandoned property."

I tapped my fingers on the bookend, still hugged to my chest. "Why should I believe you?"

"It's the truth, lady," he snarled. "Believe it or don't, what do I care?"

Actually, I did believe him. Couldn't say why. The kid was annoying, insolent, and must've suffered from a bizarre mineral deficiency. I didn't like him. And yet, I believed his story. "If you didn't kill the guy, who did?"

"Dunno." His glazed eyes fixated on the bookend and he licked his lips. "I'm still hungry. Can I have that back?"

Considering the way he kept moistening his lips, and the greedy sheen in his eyes, he must've really been hungry. For copper ore? Oh well, I'd given up on trying to understand anything that happened since I found the dead man yesterday.

I handed the bookend to Tris. He bit off a mouthful. His teeth pulverized the rock with an audible grinding noise and powdered copper dribbled from his lips. He swiped the back of his hand across his mouth.

What kind of teeth did this kid have?

I shoved the question to the back of my mind, returning to the issue at hand. "I believe you. Which means I need to ask for your help."

He made a rude noise. "I don't do favors. 'Specially not for stinking mortals."

A snide quip popped to mind, but I bit it back and tried my damnedest to look relaxed and nonthreatening. Not that anyone had ever accused me of being threatening. Just seemed like a good idea to minimize the hostility. "If I could ask anyone else, I would, but according to Nevan, you're it. Resurrect the dead man for me."

"Ah," Nevan said, a finger raised. He gave me a look that suggested he thought I was tiptoeing too close to the P-word. "Perhaps I should take over from here."

"I need his help and you said he wouldn't talk to you." I turned back to Tris. "Will you do this for me?"

"Help a mortal?" Tris cackled. Like a witch from a bad horror movie. Leprechauns were not supposed to cackle. In that moment, I realized I'd better adjust my preconceptions—or better yet, dump them altogether—if I hoped to survive in my new reality.

I raised both hands, palms together, letting my gesture beg where I could not. "Bring back the dead man and I'll owe—"

"No-no," Nevan said. He strode between me and Tris, a massive blockade composed of tight muscles and burnished skin. "She doesn't care to finish that sentence."

"Sure I do."

Nevan shot me a dark look. "Trust me. You don't."

Tris lowered the bookend, letting it rest on his thigh. He tilted his head up to glower straight at Nevan, who met his gaze with a blank one of his own. Tris spoke directly to the sylph. "Don't this broad know nothing? What kinda morons are you bringing in here these days, Nev?"

My sylph companion feigned surprise. "Now you're speaking to me, eh?"

The kid snorted. "Not cuz I wanna. But what's the point in talking to this broad when she don't even know about debts? Teach these dames the basics before you drag 'em in here."

I peeked around Nevan's shoulder. "Debts? What do you mean? Does this have anything to do with not letting me say the P-word?"

"Never mind," Nevan said, shifting sideways to keep me blockaded. "Tris, Lindsey asked for your help. Will you voluntarily perform the service?"

Voluntarily perform? I marveled at the deft way he tap-danced around these magical land mines. No please, no implication of owing anything. He asked the leprechaun to volunteer.

"What's in it for me?" Tris demanded.

Nevan gritted his teeth, blustering a breath out his nostrils. "I won't throttle you."

I curled a hand over Nevan's bicep. It bulged under my palm, hardened by a barely contained anger. His eyes fluoresced in shades of red, bronze, and white, while his skin seemed to toughen like leather stretched taut. He had the aura of a wild beast preparing to pounce. Whatever happened between Tris and Nevan must've involved way more than the sylph enjoying a simple roll in the hay with the leprechaun's sister.

I gave his arm a light squeeze. "Nevan, chill out. I can handle this."

His radioactive eyes swerved to me.

I let my hand fall away from his arm, chilled by the eerie sense of gazing into the soul of an ancient, ruthless warrior. I bit back the first word that wanted to come out of my mouth—"please"—and scoured my brain for a safer phrase.

Nevan crept closer to the leprechaun.

"Stop this," I said. "You've done enough for me and I can handle one snotty twerp. I'm grate—"

Nevan slapped a hand over my mouth.

I pushed his hand away. "What are you doing?"

"You were about to incur a debt." His gaze flitted to Tris and back to me. "All debts must be repaid, by whatever means the owed party desires."

By whatever means. He'd told me Skeiron forced him into a bargain that enslaved him to the king's whims. Nevan repaid that debt every day, humiliated by his duty. I did not care to wind up bound like that.

"You vowed to do as I asked," Nevan said. "Do not incur a debt. Obey me on this."

The gravity of his tone stopped me. His grip tightened, his nails slicing in my flesh. "Ouch. You're hurting me."

He yanked his hands away and held them in mid-air, as if he weren't sure they belonged to him. Breathing hard, he slowly lowered his arms. "I should not have held you so tightly."

"No shit." I lifted my right hand, palm out. "I won't thank anybody or say I owe them ever again. Satisfied?"

His shoulders flagged, looking suddenly weary. "Yes."

"I almost heard a thank-you in that yes."

"Owing you would not be a trial."

Tucking my hands in my pockets, I rocked forward on my toes to smile up at him. "I'll remember you said that."

His mouth slid into half smile, but then he reminded me, "No bargaining. And no gratitude of any kind."

"Got it." I angled a little closer. "You're bossy, but I've decided it's in a good way."

His voice dropped to a husky rumble. "How good am I?"

Despite the distance between us, his radiant heat soaked into me like sunshine. Our gazes intersected, drawn together by a gravitational force. My thoughts and desires revolved around him—I, the satellite trapped in the orbit of him, the planetary body. If I gave in to the pull, our passion would explode like a supernova. The mere thought of it shuddered anticipation through my entire body.

I was in so much trouble.

The leprechaun cleared his throat, regarding me with a canny gleam in his eyes.

Oh yeah, sooo much trouble.

CHAPTER ELEVEN

I DON'T GIVE A RAT'S ASS ABOUT YOUR TENDER MOMENT," TRIS AN-nounced. "If you're wanting me to resurrect somebody, better gimme one whopper of a reason. I ain't the generous type."

He dragged a finger down my arm, from the hem of my sleeve down to my wrist. I ached to drown in the fire of our kiss one more time. Instead, I tromped over to the leprechaun, who grunted his derision.

Nevan, sidling up beside me, trailed his middle finger down the back of my forearm to tease the sensitive skin of my inner wrist, unleashing a riot of sensations. My body yearned to lean back into him.

None of that now. I linked my hands behind my back.

"Well?" Tris said. "You gonna convince me or what? I told ya I ain't in the habit of doing favors for mortals."

Nevan bent forward to loom over the seated leprechaun. "You'll be wanting to grant this favor. Unless you're in the mood for a thrashing."

"Shush," I said, elbowing him in the side. "I can handle this."

He grumbled.

I turned to the leprechaun. "Someone is trying to frame me for murder."

"That's my problem how?"

"Because…" My lips moved, I knew they did, but my train of thought derailed. Nevan and Tris must've heard the engine of my mind chugging, the wheels spinning, because they both studied me with bemused humor. I bounced on my heels and told Tris, with no attempt at all to disguise my self-satisfaction, "Because Nevan'll beat the crap out of you if you don't."

Nevan balked. "Pardon me, love, but I thought you were handling the di-lemma yourself. Woman's liberation, eh? I believe that's what your kind calls it."

"Yeah, it is—and yeah, I am handling it."

"But you told him—you threatened I would—" Nevan's words dis-integrated into exasperated noises. He threw his hands in the air. I muffled a giggle, but lost the battle with my grin. My reaction seemed to smother his temper and he let his arms drop. "I will never understand mortals."

"The feeling's mutual, Mr. Elemental Spirit of the Air." I tried to glare at Tris, but the humor slowly fading out of me hindered the attempt. "Will you do the resurrection thing or not?"

Tris worked his lips as if torn by the decision. "All right. But I'm only doing this to shut up your yammering. And so's I don't gotta watch you two drool over each other anymore. I'm getting nauseous."

"Maybe it's the raw copper ore you've been wolfing down."

He fixed me with a sly stare. "You want your sack of flesh and bones brought back to life or not?"

"I do."

"Let's get on with it then."

"Thank—" I clapped my own hand on my mouth this time, cutting off my words one syllable short of thanking the weaselly leprechaun. I chastised myself silently and removed my hand. "How's it work? This resurrection thing."

Tris chomped a bite of copper ore. "Use the vortex."

"Excuse me?"

"The vortex." Tris made a swirling gesture with his hand. "The one with the big sign next to it that says *healing vortex* in big white letters."

Realization rushed through me, stealing my breath and leaving me speechless. I'd known the vortex could heal minor wounds, but resurrect the dead? Holy heaven.

Tris eyed Nevan. "She illiterate or something?"

"No," Nevan intoned, "but she can be a tad slow to comprehend. We should excuse her, since this is her first trip through the falls."

The flapping of wings made us all jerk our heads skyward. A raven orbited overhead, banked lower with each circuit of the clearing. Though ravens all looked the same to me, an instinct warned me I'd met this one before. Brennus was back.

The raven dived into a tree, landing on a low-handing branch, and cawed three times.

Nevan stared down the bird.

The creature canted its head, coughing. Brennus casually fluttered his wings.

I inched toward Nevan. "Am I right in assuming that's—"

"Brennus."

The raven launched his body off the branch. It flapped wildly as Brennus rocketed up into the heavens to circle higher and higher until his dark figure shrank into a dot, winking out of sight.

Nevan pulled me snug against his side. He didn't have to tell me Brennus's appearance signaled bad news for us. Thanks to his spy and assassin, Skeiron would soon know where we were.

Thunder grumbled. A storm cloud blossomed in front of the sun and a chilly wind whipped through the clearing. I rubbed my bare arms as my gaze drifted up to the sky and the black mass consuming the blue. A crack of thunder detonated overhead.

I jumped.

Tris froze mid chew.

Nevan scowled at the cloud, his arm clinching me tighter.

An explosion of thunder rolled across the heavens, fading into silence, but I swore I heard laughter rumbling beneath it.

Nevan's breaths heated my cheek as he hunched to whisper in my ear. "No one will harm you. Not Brennus, not Skeiron, not even one of the gods will dare lay a hand on you. I will not allow it."

I longed to believe him, but though his words carried the weight of conviction, the sight of the raven soaring across the sky had slithered doubt through my heart. Nevan would try to protect me.

He would fail.

The certainty of it shimmied a chill down my spine, despite the warmth of Nevan's arm around my shoulders. He held me fast, his arm rigid.

Tris snapped off yet another bite of copper. "What's Brennus want with you two?" Nevan opened his mouth to answer, but Tris waved a hand. "Forget it. I don't wanna know."

"Are you sure this will work?" I asked. "The resurrection thing."

"Drag the mook into the vortex and it'll heal him." Tris scratched his chin. "Probably. Depends on how long it's been since he croaked and how busted up he is. Assuming his head ain't lopped off, it oughta work."

Earlier I'd learned firsthand the vortex had real regenerative power. Still, of all the shocking revelations I'd been hit with in the past twenty-four hours, somehow the notion of a genuine healing vortex stung worse than anything else. I'd spent three months denying such a thing could exist—hell, I'd spent years denying anything supernatural existed—and now my freedom depended on mystical healing energies.

Does it spin you?

Sandy's question about the vortex echoed in my brain. Yesterday, I'd told her no. Today, I felt my head spinning at the very mention of the blasted thing.

I resisted the impulse to tap my heels together and pray to go home. Instead, I leaned into Nevan just a little. "All I have to do is drag the body into the vortex?"

"Mm-hm," Tris mumbled around a mouthful of rock. "And let me finish my lunch. Gotta get the vortex up to full power for this one." I must've crinkled my brow or given some other sign of confusion, because Tris held up the copper bookend. "I eat this, it gives me power. The vortex gets it power from me. Get it?"

No, I didn't really, but I'd take his word for it.

I considered my options for a couple seconds, then said, "You didn't have to help me, Tris, but you did. You are a much nicer boy than you want everyone to think."

He looked up at me through his eyelashes, his mouth warped into a half grimace, half smile. Couldn't expect a teenager to admit he was a good boy. So not cool.

Was he a teenager? If Nevan could change his appearance, maybe Tris was older than he let on.

Tris shrugged one shoulder, returning his attention to the copper ore. "Whatever."

I swore I detected a faint blush on his cheeks.

As Tris kept on crunching ore, I twisted out from under Nevan's arm. He raised his brows but didn't try to stop me.

Tris, mouth stuffed with rock, mumbled, "You gonna save the dead guy or what?"

"Yes. Right now." I spun on my heels and bolted down the path back to the pool and the water-spouting boulder. Another pair of footfalls clapped up the path behind me. No need to glance back. Nevan was tailing me, I knew—or rather, I *felt* it.

Breaking out of the trees, I veered toward the boulder and its burbling water, certain the way home must lie somewhere in the vicinity of the tiny cascade. I'd wound up standing in front of the rock when I leaped through the darkness into this alien place.

Great, more water.

I halted at the pool's edge, mere feet from the big rock, my eyes drawn to the fountain spurting from it. Would I have to dive into the pool? My skin crawled at the idea.

Nevan sprinted past me, straight up to the boulder. Though I panted from exertion, he hadn't even broken a sweat.

"I'm assuming," he said, "you haven't the faintest idea how to get back from whence you came."

"Nope."

"It'll be easier this time." He slid his hand into mine, lacing our fingers. "Water is the doorway. When I say jump, do it. No hesitating. It is imperative you follow my instructions."

The seriousness of his tone convinced me. I nodded, but my gut clenched when I glanced back at the water.

Nevan dipped his free hand into the little fountain. The boulder dissolved into a darkness teeming with worm-like bands of blue, green, and purple. "Jump."

Hand in hand, we jumped.

The impact as we hit the floor in the cave made my knees buckle, punching them into the stone floor, shooting pains through my legs.

Nevan landed flat on his feet, steady as a mountain.

As my vision adjusted to the dimness, I raised a hand to my forehead and strained to make out my surroundings. Ahead of me, the waterfall cascaded over the cave's mouth in a rumbling, silvery curtain, muted by…uh…magic.

I glanced over my shoulder at the portal whatsit spiraling into infinity. Would I ever get used to the supernatural being real?

Nevan crouched beside me, lashed an arm around my waist, and jacked me up off my ass. Once he'd set me on my feet, he cradled my neck in his hands. "All right, love? No permanent damage?"

A playful lift of his brow contradicted his concerned tone. He was the most confusing man I'd ever met. "I'm fine. Let's go."

To my left, a shadow stirred. My attention swerved toward it just as a figure trundled out of the darkness in the depths of the cave.

Sheriff Travis Blackwell passed in front of the curtain of water, shoulders slumped, his clothes and hair rumpled and drenched and splatting drops onto the ground. Scrapes on his arms turned the skin a raw red. His mouth was open, his breaths came hard and fast. Eyes narrowed to slits, lips compressed into a line, he planted his feet wide to bar our path out of the cave with one hand positioned on the butt of his Sig Sauer.

His voice was hushed, his tone eerily cool. "Where have you been?"

I scuffled backward, bumping into Nevan. His body pressed against my back, buttressing me there. His hands, coiled around my upper arms, staked a claim. I had no time to consider whether I liked his dominant stance or the possessiveness it communicated, because Travis intervened.

With one wide step, he closed the distance between us and stabbed a finger in the air in front of my face. "I said where the hell have you been?"

His voice boomed in the confines of the cave, ricocheting off the walls. He repeated his question, with even more volume. I suppressed a cringe—damned if I'd show him any fear, no matter how insane he was acting—and told him in a dead-calm voice, "We explored the cave."

Travis's gaze swung past me, past Nevan, straight to the disk of blackness behind us and the multicolored tendrils corkscrewing within it. His eyes flew wide, his face blanched, and the fury crumbled out of him like a fragile shell broken by the wind. His hand fell away from his gun. He rocked back on his heels.

I wondered how long he'd hidden in the shadows, how much he'd witnessed.

"What is that stuff?" Travis asked, his tone far too even.

He was putting on a front and I couldn't fault him for it. The otherworldly hole in reality had thrown me for a loop too. His voice may have been even, but his eyes beseeched me for a rational explanation.

"I saw that thing when I first came in here, chasing after you two. I tried to touch the stuff, but it—" He jerked a hand toward the whirlpool hovering in midair, his lips trembling, infecting his voice with a matching quaver. "It floated away."

"Long story." One I really, really did not want to tell him. He'd drag me off to the loony bin for sure and maybe sign up for his own stint in a padded cell.

I tracked his gaze as it zeroed in on the churning darkness and its ribbons of luminous color unreeling into eternity. The abyss telescoped down to a pinpoint and winked out with a sizzling snap and a puff of air. Where once the portal had hovered, I saw only the mottled, uneven rock of the cave's rear wall.

Travis blinked twice in slow motion. He shook his head with such ferocity his head seemed to flap like a flag in the wind. He sank his face into hands, and after a moment, looked up at me. "If it's all right with you, I'm gonna pretend I never saw...whatever I thought I saw."

"Do what you want."

He squared his shoulders, straightening. "Why'd you run, Porter?"

Just like that, we were back to the cop-versus-suspect dynamic. Not more than half an hour ago, I'd panicked when Travis whipped out his handcuffs and suggested he might arrest me. Now—backed up, in the literal and figurative sense, by a sylph who could whisk me away in a heartbeat—I discovered it had gotten much easier to defy the sheriff.

"I won't go to jail again," I informed him. "Not ever."

Nevan's fingers pressed into my skin. Whether his gesture signified support or a warning, I couldn't say for sure.

Travis drummed his fingers on his leather belt. "I offered to help you."

"You mean the way you helped last time?" I shrugged out of Nevan's grasp to take a single step forward. "Why should I trust you?"

My fingers curled claw-like toward my palms but did not ball into fists. The memory of those days, of the most horrifying time in my life, ratcheted up my tension until my entire body ached from the pressure of rigid muscles.

Nevan kissed the top of my head. His hands stroked my arms, the realness of his touch banishing the ghosts of the past. He nuzzled my hair, murmuring phrases of comfort too soft for Travis to hear.

Thank you. Did gratitude expressed in thoughts count? Nevan had said debts accrued in the Unseen realm, not here, so I supposed I was safe.

"Well, Travis?" I said. "Why should I trust you?"

He rubbed his eyes and his voice grew strained as he met my gaze head-on. "I'm sorry for how I treated you back then. More sorry than you could possibly know. Took me six months to track you down, Lindsey. I came here to try and mend our friendship. I screwed that up too. Won't ask forgiveness, 'cuz I don't deserve it, but I will say this. I failed you three years ago. I won't make the same mistake today."

I should've felt vindicated by his admission, but it left me hollow. "Why didn't you tell me any of this when you turned up in Lutin Falls two and a half years ago?"

He aimed a long-suffering look in my direction. "You wouldn't speak to me unless it was in an official capacity. I've been fixing to tell you lots of times, but I chickened out. It's still hard to admit my brother went psycho on the girl he loved more than anything in the world. Hard to admit, to believe, I didn't see it coming. He was my *brother*."

Nevan glided a hand up my back, settling his palm between my shoulder blades. I'd almost forgotten about Nevan. He had become a pillar of strength for me, and though I'd leaned into him moments ago, his presence had faded into the background of my consciousness. Another item had also lapsed from my thoughts.

The dead body.

Enough distractions. Travis's admission confused me, but I had no time to consider its implications. I moved away from Nevan, toward Travis and the waterfall behind him.

"I appreciate your honesty," I said and shoved him aside, clearing my path to the falls. "But I've got work to do."

"Work? What the blazes are you talking about?"

Spray from the waterfall misted over my face and my hair, pasting strands to my cheeks. I swiped them away. "I have a dead man to resurrect."

Travis scuffled sideways, distancing himself from me even as he glared at Nevan. I glanced around in search of the sylph and found him standing behind me, motionless and erect, his gaze remote yet fastened on Travis. Despite his aloof demeanor, Nevan's irises burned with a tempered fire. He'd withdrawn from the battle, but not from the war.

What exactly the two men were fighting for, I had no clue.

"I'll retrieve the dead fellow," Nevan said, and vanished in the blink of an eye.

Travis took a hesitant step toward me. "Retrieve? What the hell's he talking about?"

"Nevan has gone to find the body and bring it here."

Travis's mouth puckered. "He's stealing a corpse?"

"Guess so."

The vibrations from the pounding water of the falls numbed my brain, driving out thoughts. Weariness descended upon me and my shoulders caved under the phantom weight. It felt like decades had elapsed since I leaped into the other world in search of a copper-eating leprechaun. I closed my eyes, more weary in mind than in body, yearning for a rest from all this craziness.

"You were gone a long time."

I came back to reality with a mental start, rolling my eyes toward Travis. His voice had sounded too close, which made sense considering he'd crept to within a foot of me. Worry lines creased his forehead.

"Don't be so dramatic, Travis," I said. "Half an hour is not a long time."

"Half an hour?" His mouth opened and his upper lip lifted, exposing his teeth. "Lindsey, you were gone for three hours."

CHAPTER TWELVE

"YOU'RE DEMENTED." MY VOICE SPIKED AN OCTAVE HIGHER. THREE hours? No way. As a little girl I'd read stories—legends—about people who were taken by the fairies and returned years later, but they hadn't aged a day because, for them, mere hours had ticked by in the fairy world.

Travis nodded solemnly. "It was three hours."

He tipped his wrist toward me to reveal his watch, the hour hand a black sliver on the pale face. Three hours had passed. *Three hours.*

I laid a hand on my chest, over my racing heart, unable to process the shock. Time truly did move slower in the other world. No legend after all. Why hadn't Nevan warned me?

As if on cue, Nevan popped back into the cave between me and the falls, the dead man slung over his shoulder. I yelped and hopped back, my feet splashing in a puddle. "You scared me. The way you zip in and out is not good for my health."

He tilted his head down, lowering his voice to a whisper meant only for me. "You can feel my approach."

Good point. Why hadn't I this time?

I lolled my head into his chest, exhaling a soft groan. "Travis told me something I couldn't believe and it kind of knocked me off kilter."

"He did what?" Nevan enunciated each word with the hardness of an ax splitting bone.

Looking up at him, I gave his chest a light smack. "Don't go all caveman on me again. This is your fault."

"My fault?"

I backed away a few steps. "You didn't warn me time passes slower in the Unseen realm."

"Ah, that." He gave me a sheepish smile. "I simply didn't think to mention it. Besides, the time difference is usually minimal."

"Usually? We were gone for three hours."

He tapped his wrist. "Sylphs don't wear watches."

"But you knew this would happen. Why didn't you tell me?"

Travis chuckled, appearing far too pleased with himself. "Not so gaga over jungle boy anymore, are ya?"

As one, Nevan and I swung our heads toward Travis and shouted, "Shut up!"

"This is none of your business," I added, and Travis raised his hands palms out, backing away. He watched us with smug amusement.

Nevan turned his attention to me. "Time passes more swiftly in the Unseen realm when magic affects the continuum."

"You swore you wouldn't use magic on me."

He shot ramrod straight, chin up, gazing down at me over the tip of his elegant nose. "I never break a promise. Perhaps whatever allowed you to cross the veil caused time to pass more quickly. Besides, what would I have to gain by stealing hours from you?"

Good point. The missing time had served only to tick off Travis worse than before and saddled me with an absence I had to explain away. If Nevan had planned this, he would've known I'd realize how much time passed. I'd be mad at him, which I currently was. He gained nothing from the missing hours.

A nasty thought occurred to me and I whirled on Travis. "How do I know you didn't set your watch ahead three hours?"

He slapped a hand on the rock wall. "Christ, if you're gonna believe a freak who wears a dish towel for clothes, I don't know you at all."

"We finally agree on something."

Nevan hefted the dead man off the floor, slinging him over his shoulder again. "Shall we take care of your deceased friend, or should I hand him over to the sheriff?"

"Let's fix this. Please."

Nevan crossed through the falls and out of sight. I tiptoed closer to the water, envisioning the cliff one step beyond it and the roiling pool below.

"Porter," Travis grated through his locked teeth, "think about what you're doing. Who you're trusting."

"I have."

Holding my breath, I steeled myself for what lay ahead and marched through the silvery curtain of the falls.

I halted just in front of the falling water, my toes sticking out over the ledge. Nevan grasped my hand. I accepted the support and inched along behind him as he strode down the ledge with the dead man on his shoulder. When he stopped a few yards from the falls, I aimed a questioning look at him. He draped his free arm around my shoulders, snuggling me against him.

The world plunged into darkness. We sailed down, down, down into the clawing abyss, crashing through energies that scraped at my flesh. My arms bolted around Nevan's waist, I hooked my legs around his and prayed his hold on the dead man wouldn't weaken his grip on me, sending my body reeling out into the void.

Light stung my eyes. Warm, humid air clung to my skin. I blinked my blurry eyes, my arms still welded to Nevan. His muscles moved beneath me and his weight shifted as something thumped nearby, then his other arm wrapped around me. The brilliance that had blinded me diminished into sunlight streaming down through the thick canopy of foliage.

We emerged in the clearing alongside the pool. The dead man lay on the ground at our feet.

Nevan cleared his throat. "Ye might want to unhook yourself from me, darlin', before I get the wrong idea about your intentions."

"Huh?" I glanced down. My legs were intertwined with his, my arms belted around his waist, and my hips tilted into him in what might've qualified as a seductive pose under different circumstances. *Oops.* I disentangled my body from his. "Sorry. Here I order you not to kiss me, and then I go all drunken-slut-at-a-frat-house on you."

His features scrunched into the most adorable look of bafflement. "What in the name of the stars are you rambling about?"

"I—Oh, to hell with it. Think whatever you want."

Spinning away from him, I waved an arm to indicate the dead man. "Grab him and let's get moving. Travis won't be far behind."

"The sheriff is of no consequence to me, love."

His imperious tone had returned and it rankled. "Stop calling me darling and love."

"Whatever you say, dearest."

"Gah!" It was my turn to throw my hands in the air. "Maybe I'll start calling you honey-pie. How'd you like that?"

Nevan collected the body, and as we headed down the trail, I thought I heard him mutter under his breath, "Mortal women are insane."

I broke into a sprint, hurrying past Nevan, anxious to reach the vortex and resolve my legal problems. The slapping of footfalls to the rear assured me Nevan had picked up speed too and I risked a glance over my shoulder. He loped along in my wake with his usual grace and fluidity, the literal dead weight bouncing on his shoulder. Nary a speck of perspiration marred his skin.

My breasts flopped up and down with each heavy step I took, my breaths quickened into gasps, and sweat dribbled down my face into my eyes and mouth. The salty flavor made me oddly hungry. When had I last eaten? My stomach grumbled, as if answering my question with a stern *too long ago*. Every step pushed my holstered gun into my side. I'd gotten so used to carrying it every day that I tended to forget about the weapon unless I needed it.

I rubbed my burning eyes, but kept my attention riveted to the path ahead, not stopping until I reached the vortex.

Nevan laid the dead man on the ground in the center of the circle delineated by the rock benches. He lowered himself onto one of the benches, crossed his ankles, set his hands on the rock, and leaned back.

I huddled at the entrance to the vortex, incapable of moving or tearing my gaze away from the corpse. The man looked too pallid and…well, too dead to spring back to life. Tris might've lied. Or too much time might've passed.

Please, God, let this work.

The dead man groaned.

I crouched beside him, knees bent, hands gripping my thighs. *Come on, come on.*

The man's chest heaved once, twice.

Please, please. I leaned over him, counting the seconds.

The man's breathing normalized. His eyes darted back and forth behind his lids and then, as his chest rose on a deep breath, his lids eased open. He blinked slowly, gaze unfocused. Lifelike color suffused his cheeks and his lips warmed from blue to a dusky pink. Pushing up onto his elbows, he rubbed his eyes and turned to me. His dark eyes, though still a smidge bleary, shimmered with life.

The vortex had resurrected him. I sat back on my heels, lost for words.

The man fingered his earlobe, glancing from me to Nevan and back again. His gaze sharpened on me. "I remember you."

A memory of our first encounter, back in the shop when he tried to pilfer the bookends, replayed in my mind. He'd told me to go to hell, wearing much the same expression. I locked my arms over my chest.

He bared his teeth in a sneer. "You're the bitch who grabbed me in the store."

"And you're the slimy thief who tried to make off with stolen merchandise."

The shoplifter wrinkled up his nose as if I smelled awful. "What'd you do, whack me over the head and drag me out here to torture me into confessing?"

I strongly resisted the urge to slug him. *You died, you nasty little toad, and the vortex brought you back—thanks to me and my pet sylph.*

Okay, I was not going to tell him that.

Tipping backward a few inches, needing more space between me and the angry jerk in front me, I said, "Don't you remember what happened?"

"Whatever it was, must've been you did it." He scrambled to his feet, swayed for a second, and regained his equilibrium in time to snare my arm. "You had it in for me from the start. Lying bitch."

He yanked my arm.

Nevan seized the man by his shirt collar, hefting him off the ground until his toes dangled in the air. The man thrashed but couldn't break free.

For the first time since we entered the clearing, I noticed Nevan's appearance. He'd conjured up the outfit he'd worn yesterday when he corroborated my story about the dead man for Travis.

Calm as the eye of a hurricane, Nevan told his captive, "This woman knows what you are and decided to save your life anyway. Perhaps you should be grateful to her, or else perhaps I will reverse the decision."

Threatening and polite at the same time. Impressive. And the way his biceps swelled and stretched every time the toad-man wriggled, yet his grip never faltered…Well, that was even more impressive.

The toad-man went pale and limp. He dared a sideways glance at me before bowing his head to stare at his dangling feet. "Sorry."

"And?" Nevan hefted the man a little higher, extracting a whimper.

The toad looked at me. "Thank you."

Nevan dropped the man, who struck the ground on his ass, legs splayed before him, arms slack.

Since the jerk appeared suitably defeated, I offered him a hand up. He cringed as if I'd held out razor-sharp claws, or maybe he thought I'd toss him over to Nevan, but after a couple seconds he accepted the aid.

On his feet again, he scratched at his arms, avoiding my gaze. "What happened to me?"

"Someone hit you on the head."

"Hit me?" He ran a hand through his hair, catching his fingers on the blood caked there. His face blanched. His fingers came away with dried blood stuck under the nails. His brow furrowed and his eyes widened. "Why don't I have a wound? I've got blood but—"

"It was a scratch," Nevan said. "Scalp wounds bleed like the dickens."

The toad-man closed his eyes briefly, relaxing. "Yeah, that's right. They do bleed a lot."

I forced my lips into my professional smile. I did need this guy to stay grateful, so he wouldn't blab to Travis about the imagined slights I committed against him. "I'm Lindsey, and this is Nevan. What's your name?"

"Brad." He spread his hands wide, scanning the ground. "Where's my bag?"

"Your backpack?" When he nodded, I counted to five before answering. *Oh, you mean the backpack you tried to shove stolen merchandise into right before you called me a bitch?* No, that would not do. "I guess somebody took it."

"What? I had important stuff in there."

Important stuff like the bookends he pinched. I shrugged. "Maybe it'll turn up."

Brad stretched his neck, rolling his head this way and that until something cracked. Appearing relieved, he said, "I really need to get out of the stinking woods."

"Better see a doctor, just to be safe."

"No thank you. Hospitals give me the willies." He stretched again, yawning. "Besides, I feel fine."

Although I was relieved to hear it, I couldn't quite believe he felt fine. Sure, the vortex had healed my lacerations, but those had been minor. This man had died.

Brad turned his head left and right, eying the rock circle. "How'd I get here? Last thing I remember is walking out of the store, to go wait for my friends in the parking lot."

Slinking out of the shop, he meant, with his booty stashed in his backpack. Still, I had to come up with a believable explanation of how Brad wound up here.

"You must've crawled here," Nevan suggested, sounding quite reasonable, "and then you passed out. A bump on the noggin can cause short-term amnesia."

He spoke with a tone of authority, as if he knew everything about head injuries. I gave him a quizzical look, but he wasn't paying any attention to me.

"Crawled?" Brad said. Lips parted, he tapped his tongue on his upper teeth. "I suppose that could've happened."

"I'm sure that's how you got here," I said. "Nevan's a doctor. He knows all about head injuries."

Hooking my arm around Nevan's, I beamed up at him with only a hint of sarcasm.

Nevan hit me with his smoldering smile, the one that always shifted my pulse into overdrive.

"A doctor?" Brad asked. "Couldn't he look me over?"

Full of gravitas, Nevan squinted down at the other man. He laid his palm on Brad's head, patting all around his scalp, then felt under the man's chin. "You seem quite fine."

"Thanks, doc." Brad held out a hand to Nevan, who shook it once. He nodded to me. "Thanks for watching over me while I was out."

He had no idea how "out" he'd been.

Brad took three steps past us.

I whirled, capturing his arm.

"Wait, I—" *Can't let you leave because you know too much.* Oh yeah. That'd go over swimmingly. "Could you wait here for a minute? Please."

A trace of suspicion flickered across his face. "Something wrong?"

Explanations deserted me, swept away on an icy tide of panic. "Please. As a favor to me, the woman who saved your life, stick around for a minute. While I talk to my, uh, friend over there."

Nevan arched an eyebrow at my use of the term friend.

Thankfully, Brad took a seat on one of the stone benches. "Okay. I'll wait."

I moved off to the side, out of Brad's earshot, and motioned for Nevan to follow. He waved a dismissive hand, returning his full attention to the formerly dead guy, over whom he stood sentry—tall and imposing, face blank and posture relaxed, but exuding a *don't mess with me* aura. When I stomped my foot and crooked my finger at him, Nevan finally obeyed and strode toward me.

His lips quirked, anxious to form a smirk, but to his credit he suppressed the look. He made no such effort with his playful tone of voice. "Can't wait to get me alone, eh?"

Since we had more pressing issues at the moment, I ignored his innuendo. "You have voodoo powers, right?"

"I believe you're confusing me with a witch doctor. Voodoo is not among my powers, nor is it a pastime of mine."

"You know what I meant. You have magical...stuff."

He slanted closer, his voice deepening. "Stuff?"

"Come on, work with me here."

"I would, but I'm not certain what precisely you're trying to accomplish."

"We need to convince Brad to forget he ever saw us. Unless you'd care to explain to Travis how we resurrected a corpse using a healing vortex powered by a copper-addicted leprechaun. He's having enough trouble with the psychedelic light show in the cave."

"His confusion is irrelevant. I expend no energy on sorting out mortal affairs." He slid his gaze down my body and back up to my face, and in the wake of his appraisal, excitement sizzled over my skin. "Except for yours. I am acutely aware of everything to do with you."

"Brad's rebirth concerns me." All of a sudden, I could hardly catch my breath. "I need your expertise."

He edged closer, backing me into a tree, and placed his arms on trunk, bracketing my head. "My powers are bound to my duties."

Surrounded, I had no choice but to meet his gaze, inhale his scent, absorb the heat of him. "You enchant people to check for freaky supernatural thingies. Couldn't you enchant Brad for me?"

He recoiled, his upper lip twitching. After a few seconds of staring hard at me, he pushed away from the tree. "My duty does not involve enchanting men."

"I'm not asking you to kiss him. Just put him in a trance or whatever, to make him open to suggestion. You can do that, right?"

He grumbled, frowning and plucking at the buttons of his shirt.

"Please, Nevan, I need you to try. If you can't make it work, fine. But at least give it a shot." I linked my hands in a pleading gesture. "I will be forever grateful if you do this for me."

He threw a quick glance at Brad. His face pinched in disgust, but he nodded.

I hopped up to kiss his cheek. "Thank you so, so, so much."

With a grunt, he stalked to Brad. The shoplifter floundered backward a half step. Nevan snapped his fingers in Brad's face, drawing the man's attention to him. Nevan's eyes began to swirl, erupting with bright metallic ribbons of color. Brad's mouth formed an O. His eyes went wide, his entire body slackening and swaying. Lips twisted, Nevan cast me a sidelong look before he took hold of the other man's shoulders to steady him.

"Listen to my voice," Nevan said, "and look into my eyes."

His tone hushed yet potent, he spoke to Brad in a language I didn't recognize, one brimming with exotic vowels and lilting beauty. Transfixed by his voice, I studied his face and the way his lips moved as he enunciated his words, recalling those nimble lips on mine, imagining how his mouth might explore my body.

Nevan let go of Brad and said, "It's done."

"What?" Ripped from my reverie, I stared blankly at him. "Already?"

"The man was quite easy to control. Weak willed, this one." Nevan ambled toward me. "I believe I've proved I will do anything for you."

Even enchant a man, despite his distaste for the task. He'd done it for me. Because I asked. I could've kissed him—if not for my no-kissing rule.

Movement behind him snagged my attention and I spotted Brad the erstwhile thief shambling past the stone benches, down the trail to the shop. His eyes were glassy, his expression vacant.

"Is he okay?" I asked Nevan.

"He will be. The enchantment will fade within moments, long enough for him to reach the shop. He will have no memory of either of us, or of what transpired here."

"Good." I watched Brad until the woods engulfed him. "Um, are you sure he'll be all right?"

"Yes."

The syllable was clipped. I glanced up at Nevan, but he'd gone stone-faced again. He did that when he was anxious, I'd come to realize. In spite of his assurances to the contrary, he must've worried his magic might damage Brad—and maybe he worried about the same thing with Sandy, with every woman he enchanted. How could anyone, even an immortal like him, live with the consequences of wielding such power, if it might harm another? I couldn't fathom the fear and guilt it must engender.

On top of that, Nevan was bound to a nasty piece of work like Skeiron. Forced to do the king's bidding. Yet somehow, he disobeyed those orders with me. He hypnotized Brad for me too. His statement from a moment ago echoed in my mind.

I believe I've proved I will do anything for you.

Would I do anything for him? The skin at my nape prickled, the sensation sweeping down my arms. I lifted my face to Nevan's, but he was staring down the path where Brad had disappeared from view. His watchful gaze shifted to scan the woods around us, though he remained motionless and silent. He truly was a guardian. Rather than protecting Skeiron's interests, he now watched over me.

My chest seemed to swell under the pressure of a dull ache behind my ribs. My heart felt full, on the verge of overflowing with emotions I couldn't name. Wouldn't name. I'd known this man for two days. And yet…

Unwilling to finish the thought, I threaded my fingers through his. "Walk me back to the shop?"

"Anything for you."

A figure tromped out of the trees behind the vortex. Travis meandered around the stone benches, looking dazed, and turned in a circle before dropping onto one of the benches. His eyes were bleary and aimed at the spot where Brad had lain moments earlier.

He lifted his head as if it weighed fifty pounds and looked at me. "That man was dead. I saw him in the morgue. His friends identified the body."

I took a couple halting steps toward him, but his stark expression stopped me. "How much did you see?"

"Everything." Travis's unfocused gaze veered to Nevan and back to the ground. "How'd you bring him back to life?"

"With the—"

He flung up a hand. "Never mind. I don't wanna know."

Behind me, Nevan muttered with disgust, "Shall I enchant the sheriff as well?"

"No." I knelt beside Travis. "Magic is real. I know it's a huge pill to swallow, but you have to accept the truth."

"Magic?" He spoke the word in a hushed tone. "I need to be alone. To think about all this."

"Come back to the shop with us. Please."

He erupted, his race flashing red, his voice echoing off the trees. "Leave me the fuck alone!"

I jumped up, reeling backward into Nevan.

"Let him be," Nevan said quietly. "Let me escort you back to the shop."

As Nevan led me away, I kept looking back at Travis until the woods obscured my view of him. His reaction to the reality of magic was the polar opposite of mine and I couldn't understand his fury about it. His behavior over the past few days mystified me.

Well, at least he hadn't arrested me.

We crossed the rock garden in silence, our footfalls crunching on the gravel path, and rounded the corner of the shop building. His hand stayed firmly swaddled around mine. Ever the watcher, he kept surveying the woods—for Brennus, no doubt, the harbinger of everything bad.

Awareness shivered down my spine and I checked the sky for a raven, but saw nothing except a few puffy clouds. The eerie recognition of eyes tracking me slithered over my skin, so much like the intuition that affected me two days ago, right before I found the dead man, I couldn't shake the feeling I was missing something vital. In the car, I'd heard Calder's voice in my head, but that must've been anxiety induced. Not real. It couldn't have been what it seemed to be.

I stopped dead, pulling Nevan with me. He scrutinized my face, concern evident in his eyes, and said, "You've gone pale as death, love. What is it?"

What the hell. Might as well ask him, the only one who might know. "Are ghosts real?"

"Ghosts?" He brushed his thumb across my cheek. "Why would ye ask?"

"Sylphs and leprechauns are real, but ghosts can't possibly exist?"

"They exist. Not in the way mortals believe, but I fail to see the relevance."

Part of me resisted confiding in him, but most of me wanted to, badly. "Is it possible Calder, the man I shot and killed, is haunting me?"

He pulled his head back, chin tucked. "What leads you to believe he is?"

I explained what happened in the sheriff's car. "I keep having this creepy feeling someone is watching me. I'm nuts, right?"

"Never would I describe you as insane. Ghosts do not generally flit about at will, they're bound to a specific location, generally the place where they died, and only until they complete their unfinished business." He leaned in, his forehead touching mine. "However, if you sense a malevolent presence, I trust in your instincts."

"It's nice to have someone who believes me." *And understands me, and makes me feel again.* I wound a spiraling lock of his hair around my finger, loving the slick softness of it. "We have to do something about Skeiron, don't we?"

"Skeiron is my problem, not yours. Vow you will stay far from these woods until I resolve the matter."

"I am not hiding. I'm probably fired by now, so I have nowhere else to be." *Except with you.* "Take me with you or I'll sneak up behind you anyway."

"Which you did with remarkable stealth two days ago. I required mere seconds to detect your approach."

I dropped the lock of his hair. "Probably the same way I sense you coming. Magic is cheating."

"Magic is the essence of every elemental being." He patted my behind and gave me a little push in the direction of the shop. "Go. Tend to customers. And stay away from the woods."

"Ugh. You are so boss—"

An excited shriek pierced the seclusion of the garden. Raucous voices and laughter ensued, blasting over us in an auditory tide of human revelry.

Nevan gave me a questioning look. I shrugged.

Taking my hand again, he ushered me out of the rock garden and along the gravel path toward the shop. As we rounded the bend into the parking lot, I saw it was crammed with cars of varying sizes, most gray or black, the cherry red of my Malibu the only spot of color.

Well, not quite the only one.

My gaze fell upon a rainbow-colored behemoth. The motor home squatted alongside the entrance to the parking lot, behind a row of tall SUVs and pickup trucks, its garish paint job gleaming in the sun.

I shut my eyes, exhaling a whimpery moan. "They're here."

Nevan squeezed my hand. "Is it the ghost?"

"No, it's not a ghost. It's my family."

Nevan let go of my hand. "I suppose I should depart."

"Why?"

He appraised me with a curious expression. "I assumed you would not wish your family to see me. I am...difficult to explain."

At the moment, his appearance was moderately normal, though still striking. "Travis may have freaked out when he saw what you really are, but trust me. My family can handle it."

He eyed me with wary eyes. "Are you certain you wouldn't prefer I left?"

"Positive." Sort of. He expected me to shoo him away, to stop my family from seeing him. Part of me really, really wanted to sequester him from the rest of my life, but another piece of me longed to escort him straight over to the motor home, knock on the door, and introduce him to my parents.

Nevan stepped backward, shoulders square.

I recognized the movement and the way his gaze went distant, like he was visualizing another place. He intended to poof away to who-knew-where any second.

He swallowed visibly, his lips compressing.

My God. I recognized that too, a manifestation of shame, similar to what I'd witnessed when he enchanted Sandy. He honestly believed I wanted him to go, and the knowledge pained him.

Which bothered me a lot more than I liked.

Static electricity rushed over me, faint yet distinct.

Pivoting toward him, I held up a hand to halt his departure. "Wait. I said I want you to stay."

"You informed me your family could handle my appearance." He sighed with exaggerated drama. "In point of fact, you have not said you wish me to remain here."

"Stay, dammit." My turn to sigh, with irritation. "I want you to meet my family."

Laughter echoed from around the front of the building. Hand in hand, Nevan and I ventured a little further into the parking lot. A group of people milled near the shop entrance, gesticulating and smiling, their cheery voices merging into a melee of sounds. I noticed the familiar backside of a curly mass of chestnut-brown hair, attached to a woman at the center of the hubbub.

My mother pivoted our way, as if she'd sensed my approach. Delight lit up her face and she waved her hand with fierce energy.

Where was Dad? I searched the faces of the people surrounding Mom, but he wasn't among them.

Nevan grasped my arm, pulling me up short. He pointed to another, smaller throng gathered in front of the Porter family's monstrosity on wheels. "What is this?"

The half dozen people gathered there formed a semicircle around someone sitting on the ground. I tilted my head left and right, struggling to see past the bodies. A blonde young woman shuffled sideways to hook her arm around her male companion's waist. The woman was Sandy. She smiled brightly, but the person on the ground must've done something, because her eyes went wide and her mouth opened on an *oooh*. Her companion watched the spectacle, whatever it was, with equal awe.

What on earth was happening over there?

The answer revealed itself an instant later. Another onlooker moved aside, granting me an unimpeded view of the man seated cross-legged on the gravel at the center of crowd. His gray hair—cut in a short, military-type style—fringed a round face etched with wrinkles. Though I couldn't see his eyes from here, I knew they were an ice-blue echo of mine. His wrists rested on his knees, palms up, the thumb and forefinger of each hand touching to form a little loop. The lotus position. The breeze carried his litany of soft *ohmmm*'s across the parking lot.

My father was meditating in the middle of a freaking parking lot at the rock shop where I worked.

"Do you know him?" Nevan asked.

"Sort of." I watched Sandy crouch down to speak to my father, who responded with a beatific smile. "He's my dad."

Just then, someone hollered from across the parking lot. "What the hell is going on out here?"

I cringed at the sound of Stan's gravelly voice. With no explanation for my hours of being gone, I expected to be fired on sight.

Stan stormed down the path into the parking lot. His face flamed a particularly disturbing shade of maroon. His head jerked left and right until his gaze slammed into me. His arm shot up, one finger zeroing in on me. "Porter!"

His voice thundered even louder, reverberating off the trees, the metal building, the motor home. I sidled up to Nevan, grateful beyond measure when he hooked an arm around my shoulders.

My father paused in his *ohmmm*'ing to stare at Stan. Ken Porter set his hands on his thighs, fingertips curling over his kneecaps. He said something to my boss, who stopped short. Stan glanced around, seeming almost embarrassed, and squatted beside my father. After a quick discussion, the two men exchanged smiles and Stan assumed the lotus position.

Stan Lagorio was meditating. *Ohm*'s and all.

The shock of seeing blustering Stan chilling out with my dad left me immobile. I'd intended to trot over there and greet my parents, but all of a sudden I couldn't summon the will to move away from Nevan and relinquish the bizarre security he provided.

"Do you fear your family?" Nevan asked.

"No, of course not. I love them, really, I do. But they are unusual. And most people don't like unusual, especially if it comes packaged with chanting and incense burning and crystal talismans."

He rubbed my arm, the gesture so tender my heart sped up at the implications of it. I couldn't think that way, though because he was forbidden to get involved in mortal affairs.

Except he was involved in the affairs of one mortal.

Nevan tucked one finger under my chin, angling my face up to him. "I'm unusual myself, and not inclined to be judgmental about talismans or chanting."

So true. He was a supernatural being. Of course he wouldn't balk at my family's devotion to all things New Age. He was, in a way, the embodiment of their beliefs.

Which meant I was a complete jerk. I'd pooh-poohed my family's lifestyle since I hit puberty, and it turned out they'd been right. The supernatural did exist. I found myself, in this very moment, nestled under the arm of an elemental spirit.

"Perhaps," Nevan said, "you're not truly worried about my reaction to your family, but rather about their reaction to me."

Hmm, yes. There was the issue of Nevan, who even in his demure, mortalesque form exuded a sensual confidence—and oh my heavens, he was jaw-droppingly hot either way. Then there was the lingering desire that sizzled over my skin, inflamed by the slightest touch, even from his hand quite chastely holding mine or his arm looped around me.

Rein it in, Lindsey.

I bound up my sexual urges, but I couldn't bear to pull away from Nevan. No harm in accepting comfort from him.

Without moving my head, I glanced at my father, still seated lotus-style smack in the middle of the parking lot. Would my parents notice the sexual tension crackling between me and Nevan? Did it matter? I supposed I cared what they thought because I wasn't entirely sure what I was doing. Cavorting with a magical being. At least nobody had seen me with him in his natural form.

Travis had seen—too much, too soon—and it sent him on a trip to la-la-land.

He couldn't handle the truth about the supernatural. My parents were predisposed to believe.

"Would ye prefer I whisk ye away from here?" Nevan asked.

"No." Dammit, I refused to be a coward. I gripped his hand harder, maybe a bit too hard, but he didn't flinch. "I want to see them, but you have to understand. I gave up on the New Age lifestyle, then I ran off to

Texas and got into trouble and, well…It's complicated. I told them Calder dumped me for another woman. They know nothing about what happened to me three years ago."

Neither did Nevan, but in spite of the curiosity evident in his gaze, he refrained from asking.

"I'll introduce you," I told him. "Just do me a favor. Promise not to be your usual scoundrel-ish self."

"I promise to behave in the presence of your kin. I've already made the sacrifice of covering myself, so as not to embarrass you." He inclined toward me, his lips near enough to kiss. For a heartbeat, I thought he would kiss me—and he did, sort of. He pecked the tip of my nose. "I shall support and protect as necessary. You have my word."

"Thank you."

His lips contorted, as if he fought against grinning or frowning. I couldn't decide which. "You were doing so well with not thanking me. I gather your family's arrival is disquieting and has made you forgetful."

"Sorry, it comes out of my mouth all on its own. Blame my parents. Those bastards, they raised me to be courteous and thoughtful of others' feelings."

He threaded his fingers through mine, his mortalesque eyes glimmering with a hint of the sylphesque fire masked within them. "You do love your family, don't you?"

"Of course I do." My eyes found Dad again, and an old feeling resurfaced to pluck at my heart. I'd missed my family. "They've always been there for me, when I'd let them. They're good people."

"They'd have to be, to raise a daughter like you."

Aw hell. Every time he paid me a compliment, the urge to smack one on him got harder and harder to suppress.

A child's gleeful cry split the air. "Zeeeee!"

Nevan's mouth dropped open a smidgen, his eyes flaring wide for a split second as he caught sight of my little brother. Ash Porter was hurtling across the parking lot, arms flung out, a silly grin on his face.

"What is that?" Nevan said, with the disbelief of a man who'd never met a ten-year-old New Age devotee.

Before I could respond, Ash was there, hurling himself up at me. I caught my brother in midair and he clamped his arms around my neck. His golden-brown hair, cut short like my dad's, tickled my cheek.

He kicked his feet in an airborne happy dance. "Zee, it's you!"

Since Ash was all but choking me, I unclamped his arms from my neck and set him on the ground. He latched onto my left hand. I tousled his hair and he giggled. "Who else would I be, Ash? Do you throw your arms around every girl you see?"

"No, I'm not stupid," he said, rolling his eyes. "I haven't seen you in months and months and months." My brother scrutinized me with an adorable look of concentration, his tongue poking out between his lips. "You look different. What'd you do to yourself?"

"Nothing. I emailed you a picture of me last week." But I hadn't seen my family in person for over three years. Wow. Three years. "You've gotten bigger, though."

He puffed up, lifting his chin. "One point two inches taller than my last report."

"Impressive." Yeah, my brother gave me regular reports on his growth, texted straight to my phone. Little boys were weird.

Ash appraised Nevan with youthful seriousness, tongue protruding again, and crossed his arms over his chest, partly obscuring the Superman cartoon on his T-shirt. Nevan raised a brow. Ash puckered his lips. "Dude, are you Lindsey's boyfriend?"

I opened my mouth to say no.

Nevan leaped in ahead of me. "Yes, in fact, I am."

CHAPTER THIRTEEN

"MY NAME IS NEVAN." HE OFFERED HIS HAND TO MY BROTHER, WHO ACcepted it. "And you are?"

"I'm Ash. So you're, like, really Zee's boyfriend?"

"Zee?" Nevan scrunched his whole face.

I got out one syllable before my brother bulldozed over me.

"It's what I call Lindsey."

"Why?" Nevan asked.

Ash rolled his eyes and dropped his head back. "Duh, it's from her name. Lind-*zee*. Get it? Everybody should have a wicked-cool nickname. She hated it at first, but I think she's starting to like it."

"I see," Nevan said.

Ash grabbed my hand and Nevan's, leaning his weight into it as he urged us to follow him. He half dragged us across the parking, swinging our hands, skipping and peppering us with questions he rarely gave us time to answer.

"Dude, you need a nickname," Ash told Nevan. "I mean, if you're gonna be part of our family, it's kinda required."

"He's not—" I cut myself off before I rejected Ash's suggestion about Nevan joining our family. Instead, I jumped into yet another lie. "Nevan and I haven't been seeing each other that long."

Okay, not entirely a lie.

Nevan raised my hand to his lips, feathering a kiss across my knuckles. "I am, however, immensely fond of your sister."

Nevan was immensely fond of me?

"Awesome." My brother tugged our hands, ensuring we'd continue trailing him across the parking lot. He released our hands as we reached my father and his circle of admirers. "Dad, I've got totally sick news. Lindsey's got a boyfriend."

And of course, he spoke the last part in a mocking, sing-song tone.

Nevan bent close to me to murmur, "I thought he was happy about this news, but he called it sick. Does he find me nauseating?"

"To a kid, sick means it's great."

"I…see." He straightened, but seemed to have developed a permanent crease in his forehead.

Ash took off, dancing around us as we approached the motor home, taunting me with his chant of "Lindsey's got a boyfriend, Lindsey's got a boyfriend."

When my dad approached us, I introduced him to my sort-of boyfriend. After sizing up Nevan with a dubious expression, my father thrust out a hand to shake Nevan's with shocking vigor.

"Nice to meet you, son." Dad sealed his other hand around Nevan's, tugging him closer. "If you hurt my daughter, I'll hunt you down and blow a hole through your skull the size of my fist. Understand?"

To his credit, Nevan stayed placid. "You have my word, sir. I've no intention of bringing harm to Lindsey, or of letting anyone else harm her. I stake my life on that promise."

Dad scowled at Nevan for several seconds, during which my pulse rocketed to levels no human should endure. At last, Ken Porter smiled and set my would-be boyfriend free. "Welcome to the family, Nevan."

I gaped at my father. Welcome to the family? I barely knew Nevan. Yet everyone assumed this was a relationship, and more than that, a serious relationship.

The three men in my life—Nevan, Dad, and Ash—glommed onto each other, plunging into an animated conversation. Nevan laughed at some joke my father told. Ash danced on his toes.

Dumbfounded, I could do nothing more than stare at the trio.

My mom, having disentangled herself from the crowd by the shop entrance, trotted up to our group. My mind had slipped into neutral, but somehow I managed to introduce my mother to Nevan. She snared him in a bear hug.

I stood immobile, hip-deep in shock. Mom never hugged anyone except family members and very close friends. When I'd introduced her to Calder, she'd barely shaken his hand. Calder was gorgeous and charming too, yet my family never took to him this way.

Maybe they'd sensed what I'd blinded myself to—that Calder was not right, on a fundamental level. I should've seen it. Unused to the attention, I'd been snowed by his innocent sweetness, his casual confidence, and his keen interest in me. Was I making the same mistake with Nevan?

Mom finally relinquished her hold on him, chortling at whatever he'd said. I couldn't take my eyes off his face, that beautiful grin, those mesmerizing eyes.

Dad slapped Nevan on the back. Ash hopped up and down, assailing Nevan with more questions.

My mother moseyed over to me. "A boyfriend? Since when?"

"It's a recent development. Sorry I didn't tell you."

"You like him more than Calder."

"Not sure yet."

"Pshaw. It's plain to see you do." She picked lint off my shirt. Or maybe it was otherworld moss. "It's okay, I like him."

"You—do?"

"Hooey, do I ever." She fanned her face with one hand. "He is gorgeous, a real hunk. That boy could make an old woman swoon. And he clearly adores you."

"Don't you think he's...odd?"

She tsked. "I trust my intuition, sweetie. Trust yours."

My shoulders caved in, as if great pressure compressed me. "I don't know. What if this thing with Nevan doesn't work out? What if he changes, like—" *Like Calder.* But I couldn't say it, because my family knew nothing about Calder's transformation or what he'd done to me. "What if Nevan turns out to be something other than what he seems?"

"You'll leave him." She formed a gun with her fingers. "And he if lays a finger on you, I'll off him."

Yeah, my entire family subscribed to the notion of shoot first, dispose of the body later. Only in self-defense, of course, or in the defense of another. Mom told me once she believed in the essential goodness of mankind, but sometimes a man needed a reminder to be kind delivered at the business end of a Smith & Wesson .357 Magnum revolver.

Mom owned one of those. She stashed it in her purse. Cindy Porter had also given her only daughter a Bond Arms Mini derringer. For my birthday. Along with a crystal pendant designed to calm negative energies.

For the first time, I understood the juxtaposition. A woman could believe in the supernatural and carry a loaded gun inside her waistband.

My gaze drifted to Nevan, where he was still chumming it up with Ash and my father. Despite years of scoffing at New Age stuff, deep down I had never stopped believing. I let popular opinion sway me into denying it, but I'd always believed. Even before I met Nevan. That's why I'd accepted everything he told me and showed me.

And yet I'd spent years scoffing at my family.

"Jeez." I scrubbed my face with my hands. "I am such a jerk. All these years, I've treated my own family like a band of kooks. You must hate me."

Mom kneaded my shoulders, freeing tension I hadn't realized was there. "Lindsey, you are not a jerk, and of course we don't hate you."

"I'm being punished. Karma's a bitch, right?"

Her fingers stilled. "What do you think you're being punished for?"

Damn. Freudian slips were real too.

"Tell me," she said, "how you feel you've been punished."

"I meant because of this crappy job. Karma hates me. I thumbed my nose at it and now I'm suffering for my arrogance."

My mother snorted. "Poppycock."

Against my will, my lips broke into a smile. "Thanks for the vote of confidence, but I'm not sure I deserve it."

Mom swung a finger past me, off to my right. "Your karma is standing right in front of you."

Tracking the line of her finger pointing, my gaze fell on Nevan.

He sat cross-legged on the gravel, one-third of a circle completed by my dad and Ash. Eyes closed, they appeared deep in meditation. Nevan seemed more relaxed than I'd ever seen him. His serene expression triggered a pang of something I'd buried deep inside me, under a mountain of pain, locked behind that damn vault door.

Nevan opened one eye, peering at me from under lush, dark lashes. His sweet smile devastated me, tearing into the mountain inside me, easing a long-held burden. Tears pricked my eyes and I hauled in a quaking breath.

I pushed away from the motor home, a coil of dread winding tight in my stomach. Though I looked away, I sensed Nevan's gaze on me. He couldn't be my karmic reward. It was crazy.

Nevan rose in a smooth movement, spoke to my dad and Stan—bidding them goodbye, apparently, since they waved—and strolled up to me.

To my mother, he said, "May I steal your daughter for a bit?"

"Go right ahead, dear."

Nevan slipped his hand into mine, guiding me around the end of the RV and the way to the other side of the vehicle. In the shade of the behemoth motor home, he drew me into his embrace. I closed my eyes, my cheek on his chest, and sighed with a contentment I hadn't experienced…ever. Until I met him.

"I wish to be alone with you," he murmured. "Quite alone."

"Sounds good." I folded my arms around him. "Please take me away."

"My pleasure."

He whisked us both away.

—

WE TOUCHED DOWN IN THE WOODS. MY EARS RANG, THANKS TO OUR trip through the carnivorous tunnel, which had me holding my breath. Having glued my eyes shut for the journey, I wrenched my lids apart as soon as we landed on solid ground.

Nevan kept his arms around me for a few more seconds, as I regained my footing. The tips of knee-high weeds swiped across my jeans. We huddled within a grove of pines and aspens, with a solitary birch standing sentinel behind Nevan, its white bark like a beam of light in the gloaming of the woods.

He stepped back a couple paces and frowned at the weeds. "This won't do."

"For what?"

Whether he hadn't heard me or heard but chose to ignore me, I couldn't say. He lifted one hand parallel to the ground, palm down, and moved it in a swirling motion. A breeze wafted through the clearing, rustling the vegetation. The weeds collapsed to the ground, flat as they would've been right after snow melt, compressed by a winter's worth of snow.

Nevan nodded, his smile one of satisfaction.

"Worried about ticks?" I asked.

"Ticks?" He hit the word hard, as if he couldn't quite grasp its meaning.

"Yeah. Tiny, blood-sucking insects that love tall weeds and carry diseases. We mere mortals prefer to avoid them."

"I know nothing of such creatures."

Pointing at the squished weeds, I asked, "Why'd you do that?"

As he advanced on me, he raked his gaze over my body from head to toe and back again. Desire darkened his features, fired up in his eyes, and roughened his voice. "I was striving for a more pleasurable atmosphere."

I responded the only way I knew how—with evasion. "Why did you tell my brother you're my boyfriend?"

"We have kissed, and we've spent the better part of three days in each other's company. What would you call me?"

Confusing. Enthralling. Frightening, at times. "I don't know."

"You trust me. You want me. We are involved, are we not?"

Involved? The word came with so many implications. "Technically, I guess we are."

"Well then." He ensnared my wrists with his hands, rubbing the pulse points there, his eyes burning and swirling in a maelstrom of living, breathing color. "Let's enjoy the pleasures of involvement."

The heat of his skin penetrated mine, rushing up my arms and through my entire body. My breaths quickened, my nipples shot hard, my breasts felt achy and constricted inside my bra. He skimmed his hands up my arms, inch by inch, tempting and teasing along the way with light strokes of his fingers.

His hands crested my shoulders, gliding up my throat to dive into my hair. His sure fingers massaged and explored, slid down to my nape, caressed and erased the tension bound up in my muscles. I couldn't stop my head from lolling backward into his touch, nor could I silence my breathy moan. I'd never experienced anything so damn good, and yet a need swelled inside me, a craving for more than this. Much more.

Losing control, losing my mind, losing my—

I snapped out of the haze as if someone had dumped a bucket of ice water over my head. Breathing hard, I staggered backward. I'd been on the verge of letting him do anything he wanted to me, of letting him take my virginity. Hell, I would've handed it over gift wrapped with a nice little thank-you card on top. To a man—a being—I'd known for less than three days. Christ.

Nevan raised one brow, his lips curving slightly in a devilish smile.

I coughed, shifting from one foot to the other. Could he read my mind? God, I hoped not.

He strode one step closer.

I scuttled backward, and for the second time since I'd met him, backed my stupid ass right into a tree. *Gah.* Why was I backing away from him, anyway? Not because I worried about losing control at the feel of his skin on mine or the intoxicating fever of his kiss. No, not because of that.

Nevan crossed those impressive arms over his chest, inexorably pulling my gaze to the landscape of sculpted sinews on his arms, and lower, to his taut abs and the trail chiseled out by those muscles, where it plunged beneath his loincloth.

One more step. Arms falling to his sides. Tongue sliding over his lips.

Plastered to the tree, I fought to catch my breath, to take in enough oxygen, but my scalp had begun to tingle.

Another step, those hips swaying.

Breath, stolen. Thoughts, scattered. I huddled against the tree, stiff and paralyzed.

With one final movement, he penned me between his body and the tree. He planted his hands on the wide trunk of the tree, at either side of my head. My heart fluttered, my stomach too. I crooked my fingers into the bark, desperate for a handhold to buttress me.

Nevan regarded me without expression, consuming my view so the entirety of my world consisted of him and only him. "Stars in heaven, love. Ye look ready to crumble. I didn't think a mortal could be this tense."

I'd built up enough tension to hold up a suspension bridge. "I've had a rough week."

"That's not the reason." He leaned in, his chest meeting my breasts, and suddenly the barrier of my clothing seemed flimsy and worthless. "Ye weren't this tense until I brought you here. With me. Alone."

The delicate pressure of his muscles against my rigid nipples coursed a painful desire straight down to my sex. I'd never survive this if I didn't cool things down. Right. Piece of cake. Moist, decadent cake dripping with warm, dark fudge sauce.

My mouth watered. *Damn.*

I drummed my left foot on the patch of purple wildflowers beneath my boots, pulverizing the petals.

Nevan shook his head. "How can ye stand to be this pent up?"

"Excuse me?"

"Perhaps repressed is a better term."

Repressed? Pent up? I ratcheted my spine even straighter and elevated my chin. "I am not repressed."

Except I had a mental vault where I locked up my emotions. But that wasn't the same as repressing them. *Pathetic, pathetic, pathetic.*

"It was an observation," he said, "not a judgment. You conceal your most powerful feelings quite masterfully."

"Said the pot to the kettle."

"And which would I be?"

"Does it matter?"

He dipped his head to mine, his lips within licking distance. Not that I wanted to lick him—them. As if he'd perceived my lust, he wet his lips with a slow glide of his tongue. His voice vibrated through me like distant thunder. "You are definitely the pot. A kettle releases it steam, but you've got yours sealed under a tight lid."

"I'm not sure that's the correct definition a pot or a kettle."

"Ye won't distract me with semantics, love." He settled a finger on my lips. "I can feel the steam trapped within ye."

"But I'm not angry."

He dragged his finger across my mouth, swept it back to center of my lips, nudged it between them until I tasted his skin. "Not that kind of steam."

Too late I understood, and my insides went warm and liquid. My shoulders sank against the tree. My head fell back, exposing my throat. Every labored breath pushed my breasts into him, chafing my nipples, turning my nerves into high-tension wires, the current fierce and almost unbearable.

Where was the frigging grip I'd gotten hold of a minute ago? I must've dropped it here somewhere.

Fumbling for my mental armor, I cleared my throat. "Maybe I do hold things in, but you're one to talk. I'm onto you, buster. This whole happy-go-lucky Irishman thing is an act, because you're just as repressed as I am, only in a different way."

"I'm not on the brink of snapping under the pressure of it."

Couldn't help smirking. "You just admitted you are pent up."

He bent his elbows, laying his forearms against the tree, bringing his body and lips to within a hair's breadth of mine. "I maintain control because I must."

I dared not move, else I'd be kissing him without intending to. Probably not intending it. I tried to scowl, but his proximity kept me on edge—a thrilling edge, beyond which lay forbidden pleasures. Failing to muster any anger, I clutched at the tree's bark, scraping off bits. "For you, it's control. For me, it's repression. Hmph."

"Am I to know what *hmph* means?"

I squirmed and my hips rubbed across his erection. Swallowing hard, I said, "*Hmph* means if this is your idea of flirting, you need an intensive workshop in seduction."

He smiled, white teeth bared, eyes crinkled at the corners. "Seduction. Is that what you're wanting, love?"

Shit, shit, shit. Why did I never learn to shut my trap?

"No." The petulance in my voice disheartened me. I pressed myself harder into the tree, and the bark scratched at me through my T-shirt. "Not what I meant. I do not want you to…um…do that."

His fingers, poised at either side of my head, toyed with my hair. Wispy locks feathered over my skin as he rumbled, "I will gladly study your desires and memorize all the ways I might tempt you."

Had to change the subject. Immediately. "Tell me more about the Unseen realm. Are bargains and debts the only things I have to worry about?"

Interest glimmered behind the firestorm in his eyes. "Are ye planning on spending more time in my world?"

"I don't—not really. I mean, if the need arises—"

He rocked his hips into me, his arousal hard and hot against my belly. "If what need arises? Ah, never mind. I can imagine."

"Keep your *imagination* in your pants, please."

His hair tickled my face as he tilted his head to the side. He dashed little kisses over my neck, working his way back to my face until his breaths ghosted over my mouth and I swore I felt the barest caress of his lips.

My eyes flew open. I shoved my hand between our mouths. "No kissing, you promised."

"I did not kiss you." He drew his head back and frowned. "I can tell when you're thinking of him. That Calder person. I recognize the grieved look."

"I'm not sorry he's gone."

"But you grieve for your innocence. It can't be regained." Though his face had retreated, his body was still molded to mine as he circled a fingertip over my temple. "I can show you a more rewarding state of mind, and body, if you wish it. One certain to erase bad memories."

"It's not that easy."

"Nothing worthwhile ever is."

His mouth hovered close to mine, yet never touched me. He must've possessed incredible control to keep a distance of millimeters without slipping. The nearness of him, the risk of accidental contact, excited me more than I'd ever admit aloud.

"Your heart is racing," he said against my throat. "Are you afraid of me?"

"No."

"Then you must be excited."

Christ, was I ever. More than I'd dreamed I could be.

A question popped into my brain, and I had to ask, since we seemed to be constantly negotiating one thing or another. "Do bargains and debts have any real power in this world?"

"No, not here."

"Magic doesn't force you to stick to our no-kissing agreement."

"I choose to abide by it."

His admission relaxed me more than anything else he might've done. Without magical repercussions to coerce him, he nevertheless stuck to our bargain. I wondered why for a brief moment, until he silenced my inner voice, skating his hand up my arm, hovering it just above the skin, exciting the fine hairs and stimulating the nerves beneath the surface. It felt like he'd flicked a thousand tiny switches inside me, to unleash pathways never before opened. I sighed, flooded with a satisfaction so intense my body slackened.

I was aroused and unwound all at once. Electrified and soothed. Starved and sated. It seemed impossible, but like many things I'd learned of late, this impossibility proved all too possible.

"I have to go," I said, "back to the shop. My family deserves an explanation. I owe them several of those, actually." A cold blade of anxiety pierced my heart. "I need to tell them about Calder."

He watched me, immovable as a boulder, his mood unreadable.

I waved a hand. "Step aside, please."

"You'll need to release me first."

"What?"

He nodded at my hands.

They were on his hips, my fingers gripping him.

I yanked my hands away and clamped them under my arms. I flailed for my thoughts, which spun out away from me. Somehow, this man—sylph, elemental, whatever—could shatter my composure without doing a blessed thing.

"Shall I transport you back to the shop?" he asked.

I roamed my gaze over the surroundings. "How far away are we?"

"Perhaps a five-minute walk."

"I'd rather walk, if you don't mind." A little time to clear my head, away from the influence of his proximity. Unbridled desires led to only one outcome.

Pain. Suffering. Tragedy.

I ducked around Nevan, marching toward the other side of the clearing.

He cleared his throat, gesturing in the opposite direction. "It's this way, darlin'."

"Oh." I spun on my heels and stalked past him down a narrow deer trail.

Alone.

CHAPTER FOURTEEN

M Y SOLITUDE LASTED TEN SECONDS. THE SLAPPING OF BARE FEET ON earth signified Nevan had caught up to me.

I sighed when he came up alongside me. "Said I wanted to be alone."

"You said you'd rather walk. No mention of wishing me gone."

"I don't wish you gone. I wanted a little time to myself, that's all."

"Beginning to think you don't know what you really want."

Once again, he delved right down to my soul to expose a truth I couldn't deny. "Maybe I don't know what I want. But I'm too tired for penetrating insights, okay?"

He slipped an arm around my waist. "Am I penetrating you?"

"Ugh." I dared to glance at him, dismayed by his playful smile. "I just keep setting myself up for your double entendres, don't I?"

"Repressed longings are bound to slip out now and again."

Opting to let that comment go, because I absolutely did not want to discuss my pent-up emotions, I walked faster. He removed his arm but kept pace with me as we traveled in silence, his strides sure and purposeful while mine were shuffling. With anyone else, the lack of conversation would've made me uneasy, yet with him it seemed natural to be in each other's company without small talk.

A couple minutes later, as we approached the healing vortex, my gut twisted into tight little knots at the thought of what I needed to do. Tell my family about the supernatural nightmare my life had become. I resisted the urge to chew my nails, a bad habit I'd never suffered from before, and shoved my hands in my jeans pockets.

Nevan slid a hand down the underside of my wrist, easing my hand out of my pocket and into his palm.

I closed my fingers around his. "Tell me something about you. Something you wouldn't tell anyone else."

He stopped. His hold on my hand halted me too. We angled toward each other like two magnets whose poles sought to align.

"I was mortal once," he said.

"Was it a punishment, like getting suspended from school?"

"No." His fingers fidgeted around mine but he held onto my hand. "I was born a mortal and died one as well. My people had engaged in a long-standing war with a neighboring clan. I suffered a grievous injury during the last battle I fought. I was dying, I knew this." His fingers grasped mine harder, then loosened, his thumb massaging the back of my hand. "I had collapsed on the shores of a lake, my blood flowing into the waters, sinking down to the bottom where a portal to the otherworld lay. As it turned out, I had a bit of the Unseen realm in me. My blood unlocked the doorway."

Questions bounced in my head, but I squelched them. *Later.*

He raised our joined hands to his chest level, capturing me in his hold. Seeking comfort. Seeking connection. I recognized the need, since I'd suffered from it my entire life. Until I'd met this man, I'd failed to find the thing for which I longed the most. Its name whispered in the recesses of my mind, but still, I could not speak it even in my own thoughts.

No, I couldn't have fulfilled that need. Not yet. Not after three days with him.

I pulled our hands to my breast, sealing them together with my free hand. My heart beat a bit faster, with his skin glued to mine in the valley between my breasts, and my heart lightened.

Too soon, way too soon.

And yet, I could not let go of his hands.

"The sylph king, Notus, came to me," Nevan said.

"Skeiron hasn't always been king?"

"He ascended to the throne after a lengthy and violent war with Notus." A shadow seemed to fall over him—a shadow from the past. "At one time, Skeiron was an admirable warrior, the leader of the sylph army, a faithful servant to the king. Notus became depraved, though, just as Skeiron has."

Skeiron a decent guy? Unbelievable.

He appeared haggard now, burdened with the memories he recounted. "Notus offered me a choice—to die a natural, mortal death, or to be forged into a sylph. You see, elemental beings may produce offspring through biological reproduction but many deem it unseemly. We connive to increase our numbers through a method that's easier for our kind but far more perilous for the one who undergoes the forging."

I didn't like the way he said *we*, including himself in the statement. "Are you saying you've convinced mortals to go through this forging thing?"

"No." A pained look passed over his features, fading swiftly. "I would never encourage another to undertake it."

Good. I couldn't stand to think of him tricking mortals that way. Skeiron, for sure. But not Nevan. "How do elementals get people to do it?"

"We appeal to the fear of death ingrained in most humans." He gave a sharp, bitter laugh. "It worked on me. I accepted Notus's offer, though I had no notion of what it entailed. Believing in an afterlife does not, as I discovered, negate a weak soul's fear of dying."

"You are not weak." My questions must've been exposed on my face, because his mouth formed a sad smile.

"Pain and blood, that's what it entails," he told me. "The forging process demands a hefty price in suffering. I pray you never comprehend the depth of it."

My soul ached for him. The worst I could imagine was horrific, yet I sensed the truth in his prayer for me. I couldn't fathom the agony he'd lived through during his transformation.

"When an elemental offers immortality," he said, "the mortal has no conception of what awaits him."

"They leave out the bad parts, eh? Guess nobody would take the deal if they were transparent about the specifics."

"Indeed." He inched closer and my heart ticked even faster. "Since then, I've learned to be more cautious when entering into bargains."

"Why is it," I said, gazing up into his eyes, "you always smell like earth and thunderstorms?"

He extricated one of his hands from mine, plunging it into my hair to cup my nape. "I told you, I was forged from the earth and the air, imbued with everything in nature."

"There's no dirt in the air."

"Certainly there is." He tipped my head back, as if he meant to kiss me, and my lips parted in anticipation. "All of the elements are swept into the atmosphere. Water, earth, fire—you'll find particles of each in the air that surrounds, fills, and enlivens your mortal body." He dived his head down to mine, our mouths a breath apart. "Your soft, delectable mortal body."

My skin thrummed, alive with the promise implicit in his movements and his words.

He pulled away, strode backward one pace, and gestured down the trail. "After you."

Bereft of his touch, I huffed out a breath. "Do you enjoy torturing me?"

"Your ban on kissing remains in effect." His smug smile irked me. "So in actuality, it is you torturing me."

I breezed past him down the path toward the vortex. "Don't get too pleased with yourself. It's not like I threw myself at you."

"Perhaps not, but you wanted me to kiss you. Licked those ripe lips of yours and opened them in invitation."

"I did not." I had, but not on purpose. My stupid lips had a mind of their own these days.

He smiled brightly, chuckling. "Console yourself however ye like."

"Thank you. I will."

My statement garnered another chuckle. We walked in the comfortable silence I'd come to appreciate, the chattering of squirrels the only disruption to the arboreal serenity. A sky of deep azure peeked out from behind the treetops, and even the humidity sticking to my skin couldn't dampen the spark that still crackled inside me.

We passed the vortex and wended through the rock garden. Up ahead, I caught sight of the shop through the last stand of screening trees. Anxiety trickled down my nerves.

Nevan laid a hand on my wrist. "Don't go spoiling my hard work by tensing up again."

"Oh no," I drawled, "I wouldn't dream of inconveniencing you with my stark panic."

"Shall I accompany you, to offer support when you speak to your family?"

"I appreciate the offer." And I did, with all my heart. "But no. I'd better handle this on my own."

"Of course."

I glanced in the direction of the shop, its roof just visible behind the trees. "Will you be, uh, handling your own business while I'm occupied?"

He pinched the bridge of his nose. "Although I should return to my duties, I find I can't quite motivate myself."

"It's all right. I don't m—" I almost said I didn't mind, which was a lie. "I understand you have a duty and an angry king to satisfy. If you're hesitating because of me, it's not necessary. Don't let me stand in your way."

"You stand in the way of nothing."

"The men I've known would leap at the chance to kiss women for a living."

"After a century of it, they too would grow weary of the task." He kicked at a pebble half embedded in the dirt. "And it's not as if these women come to me of their own volition, or as if I choose them for myself. The desire they feel is engendered by magic, required by my bargain with Skeiron, and the kiss is vacant of meaning or pleasure."

I'd realized he hated his job, but the depth of his distaste for it never sank in until now. "You must kiss other women, for your own...enjoyment. Sexy elemental chicks must line up for the chance."

"No elemental woman will speak to me, much less proffer her lips to mine." He raked a hand through his hair. "And I suddenly find I cannot abide the notion of touching any woman other than you."

His admission stopped me. Telling my brother he was immensely fond of me was one thing. Losing interest in all other females signified a feeling deeper than simple affection, if I let myself believe it. He wouldn't lie, I knew that much.

I glanced around—looking for what, I didn't know. Anything to evade his gaze and the honesty in it. Desperate to change the subject, I asked, "Why won't elemental women touch you? Are they brain damaged, or just completely frigid?"

His dark brows elevated over his preternatural eyes. "Your confidence in me is greatly appreciated, but no. They avoid me because I engage in intimate contact with mortal woman. I am tainted."

"By measly kisses?"

"The mere touch of a hand taints me in the eyes of elemental females. What I've done with you would scandalize them."

My spirits lifted at the notion I'd scandalized supernatural females. *Score one for the mortal.* "Well, if you're not planning to fulfill your duty, what will you do while I'm gone?"

"Await you in your home." He ran a hand up and down his jaw. "If you'll permit me to enter in your absence."

"Please, feel free. I can give you a key—"

Nevan poofed away.

Politeness really was a foreign concept to elementals.

By the time I reached the RV, my parents had opened the door for me and waited on the top step.

No more chickening out.

"I need to come clean with you," I said, my voice surprisingly steady, "about a lot of things. To start with, I need to tell you the truth about Calder."

THE DOOR CLAPPED SHUT BEHIND ME AND I SLUMPED AGAINST IT, GRATE-ful for the twilit tranquility of my apartment. The draft from the air conditioning chilled my skin, drying the sweat and humidity stuck to me.

A shiver of awareness swept over me. Darkness cloaked the room, but the secondhand glow from outside filtered through the blinds, outlining a suspiciously familiar shape on the sofa.

"Nevan," I said, pushing away from the door.

Despite knowing what I'd find, when I hit the switch and light inundated the space, my pulse jumped at the sudden sight of Nevan reclined on the sofa, ankles crossed, feet braced on the worn carpeting. On spotting me, he slung an arm across the sofa's back as if waiting for me to snuggle against him.

I scuffled toward the end of the sofa. "You're still here."

"Naturally." He studied me with measured curiosity for a moment, then patted the sofa, inviting me to cuddle under his arm. "You look exhausted. Sit, before you collapse."

I tossed my purse on the floor. My car keys jangled inside it. Fatigue had seeped into every cell of my being, weighing me down and smearing grit in my eyes. Rubbing them, I clambered onto the sofa and curled up against him as he secured his arm around me. Knees tucked under me, I rested my head in the hollow of his shoulder.

"How did your confession go?" he asked, in a tone that implied he didn't care either way. Under the nonchalance, however, I discerned a sharp taint of darker emotion. Was he jealous I'd told my parents the truth and not him?

Hmm. Interesting.

I sketched curving lines on his chest with my fingertips, focused on the expanse of skin that became my canvas. "My parents needed to hear the story first."

He fiddled with the hem of my sleeve, staring into the vacant space between the sofa and my bedroom door.

"I was planning on telling you," I said, "after I talked to my family. This is after."

His gaze wandered over the meager contents of my apartment. Though he appeared unconcerned, I felt his body stiffen.

I spread my palm on his chest, propping my chin on his shoulder so I could watch his face. "I'm going to tell you about Calder, unless you're not interested anymore."

His fingers stilled. His eyes rotated my way, and though his expression stayed neutral, his lips tightened the slightest bit. "I assumed you wouldn't share the tale with me."

"You assume an awful lot, pal. Maybe you don't understand me as thoroughly as you think."

Without a trace of glibness, he said, "I admit it's possible."

"Are you offended I didn't tell you first?"

"Why should I be? I've no claim on you."

Yes you do. Sometimes I hated it, sometimes I longed to drown myself in it, but always I knew—if nothing else, on a subconscious level—he had staked a claim.

"Calder was Travis's brother, but I guess you know that already." An iron ball congealed in my gut and I laid my cheek on his shoulder, dreading what I must say. "I met Travis five years ago, when I got a paralegal job in Texas. We were friends, I thought. Not besties forever and ever, but we had nice conversations. Until his brother showed up."

This was where everything got complicated, and I took a moment to compose my thoughts. I needed Nevan to understand, maybe because I needed someone, anyone, to absolve me. As if it were possible. What I'd done could not be erased.

I snaked my arm across his broad torso, like I had any hope of holding him here if he decided to vanish again. "Calder had gone to New York after college to find himself, or some such nonsense. He came back humiliated, a failure in his own eyes. I could relate. From the moment we met, we just kind of…clicked."

Nevan stiffened a teensy bit, but he planted a tender kiss atop my head.

The story flowed out of me now, an unstoppable river of words. "I don't know why, but Travis did not like me dating his brother. He loved Calder, they'd been very close until I got in the way. Didn't mean to, but somehow I did." Memories unreeled in my mind fueling my voice with half-forgotten fears. "Calder was charming, sweet, intelligent, polite, and completely infatuated with me. I'd never been the object of anyone's affection before. He didn't even care I'm a moldy old virgin."

Nevan grunted. I hesitated, thinking he might speak, but he kept silent.

"I was with Calder for six months," I told him. "When he asked me to marry him, I said yes without reservation. Everything was good—until I decided to sleep with him."

With my ear to Nevan's chest, I counted the thump-thumps of his heart. They sped up a bit, as if he sensed what was coming. I fastened my arm tighter around him, praying his body could ground me to the present while I careened into the past.

"I told him I wanted to, you know, go all the way with him. We made a date for that night, but he stood me up, which was not like him at all." I drew me knees up, curling into myself while sheltered by Nevan. He enfolded me in his arms, the embrace protective and more comforting than I could articulate.

"He texted me," I continued, "saying he was sorry but his car broke down and he couldn't make it. We rescheduled for the next night, at eight o'clock. I went shopping in the morning, bought sexy lingerie, and I cooked a fancy meal for our candlelit date. I was so excited, so happy. But he didn't show. Again."

I crossed my arms over my knees, resting my chin on them. My insides quivered with a cold fear, a ghost of that night when everything changed.

"Take your time," Nevan murmured. "Or tell me no more. Your choice."

His understanding buoyed me to go on. "I fell asleep, in my sexy lingerie, still waiting for him after three hours. I woke up choking, with Calder's hands around my throat."

Nevan hooked a hand under my knees and eased me onto his lap. I huddled there, protected by his strong limbs, and let the tears pour out in silence. They oozed down my cheeks, hot and fast, streams of pain and regret that singed my skin. I didn't want to finish the story, but knew I had to do it. He needed to hear the rest. I needed him to hear it. Right here, right now, my future seemed to hinge on his reaction.

"Calder was all wild energy and mad conviction. I don't know how else to describe it. He'd gotten in with the key I gave him. But this wasn't the man I knew, the one I thought I loved. He was like a demon, with his crazy-wild eyes and his insane strength, and I realized he was going to rape me or kill me—or both."

Nevan caressed my hair, his face buried in the locks. The heat of his breaths rolled over my scalp.

"He tried to tie me up, to blindfold me. I kicked him in the nuts, which slowed him down for about a nanosecond. He tore my nightie, threw me onto the floor, clawed at me, and then—" I clutched Nevan's hand, but he didn't even wince when my nails cut into his skin. "He bit me. Repeatedly."

Nevan growled, a half-strangled noise, and hugged me tight.

I couldn't manage more than a whisper. "His teeth cut my ear the worst. He had his hands around my throat again, so tight I couldn't breathe. The whole time, he was babbling nonsense about blood being the key and I had to die to be stronger, to be his mate forever."

When I'd recounted the story to my parents, I hadn't cried. I'd held my emotions locked up, like always, because I never would've gotten through the ordeal of telling them otherwise. But here, with Nevan, the steel walls of my mental vault crumbled away into dust. The anguish and terror rushed through me with the same force they had that night.

"I had a semiautomatic pistol in my bedside table. When I grabbed the gun, Calder looked at it and laughed. I'll never forget the last thing he said. 'Mine forever, sweet thing, or no one's.' Then he rushed at me and I didn't have time to think, I knew I'd be dead unless—" I gritted my teeth, inhaling sharply through my nose. "I shot him seven times, six in the chest and once in the head. I emptied an entire clip into him and killed the man I was going to marry. That was the first time I saw a dead body."

The image of Brad's limp and bloodied form reared up in my mind. My stomach seemed to surge up into my throat. "When I found the dead guy the other day, I kept expecting Calder to jump out at me. Don't know why. He's gone, he has to be, I killed him."

Like a statue in an ancient temple, Nevan remained unmoving and seemingly unmoved. I knew better, though. Beneath his calm exterior, he contained a sea of emotions.

"It was my fault," I said. "I'd made Calder wait for…you know, sex. Made him wait too long and it pushed him over the edge. I wrecked him, and then I murdered him."

At last, Nevan spoke. "You murdered no one, sweet Lindsey. You shot him in self-defense. I imagine the sheriff convinced you withholding sex drove his brother to insanity."

"It's why he calls me ice princess. I'm so cold I freeze men's balls off, that's what he said at the time."

Nevan muttered something under his breath that might've been a curse in another language. "There's more, isn't there?"

A gentle query. I bent my head back to gaze at him. "After I shot Calder, I sat there shaking and crying for I don't know how long. I finally called nine-one-one, then I stumbled into the bathroom to throw up and put on some clothes. By the time the cops arrived, Calder's body was gone."

Nevan betrayed no surprise, no reaction at all, except for the gentle motion of his hand smoothing my hair, over and over, in slow sweeps. "You loved him."

"Thought I did. Not sure anymore. Maybe I don't really know what love is."

"You'll know it when you feel it." He turned me toward him so he could capture my gaze with his own. "Listen to me. Lack of sex does not compel a man to assault any woman, much less the one he claims to love. I know this for a fact."

I supposed he did, after a century of forced celibacy, but still…

As if he'd read my mind, Nevan grasped my face in his hands and said in a fierce voice, "You did not drive him mad. Besides, you were about to give yourself to him, so why would he choose that moment to snap?"

"Don't know. The snowball effect, I guess, and I decided too late—"

"No." He bent closer, our eyes level, his scorching with unnamed emotions. "You did nothing. He was weak. You are strong and good and deserve happiness."

I could no nothing except stare at him. He kept telling me how amazing I was, while I kept questioning everything, expecting him to change the way Calder had. But he wasn't Calder. Swimming in the whirlpool of Nevan's eyes, I finally understood this one fact. I knew Nevan's nature, because he'd never hidden it from me—from the jovial pseudo-Irishman to the primal warrior to the intensely sensual man, I'd witnessed every aspect of him.

I wanted to share my revelation with him, but when I opened my mouth, instead of speaking I yawned.

"Stressful day," I said around my big, loud yawn.

Nevan rose to his feet, taking me with him. In a dangerously hushed voice, he said, "If I had the power, I would travel back to that night and tear the man's head off with my bare hands before he had a chance to harm you."

I believed he both could and would do it, if given the chance. Settling my palm on his cheek, my fingertips on his temple, I felt a vein throbbing there. "The battle's long over. You can't do anything to change it and neither can I."

His eyes hooded, he turned his face into my palm. I skimmed my thumb over his mouth. His lips moved under my thumb, his tongue flicked out to sample my flesh.

Nevan stepped back, a sure sign he was about leave.

"Stay," I said. "Please. I don't want to be alone."

He nodded.

"Just let me change into my nightie first."

I hurried into the bedroom and called Nevan into the room. He strode to the dilapidated wooden chair in the corner by the window, plucked my satin robe off the seat, and lowered his lithe body onto the chair. The robe he draped over his lap, his fingers stroking the fabric.

I snatched my nightie off the bed and marched into the bathroom, kicking the door shut. I banged my knees on the sink, twice, while stripping off my clothes. The bathroom had just enough space between the sink and the wall to accommodate me, but no more than that, which was why I preferred changing in the bedroom. Not an option tonight.

When I emerged, Nevan grinned with wolfish delight.

His gaze heated when he soaked in the sight of me in my satin nightie.

The thing was skimpy, but nobody was supposed to see it. I liked the satin fabric on my skin. The spaghetti straps and mid-thigh hem kept me cool on these hot summer nights. I wore the nightie for me, not for leering sylphs.

He wasn't leering, though. He admired me, his gaze exploring the length of my body. By the time he finished his assessment, arousal had me in its velvety grip and I had to clamp my thighs together to quell the wet pulsing there. It didn't help. No man had ever looked at me the way he did. Like he wanted to devour every inch of my body.

"You are lovely," he said, petting my robe. "My tasty little morsel."

"Tasty morsel? I am not food."

"But you are delectable." He crooked his fingers into the robe, as if kneading flesh. "I know the taste of your kiss, love, sweet and spiced with all those luscious desires you keep bottled up. When you let go at last, I will feast on the rest of you as well."

For several seconds, I couldn't move or breathe. Feast on the rest of me. Though I tried so hard not to, I envisioned all the ways he might do just that.

I scuttled to the bed, flinging the covers back.

Nevan lifted my robe to his face and inhaled. His smile took on a predatory slant. "This garment smells of you, of honeysuckle and sunshine."

My knees bumped the mattress. "Baloney. Sunshine has no scent and I don't smell like honeysuckle."

"Ah, but you do. And you taste of strawberries."

Snorting, I sat on the bed. "Haven't eaten a strawberry in weeks."

"Nevertheless, you taste of them. Elementals can detect aromas and flavors mortals can't. Human men have no idea what they're missing." He frisked the satin across his lips. "You leave a fragment of your essence on everything you touch."

"Guess that means you're stuck smelling like me."

He let the robe tumble to the floor, where it puddled around his feet. "If I could, I'd bathe in your scent so I might enjoy it every moment of the day."

If he'd walked over here, I would've dragged him down onto the bed on top of me. My annoying brain, however, preferred to torture me with fear. "What about my family? Will Brennus go after them?"

My question shattered his rapture. "I don't know."

"You need to guard them."

"I will not leave you."

"Please, Nevan, I'm begging you. Watch over my family. They have no clue what's going on."

He worked his lips, finally settling on a lopsided frown. "I will not leave you alone all night, but I'll pop over every so often to check on your family. Satisfied?"

"Thank you."

He rolled his eyes heavenward. "Your manners will be the death of us yet."

I crawled under the covers, pulling them up to my neck. The cotton sheet and acrylic blanket failed to dull the effect of Nevan's gaze on me.

"Sleep well, my scrumptious mortal," he said, with humor in his voice.

"Yeah-yeah, good night."

I shut off the bedside lamp. Shadows descended, obscuring Nevan, obscuring anything that might be hiding nearby, invisible. He was a silhouette in the moonlight seeping through the lace curtains, his eyes simmering with muted amber.

Rolling onto my side, facing away from him, I began the fruitless battle for sleep. Memories of Calder and Skeiron and Brennus tormented me. With a huff, I flipped over to the other side, only to endure another replay of past horrors. I flipped back the other way. All the while, I was acutely aware of Nevan's gaze tickling my skin.

I punched my pillow. "Unh."

"Something the matter?"

"Can't sleep. No idea why, there's only a supernatural assassin stalking me at this very moment."

The wood chair he sat on creaked. As the shuffling of bare feet on carpeting came nearer, I resisted the instinct to glance over my shoulder. His presence had become a tangible thing, a light caress against my soul, both terrifying and thrilling me.

His weight settled onto the bed, rocking me a little. His firm, hot body nestled up against my backside as he sprawled an arm over my hip, letting it fall across my belly. His fingertips teased me through the fabric of my nightie.

"I will protect you," he said, "if you'll allow me to."

The strange part? Those were the most enticing words he'd spoken. "Still can't sleep."

He feathered his fingers over my belly. "I will watch over you."

My gaze inexorably moved to the deeper shadows in the corners.

Nevan withdrew his hand from under the sheet. "Perhaps a bit of illumination will ease your mind."

I expected him to switch on the lamp, but instead, he raised his hand in the air and flourished his fingers. A spark ignited in his palm, enlarging into a fist-size ball of incandescent, glittering light. He tossed the orb into the air and it hovered near the ceiling, directly over the bed, casting a delicate glow. Tiny sparks floated down from the orb, disintegrating before they touched us.

"What is that?" I asked.

"A fairy light," he said, tucking his hand under the blanket again, right over my womb. "A fae owed me a favor and gifted me with fairy lights in return. Sleep now."

The orb's glow was oddly comforting and I couldn't prevent myself from going limp as I exhaled out the tension. Cocooned by his body, enveloped in his supple flesh and tough sinew, I floated down from consciousness toward slumber.

His kiss intoxicated me. But this…I could get so addicted.

Nevan murmured to me, sweet and hushed. "Dream of me, Lindsey."

As if I could dream of anything else.

CHAPTER FIFTEEN

THE CHATTERING OF SQUIRRELS ROUSED ME AT SUNRISE. EYES CLOSED, I luxuriated in the softness of my sheets, the fluffiness of my pillow, and the whooshing of cool air through the vents. Thank heavens I'd found an apartment with central air. This heatwave would've killed me without a retreat.

Safe in Nevan's arms last night, I'd fallen into a dreamless sleep and not woken until morning. He'd said I was exhausted, and man, was he right. Soul-baring could really tax a girl. My long night's rest had recharged me for the day ahead and whatever new surprises it might bring.

I was alone in the bed this morning. The chair by the window sat empty. Nevan must've popped out to check on my family. I silently thanked him, stretching my arms above my head as I yawned.

Unease crept into me. My gaze migrated past the curtains to the gloom in the corner near the foot of the bed. I shivered at the unearthly sensation of invisible fingers probing my skin, and tugged the blanket up to my chin.

The darkness shifted.

Something is there.

I pushed up onto one elbow. "Nevan?"

Tentacles of energy, unseen and oily, stretched out to me, licking at my body as if testing the flavor. Whenever I sensed Nevan, his presence aroused and yet calmed me. This energy slithered over my skin. It seeped into my pores, infesting my psyche.

I heaved my body up into sitting position. The blanket slumped down to puddle around my hips. The tentacles fused to my flesh, to my bones, to my soul. Not Nevan. His presence activated my senses, nothing like this engulfing blackness.

"Who are you?" My voice came out strained, my throat was parched and tight.

The curtains billowed. An icy draft churned through the room.

My clammy hands dampened the sheet. The window was shut.

"Show yourself." As if I held any sway over supernatural beings. If Nevan refused to obey me, why should this entity? Still, I couldn't huddle on the bed praying the thing might vacate the premises. "What do you want?"

The darkness seethed. It siphoned fragments of light from the shaft of sunshine that warmed my skin. The bright and the black coiled, spun, coalesced into a tall figure.

A man.

I clutched the blanket to my breast, abruptly aware of the my nightie's low-cut neckline.

He moved away from the wall. His knee-length white toga swished around his thighs and the curtains fluttered behind him. Blades of sunlight scraped away the shadows enshrouding him to unmask his tall, muscle-bound frame. The light coated his olive skin with a golden sheen. His platinum-blond hair blazed as if set afire by the sunshine. Energy spun out from his body to entwine me in its frigid, slick embrace.

The being eyed me with detached interest, like a scientist examining a petri dish full of multiplying bacteria.

My ears rang. Darkness invaded my vision. I realized I'd stopped breathing and hauled in a lungful of air tainted with the sharp odor of something vile and indefinable. This was the man I'd met in the shop two days ago, the one who warned me the guardian was bound to him.

This was Skeiron, the king of the sylphs.

I fought to break eye contact but I couldn't blink, much less avert my gaze.

The immortal being before me bent his head back. "Are you the one?"

I struggled to speak, but my voice had frozen, along with the rest of me.

In one stride, he crossed to the bed. His mass towered over me, eclipsing the light and, as if on command, I raised my face to him.

He grasped my chin in one massive hand.

"You," he said, his voice cool and even, "have lured my best guardian away from his task. If you are the one, and he is concealing the truth from me…"

"Guardian?" He must've meant Nevan, the only guardian I knew, but I couldn't summon the brainpower to interpret Skeiron's words. His presence overwhelmed all else—the surroundings, my thoughts, my ability to feel anything save for his alien touch.

Skeiron's eyes shrank to slits, his mouth became a slash. "You know of whom I speak. You have spent three days with him, seducing the guardian into forsaking his duty for you."

Black hair. Swirling metallic eyes. The memory of Nevan rushed through me, sweeping my mind clean. "I haven't seduced anybody. Nevan does what he wants."

The sylph king tightened his grip on my chin the slightest bit. Flames of hellfire red erupted within his irises.

I scuttled backward, away from the pull of this creature's gravity.

Serpents of power whipped and snarled around me, unseen yet tangible, biting into my skin with every lash. I swatted at my arms and face, driven by the impulse to sanitize my flesh, but the spectral serpents tore at my flesh, firing shocks of pain into me.

The assault cut off with a jolt. The energy snapped back into the human-oid being who loomed over my bed.

Between gasps, I croaked, "I know who you are. Skeiron."

His nostrils flared, his eyes too. "A mortal may not speak my name. It is forbidden."

The nerve. I opened my mouth to spit out a snide retort, but snapped my jaw shut. This bastard stole into my home, into my bedroom, and accused me of luring Nevan away from his job of enchanting gorgeous, hapless women. Yet I was forbidden? I gulped back the hysterical laughter rising in my throat.

Skeiron exuded everything dark—anger, envy, greed, and a hunger I pre-ferred not to examine. My stomach twisted into razor-sharp knots. I clambered backward, away from him, and jumped off the bed's opposite side to barricade myself with its bulk. As if that would deter an elemental creature.

The king's top lip wrenched upward in a nasty expression. "I will root out the truth. If you are the one, I shall have you."

"I don't understand."

Skeiron flew across the bed to slam down in front me. On his knees on the mattress, inches away, he seared me with his glower. "Another seeks you, but he will not be as restrained as I."

He exploded into a black tornado the size of a man. It reeled through the room, knocking me off my feet. I cried out as my hip smacked into the dresser, my body ricocheted off it, and I crumpled to the floor.

The man-size twister plowed into the window. Glass shattered, raining into the room with a harsh tinkling sound. A final gust ripped through the space.

In the stillness that followed, I blew hair from my eyes. With both hands, I grabbed the mattress and hauled my ass off the floor. On my knees, bent over into the bed, I gaped at the shattered window. Bits of glass stuck to the wooden frame, which had splintered into multiple pieces. The curtains hung in tatters.

Nevan had alerted me to the danger, but I refused to listen. Refused to believe. Here, in my own home, the king of the sylphs had thrown down a gauntlet at my feet. And I still had no clue what Skeiron wanted from me.

Thunder boomed overhead. The building rattled around me and the floor trembled.

I staggered to my feet, bumbling sideways into the bedside table. Water sloshed in the glass I'd left there last night.

My battle with Calder nearly destroyed me, but at least my foe had been human—if deranged. This time, I floundered for the words to describe my predicament. Somehow I'd earned an enemy with unspeakable power and motives beyond my comprehension.

Skeiron's voice bellowed on the wind. "The guardian shall not have you. Your power belongs to me."

He thought I had power? This guy was terrifying *and* insane.

A bolt of dark power sliced through me. Nausea twisted my gut. Tears burst from my eyes, borne on a retching sob as the agony of Skeiron's energy clawed at my soul, and I clutched at my stomach, doubled over on another body-wrenching sob. A single thought seared my mind, a frantic call sent out through the ether, on a wavelength I'd never imagined existed. Maybe it didn't. Maybe I was freaking out from the knowledge I was about to die, but my mind—my heart—screamed the plea.

Nevan, I need you.

Thunder detonated overhead. The building trembled. Bits of paint and plaster showered down from the ceiling. The quaking escalated into a bone-jarring crescendo as framed photos bounced off the wall, striking the floor one by one. Glass cracked. The bed jounced.

The ceiling collapsed on top of me.

CHAPTER SIXTEEN

TICK, *TICK, TICK.* THE SOUND ROUSED ME FROM A FOG OF DIZZINESS and exhaustion. Darkness encased me, though I swore it had been morning a few minutes ago. My head pulsated with pain.

Flat on my stomach, I lifted my head. The floor tilted and spun.

Tick, tick.

The noise originated overhead. I pushed up onto my knees, but my muscles gave out and I collapsed again. Dust plumed up into my nose and eyes. I coughed, sneezed, panted. A heavy object pinned my feet, and though I jiggled them, I could not free my ankles. Resting my cheek on the floor, I blinked to clear the watering of my eyes. The ticking battered my eardrums like hammer blows.

I crawled my fingers across the floor, hunting for the source of the sound. My fingers bumped into a cold, metal object. I closed my hand around it and dragged the thing close to my face. The ticking got louder, its relentless rhythm apparent now. I held my alarm clock, an old-fashioned kind with hands that counted off the seconds and minutes. I was still in my bedroom.

Duh. A psycho with supernatural powers attempted to murder me, with my own bedroom as the weapon.

When I stretched one arm up over my head, my fingertips grazed popcorn-like balls. My muddled brain spit out one lucid thought. The balls came from the ceiling. Skeiron had stomped his proverbial, or perhaps literal, foot down on a pesky, eensy bug—aka, me.

I huddled under a large hunk of the ceiling. It pitched down at an angle, the higher end wedged on my bed, the lower pinning my ankles. I shoved against the ceiling chunk. No movement. I twisted around to push with both my hands, but succeeded only in punching pains into my shoulders and neck, straight up into my skull.

Trapped.

My chest morphed into a granite block crushing me. My breaths panted, shallow and unhelpful. Numbness tingled through my face and spread out into my body. I was hyperventilating. If I passed out, and the super-scary king of the sylphs came back, I'd be thoroughly screwed.

"Help!" My scream echoed in the space around me. My ears hurt from the noise. My eyes hurt too. Every muscle in my body burned or ached or quivered, or some combination of the three. My breaths puffed shallower and faster, the numbness sweeping down my limbs. "Somebody help me!"

My hoarse shriek set off a fit of hacking. I crumpled onto my stomach, cheek on the floor, hot tears streaming down my nose to drip onto the floor. No one was coming. I'd hyperventilate myself to death, if that was possible, or die in some other, more horrific way.

A weight thumped onto the pile above me. The debris shivered. Dust and fragments of plaster pelted me.

I spit out the dusty gunk that collected on my lips. What if Skeiron was back?

The ringing in my ears escalated into a chorus of off-key bells that deafened me. Black dots in my vision merged into a margin of darkness encroaching on my mind. *Don't pass out, don't pass out.*

The debris shifted. I squeezed my eyes shut against the cascade of detritus. It infiltrated my mouth, mutating into a dry, chalky paste on my tongue.

Rattling and clattering erupted overhead. A whooshing sound preceded a cracking splat.

The pressure on my ankles released with an almost painful rush. Cool air rushed over me. Light shimmered behind my lids, but I could not make my eyes open, immobilized by a primal terror. I sensed a figure above me and a familiar energy sizzled over my skin, but my adrenaline-addled brain denied my instincts, denied what I'd prayed for with the last scraps of my strength. I couldn't stop the fear from whispering in my ear a warning someone else might be impersonating my sylph, right down to the sensations I experienced when he was near but out of my sight.

When my rescuer moved closer, blocking the light, I sucked my lips between my teeth and squeezed my lids tight enough to wring tears from my eyes.

"Lindsey," a familiar voice said. "Love, can ye hear me?"

"Nevan?" I pried my eyelids apart. Through the tears and dust blending to blur my vision, I spied a person kneeling beside me. A large, bare-chested person. I inhaled, but drew in plaster dust and dirt, hacking until my throat was raw.

A hand stroked my forehead. "Shh, love, it's all right. Let me help you off the floor."

Nevan's voice flooded me with relief. The intensity of it pulverized my thoughts and wilted my body. One of his muscular arms locked around my waist to lift and turn me until he could hook his other arm under my knees. He scooped me up into his embrace, my head on his firm chest. His heartbeat hammered under my ear. My ears still rang, my breaths came quick and shallow.

"Easy now," he said. "Try to take slow, deep breaths. You're safe."

With my entire being, I trusted his words and clung to them like a life preserver. Though it consumed all my energy and concentration, I dragged in one long, slow breath after another. The ringing subsided. The numbness drained away, replaced by the warmth of his flesh against mine. I cuddled into him, relishing his earthy scent and the solidity of his body. *Safe.* Lord, for the first time in years I felt protected.

He nuzzled my hair. "Better?"

"Yeah." I dared to glance at my surroundings. Sunshine poured down through the hole where the ceiling had been, and rubble buried my bed. "I think your boss tried to smother me with a building."

He went rigid. I swung my gaze up to his face, inches from mine. The stutter in my pulse had nothing to do with shock. The stark look in his eyes, coupled with the strained slant of his mouth, pierced my heart. Without even thinking about it, I laid my hand on his cheek.

A weak smile trembled on his lips.

I caressed his face, stretching out my index finger to graze his temple. "I'm okay."

"The king spares no thought for mortals. Are you certain he did this?"

"Positive. Mr. Creepy didn't introduce himself, but I recognized him from the shop. He said a mortal shouldn't speak his name. He also said you couldn't have me."

Nevan set me down on my feet. He swept a tangled lock of hair from my face.

I rubbed my arms, overcome by an inner chill. "Your king's a real sweetheart. What's he got against me anyway? He sends a bird to spy on me, then he tries to murder me."

"If Skeiron meant to kill you, I'd be collecting the pieces of your remains from this debris."

"He dropped a freaking roof on me."

Nevan stared down at my bare feet, his arms slack at his sides.

My toes wiggled, as if they were showing off for him. Saucy little digits. I couldn't control my own toes around him.

He ground his teeth. "I failed to track down Brennus. Perhaps I could've stopped this if I had caught him."

"This is not your fault."

"It is." Nevan ran a hand over his mouth. "I've been selfish and reckless, abandoning my duty to be close to you. In the process, I've pulled you into the center of my debacle."

"Listen up." I waited until he looked me in the eye. "I wanted to be with you. I chose to go with you into the Unseen. Brennus has been spying on me, I knew it, and I decided it was worth the risk."

"To be with me?" he asked, his tone uncertain.

Just as I started to reply, a black shape spiraled down from the sky, right through the hole in the ceiling. I yelped, but Nevan glanced up with disinterest.

The grackle dove low over our heads before soaring up and away.

Nevan arched a brow at me. "Why so frightened? It was far too small for a raven."

"Excuse me for being a tad jumpy after my visit from His Royal Scariness."

"What else did Skeiron say to you?"

"Oh, nothing much." I shrugged halfheartedly, feigning indifference. "If you're the one then you'll be mine, I'm a big baddie, blah-blah-blah."

Nevan spewed a volley of what must've been curses, given his tone, but in that alien language he'd used before. He grasped the back of his neck in both hands. "Brennus may simply be observing you, but that is dangerous enough. He reports to the king. If Brennus has seen you with me, Skeiron also knows about our...relationship."

"Yeah, he probably heard you tell my brother you're my boyfriend."

"Possibly."

Boosting up on my tiptoes, I tapped my finger on his nose. "I notice you haven't asked if I'm your girlfriend."

"Such a presumption would be indelicate."

"Presuming you're my boyfriend isn't?"

"Ah..." Nevan grimaced, then swept his gaze over me. One corner of his mouth pinched.

I glanced down to discover dust and dirt coated me from head to toe and those little popcorn balls from the ceiling stuck to my skin and hair. I took hold of my nightgown between my thumb and forefinger, shaking the fabric. Dust clouded around me. Bits of debris plopped onto Nevan's feet. "If Skeiron didn't want me dead, what was the big show about?"

"It was a message. For me." Nevan focused on my shoulders, as he picked ceiling popcorn off my skin. His fingers nudged the spaghetti strap of my satin nightie. Its neckline dipped low over my breasts, exposing the upper slopes. His fingertips skimmed over my collarbone, to the juncture at the hollow of my throat. I imagined his hand dipping lower to cover my breast. My skin tightened, every nerve energized.

How could I fantasize about him touching me at a time like this?

Nevan's fingertips skated down my breastbone, into the valley of my cleavage. My nipples shot hard. His eyes widened at the sight of the taut buds poking through the flimsy fabric.

He snatched his hand away and coughed into his fist.

I rubbed my arms, shoulders bunching. "What kind of message was your king sending?"

"No matter now." He squeezed my shoulders, patted my upper arms, and lowered his hands to his sides. "What's done is done."

"Come on, I was almost a pancake. Don't you think I deserve an explanation?"

He took one big step backward, as the pained look on his face morphed into bleak resolve and his gaze focused on the wall past my shoulder. "I must leave you and I shall not return this time."

"I've lost my fascinating appeal, eh?"

"Never." His gaze fastened to mine, his eyes dazzling kaleidoscopes. "I was mistaken to believe I could have one thing for myself. How selfish I've been. I only wanted..." His hand floated up, near my arm, his fingertips teasing the gossamer hairs and triggering a flurry of goosebumps. "You'll be safe once I am gone."

A reckless impulse seized me. I grasped his hands and dragged him to me, our bodies mashed together, my breasts crushed against the planes of his muscles.

A smirk threatened to bust out, twitching his lips, but he banished it. His eyes flared hot, then darkened to a smolder. When I lifted my head, he dipped his closer to mine. Our breaths mingled, and for a blessed heartbeat I imagined our souls had mingled too. He glided his finger up my wrist, massaging lightly. Our lips hovered dangerously close.

I gave in to the lure of his magical eyes, indulged in the carnal allure of his body pressed to mine and the firm line of his erection against my belly.

"A few days ago," he murmured, his voice rough, "you ordered me to stay away. You're free of me at last. Is that not what you wanted?"

"Not anymore." I probed his eyes for some clue to his motivations, his intentions. "I am your girlfriend, Nevan. Please don't leave me."

He grazed his cheek across mine. I drank in his presence, my mind whirling from the intoxication of it. He dragged his lips down my skin, toward my mouth, and in a husky whisper said, "Goodbye, my sweet Lindsey."

My eyelids fluttered shut in anticipation of the kiss, my lips tingled, liquid fire gathered between my thighs. He wanted me. And God help me, I wanted him.

A breeze cooled my skin where his flesh had warmed me. My eyes flew open.

Nevan had disappeared.

Even as he abandoned me, apparently forever, he respected my no-kissing decree.

An unsatisfied yearning ached inside me. More than the physical need, though, I longed for the safety and connection he imbued into me. I didn't understand it. I'd never wanted it. Yet somehow, I needed it more than anything.

Sirens wailed outside, echoing the sorrow in my heart.

—

I DUG THROUGH THE WRECKAGE OF MY BEDROOM IN SEARCH OF MY robe while racking my brain for a reasonable explanation for this calamity. The sirens whined ever nearer and the cops would be here soon. When my fingers found my satin robe, I wrestled it out of the debris. Ripped and dirt-stained, it would have to do. A portion of the wall had caved into my closet and my dresser lay smashed under an avalanche of ceiling debris.

As I shook out my robe, my thoughts rewound to the first time I'd met Nevan. He caught me when I tripped. Distracted me from a dead body. Whisked me away to another world so we could get Brad resurrected. He rescued me when his king tossed a ceiling on my head. Most of all, he made me feel—period.

Car doors banged shut outside.

Pins and needles pricked at the backs of my eyes, manifesting tears. I squeezed my eyes shut, but the tears pooled anyway. I swiped at my eyes, rolled my shoulders back, and lifted my chin. I could not afford to break down. There would be questions from the authorities, most likely Travis, and I'd need all my wits to survive the onslaught. I shoved down my terror and pain, along with every other strong emotion roiling inside me, and caged them in the steel-reinforced vault of my mind, secured with three deadbolts and a massive combination lock. My passions were death row inmates.

Even prisoners condemned to death got a chance at appealing the conviction. Maybe I could, someday, release my emotions. Nevan kept encouraging me to do it, and with him I'd wanted to so badly, but I'd waited too long. He was gone, forever.

I fumbled with my robe, finally pulling it on, and clambered over the debris pile, through the doorway, into the darkened living room.

The front door quaked with the pounding of an angry fist.

"Open the goddamn door, Porter," Travis shouted. "Before I break it down."

Another blow rattled the door.

I switched on the lamp by the sofa as I hurried past it. Light flared out into the gloom, dousing the blackest shadows. I swung the door open, remembering a moment too late I was wearing my sexy nightie, with my robe unfastened to reveal the plunging neckline and high hem.

Travis's jaw dropped. His eyes all but popped out of his head. Behind him burned the sulfurous glow from the lights posted outside each door of the apartment complex. Stray beams glanced off the badge on his chest.

I whipped my robe closed, tugging the sash around my waist to knot it over my belly.

He swallowed with a visible effort. As his eyes shrank into a squint, he lurched into the doorway, inches from me. "Are you hurt?"

"No. The ceiling fell on me, but I was lucky. The bed protected me."

"What in the hell went on here, Lindsey?" He clapped his hands on either side of his head and clawed his scalp with his fingers. "How—why—" His hands fell away, his jaw trembled. The pitch of his voice rose. "Ceilings don't collapse for no reason, but I ain't seen a tornado."

A scary-angry supernatural beastie ate my house. Uh, no. Not saying that, particularly given his agitated state. I offered up the best hogwash I could. "Maybe it was a downburst or a straight-line wind."

Travis bared his clenched teeth. "How stupid do you think I am?"

"I don't think you're stupid."

He smacked his hands on the doorframe, and braced there, he pitched toward me. A current of black fury rippled through his deceptively soft voice. "Tell me the truth. After everything we've been through together, you owe me that much." He angled his neck down to level our faces. The anger radiating out of him mixed with another emotion, something far more personal. "You coulda died, and I wanna know what the fuck is going on here. The truth. *Now.*"

Or what? I didn't ask, certain I wouldn't like the answer. "It's better if you don't know."

I'd hated it when Nevan refused to tell me stuff, and here I was shoveling the same crap onto Travis. No wonder he was pissed.

He glared into my eyes. "Not good enough."

More sirens ululated outside. Past his shoulder, I glimpsed the strobing, multicolored lights of emergency vehicles. The beams lashed across the balcony to hurl their colors onto Travis with a sinister glow that matched the drilling intensity of his gaze.

I locked my hands over my belly and took one step back. "Please, Travis, let this go. It's weird and dangerous and completely crazy. You're better off not—"

He shackled his arms around me, pinning my arms to my sides, mashing me into his chest. The thick stench of booze made my stomach lurch. His mouth bore down on mine, stifling my shocked cry, the kiss hot and sloppy and soaked in alcohol. He towed me closer, his fingers punching into the flesh of my upper arms, and tried to shove his tongue between my lips.

Oh, like hell you will. I rammed my knee up into his groin.

My mouth muffled his grunt. His fingers loosened and I took advantage, slugging him in the only soft part of his belly. Air exploded from his lungs as he doubled over, and I swung my fist up into the vulnerable underside of his chin, wrenching his jaw shut with a crack. He cried out, staggered backward into the door jamb, and slumped against it. Breathing hard, he raised his face to me.

The light from outside slashed across his features, revealing tableau of drunkenness. His bloodshot eyes were glassy, his eyelids droopy. He looked dazed, his face flushed, and perspiration beaded on his forehead. His sheriff's uniform fared no better, creased with a multitude of wrinkles, his shirt partly untucked, and his belt off kilter. His holster was empty, the Sig nowhere on his person.

Travis shook his head, a palm plastered to his forehead. "Jesus Christ, what have I done? I don't know how that—why that—"

His voice evidenced the faintest slur.

Words pushed against my paralyzed vocal chords, scrabbling to get out. Angry, vulgar epithets. And a few creative suggestions for what he could do with himself.

"Lindsey," he said, reaching a hand toward me then snatching it back. "God, I'm so sorry."

I shoved him out the door and slammed it in his face.

My hand over my mouth, I fell to my knees on the rough carpeting and huddled there until the first responders banged on the door. Then I collected myself and let them inside.

Nevan did not materialize to comfort me. From here on, I was on my own.

CHAPTER SEVENTEEN

I DRAGGED THROUGH THE DAY AS IF MY FEET WERE ENCASED IN CEment and I was spiraling down into the depths of an icy river, the undertow dragging me out to sea. When I'd moseyed in at 10:14 a.m., Stan was manning the counter, his scowl entrenched deeper than usual. Catching sight of me, he trotted out from behind the counter and squeezed out a tight smile.

"How are you feeling?"

Wow, he actually sounded concerned. What alternate universe had I stumbled into? "I'm fine. Thank you for asking."

He shoved his hands in his pants pockets, danced in place, and then jerked his hands free, the fingers shimmying in a wild rhythm. He cast his gaze down to the floor. "I, uh, need to apologize to you. My wife can be difficult, even jealous, and she didn't like me hiring a woman. I took my frustration with her out on you. I'm sorry."

"Thank you," I said slowly.

"If you need a place to stay, my brother can put you up in his motel—my treat." And then he spoke the words that shattered all my previously held beliefs about the world I lived in. "I appreciate everything you do here. I know I can be difficult, but you don't complain and I'm very grateful to have you working here."

With his bombshell detonated on my head, he sprinted for his office. The door clapped shut behind him. After about an hour of pure shock, I convinced myself I hadn't hallucinated the whole encounter with Stan.

As I observed the smattering of customers in the shop, the stomping of footfalls made me glance at the shop entrance. Travis moseyed inside, halting across the counter from me. He smoothed his hands over the wood surface, studying the grain as he addressed me.

"Hey, how are you?" he asked, as if we exchanged pleasantries every morning. As if he hadn't made a drunken pass at me mere hours ago.

I had to deal with Travis eventually. Might as well get it over with.

"How am I?" I rolled my shoulders back in an attempt to iron out the kinks and appear more assured. "My apartment imploded. And what was your sympathetic response? Oh yeah. You shoved your bourbon-soaked tongue down my throat."

He tugged at the collar of his uniform shirt. "Yeah, I know."

"What the hell were you thinking last night? Drunk on the job? A sheriff's supposed to be a role model, or at least a law-abiding citizen."

"You don't know much about cops."

His superior tone ticked me off, inflaming the fury I'd bottled deep inside—only a part of it related to him, but I didn't care. Pressure throbbed in my chest. How fantastic it would be to pop that cork and spew my anger and betrayal all over Travis. Maybe it would scorch some sense into him and make me feel better.

I couldn't risk it.

"I was off duty," he said, "not drinking on the job."

"What a relief."

Color rose in his cheeks, and he coughed into his fist. "I can never apologize enough, but shit. The things I've seen, they're unreal, and I ain't handled it well."

"What you've seen? Oh, you mean when you were spying on me outside my apartment." I felt hot all over, and not in a good way. In the steaming-pot-about-to-burst way. "The self-righteous cop turned into a stalker."

"It ain't like that. Somebody's gotta protect you."

"Protect me?" His claim derailed my train of thought for several seconds, as I tried in vain to understand any of this. "You hate me. Why on earth would you be concerned with watching out for me?"

He mumbled, scratching his forehead.

"Come off it, Travis. You know what Calder did to me." I wished I had my derringer, but the holster wouldn't fit under this top. Skeiron had trashed my wardrobe, leaving me only a tight-fitting T-shirt with short sleeves, a pair of low-slung jeans, and undergarments. I'd stowed my gun and its holster under the passenger seat of my car, along with two boxes of ammo. "I shot Calder in self-defense."

Travis's head bobbed in a weak nod, his gaze still downcast.

I hesitated, gathering the right words. "When you grabbed me last night and…did what you did, it was like I'd time-warped back to that night with Calder. It's like you became him."

Travis's head fell into his hands. "Jesus. Please forgive me, I didn't think."

And therein lay the problem. He hadn't thought, because he'd been drunk. For the longest minute of my life, I glared at him and he eyed me like he'd never seen me before. With a shapeshifting assassin and his crazy king after me, I had no energy to waste on despising Travis. He seemed genuinely horrified by his actions, so I made the best decision I could.

I exhaled out my anger. "Fine, I forgive you. Let's move on."

He looked so relieved I half expected him to collapse into a weeping lump on the concrete floor. Instead, eyes shiny with moisture, he gave me a lopsided, shaky smile. "Thank you, Lindsey. God, thank you so much."

He hustled out of the shop, rubbing at his eyes.

I had no clue why he cared so much that I forgave him. Another mystery to add to my growing pile of the unsolved.

At lunchtime, my parents showed up to force food on me, which I dutifully ate despite not being the least bit hungry. The afternoon wore on, heavy and suffocated by humidity. By three o-clock, I'd begun to daydream about a double bed in a nice, air-conditioned motel room.

All the while, memories of Nevan haunted me. Memories of our...whatever it had been. The thing I hadn't wanted anyway. Or so I'd told myself. How could I grieve for a relationship that had never been? What had we shared, really? One all-consuming kiss. Flirting galore.

I wandered down the aisles of the shop, distracting my brain and my heart by reciting the names of the rocks in the bins as I tapped them. I kept my voice quiet, a tick above silence. "Snow quartz. Fossil agate. Float copper. Red sandstone."

A presence tickled my sixth sense. My pulse quickened, butterflies flapped away in my stomach. It couldn't be. But my heart whispered *please, please, please.*

"Have ye forgotten the name of this particular stone?"

My breath hitched. I knew that voice, like I knew my own thoughts.

Nevan's hands glided up and down my arms. He bent his head to my shoulder. "Well, love, do ye know the name?"

His voice in my ear sent an exhilarating shiver down my spine. "It's called star moonstone."

"And what does it signify?"

"It's associated with—" I picked up one of the silvery gray moonstones, running my thumb over its polished surface. "It signifies love and passion."

He slid a palm down my arm, past my wrist, to close his hand around mine and trap the moonstone in my palm. "I tried to stay away from you, but it's like trying to stop gravity from holding my feet on the ground. I don't understand this. I've never wanted any woman the way I want you, Lindsey. Being without you is impossible."

I leaned back into him and the steel knot of fear and anger wedged inside my heart unraveled. "You keep saying you shouldn't be here."

"Still true, but alas, I do not always do as I should. Not anymore. Not with you." His lips covered my earlobe, his breath tantalized the hairs on my cheek. "I missed you. My sweet, mortal miracle."

That broke me. I spun around and threw my arms around his neck. "I missed you, Nevan."

Had he called me a miracle? Yes, he had. *Huh.*

Nevan's arms lashed me to him. I soared on a natural high induced by the soul-stirring, utterly impossible connection that bound me to him and him to me.

The moonstone slipped out of my hand, clattering to the floor. He murmured to me in that esoteric language and I dissolved into him, my lids shuttering on their own, my thoughts scattering into infinity. This was belonging.

"Why are you smiling?" he asked.

"Am I?"

"You are. I can see half your face. It's the kind of smile that implies you've got a lovely secret." His hand roamed up my spine to the base of my neck, his fingers plied my flesh with sensual delicacy. "Care to reveal your secret to me?"

"I'm glad you're here."

"As am I." He spread his palms over my shoulder blades. "We should talk about Skeiron."

"Can it wait until after my shift?"

"I suppose it can." An exasperated sigh rushed out of him. "You are intent upon keeping this ridiculous job, aren't you?"

"It may be a crappy job with crappy pay, but it's all I've got at the moment. Stan let me come in late this morning, but I don't feel like testing his newfound generosity."

"As you wish. I will visit with your family until you're free."

"Deal." For once, I didn't overthink my actions. I simply raised onto my tiptoes and planted a kiss on his cheek.

He smirked, of course.

Reluctantly, I let go of his hand. "See you at six."

"I'll be counting the minutes."

He flashed me a sizzling smile and sauntered out of the shop.

That's when I finally registered his appearance. He wore golden brown slacks and a white dress shirt with the sleeves rolled up to just below his elbows and the top two buttons undone, exposing his tanned flesh. Though he'd once again toned down the coloring of his skin and eyes, he nevertheless made a striking figure as he exited the building.

A twenty-something girl clad in a Hello Kitty T-shirt gaped at Nevan, blinking repeatedly at the sight of him.

Yeah, those muscles were not toned down for mortal consumption. The girl looked ready to pounce on him, and I could've done the same. He was devastatingly gorgeous, even with his supernatural traits muted.

When he walked out of sight, I tried to go back to work. Worries about Skeiron chilled me, so I warmed up by engaging in some choice fantasies about what might transpire later, when I met with Nevan in private.

Make love to me, Nevan. My body ached for it. For him.

Would the damn clock ever read six?

———

I SKIPPED UP THE STEPS INTO THE MOTOR HOME, INTO THE WONDERFULLY cool air inside. I found my parents, my brother, and Nevan all seated around the dining table, laughing at a joke I'd missed. I plopped my purse onto the nearest chair.

The four of them swiveled their heads to me almost in unison.

"Your cheeks are pink," Mom said.

"It's been a long, hot day," I said, "and I'm exhausted."

Nevan uncoiled his long body and moved to my side, gathering me under his arm. I rested my head on his chest.

My mother gave me a knowing smile.

I tried to smile in return, but it came out crimped.

Her lips crooked up on one side, carving out a dimple. She appraised Nevan from top to bottom and I didn't miss the appreciative, but subtle, lift of her eyebrows. If she thought I'd had sex with Nevan, she clearly had no problem with it. My entire family adored him.

Nevan's fingers traveled up and down the bare skin of my arm. "If ye don't mind me stealing your daughter for a bit, I'd like to take Lindsey for a stroll back to the falls."

Mom's irritating, knowing smile reemerged. "Oh, how romantic."

Dad wore a smugly pleased expression. "Lindsey needs a break after what she's been through. Make sure she takes it easy."

"I'll take good care of our girl," Nevan said.

My parents nodded their approval and waved goodbye as we exited the bus. Nevan kept his arm around me during our journey across the parking lot. We passed by the concrete statues in the rock garden, picking up speed as we entered the woods. A bird screeched overhead. My stomach flip-flopped, but then I glimpsed the creature—a hawk, not a raven.

Nevan squeezed my hand. "If Brennus is in the vicinity, he hasn't located us yet. And I've thrown out a little spell to confuse him."

"Like what you did to Travis and his men?"

"Similar, yes."

We lapsed into silence, strolling along like any couple out for a romantic walk. After a few minutes, when we'd bypassed the vortex and rounded the bend just before the falls, he halted us.

"I spoke with Skeiron," he said. "He confirmed he attacked you as a message for me, though not for the reason I'd assumed. My interference in mortal affairs is trifle to him." Nevan hesitated, his gaze clouding. "He wants you."

"Why? I'm nobody."

"I've no idea why. Our conversation ended rather abruptly, when Skeiron ejected me from his fortress."

"Ejected? Do you mean physically?"

"Yes."

"Are you hurt?"

"No." He scratched his ear, glancing at the ground. "Wish I could tell you more. Skeiron wants you, that's all I learned."

He trailed a fingertip down my nose and onto my lips, his gaze fixated on my mouth. Desire sizzled on my lips, on my skin, and in the deepest, most secret part of me.

Seeming to rein in his own passions, he took a seat on the nearest stone bench and gestured toward the adjacent one.

I parked my butt on the hard rock, startled by the unexpected chill of it, and wondered if magic kept the summer heat from affecting the stone. The last time I'd sat here, an odd energy had healed the wounds Brennus inflicted on me in his raven form. Today, I suffered from the exhaustion of stress—caused by Skeiron, and to a lesser extent, Travis.

The mystical forces that lived in this place suffused me with cool, soothing currents. The first time, I'd nearly fallen down from dizziness. This time, the power of the magic flowed through me and around me, invisible yet palpable.

The healing energies wash over you like a cool breeze, infusing your body with ancient wisdom.

How many times I'd recited the spiel. Although the vortex didn't seem to be imparting any wisdom, it was washing energy into me, refreshing and gentle as a spring breeze. Though my muscles unwound, I couldn't stop worrying about what frequent exposure to mystical energies might do to me. Would I grow a second head? What if my skin turned scaly and purple? It was dumb, I knew, but the thoughts kept coming.

Nevan knelt beside me and cupped a hand over my knee. "Are you fretting about Skeiron?"

"Not right this minute."

"Why so despondent?"

"I'm not despondent." I had been after he left me this morning, and I cringed inwardly at the memory of my reaction. "Thing is, I never believed in the healing vortex. I made snide comments about it and assumed anybody who did believe was a fool. Now here I am, sitting inside the frigging vortex, feeling the exact effects I swore did not exist."

Mouth set in a hard line, he flicked his eyes back and forth, up and down, examining every inch of me.

"What are you doing?" I asked.

"You said you're feeling the effects of the vortex. That only happens if you need healing."

"I'm wiped out, that's all."

"Are you certain?"

Striving for a calming expression, I captured his hands with mine. "I didn't mean to scare you. I'm fine, I swear, no real damage. The vortex is kind of ironing out the kinks and I got a little weirded out by it is all."

He sagged a bit, shutting his eyes briefly. "Don't do that to me again, love. It…bothers me."

"Sorry." I stretched, groaning as my muscles loosened up. "Skeiron dumping a building on me was bad enough, but then Travis had to go and make a sloppy pass at me. Being kissed by a drunk was not on my to-do list."

Nevan shot straight and stiff as a telephone pole, his eyes ablaze with angry colors. He lifted his gaze above my head, shoulders back, and focused on a sight only he could see.

I recognized the signs. He was about to skedaddle, the elemental way.

"Hold up," I said.

Though he didn't vanish, he stayed in position, ready to go.

"Where are you going?" I asked.

"I shall go wherever the sheriff is and have a chat with him." He snarled the words sheriff and chat.

"No you will not."

"He must be castigated."

I jumped up. "No. He was drunk and stupid, but I already yelled at him for it—and slugged him good. I can take care of myself."

Nevan rushed to me, lightning quick. His hands grasped my shoulders, hauling me into him, and his mouth dove perilously close to mine.

"I don't like aggressive men," I said, though my body roused with a surge of desire.

He closed his lips over the sensitive spot where my jaw met my neck. He ravished my skin with all the passion and abandon he'd lavished on my mouth during our one and only lip-lock, and I threw my head back on a long, low moan.

"You're mine," he said, his mouth quivering the flesh of my throat. "You told me so."

"Goes both ways."

"Mmm…yes. I am yours, my sweet."

I groaned as he dragged his mouth down my neck, his teeth nipping at my flesh, his scorching lips journeying ever downward until they found the side of one breast. He lapped at my skin with his skillful tongue, savoring me, winding me up until I succumbed to the sheer pleasure of it, wrapping my arms around his head to hold him to my breast.

He whipped his head up, strode backward, and said, "But the sheriff must be castigated."

Before I could speak, he was gone.

The flapping of wings pulled my attention skyward. A raven circled overhead, diving low over the clearing. My instincts warned me it was no ordinary raven.

Brennus plummeted toward me with terrifying velocity.

I clambered to my feet, intending to run, but the bird's wings whacked me sideways and bowled me over smack onto my ass.

The instant his feet touched down, the raven transformed into the black-skinned, blue-tinged, monstrous man I'd met yesterday. Brennus, his face cold and hard, twisted his lips into a grotesque version of a smile. His voice boomed like nothing of this earth.

"Mortal," he said, "you have defied him for the last time."

"Get away from her."

Nevan's voice roared from behind me, invested with a rage that raised the hairs on my nape. He stalked up beside me, where I lay sprawled on the ground. With one hand, he snagged both of mine and pulled me to my feet. Cracking his knuckles, he confronted Brennus.

The raven-man smiled again.

"Guardian," Brennus said, "you have disobeyed Skeiron once too often. He sends me to deliver a final warning. Give up the mortal woman, or be forced to watch as His Majesty extracts the essence from your female and disassembles her piece by piece."

Disassemble? A gruesome image raced through my mind.

"You have until the sun sets in the mortal realm," Brennus continued. "Discard the female or Skeiron will eliminate the distraction for you."

Discard the female? I wasn't a piece of lint to be chucked in the trash.

"Deliver the woman to Skeiron," Brennus said, "or he will take her himself and his wrath shall lay waste to this realm."

I clenched my fists. "Lay waste to my world? The hell he will."

Nevan narrowed his eyes on me, rotating his head in my direction while his mouth sharpened into a scowl. Even I, a foolish and often dense mortal, comprehended his meaning—*shut the hell up, woman.*

Being foolish and often dense, however, I forged ahead anyway. "Tell your master not to bother with all the raping and pillaging, because I'm not the one he wants. He's confused me with somebody else."

The raven-man glanced at me like I was an ant crapping on his toes and told Nevan, "The king has realized she holds the power. Why else would you, guardian of the falls and seeker of the Janusite, protect this puny mortal female?"

"I will do what must be done."

A couple days ago, I might've worried Nevan had been sizing me up this whole time, to ferret out whether I did indeed have whatever power everybody wanted so damn badly. Though it made no sense, I trusted him now and I recognized he'd stated exactly what he meant. He would do what was necessary—but he'd omitted the "to protect my puny mortal female" part.

I pushed in front of Nevan, face to face with Brennus. "This *puny mortal* has a few questions."

"The deadline is sunset," Brennus said.

He shimmered and disappeared.

"Aw, come on." I spun toward face Nevan. "He can do the poofing thing too?"

Nevan shrugged.

"That's so unfair." I latched my arms around me, but my skin still crawled from our encounter with Brennus. "Am I misinterpreting this, or did a freaky raven-man just threaten to cut me up in itty-bitty pieces?"

"Skeiron would be the one to disassemble you, but only after he extracts your power."

"Oh great." I threw my hands up and let them flop back down. "Your boss wants to suck me dry and chop me up like hamburger. I feel much better. And what's the deal with Skeiron thinking I have some kind of power?"

He slipped his hand around mine, but his attention wandered, his eyes losing focus.

"Nevan?"

His gaze snapped back into focus, trained on me, and he released my hand. "I've no idea why Skeiron believes you possess great power. I've sensed something in you, suppressed and difficult to identify, yet nothing worth killing for."

"I don't have any goddamn supernatural energy inside me."

He canted his head. "Are ye certain of that?"

Was I? Despite longing to say yes, I couldn't. Not anymore. "You said a lot of humans have a touch of the Unseen in them. Maybe that's what I've got, but it's buried for some reason."

"If that were true, my enchantment would've worked."

"Maybe you're not as enthralling as you think."

He lips curved in a tender smile. "I believe we've demonstrated quite definitively that I enthrall you in other, non-magical ways."

My body chose that moment to thrust me into a whirlwind, sense-memory recap of our first kiss, segueing into a replay of his mouth on my throat earlier and the way he'd licked a path down my breast.

Nevan surrounded my hands with his and tugged me close, our hands pinned between my breasts and his torso. "You recall, don't ye?"

His voice was a seductive murmur. I struggled not to respond, but everything inside me betrayed my wishes.

"Your pupils are dilating," he said, "your breaths are quickening, and your body is yielding to me. Admit it. You are enchanted, in your own way, without magic."

"If that's the criteria, you're just as enchanted as I am."

"I'll concede the point." His voice was thick with a need rivaling my own.

My lips yearned for his. The faint caress a second ago had not been enough. I craved full contact. His lips. His tongue. His…everything.

Through the haze of desire, a thought surfaced. "What did you do to Travis?"

"Nothing. I hadn't reached him yet when I sensed you were in danger and returned."

He sensed I was in danger? I had no time to ponder the ramifications of that, because a shriek punctured the silence, ululating with blood-curdling effect.

Nevan jerked his head in the direction of the scream.

Another shriek resounded through the woods.

"That's coming from the direction of the shop," I said, overwhelmed by a mounting dread. "My parents. Ash."

Nevan hauled me into his arms and whisked us away.

CHAPTER EIGHTEEN

WE POPPED OUT WITHIN SIGHT OF THE SHOP, BEHIND A WIDE PINE TREE. In the parking lot, Sandy was gaping at the closed trunk of my car, hands raised. Her body impeded my view, but her shrill cries pierced my eardrums.

I tore down the hill into the parking lot.

Sandy's boyfriend sprinted out of the shop toward her. At the same time I reached her, he grasped her shoulders and spun her around, pressing her face into his chest, his hand cradling the back of her head.

My shoes slipped on the gravel, tripping me up.

Sandy pointed a trembling finger at the trunk, directly above the license plate.

I pushed around the young couple, tiptoeing to the trunk. A dark red liquid dripped from the undercarriage onto the gravel. Crushed in the seam where the trunk lid met the car's body was a human finger.

The world telescoped down, blackness encroaching to shut out everything except the finger jutting from the trunk of my car. The air was redolent with the stench of blood. I covered my mouth and nose with one palm, but the sheer horror of the bloody appendage and what it signified nailed me in place.

Maybe it was only a finger, not a whole body. Maybe the finger was fake.

"Porter! Open the goddamn trunk or I'll blast it open."

Travis's hollering ripped me out of my panicked thoughts, but I could not look away from the blood-soaked finger.

Nevan secured his arms around my waist, and in the back of my mind, I knew he meant to whisk me away. Numb, I wrenched out of his grasp and trudged to the driver's door. I hadn't locked the car this morning, so I swung the door out and lunged a hand under the dashboard to click the

171

trunk release. A *clunk* told me the trunk had popped open. I shuffled back to Nevan, my ears ringing faintly.

His arms came around me, pulling me into the shelter of his body.

"Don't look, love," he said. "Please don't look."

The stench of blood. The acrid taste of bile in my mouth. I couldn't stand here, immobilized, and wait for someone else to sort this out. It was my life on the line here.

I broke free of Nevan, spinning around.

Sandy fainted into her boyfriend's arms.

Travis glanced at me, his expression inscrutable but his face a touch ashen. I imagined my face must've been pasty too, and I hadn't seen what everyone else had—yet. Travis held the trunk lid at full extension, his fingers in a death grip, knuckles white from the effort. I scuffled closer, hands locked over my belly, until the trunk's interior came into view.

I reeled backward into Nevan.

A dead man lay crumpled in the trunk, limbs bent at unnatural angles, as if someone had stuffed him into the space in a hurry. But the most sickening sight was not the body. The head had been cleaved from the body.

It lay perpendicular to the neck. Blood and spinal fluid gushed out of the severed neck, filtering down through a crack in the car's metal hull to drip onto the gravel.

The dead man's face consumed my focus. His red hair. Green eyes.

"Oh shit," I croaked. "It's Brad."

Travis yanked the handcuffs from his belt. They jingled as he brandished them at me, partly due to a tremor in his hands. "Got no choice this time."

I shook my head, my gaze glued to the body. To Brad. I never even knew his last name.

Travis stalked up to me, grabbing for my wrists. "Lindsey Porter, you are under arrest for—"

Nevan threw his arms around me and catapulted us into the void.

The real world winked out as we careened in a free-fall through the abysmal tunnel, tumbling out into the world again totally out of control. Nevan lost his grip on me. I ricocheted off the ground, rolling over and over. My spine cracked into a tree. Vertigo spun my head, mutating the ground into a carnival ride.

After several seconds, the nausea-inducing motion inside my head settled down. I scrambled to my feet, a little unsteady. Nevan had come to rest a few yards away, flat on his back. I hurried to him, offering my hands. He made a face, but accepted my aid in separating his body from the ground.

We were in the woods. Where, I couldn't tell. Wild blackberry bushes bloomed nearby, their white flowers giving off a caramel aroma. The scent soothed my nerves, but nowhere near enough to obliterate the riot of thoughts in my head. Travis planned on arresting me. I understood he had little choice, but I couldn't go to jail. Whoever had framed me before had done it again, with more conviction this time.

Something Tris had told me resurfaced. He'd said Brad could be resurrected as long as his head hadn't been "lopped off." The snarky leprechaun couldn't be responsible for this. He had zero motive. The only one with a clear intent to destroy me was Skeiron.

Nevan tucked a lock of hair behind my ear. "All right?"

"I'm not going to barf or pass out, if that's what you mean." I wanted to hide under a bed somewhere, but otherwise I was peachy. "There's nothing all right about the situation, though."

Nevan's gaze hardened, his expression too. "I will not allow the sheriff to take you."

"He has no choice. Somebody put a dead—" The visual exploded in my mind as if I'd been hurled back in time to relive it. Blood. Brad. Headless. *Don't think about it.* I slammed the lid on the memory, my panic, everything. Sometimes repression was necessary. "Who killed Brad this time?"

"I've no clue."

"What about Skeiron?"

"As I said before, Skeiron doesn't muck about with corpses, much less mortal ones."

"His Nutbar Majesty wants me dead," I said. "Disassembled, remember? This might be part of his plan."

"To have you convicted of murder? What are you suggesting, he'll wait for you to be executed by the mortal system of justice so he might cackle at your funeral?" Nevan scoffed, shaking his head. "Skeiron is neither that subtle nor that patient."

"Yeah, I guess you're right." I let my head fall back, staring at the swathe of blue sky visible between the treetops. Every moment, the sun descended further toward the horizon, a silent countdown to my doom. "When is sunset?"

"When it is."

"How terribly helpful." I slouched, drained by the day's events and by our fruitless conversation. "God, I wish I had my gun."

"It would do you no good against an elemental."

"Unless you can give me an endued weapon, it's the best I've got. I bet two .357 rounds between the eyes would give him a bitch of a migraine." I gnawed the inside of my lip, chewing on the problem in a literal fashion. "If I had my purse, I could check the time on my phone. At least then we'd know how long we have."

Nevan blipped out.

Seconds elapsed, ticked off by a gigantic, phantom clock in my head. I was about to holler for him when he reappeared in the exact spot where he'd stood a moment ago. My purse dangled off his shoulder. He held my gun, in its holster, in one hand and m two boxes of ammo in the other.

"Wow," I said, smiling with real admiration, "I'm about two seconds away from having sex with you right here in the woods."

Clearly trying not to smirk, he tossed my purse to me. "Perhaps we should wait until our heads are no longer in matching nooses."

I dug around inside the main compartment or my purse for my phone. I plucked it out with an "ah-ah!" and danced it in the air in front of his face. He arched one brow and almost smiled. I checked the weather app on my phone. "Sunset is at 8:47 PM and it's 7:20 right now." I plunked the phone back in my purse. "We have a little over an hour to figure out…something."

Nevan handed me my gun and its accoutrements. By the time I'd reloaded the barrel with .357 rounds, my insides had morphed into a simmering cauldron of all my worst fears come to pass. An innocent man had died and because of me. "Somebody wants to drive me over the edge, that's why Brad was killed. If it's not Calder's ghost, I don't know who it is. Travis is having a meltdown, maybe it's him."

"Unrequited desires can turn into resentment, in a weak-willed man."

"What on earth are you talking about? Travis has no desires for me."

A muscle in his jaw ticked. "He kissed you."

"Ugh. He was drunk."

"You are blind to it, aren't you?" Nevan guided me toward a tree with a hand on my elbow. He sat down—back against the trunk, legs outstretched—and patted his thigh in invitation. I crawled onto his lap, unsure why, knowing only that I needed the contact. He linked his arms around my hips. "Think about it. The sheriff despises me. He knew you before you became involved with his brother and, by your own account, he became withdrawn and angry after his brother won you."

"Nobody won me. I'm not a raffle prize."

"You are deflecting." He gave me a squeeze, rocking my hips on his lap. "You know of what I speak."

"Afraid I don't."

"The sheriff is in love with you."

"Wha—" I jerked my head back to gape at him. "That's crazy."

Except it might not have been. When I reflected on my entire acquaintance with Travis, I recalled small clues I'd once dismissed as nothing. He had changed after Calder showed up, for reasons I never could puzzle out. He'd tracked me down in Michigan. He'd almost said he was here to protect me, before he corrected himself to say he had to protect the world from me. Travis had also pleaded with me to stay with him instead of going with Nevan, not to mention he kissed me—and begged me to forgive him for it.

Oh God. It was true.

I must've looked shocked, because Nevan smiled tenderly. "You see it, don't you? He is quite desperately in love with you. Can't blame him."

Desperately. In love. With me.

Nevan skirted my cheekbone with his fingertips. "Whatever his failings, I sincerely doubt the sheriff would harm you on purpose."

"Who then? The murderer went out of his way to implicate me. It's got to be personal."

He gazed into the distance, lips tight. "I do not believe your enemy is mortal."

"You said Skeiron isn't the guy."

"There are countless elementals in the Unseen." He lifted us both to our feet. "We should cross the veil and seek help there."

"From who?"

Nevan considered me for a moment, motionless, unreadable. He hooked his hands around my upper arms. "Skeiron must believe you are the Janusite."

"What? Why?" I clutched a handful of his shirt. "He can't. I'm not."

"It's my fault." He scrubbed his face with one hand. "When I reconsider everything Skeiron and Brennus have said, I can reach but one conclusion. Skeiron decided there is one reason and only one reason why I would shirk my duty to pursue and protect a mortal woman. You are the Janusite."

"But you can't know that, right? You said all the girls you, uh, test have to be taken to Skeiron so he can figure out if they're the one."

The sylph king's voice blared in my memory. *Are you the one?* he'd asked me. Holy hell in a giant frigging basket. He'd thought I might be the Janusite even then.

"You are correct," Nevan said, "normally that would be the case. But I took you through the falls. Brennus witnessed it. Skeiron has no idea of where I took you or why and so, of course, he's decided I spirited you away to an oracle for confirmation you are the Janusite. And now, according to his estimation, I intend to harness your power for my own gain."

"Why are you protecting me?"

Bowing his head, he scratched his neck. "I don't know."

He kept saying that, but it rang false. After I made him enchant Brad, he told me he that proved he'd do anything for me—and he swore he'd protect me from Skeiron. When he'd declared Travis was desperately in love with me, what had he said?

Can't blame him.

Goose bumps prickled my arms. I couldn't deal with another epiphany about one of the men in my life, not with Skeiron's deadline fast approaching. Whatever Nevan had meant, I had to put it aside for later.

I had more urgent questions. "You mentioned an oracle."

"Yes, the oracle is the only one who can identify the Janusite."

"When you say *the* oracle, do you mean there's just one?"

"No, there are quite a few. This oracle is the one who issued the Janusite prophecy." He frowned at the grass. "The oracle will speak only to

Skeiron. No one else is permitted to know where he lives. But perhaps I can persuade a fae to aid us, for a price."

"No bargains, remember? Bargains are bad."

"For you, yes. I have considerably more experience in negotiating them."

"Desperation is not a good starting place for making a deal, even I know that." I shoved my hands in my pockets. "Let's say you do bargain for the oracle's location and he deigns to speak to you. If he says I am the one, then what?"

"One step at a time."

"Which means you don't know."

He growled a sigh. "For once, can ye just agree and let it drop?"

"Maybe." I flashed back to the scene in the parking lot earlier today, when the Porter clan had arrived. "I can't leave my family hanging. They'll worry."

"Time is running short for us."

"We've got about an hour. Help me get to my family, let me show them I'm okay, and I'll do whatever you say."

His lips crept into a smirk. "Whatever I say?"

"Within reason."

"As you wish." When I opened my mouth, he held up a hand to silence me. "Let me check the way is clear before I take you to them."

"Hurry up."

He popped out and popped back in a few seconds later. "They are in their large, wheeled home. I instructed them to lock the door, to prevent us being surprised by the sheriff."

"You let them see you poof in?" Once was bad enough, but twice?

"They seemed well adjusted to the concept."

"Well adjusted? What the hell were you think—"

He swept me into his arms and rushed us away.

An hourglass glimmered in my mind's eye, the sand sifting away bit by bit. One hour and a smattering of minutes. One hour…

Until my personal Armageddon.

MY MOTHER SEIZED ME IN A BEAR HUG, CLINCHING ME HARD ENOUGH I expected to hear my ribs cracking. When she finally released me, I was relieved to find all my bones intact. Nevan had materialized us right in front of my parents and Ash, without bothering to ask me if I cared where we landed. Considering what I planned to tell them, I supposed it made no difference.

Besides, my parents and my brother acted like nothing bizarre had occurred, as if visitors blipped into their RV every day. For the first time in a very long time, I realized the benefits of having a family obsessed with the metaphysical.

Mom grabbed Nevan's face and smacked a firm kiss on his cheek. "Thank you for taking care of our baby."

"I am not a baby," I said. "I'm thirty-two years old. And I need to talk to you."

Nevan's eyebrows rose when I pointed a finger at him.

Snaring his hand, I dragged him down the little hallway into the bedroom my parents had allotted to me until I could find a new apartment. They'd been using the room for storage, but now it was filled with the remnants of my personal belongings. In the cramped space, made more cramped by my boxes of stuff, I couldn't get more than three feet away Nevan.

Clapping the door shut, I planted my hands on my hips, fingers tapping. "Poof in right in front of my parents? I told you not to do that."

"No, darlin', ye didn't."

He smirked with a mixture of affectionate humor and sarcasm, which made me want to kick him. And kiss him. And kick him again.

Maybe I hadn't actually told him. The past few days had become a mental blur.

"Besides, your family seems quite fine with my preferred mode of travel. In fact, they seem fine with magic in general." He rubbed his chin between his thumb and forefinger. "Why does it vex you?"

"Because it's—" I flapped my arms, as if I might pump rational thoughts into my brain. Didn't work. I threw my head back, letting my arms flop down. "Unh."

"Unh?" Nevan repeated my noise with a tinkle of amusement. "You'll have to be more articulate if you expect me to understand."

Head bent back, I let a crack in a ceiling tile absorb my focus. Thinking was too damn hard. I didn't notice Nevan coming closer until his lips brushed my throat, just below my jaw. His breaths excited my skin, unfurling tendrils of desire through my body.

"Never have I seen another mortal who contains as much stress inside as you do." His voice was sultry, his lips warm and soft, feathering across my skin in delicious little kisses. "Shall I relax you?"

He stole my breath with an open-mouth kiss on my pulse point, nipping and licking, his soft groan vibrating my flesh. I resisted leaning into him for as long as I could—about two seconds. "We have a deadline, remember?"

"All the more reason to let me give you pleasure."

"Thanks, but no." My body screamed *yes, yes, yes.*

Trailing his lips across my cheek, he took hold of my hips and rocked me into him. "Are ye certain?"

"Uh-huh." *Maybe.*

One of his large hands wandered to the small of my back, while the other cradled the back of my head, slanting it forward until our gazes converged. "You don't sound certain."

"My parents are right outside."

His fingers massaged my scalp, slow and sensual. Oh good heavens. He really did have a talent for melting me. "You're saying you would let me do this, if we were elsewhere."

Aw hell. Why bother lying anymore? "Yes."

The hand on my back skated up and over to my side, just under my breast, and with his thumb he traced the band of my bra. I barely suppressed a moan as he rumbled, "Ahhh...There is hope then."

But why was he seducing here and now? We were about to embark on Operation Destroy a Vengeful Godlike Being, which might well result in both of us being "disassembled." I couldn't fathom the impetus for his behavior, for his need to show me pleasure before we took off on a dangerous mission.

Ohhhh no. I did understand.

And the lovely fog of lust evaporated in an instant. "You think we're going to die, don't you? That's the real reason for the porn show. You're saying goodbye."

The stark sadness in his eyes told me everything I needed to know. He backed away.

Robbed of his touch, of his hands and lips and breaths on my skin, I ached in ways I hadn't known I could.

"We still have no plan," I said. "Other than going to the world of don't trust anyone, never say please or thank you, and try not to accidentally bargain your way into enslavement."

"I can think of nothing else to do." The starkness had infected his voice, but he kept his gaze squarely on me. "I will go alone. You will cross the boundary where you will be safe."

"Like I told you before, I am not hiding," I said. "We go together. Got it?"

He nodded, looking as defeated as anyone I'd ever seen. With his usual whiplash-inducing speed, he switched back into Aloof Nevan mode. Glancing around the room, he asked, "Was there a reason you brought me in here?"

"Of course." Good. I could focus on this instead of impending horrific death. I cleared my throat. "I want to tell my parents everything, which means telling them about you. What you can do. What you are."

"Do as you must."

"You don't mind?"

"No, but you clearly do."

I chewed on that for a moment before heaving out a sigh. "Might as well get this over with. Let me do the talking, okay?"

He shrugged, but the tightness around his eyes belied his nonchalance.

Pushing the door open, he swept his hand in a grand gesture for me to exit first. As we emerged into the living area, he kept one hand on the small of my back. Although my parents hadn't moved, Ash was skipping up and down the aisle. He stopped when he saw me and bounced on his heels.

Nevan lingered a pace behind me. His hand on my back comforted me more than I would've expected and I leaned a fraction into the contact, grateful for his warmth.

I drew a fortifying breath and looked at my family. "I'm sure you've noticed some strange things happening around here lately. Inexplicable things."

Ash had ceased bouncing. All three of them nodded, solemn and silent.

"Well, here goes."

I launched into a recap of the past few days, of my discovery of the body and of Nevan's first appearance, of the corpse vanishing and Nevan reappearing to corroborate my story for Travis. The raven stalking me. The leprechaun. The resurrection. Skeiron and the roof collapse and poor Brad's second demise and the Janusite and the deadline looming ahead of us. I left out Nevan's gentle seductions and the details of his "duty," though I told them he'd been tasked with finding the Janusite.

When I finished, my dad said, "Lindsey, you're in a pickle for sure."

I almost laughed. Almost.

He glanced at Nevan, then me. "How can we help?"

"Get the hell out of here." I felt Nevan inch closer, his hand drifting down to grasp my hip. I settled my hand over his. "I can't worry about you while we're off in another world searching for answers. Please, drive as far away from here as you can get."

My parents rose, Dad looping a protective arm around Mom's shoulders. "We'll leave, but we won't go too far. Our baby's in trouble and Porters don't run out on family."

Nevan whispered in my ear, "The boundary."

Oh. Duh. "Just promise me you'll stay at least one mile away from the shop."

Dad's brow crinkled, but soon realization smoothed it out. "You mean stay outside this invisible line you mentioned. The one the whatsits can't cross."

"Right."

"And water," Nevan said. "Lakes, rivers, ponds, streams, waterfalls. Any naturally occurring bodies of water may provide an avenue for a portal to open. Each has its own boundary."

First I'd heard about that. "Yeah, like Nevan says, stay a mile away from water."

"Kind of hard to do," Dad said. "This place is full of hidden waterfalls and streams."

"We'll do our best," Mom said to me. "Don't worry, sweetie."

Relief rushed through me, leaving me a bit weak. Jeez, I was massively tense, like Nevan said. "Be careful."

My mother broke free of Dad's embrace to march straight up to Nevan. Her neck craned back to meet his gaze, she aimed her sternest mother's look at him. "You better keep her safe, son. If anything happens to my daughter, I'm coming after you with every weapon in my arsenal. And believe me, I've got plenty of ammo."

Nevan wore a grave expression as he told her, "Your daughter's life means more to me than my own, Mrs. Porter. I shall protect her at any cost."

With a smile, my mother raised onto her toes to peck another kiss on Nevan's cheek. "Good boy."

She returned to Dad's side, taking his hand.

Ash stood somberly beside them. "Are you gonna come back, Zee?"

I knelt before him to level our eyes and gave him my best brave smile. "Of course I am. Don't think I'd let you eat all the chocolate pudding, do you?"

He shook his head, eyes glistening with unshed tears.

I tousled his hair and tried to sound casual. "See you later, brat."

Turning away from my family, I marched straight to Nevan. My eyes burned and my lips trembled. Nausea roiled in my stomach. If I died, at least my family would be safe outside the boundary.

Nevan enfolded me in his arms, his chin on the crown of my head, and spirited us away.

CHAPTER NINETEEN

WE REAPPEARED INSIDE THE HEALING VORTEX, THE ONRUSHING gloom of night turning the woods into a haunted forest from a Grimm fairytale. Shadows slashed across the stone benches, speckled with wan sunlight that dimmed with every passing second. Nevan kept his arms around me, holding me close. My holster must've poked into him, since it poked into me, but he gave no indication of noticing. The old stoic mask had shuttered his features.

He swallowed visibly, the solitary sign of emotion.

No, not the only sign. The way he held me, as if I might float away if he loosened his grip, it told me more than any words. I was damn glad he'd retrieved my derringer for me. If he was scared…

I looked up at the darkened treetops swaying in a wind I couldn't feel, shielded by the woods around us. "Why'd you bring us here instead of closer to the falls? We are in a hurry."

His hesitation spurred me to look at him. Though his expression betrayed nothing, his eyes were shot through with cold, pure white. "I—tried to take us there. Something prevented it."

The cold fear in his eyes seemed to rush through our touching skin straight into my veins. "Something? Do you think Skeiron…"

I couldn't finish the thought, praying he'd refute it until he decimated that hope with his next words.

"Most likely." He shut his eyes briefly and I swore his heated skin cooled a few degrees. "I sense a magical barrier walling off the falls and its vicinity. We cannot reach the portal."

"What do we do?"

He pressed a kiss to my forehead, his lips lingering there as he spoke. "Skeiron waits inside the barrier. For me."

"For us." I tipped my head back until I could see his eyes. "I'm with you. Whatever happens."

I couldn't have torn my gaze from his if I'd wanted to, but I had no inclination to sever the connection. Not for anything.

"The clock is ticking," he whispered. "Go outside the boundary. Please."

"I won't leave you to fight Skeiron alone."

Without another word, he clamped his hand around mine and half dragged me down the path toward the falls. The healing vortex receded behind us, devoured by the woods. His bare feet slapped and my boots clomped on the dirt path, a dark river ferrying us through the trees. We traveled at a brisk walk, verging on a run, with Nevan a stiff and almost robotic guide, his expression stern, his eyes focused on what lay straight ahead.

My anxiety ratcheted higher with every step, triggering a flood of adrenaline that burned in my veins and heightened my senses. Wings flapped overhead, but I didn't dare glance up, not with Nevan urging me onward at a merciless pace. The winged visitor would be Brennus, tracking us for his master.

I couldn't be the Janusite. I'd never mattered that much to the world—any world.

Nevan pulled us up short at the clearing beside the waterfall. His eyes flashed crimson and steely silver in the twilight, a muscle jumped in his jaw, and those massive shoulders rolled back in readiness for a fight.

He dropped my hand.

My throat went dry and tight. "Skeiron's here, isn't he?"

"Yes."

Wind gusted through the treetops, rattling branches and raining leaves down on us. As the greenery fluttered to the earth around us, bits catching in our hair and on our bodies, the ground beneath us quivered. A gale ripped through the clearing, and borne on the tempest, a voice deep and resonant roared.

Nevan yanked me to him, his arms steel bars around my back.

The gale blustered around us in whirling eddies. I strained to see Nevan through the ropes of my own hair lashing my face.

The wind ceased. One second blasting us, the next dead calm.

I tipped my face up to Nevan, praying he had an answer, knowing there was no magic solution this time. "I'm sorry, love. I can't take us away from here. He strengthened the magical barrier around this area to stop either of us from leaving. He banked on you coming with me."

"It's not your fault. We had no choice, Nevan."

"Where the blame rests hardly matters." He pulled his hand free and backed up two steps. With a flourish of his hand, he conjured an object.

I blinked repeatedly, sure I must be hallucinating. But it was real.

Nevan grasped a sword—long, thick, fashioned from polished, silvery metal laced with bronze. The grip was sheathed in leather, the hilt carved with ornate spiral designs. He lifted the weapon and the ambient light glinted on its blade.

"Listen carefully," he said, holding the sword at his side, blade down. "Skeiron will show himself any moment, once he's done menacing us. He will attempt to take you, but I will not allow it. I must fight him. He has an endued sword, which means I will die, but I'll make certain he goes with me."

I snaked a hand under my shirt, closing it around the butt of my gun.

"You are correct, guardian, on one point."

The voice boomed from across the clearing. Nevan and I turned as one to face the being at the edge of the pool, positioned between us and the falls.

Skeiron sneered at us, his onyx eyes seething with vile green and orange. He wielded a sword too, one forged from obsidian metal shot through with indigo. In lieu of his white robe, kilt of dark gold swathed his hips and thighs. The fabric hung low, slightly askew, exposing the top edge of his hip bones. His muscular chest rivaled Nevan's, his skin a darker shade of suntan, burnished with copper.

Heat rippled through the air, carrying with it the odor of sulfur.

"Would you care to know," Skeiron asked, "on which point you are correct?"

Nevan glowered at his king, the fingers of his free hand twitching.

"You will die, guardian," Skeiron said, "that is a certainty. But I shall not join you. The mortal wench will be mine."

The bastard called me a wench?

"If she is the one, I shall extract the power from her and discard the lifeless remnants of her pitiful—if enticing—human body. If she is not the one, I'll mine what pleasure I can from her and then slowly disassemble her mortal form."

My nails bit into my palms as I fisted my hands tight. "Like hell you will, you psychotic son of a—"

"Silence, wench!"

Ohhh, I was damn sick of him calling me that. "Somebody needs to disassemble your ass."

Nevan surged forward, sidestepping to block my view of the sylph king. Feet planted wide, he raised the sword. I swore I glimpsed a slight uptick of his lips.

"We end this the old way," Nevan said. "With physical might."

They launched into action, barreling toward each other, swords flashing. Their blades collided with an explosive clang that reverberated in the air and in my eardrums. I winced and clapped my hands over my ears to mute the crashing of their swords. Their movements came with such ferocious speed the scene turned into one big blur of motion. The clashing of metal on metal punctuated their grunts and shouts. Feet scuffled across earth, tore grass, uprooted weeds, kicked up clods of dirt.

The battle held me transfixed, my body frozen, my breaths caught in my throat. I ought to help, somehow. What could a puny mortal wench do? I'd be shredded if I dived into the melee of super-speed swordplay. What was happening? Who was winning? I could hardly distinguish Nevan from Skeiron anymore.

One of them flew backward across the clearing and slammed into a thick pine tree. The wet *thwack* of the impact echoed in the clearing.

Nevan slumped to the ground, legs askew. The sword tumbled out of his hand. His breaths panted out of his gaping mouth and blood streamed from slashes on his face, arms, and chest.

Skeiron had reopened the scar over Nevan's heart.

Between gasps, he shouted at Skeiron. "Using magic? You have no honor left, do you, Your Majesty?"

Nevan transformed the word majesty into the worst insult.

Skeiron's lips peeled back in a vicious grin, and in slow motion, his devil-bright eyes zeroed in on me.

Nevan scrambled to rise, lost his balance, clawed at the tree for support.

The king stormed toward me.

I yanked out my derringer, fired both rounds straight into his chest, and flipped open the barrel to reload.

Skeiron paused mid step, eying the wounds. He swept his hands down his chest as if brushing off insects, his eyes slitted, and rushed at me.

I jammed the rounds into the barrel and snapped it shut, but I pulled the trigger too late. A single copper-sheened hand seized my throat, knocking my aim off target. The shot punctured a tree.

Leaping to his feet, teetering for an unnerving second, Nevan snatched up his sword. "Release her."

His command thundered like the voice of an ancient god.

Skeiron strangled me. The gun popped out of my grasp. I gurgled, clawed at his hand, kicked at him, but he merely hoisted me off the ground and smiled at Nevan. Blackness licked at the edges of my vision. I battled for breath, lungs on fire, but my limbs stopped responding and my arms and legs went limp. The abyss beckoned me with sweet relief from the stabbing, searing agony. The blackness encroached further and further and—

A force hurled me sideways. The vise around my neck popped free.

I tumbled to the ground, wheezing. Brightness burst through the darkness in my vision. Ringing in my ears deafened me. I rubbed my throat, as the scene around me snapped into focus.

Nevan and Skeiron wrestled on the ground a dozen feet away. Nevan's sword lay on the grass beside me, while Skeiron's was wedged against a sapling, sharp end up. Skeiron punched Nevan in the chest. Stunned, he gasped for air.

The king pounced on the opening. He vaulted to his feet with supernatural agility and flung one hand out, fingers spread. His sword dislodged from the sapling, somersaulting through the air straight into his waiting palm. He flipped the sword vertical, blade down. Grasped it in both hands. Raised it over Nevan.

And rammed it into his chest.

"No!" I screamed.

Skeiron ripped the sword out. Blood drenched the blade, dripping off the tip onto Nevan's belly. Blood poured from the chest wound.

The drumbeat of my heart battered my eardrums. A fury like nothing I'd ever known exploded inside me, scorching and irresistible, fueling a sensation of mounting physical strength. I knew the feeling was false, but I didn't give a damn.

I closed one hand around the grip of Nevan's sword.

Skeiron was focused on Nevan, his glee enlivening his features with manic effect. He lifted the sword to his mouth and licked the blade, savoring the blood.

I pushed onto my knees and tightened my grip on Nevan's sword.

Skeiron sniggered. "Your essence tastes of weakness, guardian."

Nevan gurgled, flailing one arm. His eyes were flat, the bronze tint gone from his skin, driven out by a growing pallor. And his lips. Oh God, his lips were turning blue.

"Next," Skeiron said, "I shall taste the blood of your precious mortal wench."

I sprang to my feet, brandishing the sword.

Skeiron's gaze flicked to me, the sword, me. His eyes flew wide for an instant, but then a nasty grin split his lips.

I bolted toward him, howling with rage and terror. Before he could react, I jammed the sword into his side. I shoved with all my might until the blade sank in to the hilt and my fingernails scraped his flesh.

Hot liquid flowed over my skin.

I jerked my hand away. Blood soaked my fingers. Despite the tremors racking me, despite how the world tilted around me, I fell to my knees at Nevan's head, his crumpled body laid out before me, and thrust my arms under his. I struggled to lift him, but he was too heavy.

His hand sealed around the sword's hilt, he collapsed to his knees. "Brennus!"

The call roared on the wind that blustered over us all. A raven squawked overhead. Brennus touched down fifteen feet away, morphing into his humanoid form—but not quite as I'd seen him before. Talons curled from the tips of his fingers, sharp and glistening. When he bared his teeth, I glimpsed razor-like points.

An awareness tingled over me. Something had changed.

Nevan dragged in a breath crackling with wetness.

The world winked out.

It winked back an instant later, but we weren't in the woods anymore. Nevan had whisked us to the parking lot of the rock shop, landing us smack beside my car. The last tendrils of sunset reeled back into the horizon, casting us in sickly, ever-diminishing light. Even in the onrushing gloom, I saw the blood. The gaping wound.

"Oh God, Nevan." I clasped his face in both hands, gazing at him upside-down through a haze of tears. "What do I do? Can a doctor help you?"

"No." The wet crackle was there again and an invisible fist gripped my heart. "The barrier dropped...when you...injured him."

That was how he could transport us here. How long would Skeiron stay debilitated?

"I—" Nevan hacked, spraying bloody spittle. "Sorry I couldn't...take us further. Too weak."

Shaking my head, I stroked his cheeks. "It's okay. You did great."

He choked on a cough. Blood trickled from the corner of his mouth.

Oh Jesus, no. I had to stay calm because this was not over. Skeiron had unleashed Brennus on us and the raven would not stop until he hunted us down.

I tore off my T-shirt, leaving only my bra to cover me. I balled up the shirt and pressed it to Nevan's wound.

"No," he croaked. "Too late."

"Like hell."

In the woods, a raven screamed.

Car keys. I needed them *now*.

Fumbling in my pocket, I dug them out, scrabbled to my feet, unlocked the driver's door, and flipped the switch to unlock the others.

The flapping of wings drew ever closer.

I ripped the back door open and fell to my knees beside Nevan. The vehemence in my tone was not an act. "You are going to help me get you into the car. Understand me?"

His eye rolled shut.

I slapped him.

He cracked his lids. His lips quivered as he formed a faint smirk. "Still with the...questions. Eh, love?"

My heart swelled. If he could joke, then goddammit, he could help me move him.

I grabbed his hand and pulled. "Sit up, you arrogant sylph."

He grimaced and gasped as he levered his torso off the ground. I pulled with every iota of strength I had left, grinding my teeth against the pains webbing out through my shoulders and back. When he achieved a semi-erect sitting position, I waddled to his side and threw his arm around my shoulders, linking us with my arm around his waist.

He flailed a hand out to brace himself on the car and, with our combined strength, we hefted him to his feet. His wheezing had gotten worse. After much grunting and shuffling of feet, we got him to the back door. I pushed him inside and he flopped onto the seat on his back. His feet stuck out the door, so I shoved them inside, urging him to bend his knees.

He gazed at me with bloodshot, bleary eyes. "This is pointless. I'm... already d—"

"No. You are not dead yet, buster, so don't go giving up on me." I straightened, my hand on the door. "And that is a command."

I slammed the door.

Something whooshed overhead.

I glanced up to see a raven spiraling down toward me.

By the time I shut the driver's door and cranked the key in the ignition, Brennus had landed in the parking lot, morphing into humanoid form in a heartbeat. He positioned his gigantic bulk directly in front of the car.

I jammed the gear shift lever into reverse and floored the accelerator. The car rocketed backward. Gravel pelted the undercarriage. I jammed the car into drive and rammed my foot down, wrenching the wheel to the left as the car shot forward.

The front bumper nicked Brennus.

We blasted out of the parking lot onto the highway.

In the rearview mirror, I watched Brennus morph back into a bird and take off after us. How fast could a magical raven fly? I was about to find out.

The boundary. I only had to get us past the boundary.

Which would kill Nevan.

I pounded my fist on the wheel. What the fuck was I supposed to do?

For the first time, I prayed Skeiron was right. I prayed to be the Janusite.

A weight crashed onto the car above my head, denting it inward. A talon punched through the roof.

The speedometer breezed past seventy, then eighty, as the car rocketed down the highway. The yellow lines blurred, the trees blurred, everything mutated into a surreal blankness. Less than a mile to go.

The raven hurtled into the driver's window. The glass fractured into a gummy screen.

Through the blur surrounding the car, I spotted a familiar yellow shape. The highway sign. The mile marker.

Brennus struck the glass one more time. His talons pierced the gummy mass, then retracted.

We barreled past the boundary.

CHAPTER TWENTY

I GRIPPED THE STEERING WHEEL IN BOTH HANDS, HANGING ON AS I VEERED around a curve too fast. The car swerved over the center line, but I wrenched the wheel in the other direction, my muscles burning from the strain of it, and the car eased back into the right lane. I checked the rearview mirror.

Brennus, no longer a bird, hulked in the center of the road near the highway marker, just inside the mystical border. We'd passed the boundary—safe, for the moment.

I wrenched the wheel and jammed the brake pedal down to the floorboard. The car fishtailed and stopped amid a hail of gravel. I twisted around to peer into the backseat.

Nevan lay prone with his eyes shut and both knees bent, legs askew, one arm hanging off the seat. I snatched up his hand and felt for a pulse in his wrist. It thumped against my fingers, weak but there. What the hell was I going to do now? I'd had no time to formulate a plan. Sheer panic had driven me to action.

A healing vortex. That's what I needed.

We'd resurrected Brad with the one at the shop, but I didn't dare go back inside the boundary. Not that particular boundary, anyway. One very ticked-off sylph lay in wait for me there. I should've shot him in the head, right between the eyes. It might not have killed him, but it could've bought me more time.

Nevan had told my parents there were other portals, near other water features. I knew of another waterfall a few miles from here. Christ. *Miles*. Did Nevan have that much time?

No choice.

I floored the accelerator and the car hurtled onto the asphalt. The force of our takeoff pinned me to my seat. The car weaved, the wheel jerking in my hands, until I got a firm grip and evened out the vehicle's trajectory. Scenery zipped past. The headlights punched through the darkness like twin swords annihilating the night, though at the periphery, shadows of every shape and size lurked. They seemed to writhe and jump from the car's dizzying speed. At first, I jumped at each faux surprise—until a strange numbness set in, affecting me down to my bones. I navigated on autopilot, my mind incapable of any thought except getting to the waterfall.

Roaring around a curve, I spun the wheel to slalom my car around another vehicle. My body was slung one way, then the other. Back in my lane, I risked a quick glance into the backseat.

Nevan was sprawled as before. Eyes shut. Lifeless.

No, not lifeless. Unconscious. *Remember that. You can't afford to freak out every time you look at him.*

I concentrated on the road, both hands on the wheel, my knuckles white. Nobody was losing anybody tonight.

How far had I driven? The miles blurred the same as the road. I let up on the gas pedal and the speedometer eased downward. Seventy. Sixty.

The landscape was familiar. Not far now.

Nudging the accelerator, I pushed the car back up to eighty. The road curved left and right, forcing me to ease off the gas. My heart pounded. A cold sweat dribbled down my temples. Almost there.

The headlights flared across an asphalt driveway up ahead. A big, blue road sign announced "Rest Stop." This time I stood on the brake pedal, terrified to miss the turn and have to double back in the dark, on this narrow highway. I veered the car into the semicircular drive and parked it in front of the shed that housed the restrooms. The car was angled across three parking spaces, but nobody was here in the dead of night. By rote, I shifted the car into park, shut off the engine, and stuffed the keys in my pants pocket. The headlights stayed on, but outside their reach, full-on dark had swallowed the earth.

I retrieved a flashlight from the glove compartment, kicked the driver's door open, leaped out, and tore the passenger door open.

Nevan lay so still. His head lolled. One arm dangled off the seat with his fingertips grazing the floorboard. Blood still trickled from his wound, down his side and onto the floor.

When I shoved a finger into his neck at the pulse point, a weak beat pushed against my flesh. Relief nearly toppled me to the ground.

I needed to move him, but how? I hadn't been able to carry him by myself before, and even with his aid it had taken all my strength. A fatigue deeper than any I'd known before weakened my limbs, far worse than before. The adrenaline spike I'd experienced back in the clearing had drained away when I needed it the most.

"No!" I screamed it into the night, collapsing against the door, and glared up at the stars. "I could use some fucking help down here!"

As the echoes of my screams spiraled down into silence, I detected another sound.

The soft rumble of a waterfall.

I jerked upright. *Of course, you moron, that's why you came here.*

To heal Brad, we'd required a leprechaun's help. And elementals—fae, whatever—possessed far more strength than I did, not to mention nifty magical powers for zipping here and there. Locating a leprechaun meant traveling into the other realm on my own. Could I even open a portal without Nevan's help?

Well, I'd transported Nevan across the boundary and he was still alive. Maybe I was the Janusite, or maybe things weren't as black-and-white as these supernatural types believed. I had to try.

My gaze lanced down to Nevan. I'd have to leave him here, alone, while I hunted down a willing elemental.

A sharp pain stabbed at the back of my throat.

Bent over the seat with one knee on the floorboards, I brushed my fingers over Nevan's cheek. My hair fell around his head like a curtain. His customary heat was fading, with a chill seeping in behind it.

"I'll be back soon. Don't you go anywhere." Though his face was blank, I imagined his smirk and that sultry chuckle every time he'd teased me for saying dopey things. I touched my lips to his forehead. "I'll fix this, promise."

Without allowing myself to think anymore, I shut the door and clicked on the flashlight as I ran for the waterfall. No trail led down to it. Instead, a railing made of driftwood barred the way and a big wooden sign offered historical information on the site. I clambered over the barrier. My left boot caught on the uneven wood. I cursed, the noise bouncing off the trees, and shook my foot loose.

I bolted toward the falls. The water cascaded down from maybe ten feet above the ground, onto a flat landing of sorts that tapered into a small, shallow pool.

My boots slid on the slick rock as I sidled across the landing, my back flat against the cliff. In my left hand I clutched the flashlight, while with my right I clawed at the rock wall in search of support I didn't really need. At the falls, I stepped away from the cliff and squinted into the darkness. My flashlight penetrated the thin veil of water.

No cave. A solid wall of rock backed the falls.

My head spun, and for more seconds than my wits could stand, I waited out the vertigo. I still felt lightheaded, but at least I wouldn't trip and crack my skull on the rock landing.

You should exercise more care, darlin', or you'll crack that lovely head of yours.

Nevan's words to me the first time I'd seen him replayed in my brain. A sharp sob burst out of me. The flashlight clattered to the ground. I slapped both palms on the cliff face, through the water, oblivious to the cold liquid that sprayed up in my face and inundated my hands, my arms, my ankles, my boots.

Water is the doorway. Nevan had said that too.

Not *the waterfall is the door,* but water itself. Had that been what he meant?

I pushed away from the wall. Snagged the flashlight. Clamped my hand around it. Turned away from the falls.

The pool appeared shallow, probably similar to the deep end of a swimming pool. I really could crack my skull, if I was wrong about this. Time for a genuine leap of faith.

Drawing in a long breath, I held it. Now or never.

I leaped into the water.

My feet punched through the surface. Water erupted around me. I plunged into the pool, sinking deeper and deeper, flailing my arms, struggling against the overpowering urge to suck in a breath.

Up, down, left, right—my mind fought to sort out the directions but failed. I twirled round and round, starved for air, chest aching from my thunderous heartbeat and the urgency to breathe. Oh God, I would die here, in this pool, alone.

Images flashed in my mind, bright and fast. My parents. My baby brother. The rock shop. Travis. Nevan.

He would die because of me. Because I failed.

My lungs screamed for oxygen. I released the breath I'd held, shooting out a cloud of bubbles. Pressure built inside me until I feared my lungs might explode. One final, anguished plea echoed in my mind. *I don't want to die.*

A vision of Nevan's face hovered in front of me, glowing with ethereal light. The soothing energy of his presence streamed into me.

The beam of my flashlight, still gripped in my hand, speared down to the pool's bottom.

I fought the impulse to inhale, but it grew stronger every second.

Open up, you stupid portal.

As my body dived toward the bottom, the ground crumbled away below me. An oily blackness churned like a whirlpool, its spiraling eddies interwoven with iridescent green and purple. The pull of the portal dragged me down faster, faster, as my limbs stretched taut and pain coruscated through me. Just as I lost the battle to not breathe, I launched through the surface into the open air, bobbing like an empty bottle. I gulped in mouthfuls of air. Nothing had ever tasted so delicious or felt so wonderful. Water streamed off my hair, rolling down my face in rivulets. I blinked to clear my eyes.

Night enveloped me, but a faint, milky glow sifted through it.

Head bent back, I panted and stared at the double moons—one large, one small—smiling down at me from a sky speckled with more stars than I'd ever seen from the mortal realm.

I swam to shore. My flashlight lanced across the alien landscape and straight up into the sky. A new burst of energy shored up my body, fueling my muscles as I hauled myself out of the water and onto my feet.

Now to find a damn leprechaun.

My jaw hurt, which made me realize I was gritting my teeth. I chewed my lip instead, drilling my brain for answers. I knew of one leprechaun, but we'd found Tris by going through the other waterfall. Everything looked different here.

When I'd screamed for Nevan, he'd heard me and come to my rescue. Might the same tactic work with a different elemental?

I threw my head back and yelled, "Tris, you obnoxious little twerp, get your ass out here this instant."

Seconds that dragged like minutes ticked by on my mental clock. Ten. Fifteen. Nothing happened.

Nevan was dying, all alone on the other side. I'd gotten him past the boundary, halting Brennus's pursuit.

The boundary.

Everything inside me froze. Since I'd brought him to another waterfall, that meant we'd traveled inside another boundary. Brennus and Skeiron might've found him already.

No. They couldn't have guessed which waterfall I'd taken Nevan to, or that I took him to any kind of portal. I needed to cling to the positive thought, because otherwise I'd fall apart.

I shined my flashlight into the inky woods. No leprechaun yet.

Screw this.

I screamed, like a teenage girl riding her first roller coaster. I shrieked Tris's name, railing epithets into the night.

My cries slid back into wordless, blood-curdling screams, the likes of which had never busted out of me before in my life. I screamed until my throat burned, until my voice cracked, until—

Tris materialized in front of me.

Gasping for breath, I choked off my wail. My throat scorched like sandpaper set on fire.

The leprechaun screwed up his mouth, brows knit and lowered in a sullen expression. "What the hell do you want, lady? You're waking up the whole neighborhood."

"To hell with your friends," I croaked. "You're the only one I need."

"Here I thought you were hot for the sylph. Hate to break it to you, sister, but you ain't my type." He waved at my breasts. "Too busty."

"You little worm." I stomped straight up to him, stabbing my finger into his chest. He winced the tiniest bit. "I don't have time for your bullshit. Nevan is dying."

His brows smoothed out and an emotion flickered across his face, but I had no brainpower left to decipher it. He stuffed his hands in the pockets of his ripped jeans. "What's it got to do with me?"

I bent to glare into his eyes, our faces so close my breaths reflected off his skin. "You are going to heal him with the vortex."

"Ain't no vortex here, lady."

I shuffled back a step. "What?"

"No vortex." He enunciated with exaggerated care, as if speaking to a dimwit.

I felt dimwitted at this moment, and devoid of all hope. But I could not—would not—give up. "There's a waterfall. I brought him here, I nearly drowned crossing the fucking veil, and you're telling me it was all for nothing?" I grabbed the collar of his flannel shirt, hauling him into me. My lips scraped his as I hissed words at him. "You find a way to heal him or I will rip your dried-up, repulsive, festering little heart right out of your chest."

He stopped blinking. Stopped breathing. Stopped fighting and just stared at me.

"Do you hear me?" I shook him hard enough to rattle his brain. "Do you?"

"Yeah," he said slowly, his voice hushed. "I hear you, but..."

"What?"

He shrank a little, shoulders bunching. "There really ain't a vortex here, I'm sorry. We'd have to somehow get him to where there is one."

"Not the one where I first met you. Skeiron is there, or he was, and he's pissed." Understatement of the millennium. "I don't think Skeiron's dead, but even if he is, Brennus would be waiting for us there."

"Skeiron? Brennus? Holy cripes, lady, feed me to the hell hounds and get it over with. I can't fight those two."

"You don't have to." A retched thought took hold and I squinted at Tris. "Are you working for Skeiron? Is that why you won't save Nevan?"

"Working for him?" Tris blew air through his lips. "He massacred a whole coven of fae witches to steal their power. No fae helps him—ever."

"Unless he tricked you into a bargain."

One corner of his mouth ticked up in a half smirk. "He can't. We made a group bargain not to deal with Skeiron, and trust me, we worded it so no stinking sylph can get around it."

Though I couldn't focus on his words, though part of me understood.

I shoved him away. "Get Nevan to another vortex and *fix him*."

"Yeah-yeah, okay." Tris raised his hands, palms out. "I know of another one, a good strong vortex. I'll have to, um..." He twirled one finger in the air. "You know, uh, kinda get us there the magical way."

"Whisk us through the tunnel thingy. Fine, I don't give a damn, just do it."

"Well, ya see, I ain't eaten lately."

I shook my fists in the air. "Then eat some goddamn copper."

"Got none."

"Nevan is dying."

"Sorry, I can't do nothing without fuel." He cringed, as if expecting me to explode.

Which I'd done constantly since summoning him. I drew in a breath, letting it out little by little, and fought for self-control. Easier said than done. My entire body had begun to shake with a combination of terror and fury. Still, I managed a calmer tone when I spoke again. "Zip over to the rock shop, you'll find plenty of copper there."

"All right." He eyed me askance, leaning back. "You better come with me. Never know who you might've woken up with your hollering."

The thought of Nevan breached my panic. He'd be as safe where he was as anywhere, and besides, I had no other options.

Tris cautiously stretched out a hand to me. I took it. Nevan had always embraced me for traveling this way, but the instant my hand touched Tris's, he zipped us away. We materialized in the darkened shop, my flashlight illuminating the interior.

My trip with Tris proved Nevan hadn't needed to hug me for traveling. He must've wanted to do it that way. The realization made my chest ache.

Tris and I scurried around the shop gathering every kind of copper available—nuggets, fist-size chunks, jewelry fashioned from the stuff, and a pair of copper ore bookends like the ones Brad stole.

Brad. He was dead forever this time.

Nevan would be soon too, if we didn't hurry the hell up.

In one hand, Tris grasped the plastic shopping bag we'd laden with copper items. Before I could pester him, he snagged my hand and transported us to my car, where it was parked at the rest stop. I tore the back door open and knelt at Nevan's head. Tears fuzzed my vision and tightened my throat. I clamped my teeth over both lips, clasped Nevan's cold hand in mine, and looked at Tris. His hand still held mine.

"The vortex," I said through my teeth. "Now."

No griping. No eye rolling. He zipped us away from the car, into a forest much like the one around the shop and the other waterfall. Were we still in the Keweenaw? In Michigan? I didn't give a crap anymore. Nothing mattered except saving Nevan.

He lay at my feet, crumpled on the ground. The moss-covered earth squished under my boots as I moved to Nevan's side and crouched there, his hand still enclosed in mine. I clasped our hands to my heart.

Tris inched backward away from me.

Wherever we were, this clearing had no sign declaring the area a healing vortex, no stone benches, nothing except empty space ringed by the woods.

The leprechaun squatted, ripping open the shopping bag. He wolfed down copper ore in whole chunks, only resorting to biting off mouthfuls when he got down to the bookends. Ore dust rained from his lips, coating his clothing and sprinkling onto the mossy ground, as his teeth pulverized the rock in quick time. When he'd finished, he wadded up the bag and jammed it in his pocket. Then he rose and rolled back his shoulders.

His blue eyes gleamed, twin supernovas of cobalt blue.

And he just stood there.

My frustration exploded out of me on a breath. I flapped my arms, trying to get his attention, but he gazed off into nothing. "What is wrong with you? Wake up, dammit."

"Something hinky's going on," he said, sounding drugged. "Funky energy's interfering, and I can't get past it." His gaze cleared and zeroed in on me. "It's you."

"That's—" I stopped, my mouth still open. Nevan said time passed slower in the Unseen because magic must've been interfering with it. He'd suggested the energy he sensed in me had been responsible. Now Tris made a similar claim, but I didn't give a damn what the cause was. "How can we fix this?"

"No frigging clue. Maybe a b—" The color flooded out of his face. "Forget it. There ain't no way."

I slunk closer to him. "A bargain. That's what you almost said."

"No way." He blundered backward, tripped on a rock. "If I power up the vortex from this side of the water, I have to pull in a piece of the Unseen realm to do it. In essence, we are in my world."

So a bargain…*Shit.*

"Can't let you do it, lady." He twisted his shirt around his fingers, glancing down at Nevan. "He'd kill me if I did."

My gaze fell to Nevan. His pale face. Those sensual lips now a frightening shade of blue-white. The blood on his chest. The gaping wound.

Flashbacks raced through my mind. Nevan taking me away when Travis was chasing me. Nevan's body curled around mine as I slept. The way he insisted I eat and brought me tempting foods to ensure I did. His lips on mine, tender and then ravenous with passion. The vow he'd made to my mother, that he would protect me at any cost. I squeezed my hands around his. If his death was the cost, I could not let him pay it. My hands trembled. *Nothing else matters.*

I rolled my eyes up to fixate on Tris. "If you heal him, I will give you anything you want."

"Aw, lady, are you nuts?"

"Probably. Do we have a deal?"

Tris's gaze darted to Nevan and doubt flickered on his face. His shoulders hunched. "Oh man, if I let you do this, he'll murder me for sure."

"I won't let him." I lifted my chin, trying for self-assurance I didn't feel. "Here's the bargain. If you restore Nevan to his normal state, healing all his wounds and bringing him back to consciousness, I will give you anything you want and I'll stop Nevan from hurting you. Agreed?"

"You sure about this?"

"Quit hemming and hawing."

He gave a curt nod. "I accept your terms."

A tether of power whipped between me and Tris, the unseen ends latching onto us with a jolt. Bargain sealed.

"Do it already," I said. "Uphold your end."

Tris closed his eyes.

Energy roiled off him in coppery, glittering tentacles. They nipped at my skin, zapped into me down to the core of my being. The tentacles gyrated around the three of us, diving into the ground, spewing out of it again, encompassing Nevan until the shimmering energy obscured his entire body, except for the arm I clutched to my breast.

I shut my eyes and prayed, like I never had before. I infused my silent prayers with every ounce of anguish and hope I harbored inside me.

Nevan's hand warmed in mine.

The snapping energy dissipated.

I cracked my eyelids to peek out through my lashes. Nevan rested on the ground as before, but his bronze coloring had returned. His hand in mine had grown warmer, feeding into me that precious, intoxicating heat.

My tears flowed, unfettered.

Tris cleared his throat. "Seeing how my job's done, I'm gonna split. He can get you wherever you need to be."

Without looking away from Nevan, I said, "Okay. Thank you."

"For crying out loud, lady. Gratitude too? You better keep up your end, 'cause if he comes after me, I'm calling in your debt."

He vanished.

Nevan's fingers twitched. I lifted them to my lips and kissed them one by one.

A moan emanated from him.

Was he still injured? Damn that leprechaun. I spread my palms on his chest, running them over his skin in broad circles. The wound was gone. Only the old scar over his heart remained.

My tears splattered onto his chest.

"Why are you crying, love?"

At his words, I burst into a fit of weeping.

Nevan sat up, folding his arms around me, and pulled me onto his lap. I hugged my hands to my chest, burying my face in his neck, and let his heat banish the chill. He stroked my hair and rocked me as he murmured soothing sounds. Gradually, my weeping subsided. He kept rocking me, his arms firm but gentle around my shoulders.

His body squashed my arms to my chest. I wrestled my hands free to hold his face in my palms. "You're alive."

"Was I dead? Didn't feel like it."

"Not quite, but—" His hands traveled down to my hips. I couldn't move my hands, his skin felt too good under them. "It took so long to get you here, to this vortex. I got us away from Brennus, but then I had to find Tris and he needed copper and—"

His fingers kneading my flesh scattered my thoughts.

"It's all right." His voice was a low rumble, unbelievably sexy. "I'm quite impressed you got me here without Skeiron beheading us both." He ran his hands over my shoulders and down my arms—searching for wounds, I supposed. "Did he or Brennus hurt you in any way?"

"I'm fine." I raked my hands up the back of his neck and into his hair, my fingers splayed over his scalp. "How are you?"

"I feel quite well, very alive."

The way he accentuated the last word flashed heat through me, from my lips straight down between my thighs. I wriggled on his lap, relishing the sensation of hard muscle as it rubbed against my aching core. An impulse hit me and I had no willpower left to resist.

I drew his head down to mine and crushed my lips to his. He yielded to me without hesitation, his lips parting for me. I forged deep inside, lost to the sensations of his tongue, his mouth, his hands anchoring my waist. He groaned into my mouth. I devoured him as if our essences could merge through our lips joining and our tongues tangling. I kissed him like nothing else in the universe mattered to me, nothing except him and this heady passion.

He broke the kiss, his flaming eyes locked on mine.

Dazed, I couldn't prevent the words from spilling out unbidden, hushed enough he couldn't have heard. "Rein it in, Lindsey."

He leaped to his feet, carrying me up with him. I landed flat on my feet.

The flashlight's beam sprayed across the ground in a wedge of illumination, aimed right at Nevan. I backed away, bereft from the loss of contact, but I needed to see him, all of him, to be sure.

The flashlight flickered and extinguished. I snatched it up, shook it, thumped the heel of my hand against it. Nothing. I made an unladylike, disgusted noise.

"What is the matter, my sweet mortal morsel?"

"Flashlight's dead. I can't see a thing."

"I can see you." The statement, his teasing but sensual tone, tickled me in the most intimate way.

"You might still be injured. I need to…" How could I phrase this without sounding salacious? Oh hell, who cared. "I need to get a good look at you. Please."

"If you insist."

Balls of light popped into existence in his palms. They swelled into softball-size orbs, bluish and sparkling with the purest white.

Fairy lights.

He tossed them into the air, where they floated above our heads. He conjured a half dozen more, tossing them into the air so we were immersed in the shimmering glow.

And I saw him. All of him.

"Here I am, love," he said, devouring me with his hot gaze. "What will you do with me now?"

Chapter Twenty-One

THE FAIRY LIGHTS TWINKLED ABOVE OUR HEADS, BATHING US BOTH IN silvery light. The six feet of space separating us glittered with incandescence, from the droplets of energy showering down from the lights. The air sizzled faintly.

And there, like a mirage in the forest, stood Nevan.

I roamed my gaze up and down his length, soaking in every muscular inch of bare flesh. I'd intended do nothing more than verify his wounds had healed, but I couldn't stop the heat pooling inside me, low down, in places I'd ignored for far too long. My attention wandered to his chest, that dazzling expanse of bronzed skin. My hands ached to explore him, to map out the contours of his body with my fingertips. I licked my lower lip, slowly, envisioning my tongue on his neck, licking my way down to—

"Are ye quite finished, love?"

Nevan's voice, rife with self-satisfaction, snapped me back to reality. Sort of. The damned fire in my nether regions had coalesced into a deep, throbbing tingle. The sensation robbed me of my breath and stripped away my senses, until I had a hell of a time hauling my mind out of the fantasy. Maybe it didn't have to stay a fantasy. Just for tonight, maybe I could release my fears and dive into Nevan's embrace, into his kiss, into…everything. Maybe.

An old saying popped into my head, the phrase sailors of the olden days used to describe what lay beyond the horizon—*there be monsters here*. The ghost of Calder, real or imagined, was my monster. Nevan was my horizon, but I was too chicken to go there.

I folded my arms over my chest, proud of my physical composure in the face of hormone overload, and gestured at him with one finger. "You look fine."

But oh, he looked way better than fine.

A memory exploded in my mind—Nevan, prostrate on the ground, a sword jammed into his chest, blood pouring out. A jolt of dizziness rocked me and I zeroed in on his torso again. Though I saw nothing aside from his scar, not a scratch or scrape, doubt niggled in my gut. "Is the pain gone? Are you sure you're completely healed?"

"I told ye already, I'm quite fine." He flashed a wicked grin. "But hadn't ye better check for yourself? I understand mortals conduct physical examinations after an injury."

"I—well yes, but—" A blush fired up in my cheeks, so hot aliens on distant planets must've spotted the glow. *Rein it in, Lindsey.* "I'll take your word for it."

Nevan shook his head, rolled his eyes, and sighed. I struggled to hold back a smile. He did "exasperation personified" so well.

Hands clasped behind his back, he began to pace in a circle around me, his strides long and purposeful, fluid and masculine. The hunter stalking his prey. He watched me with each step, and even when he crossed behind me, his gaze flared across my skin, stoking an awareness deep inside. Half of me relished the thought of being the sole focus of his concentration. The other half wanted to bolt, hide, pretend I hadn't broken my own decree that we never kiss again. I'd thrown myself at him in the most humiliating way. I'd done more than kiss him. I'd drowned myself in him.

And lord, had it felt *good.*

But it was a mistake. Calder had taught me that lesson.

Nevan's footfalls shooshed on the grass, the skin of his ankles glistening with dew. He circled around me again, and again, and again, inching closer with each circuit. The playful sylph had retreated, submerged beneath the ancient warrior. Though I'd glimpsed this part of him a few times, when others provoked him, now I had triggered his feral, possessive instincts.

I fidgeted, but did not move my feet. "What are you doing?"

"Thinking."

"About…"

"You." He smiled, that thousand-watt smile, the one that zapped me with an electrical shock every time he beamed it at me. "I've thought of little else since first I saw you."

"Which would be three months ago, when you were pretending to be somebody else."

"Nice try." He crossed behind me, out of sight, yet I felt him prowling ever closer. "I won't let you reshape this conversation to your own comfort. This will unfold as I design it, not you."

"Whatever you say, Mr. Bossy Pants."

Though he arched an eyebrow, he kept pacing. *Shoosh, shoosh, shoosh.*

I let myself admire the view when he passed in front of me again. Never before had I enjoyed an unimpeded, uninterrupted view of him in motion, those muscular thighs working, his loincloth shifting a little with each step, stretching taut over the bulge of his cock.

The shooshing stopped. He stopped. Behind me. Watching.

Every cell on the backside of me electrified, a million microscopic circuits zinging an erotic current straight down to my core. I gulped, not sure why, and bundled my arms around myself, then dropped them to my sides, my fingers twitching in a restless rhythm. "What are you doing?"

"What would you like me to be doing?"

"I don't know."

He stepped into my peripheral vision. I wanted to look, but my head refused to budge. He exhaled a long, languid sigh that rippled shivers down my spine. When he spoke, his tone was thick and molten. "You kissed me."

I snorted out a nervous laugh. "Yeah, I'm aware of that."

Damn if my voice didn't quiver the slightest bit. *Get a grip, woman.*

In two long strides, he moved in front of me, turned, and whirled on me. Ten feet, maybe twelve, separated our bodies, yet the gravity of his presence pulled at my atoms.

He canted his head. "You made me vow never to kiss you again, to keep my lips away from yours at all times. Then you kissed me, and not a simple kiss, but the wanton kind that compels a man to reach certain conclusions."

"I didn't mean to lead you on."

"You've led me nowhere. I've been dragging you here by the hair."

I did a double take. Seriously, I did. He dragged me? Never. He'd been gentle, careful, respectful. And yes, erotic as hell. But never, ever rough with me. Yet to him our little dance had clearly seemed like an ordeal. He didn't look annoyed, though. Curious, maybe. Predatory. Possessive, in a way that liquefied my resolve.

He ran his tongue over his lower lip, slowly, sensuously. "You broke your own vow. I want to know why."

"Maybe I changed my mind."

"You realize what this means."

Yeah, I'm a lust-drunk moron. "Why don't you spit out whatever it is you're trying to say and stop making me guess."

"You want me."

I laughed, but it came out as a frantic giggle. Even the densest man would've picked up on the subtle clues to the non-mystery of my attraction to him.

He shrugged one shoulder, undulating all that taut flesh. "It's all right. I want you too. Which is why I'm not letting you 'rein it in' this time."

My heart stopped. I know it did. I'm pretty sure every clock on earth stopped ticking too. He must've heard me mumble those words—*rein it in*—under my breath, to myself, after I kissed him.

"Let it go." His voice was the purring of a cougar.

My heart started up again with an agonizing thud.

Nevan strode toward me, narrowing the gap between us to inches. The vision of him, of his muscles pulsating with each movement and the tiny loincloth straining to cover him, devoured my focus. For the first time in my life, I craved a man with a passion so intense nothing could quench it. Nothing except for his body.

An icy ribbon of fear unfurled in my chest. I teetered on the precipice, more than ever before, nudged there by lust and…affection? Yeah, okay, I liked him. Hard not to like a man who'd taken a sword to the chest for me. It was nothing more than…a mild fondness and immense gratitude. Expressing either sentiment posed risks I didn't care to take.

He lifted a hand, grazing it over my arm with the barest touch, and my breath caught. The heat of him radiated over my skin as he wrapped his arms around me, tugging me tight into his lithe, firm body. I drew in a long breath, savoring the scent of him—earth and grass, with a hint of sharp sweetness evocative of onrushing thunderstorms. He always smelled of the elements, but then what did I expect from a sylph? He was, he'd told me, forged from the air and earth. I should've pulled away, the impulse pulled at me, but a stronger need overpowered it. The need to relent. Drop those blasted reins. Give in.

His breaths caressed my ear as his voice murmured, "You're tensing up again. Why must you do that? Do ye really believe I'll harm ye?"

"No." I said it without thinking. And my eyes were closed. Damn, when did that happen? I commanded my lids to open, but they disobeyed.

His lips brushed the shell of my ear, his breath teasing the inside, while his hands skimmed the hairs on my arms. "You are glorious, Lindsey, a goddess in disguise. Instead of hiding under this brittle armor, you ought to shake it off and bask in the sun. With me." His mouth slid lower, his teeth nipping my lobe. "How about it?"

"I—" Christ. I'd made so many mistakes, survived too many disasters, to believe losing control had no consequences. "You might change your mind."

"About what?" His voice was low, sultry.

"Me. I'm not…like this. Not like all those other women you've been with."

"The others were nothing compared to you."

"I'm a repressed, scaredy-cat virgin. Remember?"

He laughed, his lips trembling over the skin under my ear. "You are strong and clever, braver than the most powerful elemental, and—" He cupped one hand on my right cheek, turning my face into his. My lips met his cheek, sending a flaming shudder down my body. "And you are the most desirable woman in any realm. If you stop holding back, you'll realize just how glorious you are. Unleash your passion. I won't let you fall."

My heart pounded so hard and fast I thought the blood might burst my veins. "You don't know what you're asking. I'm not capable of it."

His head moved, his hands too, releasing me. "Open your eyes."

I did. Though measured in inches, the gulf between us seemed wider than the universe.

Nevan studied me with thoughtful interest, his gaze roaming the length and breadth of me. "You seem quite capable to me."

His eyes lured me in and bound my focus to him.

I stuffed my hands in my jeans pockets. Anything to stop my fingers from stretching out to explore his flesh. I had to step away, right this second, but my legs disagreed. "Look, I know you'll panic if I express any you-know-what, but you did save my life and, well, I..." Struggling for a way to thank him without thanking him, I grumbled. "Screw this. We're still in my world, so I'm going to say it. Thank—"

His mouth smothered my words. His lips moved over mine, pressing and releasing, capturing my lower lip, then setting it free. My traitorous hands twitched in my pockets, hungry for the feel of his skin. I wanted him. I needed control. I ached to unleash my body and soul. I had to shield myself.

Nevan parted his lips from mine, though just enough to speak. "Do you recall the pot and the kettle?"

"Yes." Our previous conversation, about pots calling kettles black, didn't seem relevant here.

He backed away one pace. I fought the urge to haul him back, and as if he sensed my inner battle, his mouth slid into a knowing smile. "What does the kettle do, love?"

"Huh?" In my head, I ran a quick replay of our earlier discussion. "Oh. Right. It steams. But I don't understand why we're talking about this."

"That's why. Because you don't understand." He slanted his head, eying my breasts with a ravenous gleam. "A kettle releases its steam. You're a pot, keeping everything locked under a tight lid, boiling away, building up pressure. What you don't seem to comprehend is that you've got to let some of it off, or the pressure will blow you apart." His focus shifted to my eyes, intent and unwavering. "I'd hate to see that happen to you."

"I can't change what I am."

"Sure ye can. Decide to become a kettle."

I huffed out an annoyed sigh. "This is the most ridiculous metaphor ever and I'm sorry I ever mentioned pots or kettles. I'm a person, a very, very screwed up person who can't just decide to become a—" I threw my hands up. "A kettle or whatever. Pots are pots, end of story. I wouldn't even know how to do what you're suggesting."

"Losing control is easy, darlin'. With the proper motivation."

Without taking a single step, he reached across the distance and dragged me into his arms, pinning my hands to his chest between our bodies. One of his arms locked me there. The other raised as he thrust a hand into my hair and forced me to look up at him. "You, my glorious goddess, can be anything you choose to be."

"Why do you care what I am?"

Amusement sparkled in his eyes and dimpled his cheeks. "Because you matter."

I yearned to believe he meant what my heart prayed he did, but his vagueness left too much doubt. "I matter because your king wants to kill me. Otherwise, someone like you wouldn't look once at me, much less twice."

"I've looked at you a thousand times, seeing the woman, the goddess, the frightened little rabbit, and everything else in between."

"But why? Why me?"

"I'll tell ye later, when you'll be receptive to the answer." His tongue danced across my lips.

"Uhhh…" It was all I could manage to say.

All around us, a breeze rustled the aspen trees. Their leaves rattled, pattering like rain. The sensual sound rippled the tingling through my entire body, from my loins to my scalp, and straight down to my toes. His fingers massaged my scalp in lazy, gentle strokes. His voice dropped to a seductive whisper. "Steam for me, Lindsey."

I drank in the sound of the words, letting them course through my veins, intoxicating me with every syllable. *Steam for me.* The heat pulsed inside me, a driving force too powerful to fight, and I didn't want to anymore, the craving was too intense, the pressure more than I could stand. I let his body brace me, my knees trembling, and for once, I didn't even try to clamp a lid on the passion escalating inside me.

Nevan stroked his hands up and down my back, dipping his head to whisper his breaths over my mouth. I lowered my head to his chest, grazing my lips over the centuries-old scar across his heart. He shuddered. This big, strong, elemental man—my bronzed god, the hero who'd saved my life over and over—shuddered at my touch.

I tilted my head back to gaze at his face, at the lines fanning out from his half-closed eyes. He'd gone stiff, his hands tense as they settled on my hips. Maybe I'd embarrassed him by touching his scar in that way. But no, I could not believe I had the power to embarrass a man who lived in a loincloth and excited every nerve in my body simply by speaking my name in a sultry, husky voice. Just in case I was wrong, in case he was the one in need of relaxation this time, I tapped his chest with one finger. "Is your heart still in there? I mean, you said Skeiron cut you when he cursed your heart, so…"

His chuckle rumbled in his chest, vibrating into me. The tension softened, his hands tugging my hips into him. "Yes, darlin', I've still got the bloody thing."

"Why is your heart a bloody thing?"

"Because it's given me naught save agony. Until tonight." He hooked his thumb under my chin, lifting it, and ducked his head near to mine. His breaths, hot and enticing, teased me and I burned to taste him, to take his breath into my body and meld with him. He bent closer, our lips brushing. "Let's not start with the questions again. I can think of other, more interesting things we might do together."

No words. No thoughts. Only him.

"Say it, love."

"What?"

"You know what. The words I told ye never to speak again unless you agreed with my interpretation."

"Don't remember the words."

"Yes you do." He slipped his tongue between my lips, then withdrew. "Say it."

I did know what he was asking. He'd promised me if I spoke a certain phrase one more time, he'd accept the offer, though at the time I hadn't meant the words the way he'd implied. Right here, in this moment, I understood exactly what he needed from me. Permission.

A choice. A precipice.

I jumped.

"Nevan…take me."

His voice growled, his lips dangerously close to mine. "I will do just that, for as long as it takes, as many times as it takes, until you break apart for me and only me. Not because your fear has cracked you, but because I have won you, body and soul."

Need catapulted through me with such force I swayed in his arms. He clinched me tighter against him. His flesh scorched mine through the fabric of my T-shirt, exciting my every nerve, until my nipples hardened against him. For the first time in—oh God, how many years?—I confronted the hunger burgeoning inside me without a shred of shame to taint it.

No more fear. This is your chance to come alive again. Seize it.

I bent my head to scrape my tongue across his scar.

He tensed again.

Don't chicken out now. I dragged my tongue across the faint line of rough skin once more, tracing a damp path up his chest, over his collarbone, into the hollow above it.

He groaned.

A thrill coursed through me. He liked it. No, he *loved* it. I held power over him, despite the glib facade he often retreated into, despite the fact he could crush me with his elemental magic with a single flick of his wrist. In this moment, *I* controlled *him*. My touch ignited his passion. Why he was rock hard, and not in the way I wanted him hard, baffled me. I'd given in, hadn't I? That's what he wanted.

I skated my hands up his chest. "Shall I help you…relax?"

He hissed out a shaky breath. I had no doubts he remembered the precise context of the moment when he'd posed the same question to me.

Still, he said nothing.

I bounced up onto my tiptoes. Our eyes leveled. Currents of bronze, gold, and silver swirled within his irises, a vortex of molten metal sparking with bright red pinpoints. I let the sight entrance me for a moment, reveling in the strange beauty and naked desire in his eyes. Then I draped my arms around his neck. Shut my eyes. Hauled in a deep breath. And crushed my mouth to his.

His teeth clamped shut, blocking my tongue.

I peeled my mouth away and squinted at him.

"No," he said, without a hint of emotion.

My heart thudded and my head reeled, but not from desire. A cold emptiness sucked all the passion out of me, leaving me speechless.

His expression softened, his body relaxing at last. "I didn't mean no, darlin'."

"Well, you *said* no. And I swear if you start arguing semantics with me—"

The tips of his fingers sealed my lips. "I meant not this way. You're trying to control the situation again, and while I enjoy your efforts immensely, we're doing this my way." He danced his finger over my mouth, as his other hand massaged my hip in an intoxicating rhythm. "You, my little kettle, will be the one losing control. This time."

He skimmed his hand across my cheek without touching my skin, his fingers awakening every little hair, and I turned my face into his palm, flicking my tongue across it. He shifted his hand down to my neck, hovering his flesh an aching millimeter from mine. Last time, I'd stopped him. This time...

This time. He'd said I'd be the one to lose control this time. Did that mean next time—

He swept his lips across mine, shattering my thoughts. His mouth claimed mine, and with one thrust of his tongue, I was gone, consumed by the passion exploding between us. He sank his hand into my hair and bent my head back, delving deeper into my mouth, his tongue soft and slick, demanding my surrender. I relinquished everything to him, giddy with the freedom of it, exploring him with wild strokes of my tongue.

He released my hair and grasped my buttocks. His mouth fused to mine, he hoisted me off the ground, my hips pinned to his groin. A long, low moan resonated inside my chest, up my throat, straight into his mouth. His chest heaved. One of his hands lunged under my shirt. The rasping of his palm against my skin shot a white-hot bolt of desire into my core. I raked my hands through his hair, gripping the back of his head, forcing him closer as I feasted on the flavor of him.

His arousal swelled against my sensitive mound, activating all my nerves at once. I flung my legs around him, desperate to take him inside, even through my jeans. I didn't care, couldn't think, my every inhibition flapping around me in tatters.

He tore his mouth from mine, panting, his cock jutting into me. "This won't do at all. Can't have ye screaming my name in the woods again, for anyone to hear." He ground his hips into me and I gasped. "Only for me."

The world vanished. He whisked me through the tunnel of clawing darkness, so fast I had no time to process the journey, and out again into the moonlit night. Droplets of cold water sprayed our bodies as I clung to him. The falls rumbled beside us, silencing any question I might've asked, if I'd retained the capacity for speech or rational thought. Gripping my bottom with one hand, he slid the other up my back to secure me to him. In one swift motion, he turned and leaped through the cascade.

We touched down in the cave. Or he did. My feet dangled above the stone floor. He set me down, freeing one hand, but maintained his firm grip on my ass with the other, staking a claim and ensuring I wouldn't forget his intentions. As if I could. The proof of his intentions rubbed against me.

He waved the fingers of one outstretched hand. The doorway to the Unseen realm spiraled open, swelling and roiling. The sight of the oily, writhing blackness, and its iridescent curls of energy, constricted my throat. I'd seen it before, walked through it with him, but the portal still creeped me out.

I jerked out of his grasp. Bad idea. Now I could see every glistening inch of him, as well as the beads of water rolling down his body to drip onto the floor. It took all my willpower to resist the urge to dry him off with my mouth. "Where are you taking me?"

"To my home. Where I can keep you safe."

"You have a home?"

He glanced at me sideways. "Did ye think I lived in the bushes?"

"I never actually thought about it." Too distracted by sensual fantasies, and the occasional threat of imminent death. "Is it like a house or a cave? Maybe an underground lair?"

His full attention snapped to me, my stomach fluttering at the intensity of his stare. He curled his fingers closed. The doorway telescoped shut.

I cleared my throat. "Uh, you know, I don't think this portal thingy likes me, so maybe we should go back to the woods. Or forget the whole thing. Yeah, that's the smartest move, let's shake hands and say good night."

"No." His tone brooked no argument.

But I argued anyway. "We barely know each other, and as you've pointed out so many times, I'm horribly pent up. We should think about this."

"That's the problem. You're thinking too much." He marched to me, grabbed my ass, and hefted me off the ground. "I can remedy that."

A chill washed over me, eradicated in an instant by the fire of his flesh against my bare skin.

My bare skin? What?

I glanced down. "Oh!"

My clothes—every scrap, from the T-shirt to my panties, even my boots and socks—were gone. His loincloth had melted away too. I wobbled in his grasp and locked my arms around his shoulders for support. The friction of his skin on mine unfurled sinuous tendrils of desire in me. I was naked. With him. Against him. On him.

He exerted a light pressure to spread my thighs a few inches. It was enough. His erection slipped between my already damp thighs, torturing the swollen, aching flesh at my core. I gasped, digging my nails into his shoulders. He rocked his hips to torment me more. I tried to open myself to him, but his hands kept me locked in place. His face had turned to a mask of control, his eyes narrowed, the rest of his body as rigid as his shaft.

"Nevan." I whimpered his name.

With a faint groan, he rushed forward until my back slapped against the rock wall. His teeth nipped at the hollow of my throat, tracking down my skin with every little nip, edging nearer to the swell of my breasts. He let go, bent his head, and covered my nipple with his mouth, suckling fiercely, stunning a cry out of me. He nipped me, laved his tongue over me, sucked so hard the pleasure burst through my sex like fireworks inside me. I arched into his touch, expecting—praying—he would drive into me at long last and end my torment.

Instead, he took hold of my left thigh and hitched it over his shoulder, then did the same with the other leg. Perched on him, his face perilously close to my throbbing core, I slapped my hands on the wall, clawing for purchase but finding none. He eased me toward him, his mouth so close to my flesh, excitement intensifying every sensation. What the hell was he doing to me? I tried to squirm out of his grasp, but he held on.

"Nevan?" Fear tightened my voice.

His eyes met mine, burning, swirling, promising everything I'd denied myself—and he uttered two syllables that annihilated my inhibitions. "Trust me."

I stopped squirming. Let my body go limp. And closed my eyes.

He cradled my hips in his hands, tipped me toward him, raked his tongue across my rigid nub. Pleasure broke through me, so hot it almost hurt. His tongue licked and stroked with merciless precision, and his mouth closed over my nub to suckle with ruthless strength. I bucked against him, clutching at him, my hands digging into his hair, his scalp, urging him deeper into me. He worked his way down my cleft, inch by inch, stroke by stroke, traversing the length of me with his lips and tongue. I lost all sense of reality, as my guttural moans and feral cries echoed off the walls. Pressure escalated inside me, squeezing out whimpering pleas. His tongue thrust into me and twirled, propelled me higher, consuming me with one thrust after another, delving deeper and harder as my nails scraped his scalp.

My body convulsed with a thunderous orgasm, wave after wave of earth-shattering ecstasy ripped through me. As the exquisite pleasure settled into a dull ache, I floated away on a cloud of endorphins, higher than the moon. I was dimly aware of Nevan moving, picking me up, carrying me. By the time I drifted back down, we stood before the pulsating doorway, with me cradled in his arms. Still naked.

"Where are my clothes?" I asked absently, not really caring anymore.

"I sent them to my home. But you won't be needing clothes tonight."

My body responded to his promise, but my head battled to sort out what I'd just done. Or rather, what I'd let him do. "That was…I don't know what it was, actually. Unexpected, for sure."

"Lindsey, my love." He kissed the tip of my nose. "That's how you let go."

I grinned. Couldn't help it, though I must've looked like an idiot. I was beyond caring. Nevan had liberated me from a terrible burden, and tonight I soared with a freedom I'd never known before.

The grim concentration on his face told me how much he'd restrained in the last few minutes. I brushed my hand over his cheek. I needed to tell him something before he took me through the veil and I couldn't say it anymore. "This might sound idiotic, but I'm going to say it anyway. Thank you."

He smirked with what I took for masculine satisfaction. "Save the gratitude for after I'm finished with you."

"Finished?" It came out whiny. "Are you…That sounds kind of final."

"Ye must stop thinking the worst. I meant finished for tonight." He adjusted my weight in his arms and his erection grazed my buttocks. "I'll never be completely done with you, not if we both live to eternity."

"Okay." Two distinct syllables, divided by my crumbling will.

"What happened a moment ago, that was for you." His voice had grown raspy, strained. "Now it's my turn."

He strode through the portal.

Chapter Twenty-Two

WHISKED AWAY THE MOMENT WE EXITED THE PORTAL, I SQUEEZED MY eyes shut against the gnawing chill of the tunnel. Nevan's arms bound me to him, cradling me to his body, and I knew without any doubt he would keep his vow and never let me fall.

Light extinguished the darkness as we exited the tunnel, into the Unseen realm. Radiant warmth washed over me.

I cracked my eyes open. We stood inside a windowless room, hewn from solid rock, with smooth walls and an earthen floor. Oil lamps affixed to the walls kindled a golden glow within the space, but shadows lurked beyond the doorway at the far end of the oval-shaped chamber.

Nevan settled me onto a long bed precisely the size of one tall, sexy sylph. My feet hung suspended several inches above the floor. My bottom sank into the bedding, fashioned from something thick and plush, with a fur blanket on top. I combed my fingers through the lush, silky hairs of the blanket, loving the way my skin sensitized at the feel of it. I registered nothing else beyond the bed, thanks to the man poised before me, an arm's length away.

With no conscious intent, I touched my fingertips to my lips. The faint rush of air escaping them tickled my skin. I beheld him with unabashed fascination, taking in the panorama of his stunning, nude body and the luster of water droplets that clung to him. The flames of the oil lamps licked at his skin, exactly the way I wanted to lick him. Everywhere. Over and over. *Right now.*

His rigid shaft rose up at my eye level. Desire shimmered through me, warm and familiar, electric and silken at the same time. God, I wanted him. And after what he'd done to me—for me—behind the falls, I'd shed any guilt or shame about craving this man. This elemental spirit. My Nevan.

Mine.

The thought fired an erotic missile down my body, from my lips into my nipples, and straight down to my sex. No wonder he relished calling me his, if he experienced anything like this when he spoke, or even thought, the word.

He delved a hand into my hair, stroking my scalp. I leaned into his touch, eyes half closed, but the bliss disintegrated with a single memory that slashed through my mind. Skeiron. A sword. Blood.

"You're thinking again, love." Nevan's voice lured my gaze to his with an inexorable pull. "You're thinking of reasons to stop."

His fingers trailed down my neck, across my shoulder. I longed to tilt my head back and offer my throat up for his ministrations, but he was right. The memory of Skeiron's attack had me doubting everything again.

Nevan dragged the backs of his fingers down my arm. "You're not stopping now."

I wanted tonight to stretch on to eternity, with the two of us holed up in his lair, entangled in every way. But could we afford to ignore the threats looming outside this protected haven?

"Skeiron," I said, battling to ignore the storm of sensations triggered by his fingers as they skated down to wrist. "He's out there, hunting for us."

"Not yet." Nevan lowered onto one knee, his face level with mine. He took my hand and feathered kisses across my knuckles one by one. "The king was grievously injured, at the hand of my courageous love, and he will require a good deal of time to recover."

"Tris told me the fae won't help him, because he murdered their witches."

"It is true." Nevan turned my hand over, flittering his lips over my palm, up to my wrist. His tongue teased my tender skin, and all the while, his gaze held mine. "But I would rather discuss what I want to do to you tonight."

"Oh." I couldn't break eye contact, my body overwhelmed with a riot of sensations set off by every word he spoke and every whisper of his skin on mine. "Tell me."

"Perhaps I should show you." His thumb massaged the inside of my wrist, while his other hand coasted up and down my arm. He pressed a damp kiss to the hollow of my shoulder and I sighed with pleasure, helpless against the onslaught of his touch. His lips curved up in a gentle smile. "You, my little kettle, truly could drive a man mad by looking at him the way you're looking at me."

His hand on my wrist moved up to my inner elbow. His thumb manipulated the flesh there as his lips found my throat, lingering on my skin until I let out a long, breathy moan.

"Forget Skeiron," he breathed onto my throat. "Forget everything for this one night. You hunger for me and I hunger for you—your mind, your voice, your lips, every part of your luscious body."

"Me too," I groaned. "Want yours, I mean."

His chuckle liquefied what little remained of my willpower. He ran his tongue up my throat to the spot just under my ear, then took my lobe between his teeth, flicking his tongue across it. I sagged into him, powerless to move or speak or breathe as he breezed his lips down my jaw to my chin. He pulled in a harsh breath, his voice going rough with barely contained passion. "I need to be inside you."

"Oh…" I arched my back as his lips found the corner of my mouth. "Nevan, yes, now."

"On your back, love." He drew his head back to meet my gaze. "Please."

An odd sensation rippled through me, a cross between static electricity and faint needle pricks. I stiffened. "What was that? Did you feel it?"

"Yes." He nuzzled my cheek, my hair, my neck. "Don't worry. I asked permission, which is a kind of debt—a very small one."

"Permission. You mean saying pl—the P-word?"

"Correct."

"Why would you do that?"

I felt him smile against my throat. "You seem to have an obsession with politeness." He swept a hand up my belly, between my breasts, to spread his palm over my heart. "And I need to make certain you feel no compulsion to give yourself to me."

A tendril of ice coiled around my heart. "Magic?"

"No." His hand stayed on my chest, its heat penetrating my skin, but his lips ghosted over mine in brief, light kisses. "As you may have noticed, I can be rather demanding."

"Right." I dared to rest my hands on his back, sliding them over taut muscles. "You are bossy. But since you asked nicely…"

I stretched out on the bed with my arms above my head, exposed more than I'd ever been before, with anyone. "You're the first man who's seen me naked."

His tongue slicked over his bottom lip, his eyes burned a brilliant shade of brandy. "I want to be your first and your last. Your only lover."

I linked my hands over my head, wondering how I could ever be with another man after him. He did things to me, without removing a stitch of clothing, I couldn't have imagined were possible. Not because he was a sylph. Because he was Nevan.

His weight settled onto the bed, eliciting a soft creak, as he straddled my legs. The entirety of his body towered above me, transformed into a golden statue by the sensual lighting and the tension in his muscles. Soon he would touch me, take me, do everything I'd longed for him to do to me.

My mouth went dry. Sex with a supernatural being. Was I ready for this? Was it safe?

Nevan's gentle smile slanted downward. His brow crinkled. "What is it?"

Hugging myself, I averted my gaze to the wall beside us.

Nevan kissed my forehead, the bridge of my nose, the tip of it, the little dent above my mouth. I couldn't stop my eyes from seeking his, but a pang pinched the back of my throat.

"Tell me," he said, without a trace of demand, only a tenderness infused with an unspoken plea.

Hands joined over my belly, I caught my bottom lip between my teeth. If I wanted him to make love to me, if I wanted some kind of relationship with him, I'd have to learn to express my concerns. Not my strong suit. "Well…I was wondering if it's dangerous for a mortal to have sex with an elemental."

Gold and silver flecks glimmered in his irises as he tugged at my lip with his teeth, encouraging me to free it. When I at last loosened my hold on my lip, he drew it into his mouth, swiping his tongue across it, releasing it little by little—so gradually I felt his smooth flesh sliding over mine. "Ah, you do fret about everything. Don't ye, darlin'?"

"And this is news to you?"

"Hardly." He hooked an arm under me and flipped us over. I yelped, suddenly on top of him. The lightning-fast movement ensured I wound up straddling him with his knees bent behind me for support. His rock-hard arousal was trapped underneath me, between my thighs, the ridge of it pressed into my cleft with the head jutting out over his stomach.

He hit me with that devastatingly wicked grin. "You're in control, to do with me as you wish."

My mouth opened, but my voice had abandoned me.

His big hands came up to curl around my hips. "No harm will come to you. Countless elementals have bedded countless mortals. Even gods may engage in relations with humans."

My hands rested on my thighs, though I yearned to explore his body. "You're at my mercy?"

"I am." He rocked my hips forward, pushing my swollen flesh into his shaft. "Do with me as you will."

"That may be the hottest thing anyone's ever said to me." I gazed down upon the raw maleness laid out beneath me and wrung my brain for some sexy thing to do, but I came up empty. *Dammit.*

"You look perplexed, love." He frisked his hands down my thighs to where my hands rested, encircling my wrists, lifting my hands, threading his fingers loosely through mine. "Touch me."

I stared at his chest, longing to do as he suggested but uncertain how to do it. I had no experience with seduction.

He let go of my wrists and curled his hands over my hips again. "You've avoided touching me, for the most part. But when you did, you drove me wild." He rotated his hips, grinding his arousal into me. "Give it a go."

Excitement rushed over my skin, raising the fine hairs, as I splayed my hands over his chest, relishing the feel of his smooth, supple skin contrasted with firm sinews. *Do with me as you will,* he'd said. All right then.

I spread my hands and began painting swirls on his pectoral muscles with my palms and fingertips, exploring the canvas laid out beneath me, a masterpiece of muscle and skin and bone. For the second time tonight, I set my mind loose, shedding all my worry, doubt, and inhibitions. I let my body take over, moving without conscious thought. My hands wandered up his throat to his face, my thumbs glanced over his lips before my fingers covered his mouth, the tips playing with his pliant flesh. His lips were warm and full, sinfully lush. His breaths whispered over my fingers, sneaking out between his slightly parted lips, and when his tongue flicked out to taste my fingertips, I froze for a moment, paralyzed by the sudden rush of liquid fire between my thighs.

He must've felt my wetness on his erection, nestled against my sex, because he groaned softly, his eyes fluttering half closed and his breaths growing heavier.

My body had come alive from head to toe, awakened to every sensation like never before. I plowed my hands into his hair, plying his scalp, delicately at first, but then harder and faster in time with my quickening pulse. I skimmed my fingers down his face and throat, into the uncharted territory of his body. Earlier, I'd fantasized about mapping out his flesh. Now, I charted every inch of his sculpted muscles and soft flesh, kneading and stroking, as stimulated by it as he was—evidenced by his pulsating shaft and shortening breaths. His eyes, though hooded, ignited with fiery shades of scarlet and amber.

I moved to elevate my hips, but his hands bound me to him.

"Not yet," he rasped.

"You're a glutton for punishment?"

He rolled my hips forward, grinding my sex down on his cock, choking back a hoarse groan. "Your naked body on mine is not punishment. It…Ahhh, it is the most exquisite reward."

Another rock of my hips. His fingers sank into my hips, urging me into a rhythm. My slick flesh slid over his shaft, back and forth, inflaming my need and propelling my body toward climax. Panting, gasping, I slapped my hands onto the blanket at either side of his head and dived my head down to his. Our lips collided. We ravished each other's mouths with velvet strokes and desperate moans, starved for the taste of each other, lost to the craving that would not be denied. His hands raked up my back. I crushed my body to his, my taut nipples scraping on his skin as everything inside me clenched, hurtling toward release.

I wrenched my lips from his, breathless, aching and throbbing deep inside for a the release I'd denied us both. "Not like this."

Nevan growled, "Like what?"

I swatted his chest. "Don't get grumpy."

He took a long breath, seeming to collect himself as he exhaled. "What is it?"

"You said—" My panting derailed my words. I took a few precious seconds to catch my breath. "I thought we were going to, you know, have sex."

"That's what we're doing."

"No, I mean…" I leaned back against his raised knees, needing the space between us but hating it at the same time. "I don't want it halfway. All the way or nothing."

"We'll get there." He walked his fingers down my thighs. "We have all night."

"I know you like to play, but I've been waiting a long time for this."

Understanding curved his lips and lit his eyes. "And you want to get right to it. Play later."

"Exactly."

He raised onto his elbows. "I've no objections to taking you right now."

The sheer sensuality of his tone made my sex throb. But I had one more matter to settle first. "I need to ask a very important question."

His groan resonated through his torso, straight into my groin. "If you must."

With a little huff, I shifted my weight to ease the tension building again between my thighs. The movement did not help. "In my world, we have something called safe sex."

"I told ye, my kind and yours enjoy pleasurable relations with no injury—"

"That's not what I meant." I screwed my face up with irritation, which made him grin. "Do elementals have birth control? You know, ways to prevent pregnancy."

"Ah, I see." He boosted his hips up, rubbing his erection into me. "I can't impregnate you without exercising a conscious decision to do so."

"Really?" When he nodded, I couldn't help laughing. "Damn. Wish we had that option over on my side of the falls. For mortals, it's very complicated. I mean, there's pregnancy and then you have STDs—sexually transmitted diseases."

"No wonder your kind are so repressed. It's a wonder you ever loosened up for me."

"Watch it, buddy." I thumped his thigh, but that only made his grin broaden and his eyes twinkle. "So about diseases…"

He pushed up on one arm, half sitting, and captured my wrist with the other hand. Drawing it to his mouth, he tormented the inside of my wrist with his deft tongue. "I'm immortal, love, which means I suffer from no natural diseases or illnesses of any kind."

"Oh. Good." I felt my lips pucker. "But you're not invincible. You could catch a magical disease."

He slapped a palm on his forehead. "Thunder and hail. Do ye ever quit the worrying?"

"Not really."

"Hmm." Both hands on my back, he hauled me down to his chest and murmured seductively in my ear. "In that case, you know what I have to do."

With dizzying swiftness, he flipped us over and took my mouth in a sweet, sensual kiss that went on and on. When he pulled away, he lowered his body over me, bracing himself with both hands at either side of my shoulders, his neck inches from my face. The heat and scent of him radiated across the gap between us and I couldn't breathe, overwhelmed by the knowledge of what was to come. I knew, but lord, I didn't know. How he would take me. How he would stoke me. How his shaft would fill me to bursting. How I would fling my self-control out the window and cling to him with all my strength, riding out the storm.

These were fantasies, nothing more. Any second, I would experience the reality.

When he nuzzled my ear, I sucked in a lungful of blessed oxygen, arching into him as his hair tickled my skin. He moved lower, peppering feathery kisses across vulnerable flesh, eliciting sighs from me that ruffled his hair. He raised his head to gaze at me with a tenderness that floored me. Not just sex. Not for either of us.

He kissed the corner of my mouth. "Everything with you is a revelation. *You* are a revelation."

"What does that mean?"

"It means shut up, Lindsey." He uttered the decree without a hint of sarcasm or annoyance, but with a gravelly tone that testified to the passion flaming in his eyes, darkening his expression, tensing his body.

I shut up.

He levered himself up on one arm, his erection skimming my belly, and settled a hand on my throat, the fingers loose and relaxed. I must've flinched a bit at the position of his hand, because he murmured wordless encouragements. My muscles slackened of their own volition, my body answering his every call without hesitation. He covered my body with his, easing my thighs apart with his knees. His head was above mine, his cheek against the crown of my head, so that my hair muffled his voice. "Are you ready?"

Helpless to speak, I answered by throwing my arms around him, my hands on his back fisting and loosening, fisting and loosening, my mind senseless from the feel of his muscles undulating beneath my palms. I buried my face in his neck, nibbled his shoulder, crooked my fingers until my nails dug into his skin.

"Take that as a yes," he said, his cracking from the sheer power of his need.

"Nevan." His name tumbled from my lips, chased by breathless little noises. "Yes."

Poised above me, propped on his straight arms, he admired me with rapt wonder, as if my body offered the solution to a great cosmic mystery. I started to ask a question, but he stunned me into silence with a punishing kiss, ravaging my mouth with his tongue and his lips, at once enticing and demanding. Without a word, he pulled away and lifted my hips off the bed. Exhaled a raspy breath. Rolled his hips back. And finally, plunged into me.

He moved inside me, delicate and slow, rocking in and out in with a purpose and strength that stripped away every vestige of my inhibitions. The velvet softness of the bedding electrified my bare skin with each movement. He bent to suckle my earlobe, his breaths soft groans against my flesh. I clenched his hair in my fist, arched my neck to inhale the earthy scent of him. The silky texture of his hair sparked through my nerves, spurring me to unleash a string of mindless noises. He showered kisses down my neck, across my throat, up the opposite side to nip at my jaw, and all the while he thrust in and out, each stroke forceful and controlled.

"Lindsey, my love..."

A strange pain gripped my heart. He was mine and I was his. All the pain of past betrayals fled the instant he'd spoken those two beautiful words. *My love.* I'd barely noticed the first time he spoke the phrase back in the cave, but in this moment the lilting declaration struck me full force. My hands fell to his shoulders, squeezing and releasing in a fierce rhythm, in time with his thrusts.

"Nevan." His name was a plea and a demand, punctuated by my teeth rasping across his shoulder. "Don't hold back. I let go for you, and oh God, I need you to let go for me."

A guttural, almost feral sound rumbled in his chest. I crushed my open mouth to his throat, to take in the vibrations of his vocal chords, seized by an insatiable need to merge with him in every way imaginable.

Nevan rose into a crouch, pulling out of me, running his hands down the insides of my thighs to my knees. "I cannot deny you anything."

He braced his hands at either side of my shoulders and drove into me, filling me with exquisite pressure, diving deep with one breathtaking thrust. I trussed my legs around him, secured by my locked ankles, and held on for the ride. His length consumed me as he pounded into my flesh again and again, sweat beading on his forehead. I nearly shattered into a million shards, writhing against him like a wild thing, heedless of the senseless pleas bubbling out of me, the speed and desperation of my cries quickening along with his movements until the bed thumped against the floor, counting out the frantic pace of our love-making.

Dropping onto his elbows, his mouth against my ear, he whispered exotic words I couldn't decipher. The beautiful phrases flowed into me like warm liquid, softening my need just enough to keep me teetering on the edge.

My gaze was riveted to him, my mind exclusively focused on the experience of his body—hips pumping, muscles straining, burnished skin glistening—as he tortured me with an ecstasy beyond comprehension. I bucked my hips to force him deeper, lost in the fervor he conjured within me, clawing at his back to pull him closer.

My release racked my entire body. I screamed, heart thrashing in my chest as he shouted with his own climax, plunging into me once, twice, three times before collapsing on top of me, startling a strangled cry from me. He rolled onto his side next to me, balanced near the bed's edge.

Robbed of breath, I struggled to compose myself, to no avail. This man had wrecked me. My self-control, gone. My inhibitions, gone. My fear and shame, gone.

My heart…gone. I'd handed it over to him, without even realizing it, the second I granted him permission to ravish me. And oh boy, had he ravished me thoroughly.

His arm around my waist, Nevan pressed his lips to my forehead. "You are indeed a revelation, my sweet mortal angel."

I felt a smile stretch my lips and dimple my cheeks. "No one's ever called me an angel before. I like it." I roved my hand over his muscular arm. "But I'd really like to know what you mean when you say I'm a revelation."

"You've performed a miracle. You resurrected my heart."

My pulse stuttered. For several seconds, I stared at him. My face probably resembled a cartoon character's version of shock, though his expression revealed no disgust or amusement, only adoration.

He guided my hand to the scar on his chest, my fingers over the mark. "I thought Skeiron destroyed my heart forever. For a century, I felt nothing more than surface emotions. No passion, no fire, only an emptiness that made me ache for what I knew could never be." He brought my hand to his lips, kissing my palm. "You proved me wrong. You awakened my heart and showed me how to care for another above myself. And you introduced me to true passion, like none I've experienced in my entire existence. That is why you are a revelation."

Speechless, I could do no more than gape at him.

"No need to speak." He held my palm to his cheek. "I wanted to tell you, that's all, to help you understand why I'm here with you."

My brain sputtered to life at last, spitting out a jumble of thoughts. "Is this the thing you wouldn't tell me until I was receptive to the answer?"

He shook his head once.

I turned onto my side, facing him, and looped my arm around his back to pull him close. He obliged, molding his body to mine. I snuggled my face into his neck. "Mmm…Tell me the other thing. I'm feeling very receptive at the moment."

"Later. Sleep, love. You're exhausted." He pinched my bottom. "Partly my fault."

"Don't think I can sleep."

"Try."

His hands caressed my back in slow circles, light and calming. I relaxed into him, into the fur beneath us, and—despite myself, despite the horrors lying in wait outside this little sanctuary—I slept.

CHAPTER TWENTY-THREE

I WOKE ALONE IN THE NEVAN-SIZE BED, THE FUR BLANKET ENSHROUDING me. Yawning, I sat up and stretched. The blanket slipped off to gather around my waist. I flipped it away, to the foot of the bed, and swung my feet over the side. Despite my nudity, I felt no chill. The air inside this underground bubble stayed skin temperature, apparently. My skin temperature. Nevan must've adjusted his…thermostat, for lack of a better term, to suit my body. His flesh ran considerably hotter than mine.

Hot skin. On me. His body pinning me into the bed. His hips undulating, driving him deep inside me. My body sizzled from the memory, a damp ache burgeoning between my thighs.

Last night, when he lay on top of me with our bodies in full contact, he'd shown me astounding passion and a tenderness that stirred a silly, girlie part of me to wish for things I couldn't have. He was a super-powerful sylph from a world of magic, I was an underemployed ex-paralegal from plain old Earth. Where could this go? Nowhere.

I rubbed my arms, but the chill frosting through me originated within, not without. Skeiron was still out there. If we survived his wrath…

We still came from different worlds, literally.

I glanced around the softly lit room, wondering where the source of the light was, unable to trace the diffuse glow to any particular spot. But I wondered about something else with more urgency. Where the hell was Nevan?

What if Skeiron exerted his magical influence to drag Nevan away from me? Or what if Nevan went willingly, to conspire with his king? No, I refused to believe that. Yet his bargain with Skeiron bound him to do his king's bidding, and really, I knew so little about the immortal warrior who'd become my lover. I couldn't compete with supernaturally enforced fealty. I needed to know either way.

I took a big breath and shouted with all my lung power. "Nevan!"

Silence, broken only by the thumping of my heartbeat.

If Skeiron had lured Nevan out into the open…Last time they'd fought, Nevan got skewered and I almost died saving him. Skeiron might kill him this time, for good, with me locked up in this underground hole and helpless to stop it. *Not again, please, not again.*

"Nevan!" I shouted.

This screaming-for-my-man stuff was absolutely not me, yet I'd resorted to it more than once in the past few days. Maybe I didn't know myself as well as I thought. Then again, it was the only method at my disposal for contacting Nevan.

I hollered his name once more, empowering the cry with all my frustrations.

Nevan winked into view right in front of me, his loincloth-clad groin smack in front of my face. He crouched down, his hands coming to rest on my thighs. "What is it?"

"Are you serious? Asking what's wrong?" I kneed his chest, but he didn't react. "I was afraid Skeiron tricked you into meeting him and he—You weren't here and I didn't know what to think."

His left hand lingered on my thigh as the right one cradled my cheek. "You worry far too much."

"Yeah, we've had this conversation before." I shut my eyes, leaning my face into his touch. "I can't stop worrying until we've dealt with Skeiron and all this Janusite crap."

"I know." His thumb traced the seam of my lips. "I hate to see you tying yourself up in knots again, after I worked so diligently to unravel them."

The sincerity in his tone, and the sensual promise implied by them, unraveled me all over again. Enveloped in his presence, I reveled in the sense of safety he'd imbued into me last night, with his body and his words. One thing I knew for certain. This man could never turn on me, not willingly, and even under duress he'd fight it to his last breath.

"Did you believe I'd abandoned you?" he asked, without inflection, his face unreadable.

"Of course not. I don't want to have to save you again is all." My teasing tone must've bypassed him, because his expression fell into resignation and his head drooped, leaving me to gaze at his hair. "That was a stupid joke, my backwards way of saying I was worried about you. I know you wouldn't abandon me. I trust you."

His head sprang up, making my hand slip down to his cheek. "You must never trust me."

I went cold inside at the finality of his tone. "Last night, you asked me to trust you. This morning, you tell me not to. What gives?"

"Then, we were in your world. Now, we are in mine." He fastened his hands around my waist and brought us both to our feet, keeping me close. "Vow you will never trust me on this side of the falls."

"I won't say it. I can't."

"Lindsey."

"Don't *Lindsey* me." I shook off his hands. "It would be a lie. I will trust you, no matter what."

"Then you will die."

"Stop being so melodramatic." I squared my shoulders and lifted my chin, which probably didn't look as resolute when I was naked. "The subject is closed."

He blew out three short, erratic breaths, his gaze bouncing around the room as if he couldn't quite focus on any one thing—until he aimed his eyes, now flat and dull brown, at me. "Fine. We must talk about our other problems."

At the moment, he seemed anxious and irritated with me over my refusal to un-trust him. Yesterday, he'd told my brother he was immensely fond of me. Last night, he claimed I'd resurrected his heart, though I'd seen zero evidence his emotions had ever shriveled up, mummified by the so-called curse. Skeiron might've lied about imprecating Nevan's heart. Since Nevan disliked talking about it, I was left to draw my own conclusions.

Skeiron was a mass murderer. I could totally believe he'd lie about cursing someone.

The truth might lie in whatever it was he'd refused to tell me last night.

I crooked my fingers around the bed's edge, one finger tapping. "Are you sure Skeiron cursed you? I mean, what proof did he have?"

"It was magic, love. There's no concrete evidence. The proof was in my inability to feel for a century." He caught my hands, gently prying them from the bed's frame to surround them with his hands. "Until you, that is."

"Oh please." I tried to lean away from him, but his hold on my hands inhibited movement. "I'm not convinced you ever were cursed. I think Skeiron played on your guilt about his daughter and used the power of suggestion to make you believe he'd stripped you of your emotions."

He scrutinized my fingers, brushing his thumbs over my knuckles. "Perhaps."

"What does it take to imprecate a heart, anyway?"

"I'm not certain." He pursed his lips as if deep in thought, silent for a moment. "Fae magic, I presume. A great deal of it."

"Ah-ha." At his dubious look, I straightened and lifted my chin. "Tris told me Skeiron massacred the fae witches and no fae is allowed to help him. You confirmed that. So how could he get his hands on a fae curse?"

Nevan's face blanked and his hands fell away from mine, and for several seconds I thought he wouldn't answer. At last, he leveled his shocked gaze at me and spoke. "He couldn't."

"See." I sat back, arms folded over my breasts. "I was right."

His smile was shaky, as if he couldn't quite believe I'd been correct on this. Or maybe he couldn't quite believe for a century he'd languished in the self-delusion, instigated by Skeiron, that he'd been cursed.

"By the stars," he said in a hushed voice, gaining strength with each word. "I've been such a bloody fool, all these years."

"Hey, don't beat yourself up about it. Skeiron is one wickedly scary son of a bitch." I laid a hand over my heart. "If he told me he'd cursed my heart, I'd probably buy into it."

"Still, I might never have realized the truth without you."

"I don't know about that. Some other chickie would've come along eventually and—"

"No." The force of his declaration resonated within the room.

"Take it easy." I lowered my hands to my bare thighs. "It doesn't matter either way. You were never cursed."

"It does matter." In one stride, he bridged the gap between us and dropped to his knees before me, settling his hands over mine. "You matter."

I squirmed, searching for the courage to ask the question that plagued me. "Will you tell me the thing you wouldn't say last night?"

"Perhaps you are receptive."

"Let me decide that." I slanted toward him, my breasts waving above his face. "I'm receptive."

He stared at my breasts, the tip of his tongue slipping out between his lips. My nipples went taut under his intent gaze and he swallowed visibly. I leaned back, which seemed to break the spell.

Nevan clasped my hands to his heart, right over his scar. "You saved my heart and my life. I would've died, but you risked your safety to restore me."

His voice had gone husky—this time, with deep emotion rather than lust.

I couldn't speak or tear my gaze away from his.

"My heart may not have been cursed, but I'd been unable to care for anything or anyone, trapped in a hell of my own making." He let his head fall forward onto my lap. But then an uncertain laugh rumbled out of him and he tilted his head to gaze up at me. "You saved my soul, Lindsey. I owe you a debt I can never repay, though I'll spend the rest of my existence trying to."

A tether snapped taut between us, pulsing with fervent energy. I'd felt a similar, but far less intense, binding when I promised Tris anything if he'd save Nevan. This time, the energy burned with more than the power of a debt. It shimmered with the unquenchable fire of passion and devotion.

Nevan mashed my hands into his flesh. "Thank you."

The tether pulsated, hot and hard, driving his commitment into me with such force I lost my breath. No, my debt to Tris couldn't compare with this. Nevan owed me his heart, his life…his soul.

A one-sided commitment meant nothing. I owed him everything. "You've saved me too, Nevan. I owe—"

He silenced me with two fingers on my lips. "Don't. Let the debt stand, love, please. You may need it."

"I don't understand. Why can't I express you-know-what like you did?"

"Because when two parties each owe the other in equal proportion, it cancels out both debts. I do not believe your gratitude to me is equal to mine, but I won't risk it. You may soon have need of the bond."

"You've said that twice. Why would I need you to owe me?"

"It's a life debt. The most potent sort." He rose and took a step backward. "A life debt supersedes all other obligations and bargains. In fact, there is little else capable of overriding the debt levied by saving a life—except accomplishing the same feat in return."

"You would have to save my life the way I saved yours."

"Precisely. A life for a life."

"And you're sure," I said, "nothing else can override it."

His forehead crimped into deeply etched lines. "Once, I would have said no without hesitation. But I'm beginning to wonder if there is another force more powerful than any debt."

"Like what?"

He gazed at me with what I could only describe as longing. "I'll let you know when I figure that out."

Realizing he would say no more, I heaved my body off the bed and rubbed my temples. My brain was starting to hurt. "What kind of influence does the person holding the debt have over the person who owes them?"

"You will have nearly unlimited sway over me." He moved closer, his hands coming up to grasp my hips. "I am at your command, a virtual slave to your desires."

A languid, molten heat unfurled through my body, pooling low in my belly. Oh God, how did he infuse every syllable of that statement with simmering sensuality?

Because he was Nevan, that's how. And I loved everything he did to me. No more denials.

I wound my arms around his waist, my body flush against his. "My slave, huh? Think I'm going to like this life debt stuff."

"A debt has never been so pleasurable." He rubbed his hands up my back and down again to the upper curve of my buttocks. "But beware. Even if another saves your life, you must never admit to the obligation or you will be at the whim of the debt-holder forever, unless they incur an equal debt to you."

"Yes, sir. Any other orders?"

"Several come to mind, but we haven't the time. "

Memories of last night—of our bodies entwined, of the rapture he'd given me—replayed in my mind, too vivid to allow coherent thought. With a great feat of willpower, I ignored the fresh desire smoldering within me. "How does it work? This debt thing, I mean. If you're a slave to my whims, do I just holler your name and, whoosh, you appear to do my bidding?"

"Whoosh?" The laughter in his voice matched the affectionate amusement on his face.

"Yeah. Whoosh." I rolled my hips into him and he winced, though I recognized it had nothing to do with pain and everything to do with his swelling erection. "Is that how it works?"

"Essentially, your colorful description is accurate." He palmed both my buttocks, kneading my flesh. "The owed party must consciously invoke the debt and speak the words in the form of a command. Then and only then will the full magical power of the debt be invoked."

"Hmm. These magical rules are damn confusing." I freed one arm, reaching up to comb my hand through his hair. "If I can't use the G word or the T phrase, then I'll have to be more creative. I was a terrified, pent-up mess. You should've walked away, but you didn't. You freed me from a burden I've carried for way too long, and oh yeah, you rescued me—repeatedly. You're my hero."

He groaned, scrunching up his face.

I tickled his scalp.

His lips ticked up at the corners, but he pulled away, turning his back to me. "We should be talking about your future."

"What about it?"

"Your future is uncertain as long as you stay in my world, or within the portal boundaries in your world."

"Why bring me here if it's so dangerous?"

I couldn't see his face anymore—confronted with his uninformative, though mouth-watering, backside—but I spotted the slight hunching of his shoulders and the way his head lowered a smidgen. He spoke in a quiet voice I had to strain to hear. "I tried to let you go, Lindsey, but I cannot do it. Skeiron has attempted to kill you twice and yet I cannot push you away. My sanity has left me, but I don't care, so long as I have you."

I padded up behind him to drape my arms around his waist, my cheek on the rippling muscles of his upper back. His chest inflated on a deep breath, then deflated as the air hissed out of him.

Rubbing my cheek on his skin, I said, "Can't let you go either. When you were dying, I wanted to die too. I did some stupid things, I almost killed us both by losing control of the car, but I had to make it to another waterfall. It was the only chance." I hugged him tighter, needing the intimacy more than ever. "So you see, we're both a little crazy."

He spun around, grasping my shoulders. His eyes darted back and forth, hunting for something in my expression or my eyes. His mouth had set in a stern line.

I tried to smooth away the lines on his forehead, but they were too entrenched.

"Tell me," he said, "exactly what happened after Skeiron defeated me."

A storm cloud had invaded his eyes. They darkened, the colors washed out by a cold, gray fear. He squeezed me until I flinched, then loosened his grip just enough to let me breathe again.

I touched his cheek. "What's wrong?"

"You mentioned another waterfall. When I woke, I assumed we were in the same woods as before."

I thought back to last night, after Tris left us. Nevan and I had been in the throes of passion, clamoring to get inside each other, and he had whisked me away to the waterfall. Our waterfall. Not the one I'd penetrated to get to the Unseen realm and beg Tris for help. Nevan took me to the falls behind the rock shop, because he hadn't realized we were in a different place.

Guess sylphs didn't have GPS.

Nevan pulled me close, his gaze boring into me. "There is no other waterfall within one mile of the falls I guard."

"Duh. You whisked us to my car and we got you inside, remember? You passed out, I think. I improvised."

"Crossing the boundary should've destroyed me."

"It didn't and I had no choice, what with Brennus on our tails. You were bleeding to death and I drove super-fast. Maybe we outran the boundary thingy." Idiotic, but all I could think of to explain it. Except for the option I still could not accept.

Nevan had the grace to ignore the obvious conclusion, for the moment.

His eyes narrowed. "What else did you do to save me?"

Uh-oh. "What do you mean?"

"You mentioned doing stupid things, plural." He angled his head until our lips grazed each other. "What else did you do?"

His proximity overpowered my brain, my body, everything. He knew the effect he had on me and exploited it to his advantage whenever necessary. I had to admire his tenacity, but in this moment I could've slugged him for it. If I'd retained control of my limbs. Which I hadn't.

Without meaning to, I melted against him, my chin braced on his chest, slanting my face up to bring our mouths into full contact.

He rasped his tongue across the seam of my lips. "Tell me."

"I…made a deal with Tris."

His head jerked up, eyes flaming. "You what?"

I studied the scar on his chest and nibbled my lip. "You were dying. I couldn't stand by and let that happen. I couldn't lose you. But the only way I knew to save you was a healing vortex and I couldn't go back to the one by the shop because Skeiron might've been there, or Brennus, so I took you to another waterfall in hopes it also had a vortex and a doorway." I inhaled, breathless from my long-winded explanation. "Somehow, the portal opened for me, even without you there to do it, and I went through."

No need to mention the almost-drowning portion of my evening, I decided.

Frowning, Nevan held perfectly still.

"And then I found Tris," I said. *Screamed his name until the blasted leprechaun paid attention.* "I begged him to heal you. I said I'd be, um, grateful."

Nevan shut his eyes, his mouth twisting into a grimace. "How grateful?"

"I may have promised him anything if he healed you."

"Anything?" He gaped at me as if I'd vowed to have kinky sex with the leprechaun and bear his arrogant little spawn. "Were those your literal words? You would give him *anything*?"

"I said, and I quote, if you heal him I will give you anything you want."

I watched Nevan's jaw grind. His nostrils flared.

"You have no right to be mad," I said. "You'd be dead if I hadn't bargained with Tris."

His shoulders flagged, a breath rushing out of him, and he let his head fall onto my shoulder. "I am not mad. I'm afraid for you."

"I won't apologize. Given the same choice, I'd do it all again."

"You've indebted yourself to a powerful elemental. Tris may call in the debt anytime he likes, in whatever manner he likes."

"I really don't think he'll do anything bad."

"You've known him for less time than you've known me. How can you be certain?"

"Intuition." And yeah, I believed in that crap now. "I was right to trust you, and I'm right about Tris. He's not as bad as he wants everyone to think. In fact, he seemed genuinely upset at the idea of you dying."

Nevan barked a derisive laugh.

"You used to be friends," I said. "Why is it so hard to believe he still cares if you live or die?"

"Perhaps he does. Satisfied?"

"Yes."

Nevan stared past my head, his gaze distant. "Did you say the portal opened for you?"

"Yep."

"Are you certain Tris didn't open it? I imagine you were screaming *his* name this time."

"Jealous?" I teased. "But no, I didn't yell for him until after I went through."

His gaze swiveled back to me and he pushed me away, only a matter of inches, but enough to get my attention. He kept his hands on my upper arms. "Are you certain? The portal admitted you without any magical being to assist you?"

I flung my arms out, forcing his hands away. "Yes, dammit, I'm certain. What's wrong with you?"

He opened and closed his mouth several times before finally speaking. "I know of but one way it could be possible. Even mortals with a touch of the Unseen in them can't command a portal to open."

"Okay. How'd I do it?"

"Lindsey…you are the Janusite."

Chapter Twenty-Four

Nevan insisted we eat before discussing his outrageous claim any further and my stomach had chosen that moment to growl, so I deferred to him this once. He took me into his kitchen, where I observed from atop a high stool while he moved this way and that, preparing a meal even more enticing than the one he'd brought me that first night.

I couldn't remember the last time I'd eaten, or what I'd eaten. The meal he whipped up for me this morning roused my taste buds with decadent flavors and sumptuous textures, laced with hints of the exotic, every bite of it designed to make me moan with pleasure. Lord, the man could cook.

Throughout the meal, he picked at his food, pretending to partake—for my benefit, no doubt. He kept frowning, only for a second each time, and rubbing the back of his neck. The tension mounting in him was subtle yet definite, but I was too starved to pause for an interrogation. Once I'd wolfed down the last of my meal, I wiped my mouth with the silky napkin he'd provided, realigning my butt on the stool to face him.

"Something's bothering you," I said, setting the napkin on the counter. Yeah, I was avoiding the Janusite discussion, but for a good reason. "What happened while you were gone earlier? Where did you go?"

He turned away, leaned against the counter behind him, and clamped his fingers over its edge.

I watched him stand there like a statue for several minutes, his profile offering no clues to his agitation, until I could take the silence no longer. "You need to practice your sharing skills."

He grunted.

Jumping off the stool, I marched in front of him. "Explain."

I phrased it as a command rather than a request, to sidestep the danger of saying please and all that craziness. Besides, I was getting damn tired of begging him to be honest with me.

Nevan let his head fall back, his eyes directed at the ceiling but his gaze retreating somewhere much further away.

I roped my arms around his neck, my hands at his nape, and pressed my entire body to his. God, the feel of his skin on mine never failed to crackle desire through me.

His breath hitched.

I lavished an open-mouth kiss on his throat, determined to lure him back from his thoughts, rewarded by his eyes homing in on mine. "Come on, you know I won't back down until you tell me."

After a pause, he said, "I went out to assess the danger, to determine if Skeiron has healed yet. I came upon a battalion of his soldiers."

When he fell silent again, I prodded, "And?"

"I overheard them discussing the king's swift recovery and their orders to hunt down both of us. I was about to leave when—" He squeezed his eyes shut, grimacing. "One of them spotted me. I'd cloaked myself, becoming invisible, but the glamour must've slipped. Or I slipped." He opened his eyes and shook his head. "I failed you yet again."

"You have never failed me."

His hands fell to his sides, his entire body slumped. "They nearly caught me. I escaped, as your kind would say, by the skin of my teeth."

"But you did escape. That's the important thing."

Though he nodded, my gut told me he didn't truly believe it.

He stomped out of the kitchen.

Totally confused, I stared after him for a moment before I took off at a trot to catch up. He'd gone into the living area, halting at its center. My gaze wandered to the bed, rumpled from our passion the previous night.

Nevan stood tall and stiff, hands fisted at his sides, his jaw tight enough to grind diamonds to powder. "Skeiron is hunting for us as we speak."

I approached him from the side, reaching out a tentative hand to touch his arm. "We'll face him together."

"You will stay here." He rolled his shoulders back, lifting his chin to stared down at me. "I will destroy him. Alone."

"You tried that already. He came way too close to killing you." Realization raised all the hairs on my arms. "Quit trying to get rid of me. I won't hide. And you can't seriously expect me to stay here, in this underground lair, while you go fight the bad guys."

"I do. And you will."

"Like hell I will." I tipped my own chin up. "I am going with you."

"No. I will not permit it."

I drew back, feeling as if he'd struck me. "You will not permit it? I'm not your sex slave, who you can lock up in this dungeon until the next time you get horny."

"Lindsey—"

"Quit saying my name like that." I jabbed a finger in the air near his chest. A different kind of fire raged inside me, one borne of fury. "I'm not a child. And I make up my own mind about what risks to take."

"You are only safe as long as you remain within the wards. They are magical spells that prevent anyone else from entering my home." He threw his hands up, eyes going wild and sparking with electric blue and searing white. The colors of fear. He shook his head and his dark hair quivered around his face. "I cannot protect you out there."

"You said you'd never abandon me."

He jerked his head up, eyes intent on me. "I will return for you."

I moved closer but did not touch him. His fear unnerved me, and a compelling urge to soothe him flowed through me, softening my voice. "Nevan, think about it. What happens if Skeiron kills you this time? I'll be stuck here with no way out."

Though he didn't react, I glimpsed something indefinable in his eyes that told me he'd recognized the truth of our situation and knew I was right.

I reached for him, but he spun away from me, clutching his head in his hands as he stalked back and forth across the room, his pace increasing with each circuit. He thrashed his head, muttering things I couldn't make out. He might've been speaking another language, or just mumbling nonsense. When his pace turned frenetic, I thrust out a hand to halt him.

My fingers curled around his bicep, I stroked my thumb over his skin. "There's a risk either way. If I go with you, at least I'll know what happens to you—and vice versa."

He turned his face up to me, the anguish there tearing at my heart.

I threaded my fingers between his. "I want to be with you, whatever happens."

A moment—maybe two or three or ten—in which neither of us spoke or moved. We regarded each other, fingers and gazes entwined, unwilling to sever the connection yet unable to bridge the gap between us. Just when I feared he'd zip away, leaving me here alone, he folded me into his arms and said, "I wish to be with you as well. Whatever comes."

"Good. Because I'm way too stubborn to let you have your way."

"I suppose I must accept that." He swaddled me tighter in his arms. "You cannot ignore the truth any longer. You are the Janusite."

"That's ridiculous." Plastered to him, I suddenly became aware of our nudity. Of my nudity. I scrambled out of his embrace and said, "I can't fight Skeiron in the buff. Where are my clothes?"

He waved toward a cushy chair. My clothes were stacked on the seat, neat and clean.

As I hurried toward my clothing, Nevan remained glued in place. I yanked my clothes on with violent movements, my hands shaking faintly—whether from fear of the battle to come or fear of considering the possibility I was the Janusite, I couldn't say. By the time I had my boots laced, I remembered my derringer and began frantically combing the room for it, going to so far as to drop to my knees and peer under the bed. When I came up empty, I clambered to my feet and muttered. "Shit."

Nevan flew to me—whoosh, he was there. "What is it?"

"I lost my gun."

He held out one hand and my gun poofed into his palm, tucked inside its holster.

I plucked the holster from his hand, slipping it inside my waist band and clipping it onto my jeans.

"You feel safer with it," he said.

"Sure. I like my gun." I rose onto tiptoes to peck his cheek. "But I don't really feel safe unless I'm with you."

He studied me as if I'd babbled in gibberish.

I smoothed my shirt, but the outline of my holster still showed. "Time to fight Skeiron, eh? Guess we better get moving. Don't suppose you have a plan this time."

"In a manner of speaking." He cranked one corner of his mouth into an expression of dismay. "I rid the world of Skeiron whatever the cost, and if necessary, I will bargain with him to save you."

"Bargain? No. I forbid you to do it."

"Alas, I don't always do as I'm told." He ran a finger down my jawline, to tap my chin. "I will give up my freedom, my life, my soul, for one reason alone. For you."

"I don't want you to. You're already enslaved, who knows what Skeiron would demand for this. And if I'm the Janusite, he won't bargain at all."

"Perhaps. But I will try—for you." He edged closer, until I had to bend my head back to meet his gaze, and said, "Not for the Janusite. For you. Lindsey Astrid Porter."

I screwed up my mouth. "How do you know my middle name?"

"Your mother told me."

"Never say it again. It's goofy."

"But it's charming. Do you know its meaning?" When I shrugged, he told me, "It means beloved goddess."

"If you say so."

"You are a goddess," he said, "in every way. And you are beloved, by your family and friends."

His eyes grew…misty? Dear lord.

"And by me as well," he added.

Nevan's confession set my stomach to fluttering, hardly a useful state to be in considering the upcoming battle. "Getting back to Skeiron, we need some kind of plan."

Nevan let out a frustrated grumble. "What would you have me do? I have no chance of acquiring an endued weapon before we encounter Skeiron."

"I'm not exactly unarmed." I patted the holster inside my jeans. "I know you'd rather I hide under the bed, but I was helpful last time you went to war with Skeiron."

"Helpful? You came close to dying and indebted yourself to a leprechaun."

"Well," I said, "have you got a better idea?"

"I have no ideas."

He sounded so desolate, I longed to pull him into my arms and kiss away his anguish. "How about if I give you permission to whisk me away anytime you deem it necessary, provided I'm in serious danger?"

"That would be acceptable, though not preferable."

"In that case, you have my permission—exactly as I outlined it." I considered my options for a moment, then said, "I've got an idea."

One of his brows arched. "I imagine I won't approve."

"Probably not." I slanted toward him, angling my head back to meet his gaze. "But look at it his way. You've got no other options, so you might as well try my crazy idea."

"Which is?"

"Gather *my* allies."

His lip curled as his head popped backward. "Mortals? Against the king of the sylphs?"

"Hey!" I nudged his shin with my boot. "This mortal saved your ass. Don't get snooty about it."

"Snooty?"

"Yeah, it means uppity." I lifted my shirt hem to reveal my holstered derringer. "I have a gun and my parents are well armed. The sheriff owes me a big one. Hell, we might even get some heavy artillery, if I play the guilt card heavy enough."

"Four mortals will not be enough—"

"And there's Tris." At Nevan's disbelieving look, I explained, "I'm positive he will help. The kid's not all that bad."

Nevan sniffed, with a haughty bob of his head. "I stand corrected. Four mortals, an irritating fae, and me. Salvation, at last."

"Better odds than last time, at least."

He scratched his head. His face twisted into a mixture of agony and severe annoyance. Finally, he threw his head back and groaned. "All right. We try your plan."

"Good." I extended my hand to him. "Let's go."

"One moment."

I started to balk, but his look of intense concentration stopped me. He stared into nothing, eyes distant, body taut and erect.

Metal plates materialized around his limbs.

I choked on a gasp. He'd conjured a freaking suit of armor.

The metal shone bright silver, with feathery veins of bronze and gold shot through it. A matching helmet appeared on his head, with the face plate flipped up, and leather boots affixed with plates forged from the same metal encased his feet and ankles. His sword, the one I'd used on Skeiron, took shape in his hand.

I slid my tongue over my lower lips as I scanned him from head to toe. "If you want to have sex again before we go, I'm game."

His smile was sensual and very, very intimate. "Later."

When he held his hand out to me, I took it. He zipped us out of his home.

My feet touched down on solid earth, in the woods, at the base of a low hill. "Barely even felt it this time."

"Perhaps you are adjusting."

I squinted into the darkness. "Where are we?"

"Outside my home." He hugged me tight. His armor fit so well it was like a much harder version of his skin. "We should have appeared at the portal."

His confused tone rippled dread through me.

"Why didn't we?" I asked.

"I've no idea." He canted his head, as if listening. "I felt energy fire through me. Only once before have I experienced anything like…"

"What is it?" I whispered, though I wasn't sure why.

"We must go."

He vanished.

I staggered a step, off balance from the loss of his support. Even more than his body, though, the loss of him echoed through a hollow space in my soul. He'd abandoned me.

No. He would not desert me.

I felt energy fire through me, he'd said.

A surge of air blasted over me, setting off an electric thrill of anticipation. "Nevan!"

I whirled around—and came face to face with Skeiron.

The king of the sylphs regarded me with a warped smile and eyes bright with cold blues and greens. "I'm afraid Nevan cannot return to you. Unless I command it."

I spun away.

He catapulted his body toward me. His arms cinched tight around my torso, strapping my arms to my sides. "Nevan, come here."

Nevan materialized in front of us, his armor gone.

Posture stiff, face blank, eyes dull and still as a stagnant pond, he directed his gaze at his king.

Awaiting orders. Bound to heed his master's whims.

I struggled in Skeiron's grasp, but he only tightened his arms around me.

"You see," he said, "Nevan belongs to me. He serves my will, not yours—and not his own."

Skeiron shoved me toward Nevan. "Hold her."

Nevan shackled me in his brawny arms, and for the first time, being pinioned to his body shot an arctic chill through me.

The sylph king waved a hand. "Strangle her."

Nevan clamped a single hand around my throat and squeezed until I sputtered, choking on every attempt to inhale. Stars burst in my vision, but blackness swept in from the edges to consume my vision bit by bit. I clawed at Nevan's hand, kicked at his shins. He lifted me off the ground, cranking his hand tighter and tighter. I couldn't breathe, couldn't gurgle, couldn't shake his grip no matter how hard I thrashed. A final, desperate ploy exploded like a bomb in my mind.

Stop, Nevan, you're killing me.

When Skeiron dropped a ceiling on me, I'd called to Nevan with my thoughts and he rushed to my side. Now, the solitary response was a weak flicker of red in his eyes and a slight downward tick of his mouth.

My lungs were on fire. My vision telescoped down until all I could see was Nevan's eyes.

"Enough," Skeiron said, his tone bored. "I need her alive."

Releasing my throat, Nevan restrained me with his arms again, holding my feet off the ground. I hacked until my chest throbbed, knowing I could not escape.

"Show her to me," the king said, and damn, did he have the authoritative, kingly arrogance thing down pat.

Nevan flipped me around, barring one arm over my hips and the other across my chest, buckling my arms down. I had no leeway to struggle, except with my feet. When I thrashed them, he locked one powerful leg around both of mine, constraining me while balanced on one foot. If he were mortal, I could've knocked him off balance, but his preternatural agility kept him steady even when I struggled in his grasp.

Skeiron sauntered to us, his freaky eyes on me. "Are you the Janusite?"

"Does it look like I am?"

One side of his mouth slanted upward as he slid a finger down my jaw. "Mortals are so predictable. Fighting the inevitable, believing they can win."

"What about you? Searching for a lowly human female to escort you across the boundary, because you're too impotent to do it yourself."

"Watch your tongue, mortal."

"My name is Lindsey Astrid Porter."

Skeiron kept his gaze nailed to mine but no longer spoke to me. "Nevan, have you witnessed any evidence she is the Janusite?"

Nevan's muscles went rigid around me, his fingers crooking into my flesh. In a dead voice, he replied, "Yes."

"Tell me."

One of his fingers jerked, pressing into my hip. "She—transported me across the boundary."

My stomach plummeted through the ground, but then I heard the faintest wisp of tension in his voice and hope sparked to life inside me. Though he'd ratted on me, he hadn't mentioned I wasn't touching him when we crossed the boundary. Important or not, the fact would've interested Skeiron for sure. Maybe Nevan was fighting his bargain after all.

"What else?" the king asked, his voice hushed but thick with a seething fury.

Nevan's foot fell away from my legs, no longer binding them. "She opened a portal without assistance."

"Is that all the evidence you've seen which identifies her as the Janusite?"

"Yes."

The spark of hope blossomed into a full-blown flame. He hadn't said a thing about the strange energy he sensed in me, or about me calling Tris to help resurrect him. He was still in there, rebelling against his king's hold on him.

It wasn't enough.

"Take her to the dungeon," Skeiron said.

Nevan rocketed us away.

CHAPTER TWENTY-FIVE

A HORDE OF FOOTFALLS THUMPED FROM SOMEWHERE IN THE DIS-
tance, growing nearer with every *thud-thud* of synchronized feet. I
stared at the doorway of my cell, a gaping maw in the smooth walls hewn
from pale bedrock. Were they coming for me?

Goose bumps prickled my arms and I swept my hands up and down
them to banish the chill. A few minutes earlier, after Skeiron and Nevan
left me alone here, I'd tried to walk out the doorway—only to smack into
an invisible barrier. My head still hurt from the impact and the strangely
electrical jolt it zapped through me.

I was a prisoner. Nevan had brought me to my cell.

You must never trust me, he'd told me this morning. *On this side of the
falls* had been the qualification. I'd scoffed at the idea because, though he'd
confided the details of his bargain with Skeiron and warned me about magical debts, part of me still couldn't accept the reality of it all. Mortals broke
their promises every day. No one died from it.

But I might die today. And Nevan might be forced to kill me.

I paced the length of the oval room, maybe a dozen feet across, my
body crackling with nervous energy as the thudding footsteps outside receded. *Relax*, I commanded myself. As if that ever worked. Minutes ticked
by in my head, each second pounding like a hammer striking an anvil. I
checked my watch each time I reached the doorway, before I spun on my
heels and started the circuit over again. Ten minutes bled into twenty,
then thirty.

I tried shouting for Nevan. No response.

Forty-three minutes into my incarceration, my feet aching from repetitive
impacts with the hard stone floor, I gave up and slumped against the wall.

Had I lost Nevan for good? He belonged to Skeiron, or so the king
said. But Nevan had defied his king at every turn since the moment we

met—until today. I longed to believe his bargain with Skeiron had weakened somehow, granting him a measure of freedom, but then I flashed back to his vacant face when he shackled me in his arms and abducted me to this hellhole—all because the king commanded it.

Christ, I didn't understand this magic malarkey anywhere near good enough. I was lost in this world.

Weariness engulfed me and I sank down the wall to the floor. Knees bent to my chest, I let my head droop.

Thunderous footfalls reverberated in the corridor, growing louder and sharper, advancing on my cell.

Pushing up onto my feet, I pressed my back to the wall and sneaked a hand under my shirt to rest it on my derringer's grip. Skeiron either hadn't known what a gun was or dismissed it as no threat, since he'd given it no more than a cursory glance. I'd considered firing a shot at the force field in the doorway, but decided I'd accomplish nothing except deafening myself for several minutes. If the soldiers, or whatever they were, approaching now stopped in for a little chat, maybe I could blast holes in their foreheads and at least incapacitate them long enough to escape.

I had two rounds in my gun, having lost my ammo boxes somewhere along the way. Based on the racket out there, I was dealing with more than two sylph soldiers. I inched closer to the doorway to peek outside.

Two by two, the soldiers tromped past my cell door, clad in obsidian armor gilded with metallic ruby streaks. Matching helmets with face shields disguised their faces, and not one of them deigned to glance at me. Maybe Skeiron had tricked all of them into bargains, making them automatons bound to his will.

Nevan had looked like that. Robotic. Dead. I knew what he was, but he'd never seemed inhuman—until today.

Soldiers filed past.

I counted fourteen, every one as tall as Nevan, some taller, and every one of them built like a pro wrestler on steroids.

For once, I was quite happy to be ignored.

As the last pair goose-stepped past, an image flared in my mind—Nevan in his armor. It had glistened with bright colors, with life and light, not the obsidian darkness of Skeiron's army.

I trudged to the center of my cell, turning in a circle, studying the smooth alabaster of the ceiling.

Why hadn't Nevan come when I hollered? He owed me a life debt. That superseded all other magic, according to him, which should've meant he could penetrate any protection ward Skeiron erected around this underground bunker. Yet Nevan ignored me.

He wouldn't. If I called, and if he could come, he'd be here in a flash. *If he could.*

I struggled to recall everything he'd told me about life debts. Only another life debt could erase it, and the debt-holder had nearly unlimited power over the debtor. *A virtual slave*, he'd said, which sounded sexy as hell at the time. He'd cautioned me to never admit to such an obligation or I'd be at the whim of the debt-holder forever, unless they owed me an equal debt in return. Nevan had sealed his life debt to me with his beautiful words of gratitude and he hadn't saved my life since then. No equal debt.

He still owed me. He was bound to me, at my command.

I'd asked how it worked, if the debt-holder simply thought about the debtor would the other person appear, like whoosh, to do their bidding. I remembered Nevan's laughter at my use of the word whoosh, his face full of affectionate humor.

My throat tightened. What had Nevan said after that?

The owed party must consciously invoke the debt and speak the words in the form of a command. Then and only then will the full magical power of the debt be invoked.

Duh. I'd screamed his name, but not invoked the debt. Back in his cave home, I'd told him to take me with him, but I hadn't consciously invoked the debt then either.

I threw my head back, shook my fists in the air, and shouted so loud my throat burned and my voice cracked.

"Nevan, you get down here this instant! You owe me and I command you to poof your freaking ass in here immediately, don't care what you're doing, just get your goddamn self here!"

Breathing hard, pulse pounding behind my eardrums, I dropped my arms to my sides and listened. Waited.

After a couple agonizing seconds, I could take it no longer. "Nevan! I said get your—"

"There's no need to shriek at me, love."

I yelped and spun around.

Nevan leaned against the wall, arms crossed over his chest, head cocked and lips ticking up at the corners.

I wagged a finger at him. "You scared me half to death."

The little smile faltered. "Don't speak of death, even in jest."

A knot inside me loosened at the sight of him, sagging my shoulders. "I finally figured out how to make you do what I want."

With one thrust of his arm, he separated from the wall and spanned the distance between us. His hot gaze liquefied me but he held back, by a degree of inches. His hands floated up, as if to touch me, but flopped down to hang at his sides. "I've been waiting an eternity for you to call me."

"I only figured out how to make it work a minute ago. Doesn't Skeiron have wards? How'd you get through them?"

"I was still within the wards. Awaiting the king's next order."

"Well, you're free of him now." I swung my gaze to the doorway, then back to Nevan. "I saw a bunch of soldiers go by. Is Skeiron preparing for war?"

"A king is always preparing for war. Another sylph might rise up to usurp the throne, as Skeiron did to Notus. Then there are the other elementals and, of course, the troublesome fae."

"No rest for the wicked, eh?"

"Even the righteous must be ever vigilant." He watched me for a long moment, uncertainty flickering in his eyes. "I would have killed you, Skeiron commanded it." He gritted his teeth, unwilling to meet my eyes. "If I had taken your life, I would never have forgiven myself. Lindsey, I—"

"Shut up. I'm not forgiving you because there's nothing to forgive. You were enslaved to his will."

"Until you freed me." At last, he enfolded me in his arms, surrounding me with his strength and warmth and earthy scent. My eyelids closed and I nestled into him, cheek to chest. He threaded his fingers through my hair, stroking my scalp, feathering hair over my neck. "What will you have me do next?"

"If I ordered you to raze this creepy compound, could you do it?"

"Given my life debt, I would be forced to try. However, I am not an earth elemental. I lack the power of a gnome, the only type of creature that might succeed in destroying Skeiron's palace."

"Palace? It's drafty and barren, not opulent."

"You have seen but a portion of it." He kissed the top of my head, and I heard a sniff as he sampled the scent of my hair. "As always, you smell of everything sweet and wonderful."

Propping my chin on his collarbone, I gazed up at him. "What should we do?"

"I don't know. For days, I should've been formulating a strategy, but I could think of nothing outside of you."

"Well…I have an addendum to my original plan."

His mouth compressed. "I imagine I won't approve of this idea either."

"Probably not."

"No more of your schemes. Now that you have freed me from his control, I will confront Skeiron."

"Screw that idea." I placed my hands on his shoulders. "You're a virtual slave to my will, right? So listen up. You will not fight Skeiron unless he attacks you first. That's an order."

He bared his clenched teeth. "Lindsey."

"I mean it. Keep away from Skeiron."

Another voice chuckled from the doorway. "Sage advice from your mortal whore, guardian."

I whirled on Skeiron, fueled by a sudden and irresistible rage. "I am not a whore, you whacked-out son of a bitch."

Skeiron waved a hand, the invisible barrier glittered, and he strolled into the chamber. "You've brought the guardian to me. Excellent." He flashed me a sneer at me and focused on Nevan. "You will suffer for your disobedience, old friend. And you will watch as I strip the power from your mortal plaything."

I seized Nevan's hand. "Get us the hell out of here."

He pulled me into his arms.

Skeiron raised a single finger. "I have your brother, Lindsey Astrid Porter."

Clinging to Nevan, I glowered at Skeiron. "You're lying."

"Ash—that is his name, is it not?—sits in my bedchamber, guarded by my most steadfast follower, Brennus."

"I don't believe you."

He motioned for me to exit the room. "Come. I will show you."

Nevan clenched me tighter.

Skeiron arched a brow. "You may always command your slave to remove you from this place at any time. He clearly owes you a debt of overarching magnitude." He made a disgusted little huff, throwing a sidelong look at Nevan. "What service did she perform to earn such gratitude?"

Nevan squinted at his king, anger flaming in his eyes. I curled my fingers on his chest, scraping my nails to gain his attention. When his eyes flicked down to me, I said, "Let it go."

He acknowledged the command in my voice with a curt nod.

Skeiron strode out the doorway. Nevan gathered me under his arm and led me out into the corridor under the shield of his body.

"You have my permission," I whispered to him, "to get me out of here whenever you feel it's appropriate—once we get my brother."

He gave me a quick squeeze, the only indication he'd understood me. His gaze was nailed to the back of Skeiron's head as the king ushered us down corridor after corridor, and finally, up a sloping passageway. The cold, pale rock of the lower level segued into a rich, brown stone shot through with green veins. The walls were still smooth, but here polished so the oil lamps on the walls shimmered golden light across the surface. The further we traveled, the drier my mouth grew. I sensed...I don't know. Something very bad on the way.

Ash was not here. He couldn't be. My parents took him outside the boundary.

Skeiron shepherded us around a curving corner. We halted in front of a wooden door engraved with symbols I didn't recognize and Skeiron twisted the knob to swing the door inward.

Unease crawled over my skin, pricking like a thousand tiny claws.

There, perched on the edge of a large bed, sat my brother.

Ash swung his head up, training his gaze on the doorway. His face lit up with relief and excitement, and he propelled himself off the bed toward me.

Brennus the raven-man sprang out from beside the doorway, inside the room, to block Ash's path.

My brother hopped up and down, trying to see around the massive shapeshifter. "Zee! Are you okay? Where are Mom and Dad?"

"I'm okay." I tried to move toward him, but instead of letting me go, Nevan inched us both closer to the door. I forced a smile for Ash. "Everything'll be okay, I promise. I'll find Mom and Dad. I'm sure they're okay too."

If I said "okay" one more time, it would stop sounding like a word.

Skeiron nodded to Brennus. The raven-man slammed the door shut in our faces.

Ash shouted to me, his cry muted by the wood. "Lindsey!"

I wanted to attack someone, anyone, or at least beat my fists on the door. It would do no good. Channeling my anguish and fury into something useful, that was a better option.

Confronting Skeiron, I demanded, "What did you do to my parents?"

"They remained on the other side of the boundary." His arrogant smile had me battling not to whip out my gun and shoot him between the eyes. "Your brother's room in the—what do you call such establishments?—in the motel was a few feet within the limit." He gave me look of mock pity. "You see, there is more water in your world than you recognize. The motel lies near a spring which is hidden from view in a remote section of the forest."

Hidden springs? How the hell was I supposed to protect my family when I couldn't see the dangers?

Skeiron's arm shifted. Metal glinted.

He'd conjured a goddamn sword. The one he'd rammed through Nevan's chest.

In a heartbeat, I understood his intention.

Shoving Nevan away, I commanded him with every ounce of conscious effort I had. "Get out of here!"

He vanished, the instant before Skeiron's sword slashed the air where he'd stood.

Skeiron seized me by the throat, yanking me off my feet. "Clever wench. I will destroy him, but first I will drain you of every trace of Janusite magic."

We teleported us away from the room where Ash was held, into a dank and gloomy chamber with rough walls. The air was redolent with the stench of blood and pain.

He dropped me.

I stumbled into a hole, regained my footing, and whirled on the sylph king.

With a flourish of his hand, he summoned another man who emerged from the shadows behind him.

"This," the king said, "is the mage who will extract the power from you. It will be painful, and it will not end until you are dead."

The mage shuffled toward me, his grimy hands outstretched. His stained, red robes dragged across the floor. Scars etched across his face cinched his eyes and mouth into a perpetual grimace.

I snaked a hand under my shirt's hem, going for my derringer.

Skeiron flicked his wrist.

An unseen force hurled me into the wall, suspending me there, my feet off the floor.

The mage shambled to me. He grasped my head in hands that stank of filth. His fetid breath choked me. His purple eyes seared into mine, his irises shot through with a dark light dredged from the depths of the grave. My grave.

He spewed a string of noises, some kind of incantation in a long-extinct language.

A million tiny teeth tore at my brain.

I refused to scream. No way would I give Skeiron the satisfaction. Agony shredded me, from my head down to the soles of my feet, in slicing waves that wrenched my body, but I gritted my teeth and clenched my fists until my nails punctured my flesh. Blackness pitted my vision, the room twirled around me, and I knew I would die here—buried inside the earth, with a skeletal mage sucking my soul dry—unless I mustered the brainpower to save myself.

I longed to call for Nevan, but I could not risk Skeiron attacking him. The fates of two worlds depended on one of us surviving, and with his powers, he was far more useful than I was.

Save the worlds, Nevan, for me.

It was my last thought, as a final wave of magic towed me under to drown.

The mage gasped. His hands flew away from my head and he staggered backward, eye bulging.

My agony relented, permitting me one long inhalation, a breath so cleansing I nearly sobbed from the bliss of it. The ringing in my ears waned and the blackness receded.

The mage lifted one long-nailed finger to me in accusation. On a wheezing breath, he said, "The power, she protects it. She hoards it. No magic of any realm may breach the mind of the Janusite."

Skeiron punched his fist into the wall. Chunks of stone crumbled away to patter on the floor.

My knees buckled as the mage's hold on me evaporated, and I flailed at the wall for support, my hand at last slapping flat on solid rock. Damned if I'd collapse in front of Skeiron.

"You swore to me," the king said, seizing the mage's robes with both hands, "you could extract the power and feed it into me."

The mage sputtered. "I tried, your majesty. But she is neither elemental nor human. A fragment of Janus's essence lives inside her." His pallid face turned sickly gray when Skeiron clamped a hand around his neck. "My liege, it took the combined power of the gods to scatter Janus's energy to the Four Winds. Perhaps they could..."

Skeiron rattled the mage with a violent shake. Spittle sprayed from his lips as he said, "You suggest I appeal to the gods?"

"N-no." The mage mewled. "I tell you what I learn from her, nothing more. Please release me from my bargain. I've done all you required of me."

"Have you?" The king sneered, his tone caustic. "Our bargain was for you to mine the Janusite's power and transfer it to me." Skeiron cinched his fist tighter around the mage's neck, making the man gurgle. "You have voided the bargain. Your life is forfeit."

With a sickening crunch, Skeiron crushed the mage's windpipe.

I winced, shutting my eyes until I heard the mage's body thump to the floor.

The sylph king rounded on me.

Without a thought, without conscious decision, I tore the gun out of its holster and fired both .357 rounds into Skeiron's chest. I'd almost aimed for his head, but I wasn't sure I could hit the target with adrenaline ripping through my veins.

The rounds slammed into his chest. Blood spurted.

He jerked, stumbled away from me.

I opened my mouth to shout, but got out only a squeak.

Nevan appeared beside me. He collected me in his arms and spirited us away. High-voltage shocks racked my body, snapping and crackling around and within us both. This was not the rollercoaster through hell. It was a torment of fire and power that tore at the center of my being.

We landed in the forest. I didn't know where and I didn't care.

Shoving away from Nevan, I said, "Go get my brother. Hurry!"

He shook his head, his mouth a grim line.

"Nevan, I command you to retrieve Ash."

He shut his eyes for heartbeat before zeroing in on me. "I can't."

I beat my fists on his chest. "Save him, dammit. Save my brother."

"Lindsey, I—" His shoulders caved in and the misery on his face stopped me. "Oh, love, I can't save anyone."

I slapped him in the face. He did not move or react. I slugged him in the jaw. "Are you working for Skeiron? Is that it?"

"No."

"Then go get my brother."

"I cannot." His tone was solemn and heartbreakingly certain. "I would retrieve your brother, you know I would, but I can do nothing anymore. I'm prevented from action."

"But this fucking debt overrides all magic. You told me that. You swore it."

"I was truthful but—You must have felt it during our transit. The energy firing through me must have affected you as well." His glowing amber irises had faded into a dirty brown. "We barely made it here. Skeiron stripped my powers."

The seconds ticked by, counted out by the rapid beating of my heart. Reholstering my gun, I stomped back and forth across the little clearing, faster and faster with each ten-foot circuit, perspiration oozing down my temples.

I should never have let Nevan take me out of there. I should've commanded him to retrieve Ash first, then get me. What kind of a sister abandoned her baby brother in the lair of a psycho elemental being?

Nevan had shown up before I called him and took me away before I had a chance to demand he get my brother first.

"Why did you command me to leave you with Skeiron?" Nevan asked.

"He had a sword. He was about to skewer you again." I kicked a tree so hard the concussion lanced up my ankle into my shin. Dancing on one foot, I cursed myself blue. "You should've taken Ash, not me. He's just a kid."

"I sensed your suffering. You had granted me permission to remove you from the palace if I deemed it necessary, if you were in danger, but I had no power to pierce the ward caging in your brother."

"Did you even try?"

Nevan took hold of my shoulders, rotating me toward him. Despite his haunted expression, a hint of the old confidence sparked there. "We will rescue your brother. I vow it."

A metaphysical bond, more slender than the life debt but still palpable, snapped taut between us. He'd cemented his vow with magic, willingly.

God, I loved him.

And the revelation didn't even scare me. I was in love with a sylph from another world. Maybe it never could work out between us, but for this one day, I'd welcome the experience of loving him.

Hands crossed over my chest, I leaned into Nevan, resting my cheek on his skin. "I am the Janusite. Skeiron brought in a mage to prove it. Turns out I've got a piece of Janus's essence inside me, though nobody seems to know what that means." Entranced by the thumping of his heart, I relished his warmth. "We're screwed, aren't we?"

The sunlight percolating through the treetops speckled his skin with light and shadow. He fastened his arms around me. "Forgive me."

"For what?"

Nevan released the longest groaning sigh I'd ever heard. "I cannot whoosh you anywhere, or conjure anything, or protect you in any manner. I am impotent and utterly useless."

"Bullshit."

He scuffled away from me. "We are far from the portal to your world and the only way back is to walk. Skeiron will have his army searching for us. Leave this place. Quickly. You may make it to the portal before Skeiron catches up to you."

"And what about you?"

"Since I am of no further use, you must leave me here. I have vowed to retrieve your brother and I shall keep my promise."

"Your plan sucks," I said. "I veto it."

He hissed a breath out his nose, eyes squinted. "I am useless."

"You, Nevan, are not in any way impotent, with or without magical abilities."

"Currently, I am but a man. Unable to defend you."

"Oh please." I shook my head. "You are not a man, as you've told me so many times. You're a hot sylph with cool armor and a wicked sword."

"Even if I had my sword and armor, without powers I am—"

"Not useless." I punctuated each word with a thump of my fist on his chest. "I need you in warrior mode, not moping like a fairy."

A small, tight smile stretched his mouth. "Warrior mode is pointless without armor and a sword."

"Maybe I can help you with that."

His smile changed into one of bemused interest. "In what manner?"

"Well, I've got all this power, right?" I swept a hand up and down, indicating myself. "I'm so strong, the mage couldn't suck the magic out of me. I've got serious power."

Nevan got that dubious look again, the one that said he knew I was about to suggest something wacky and he wouldn't like it, but he'd give me a chance to explain anyway. "Janus was the god of doorways, which is why you can open the portal and transport immortals across the boundaries in the mortal realm. Not helpful in—"

"Shush." I took a breath, rolling my shoulders back. "Think. I have Janus's power. He was the god of doorways, yes, but also of beginnings and endings, and of transitions."

"Information I gave you."

"Zip it. I'm not finished."

He mimed zipping his lips shut. Cheeky sylph.

"This Janus guy was tough, right?" I gnawed the inside of my cheek, flipping through the pages of my mental book for answers. "You said Janus was so powerful the other immortals feared him and so the gods banded together to destroy him. But they couldn't get rid of his power, so they scattered it into the winds."

"The Four Winds, which are not winds as you know them. They are both avatars and guardians of energy and magic."

"Doesn't that mean they must've been the ones who put Janus's essence inside me?"

"I suppose," Nevan said slowly. "Not directly, however, since Janus was destroyed eons ago. They must've set things in motion. Why does it matter?"

"They imbued me with magical powers, right?"

"Yes."

"Here's my plan." I paused—not to be dramatic, but because I also feared my plan might be too crazy. "Step one, I make use of my Janusite magic to re-empower you."

From the look on his face, I could tell he really, really wanted to *Lindsey* me. "I doubt that is possible."

"You're awfully pessimistic at the moment, so I'll go with my instincts this time." I walked straight up to him, bounced up on my toes, and leveled our gazes. "I'm giving you back however much of your power I can, whether you like it or not. The life debt ought to smooth the way."

His arms went limp as he gave a tiny shake of his head. "I've come to realize I cannot stop you, when you've set your mind to a task."

"Smart man."

"Do I want to know about step two?"

I sank back down onto my heels, patting his chest. "Step two, I'm going to give Skeiron exactly what he wants."

Nevan flinched away as if I'd shot him. "You will not surrender to Skeiron."

"I have to. He has Ash." I tugged his hands and he shuffled closer. "Besides, after I've shared my magic with you, I'm counting on you to crash through the wards, empowered by your debt to me. In fact, I hereby command you to rescue me and Ash once I've found him."

"Let us pray the life debt is strong enough for that. What is the rest of your plan?"

"I invite Skeiron to take a jaunt across the boundary with me. If we pull it off, this little field trip will be one Skeiron won't enjoy."

He covered his face with his hands for a second, and then let them drop away. "Your plan sounds exceedingly dangerous—and it requires you to be alone with the king. Even with an infusion of your power, I rather doubt I'll be strong enough to aid you if things should go awry."

I placed a kiss over the scar on his chest. "You are smart, resourceful, stubborn, and brave. With or without magic, you have what it takes to help me defeat Skeiron."

Nevan stopped blinking, his cheeks faintly pink. "I am yours to command."

We stared at each other, unspoken things hovering between us, things we both wanted to express but each held back for different reasons. Or maybe the same reason. Fear.

At last, he said, "Explain to me how transporting Skeiron across the boundary will end anything. You took me through the barrier and I am quite alive."

Okay. Honesty time. "We both know why I was able to take you over the boundary, without even touching you."

"Do we?"

I didn't pull away from him, but I did squirm and start counting the swirls in his eyes. "It's not about sex, Nevan. It's about you. How I feel."

He searched my face, his brow pinched above his nose.

"The point is," I explained, "I could take you over the boundary because we have a…um…"

"Connection." No inflection, no smirk, a simple statement of fact.

I nodded. "My magic was awakened by my desperation to save you. I don't have that connection with Skeiron. If I take him across the line—"

"He will be destroyed."

"That's the idea. He doesn't understand why my powers worked with you. He believes I can take him over the boundary."

Nevan gazed at me with admiration. "You are a genius."

I rolled my eyes.

He kissed my forehead. "I will do as you ask."

"About damn time." I ran my hands over his chest. "I wish I could give you all your powers back. Make you whole again. But I think partway is the most I can do."

He thrust a hand into my hair, angling my face up to his. "I was whole again the moment you looked at me in the forest that first day, when you saw me as I truly am and looked on at me without fear or disgust."

"That moment changed me too." A better confession clamored to get out and I no longer saw any reason not to tell him. "I love you, Nevan."

"I love you, Lindsey Astrid Porter."

He kissed me long and slow, with a tenderness and yearning equal to mine, and I relinquished my body and soul to him yet again, within the confines of this bubble we always erected around ourselves whenever we touched. When our lips parted, I cleared my throat, still feeling the slickness of his mouth on mine.

Energy tingled over my skin, diving under the surface to suffuse my entire being. I crushed my mouth to his again, willing my power to infuse him too. He made a surprised noise deep in his throat, his body tensing and then relaxing.

Metal materialized between us.

I moved back a step, smiling when I caught sight of the armor shielding his body and the sword gripped in his hand.

A rustling, faint but distinct, lured my attention to the woods behind me. An instinct stirred inside me, warning of Skeiron's approach.

"Go," I told Nevan. "Skeiron's almost here, I can feel it. Find Tris, he'll help. Find my parents and Travis. Gather our allies, Nevan."

"I will." He laid a hand on my cheek. "Be careful, my love."

He turned and jogged off into the woods. Despite his armor, he made little noise as he slipped away into the night.

I walked in the opposite direction, into the deeper shadows where the forest canopy thickened. Strange insects chirped, orange specks danced in the bushes and trees, and the moss-like ground cover squished under my boots. I ducked a hand under my shirt to touch my holster. With no bullets, the gun was useless—yet reaffirming its presence comforted me somehow.

A raven swooped down from the trees to land in front of me.

Brennus rose, a rippling, roiling shadow that transformed into a man-like creature. His black eyes locked on me. "You are without your guardian."

"And you're without your king."

The weight of another gaze prickled my skin. I spun to face Skeiron.

"He is my scout," the king said. "But never out of contact with me."

"Does he want to serve you, or do you have something on him?"

"There is no difference." Skeiron strode up to me. "Your guardian will not save you this time."

"Don't count him out yet. You may have stripped his magic, but he's still ten times the man you are."

"He is powerless, no better than a mortal." Skeiron nodded to Brennus. "Find Nevan and kill him."

The assassin morphed back into a bird and launched into the sky. His cackling echoed down through the forest.

Nevan, please, run fast.

Chapter Twenty-Six

Skeiron zipped me back to his subterranean palace, straight into the room where he was holding Ash. The instant we materialized, my brother flew off the bed where he'd been sitting cross-legged and tackled me. I staggered backward but clung to him as fiercely as he clung to me.

"Zee!" Ash clinched me hard enough to make me gasp. "I knew you'd come back. Can we go home?"

"Soon, I promise."

His saucer eyes latched onto my gaze. "I don't like it here."

"I know." With a pointed look at Skeiron, I told Ash, "I have to talk to our host first, but then we are going home."

Possibly to die.

I pulled Ash tighter to me and kissed the top of his head. Then I said something I'd never said before to my brother. "I love you, Ash."

His head popped up again, his eyes no longer wide but squinted with befuddlement. I tried to clap the old lid on my emotions, but my hazmat-level containment had fractured. My face must've revealed everything—my guilt at failing to protect my family, uncertainty about what was to come, and so much more—but my brother noted only the fact of what I'd said.

A grin broke out on Ash's face. "I love you too, Zee."

I mustered a smile, weak but genuine. "I need you to trust me, sweetie. I will get you home, but first, I have go outside for a few minutes."

His eyes widened again as he bit down on his lower lip.

"I'll be back," I said. "Just a few minutes."

Ash nodded, eyes glistening with unshed tears. He scampered over to the bed, hopped onto it, and dangled his feet over the edge. The heels of his sneakers bumped the wooden bed frame with each swing of his feet.

A shadow shifted in the far corner, and I abruptly noticed the obsidian-armored sylph posted there.

I led Skeiron out into the corridor.

He shut the door. His expression revealed nothing, but he watched me as if waiting for me to initiate our discussion.

Trying for nonchalance, I let my arms hang slack, my shoulders relaxed and rolled back, resting my weight on one hip. The mistake I'd made before was allowing Skeiron to witness my fear and anger. *Time to rein it in again, Lindsey.*

This part of my plan required cool detachment and clear thinking. I hadn't shared the details about this phase with Nevan, because he would never have agreed to my surrendering to the king if he knew. I needed him far away, gathering our allies in the relative safety of the mortal world. Of course, he couldn't breach the boundary on his own, which left him vulnerable.

To Brennus. To whoever framed me for murder. To Skeiron and his freaking army of sylph warriors, all armed with magic while Nevan had none.

Focus, Lindsey. You've got the power here, remember?

I deliberately met Skeiron's gaze, ignoring the cold that slithered through me at the eye contact. "I want to make a bargain with you."

No reaction. "What sort of bargain?"

"You want me to help you cross the boundary." My fingers had started to twitch. I closed them into loose fists. "I want a few things in return."

"Bargains are formal agreements with magical power."

"That goes both ways, you know."

He crept closer, bending forward to loom over me.

I squelched the impulse to back away. This was it.

His eyes glinted with pure white and seethed with putrid green. "Speak your demands."

"You release my brother and agree to never kidnap, harass, injure, or kill any member of my family ever again. They are safe from you and everyone who is, was, or will be associated with you."

He slanted lower, descending over me. His odor, sharp and sulfurous, suffocated me. I fought back a retch as he plunged his head down to sear his gaze into mine. "In return, you will share the power of the Janusite with me and only me. You serve my will, without question."

"As long as you're king."

He blew a breath out his nose. "As long as I am king. You will also remain with me, physically present at my side, for the remainder of your life."

"Or the remainder of yours, whichever ends first."

"Agreed." He smirked, clearly certain he'd outlive me.

"One more thing." I resisted the urge to scuffle backward, to escape his vile presence. "You will call off Brennus. No harm will come to Nevan for the rest of his existence and you'll return him to his full power, releasing him from any and all bargains he made with you, as well as from the curse on his heart."

I didn't believe Skeiron had really cursed Nevan, and Nevan believed I'd broken the curse anyway, but I wanted nothing omitted from this bargain.

Skeiron's tongue snaked out to moisten his lips. "Nevan has no value to me anymore, so I accept your conditions. In return, you will have no contact with Nevan for the duration of your bargain with me." He snatched up a lock of my hair, coiling it around his index finger, and pulled it taut. "Our bargain will last forever, you realize, as I am immortal."

But not invincible. The king had no idea Nevan apprised me of that fact.

I squared my shoulders, clearing my throat. "Do we have a deal? Based on the parameters we've outlined since the moment I initiated the process by stating my clear intention to strike a bargain."

He brought his finger to his lips, my hair wrapped around it, and inserted his long finger into his mouth, lips puckering around it as he sucked. His face contorted in disgust. He spit out my hair. "You taste of *him*."

"Do we have a deal, Skeiron?"

He straightened, a tower of muscle and menace. "Yes. A bargain is struck."

Magic shot through me, fire lashed with ice, electricity sparked by rain. The ground trembled, or maybe my legs quivered. I struggled to keep my footing as the power of the bargain coursed through me.

The energy faded into a simmering discomfort and I regained my equilibrium.

Brennus appeared beside Skeiron. "I was a feather's breadth from capturing the guardian. Why have you commanded me to return?"

"I have struck a bargain with the Janusite."

Though I supposed Janusite was an improvement over wench, I still fumed at the moniker. "I have a name."

Skeiron sniffed. "I've no use for mortal names. You are a tool, not a comrade."

A tool. Fabulous. I prayed I'd done the right thing, instead of just royally screwing myself and everyone who mattered to me. The one thing I'd most wanted to ask for had been the one thing I could not request.

That he leave the mortal world alone.

Skeiron would never have made such a vast concession, what with multiworld domination tops on his to-do list. Saving my family and Nevan was the most I could ask for and I was banking on my ability to craft a solid bargain— and on the hope Skeiron wouldn't finagle a way around my terms. I bore sole responsibility for saving the world.

Not entirely accurate. I had my allies. My well-armed family, a tough sheriff, and one testy fae. My best hope for rallying those allies lay with a singular sylph clad in armor, who wielded a magnificent sword.

Nevan believed his current lack of power made him useless. I would've bet on him in any fight—unpowered, unarmed, with both hands tied behind his back. But my deal with Skeiron, sealed by our mutual agreement, ensured Nevan would regain his full power.

I pointed toward the doorway. "My brother."

"Will accompany us to the portal, which you will open. Once we are through, your brother may return to your family."

"And Nevan?"

"He has been restored."

I'd have to trust him on that point, since I'd agreed to stay away from Nevan for the duration of our bargain. An ache throbbed in my chest, squeezing my heart. I'd couldn't see Nevan again, much less touch him. And God, how I yearned for the comfort of his arms around me. *Out of reach forever.*

Unless I succeeded. Unless I liberated two worlds from a tyrant.

Me. The one-time man-killer who'd hidden out in a rock shop for three years, too afraid to deal with the past.

Nevan's voice echoed in my mind. *You are a goddess, in every way.* Time to act like one.

I was more than the frigging Janusite. I was Lindsey Astrid Porter, daughter of gun-toting hippies, girlfriend of an immortal elemental warrior from the Bronze Age, and the tough chick who'd blasted .357 rounds at a sylph king and bridged two worlds to resurrect my lover. Plus, I'd talked a powerful being into agreeing to every one of my demands.

No time for basking in my accomplishments. The greatest risk of all was ahead of me.

The door pivoted inward and Ash trotted out, escorted by his sylph guard.

"Let's get moving," I said. "We've got a boundary to cross."

I PUNCHED THROUGH THE FALLS AND SIDESTEPPED ONTO THE LEDGE, MY hair glued to my face and my clothes dripping. Goose bumps pebbled my skin, chilled by frigid water. I threw a hand up to shield them from the brilliant sunlight, as my eyes slowly adjusted. Humid summer heat blanketed me, turning my drenched self into a clammy mess.

Ash tumbled out of the falls. I snagged his hand and urged him onto the ledge beside me, scooting sideways to make room.

Skeiron leaped out next, lithe as a cougar, far more agile than either of us mortals. With one smooth stride he penetrated the cascade and pivoted to march onto the ledge, pushing past me and Ash. We crushed ourselves to the cliff to avoid getting shoved off into the deep pool below us.

When Nevan had taken me through the waterfall, he whisked me onto and off of the ledge. Skeiron made no effort to aid us. He leaped across the wide gap between the ledge and the wooden railing, vaulting over the barrier onto the dirt path where I'd first seen Nevan. Hand in hand, Ash and I inched along the shelf.

Brennus hurtled through the cascade in raven form, wings spread wide, water spraying out. His wings whooshed as he soared past us, high into the sky and out of sight behind the trees.

Ash and I reached the ledge's limit. A good fifteen feet out and six feet down separated us from solid ground, with the railing in the way. Skeiron waited on the path, gaze fixated on me.

"Need a hand?"

I yelped at the familiar voice. Ash jumped, reeling into me, and the momentum thrust us forward, our feet skidding on the wet stone.

A rangy body swung out in front of us, halting our fall.

Tris frowned at me. "So ya do need a hand. Eh, lady?"

"You scared the hell out of us." I slapped his arm. He moved past me to hover in the air just beyond the ledge's end.

He was floating. Actually *floating*.

"Whoa," Ash said, staring wide-eyed at Tris. "Who's he?"

"A leprechaun," I told him. "Tris, about my brother…"

"Got a safe place to hide him." Tris rubbed his neck and grumbled. "Nevan wanted to come get you, but he couldn't. Something about bleeping foolish mortal women. I'm paraphrasing. Nevan's powers are back, but cripes, that dude still has issues—and he knows about your new bargain."

The deal with Skeiron prevented me having any contact with Nevan. He must've sensed the prohibition, much the way he sensed when I was in trouble back in the palace. "Nevan sent you?"

"Yep." Tris offered me his hand. I took it, and since I was holding Ash's hand, the three of us winked out of and back into the real world, our feet now on the path about twenty feet from Skeiron. Tris cast a wary glance at the king and hunched his shoulders, jamming his hands in his jeans pockets. "Nevan don't know the details of your bargain, but he ain't a happy camper."

"Tell him to trust me, stop bitching, and do what I told him."

The leprechaun grinned. "Sure. Love to."

Without so much as a wave goodbye, Tris grabbed my brother's arm and they vanished.

The sylph king watched with arrogant satisfaction as I approached him. "Your fae friend will not save you. Nevan cannot save you. The bargain you entered into binds you to me forever."

Our deal stated it remained in effect until one of us died. He assumed I'd die first and my enslavement would last essentially forever, in mortal terms. Good. My plan relied on his misconceptions.

Skeiron herded me down the path, past the vortex, and through the rock garden into the parking lot. The Porter family motor home hunkered there, parked near the exit onto the highway, but the shop seemed oddly deserted. I wondered why he hadn't poofed us straight to the boundary. This death march of ours made worms wriggle in my gut.

But it was more than the walk. Everything seemed off. I struggled to figure out why, when the truth hit me.

Silence. No birds twittered. No cars hummed on the highway. Even the rumble of the fans inside the shop had gone quiet.

The door of the motor home burst open. My parents rushed out, their arms loaded with—well, arms. My father had slung a rifle over his shoulder and wore a gun belt with a holstered semiautomatic pistol on his hip and extra ammo clips attached to the belt. Mom gripped a shotgun, with her favorite .357 revolver and its speed loaders clipped to her belt, ready to reload on the fly. She had another handgun berthed in a shoulder holster, while Dad carried a second rifle in a sheath strapped to his back.

I'd never loved them more than in that moment.

My parents stopped halfway across the parking lot, their stances wide, their gazes and expressions hardened into steel.

Skeiron tipped his chin up, sweeping his haughty gaze over them. "If you wish no harm to come to your daughter, lay down your weapons."

Mom targeted her 12-gauge shotgun at Skeiron. "Touch my daughter and I'll blow enough holes in you to make your head spin for a good long while."

"He won't hurt her," Dad said, resting his hand on his holstered pistol. "He needs her alive. We're just here to make a point."

"And what point is that, puny mortal?" Skeiron asked.

Nevan materialized in front of my parents. His impressive armor glittered in the sunshine. He set his mouth in a determined line, his eyes twin supernovas, his body a vision of sinuous muscle and contained fury.

"The point," Nevan said coolly, "is to show you Lindsey will never be alone."

How the hell was he here? The bargain—

Nevan winked at me, his eyes glittering.

And that's when I understood. He held a trump card nothing could outplay. He owed me his life. Though I remained bound to Skeiron, the part of our deal forbidding me from seeing Nevan could not override the life debt. I'd granted him permission to come to me whenever he deemed it necessary.

A flash of movement drew my attention to the shop's entrance.

Travis sauntered down the walkway, his strides long and purposeful, one hand firmly on the gun on holstered on his hip, the other gripped around the barrel of a rifle. He wore his sheriff's uniform and his eyes were clear, his face molded into a stern expression.

Stan marched out of the shop behind Travis. His tie-dyed shirt and rumpled khakis clashed with the M-16 rifle he held in both hands.

My allies. My army. Pride swelled in my chest for this ragtag group of family, friends...and Nevan.

Without thinking, I took a step toward him.

An invisible force yanked me back. I grunted in surprise, stumbled, caught myself.

Skeiron sniggered. "You belong to me, wench."

Wench again? Oh, he'd suffer for that. "Let's go to the fucking boundary already."

"Not yet." His arctic smile frosted my blood. "It's time to teach you a lesson about bargains."

I recoiled a step, gravel crunching under my boots.

"Did you believe," he snarled, "*you* could outwit *me*, the king of the sylphs? I have negotiated bargains since before your kind learned to paint outlines of their hands on cave walls."

My gaze shot to my parents and then to Nevan, who'd switched into warrior mode, stoic and rock-still.

"Your family is safe from me and my associates," Skeiron said. He pointed a finger straight up, indicating the sky. "But not from the elements."

I stared up at the heavens, a ceiling of deep azure arching over our heads. A gray blob appeared, swelling and churning, transmuting into a writhing mass of purple and black. The air thickened, charged with a faint current that crackled over my skin. The humidity choked my lungs.

The storm cloud swallowed the sky, plunging us into a false twilight. Lightning slashed the air. Thunder detonated, the ground shook, and balls of sizzling, white plasma disgorged from the clouds. They bounced along the gravel to fizzle out at our feet.

I waved my arms above my head. "Get inside!"

My parents retreated into the RV. Travis and Stan bolted for the store.

Nevan remained steadfast in his position twenty feet from me and Skeiron, the sword in his hand, its tip directed at the ground.

The storm unleashed a torrent of rain. It inundated us and clogged my vision, but bound to Skeiron, I couldn't move unless he bid it. Tiny hailstones pecked my face, arms, chest, stinging my skin.

The sky mutated to grayish green, washing the world in an eerie light, and a clattering, rumbling racket erupted overhead.

Skeiron seized me, and in the instant he teleported us away, I glimpsed the source of the tumult.

A tornado was descending on the heads of everyone I loved.

CHAPTER TWENTY-SEVEN

WE CRASHED DOWN ON U.S. 41, SMACK ON THE DOUBLE YELLOW LINE. SKEIron was behind me, his hands shackling my upper arms. He yanked me back against his body, the fabric of his toga scraping over my exposed skin.

Straight ahead of us, sunlight set the mile marker sign ablaze.

Behind us, thunder boomed. Lightning cracked. I twisted my head around to look back and panic surged in my chest. The thunderstorm overwhelmed the horizon and half the sky above us, and I could just make out the gray-blue rope of the tornado whipping side to side, spiraling ever downward.

Skeiron spun us both around to face the storm. "Your loved ones will be destroyed in a matter of moments. Know you belong to me and there is no one left in any realm who can rescue you."

Metal screeched and clanged. Wood cracked. I couldn't see the shop or the RV, but I realized the tornado was chewing them up. It spat debris in a whirling-dervish cloud. My mind jumped to the worst conclusions, but I did what I do best. I bottled up the terror, the images of mangled bodies, and locked it all away in my mental vault.

Tears streamed down my cheeks, but I hauled in a breath and steeled my soul. I had to finish this.

Power sizzled in the air.

A phalanx of black-armored sylph soldiers materialized before us, two rows of ten each. Another phalanx appeared beside the first. Then another. And another. I counted the groups as they popped into view, until the last one emerged and Skeiron leaned in to growl in my ear.

"This is one battalion. I have twenty more."

I'd counted a hundred soldiers in this battalion. Twenty more? That would make...

Two thousand soldiers.

If they survived the tornado, I had my parents, Nevan, Travis, Stan, and—if he showed up—Tris. Seven of us against way too many of them. If any of my family and friends were still alive.

My gaze flew to the tornado. The ripping, banging, freight-train racket reverberated in my ears.

Skeiron wheeled us back around toward the mile marker sign. "This is the boundary, delineated by the post there. The energy licks at me even here, thirty paces from the line." He thrust me toward the sign, making me stumble a few steps. "It is time, Janusite."

A *pow* ripped through the air, originating from the sky behind us.

I whipped my head around.

The tornado scattered. The thundercloud dissipated, like smoke blown away by a hair dryer.

Nevan. Somehow I knew he was responsible, though I had no clue how.

Skeiron clapped a hand on my shoulder, wrenching it backward. I bit back a grunt.

"The boundary," he said. "Now."

Oh God, please let this work.

I took a deep breath, straightened, lifted my chin, and marched down the highway with Skeiron trailing behind me. When we reached the mile marker sign, I hesitated long enough for him to catch up. I took hold of his hand, cringing inwardly at the contact, and led him across the boundary.

Heat flashed over me. I tripped, halted, gasping for air as pressure mounted in my chest.

Skeiron freed my hand and clutched his head in both palms. His eyes went wide, his mouth was agape, and his entire body shuddered violently. Sparks of energy seared his skin.

He crumpled to his knees, his features distorted in agony.

I scrambled away from, toward the boundary. A bizarre mixture of glee and horror tore through me, propelling me forward again to crouch beside Skeiron. I didn't care that my voice came out harsh, not like me at all, rife with an anger I'd suppressed for too long. "I promised to stay with you as long as you're alive and still king."

He bellowed at me.

"Sucks, doesn't it?" I bent closer and the power ripping him apart singed my skin. "You made a bad bargain and you made one too many assumptions. You should've asked me how I managed to take Nevan across the line."

Energy arced over his flesh, into his nostrils and open mouth. He gagged. "You will suffer. My army—"

"Will be stuck on the other side of the boundary, you stupid bastard." I gulped down my gorge, sickened by the blood pouring from his nostrils. I forged on anyway, hungry for a vengeance I hadn't realized I needed. "Let me tell you how this works. I brought Nevan across the line because he matters to me. Love empowers my magic, you sadistic bastard."

The king screamed.

A curtain of white, electrical energy enveloped him. His body seemed to blur and boil, bits of him splitting off to spiral out into the air, forming an ever-growing mist. The realization of what I was witnessing struck me. I staggered backward a few more steps, my hand flying to my mouth.

His body was being disassembled atom by atom.

Thunder exploded just down the road behind me.

As the remnants of Skeiron drifted into an amorphous cloud above my head, I risked a glance back down the highway.

The sylph army was advancing on me, swords brandished.

Gulping down the lump in my throat, I stared up at the cloud composed of Skeiron's essence. It floated up, expanding, dispersing. A gust of wind worthy of a hurricane blasted over me. I teetered toward the boundary but held my ground.

The wind scattered the cloud, scattered Skeiron to the Four Winds.

Gone. No longer king, no longer alive.

Our bargain shattered with a palpable tearing sensation. I hissed at the pain, though it was blessedly brief.

The sylph army halted at the boundary, an arm's length from me.

I raised an arm to indicate the last vestiges of the Skeiron cloud. "Your king is gone. You can't cross the boundary, which means there will be no conquest of the mortal realm. Go home."

They didn't move.

What did I have to do to get rid of these creeps?

"It doesn't work that way, love."

Relief gushed through me at the sound of Nevan's voice. Moving only my eyes, I searched the area for Nevan and found him a few feet to my left, angle sideways to me on the opposite side of the boundary. His armor glistened and sunlight bounced off the blade of his sword, gripped in his muscular hand.

"Need a bit of help, darlin'?" he asked with a grin.

"The damn army won't go away."

"I'm afraid they'll have no intention of giving up." He swept his gaze over the army poised a dozen feet from him. "They will complete their mission, even without a king."

I nabbed his hand and towed him over the boundary. As I twined my fingers tightly with his, I said, "It's safer over here. Is my family okay?"

"They are unharmed, as is your employer." He hesitated, then added, "And the sheriff."

"What got rid of the storm?"

"I did."

"I knew it." Though I longed to kiss him, I wouldn't do it in front of the sylph army. "How did you do it?"

"I am an air elemental—and my full power has been restored, which I believe you are responsible for. Aren't ye?"

"Absolutely." Hell with the army. I sealed my lips over his for a firm kiss. "Best deal I ever made."

He brushed the backs of his fingers down my jaw. "I underestimated you. What you did, crafting such a cunning bargain…You will do fine in my world."

"Thanks." A warm glow enveloped me from the inside out. The glow of victory, yes, but mostly it stemmed from his compliment. "I never realized how incredibly powerful you are in your full glory. You are magnificent, Nevan."

He puffed up a little, his closed-mouth smile one of pride and well-earned satisfaction.

My gaze wandered to the army standing motionless mere feet from us. "What mission are they waiting to finish?"

"To destroy me and your family, then take you back to the Unseen realm. They must avenge their king."

"I thought killing him would end this."

"Sorry, love." He sighed. "It's only the first stage."

"What else is there? Do you have a plan?"

"Nothing as foolhardy as yours." He sounded annoyed but his gaze was soft, his eyes muted by worry.

"My ideas are always crazy," I said. "But it worked. Skeiron is no more."

"Yes, I saw what you did." He let out a long sigh, and I swore a burden physically lifted from his shoulders, squaring them. "You freed me, Lindsey. Thank you."

"Are you back at one hundred percent? I mean, did my bargain with Skeiron get undone when I undid him?"

"Agreements previously fulfilled remain and we are both freed from our vows to him. But for the record, you have not yet experienced my full glory." He hit me with his best sensual smile and a pulse of sweet, erotic energy shot through me. "I'll demonstrate it for ye later, in private."

If what he'd shown me so far represented less than his full glory…Another pulse of desire rippled through me.

He dipped his head and pulled me closer. "Think ye can handle me, unrestrained?"

"Absolutely." I swept my hand through the air, indicating the sylph battalion. "You had a plan?"

A soldier separated from the throng and approached the boundary. His face shield revealed only his eyes, but he spoke in a voice gravelly and cold. "Surrender the Janusite or we will slaughter every human within the confines of the boundary."

Without releasing my hand, Nevan rose to full height, shoulders back, head high. He looked so regal, so powerful, so virile. *Magnificent.*

I observed him—okay, gazed in rapt adoration at him—as he addressed the army.

"Skeiron is no more," he announced, his voice echoing off the trees. "He cannot protect or empower you. All of you have seen what the Janusite can do. The king possessed more power than all of you combined, and yet she—" Nevan swept a hand in my direction, flashing me a surreptitious wink. "—destroyed him without a single weapon, wielding only the power of the Janusite. Do you dare challenge her?"

All but a dozen of the soldiers vanished.

"If you will not surrender," the leader of the army said, "the battle begins."

Nevan's posture went taut, his demeanor shifted into predator mode. His voice became a soft threat. "So be it."

I nudged him with my shoulder. "This is your plan? Interdimensional war?"

"Trust me." He voiced it as a statement, but uncertainty flickered in his eyes, as if he still couldn't quite believe I did trust him.

"I was just curious," I said. "But I've got complete faith in you."

"As do I, in you."

Someone blipped into view to my right. I blinked at the late-comer.

Tris slouched with arms slack at his sides and scowled at us. To Nevan, he said, "We doing this or what?"

"We are."

I glanced from Tris to Nevan three times before pinning my gaze to the sylph holding my hand. "What the hell is going on?"

At least a dozen men and women appeared, one after the other, individuals of various ages, shapes, and sizes. They wore casual attire, as if they'd just come from the mall—everything from jeans and T-shirts to crop tops and corduroys. One young woman sported a mini skirt.

Every one of them carried a weapon. Daggers. Maces. Swords. Bows and arrows.

"We got this covered," Tris said. "We've endued your team's weapons, temporarily, to give you mortals a leg up with the sylphs at the shop. Ya might wanna go help them, while me and my team cast a little spell."

"A spell?" I said, totally confused.

Nevan hooked an arm around my shoulders. "They will erase the soldiers' memories so they forget both their mission and why they sought you."

"Ah…" I looked at Tris, speechless.

Nevan spoke for me. "She's trying to say she appreciates the fae's assistance."

Tris shrugged, making a noncommittal noise.

"Don't worry," Nevan murmured to me. "Only Tris knows you are the Janusite. The other fae have no idea."

Thank heavens for that. I glanced up at the sky, issuing a prayer for more good fortune. "I need to see my family. Take me, Nevan, please."

He took me. And he didn't even make an off-color joke about my word choice.

The gunshots battered my eardrums in the instant before the world blurred into view. The explosive noise made my ears ring, deafening me.

Over by the RV, Mom and Dad unleashed a volley of gunfire at two sylph warriors. The soldiers flinched at the impact of the bullets but did not relent as bore down on my family.

Stan huddled against the shop building, pinned down by a trio of sylphs. He squeezed off round after round, sweeping his M-16 left and right to hit all three soldiers. One dropped to his knees and clutched at his neck, blood streaming out from between his fingers.

A weak spot. Hallelujah.

Stan's lips moved as he shouted something to Travis and my parents.

From his vantage in the driveway, Travis fired off a shot. The sylph in his path lunged at him, clamping one hand around his shooting arm and wrenching it. Pain contorted his features. He must've cried out, but I couldn't hear a damn thing. The gunfire ricocheting off the metal shop building reverberated off the trees in a feedback loop that amplified the ringing in my ears.

Nevan threw an arm around me, his sword brandished in his other hand. My own voice sounded muffled when I told him, "Go. Help them."

I had no idea how sylph hearing worked but I prayed he could still make out my words, by lip reading if nothing else. He nodded, started to leave, and turned back to me. He offered his open palm to me and two objects appeared in his hand. A box of ammo for my derringer. I took the gift.

Nevan stalked off into the melee.

Heart pounding, I yanked my gun free of the holster inside my waistband, popped open the barrel, dumped out the empty shells, and dropped in two .357 shells. As I clicked the barrel shut, I caught sight of Nevan.

With his back to me, he clashed swords with a sylph taller and broader than he was. Their blades locked as the soldier drove Nevan backward.

My mom shot a sylph in the neck. Blood spurted. The warrior tumbled backward onto the ground.

The gigantic soldier battling Nevan swung his sword back and slashed it at Nevan, who thrust his own blade up to meet the assault. The other sylph pounded his sword into Nevan's with brutal force, knocking Nevan off balance. He lost his footing and his knees smacked into ground.

With deadly precision, the other sylph hefted his sword up, aimed the tip down, and drove the blade toward Nevan's throat, exposed above his metal breastplate.

I pulled the trigger on my derringer, slamming both .357 rounds into the soldier. One round fractured his collarbone, blood running down his breastplate. His head jerked as the second round slammed into his neck. His sword veered sideways to puncture the ground beside Nevan's head.

The warrior collapsed, face down in the gravel.

With one hand, Nevan braced his sword on the ground and levered his body off the gravel. I rose with him, oblivious to the battle raging around us.

Nevan shoved me behind him and thrust his sword straight into the sylph who'd been targeting me with his own blade—the soldier I hadn't seen coming. Nevan's blade pierced the warrior's neck, nearly decapitating him, and he fell down dead.

Travis dispatched the last soldier with a shot to the larynx.

Blood stained Nevan's armor and his sword. My gaze traveled around the parking lot, taking in the blood pooling around the dead sylphs, the red stains on the clothing of my friends and family. I was the only one not marked by the battle. My stomach twisted, at the gore and at the realization the ones I loved most in the world had risked their lives to protect me.

Even Travis, the man who'd harassed me for three years, had stood by me in this fight. Of course, I now realized he'd been in love with me for years. I scratched my arms, plagued by a sudden itching all over me. Travis loved me. I had no idea how to deal with that, but the time had come to stop hiding from life and the problems it handed me.

I holstered my gun.

None of this would've happened if I weren't the Janusite. Nobody asked me if I wanted this burden. I was stuck with it, though, and I still had no conception of what the job entailed—or what I might become.

Shedding his armor, vanishing it to wherever he sent his possessions, Nevan drew me into his arms. I wrapped mine around him and buried my face against his chest, the heat of him comforting me like it always did, though I needed it even more today. The ringing in my ears died away and I noticed sounds. My parents, Travis, and Stan chattering. The *ka-chunk* of rounds being chambered into firearms. The *thump-thump* of Nevan's heart.

We both needed a cuddle. And damn, we'd earned it this time.

"Is everyone okay?" I called out, unwilling to peel myself away from Nevan yet.

"Fine," said Mom, Dad, Travis, and Stan.

My head shot up and, without relinquishing my hold on Nevan, I twisted my head around to study my parents. "Where's Ash?"

On cue, Tris and Ash poofed in. The leprechaun shrugged and poofed out again, as my brother exploded with glee. "Whoa, Zee, that was awesome! Teleportation rocks."

I resettled my head on Nevan's chest. Warm. Solid. Velvety against my cheek. "Thank you, Nevan. For saving my life—again."

"You saved my life as well." He combed a hand through my hair. "Once again, we're even on the gratitude front."

"I like equality. Then I know you're here because you want to be, not because you owe me."

"Never doubt that, love."

"But we need to zip on over to the other side of the falls and officially cancel out your life debt."

"We will. Later."

A *whoosh-whoosh-whoosh* made all of us glance skyward.

Brennus, the raven, soared overhead in a wide circle.

My dad swung his shotgun up and loosed three rounds. The bird cackled and swerved out of sight behind the trees.

We'd forgotten all about Skeiron's pet assassin.

The raven swooped down with stunning speed, his body a blur of motion. His talons sank into my shoulders. I clawed at them, but as swiftly as he'd descended, Brennus ripped me away from Nevan and launched into the sky with me in his clutches.

CHAPTER TWENTY-EIGHT

I SHUT MY EYES AGAINST THE WIND SCOURING MY FACE, GRABBED onto Brennus's talons, but no amount of scratching and pulling loosened his grip. I couldn't fight off a damn bird? So much for me being the most powerful muckety-muck ever. Plummeting to death from high above the earth appealed to me a hell of a lot more than whatever Brennus had planned. Daring to open my eyes, I choked back a scream.

We plunged through the sky, toward the woods below. My stomach heaved at the sudden drop. The air bit into me like teeth and lashed my hair around my face.

Brennus flew us straight toward a waterfall secluded deep in the overgrown forest. It stretched higher than the falls behind the rock shop. This cataract rumbled with menacing vigor, its water spraying up in a low-hanging cloud.

We plummeted into the cascade. I gagged as water pierced my nostrils and throat.

The raven-man released me. The momentum of our flight hurled me across the cave behind the falls, straight into the rear wall. My bones cracked against solid rock, my nerves screamed from the agony. The tang of blood dribbled down the back of my throat, into my mouth. I toppled backward onto the floor, striking with a lesser, but no less excruciating, blow.

My entire body burned, ached, throbbed in the worst way. I was fairly certain I'd broken multiple bones. I tried to move my legs but they didn't budge. I managed to lift my arms and palpate my head. My scalp was moist with a warm, viscous liquid spreading through my hair. I fought for each breath, wincing at the pain in my chest.

Brennus landed by my feet. He squawked once and morphed into his humanoid form, rising above me, his head inches from the high ceiling. He dragged me by my feet into the center of the cave. His black eyes, cold and empty, bored into me.

"You must die," he said, sounding vaguely regretful about it.

I rolled my eyes to glance around the cave. Based on my glimpses of the area outside, I'd determined this wasn't the falls behind the shop. Brennus had taken me far away and I had no idea how long it might take Nevan to find me.

I was a self-reliant woman, right? I could save myself.

Except I couldn't move my legs. Or my arms. Turning my head, even a smidgen, shot searing pain through my skull.

Brennus tilted his head side to side in a bird-like mannerism. "Thank you."

I stared at him, unblinking. "Excuse me?"

The wet rattling in my voice made my gut clench. *Running out of time.*

"You killed Skeiron," he said. "I was bound to the king by a bargain he tricked me into, which prevented me from harming him. Skeiron commanded, and I had no choice but to obey." He swiped a hand over his bald head. "He is gone, thanks to you. But, I'm afraid, you still must die."

"Why? You're free to do what you want." I coughed, spitting blood onto my chin. "I've done nothing to you."

He gave a slow nod that turned into a shake of his head. "Another has bound me with a debt beyond all others. He spared my life once and forced me to admit the debt I owe him." Brennus knelt beside me, laying a hand on my stomach. "For a thousand years, I have served the will of my king. But on this day, I must enact the will of my true master—as I did when I terminated the life of the red-haired mortal."

The truth shivered through me. "You killed Brad."

His eyes narrowed. "Brad? Was that the mortal's name?"

"Yes." I pulled in a crackling breath, my chest on fire with pain. "Who made you do it? Who is your true master?"

He shifted over me, straddling my thighs. "Enough of this talk. You must die, but first I must know. Will your power be scattered or will it be destroyed forever?"

"No fucking idea."

He grasped my chin and yanked my head left and right, inspecting me with a ruthless focus. "I cannot perceive your magic. Only the guardian was permitted that right." His nails dug into my skin, triggering the hot sting of blood. "I must risk it. He commands me to do so."

Brennus drew back one huge hand, like a baseball player about to pitch a ball. His fingers slimmed and sharpened into black talons.

You've got magic, girl. Use it.

Fueled by desperation, I reeled my thoughts back to the moment when my power first emerged, when Nevan kissed me in the woods to test me. The passion, the freedom, the burning connection between us—those elements awakened the magic. But it was trust and love that liberated my powers.

Brennus shredded my shirt with his talons. He tapped the curved point of one talon on my chest, over my heart. "I will take your heart and hex it to bind your magic to the Four Winds. No one shall ever recover your power."

"What is it with you guys and cursing hearts?"

"The heart is the seat of the soul."

He drew a circle on my flesh, marking out his path.

I concentrated all my thoughts, all my desires, on one objective. *I love you, Nevan.* Could he hear me? I didn't know, but the declaration blazed through me. The potency of it wrung tears from my eyes and flooded me with energy. Hot, snapping power. It scorched my veins, energized my body, overwhelmed the pain. The doors of my mind and my soul flung wide. I might die in a few minutes, but in this moment, I was empowered.

Brennus pressed his talon down to pierce my skin. His eyes rapt on the task, he parted his lips as if admiring his handiwork.

He drove his talon deep into my chest.

I swallowed my scream, because goddammit, I would not give him the satisfaction.

Nevan's energy poured into me. Warm. Spicy. Earthy. Just like him.

The talon fractured my ribs. I screamed and hurled everything I had at him, uncertain of what I was wielding or how it worked. A wave of glittering, ice-blue magic collided with the raven-man. His body jerked. His talon popped out of my chest. Another, stronger wave—a tsunami of power—bowled him over backward. He flipped end over end, flying through the air, to wham into the wall.

"Nobody curses my heart."

Speaking sent me into a fit of wet hacking. Liquid dribbled from my lips, accompanied by the bitter taste of blood. Blackness invaded my vision.

Nevan blipped into view beside me, his face wrenched with grief.

Yeah. I was dying. The idea bothered me less than I would've expected, lost as I was in a haze of numbness. I wanted to see my family, to be held by Nevan one more time.

From far away, I watched Nevan produce his sword, targeting Brennus.

"Don't kill him." I spoke the words, my voice rattling, though I felt detached from my own voice. "Someone else made him do it. A bargain."

Nevan stopped with his sword still raised over the assassin and glanced at me. "Who?"

Another figure materialized near my feet, on a diagonal to Nevan and Brennus. In a throaty Texas drawl, the newcomer said, "I made him do it."

A chill like none I'd ever experienced froze me from my skin straight down to my soul. I croaked, "Calder?"

"Howdy, angel." Hunched over, as if his spine had been permanently crooked, he extended a bony hand to point his claw-tipped finger at me. His eyes had no whites, only golden brown irises that filled the orbs, with black pupils dilated by the gloom in the cave. "Took me a long time to figure out how to get you, how to get the power to do it. You got no clue how many bargains I had to make."

Calder's voice scraped like sandpaper on granite. Long, wiry hairs sprouted from his arms, exposed by the ripped and filthy short-sleeve T-shirt that hung on his emaciated torso.

Nevan let his sword-holding arm fall, the tip of his blade lodging in the dirt. "This is Calder?"

My formerly dead ex-fiancé laughed, the sound sharp and rough as broken glass. "And you're her new honey. Sorry, but you lose. She's mine, forever."

Nevan gritted his teeth, forcing words out between them. "You made it appear she had murdered that man. Why?"

"You oughta know how it works." Calder dropped into a crouch, running his teeth over his bottom lip, revealing two sharp canines, inhuman in size and shape. "The forging has to be entered into willingly. She's gotta want to die."

I tried to sit up, but pain racked my body and forced me down again. "Forging? What are you talking about?"

"Why d'ya think I did all this?"

"Revenge. I shot you."

"Nah, you got it all wrong, sweetness." He trailed one claw up the inside of my calf, raking it over the denim of my jeans. "I was trying to tell ya that night. We can have eternity together, but only if you go through the forging. Like I did."

The forging. Puzzle pieces clicked into place in my mind, forming a vivid picture I'd never wanted to see. Nevan had told me how, as his mortal body lay dying, his blood had opened a portal and drawn the sylph king Notus to him. On the night I had shot Calder, he kept saying my blood was the key, and if I died, I'd be strong enough to become his mate forever.

Oh God. His mate.

I focused on his eyes, the odd coloring and the lack of whites. His wicked canines. The long hairs on his arms. He wasn't human anymore. He wasn't a ghost either. Nevan had told me it took enormous strength of character to survive the forging process intact. Why on earth would Calder have volunteered for it?

"I was attacked," he said, curling those clawed fingers over my knee. "I can tell you're wondering why I signed up for this. Well, I didn't—exactly. I went hiking in the woods and a damn cougar got me. I was dying, but I'd fallen next to a stream."

Water. A portal.

"All of a sudden," Calder said, "this man was there. Offered me a chance to live, but in a different way. I'd be immortal and powerful, practically invincible, and he swore I could still have you. But only if you went through the forging."

I coughed, wheezing for air, dizzy from blood loss and pain—and the stark reality of everything Calder had done. For me. No. For himself. "If you loved me, you would've let me go."

Nevan fell to his knees beside me, laying a palm on my forehead. He eyed Calder sideways. "She needs healing."

"Uh-uh." Calder flicked one claw at Brennus, who conjured Skeiron's endued sword and wedged the tip at the base of Nevan's skull. Calder wagged a finger, tsking. "She has to die, you know that. I'm getting my mate back and this is the only way. She's gotta be forged and become like me—like us."

Nevan's lip curled. "You and I are nothing alike. I'm a sylph. You are one of the kerkopes, a filthy shapeshifter, a monkey in a man's body. I can see why you chose the species, they are as vile as your soul."

Calder slammed his fist onto the rock floor. "Shut up! Lindsey was mine way before she ever met you. She wore my ring."

Nevan arched one eyebrow. "And yet she remained a virgin while with you. She gave herself to me after four days." His hand still on my forehead, he bent his fingers to caress me in a soothing gesture. "We both know which of us she chooses."

Calder leaped up, his bare feet lifting off the floor and smacking down again. His feet bracketed my thighs, inches from Nevan. Calder bent, then flexed, his fingers. "Lindsey, tell him. You choose the forging. You choose me."

My voice thin and reedy, I said, "Brennus said you wanted me dead."

Throwing his head back, Calder groaned. "The bird's being too literal. You have to die to be forged."

Nevan winced as Brennus prodded his neck with the sword. "She does not want—"

"Shut up!" Calder screeched, clutching his head in both hands, eyes wild. "You don't get to choose for her."

"And you believe you do?" The cold hatred in Nevan's voice made me look at him, but his face gave away nothing.

"I love her," Calder growled. "It's my right."

"Nobody decides for me," I said, lifting my head to meet Calder's gaze. "You tormented me for days, framing me for murder and sending Brennus to stalk me. You must've known Skeiron was after me, but you didn't do a damn thing about it. Guess who did." I smiled weakly at Nevan, then turned back to Calder. "Why on earth would I ever choose you? I'm sure as hell not dying to be with you, turning myself into a giant monkey-thing so I can be your mate."

Calder backed away from me, past my feet, hiding near the wall. "Then you die. For good, for real, no take-backs."

Nevan squinted at Calder. "I will never allow it."

"That's why you die first, lover boy."

Calder nodded to Brennus.

The assassin sliced Skeiron's sword down at Nevan's neck.

Nevan rolled out of the blade's trajectory, kicking at the sword with such strength it popped out of Brennus's grasp. Nevan snatched it up, bounded to his feet, and slashed the blade toward Brennus.

"Stop!" I said.

Nevan hesitated, the blade nicking Brennus's skin. A droplet of crimson blood trickled down the iridescent blue-black flesh of his throat. Nevan looked to me, a question in his eyes.

He'd stopped because he had to, thanks to the life debt.

"Don't kill him," I said. "You of all people should understand it's not his fault."

"But he'll kill us both. His debt to this one—" Nevan pointed the sword's tip at Calder. "—coerces him to do so."

I summoned the last ounce of my life energy, though it drained away on every drop of blood, to push up onto my elbows and address Calder. Pain coruscated through my nerves, my bones. "You signed up for the forging because you wanted power, didn't you? Not for me. Not out of love or a desire to stay with me. Anyone who loved me could never ask me to give up my humanity. And you're not even asking, you demand it."

Calder inched toward me. "If you love me, you'll do it."

A great sadness filled me, part grief over what had become of Calder, part regret for what I needed to say. "I never loved you, Calder. I wanted to, tried to, thought I should and even convinced myself I must have. It wasn't real. I'm sorry, but it's true."

He leaped forward in a crouch to squat on my midsection.

Nevan rushed toward me, but Brennus punched him in the chest, hurling him backward into the cave wall.

Calder scraped a sharp claw lightly down my throat. "You're dying, baby. Let me help you be reborn."

"I'm the Janusite. How do you know I can be forged?"

"Worth a shot." He leaned down to press his rough, cold lips to mine. "The sylph must've put a spell on you, to make you forget how much you love me. It's why you ran away to this nowhere place. But you can't escape destiny. The forging will free you."

The man I'd known—the sweet, charming man who swept me off my feet—had died three years ago, before I shot him. He chose eternal life and immense power over the peace of natural death. If I died here in this cave, my soul would move on and I would leave this world certain I'd achieve immortality through the memories of my family, my friends, and Nevan.

He'd shown me real love, forged from trust and respect—not a need to control and possess.

"Kill me," I said, "but I will never submit to the forging."

Chin quivering, Calder shook his head. "You'll change your mind when the time comes."

"I won't."

"You will." He raised his hand and his claw elongated, the tip sharpening into a thin, double-edged blade. "You will."

He lanced the claw across my throat. My arms gave out. I collapsed onto the floor, my head thudding on the stone floor. Lights flashed in my vision, then fizzled out.

Nevan roared. He tackled Calder, the two wrestling and grunting and thrashing their limbs.

My body had gone numb, the only sensation that of hot blood streaming down my throat. As my eyesight waned into a deepening darkness, the shapes of the battling elementals faded from view. The noise of their scuffling seemed far away.

Crunch.

Silence.

A final thought flitted through my mind. One of the men had snapped the other's neck, and somehow, I knew Nevan had emerged victorious.

The living world spun away from me as my consciousness receded toward a blessed emptiness and the void claimed me.

Chapter Twenty-Nine

S ENSORY DETAILS PIERCED THE NUMB HAZE ENVELOPING ME, ONE AT A time. Pins and needles prickling my flesh from head to toe. Cool air on my skin. Soft, damp grass under my body. Voices, their words indistinguishable.

A singular voice broke through, low and fierce. "Come back to me, love. Please. I need you."

Nothingness overwhelmed me.

Time passed—minutes, hours, days, who knew. My consciousness seemed to float back down into my body, and my mind roused from the deepest slumber. My eyes stayed closed, my lids too heavy to move.

Soft fabric slid across my bare arms as I shifted position, and a puffy pillow cradled my head. Warm light glowed beyond my eyelids and warmed my face. Traffic rumbled nearby, muffled and intermittent. I pulled in a long breath and exhaled bit by bit, cleansing some of the grogginess. A tentative stretch of my entire body brought no pain.

The scent of thunderstorms wafted over me.

A smile parted my lips as I cracked my lids open. Nevan reclined in the padded wooden chair in the corner of my bedroom in the motor home. His eyes were shut, his head leaning against the wall, both arms slack with one hand on each thigh. He wore his khaki pants and polo shirt. I lay on the bed, beneath the blue-and-green quilt.

I tossed the covers off me.

Nevan's head sprang up, his eyes flew open. His lips trembled with a smile struggling to form, hindered by the concern evident in his gaze as he surveyed my body.

Sitting forward, he asked in a tentative voice, "How do you feel?"

I stretched again, with more vigor, swiveling my hips and thrusting up my breasts. "Mmm. I feel wonderful."

And I did. How odd.

The image of Brennus shredding my shirt and ripping into my chest exploded in my mind, followed close behind by the memory of Calder slashing my throat. My ex had turned into a shapeshifting monkey-man. I rubbed my chest, uneasy at the memory, then noticed a sky-blue cotton shirt and gray sweatpants covered me—and my wounds had healed completely.

"How long—" Realization struck me, ushering in a relief that slackened my tight muscles. "The vortex. You got Tris to heal me."

"Yes. Repairing the damage required a great deal of energy. Tris will be resting for days to regain his strength, but he was more than willing to help." Nevan watched me as if I might disintegrate, as if he'd imagined me. "Are you certain you feel no pain? No remnants of your injuries?"

"Positive." I spread my arms wide, luxuriating in the softness of the satiny sheets. I felt alive, awake, vital. "Never felt better."

"Glad to hear it."

"Um…" I recoiled from the need to ask, but I had to know. "Is Calder dead? I mean, really dead?"

Nevan nodded, eyes downcast. "I snapped his neck, then Brennus handed me Skeiron's endued sword and I drove it through Calder's heart. He will never haunt you again."

"I hope he's at peace." I rolled onto my back, picking at the hem of my shirt. "Christ, I can't fathom why he volunteered to become a monkey-thing."

"Doubt he knew precisely what he'd become."

"What are kerkopes, anyway?"

Nevan braced his elbows on his knees. "The first kerkopes were a pair of mortals who angered Zeus and were cursed to become shapeshifting monkeys. Over thousands of years, they've recruited more humans through the forging process."

I considered his words for a moment. "Brennus is a shapeshifter, but he looks essentially human—except for his shimmery skin. Why did Calder seem so different?"

"Kerkopes inherit their physical traits from the original curse. They are unable to completely shift back into humanoid form."

"Creepy." I stretched my whole body, arms above my heads. "Let's talk about something more fun."

In the literal blink of an eye, he lay on top of me, kissing me, running his hands up and down my sides. "No talking."

His left hand grasped my hip, his right kneaded my breast. His mouth devoured me with a hunger borne of fear and desperation but fueled by joy, his tongue sweeping over mine, coiling around it, firing up my libido with record speed. I wrapped my arms around him and gave in to the passion, our bodies molded together, limbs entwined. My fingers wended through his hair. I inhaled his scent, savored his taste, thrusting my tongue into his mouth as he delved deep into mine.

The door latch clicked. "Oops!"

At the sound of my mother's voice, Nevan rolled off me onto his side, head bowed. I flailed for the covers—to hide myself, because in his fondling he'd shoved my shirt up and tugged one breast out of my bra.

I aimed a sheepish look at my mom, but I couldn't meet her gaze. Sheesh, I was like a teenager caught making out with her boyfriend. My lips still burned from the intensity of Nevan's kiss.

"I came to see if you're awake and I see you are," Mom said. Her gaze switched to Nevan and back to me. "I take it you're feeling better."

"One hundred percent."

"You must be starving." Her tone conveyed motherly concern, but her faint smirk suggested she knew exactly what would've happened if she hadn't interrupted us. "It's blueberry pancakes this morning."

She shut the door.

"Morning?" I pushed up onto my elbows. "How long was I asleep?"

"The remainder of yesterday and all night." Nevan traced a fingertip over my collarbone. "I feared you might never wake, in spite of Tris's valiant efforts."

I opened my mouth in a mock gape. "Did you just call Tris, the vile leprechaun, valiant?"

Nevan rolled his eyes. "You will not hear me speak the words again."

"Do you like blueberry pancakes?"

He stared at me for moment, as if I'd spoken a foreign language. Leaning down, he teased my mouth with swift brushes of his lips and quick laps of his tongue. "I will eat whatever your family offers me, because pleasing them pleases you." He nipped my lower lip. "And pleasing you is my prime objective."

I didn't know what to say to that, so I straightened my clothes and led him out into living room. We ate pancakes while my brother peppered us with questions about the Unseen realm, my status as Janusite, and the details of Skeiron's death. Nevan wolfed down the pancakes with obvious relish, even groaning his approval, and downed what must've amounted to a half gallon of milk. My mother kept offering him more of everything and smiled every time he complimented her cooking, her housekeeping, and especially her marksmanship and courage during the sylph battle.

When my dad started his interrogation, Nevan didn't even seem irritated at the questions. Dad asked if Nevan had used his "voodoo spells" to control me and even that question didn't faze my sylph. He simply stated, "I would never betray your daughter in such a way. If I can't win her without magic, I do not deserve her."

I couldn't stop watching him. His easy smiles, his honest answers, his charming quips and his obvious affection for my family. He handled my brother expertly, in spite of his incessant quizzing about the other world.

Nevan cared for my family. There was nothing sexier in the universe.

Mom noticed my infatuated stare and gave me one of those smiles only mothers could pull off, the kind that said she recognized the depth of my attachment to him and she approved.

After breakfast, Nevan and I wandered outside. The shop building had suffered worse than any of us. The roof had caved in and a big hole gaped in the wall facing the parking lot. Through the gap, I spied overturned tables, the contents of their bins scattered over the floor.

Things could be replaced. Saving lives, saving the ones I loved, that mattered more than property damage.

We met Stan and Travis on the path to the shop door, where the two men were talking and gesturing at various wounds on the building. Instead of his sheriff's uniform, Travis wore jeans and an Aerosmith T-shirt. He looked different in civilian clothes, younger somehow, and more like the man I'd been friends with for years, back before Calder wrecked us both.

I'd found my redemption. Maybe Travis would find his one day.

Nevan slipped an arm around my shoulders. "Are you disturbed?"

"Bad memories, that's all."

As if he sensed my attention on his back, Travis turned toward us. He looked frightened for a moment, but regained his composure and traipsed over to us. He flashed me a tight smile. "Lindsey."

One word conveyed more than I could interpret. Regret. Sorrow. Guilt. Maybe a tinge of hope.

He offered his hand to Nevan. After a quick shake, both men jerked their hands away. Not exactly friends, but no longer enemies.

Travis shifted his weight to one foot, then the other. He hooked his thumbs in the waistband of his jeans, hunching his shoulders. His gaze flitted from the ground to me, back and forth several times, before settling on my face. "Lindsey, I need to apologize, again. I got no excuse and you know I ain't a drinker under normal circumstances. I don't expect us to be friends, won't ask for it but—"

"Stop." I couldn't take his rambling. It made my skin itch. I realized what he wanted and I realized I needed to give it, for both our sakes. "I forgive you. Let's move on, okay?"

His shoulders relaxed. "Okay. Thanks."

I let Nevan shepherd me away. Stan smiled and waved, and I reciprocated. This whole craziness had brought positive changes to my life, like the way my relationship with my boss had improved.

Nevan and I moseyed down the trail to the falls, his arm around my shoulders, mine draped around his waist, my head on his shoulder. The normalcy of our stroll, of our comfortable intimacy, made warmth swell in my heart. I'd thought I would never find this, but it found me. And at last, I understood what it was.

We halted at the wooden railing that hemmed in the pool and the falls. The spray misted over us, dampening our skin and hair. Nevan pulled away to move in front of me, face to face. His expression was serious, almost wary, as he stroked his palms up and down my arms, the droplets from the falls lubricating the motion.

Nevan dragged me into his arms, but rather than kissing me, he zipped us to the ledge beside the waterfall and jumped through the water with me snug against him. We lighted on the rock floor, dripping, my short breaths heaving my bosom into his chest. He ravished my mouth with passion and hunger, our kiss a mutual declaration of everything we couldn't express in words. The kiss heated swiftly, our hands groping, our bodies melting into each other, desire bursting inside me in tiny explosions of pure pleasure.

Our lips still molded together, we dived through the portal and he whisked us to the clearing outside Nevan's home. He broke away, backing up several feet.

I waved toward the slope that concealed his lair. "Why didn't you blip us inside?"

"Blip?" His mouth quirked. "You do come up with the most interesting descriptions."

"It's a gift."

He ducked his head, scrubbing both hands in his hair. When he raised his head again, his face had gone impassive. "Stay with me."

"Are you asking me to move in with you?"

"Yes."

I was mute for several seconds, my thoughts adrift. "I can't live with you."

"Why not?"

"I've never lived with anyone other than my family. And besides, we hardly know each other."

His mouth tightened, his hands fisted. "But you love me."

"That doesn't mean I'm ready to move to the Unseen realm and shack up with you."

Nevan threw his head back and let out an exasperated growl.

"Ugh," I said. "You are so melodramatic when you don't get your way."

His gaze homed in on mine and his flaming eyes sent an erotic shiver through me. "I want you with me always, love. You feel the same, you told me so. Stay with me."

The intensity he imbued into the last sentence shot heat through me, a lightning bolt of desire that throbbed in my sex. I longed to say yes. The word lodged in my throat and I swallowed. "This is a big decision, Nevan. We've known each for what, a week? I need time."

One corner of his mouth ticked downward. "Time for what?"

"To think, dammit. I need time to think about this, about you, about us."

He nodded. "How much time?"

"I don't know."

Sighing, he shook his head. "I will grant you time to think. How much do you require?"

"Are we negotiating a bargain?"

His head drew back, his eyes narrowing. "You believe I would trick you into a bargain?"

"No." I rubbed my temples. "I'm sorry. You wouldn't do that to me."

"I simply want to know how long I must wait." His fingers wriggled, as if working out a muscle spasm. He was anxious. This powerful warrior from another world fretted about my answer to his request. He cleared his throat. "I promised you once I would never use magic on you without your express permission. You know I keep my vows."

And I did. Even without magic to bind the promises, he kept them anyway.

He coughed, glanced around, fixed his attention on me again.

I gathered my sopping hair in both hands and wrung it out. Water splattered the ground. "Two weeks."

The breath he must've been holding rushed out of him. "May I see you during this period?"

"Of course. That's kind of the point." I wrung out my shirt's hem. "I want us to get to know each other."

The old playfulness returned, sparkling in his eyes. "Starting now?"

"Sure." His tongue darted out to moisten his lips, his eyes zeroed in on my breasts, and I knew what he was thinking. "Oh no. There will be no sex today."

Disappointment flashed across his face for an instant. "Perhaps tomorrow. Or the next day."

"You don't mind waiting?"

I hadn't noticed when he'd switched his Eddie Bauer outfit for the loincloth, but I suddenly became aware of his near nudity. My cheeks heated. Ridiculous, after everything we'd done together while buck naked.

He cocked one hip, stretching the loincloth taut over his groin, reminding me of what he could do with the asset hidden beneath the scrap of fabric. "Lindsey, my love, I am an immortal spirit. I have all the time in the world and I would wait until eternity for you."

"Tha—oops." I slapped my palms on my thighs. "Gah. Almost said the T-word. I've got work to do on the gratitude front."

"You'll be fine." He gave me an appreciative look. "Your bargaining skills have certainly improved. You outwitted Skeiron."

I squared my shoulders. "I did, didn't I? Maybe I am awesome after all."

"You awe me at every turn." He roved his gaze down my body and back up to my face, his lustful expression shifting into concern. "You seem worried."

"It's the debt. I don't want you staying with me because you have to come whenever I call."

"Never mind that."

"I will mind whatever I like." Hands on my hips, I drummed my fingers. "No more debts between us. You saved my life when Calder slit my throat. I owe you my life, just like you owe me yours. We're even."

The tether binding us in a one-sided debt snapped. The dissolution hit me with a jolt, like I'd touched an electrified fence. It passed in a split second, leaving behind a new, much softer bond. A genuine one, formed out of emotion.

"There," I said, letting my hands fall to my sides. "That's a relief."

Nevan swept me into his arms. His lips descended toward mine and I slapped a hand over his mouth. "No sex, remember?"

He licked my palm with leisurely strokes of his warm, slick tongue. When he peeled his mouth away from my hand, he left a damp trail across my skin. "I can do a great deal without removing your clothing." He slid my middle finger into his mouth and sucked. "Without even touching you."

I looped my arms around his neck and surrendered to his kiss. By the time we parted, I was breathing hard, flushed all over, and my swollen lips tingled. I pressed my lips to the corner of his mouth. "Show me your world."

A smile of unbridled elation illuminated his face. "My pleasure."

CHAPTER THIRTY

For two weeks, I traveled back and forth between the worlds—but only during my off hours. My job mattered to me, and despite his grumbling, Nevan did not try to convince me to quit. When Stan offered me a promotion to assistant manager, after a moment of head-spinning shock, I accepted. When Stan informed I'd get a big raise, bumping my income up to twice what it had been, I stopped breathing for so long my ears rang.

Everything had gotten better these days.

Every few days, Travis stopped in at the shop to say hi. At first, we endured awkward conversations about the weather, but eventually we found a new dynamic for our relationship. We didn't talk about *that* night, or about Calder. Travis and Nevan learned to tolerate each other, though I held out no hopes they'd become best buds. As long as they weren't killing each other, I was happy.

Nevan popped in everywhere I went—the shop, my parents' motor home, my new apartment, the freaking grocery store. At least he had the sense to wear normal clothes in public, but in my apartment, he made no efforts to conceal his sylph-ness. I didn't want him to anyway. I'd grown rather fond of his loincloth.

And yeah, we discovered I didn't need to escort him over the boundary as long as I was somewhere in the mortal realm at the time. When I asked him how that could be, he'd given me the sweetest smile and explained.

"You asked me once," he said, "if anything is stronger than a life debt. I suggested one thing might be."

"I remember."

He touched his forehead to mine. "It's love, Lindsey. The force more powerful than any magic. The one that allowed me to forgo my duty and defy Skeiron. You told me love empowers your Janusite magic, and that's because it is the only unbreakable bond in the universe."

I almost balked, but my heart confirmed what he'd suggested. I no longer needed or wanted to deny the power of what we felt for each other. He was right, and the realization imbued me with a heady sensation of freedom and exultation.

At work a few days later, while Nevan was off with Ash and my dad doing heaven knew what, I looked up from restocking the fossil agate bin to find Tris observing me from the opposite end of the aisle.

Hand raised, I waggled my fingers at him. "Hi."

Tris scowled, glancing around as if afraid of getting caught. By mortals or his ilk, I had no idea. Apparently satisfied, he moseyed to me.

"Guess the healing stuck," he said.

"If you're asking how I am, I'm great. Thanks for your concern."

He flinched, probably more at my use of the dreaded T word than my sarcasm. "Yeah, whatever. Just don't go getting yourself mortally wounded again, pun intended. I ain't got enough energy to keep up with you and your boyfriend."

"I'll try." I patted his cheek. "You're very sweet to come check on me."

Tris scowled again, though with less sincerity.

"I've been wondering," I said, "why you got so wiped out from healing me and not from healing Nevan."

"You were way more damaged than him. Besides, repairing two almost-dead people in less than a day will tax any leprechaun."

"Ah." I'd forgotten how close together our near-deaths had come. "I appreciate you risking your own skin to save us. You're a good boy."

"Jeez, lady." Tris did an excellent impression of a snottily embarrassed teenager. "Quit calling me nice things. I got a rep to uphold."

"I'll be sure to spread it around you're a heartless little bastard."

He smiled, for real. "Could ya?"

"Absolve her this instant," said a deep voice from behind me.

My body awakened, responding to Nevan's voice even before I turned sideways to stay in view of both Tris and Nevan. My sylph wore tight jeans and a tan T-shirt, his every muscle on display.

I clasped his hand. The action had become instinctive. "What are you mad about this time? Tris hasn't done anything. Today."

"Hey!" Tris complained.

Nevan glared at the kid. "He's been hiding from me for days, because he knows what I'll do if I catch him. You still owe this leprechaun a debt."

"Don't care. Leave him alone."

Tris snorted. "I can handle a frigging sylph. They ain't so bad-ass as they think."

Nevan's voice dropped to a menacing whisper as he slanted forward just enough to loom over Tris. "I'm at full power, tiny fae."

I slapped a hand on Nevan's chest. "Cut that out."

He drew back, but the murderous glint in his eyes remained.

Tris hunched his shoulders, his gaze on the floor. "Chill out, Nev. I absolved your girlfriend right after I left her at the vortex with you, when you was still out cold after the healing." He looked straight at Nevan. "You two better get more careful."

I gave him a sly smile, a trick I'd learned from Nevan. "Why? Are you worried about us?"

"No." The petulance in his tone sounded forced.

Nevan squinted at Tris. "You truly absolved Lindsey of her entire debt to you?"

"Yeah-yeah, like I said." Tris nodded to me. "She'd feel it if she still owed me."

Thinking back to when my debt to Tris was sealed, and recalling the similar sensation when Nevan indebted himself to me, I recognized the truth. "He's right, Nevan. I don't feel it anymore."

Nevan relaxed, pulling me against him.

Tris shook his head. "I'm outta here. I'll spew copper sludge all over this floor if I have to watch you two make out."

He made a beeline for the back door. Once the leprechaun had walked out of sight, Nevan's lips found mine. His kiss was playful, sweet, and restrained.

Probably because we were in public and I'd chastised him for trying to ravish me in any way—with his mouth, his hands, or his other assets—in view of other beings, in either realm. He'd clearly disapproved of my need for privacy, but acquiesced to my demand.

These days, when he caved to my will, I could rest easy knowing magic played no part in his decision. He did it because he loved me.

He bent his head back. "Why are you smiling?"

"I need a reason?"

"No, I suppose not."

But it irked him not to know. I'd learned this about him over the past couple weeks.

"If you must know," I said, "I was thinking how wonderful you are."

A naughty grin spread across his face. He reached down to cup my behind with both hands. "What else were you thinking?"

I poked Nevan in the ribs. "No monkey business in public, remember?"

His lips flattened, but he removed his hands from my tush.

"About what I was thinking," I said, resting my hips against the bins. "Would you like to sleep with me tonight?" When his expression brightened, his eyes flaring hot, I amended, "No sex. Just sleep. With me."

I'd expected his excitement to wilt, at least a tad, but it didn't.

He cupped my cheek—the one on my face this time. "I'd love to sleep with ye, darlin'."

That night, I slipped into my slinky nightie and slid under the covers beside him. He enveloped me in his body, one arm draped over my belly, his fingertips dancing over the fabric to tease my skin, as he'd done the first night we slept together.

I awoke the next morning to the silky brush of his lips on mine. He kept it chaste, but even the light touch, the gentle questing, stoked me to white-hot awareness. I plowed my fingers into his hair and pulled his head closer. He groaned as I plunged into his mouth, intoxicated by the scent and flavor of him.

We kissed for an hour. I was late for work, but Stan made no comment, accepting my apology.

The fourteenth day arrived.

Nevan materialized at the foot of my bed at six a.m., his approach waking me before he entered the apartment. I switched on the bedside lamp and froze when I saw his face—the tension lining his forehead, the haggard tint of his skin, the dimmed colors in his eyes.

"I've been summoned," he said. "By the tribunal."

"The what?" I scrambled across the bed to kneel at the footboard where he stood. "I don't understand."

"My people are without a king. The tribunal demands a full accounting of Skeiron's demise and my role in it, before they appoint a new ruler."

"A full accounting?" I tried to lay my hands on his bare chest, but he shuffled backward. "Are you in trouble?"

"I aided in the demise of a king. I abandoned my duty and consorted with a mortal."

Though he kept his gaze squarely on me, the starkness in it carved a gulf between us. He'd done all of those things for me.

I slid off the foot of the bed to close the distance. "We can hide across the boundary."

"No, love." He ran his hands up my arms, drawing me closer. "We can't hide from this. I must confront the consequences of my actions."

I blinked away the first sting of tears, desperate to prolong this moment, to keep him here as long as possible. "Will you come back?"

"You have my vow, I will return."

"When?"

He pulled me into him, my face buried in his neck, his arms pinning me. "When I can, love. When I can."

"What if—"

Slanting my head back with a hand on my nape, he silenced my unfinished question with a tender kiss. "Hush, Lindsey. I will always come back to you, whatever the cost."

Before I could respond, he vanished.

Days crawled by, one after another after another. I crossed them off on the calendar in my kitchen, and with each stroke of my pen, a new pang lanced my heart. Five days and no sign of Nevan. Six days. Seven.

On the eighth day, I sat alone inside my parents' motor home, in a chair that swiveled left and right with the restless movements of my feet. I'd finally convinced my parents to go home to Kentucky, where they owned an actual house—the kind with a foundation and everything. Besides, this was August and the approach of autumn signaled the close of their annual summertime sojourn.

Nevan was gone. My parents and my brother were leaving. I had Stan and Travis, but as much as I liked them—yeah, I even liked Travis again—they served as pale substitutes for the people I loved.

I clapped my feet down on the floor. My chair halted with a creak. I slumped until my butt started to slide off the chair, staring vacantly at the breakfast nook across from me.

A familiar sensation rippled through me from deep within, triggered by the pulsating tingle of magical currents in the air. The fine hairs on my arms lifted as the aroma of earth and thunderstorms tantalized my senses and anticipation enlivened every cell of my being.

I bolted upright in my chair, hands clamped over my knees. A lightness rushed through me, banishing the malaise, and my gaze rotated toward the open doorway of the motor home.

A shadow elongated through the opening.

I leaped up, kicking over a pile of comic books on the floor, and sprinted for the stairs. I stopped short, my heart soaring at the vision awaiting me at the bottom of the steps.

Nevan grinned at me with the most brilliant joy I'd ever witnessed. Though he wore his toned-down-for-mortals glamour, he looked so good I wanted to throw myself at him and lick him from head to toe like a delicious, man-size lollipop.

"There ye are, darlin'," he said. "Aren't ye glad to see me?"

Glad? The term fell woefully short of describing the overpowering high hurtling through me at the sight of him.

I held off on the licking thing, but I hurled myself at him, sailing across the distance without touching one toe on the steps. He caught me, staggered backward, and whirled us both around with my feet flying through the air.

Our lips found each other in a kiss of sheer, unbridled passion. His tongue thrust into my mouth, devouring me with powerful strokes until I went soft in his arms. When we finally broke the kiss, he held me tight with my feet still off the ground. After a few minutes of silent rapture, basking in the feel of each other, he set me down. His hands lingered on my back, cradling me.

I splayed my hands over his chest, on the pale green shirt that disguised his jaw-dropping physique. Sort of disguised it. "How'd the meeting go?"

His lips kicked up, but he ironed out the amusement. "The meeting, as you call it, went much better than expected."

"No disassembly required?"

With a soft chuckle, he shook his head. "No punishment whatsoever. In fact, the tribunal was pleased to be rid of Skeiron."

A selfish thought reared its head and I had to ask, though I bit my lip and focused on the buttons of his shirt, fingering one. "Um, do they know I'm…"

"The Janusite?" At my anxious nod, he pressed a kiss to my forehead. "No one knows except you, me, Tris, and Brennus."

"No one else?" I pulled my head back, squinting up at him. "But the entire sylph army—"

"Only one battalion knew your identity and they have since forgotten, as ensured by the fae spell. The tribunal believes the Janusite is a myth."

"Thank heavens. I'd still like to know what being the Janusite means, in terms of the bigger picture."

"We will discover the truth together. I promise you this."

I cuddled up to him, my head on his chest, listening to the beat of his heart and the steady rise and fall of his breaths. We held each other for several minutes, silent and content in the warmth of each other. He moved his hands in slow circles on my back. I swirled my fingers over the back of his neck.

Finally, I said, "I owe you an answer."

"No, love. You owe me nothing."

"You're getting it anyway."

I ushered him into the motor home, shutting the door for privacy, and gestured for him to take a seat in the breakfast nook. I slid onto the bench beside him, our thighs pressed together. Hands on my lap, I braced for his reaction to what I was about to say.

"I can't live with you, Nevan."

Though his expression stayed placid, icy blue flashed in his eyes. "I see."

He moved to get up.

I grabbed his arm, urging him back down. "I'm not finished."

Mouth tight, he sat beside me again, stiff and straight, his eyes aimed out the windows across the aisle.

I scrubbed my hands on my thighs to wipe away the clamminess.

Nevan did not look at me, though one finger tapped on his thigh. "Continue."

His imperious tone bristled, but I recognized he was trying to appear unaffected because he was, in fact, very affected by my announcement.

"My family is in this world," I said. "I can't abandon them, but I want to be with you. I want us to have a relationship, like normal people."

"We are not normal."

"Yeah, but we can follow some normal customs." I grasped his hand, stilling his nervous finger. "This is called compromise, Nevan. If you want to be with me, you have to give a little."

His hand clinched mine. "All right. Compromise."

I let out the breath I'd been holding.

Angling sideways on the bench, he pulled me onto his lap. "You will spend every other night with me, in my home."

"Weekends only."

"I'll agree, as long as I spend the weeknights with you in your apartment."

"No." I rapped a finger on his chest. "That's living together."

Both hands on my hips, he tipped them into his burgeoning arousal. "I enjoy bargaining with you."

"I can tell." I wagged my finger at him. "Behave."

"Make your final offer."

"Weekends at your place. On weeknights, you can stay with me if I ask you to." I leaned in until my nose bumped his. "Agreed?"

His gaze seared into mine and a single word rolled of his tongue with sensuous promise. "Agreed."

"Thank you. Now please take me home and make love to me."

"My home or yours?"

"Don't care. Just take me."

He whisked us away. We emerged in my bedroom, where the closed curtains kept the room in twilight, even at midday.

"Tell me," he said, toying with the rivet on my jeans, "would you like to experience my full glory?"

The question rocked me. "Yes."

"I've never made love to a woman before."

"What?" I made an unladylike face. "You've been with lots of women—including me."

"I have enjoyed carnal relations with many females." He unhooked the rivet and eased the zipper down, the sound alone making my sex pulse. "I made love to none of them, because I loved none. Until you."

His hand stole inside my jeans, gliding inside my panties to palm my mound. One finger parted my folds and traced circles around the bundle of nerves at the apex of my thighs. I sucked in a breath.

"I am yours alone," he rasped, his breaths heavy. "Are you mine?"

"You know I am."

"Mmm," he murmured against my throat. "Will you be mine once I become king of the sylphs?"

Drunk on lust, I needed a few seconds to process what he'd said. As the meaning and import of it sank in, I caught his head in both my hands and forced him to look at me. "When you what?"

He moved his hand to cup my breast, and suddenly my bra felt constrictive. "The tribunal asked me to assume the mantle. I will ascend to the throne in a ceremony three days hence."

"Three days?" I tugged his face closer, peering into his eyes. "Will they let a king consort with a mere mortal?"

"I agreed to their proposal with one condition. They must accept you."

"And they said yippee, sure thing?"

"Not precisely." He raked his thumb over my rigid nipple. "But they acquiesced to my terms."

"Wow." I ran my hands down his neck, over his shoulders, fondling the muscles of his chest through his shirt. "I'm sleeping with a king."

His lips curved in a mischievous smile. "Shall I undress you slowly?"

That devious finger of his, wedged inside my panties, rubbed with strong, but mercilessly unhurried, strokes. His lips swept back and forth across my cheek, as I writhed in his hold, grinding my hips into him.

"Dammit, Nevan, vanish our clothes."

"Anything you wish, my sweet mortal goddess."

Our clothes dissolved. Cool air kissed my skin, tormenting my taut nipples. His hand dived lower and his thumb flicked across my nub, as his fingers explored my opening.

I moaned. Loudly.

He zipped us onto the bed, his hard body on top of mine. "It's time to show you all of what I can do."

Chapter Thirty-One

His kiss was deep and all-consuming, rich with hunger yet softened with tenderness. A contradiction, just like him. Warrior and jovial sylph. Bone-melting passion and aching gentleness. Eyes closed, I surrendered to anything he gave me.

Inch by breathtaking inch, he slid his swollen shaft inside me, penetrating my throbbing core. I arched into him and panted, "Faster."

His mouth consumed my protests. I clamped my arms around him as his shaft filled me to the hilt. He froze mid kiss, our tongues entangled. I clawed at his back, strapped my legs around his, and thrashed beneath him.

"Always eager," he growled. "I love your passion."

He drove into me, pounding into me with reckless desire, and I bowed up into each thrust, desperate to take him into me as far as possible. Locked in a fiery kiss, we were joined on every level. Even our powers were drawn to each other, the magics twirling around each other in a supernatural tango, colliding and separating in rhythm with our love-making. Through my eyelids, I spied a rainbow of lights exploding and sparkling around us, and I opened my eyes to see a constellation of fairy lights dancing around and above us, their sparks wafting through the air.

Even gravity seemed to give way to our passion and a lightness overtook me, a sense of weightlessness that amplified my arousal. His arms slipped under my body to bolster me as a climax of explosive power shattered me.

My cry wrenched our lips apart. I threw my head back to scream again, the ecstasy crashing through me again and again. At last sated, I clung to him as he plunged into me once, twice, and on the third thrust found his release. His own cry was half groan, half shout.

I shut my eyes, for fear I'd do something idiotic like weep. I'd never felt this close to anyone—and it wasn't only from the mind-blowing sex.

"Damn." My voice was breathless, my body tingling. "I hope that was your full glory, because anything more might kill me."

"Look down, love."

"Why?"

"Please, once, do as I ask without questions. You won't regret it."

I pried my lids apart, turned my head, and gasped. I belted my limbs around him. No way was I letting go.

We floated atop a white cloud outlined with silvery gray. The literal air bed hung suspended high above the earth, so far up I could glimpse Lake Superior, which lay twenty miles from my apartment complex. The building was tiny from this vantage, like a child's toy.

"Loosen your grip," Nevan said, his voice tight, "before I lose mine."

I struggled to make myself relax. "Better not drop me."

"Never. I meant I'd lose my grip on the magic that's holding us up here." He pecked a kiss on my lips. "Thank you for loosening up."

"You mean just now, or in general?" I gingerly stretched out one foot and tapped my big toe on the cloud. It billowed around my foot. "This isn't solid."

"It is and it isn't." He swept his fingers through the gaseous bedding, swirling it with ease. "And to answer your question, I meant both. If you hadn't loosened your grip, I might've sent us both plummeting to the ground. But I'm also grateful you let go of your emotions."

The cloud captured all my attention. "What do you mean it is and it isn't solid?"

"It's magic, my love. You'll have to get used to the contradictions."

"Will the cloud support me?"

His smile was as cryptic as his words. "It will and it won't. Go on and try it out. I won't let you fall."

I hesitated, then lowered one leg onto the cloud. My limb sank in a little, but somehow the cloud buoyed it. I let me other leg relax onto the billowy bed. Nevan's arms slackened around me and my whole body sank onto the cloud. It felt like the best waterbed ever, without the sloshing.

Nevan moved to roll off me. I stopped him with my arms around his back.

He gave me an odd look, a mixture of confusion and amazement. "Aren't I—how do you phrase it?—squishing you?"

"A little, but I like it."

"What would you have me do then?" He palmed one breast. "I am at your command."

"Make love to me again. And again." I swished my hand through the cloud. "And maybe again after that."

He laughed, the full-throated kind rife with such joy I couldn't help joining in. When our laughter faded away, he took my face in his free hand and stared into my eyes. "Are you sure you wish to have a relationship with me?"

"I hate to break it to you, but we're already having one."

His other hand kneaded my breast, his thumb raking over my nipple. "You know what I mean. Life with me will not be simple."

"You've got yourself a handful too."

Thunder rumbled in the distance. I glanced left, spying a storm cloud on the horizon. Lightning lanced up from the cloud top, straight out into space.

I slapped his behind. "Is that you? The thunderstorm?"

"Possibly. It won't be severe, nothing but a light show with some much-needed rain. This is my power. And you fuel it."

"Oh. That's, um, sweet. I think."

"Sweet is not the compliment I'm seeking at this moment." He ducked his head to capture my nipple in his mouth, giving it quick pull. "Would you care to amend your statement?"

"Arrogant sylph."

"I'll accept that."

By the time we came down, from the skies and from our next round of full-glory sex, the sun had dipped below the horizon. Lightning coruscated across the sky, the bolts slender and white-hot.

In my bed again, we snuggled under the covers. Nevan's thunderstorm produced a soft, steady rain that pattered on the roof.

From here on, our lives were merged and time itself could not sever the unbreakable magic of our love. Me and my sylph warrior, on a journey with no itinerary, because we'd make it up as we went along. With my ear to his chest, I counted the time between lightning bolts and thunder by the clock of his heartbeats.

However fast or slow the clock ticked, for me, he had nothing but time.

Aꜰᴛᴇʀ ᴛʜᴇ Fᴀʟʟs

TWO DAYS AFTER

I RECLINED ON TOP OF A HILL IN THE UNSEEN WITH THE SOFTEST BLANKET I'd ever felt beneath me and the unearthly sapphire sky above me. The orb of the sun blazed bright and tiny, flame-like jets flickered around it. Yeah, I would need time to adjust to the strangeness of this parallel world. It helped to have a native here to guide me. Nevan lay stretched out on his side facing me, his head held up with one hand. He wore the familiar loincloth.

Tomorrow, he would become king of the sylphs. I was sleeping with a king. How weird was that? My ex-fiancé had become a monkey-thing, and now I was the girlfriend of an otherworldly monarch. Me. Lindsey Astrid Porter.

What if the other sylphs refused to accept me?

Nevan touched the spot between my eyebrows. "This furrow tells me you are fretting again. What bothers you, love?"

"Your coronation is tomorrow."

"I am aware of that."

Biting my lip, I flipped onto my side to face him. "What if they won't accept me? What if they force you to choose between me and being king?"

"Then I will choose you."

"You shouldn't have to give up being king for me."

He dragged his finger down the bridge of my nose. "I can live without the crown, but I cannot do without you in my life, Lindsey. There is no decision. If I must choose, I will stay with you."

I flopped onto my back again, groaning miserably. "Maybe we should tell all your sylph buddies I'm the Janusite. They wouldn't dare reject me if they knew."

"No one must know."

"But it might help."

Nevan sprang into a sitting position. "No, Lindsey. We will never tell another soul what you are. Skeiron tried to steal your power, and I will not have you endangered again simply to make my ascension to the throne easier."

I picked at the blanket and screwed up my mouth, but I couldn't think of a comeback that might convince him. He was right, anyway. If we shared the Janusite news with the sylphs, it wouldn't end there. Someone would blab to somebody else from another elemental kingdom, and soon, everybody in the whole damn Unseen would know. I really didn't want to ask Nevan to erase the memories of more sylphs. What if they got brain damage from it?

Nevan leaned in to kiss the spot between my eyebrows. "What can I do to ease your mind?"

"Oh, don't worry about me. I'm sure this whole coronation thing won't be as uncomfortable as I worry it will be. Anticipation of a stressful event is always worse than the actual event."

"True." He kissed a path down my nose and pressed his lips to mine. "There are pleasurable forms of anticipation."

I thrust my fingers into his thick, silky hair. "Yes, there are."

THREE DAYS AFTER

CORONATION DAY. AFTER SPENDING THE NIGHT AT NEVAN'S LAIR, I ENJOYED the sumptuous breakfast he prepared for me and showered in the waterfall in his bathroom. Once Nevan had dried off my body with a towel—taking more time and care than was strictly necessary, seeming to enjoy teasing me with his sensual pat-down—he summoned a burst of air to dry my hair. It came out perfectly bouncy and wavy. I applied some subtle makeup and put on the dress I'd bought yesterday. It was a tasteful blue number with frilly short sleeves and a hem just below my knees, along with a pair of equally tasteful blue pumps and a pair of dangly, pale-blue earrings. Surely, the sylphs couldn't find fault with my wardrobe. As for me…If they didn't like this mortal chick, they could shove it.

I twirled in front of Nevan. "Well? How do I look?"

"Utterly delectable, my sweet mortal morsel." He slung an arm around my waist, and his mouth descended toward mine.

Shaking my head, I shoved a hand between our lips to stop him. "Uh-uh-uh. Don't smear the war paint."

His brows crinkled. "War paint? There will be no battle today."

"It's a mortal saying. Means I got all gussied up to impress the bejesus out of these sylphs so they'll think twice before messing with me."

"At least you are no longer fretting. I suppose war paint is a preferable alternative." He stepped back to admire me from head to toe. "You are luscious. I pray I can restrain myself until after the coronation. The moment

I am king, I'll be whooshing you to the nearest bed to ravish you for the remainder of this day and all night."

My body responded to his sultry declaration with a tingling shiver that lifted every fine hair on my body.

I reached out to tickle his cheek. "You said 'whoosh.' That's a Lindsey-ism."

He clasped my hands. "It is. I've come to appreciate your odd terms for…everything."

"What else do you appreciate about me?"

"Everything." He pulled me against his body, his hands on my bottom. "How will I survive this bloody coronation? I have to look at you through the whole ceremony."

I looped my arms around his neck. "We could skip it."

"Mmm, yes." He squeezed my ass, tugging me into his growing erection. "Perhaps we should skip it."

Just when he dipped his head to kiss me, he jerked and froze. His eyes widened for a heartbeat, then he shut them briefly and groaned. His body slackened, and his hands fell away from my behind.

"What is it?" I asked.

"The tribunal summons me for the coronation."

I drew back. "They summon you? How? I didn't hear anything."

"You wouldn't. It's magic, not a worldwide radio broadcast."

Ah yes, I had explained radio transmissions to Nevan yesterday. After our time on the hilltop in the elemental world, I'd taken him for a drive in my Malibu to show him the Keweenaw. He had marveled at the car's radio and asked questions about how it worked, how the transmissions were sent and received, how far the signals could travel. I gave as much information as I knew, but I was no radio engineer or whatever they called people who understood that stuff.

Nevan pulled away from me, took my hand, and whooshed us away.

We materialized in a hallway inside the palace, two paces away from of a set of closed double doors. Nevan's armor had materialized on his body.

Two sylph warriors guarded the doorway. I remembered this place from the one and only other time I'd visited it, back when Skeiron had abducted me, locked me up in his dungeon, and got a mage to try to suck my brains out.

"You are fretting again," Nevan said.

I leaned in to whisper, "When you're king, will you be living here? In the palace?"

"I have not considered living arrangements." His hand tightened around mine. "Let us get through the coronation first."

"Sure."

We stepped toward the closed doorway.

Both sylph soldiers took sideways steps to block our way.

Nevan squared his shoulders, his jaw set. "What is the meaning of this? You dare bar the path of the one who will be your king in a matter of moments?"

"I regret the need," one soldier said. "But your mortal plaything may not enter the throne room."

Mortal plaything? Was this guy serious? I'd saved two worlds from the wrath of Skeiron, but of course, nobody knew about that. Protecting my identity as the Janusite had taken precedence over getting the credit.

"Lindsey goes where I go." Nevan narrowed his gaze on the soldier who'd spoken. Through clenched teeth, he said, "Move aside."

The soldiers held their ground.

Nevan's nostrils flared the slightest bit, a sure sign he'd had enough of this.

"I can wait out here," I said, hoping to defuse the situation. Starting his kingship with a fight seemed like a less-than-auspicious beginning. "It's okay, really."

"No," Nevan snarled, "it is not okay."

He flicked his wrist.

The double doors exploded inward, whacking into the walls inside the throne room. The two soldiers flew backward and tumbled across the shiny stone floor.

I got the briefest glimpse of five beings dressed in golden robes before they winked away.

Nevan half dragged me into the throne room, straight up to the vacant bronze-and-gold chair positioned atop a dais. The crowd gathered within the room hustled out of our way. A solitary sylph, clad in bronze-colored robes, lingered beside the throne. His wrinkled face and salt-and-pepper hair surprised me since sylphs were immortal, but I'd have to ask Nevan about that later.

The robed sylph gestured toward the floor. "Kneel."

Releasing my hand, Nevan knelt before the older being and bowed his head.

Apparently older. Whatever.

The robed sylph, who I decided must be a priest or something, withdrew a scepter from inside his robes. He intoned words in another language that sounded like the one I'd heard Nevan speak a few times. The priest touched his scepter to each of Nevan's shoulders, then tapped it on top of his head.

Stepping back, the priest nodded.

Nevan got to his feet, seized my hand, and marched up to the throne. He settled into the huge, shimmering bronze chair. Chin lifted, he surveyed his subjects.

The priest announced, "All hail King Nevan, liege of the sylph kingdom."

Everyone except me dropped to one knee, lowered their heads, and murmured, "All hail King Nevan."

"You may rise," Nevan said.

His subjects rose.

The king snared my waist and pulled me onto his lap. I squelched a yelp and forced a smile as all the sylphs in the room swerved their gazes to me.

I waved. "Hi."

Nevan's lips twitched up at the corners, but he managed to maintain his kingly expression of austere authority. "Lindsey is mine. No one shall dare question her right to be at my side or her place within this kingdom. She is my mate."

His mate? I knew he loved me, but we hadn't discussed our official status. Did we have an official status? It seemed like we did now. He'd announced it to a roomful of sylphs. He'd made a royal proclamation that I was his mate.

Nevan flourished his hand in the air. "Let the celebration commence."

Some of the sylphs picked up instruments I hadn't noticed before and began playing a boisterous tune. The others started to dance, hooting and hollering.

More sylphs streamed through the open doors carrying trays full of food.

Nevan whisked us away from the party, straight into his underground lair and onto the bed with me underneath him, both of us naked. Yeah, he didn't believe in wasting time.

He pressed his lips to my throat, kissing a damp trail down to my breast.

I grasped his head and forced him to look up at me. "Not yet."

With a growly groan, he rolled off of me. "I imagine you want to talk."

"Yes." I sat up. "The coronation ceremony was kind of…anti-climactic. Guess I was expecting more fanfare. And who were those guys who skedaddled the second they saw us?"

"They were the tribunal." He shifted uncomfortably on the bed. "They disapprove of the king consorting with a mortal and decided to show it by refusing to attend the coronation when they realized I had brought you."

"I wonder who came up with the label of mortal plaything." I drew my knees up and hugged them. "Sounds like this tribunal hates me. Won't that make your job harder? I mean, the tribunal is like an oversight committee, right?"

"They are."

"Why do they hate me?"

"Because they are imperious and officious, that's why." Nevan pushed up into a sitting position and placed a hand on my arm, stroking it up and down. "Forget what anyone else says. You are my mate, and I have no intention of giving you up merely to satisfy a few small-minded individuals."

"Glad to hear it." A memory of the coronation flitted through my mind, and I had to ask. "The sylph who performed the ceremony seemed older than everybody else. How does an immortal being get gray hair?"

"It is sometimes conferred on an individual as a sign of respect."

"Magically made gray hair? Most humans try to avoid looking older."

Nevan lifted one shoulder. "To an immortal, signs of age are a novelty."

"Guess that makes sense." I glanced around the warm and welcoming space that was Nevan's home. "You didn't answer my question yet. Will you be living in the palace?"

I got a chill just thinking about it.

Nevan enfolded me in his arms and his warmth. "You dislike the palace. Because of your experience with Skeiron and the mage."

"Yes, but I'm sure I'll get over it. If you need to live in the palace, I will adjust."

"There is no law which requires the king to be in residence there." He combed his fingers through my hair, down to my nape. "I may live wherever I choose."

"Won't the tribunal gripe about it?"

"Naturally." He bracketed my face with his hands. "I care nothing for what others think. You will be with me always, and I will live wherever you are comfortable."

"I appreciate that, but I don't want you to get in trouble because of me."

He swept his thumb out to seal my lips. "Hush, love. It's settled. I will live here and visit the palace when necessary."

I smiled against his finger.

At lightning speed, Nevan repositioned us on the bed with me beneath his big, muscular body. The weight of him bore down on me, but I didn't mind at all. I loved the feel of him on top of me.

Nevan slipped a hand between our bodies, between my slick folds. "This is how I wish to celebrate my coronation. Here, with you. Alone. Naked." He dragged his finger up and down my cleft, eliciting a gasp from me. "What should I do to you first?"

"Anything you want, Your Majesty."

Whatever the tribunal might do or say, I knew one thing without a shred of a doubt. Nevan would always fight for me, for us.

I moaned when he found my taut nub and massaged it with his thumb. "You're my mate too, Nevan."

"Good." He caught my bottom lip and released it little by little. "Let's demonstrate our devotion to each other."

We did. For the rest of the day and night until we both collapsed on the bed, too spent to stay awake. Let those officious sylphs call me the king's mortal plaything. Why should I care? I loved the way he played.

THE MORTAL FIRES

Undercover Elementals, Book Two

Chapter One

"I AM NOT YOUR SUPERNATURAL TAXI SERVICE." I LODGED MY HANDS on my hips and tried to frown at the leprechaun in front of me, but his pseudo-pleading look turned my frown into a half-suppressed smile. Tris was no stereotypical leprechaun. He wore no green felt hat, looked like a teenager, and stood average height—with a rangy build, buzz-cut brown hair, and bright blue eyes that glimmered with an uncanny light.

"Are you discriminating against leprechauns?" he asked in his very human accent, a cross between Chicago and the Bronx despite the fact this elemental being lived in a parallel world.

"Oh please." I lolled my head back, rolling my eyes at the heavens. It wasn't my fault somebody a long, long time ago created magical barriers to stop elemental beings from traveling more than one mile from any interdimensional portal. "Claiming discrimination is not going to make me do what you want. If I take you across the boundary, you might die. For real, for good, no coming back from it—not even for an immortal being like you. Getting my friend ripped apart at the molecular level would really ruin my day."

Tris had ambushed me outside the rock shop where I worked as assistant manager. I may have been the Janusite, a mortal gifted with the powers of a Roman god, but I still had to pay the bills.

I glanced at the corrugated metal building that hunkered alongside U.S. Highway 41 in a remote section of rural Mandan County, in the heart of the Keweenaw Peninsula. A colorful sign pronounced the shop "Rock the Keweenaw: Upper Michigan's Premier Geology Superstore." The building sported a fresh coat of barn-red paint. I'd come here on my day off to head for the Unseen realm and try to discover more about what being the Janusite meant, but the leprechaun had waylaid me.

"Come on," Tris whined. "You take Nevan over the boundary all the time."

Ah, Nevan. I couldn't help smiling every time I thought of my boyfriend. My immortal boyfriend. A sylph, no less. My mind rewound to last night, and the hours I'd spent ensconced in Nevan's underground lair in the Unseen realm, naked and wrapped in his big, muscular body, kissing and touching and—

"Hey!" Tris snapped his fingers in front of my face. "Don't go getting that dreamy look on your face. I'm talking to you, lady."

I folded my arms over my chest as a car whizzed past on the highway, twenty feet behind me. The morning sun glared in my eyes, peeking over the treetops and the roof of the rock shop on its daily journey across the sky. "I don't care to test the limits of a magical barrier or of my powers."

"You're gonna make me beg, aren't you?" Tris grumbled, screwing up his mouth, then sighed. "Lindsey Porter, would you pretty please take me over the boundary so I can check out your world?"

A warm tingle rushed through me, an awareness of a particular elemental approaching. My heartbeat accelerated, the fine hairs on my arms and the back of my neck lifted. Nevan was on his way.

"Sorry," I told Tris. "Gotta go."

Without waiting for his complaint, I sprinted around the back of the shop building, through the rock garden and past its concrete statuary of fantastical creatures, and straight down the trail into the woods. I reached the healing vortex, halting at the bench-shaped stones arranged in a semi-circle around the empty space that contained invisible, healing energies. I'd once believed the vortex was a hoax, nothing more than a fiction to attract tourists, but I now understood it was real. The vortex could heal wounds and promote mental well-being, but it could also do so much more. It could resurrect the dead.

The warm, liquid tingle that heralded Nevan's approach mutated into a chill slithering down my spine. Not Nevan.

A breeze wafted past me, carrying with it a faint and unpleasant odor reminiscent of ammonia. It dissipated in seconds, though, and I hadn't gotten a good enough whiff to identify the smell.

I turned in a circle within the vortex, scanning the woods for the source of the false sensation that had drawn me here. The woods were quiet—too quiet. No chattering squirrels or rustling of the wind through the leaves.

How could someone or something fool me into thinking Nevan was coming? My connection with him fueled the sensation. I had no similar connection with any other living thing. Of course, I was living among magical beings who sneaked into the mortal realm undercover, often posing as mortals. I had no clue how many elementals walked among us mere mortals.

Twigs cracked at my left one after another, amid stumbling footfalls and the panting, whimpering breaths of a distressed individual.

I spun toward the sound and shoved my hand under my shirt to close it around the grip of the handgun holstered inside the waistband of my jeans. The Bond Arms Mini derringer was small enough to fit inside my palm but let me fire .357 rounds as well as shotgun shells, thanks to its interchangeable barrels. I hoped I wouldn't need either today, but I rested my hand on the gun just in case.

A girl staggered out of the woods and stopped several feet away, her body shaking, eyes wild and golden brown hair disheveled. Her large blue eyes flicked to me, and she froze. Her pallid skin grew whiter.

"Lindsey," the girl said, her voice dry and brittle.

"Do I know you?" Pretty sure I didn't, but she gaped at me like I was her long-lost relative.

A chill swept over my skin. This girl resembled me. Not like we were twins, but enough we could've passed for sisters. The pale girl gasping for air was more slender, where I had curves, and looked younger but otherwise…

The girl scuffled closer and stretched out one ghost-white, dirt-encrusted hand to me. Her face had transformed into a mask, as if she were drugged or entranced.

"You don't belong," she intoned. "You never will. Accept your fate or the forces allying against you will consume your power and your soul."

My power? She couldn't know about me being the Janusite.

The girl's knees trembled. She swayed on her feet, eyes rolling back in her head for a couple seconds before she seemed to return to reality, her gaze suddenly sharp and clear and locked on me. "You can't win. He won't choose you this time."

"What are you talking about?"

"The one you love. He won't choose you."

Finger-size marks bruised her neck.

I took hold of her shoulders. "Did someone hurt you?"

"He sent me to tell you. He made me come." She shuddered. "Swore he'd punish me if I disobeyed him. The way he punishes…"

She bit down on her lip, tears gathering in her eyes.

I studied her face, her bloodshot eyes, her skin that seemed drained of life. No human whackjob had done this to her. "Who hurt you?"

The girl swayed again, her eyes unfocused. "He calls himself N—"

She fainted into my arms. I hugged her to me with one arm, feeling for a pulse in her wrist with my free hand. The rhythmic surge of blood pushed against my finger, weak but there. I fumbled in my pocket for my cell phone, then remembered I'd left it in my purse back in the shop. *Dammit.* I shouted with all the volume my lungs could muster.

"Help! Somebody, help!"

Tris blipped into view beside me. One second not there, the next visible.

I jumped, my heart racing. "Thank God. Help me get this girl back to the shop. She's not well."

Tris glanced at the girl and his lip curled. "Cripes, lady, what'd you do to her?"

"Nothing. I found her this way." I glared at him and said, "Help me."

He slapped a hand on my shoulder and we zipped away, emerging a split second later on the gravel path right outside the shop's main entrance.

"There," Tris said, "that's my good deed for the day. I can't take you to the hospital, seeing as it's past the boundary."

"What about the vortex?"

His nostrils flared as his gaze bounced from the girl in my arms to the woods and back again. "Dark magic did this, I can taste it. Ain't no coming back from this kinda sickness."

"Please, Tris, can't you try?"

"Can't. Too dangerous." He gulped, his own face paling when he glanced at the girl. "I'm sorry."

The leprechaun vanished.

Motion in the trees snared my attention.

A tall, black-robed figure loitered at the edge of the woods, at the periphery of the parking lot. The hood of the figure's robe concealed his face.

Before I had time to wonder why I assumed it was a man, the figure winked out of sight.

In my arms, the girl began to twitch, foam spilling from her mouth.

"Stan!" I shouted. "Call nine-one-one! Hurry!"

CHAPTER TWO

HE AMBULANCE RUSHED OUT OF THE PARKING LOT AND DOWN THE highway, taking away the sickly girl. I turned away from the road, my shoulders flagging. While I'd watched the paramedics loading the girl into the ambulance, I'd kept wondering what on earth had gone down here. Did the black-robed figure have anything to do with the girl's illness?

I'd stopped believing in coincidence the day I'd discovered the Unseen realm existed.

A tepid breeze ruffled my hair around my face and rattled the leaves of nearby quaking aspen trees. The sound imitated the pattering of a light rain, a strange contradiction to the clear blue sky above. My gaze drifted to a couple and their two small children navigating the path to the rock garden. It led up the hill into the woods and straight to the waterfall where I'd first met Nevan six weeks ago.

Why had I sensed him, if he wasn't in the vicinity? Another unanswered question.

"Am I boring you?"

Torn from my thoughts by the gruff voice, I turned to face the man behind me. Sheriff Travis Blackwell stood with hands on his hips, thumbs hooked inside his belt behind the .40-caliber Sig Sauer berthed inside a leather holster. Not long ago, I would've felt intimidated by his stance and the ease with which he could've whipped out his gun to threaten me. These days—thanks to both of us coming to terms with what really happened to Travis's brother, my fiancé Calder Blackwell—the sheriff and I had reached a state of tentative friendship, almost a return to the way we'd interacted before I met Calder.

It helped that Travis wasn't calling me ice princess anymore.

"Well?" Travis said. "You paying attention or what?"

His Texas twang truncated some words, turning *paying* into *payin'*, but elongated others.

I sighed and rolled my shoulders back. "I'm listening. You're sure the girl's okay?"

"EMTs said she's severely dehydrated and exhausted, but the bruises don't look recent. Docs at the hospital will check her out to make sure, but yeah, they think she'll be fine once they get plenty of fluids into her."

"Thank heavens." I rubbed my neck, because it had begun to ache. I had a feeling I'd been gritting my teeth ever since I found the girl. "Did she say anything?"

"Just her name. Megan Kozlow. And the number for her parents. I called 'em and they're coming to pick her up." Travis frowned, shaking his head. "Damnedest thing. They say they last saw her in Copper Harbor, a good hour's drive way. The family was in an ice cream shop two days ago when she went to the bathroom and nobody saw her again. They reported it, but the Keweenaw County guys couldn't find any sign of the kid. Copper Harbor ain't exactly New York City, so I got no idea how somebody took her without anyone seeing."

"Was there a body of water nearby?"

"Lake Superior's a block away from the shop." One side of his mouth crimped. "Please don't tell me this has something to do with…all the freaky shit."

"That close to a body of water, any elemental could've abducted her. She was well within the one-mile limit." Natural water features concealed portals to the Unseen realm, but no elemental could travel beyond the one-mile boundaries that encircled every body of water on earth. With my newfound abilities, I could take elementals across the boundary, but only my closest allies knew about my skills. "Disappearing without a trace, in the blink of an eye, is a hallmark of the elementals."

"One of them must've taken her." Travis groaned, looking utterly miserable. "Wish to hell that was a surprise."

The girl's words to me replayed in my mind and a chill swept over my skin. I hugged myself, to no effect. The chill refused to leave. "How old is she?"

"Nineteen."

Christ. So young. I couldn't bear to think about what her unknown abductor had done to "punish" her, or that he seemed to have done it as part of a scheme to frighten me.

Travis let his arms drop to his sides, his shoulders slumped. "Did the girl say anything to you?"

I told him everything about my encounter with Megan, from the moment she staggered out of the woods until she collapsed in my arms.

Travis's eyebrows knit together. "Somebody whose name starts with N did this."

"Apparently."

He shifted his weight from one foot to the other, grimacing and scratching his cheek. "I hate to say it, but you and me, we do know somebody whose name starts with—"

"Nevan did not do this." Never mind that his name started with N, and that I'd sensed his presence right before Megan stumbled into me.

Travis held up his hands, palms out. "Hold up, Lindsey. I'm not saying it was Nevan, and you gotta believe me, this ain't jealousy talking anymore. I'm only looking at the facts we've got."

"I understand you have to consider it." Hugging myself tighter, I swallowed against a sudden tightness in my throat. "But you don't know Nevan like I do. He's a good man and he would never, ever hurt an innocent girl."

"Okay," Travis said slowly, "I get it. But listen, he was under some kind of spell when you met him, one that made him do things he didn't want to do."

"It was the result of a sucky bargain. And even when Skeiron had an iron grip over him, Nevan resisted the king's worst commands. He fought it with every ounce of willpower he had in him. Besides, Nevan is not bound by a magical bargain anymore."

"Are you sure?"

I tried to respond, but my voice refused to function. A cold fist gripped my heart. I knew Nevan wouldn't hurt an innocent willingly, but could I ever know for certain he hadn't gotten roped into another magical trap?

Travis settled a hand on my shoulder, his touch and his voice gentler than I'd ever known him to be. "I'm sorry, Lindsey. I'm a cop, and I gotta look at the simplest explanation first."

"Magic is the simplest explanation?" I almost smiled to hear Travis the logical cop suggest such a thing, but the worry gnawing at my gut squelched any humor.

"Crazy, ain't it? Guess I'm getting more used to this freakiness than I thought."

"Amazing what you can get used to when you have no choice."

Travis kicked at a rock. "I better get back to the office."

"Yeah."

He ducked his head and looked at me sideways. "You ever think about Calder?"

I shoved my hands in my jeans pockets and hunched my shoulders. "Yeah, I think about him sometimes."

Too often, actually. I had nightmares about my former fiancé, but I also suffered the occasional thought about what might've been if Calder hadn't stumbled onto a cougar and sustained fatal wounds from the attack, if he hadn't died and been reborn as something else. That sequence of events had altered my life too—and Travis's.

"You ever wonder," Travis said, "if we could've saved him?"

I shut my eyes. "Your brother was going to kill me. Nevan had to take him out."

"But you guys didn't even try to resurrect him. You brought back a frigging shoplifter, but you left Calder dead."

His words might've sounded angry, if not for the strain of grief in his voice.

I met his gaze, refusing to shy away from this moment. I'd known it would come sooner or later, when the shock of recent events dimmed and the consequences became baldly evident.

"Travis." I moved closer to light a hand on his arm. "We couldn't bring Calder back even if we'd wanted to, I'm sorry. There was no time. Nevan and Tris had to rush to get me to the vortex and heal me."

Travis nodded, his eyes glistening. "Can't believe my kid brother turned into a shapeshifting demon monkey."

"Neither can I." Unsure what to do with my hands, I stuffed them in my pockets again. "I wish we could've saved him, could've turned him back into himself. He didn't give us a chance to try. You know I would've saved him if I could."

"Yeah, I know."

I wanted to hug him, but that would've been weird. Travis had kissed me once, when he was drunk and freaked out by supernatural occurrences, and I didn't want to give him the wrong impression.

A familiar wave of warmth crested over me. Unlike what I'd felt earlier, this was strong and right and unmistakable.

"I have to go," I said. "Nevan's coming."

I bolted across the parking lot and through the rock garden, up the hill to the vortex. Just as I sat down on the nearest stone bench, Nevan poofed into view at the other side of the vortex. I'd gotten accustomed to the way elementals could poof in and out whenever they liked, and at times I envied that ability.

Nevan wore his favorite attire, a tan loincloth plastered to his hip and groin, the fabric seeming to blend into his bronzed skin. When he sauntered toward me, taut sinews flexed in his powerful thighs and across his sculpted abdomen. The sunlight glistened on his body, highlighting the metallic bronze sheen of his skin and the paler track of the scar that lanced across his heart.

I melted from the inside out, captivated by the sight of him. Would I ever get tired of admiring his exotic beauty? A sigh of appreciation whispered out of me. No, I never would.

He dropped onto one knee, settling his hands on my thighs. When he spoke, his Irish brogue lilted the words into a hypnotizing melody. "Good morning, love. Didn't want to leave while ye slept, but the tribunal—"

"Ugh. Can we not talk about the tribunal?" My thighs parted of their own volition, my body anxious for him to get closer. "I'm starting to think the tribunal keeps calling you in for meeting after meeting for the sole purpose of keeping you away from me as much as possible."

"Perhaps they do." He slid his hands up and down my thighs, and even through my jeans, his touch excited my skin. "But I have returned. As I always do."

My mind struggled to remain lucid, but the unnatural heat of his body enveloped and distracted me. I longed to plaster myself to his nakedness. "You could've woken me up to say goodbye, instead of dropping me off in my apartment while I was still asleep."

He smiled, one of those slow and sensual smiles he'd perfected, and eased my thighs apart to move his body between them. "You're angelic in slumber, and your snoring is adorably nasal. I hadn't the heart to disturb you."

"I'll ignore the snoring comment and forgive you anyway." I looped my arms around his neck and he slipped his arms around me, his hands roving my back. "How was your meeting?"

"Pointless."

"Sorry to hear it." The events of the day resurfaced in my mind, and I said, "A weird thing happened earlier. This girl—"

"Later." He nuzzled my neck, his breaths teasing my skin. "I would rather spend this time making love to you and convincing you to live with me."

"But the weird thing—"

"Tell me after, darlin', when we're both relaxed and thoroughly sated." His voice had lowered into a sultry register that never failed to arouse and entrance me. "First, tell me again why ye won't live with me."

The intoxicating nearness of him and the subtle, sensual way he touched me threatened to obliterate every thought in my head, but I couldn't let it. Not yet.

"Listen to me, Nevan." I planted my hands on his chest to keep him from cocooning me with his body and his mind-scrambling presence. "Something happened that's got me spooked, and it should have you spooked too."

He went still, his gaze searching mine. "Tell me."

I related my encounter with the dazed girl. "I don't know who this N person is or what exactly he did to her, but this was a message for me."

"No one will harm you, not as long as I live." He enveloped my hands with his. "And you have proven capable of defending yourself, as well as others. We will discover the culprit of this attack on an innocent girl, together."

"It's what we do, right? Hunt down evil." I suddenly recalled a part of the story I'd forgotten to mention. "Right before the girl showed up, I swore I sensed you coming."

"You would have. I had already crossed the veil at that point, and I paused in the cave to speak with Brennus. He had questions about his new duties as guardian of the falls."

"But you didn't find me until just now."

He raised our joined hands and kissed my knuckles. "I wanted to come to you immediately, but Brennus believed someone had breached the portal while he patrolled the woods. I returned to the other side to investigate, but found no evidence to support his concerns."

"What kind of evidence were you looking for?"

"Remnants of the magic used to open the portal or perhaps footprints."

"Somebody did come through. The man in the black robe."

Nevan's hand tensed around mine. "You believe Brennus detected his arrival, yet somehow the robed man concealed the magical evidence of it."

"Is that possible?"

"You should know by now, anything is possible."

"Sherlock Holmes would have an aneurysm if he were in my shoes, because logic has no bearing on the elemental world."

Nevan glided his hands up my arms and around to my back, roaming them in slow circles, urging me closer to the inviting heat of his body. "Before we delve into the riddle of the man in black, I would like to solve another mystery. Why will you not live with me?"

Pressed against his firm body, I threaded my fingers into his hair and moved them in lazy circles on his scalp. "We've been through this before. I'm not ready to relocate to the Unseen and shack up with you. I need more time."

Though I loved Nevan, like I'd never loved Calder, I'd known Nevan for a matter of weeks. He was immortal, insanely hot, and recently crowned king of the sylphs—all things that complicated our lives.

Nevan fixed me with his steady gaze, his amber eyes glowing from within and swirling with metallic shades of bronze, gold, and silver. "You still think of Calder, don't you?"

"Well...yeah." I hunched my shoulders. "He turned into a monster, literally."

"You fear I will do the same."

"No. Maybe. I don't know." Letting my head fall back, I growled in frustration. "I'm confused, okay? I've got a new job and my Janusite powers to figure out. I've been researching the mythology of Janus, but I need your expertise here. Then there's the tribunal, who want you to dump me. Most everybody in your world agrees with them I'm a filthy, worthless mortal."

His fellow sylphs called me "the king's mortal plaything." Only three elementals knew I was the Janusite—Nevan, Tris, and the shapeshifter Brennus—and the rest of them dismissed me as a puny, insignificant human. They had no clue I was a mortal gifted with the powers of the Roman god Janus, the only being in either world who could take elementals across the boundaries in this world.

"I will never leave you," Nevan said, "no matter what the tribunal or anyone suggests."

"You might be better off without me. Not that I feel unworthy, but really. How many times did you have to save my life when Skeiron came after me?" I dropped my chin to my chest, then lifted it again to gaze into his whirlpool eyes. "Like I said, I'm confused and I need more time. Please understand."

"I do understand." He peppered kisses along my throat. "But how much more time do you require before making up your mind?"

"Don't know. I…" My voice trailed off, thanks to Nevan nibbling at my earlobe. I tilted my head to the side, exposing my throat to his ministrations. He dragged his lips down my neck, his hands skimming up my back to splay over my shoulder blades, urging me closer until my taut nipples pushed against his bare chest through my shirt and bra. "This is so unfair. You know I can't think when you're—Oh."

With my arms around his head, holding him to me, I arched into his body as one of his hands drifted around to my breast.

"My sweet Lindsey," he murmured into my ear, "I want your delectable skin on mine while I dive into your slick heat."

Oh God, I wanted that too. "Right here in the vortex? What if a tourist shows up?"

"Then I shall whisk us away." He drew my earlobe into his mouth, suckling briefly before releasing it. "The healing vortex does more than heal. It can strengthen our bond and heighten our pleasure."

"Are you serious?" I pulled my head back, brows raised. "You never mentioned that before."

"Never had you soft and willing inside a vortex before."

I was soooo willing. Since the moment I'd given up resisting his seductive charms—on the fourth day we'd known each other—I couldn't say no to him. Didn't want to. He set me on fire, and I dissolved into him every time.

The crunching of footsteps on the fallen autumn leaves interrupted our interlude. Nevan leaned back, twisting his head around to glance in the direction of the sound. I slanted sideways to peer around his large body.

A woman traipsed out of the woods to the left of the trail and stopped at the edge of the vortex. The gossamer layers of her flowing gray dress obscured, but did not fully conceal, the curves of her body and the perky globes of her breasts. The leaves remaining on the trees softened the sunlight, making her alabaster skin glow in contrast with her rosy lips and fiery red hair.

A belt fashioned from silver links encircled her waist, hanging low in the front, weighed down by a green pendant. The slender, cylindrical pendant featured a flared top and tapered down to a point. A series of chevron marks decorated the flared cap, while horizontal lines wrapped around the cap's base. The shape seemed familiar, but I couldn't quite place where I'd seen it.

The woman's emerald green eyes glinted with specks of silver as she smiled—at Nevan.

I blinked rapidly, confused by the familiar way she smiled at him, like she knew him well and was quite fond of him. Like she *really* knew him. Like she'd…slept with him.

Nevan sprang to his feet, nearly bowling me off the bench. He left me to regain my balance on my own, since he was too busy striding toward the strange woman. Halting several feet away from her, with a stone bench between them, he gaped at her with a faint pallor under the bronze gilding of his skin. His eyes had gone wide, the swirling in them gone.

The woman stretched a pale, slender hand out to him. "I've found you at last, Tuathal my love."

She spoke with an Irish accent, like Nevan's but more pronounced.

"Ceara," Nevan whispered, stumbling backward a step. "You are…alive?"

Her laughter tinkled like tiny bells. "As I am here, clearly I live."

I hefted my body off the bench, inching closer to Nevan. When I touched his arm, he flinched, his gaze darting to me before zeroing in on the other woman once more.

"Nevan," I said, giving his bicep a gentle squeeze. "Who is this?"

The woman arched a single, elegant brow but did not glance at me for even a nanosecond. "Nevan? Is that what you call yourself in this life, Tuathal? I hadn't heard, but then, I've been indisposed for quite some time."

Nevan and the woman stared at each other, he with shock, she with amused interest. It was like I didn't exist anymore.

I shook Nevan's arm. "What's going on?"

He blinked slowly, as if emerging from a trance, and turned toward me. "This is Ceara. My wife."

CHAPTER THREE

WIFE. THE WORD GOT WEDGED IN MY BRAIN, IN THE GAP BETWEEN hearing and comprehending. For the past six weeks, Nevan and I had shared more than hot sex. We'd shared the details of our lives, past and present. The future had been uncomfortable to discuss, given the uncertainty of his position as king and my newfound powers, the ones I still didn't understand and wasn't sure I wanted.

Nevan and I had agreed we needed to be totally honest with each other. I'd assumed he told me everything that mattered.

Until I'd been confronted with the ethereally beautiful woman he called his wife.

Nevan watched me with haunted eyes, the spinning colors of his irises duller and almost motionless, with only the faintest motion within them. His expression had gone stony. Though his shoulders slumped a little, a distinct tension made his body rigid.

I moved toward him, instinctively reaching up to lay my hands on his bare chest, needing the comfort of physical contact.

He backed away a single step.

A pang lanced through my heart. I was losing him, in the space of a few seconds. One minute, he was seducing me and the next…

Who the hell was this woman, this wife of his?

After everything we'd been through together, this was not how it ended. I'd almost died for him, he'd almost died for me, we'd fought an entire goddamn army of brainwashed sylphs together. He'd asked me to live with him, though I'd insisted I had to spend part of the time here in my world.

A sick feeling churned in the pit of my stomach. I'd never wondered why he didn't ask me to marry him. Hadn't known if elementals did that sort of thing. Maybe he hadn't asked because he knew his wife was still out there.

Christ. I could spin my brain in dizzying circles wondering and worrying, or I could make him talk to me.

Ignoring the eerily serene woman behind him, I closed the distance between us and raised onto my tiptoes. He held stone-still as I locked my hands behind his nape, forcing him to meet my gaze. Threads of bronze whorled in his irises, bright and alive, but only for a moment. My breaths reflected off his face, back onto mine.

"Tell me what's going on," I said.

When he spoke, his voice was a smidgen above a whisper, his words meant only for me. "Not here. Please."

His hands came around my waist, as if he needed to anchor himself to me.

"Tuathal," his wife said, "we must speak. Alone."

A knife-like edge sharpened the last word. I peeked over his shoulder at Ceara, who glared at me with eyes now transformed into twin disks of pure, shimmering silver. Something about the metallic color, the way it swallowed up the whites of her eyes, rushed cold through my veins. Her lips had flattened, her fingers had curled into her palms.

I sensed, on a level deeper than conscious thought, that she despised me with a seething intensity.

Nevan brushed a kiss on my lips, released me, and spun on his heels.

The instant he faced Ceara, the woman's eyes returned to brilliant green flecked with silver. She reverted to saccharine smiles and ethereal grace as she sashayed closer, stopping an arm's length from Nevan.

I clenched my fists and my jaw. This woman was married to my boyfriend. Didn't that make me his mistress? Oh great. In a heartbeat, I'd gone from girlfriend to adulterous lover.

Ceara deigned to shoot a haughty glance my way before she proffered one elegant, pale hand to Nevan. "Come with me, my love. We have much to discuss."

"Whatever you have to say," Nevan told her, "you will say in front of Lindsey."

Ceara lifted her perfect little nose and sniffed. "Very well, as you wish."

Nevan tensed, but he pulled in a deep breath and relaxed his posture. "Speak and be done with it."

"I've heard you became king of the sylphs. Congratulations."

Shoulders bunching, Nevan hissed out a breath.

Ceara's lips kinked into a smug smile. "Since you and I are still married, technically, this means I am your queen. I intend to claim my rightful place and rule by your side."

Nevan flinched as if she'd struck him but covered up his response in a heartbeat. "I choose my own mate. Lindsey will rule with me."

"Will she?" Ceara tapped her chin with one finger, then wagged it at Nevan. "Oh, but Tuathal, the council has not approved your selected mate. They have, in fact, resisted it. A mortal as queen, or even consort to the king, proves a bitter pill to swallow, does it not?"

"I am king." A muscle in his jaw ticked. "The council will accede to my will."

Ceara circled around Nevan, pushing between me and him, and trailed a finger down his bicep. When she crossed in front of him again, she tilted her face up to capture his attention. "Over all these thousands of years, have you spared a single thought for Daráine?"

Nevan swallowed visibly, his eyes darting away from Ceara and back to her again. "Of course I have. Her fate is unknown to me."

His wife leaned in, tipping her head back further to maintain eye contact. "Why did you never return to check on either of us? Once you achieved the forging, did your mortal life no longer matter? Did we no longer matter?"

"I—" He turned his head to the side. "The bargain I struck with Notus, to become immortal, forbade me from having contact with anyone from my mortal life or from looking in on my former life. I longed to make certain you and our daughter had survived the attack, but I could not."

Bargains wielded real power in the Unseen realm, power that could extend into the mortal world once the deal was struck. A nasty bargain had forced Nevan to search for the Janusite for a century and to do Skeiron's bidding.

Wait. Had he said daughter? I opened my mouth to speak, but words failed me. Nevan had neglected to mention both his wife and his daughter.

Ceara snapped her fingers in Nevan's face. "Look at me, Tuathal."

He turned his head toward her again, his face blank.

"You abandoned us," she said. "You ran away to fight the enemy and left me and our daughter unprotected."

"I instructed you to flee into the woods, to seek shelter far from the battle."

His voice sounded as dead as his expression.

"Ah yes," Ceara scoffed. "You told us. But we had no time to run, the enemy came too soon. When I saw them approaching, I distracted them so Daráine would have time to escape into the woods."

His gaze pinned to her, Nevan stood motionless, as if unable to tear free of her hold. "How did you—"

"Become an elemental?" She slashed her nails down his jaw, drawing a thin line of blood, then seized the back of his neck. "I sacrificed myself to gain Daráine time to flee. I had only a dirk, but I charged at the enemy screaming like a banshee and waving my dagger at strong men armed with swords. An enemy soldier cut me down within moments."

Nevan stumbled backward a half step. "Daráine?"

Ceara tipped her head, eyes narrowed, and studied him for a long moment. "She lived on. A family from another clan took her in and raised her as their own. She was, so far as I could tell, happy in her new life. Later, she wed and bore children of her own. Our line has survived the ages, Tuathal. Our descendants live today."

My brain, discombobulated by so many revelations, latched onto a crazy notion. What if I was one of Nevan's descendants? *Ew.* I couldn't think about that right now. Besides, Nevan had died five thousand years ago, which meant for all I knew, he could've been an ancient ancestor to ninety percent of the humans on earth.

Nevan lurched backward into the stone bench, his knees buckled, and he thumped down onto the hard seat. "You were permitted to watch over Daráine?"

Hands linked behind her back, Ceara rocked back on her heels with her nose held high. She kept her glacial gaze trained on Nevan, but he seemed to have retreated into the mire of his own memories.

I wanted to go to him but feared I'd be intruding. This was his wife, after all, and they were discussing their daughter. Their descendants. I couldn't fathom the span of time they'd both lived through, or the horrors they'd experienced.

Ceara sighed with exaggerated wistfulness. "The one who made me what I am was a master sorcerer, born of the fae but transmuted by his power into more than a solitary being. Shortly after my revival, when I was weak and confused and in terrible distress, he took pity on me and showed me Daráine. She never saw me or knew I had visited her."

I couldn't keep my mouth shut anymore. Nevan looked about to go catatonic, and I wanted some goddamn answers. Whatever Ceara wanted, it was more than to become queen of the sylphs. My gut told me everything about her indicated a calculating being who had plans. Big plans. For my honey.

Not on my watch, sister.

Stomping up to Nevan, I settled a hand on his shoulder. His usual heat had lessened into a warmth like that of a mortal body. Not good.

I cleared my throat, catching Ceara's attention. "What is it you want with us?"

She laughed softly, with no small measure of derision. "I want nothing from you, mortal. Tuathal is my husband. I hereby claim him and all rights inherent in our bond, sealed by handfasting."

"Five thousand years ago, when you were both mortals." I flapped a hand, as if might shoo her away. No such luck. "The forging changed you both. You can't hold him to a promise he made in another lifetime."

"Soul bonds are forever, child." She bared her teeth on the last word, a flash of white in the muted sunshine, then switched her focus to Nevan. "I will give you time to absorb all that I've told you. However, I shall not relinquish my claim. Not as long as I live, which will be for eternity."

Ceara vanished.

Chapter Four

Nevan and I faced each other—in silence, our gazes fused together—for a minute, maybe longer. Neither of us knew what to say. I sure as hell didn't, and based on his blank expression, he didn't either. He had a wife? From his mortal days?

And she'd come back for her husband.

Not quite right. She said she'd returned to take her "rightful" place as queen, which meant she'd come back for the power now bestowed on Nevan as king of the sylphs. But did she still love him? Had she ever loved him?

Did he love her?

"Talk to me," I said, my throat suddenly tight, my mouth parched. "Please, Nevan."

He covered his face with both hands, his muscular shoulders drooping.

The air around us grew colder and chilled the bare skin of my arms, exposed by my short-sleeve T-shirt. The cooling was distinctly unnatural. I had no idea if Nevan, as an air elemental, had the ability to alter the temperature in his vicinity, either by accident or on purpose. I did know he could create thunderstorms, so it seemed plausible he could affect the air temperature too.

Both of his hands swept up his face and through his longish hair, tousling the wavy, obsidian locks. Still slumped, he looked at me. "There is much to explain."

"No shit." Despite my harsh words, the bleakness in his eyes spurred me to take his face in my hands and feather my lips over his. "It's okay. Whatever it is, I can handle it."

What if he confesses his undying love for his eerie wife, can you handle it then?

My heart clenched, my chest ached. I'd have no choice but to deal with it. Though we'd known each other for six weeks, I couldn't imagine the rest of my life without Nevan.

"Not here," he said. "Never know when there may be prying eyes or ears about."

Yeah, like shapeshifting assassin-spies. Sure, Brennus the raven-man had become an uneasy ally in the wake of Skeiron's death, and the new guardian of the waterfall behind the shop, but I still preferred to steer clear of him. Brennus had slit my throat, though he'd done it because a bargain forced him to follow his master's orders. And his true master had been my ex-fiancé, Calder Blackwell, a newly forged elemental.

God, my life was so freaky these days.

Nevan gathered me into his arms and whisked us away. To the rest of the world, we would've appeared to vanish into thin air as we traversed a kind of interdimensional superhighway in the space of a millisecond. We emerged on the natural ledge of a red sandstone cliff some thirty feet high, alongside a waterfall that spilled down into a twenty-five-foot-deep pool. A wooden railing hemmed in the pool, with a quaint wooden bridge stretching across the far end of the little pond. My gaze wandered to the right, past the railing, to the small clearing where I'd first met Nevan. It felt like ages ago, so much had happened since that moment.

His arms still around me, Nevan leaped through the falls.

I gasped from the deluge of cold water that drenched us, soaking me to the skin and gluing my hair to my face. We whomped down inside the cave behind the cascade. Though the waterfall rumbled behind us, the magic invested within the cave muted the noise. The faint prickle of supernatural energy swept over my skin. I shivered from the mixture of cool, damp air in the cave and the cold water that had soaked me and my clothes.

Nevan released his hold on me, though he kept his body in contact with mine. He frisked his hands up and down the length of our bodies, his palms not quite touching me, and warm air rushed over us both. My clothes dried in an instant, my hair too. The droplets clinging to my skin evaporated. Nevan was dry as well, his hair restored to its perfect, wavy state with the locks kissing the shells of his ears.

I looped my arms around his neck and wound my fingers into the hair at his nape. "I appreciate the warm-up, honey."

He winced.

I'd started calling him honey a couple weeks ago, unconsciously at first, but his usual response was to smirk and kiss me senseless. Wincing seemed like a bad sign. If I'd said the dreaded T-word and thanked him, I might've understood his reaction. Though gratitude held no power in this world, he preferred I didn't say "please" or "thank you" at all. I needed to train myself to avoid incurring debts, he said.

Since I'd avoided the P – and T-words, why was he uncomfortable? Was he trying to figure out how to dump me graciously?

Ugh. I had to stop fixating on the worst-case scenarios. Nevan loved me, I knew it, he'd proved it to me over and over again. Still, I had good reasons for my angst about our relationship. My last boyfriend had turned into a monkey-man, framed me for murder twice, and sicked a raven-man on me to force me into accepting the forging. A girl had a right to some relationship paranoia after all that. The fact I'd met Nevan barely more than a month ago didn't soothe my innate tendency toward worrying. How much did I really know about the man whose bed I shared? The man to whom I'd gifted my heart and soul?

He'd told me everything about his past as an elemental. His mortal life remained a mystery, one he avoided talking about whenever I asked.

Nevan rotated us sideways to the falls and extended a hand toward the cave's back wall. With a flourish of his wrist, he accessed the veil between the worlds, between the land of mortals and the Unseen realm where elementals and gods reigned. The portal spun open to fill the rear of the cave. Its abyssal, inky blackness writhed with ribbons of red and purple.

Clutching me to him, Nevan leaped through the portal.

The instant we exited on the other side, he zipped us away. I had time only to glimpse the boulder that marked the portal on the Unseen side and the water burbling out of its top, tumbling down into a ten-foot-diameter pool. Next thing I knew, we stood at the base of a mountain sheathed in unnaturally green grass, surrounded by trees laden with moss instead of leaves. I bent my head back to gaze up at a swathe of the teal-colored sky. We were outside Nevan's home, his underground lair hidden inside the mountain and protected by magical wards that prevented anyone but him from entering.

No one else knew about his home. I could enter it only if he escorted me. He wanted me to live with him, but I couldn't get here without his assistance.

We poofed into his lair.

Nevan's arms fell away from me as he stepped back a few paces.

The air inside the chamber stayed a comfortable temperature for me, despite the fact his body temperature ran hotter than mine. I appreciated his thoughtful concession to my needs. Smooth walls carved out of the mountain's pale stone lightened the room, as did the gentle glow emanating from everywhere and nowhere. Chairs and tables sat here and there. At the far side of room, tucked into a cozy corner, hunkered the Nevan-size bed.

I'd spent countless hours in that bed, beneath the lush fur blanket, luxuriating in the afterglow of our love-making or simply relishing the serenity of lying in his arms. My body softened at the memories.

"You're smiling," he said, his brows crinkled.

"Am I?" Tearing my gaze away from the bed, I relinquished the memories and returned to the present. "Why didn't you tell me you had a wife?"

He ran a hand over his mouth, eyes averted. "It was a long time ago. I was, quite literally, a different person—a different being. The life I lived then became irrelevant the moment I underwent the forging, and I have spared no thought for it in many eons."

"But you had a wife and a daughter."

"They were lost to me after the forging." He began to pace, his posture tense, his focus somewhere else. "When the king, Notus, offered me immortality, he established a condition. I must never again have contact with my anyone from my old life, and I must never attempt to look in on them or visit the portion of the mortal realm where I had lived and died. The break must be clean, he said. I must commit to a new existence without looking back on my old one."

"But Ceara claims she was allowed to look back. She at least took a peek now and then, even if she didn't interact with anyone."

Nevan wheeled sideways in front of me. "Ceara was always stronger than I. She must have rejected the condition of no contact." He grimaced, fisting his hands. "I gave in to whatever requirements Notus demanded. Evading death was all that mattered to me."

"Stop it." I moved toward him and closed my hand around his bicep. Well, as much of his bicep as I could manage to grasp, given the extraordinary girth of his upper arm. "You were dying and Notus took advantage of that vulnerability. Besides, you have no idea what Ceara might've agreed to when somebody offered her the forging. You don't even know if what she's told you is true."

He shut his eyes. "Why would she deceive me? When I knew her, Ceara was a kind and loyal wife, a sweet girl."

"She's not a girl anymore. She's—" *An elemental bitch with a hidden agenda and designs on my man.* "She's different now. You told me the forging changes a person, and only someone with a strong will can survive it intact. That's why Calder came out wrong, because he wasn't as strong as you are. The weakness in his character meant the forging fractured him. Maybe the same thing has happened to Ceara."

"Perhaps." He sounded less than convinced.

Nevan had told me once the forging demanded a hefty price in blood and suffering. From what I'd gathered, the process of transforming a mortal into an elemental destroyed the human body at the molecular level and reshaped it into an altogether different form. Elementals considered pregnancy and childbirth to be unseemly. In Nevan's words, they connived to increase their numbers by preying on the fear of death to trick mortals into undergoing the forging.

But a weak human soul made for a twisted elemental being.

Case in point: My ex-honey, Calder Blackwell.

"Either way," I said, "Ceara's not the girl you knew."

He sighed, his entire body seeming to deflate. "But she is still my wife."

"Is she?" I crossed in front of him. "You both died thousands of years ago. The man and woman who married are long gone."

He still wouldn't look at me.

I cradled his face in my hands once again, hoisting up onto my toes to draw his attention to me. I spoke only when his eyes, swirling with hazy colors, zeroed in on mine.

"You said yourself everything from your first life is irrelevant. I heard what you didn't say, though. Your old life isn't irrelevant because it meant nothing to you, it's irrelevant because you are a different man." I locked my arms around his neck to lift myself higher, our lips a breath apart and our eyes level. "No one can hold you to a marriage vow you made in another life, because that man wasn't you."

Praying I was right and not merely desperate to eradicate the competition, I waited for his response. Seconds ticked by, counted on the metronome of my heart as he stared into my eyes, transfixed by thoughts I couldn't comprehend.

His arms came around me, tugging me tight against his firm body, the sizzling heat of his skin warming me.

"Lindsey, my love," he said in that rumbly, sexy tone he'd perfected, "you amaze me at every turn. Your strength and determination remind me of why I love you so deeply."

His words dissolved me and, eyes half closed, I inhaled the earthy scent of him. "I love you too. No matter what."

"You are a miracle." He flattened his palms on my back and crushed me to him, his mouth devouring mine, our tongues lashing and coiling around each other. The flavor of him, sweet and spicy and all Nevan, suffused my being like a magic spell, enchanting me like nothing else on earth could. The world spiraled away from us, as if we hovered inside our own bubble of reality. Pleasure rippled through me, hot and tempting, urging me to take more, give more, and never stop until we were naked and entwined in the fur blanket of his bed enjoying post-coital bliss.

Nevan severed the kiss, breathing hard. The vibrant colors of his eyes had flared to life again, a kaleidoscope of fire and molten metal.

Breathless, I could do nothing except gaze at him with shameless adoration. He had that effect on me every time he kissed me. What thrilled me most, though, was realizing I had the same effect on him.

I combed my fingers through his hair, loving the silky softness against my skin. "You know how much you mean to me, Nevan. I want to be with you and only you forever. But the only way this will work is if we're honest with each other, all the way. I've told you everything about my life, even the embarrassing stuff and the painful things I'd rather forget. I need the same from you."

He rested his forehead on mine, eyes closed. "You want to know about my mortal life."

"Yes." I let myself sink into the intimacy of the moment, the incredible bond I shared with him, one borne of love and passion and trust. "It's important because I want to understand you, but also because your former wife is butting into our lives. Do you think she can really make a claim? I mean, would the tribunal listen to her and—" I bit down on my bottom lip, raised my head, and dared to ask. "Do you think there's a chance they'll order you to take her as your queen?"

"I am king." He straightened, his jaw set. "They will not command me."

"You're king because they made you king after Skeiron was destroyed. What if they…I don't know, coerced you into a bargain with some kind of leverage as bait."

"Leverage?" He drew his head back, squinting at me. "You think they might use you as leverage to force me into a bargain, one in which I take Ceara as my queen."

"You can't tell me they aren't capable of doing something like that. The dirty bastards won't even let me into their powwows with you. They've refused to even meet me." I slid my hands down to his chest, my fingers crooking into his skin, and studied the lines of his muscles. "They'll never accept me, a puny mortal, as your…consort. I'm sure they'd jump at the chance to have an elemental woman on the throne."

He kissed the tip of my nose, his lips curving in a sweet smile. "You are many things, darlin', but puny is not one of them."

"Most folks in the Unseen think mortals are weak and useless."

Nevan crooked a finger under my chin and tipped my face up to his. "When I take a queen, it will be you. The tribunal will either accept you or suffer my wrath."

I'd witnessed firsthand what his wrath could do, but a simple fact remained. "You aren't as powerful as Notus or Skeiron. They ruthlessly pursued power at any cost and amassed enough to keep anyone from trying to oust them."

His mouth compressed into a line. "You believe me too ineffectual to rule."

"No, of course not." Groaning, I let my head fall onto his chest. "I'm saying this all wrong. What I mean is, they don't fear you the way they feared Skeiron, and Notus before him."

"If they try to keep me from you," he said, his voice tough as steel, "they will fear what I will rain down upon them. Heads will roll, in the most literal and graphic manner."

Craning my neck back, I rested my chin on his chest and smiled up at the man I adored. His threats of violence on my behalf never failed to give me a warm, fuzzy feeling. "Aw, honey, you always say the sweetest things."

"No one takes you from me. No one."

"Same goes for you. Any elemental hussy who tries to steal my man has a bloody fight on her hands."

A grin, slow and heated, spread across his face. "I do love your bloodthirsty side."

I laid my cheek on his chest, relishing the warmth and comfort of him even as an idea sparked in my mind. "Do you still glamour? I only saw you do it once, when we first met. It's still one of your powers, right?"

"It is. But I have no desire to utilize it. After a century of deceiving mortal women by disguising my appearance, I've had my fill of glamouring."

Yeah, I could understand that. Still, my curiosity about his past got the better of me. "Show me what you looked like as a mortal."

With a restraint that surprised even me, I kept from saying "please."

He cringed away from me, backing up a few paces, his gaze on the floor and his features slack. "You don't want to see it. I was not the man I am now, and the past matters nothing to our future."

"Beg to differ." I moved toward him but halted a couple feet away. "Total honesty, Nevan. I told you we both need that for this to work between us. Honesty means total trust too, and if you can't trust me to see the old, mortal you without judging—"

"I trust you." He cupped his hands around my upper arms, stroking up and down. "In every way, I trust you. But my human life—"

"Is a part of who you are today, whether you want to admit it or not. You're a different man since the forging, but your previous life influenced who you became after the transition. To have a future with you, I need to understand your past." I sidled up to him, snuggling into the hollow of his shoulder. "Don't make me say the P-word."

He groaned with resignation, his body slouching against me, then pushed away and adopted a regal, erect posture. His image shimmered and shifted, but I realized this was just a facade, not a genuine transmutation. Glamour allowed him to assume a different appearance without altering his actual form. I watched with amazement as his bronzed skin grew paler and his body adjusted to a new—or rather, old—version of him.

The mountainous muscles that made him an impressive and striking figure had shrunk to a more subdued kind of buffness, akin to an average Joe who earned his muscles through hard labor rather than gym workouts. He seemed shorter too, by maybe a few inches. His hair had become longer, dulling from its usual glistening onyx to a dark brown and losing most of its waviness.

And his eyes. The churning, metallic hues had vanished, replaced by a hazel shade that was striking but not as arresting as his normal colors.

I angled my head side to side, examining this alternate version of him. After a moment, I strolled up to him, hooked my arms around his neck, and kissed him thoroughly. Though he tried to remain stock-still and unaffected, he couldn't resist giving in to the demands of my lips and tongue. The kiss was slow and hot, charged with every emotion we harbored for each other and with the passionate devotion and scorching desire we shared.

When we uncoupled our lips, I gazed up at him with all the ardor he inspired in me, as entranced by the mortal Nevan as I was by the immortal sylph. "I love every version of you. I love what's inside you, your heart and your passion, and your determination to always do the right thing. I love your heroic side, your tender side, even your insecure side. The whole package. That's the real you, the rest is just wrapping paper."

Right there in my arms, he morphed back to his usual self.

"Wrapping paper?" he said with a smirk.

"You know what I mean."

"Indeed I do." He slanted his head closer to mine, his pupils large and his lips parted in disbelief. "No one has ever seen all of me and accepted it. But you accept me no matter what, and I love you all the more for that."

I placed my cheek on his chest. "You don't have to be afraid to share your past with me."

"I realize that now, and I cannot believe I ever doubted it." He caressed my hair, his thumb grazing my cheek. "You worry about the robed man and the girl he harmed, don't you?"

Unwilling to peel my cheek away from his skin, I splayed a hand over his chest "There's Ceara too. All of this is beginning to feel like a replay of six weeks ago, like somebody wants to drive me crazy again the way Calder tried to do."

"They may try, but you are far too strong to crumble."

"I'm scared, Nevan. This all feels much worse than what happened before, when Skeiron was hunting for the Janusite—for me. You're king, but the tribunal doesn't trust you. Somebody sent an abused girl to deliver a message I don't understand. Your dead wife shows up not dead but immortal and scheming to be your queen." I listened to his heart beating, the sound so close to my ear it felt like our bodies had melded. "I can tell you're more worried than you let on."

"There is reason for concern, but I will never let any harm come to you as long as I am alive and able to prevent it."

"I know." I pushed away from him, though his hands lingered on my waist. "But it's time, Nevan. I need to know about your past. Your human past."

He nodded grimly. "Perhaps I should start with end. The battle that altered my fate."

"Okay." I tromped over to the nearest chair, one fashioned from a honey-colored wood, and settled my behind onto the plush cushioning of the seat. The chair dwarfed me, since it was sized for Nevan. An odd anticipation zinged through me, along with an icy current of dread. He was about to reveal all to me and I wasn't positive I'd wanted to hear it. His reluctance to tell me made me wonder what awaited.

Nevan lowered his big body onto the chair beside mine. His arms went slack, his hands dropped onto his lap. "My people, the Partholonians, had lived in peace for many years, keeping to ourselves and away from other tribes. One day, a clan from far away landed on our shores and set to destroying us. The Fomorians cared for nothing but conquest. We stood no chance against them, with their overwhelming numbers, but we had no choice except to fight."

He leaned his head against the chair's back, his gaze directed at the ceiling. I wanted to take his hand in mine, to offer comfort, but understood this wasn't the time.

"When the alarm call was sounded," he continued, "the enemy had already breached the outer regions of our lands. All the men, including myself, rallied to defend our village. I believed my wife and daughter would be safest in our home, and so I left them there alone. Ceara is right, I abandoned my family."

I could keep silent no longer. Folding my hand over his on the arm of his chair, I leaned toward him and spoke with quiet determination. "I know you like to blame yourself for anything bad that happens, but sometimes bad things just are. We can't stop them no matter how hard we try. You did the best you could under the circumstances and if that b—" I caught myself before I called her a bitch. The woman gave me a serious case of the heebie-jeebies and I didn't trust her, but name-calling wouldn't help Nevan. All I cared about in this moment was protecting him. "If Ceara really cared about you, she wouldn't be packing your bags for a round-the-world guilt trip. Please don't see her again while you're feeling this way. It could be dangerous."

Without moving his head, he glanced my way. "You believe Ceara has ill intentions."

"Don't know. And neither do you." I squeezed his hand. "All I'm saying is be careful. When you do see her, make damn sure you don't get guilted into a bargain or debt."

He drummed the fingers of his other hand. "I have been dealing with magical bargains and debts since before your civilization existed. Never have I accidentally indebted myself or stumbled into a disadvantageous bargain."

"Except with Skeiron."

A dark look overtook his features. He glared straight ahead into empty space for a moment before he launched out of his chair. "That was different."

"Right." I rose too, moving in front of him. "Skeiron pushed you into a crummy deal by using your guilt over sleeping with his daughter against you. He threatened to murder her unless you did exactly what he wanted. How did that turn out for you?" I raised my eyebrows. "Oh yeah, you were enslaved for a century, forced to hunt down mortal women who had a 'touch' of the Unseen in them, and take them straight to Skeiron. You still have no clue what he did to those women before he sent them home, rejected because they didn't have the Janusite power."

Nevan scratched the back of his neck, his face pinched.

I was right, and he knew it. Being right failed to make me feel better, though, because it meant he was in danger if—when—he met with

Ceara. I realized I couldn't stop him from seeing her, but I wished to hell I could convince him of the risk.

Grasping his hands in mine, I held them to my chest. "I'm begging you, Nevan, be careful. Better yet, let me go with you when you see her."

To my surprise, he nodded. "Yes, you should accompany me. We share our lives, which means what affects me affects you as well."

"Yes, it does." I let go of his hands and draped my arms around his waist. "Nobody messes with my boyfriend."

Folding his arms around me, he teased my lips with his own. "Anyone who attempts to disunite us will pray for death."

"I love your bloodthirsty side too. It's oddly hot."

He took my bottom lip between both of his, releasing it little by little. "Remain here while I conduct an errand. I'll return swiftly, you have my word."

"Where are you going?"

"I've procured a surprise for you, but I must retrieve it." He glided his hands up and down my back, his fingers spread wide. "Two surprises, in fact."

"Mm, I love presents." I dragged my lips across the scar over his heart, flicking my tongue out to sample his skin. "But right now, I want something else more."

He slid his hands onto my ass, cupping both cheeks. "Wait for me in bed, love."

A sudden draft whispered over my skin from head to toe. I grinned, knowing without looking that he'd vanished my clothes. My bare nipples scraped on his chest and went rigid from the sensation of his velvety flesh on mine. His strong hands squeezed my behind. I almost moaned from the bliss of skin-on-skin contact.

His loincloth in place, he stepped back and went still, the precursor to his poofing away. Before he winked out, though, he hit me with his most sensual smile. "In bed, love."

The second he disappeared, I padded over to the bed. Slipping under the fur blanket, I imagined all the wonderful, erotic things we'd do together as soon as he returned. Visions blazed in my mind, of a nude Nevan on top of me, his hands everywhere, his mouth licking and nibbling wherever he could find a sensitive spot to tease.

Minutes ticked by. Lots of minutes.

The lovely state of arousal I'd reveled in began to wane, replaced by a gnawing pain in my gut. I climbed out of bed and found my clothes neatly folded and stacked in a corner, the same place Nevan always stashed my clothes when he blipped them away for me. Because I didn't have my purse with me, I couldn't check the time on its clock, so I had no way to gauge how much time had passed since he left. It felt like hours.

After dressing, I could do nothing more than pace the room, pop into the adjacent kitchen now and then, and wait. I paced until my legs ached and my eyes felt gritty, until my yawns became frequent and my eyelids grew heavy. Finally, I lay down on the bed on top of the blanket, with my clothes and boots on, too exhausted to stay awake any longer.

I spiraled down, down, down into a restless sleep.

Chapter Five

Sometime later, I woke to a fluttery sensation of feather-light kisses on my neck. Before I opened my eyes, I sensed Nevan's presence. Sure, he was the only being permitted through the lair's wards, but if we'd been at my apartment I would've recognized his approach all the same. From the day we met, I'd been able to sense him before he even appeared in front of me.

Driven by instinct, I thrust my hand into his hair and moaned my appreciation as he licked his way up my throat and over my chin. When he paused there, I made a disappointed noise.

"Soon, love," he murmured, his breaths tickling my lips. "But first, I have your surprises."

The haze of sleep evaporated as I recalled how long I'd waited for him to come back to me. I pushed up onto my elbows. "Where have you been? I was worried sick. Not to mention trapped in your lair."

"Our lair." Nevan straightened. His legs hung over the bed's edge with his hips alongside mine. He swept an errant lock of hair from my face. "I was unavoidably detained. I had no desire to cause you stress, please forgive me."

His use of the P-word zinged a magical current through me, faint but detectable, the unmistakable portent of a debt on the verge of being sealed.

I sat up, searching his face for some clue to his behavior. "You said the P-word. You never, ever say that. What's wrong?"

"Nothing." He hesitated, his expression unreadable, but then he smiled and chucked me under the chin. "The fae witch who helped me with your surprise took a bit longer than expected to finish the task."

"You said you had to retrieve my presents." The sharp tang of anxiety infiltrated my mouth, and I gripped the fur blanket. "Now you're saying you had to get them made. Why do I feel like you're hiding something? You never lie. Not to me."

"I am not lying. I believed your surprise would be ready when I met with the fae witch, but she informed me the magic involved was more complex than anticipated. Since I very much wanted to give you the gifts tonight, I decided to wait for her to finish."

His explanation made sense, and combined with his earnest expression, it eased my anxiety somewhat. Nevan would not lie to me, not willingly. He had disappeared for a long time, though. With Ceara out there, intent on becoming his queen, I had to wonder if she might've gotten to him. Tricked him. Guilted him into a bargain.

Nevan reached down to the floor, producing two wooden boxes, each fashioned from a rich, golden wood and engraved with ornate, decorative figures. He offered me the larger box.

I needed both hands to hold it. A small gold latch fastened the lid shut.

"This," he said, "should ease your worries about your safety."

My safety? I was freaked about *his* well-being. Still, I smiled and unhooked the latch, swinging the lid up to reveal…"Is this my gun? It looks like it."

Inside the box, nestled on a red velvet cushion, lay a Bond Arms Mini derringer. The tiny gun seemed even smaller in the large box, but the container also held two boxes of ammo.

"Not your gun," Nevan said, "but an identical weapon. I asked your mother where I might obtain such a firearm and she directed me to a website." He enunciated the word like a man who'd never seen a computer, much less visited a website. Which he was. "I asked if she might help me purchase the weapon. She did, and I had it endued."

"Endued?" I couldn't suppress the wonder that infused my voice. An endued weapon was imbued with powerful magic that enabled it to kill an immortal being. Nevan had acquired a new endued sword a few weeks ago, to replace the one he'd appropriated from Skeiron. Keeping the black sword of the man who'd enslaved him had been too weird for Nevan. He needed an endued weapon, though, to protect himself from whatever threats might crop up.

Now I had an endued handgun.

God, I loved this man.

Nevan picked up one of the ammo boxes. "I also had the witch endue the ammunition for your weapon, both the smaller ones and the large cartridges."

My mouth probably fell open as I ran my fingers over the box of shotgun shells. Nevan held a box of .357 rounds. The interchangeable barrels on the derringer allowed me to load either type of ammo.

And that's when I spotted the other barrel tucked behind the gun, the barrel sized for shotgun shells. I touched the metal. "Is this endued too?"

"Naturally."

I flung my arms around his neck and showered his face with kisses. "I love my present. I love it, I love it, I love it."

He chuckled softly. "I'm pleased you're pleased, darlin'. But I've got something even more important to give ye."

"Better than my very own endued weapon?" I sat back and rubbed my palms together. "Gimme, gimme."

"You are utterly adorable when you're excited this way." He handed me the other box, slanting toward me to murmur, "Though I look forward to exciting you in other ways."

Desire arced through me like electricity, triggering a dampness between my thighs, but nothing could distract me from my second present. I popped the little gold latch on the palm-size box and flipped it open. Inside, nestled on a crimson cushion identical to the one in the gun's box, lay a small, cream-colored stone.

"Pick it up," Nevan said, his voice deep and sultry. "You'll enjoy the sensation."

I plucked the stone from the box, cradling it in my palm. The stone warmed my skin, sending a pleasant tingle through my hand and out into my body. The tingling suffused me with a familiar, arousing sensation.

He cocked his head, his expression expectant. "Do you feel it yet?"

The warmth the stone conferred swelled into a rush of intoxicating heat.

Sucking in a shaky breath, I eyed Nevan. "It feels like…you."

"Because it is me." He surrounded my hand with his and eased my fingers closed around the stone, sealing it in my palm. "This is a soul stone."

"Which means?"

"Soul stones are indigenous to the Unseen realm. For one who knows how to tap into them, they absorb a piece of that individual's magical and spiritual essence—their soul—which may then be transferred into the recipient. It's considered a priceless gift."

I held a piece of his soul in my hand? The intimacy of his gift startled me. I must've looked it too, because he turned his face away.

"If you're offended by the stone," he said, "I will understand."

Offended? Hell, I had half a mind to sleep with the blasted thing duct-taped to my, um…chest. Yeah. My chest.

Not that I was going to do it.

Since his hand still enveloped mine, I laid my other hand atop his. "I love your gift."

"There is more to it." He gazed into my eyes, his aflame with brilliant colors. "I could have conferred my essence into the stone myself, but I required the help of a fae witch to bespell it with the appropriate magic."

"Appropriate for what?"

"To grant you access to our home. The soul stone also will open a hidden doorway so you may breach the wards and enter this place." He brushed the backs of his fingers up and down my cheek. "I want you to feel this is our home, not mine. With the stone, you may come and go as you please."

"It's a key to your place? I'd offer you a key to my place, but you zip in and out whenever you like."

"With your permission. And thanks to your powers, which let me cross boundaries as long you are in the mortal realm."

"Of course." I plucked at the hairs of the furry blanket. "Um, what happens if I accidentally misplace the soul stone? Could someone else take a piece of your soul?"

"You never do cease worrying, love." He pecked a kiss on my lips. "The stone is attuned to you. If anyone else should touch it, they would feel nothing."

I exhaled a relieved breath. "Good. Can I give you one of these soul stones?"

"I don't know if a mortal soul could interact with one of these stones. They are designed to work for elementals, not humans, and our souls are far more potent and rich with innate magic." He slipped an arm around my waist and pulled me into him, vanishing our clothes at the same instant. "Besides, I need no magic to feel the essence of you. Our souls merge every time we make love. I know you feel it, my sweet, mortal soul mate."

Oh yes, I felt it. The intense pleasure of our love-making generated more than mind-blowing orgasms, it also fueled a connection beyond anything I could've imagined might exist before we found each other.

His exact words finally hit me, and my breath hitched. "Did—did you call me your soul mate?"

"Naturally."

"You've never said that before. Do you mean it literally, or is that another endearment?" My heart began to race and my head grew light, as if the fate of universe depended on his answer.

His smile was tender and the tiniest bit sad. "I mean it, Lindsey. Why else would I gift you with a fragment of my soul? It's because you already possess all of mine."

I couldn't catch my breath. No one had ever expressed to me a sentiment anywhere near the depth of what he'd confessed. "My soul is yours too. A couple months ago, I didn't believe in soul mates or magic, but now I understand all of it exists. What we have, it's real and powerful and forever."

He scooped me up and lay me down on my back atop the blanket, covering my body with his. "At last you see, we belong to each other and no one may break the bond. Not the tribunal and not Ceara."

"I know you mean that." I chewed the inside of my cheek. "But something will come between us. I'm not immortal. You'll be forced to watch me slowly wither and die."

Lines etched across his forehead. "Why should I think of that? I will take whatever time I have with you."

"And then what? I'll be gone, but you'll live forever."

"What precisely are you trying to say?"

I shrugged, as much as I could with him on top of me. "Maybe the tribunal has good reason to disapprove of our relationship. I know how I felt when you almost died. Maybe it's selfish of me to hold onto you, knowing how devastated you'll be when I die. And I will die. That's kind of the defining trait of mortals."

He raised onto his elbows, gazing down at me with confusion. "Do you believe I will abandon you when you begin to age?"

"No, I'm positive you'll stick it out no matter what." My mind traveled back to the moment when he lay half dead before me, his chest punctured by Skeiron's endued sword, blood pouring from the wound. Tears pricked at the backs of my eyes. I blinked them away, a sudden ache burning in the back of my throat. "I'm not sure you should stay with me. Loving me will only cause you pain in the end, and I never want to be the source of your suffering."

"You could never be the source of pain for me." He bracketed my face with his hands, his thumbs resting on the corners of my mouth. "If losing you one day is the cost of loving you, then I will pay it gladly."

"It has to be tempting, though, what with your wife alive and immortal."

"What do you mean?"

"She can offer you something I can't. Eternity."

His expression hardened. "There is no temptation. I will take a lifetime—a mortal lifetime—with you over eternity with anyone else. You are my soul mate."

My heart swelled, even as my fingers went cold. In a small voice, I asked, "Did you love Ceara?"

"Until you, I had loved none but my mother and father, and they died so long ago I could scarcely recall the feeling." He his mouth twisted into a rueful smirk. "Some would've said I loved myself with unwavering commitment."

I made a rude noise. "You are not egotistical."

"Your faith in me is heartening, but I haven't answered your question yet." His focus drifted away from my face. "It was an arranged marriage, entered into according to the customs of my people. Ceara and I did not love each other, though we achieved a kind of awkward friendship."

"Obviously, you had sex with her."

"Three times only. As soon as she became with child, Ceara told me she would not engage in carnal relations again, that she did not enjoy the act the way a wife should, and she deeply regretted her shortfall. I assured her she owed me no further...interactions. I would not force my attentions on her."

"You were celibate after that, weren't you? I mean, you're not the type to screw around on your wife, even if you didn't love her."

A ghost of a smile curved his lips. "You truly do understand me."

"Well, we are soul mates." I walked my fingers down his naked chest, inch by inch, ever nearer to his groin. "After your forging, you didn't exactly abstain anymore, did you?"

"You already know this. I've told you I…dallied a great deal."

"Until you slept with Skeiron's daughter, and he found out. Yeah, I know the story. Thanks to the crazy king and his nasty bargain, you were enslaved for a century."

Nevan bent to rub his lips across mine once, twice, three times, before he murmured against my lips, "You freed me, my love, and I will never stop showing you how grateful I am."

"You freed me too, honey." I glided my hand down the length of his growing erection, curling my fingers around its rigid girth. "Let me express my gratitude."

I captured his lower lip between my teeth, sucking it into my mouth, while I pumped my hand up and down the sleek flesh of his cock. He hissed in a breath, his back arching. While I released his lip slowly, I grasped the nape of his neck to pull him in for a kiss. He devoured me with deep, lush strokes of his tongue and groaned into my mouth as I milked his erection.

He broke the kiss and locked his hand around my wrist to halt my intimate massage. "You first."

"Mm, I want you to pop your cork first this time."

With a gentleness that seemed incongruous with the heated tension in his body, he lifted one of my hands to entwine our fingers and press my hand into the plush blanket. "In my entire existence, I have loved only one woman and I intend to prove it to you every single time I thrust into your sweet body. That is why your pleasure always comes first."

I undulated my hips, grazing his swollen shaft. "When you put it that way…"

He showered my throat with light kisses, working his way down my chest toward my belly, his hands sliding down my arms with aching slowness. Every cell in my body tingled with anticipation. My back bowed up as he kissed and licked his way down my belly, inching ever closer to the hairs at the apex of my thighs.

"Oh Nevan," I moaned and rocked my hips toward his waiting mouth. "I've never loved anyone but you, and I never will. But God, right now all I want is you inside me."

"Easy, love." I felt his lips tighten against my skin, a sure sign he was smirking. "I see I still must teach you patience."

"Some other time. Right now, just—" I lost my voice, my breath stolen by the sensation of his lips edging nearer to where I most needed them.

Nevan froze. "Bloody hell."

He spat the curse, hoisting himself up on his arms, his face wrenched into a scowl.

"Oh no," I said, shaking my head, "don't tell me—"

"The tribunal is summoning me."

"Can't you ignore them?"

He rolled to the side, his legs swinging off the bed to touch down on the floor. With his back to me, shoulders slumped forward, he let out the most frustrated sigh I'd ever heard. "They won't stop calling until I go to them."

I elevated myself on my elbows. "Please tell me they can't see what we were doing."

Nevan rose to his feet, the loincloth materializing around his hips. "They cannot see where I am or what I am doing."

"Thank heaven for small mercies." I swung my legs off the bed, but they dangled several inches above the floor. "I really don't want elemental perverts getting their rocks off by peeping on us."

"I do love your colorful language." Nevan's smile, though closed mouth, brightened his face and carved out cute little divots in his cheeks. He bent over to kiss my forehead. "Wait here if you like, or return to your home and I will find you there once the meeting is over."

"What do you think they want? Considering your wife turned up today…"

"You believe the tribunal wants to speak with me about her." He scratched his head. "Perhaps they do, I have no idea."

"Take me with you."

"Lindsey."

I tilted my head back to meet his gaze and raised my eyebrows. "Don't *Lindsey* me. If your formerly dead wife is involved, I should be there."

"The tribunal will not admit you into their chambers, and I will not abandon you in the woods." He knelt in front of me and clasped my hands in his. "I will come back to you as soon as the meeting is over. Trust me to handle whatever matters might arise."

How could I say no to that? I trusted him with all my heart and soul, but I also understood the power of his guilt. It had gotten him enslaved once before. Still, I had to trust he wouldn't make the same mistake again. "Okay. Go to your meeting and come find me after. Think I'll head home and see what time it is in the mortal realm, in case I'm late to work or something."

Time could pass differently here in the Unseen, though I'd experienced the phenomenon only once. On that occasion, three hours had elapsed while I thought it had been half an hour.

"Before I go," he said, "let's make certain the soul stone works."

"Good idea."

He grasped me around the waist and hoisted me off the bed onto my feet. My clothes materialized around me, wrinkle free and perfectly positioned. I did note my T-shirt had wound up pulled lower in the front to expose more of my cleavage. Ah, my Nevan. He just couldn't help himself.

I extricated the soul stone from my jeans pocket. "What do I do?"

"Approach the outer wall." He gestured toward the smooth-hewn rock behind him. "Then simply instruct the stone to open a doorway."

"Instruct it?" Rolling the stone in my palm, I trudged to the wall. Instruct the stone. Sure, I could do that. I raised my hand, palm up, the stone cradled there. "Open a doorway, little soul stone."

Nothing happened.

He grinned and chuckled at my attempt. "Not like that, darlin'. Use magic to command the stone."

"Terrific." I let my head fall back and gave a piteous moan. "Magic hates me. It'll never work when I want it to."

"On the contrary." Nevan strode up behind me, encircling my waist with his arms, dipping his mouth close to my ear. "Magic adores you, and like me, it cannot resist your desires."

"Mm." I couldn't think of anything coherent to say, not with him teasing my senses with every whisper of his breath on my ear.

His fingers fanned out over my belly, tugging my backside into his front side. "You tap into the magic with so little effort, without intending to. It bends to your will, shifts and reshapes itself to ensure your happiness. When I was enslaved to Skeiron, you gave me the power to disobey him. Time itself loses its way around you, as enchanted by you as I have always been."

I covered his hands with my own, relishing the feel of his muscular form molded to my willing flesh. "If this is your plan, it's got a flaw."

"What is that?" he asked, licking at my earlobe.

"If I have to get turned on in order to use my powers, I'll be screwed when you're not around to get me hot."

"You've got it backward, darlin'." He fitted his mouth over the hollow my throat for a wet kiss. "The screwing happens when I'm here."

He stepped away, robbing me of his heat and tempting muscles.

I closed my hand around the soul stone and focused all my mental capacity on one command. "Open sesame."

Blue magic glittered in the air before the wall, spinning in iridescent whorls. The rock blurred and rippled, then poof, a me-size hole appeared. Beyond the opening, I spied the woods that surrounded the mountain.

I tossed the soul stone in the air and caught it in my palm, quite pleased with myself. I'd tapped into the magic at will—and not out of desperation because I was dying from a slit throat. Not this time, anyway.

Scrutinizing the opening, I said, "I thought we were deeper inside the mountain, but we're only a foot in."

"Have you not yet learned to take very little at face value?" Nevan pointed at the doorway, and in a patient tone said, "You compressed the distance."

"I did?" Tilting my head to the side, I eyed the doorway. "Cool."

We walked outside hand in hand, and the doorway telescoped shut behind us. Nevan hauled me into his arms, zipping us to the boulder that marked the portal. Nevan waved a hand to open the doorway to the other side.

"I will return to you," he said, "that is a p—it is the truth."

He'd almost promised it, a big no-no here in the Unseen, far too close to a debt. Though he had no qualms about indebting himself to me, he knew the idea made me uncomfortable. Once, he'd sealed a debt to me on purpose—but only to give me leverage to undermine Skeiron's hold over him.

"I'll be waiting for you," I said.

"And worrying, no doubt."

"Yeah, probably." I hunched my shoulders, feeling sheepish all of a sudden. "I can't help it. Worrying is my thing."

Nevan kissed each of my hands in turn, then let go of them and stepped away from me. "All will be well, my sweet love. Trust me on this. Now, through the portal with you."

I turned and crossed the veil between the worlds. Just as the portal began to telescope shut, I glanced back.

Nevan winked at me and vanished.

The portal spiraled shut.

I was left with a hollow ache in my chest and the niggling sensation I'd overlooked a vital clue somewhere in the course of this day. Nevan would be careful. But if Ceara played the guilt card, would he call her bluff or fold?

Please stay strong, Nevan.

Chapter Six

I DISCOVERED IT WAS THREE A.M. IN THE MORTAL WORLD, PROBABLY thanks to the way my powers screwed with time in the Unseen, making it move slower. The phenomenon hadn't happened in weeks, but the stress of today must've triggered a recurrence.

Since I had no idea when Nevan might return, I changed into my nightie and curled up under the sheets of my very ordinary bed in my very ordinary apartment. My next-door neighbor snored like a rusty chainsaw, the noise vibrating through the walls. But it wasn't the snoring that had me tossing and turning, getting tangled in the sheets in a totally non-sexy way. Anxieties about Nevan, the tribunal, the kidnapped girl, and everything else about my bizarre life bounced around in my brain pinball-style.

For hours, I struggled to sleep. The best I could manage was a fitful doze.

After an oh-so-refreshing forty-five minutes of naptime, I downed a bowl of cereal and drove to work, shambling into the rock shop while stifling a yawn. Stan, my boss, squinted at me but made no comment on my state. My clothes were clean and fresh, though I felt nothing close to cleansed or freshened. My new, endued derringer nestled against my hip, tucked in its waistband holster and loaded with my spiffy endued ammo. Today, I'd opted for .357 rounds.

The morning dragged by like pine sap in winter. Despite cradling the soul stone in my hand every fifteen minutes, the reassuring sensation of Nevan's peaceful essence failed to reassure me. I hadn't thought to ask if the stone offered a real-time glimpse of his well-being, or if it was a one-time snapshot. The thing was designed to get me into his home, not to connect us across time and space. Or that's what I thought. He hadn't mentioned any other capabilities of the stone. Next time I saw him, I'd ask.

If I saw him.

Dammit, I would. The tribunal could be real asses, as far as I could tell, demanding an enormous amount of Nevan's time. He was king, for crying out loud. They should bow down to him, not the other way around.

Nevan would give them a good dressing-down, for sure.

I skipped lunch, ignoring Stan's insistence that I needed to eat or I'd pass out—and then I'd be no good as an employee. These days, I understood his gruffness covered up the fondness he had for me, which he was too macho to admit. I'd grown rather fond of him too. Watching the guy battle immortal sylphs had given me a new perspective on Stan Lagorio.

Just past two in the afternoon, Travis showed up to update me on Megan's condition.

"She's okay," he said, leaning one hip against the checkout counter across from me. "Physically, anyhow. The bruises are old and pretty minor. She's got no internal injuries, but the docs can't say how she got so severely dehydrated. And the poor kid won't say a word about the bruises, panics if anyone asks."

"Is the hospital outside the boundaries?"

He screwed up his mouth, fidgeting. "As far as I can tell, the hospital's safe."

"Thank goodness for that."

"She wants to talk to you."

I paused in sorting through a stack of receipts. "Me specifically?"

"Ain't that what I said? Kid says she wants to talk to Lindsey Astrid Porter." He eyed me sideways. "You know this Megan girl?"

"No, of course not."

"Well," Travis said, gesturing toward the shop's entrance, "let's find out what she knows."

"Right now? I'm in the middle of my shift."

"I'll tell Stan it's official police business."

"Oh great." I let my head fall back, staring up at the bare rafters below the corrugated metal ceiling. "Just what I need, my boss thinking I'm a suspect in a crime—again."

"Relax, I'll make sure he knows it's nothing like that."

He marched straight to the door to Stan's office and, without knocking, strode inside. His presumptuous actions irritated me, but my brain had no room for it. I was too consumed with thoughts of what happened to Megan and who had sent her to me, not to mention why.

Travis traipsed out of Stan's office. "All fixed up. Let's go."

I snagged my purse and followed him out the door.

We had reached his vehicle, a Ford Expedition emblazoned with the logo of the sheriff's department, when Travis's phone warbled. He held up a finger in a silent request for me to wait, as he answered the call. His features shifted into stoic cop mode.

I leaned my back against the vehicle and rested my head on its hard metal. The morning sun unfurled streamers of pink and orange across the blue sky, igniting a smattering of puffy little clouds.

Something flickered on Travis's face, something like surprise mixed with anxiety. He resumed cop mode, though, and walked away from me to continue the conversation out of my earshot.

A moment later, he strode back to me. "Megan's gone."

I jerked upright, slammed with a wave of cold. "How?"

"You tell me." He pinched the bridge of his nose, eyes crimped shut. "I had a deputy posted outside her room, and the windows inside don't open. Another deputy was posted in the parking lot, in clear view of those windows. Nobody saw or heard a damn thing."

My blood seemed to have iced over, chilling me from my skin down to bones.

Travis flung hand up and then let it fall slack at his side. "She disappeared into thin air."

"We both know what this means."

"But there ain't no water near the hospital."

"Are you sure?" I stepped up to him, my head craned back to look him in the eye. "I thought my brother was safe, but Skeiron found a hidden spring that let him sneak into the mortal world and abduct Ash. The man in black must've found a similar opening. Any natural water feature, no matter how small, can serve as a portal between the worlds."

"Dammit!" He punched his fist into the Expedition's hood. Wincing, he cradled his hand. "I fucked it up again, didn't I?"

"Not your fault."

He scowled at the small dent he'd left in the vehicle's hood. "Doesn't matter whose fault it is. The girl's gone."

Taken by an unknown enemy, for unknown reasons. Yet Megan had told me herself this was all connected to me. She resembled me. She was forced to deliver a message to me.

I could think of only one reason for someone to target me. They knew I was the Janusite.

And I knew of only one way someone could learn that fact.

One of my allies had betrayed me.

CHAPTER SEVEN

I HEADED INTO THE WOODS A FEW MINUTES LATER, DETERMINED TO FIND Nevan or…I didn't know what. Take action. Stop waiting for another bad guy to hunt me down. Travis had rushed off the to the hospital to examine the scene of the crime. I had zero expectations he'd find concrete evidence. The man in black covered his tracks too well.

My boots made little sound as I marched past the vortex. I had no idea what I'd do once I crossed the veil into the Unseen. Wing it, that's what I'd do.

The sounds of the woods faded into a hush so unearthly it stopped me. I turned my head left and right, listening to the absence of noise. In the moments before Megan staggered out of the woods to deliver her message, I'd perceived the same kind of hush.

I held still, expecting…something. The stench of ammonia, akin to cat urine, drifted on the barest of breezes. I crinkled my nose, but then I remembered smelling the same odor the last time the woods had gone quiet, and goose bumps prickled my arms.

A crack and a whoosh pierced the preternatural silence.

My body tensed. My senses heightened, amped up by the adrenaline coursing through my veins.

Crackling. Crunching.

The noises originated further down the trail.

Slipping the derringer out of its holster, I held the gun muzzle down and trotted in the direction of the sounds. The source came into view when I rounded a curve in the path, emerging into the clearing beside the waterfall.

Fire had engulfed a bush.

The flames licked upward, stretching ever higher as if striving to reach the sky. Before I could consider the reason for the fire, a shape on the ground snared my attention. The bush partially concealed the object, so I sidled past it for a clearer view.

The gun tumbled from my hand, thumping onto the ground.

A girl lay prone beside the bush, her eyes wide and unseeing. A few feet away, behind the bush, another girl lay sprawled on her back with lifeless eyes aimed at the heavens.

I stumbled backward a step. No need to check for a vital signs, the truth was evident.

The girls were dead.

My skin crawled as I took in the totality of their appearance. Both girls had golden brown hair, blue eyes, and similar features. Not just similar to each other, but comparable to my hair and eyes and face.

Someone had murdered two young women who looked like me.

"Please, no."

A female voice whimpered the phrase from behind me.

I snagged my gun from the ground and whirled around.

A black-robed figure clutched a young woman, one arm around her waist and one pale, bony hand bolted around her throat.

Megan Kozlow whimpered again. "Please help me."

The man in black flicked one finger in my direction.

"There ye are, love," he said in a good approximation of Nevan's voice and accent, but without the indefinable element that made Nevan…Nevan. "I've been searching for ye."

I gripped my gun tighter. "If you're trying to convince me you are Nevan, you're doing a horrible job of it. Nevan is broad and muscular. You're skin and bones."

"A glamour, naturally."

His imitation of Nevan's voice came so close to the real thing that a weight of doubt settled in my gut. This was not Nevan. The creature before me must have no idea I could sense Nevan. I'd detected his approach right before Megan found me earlier, but I had not sensed Nevan this time. Yet the robed being wanted me to believe he was my lover.

Why?

He chuckled, nearly the way Nevan might, but with a thread of menace in the sound. "You've always worried you can't trust me, that I might be entrapped by another bargain. Now, you wonder if I'll choose Ceara instead of you."

Good guesses. He must've sent Ceara, and it didn't take a genius to figure out her rebirth would put stress on both me and Nevan. His assumption it weakened our relationship was dead wrong. This being had no clue about the depth of the connection Nevan and I shared.

Tears streamed down Megan's cheeks. She sniffled, whimpering again. "Don't punish me, please."

Bastard. He had to pay.

"What do you want?" I asked.

"To whittle away at your soul until nothing remains but fear and regret."

I hooked my finger over the derringer's trigger, poised to fire. "What's with the girls who look like me?"

He caressed Megan's neck with one finger, its sharp black nail grazing her skin. "Offerings to you, sweetness. To prove my devotion."

Megan sobbed.

I gritted my teeth but then forced myself to relax as much as possible under the circumstances. Getting this bastard to let the girl go had to be my priority.

"Listen," I said, edging a little closer, "you don't need another offering. I believe you're devoted to me. Let the girl go. You have me, you don't need her anymore."

"But you need the reminder."

He slashed his fingernail across Megan's neck, slitting her throat, and tossed her body to the ground. She gurgled and twitched.

I raced toward her.

And crashed into an invisible barrier.

Careening backward, I lost my grip on the derringer. It popped out of my hand and hit the ground with a thump.

I caught my balance, too late.

The robed being kicked Megan's body to flip her onto her back. Her eyes stared into eternity, her gaze as dead as her body.

I shut my eyes. Three girls dead because of me.

That was the point. This being wanted me to feel the guilt of their murders, as if I held some measure of culpability.

No, this was not my doing. It was all him.

And he would pay.

My trigger finger itched to fire an endued round straight into the robed bastard's head. But he'd erected a ward between the two of us, and I doubted even an endued bullet could penetrate it.

One way to find out.

I swung the gun up and pulled the trigger.

The shot boomed, reverberating off the trees and the sandstone cliff of the falls, but the .357 round ricocheted off the ward. It struck a tree, splintering bark off the trunk.

The robed being laughed.

Blood pounded in my ears. My body quivered with the rage building inside me, and I unleashed a guttural roar.

"What the hell do you want?" I demanded. "Murdering girls? For what? I know you're not Nevan. Who the fuck are you?"

"The one you love," he said. The Irish accent was gone, and his voice had lost the depth and vigor instilled in his imitation of Nevan. His voice took on a hoarse and brittle quality. "These three died the way you should have. Only when you've learned the lesson will you be ready for the truth."

His robes dragged on the ground as he crept toward the invisible wall between us. A single, sinuous finger stuck out of the robe's long sleeve to point at me.

"You," the being said, his voice disconcertingly calm and even, "are the key to everything. I feel no danger in telling you this because you cannot stop what is to come. When you realize the futility of fighting, you will join me."

The ward tumbled down with a flash of white energy.

I'd gone numb all over, from my skin down to my soul. "Who are you?"

"One who has waited eons for retribution." He raised his arm, stretching out his finger to touch my chin, sending a cold charge into me. "The girls, what I did to them. It was all for you, to prepare the way. Together, we will change the worlds."

The frigid touch of his finger shot a hard shudder through my body. I staggered backward. Even with shock muddling my thoughts, I latched onto a memory.

"Ceara called you a sorcerer," I said. "You're the one working with her."

"I am a sorcerer of sorts." He lowered his arm. "But you know nothing of my plans or intentions. Only when you enter the fold will I reveal my secrets to you."

"Never going to happen." I noticed a dark shape on the ground and marshaled enough wherewithal to grab the derringer and aim it at the sorcerer's head, smack between his eyes. "I won't let you hurt anyone else."

I fired the second, and last, round.

The bullet bounced off his forehead.

A personal ward around his body? *Shit.*

"You can't stop me," he said, and leaned forward. The hood still concealed his face, the sun too low in the sky to penetrate the shadows. "Unless you nourish your power and achieve the full potential of the Janusite. Then, you and will be equals."

"And then I will destroy you."

"No." He straightened, and his voice took on the bright lilt of half-suppressed laughter. "And then you will gladly join me."

"You're insane."

"If I am, you made me this way." He backed up to the edge of the clearing. "You don't belong in either world, Lindsey, and you never will. Nevan won't save you this time, because he won't choose you. Accept your fate or we will consume your power and your soul."

The sorcerer vanished.

I stood there, too numb to think or move, overwhelmed by the sensation nothing around me was real.

A raven squawked overhead and swooped down to land in front of me.

"Brennus?" I said. My solitary thought was that I'd imagined the bird. I still suffered the unsettling perception of unreality.

The raven rippled and shimmered, enlarging into a manlike outline. The shape resolved into a mountainous being, packed with muscles bigger than Nevan's and ebony skin tinted with a blue sheen.

Brennus fixed his coal-dark eyes on me. "My lady."

His voice was deep and resonant, and it always gave me the willies. He always gave me the willies. He'd started calling me "my lady" after Nevan became king, though no one else in the universe called me that.

The raven-man tilted his head in birdlike jerks. "You are unwell."

"No, I'm—" *Totally freaked out.* Willing myself to get a grip, I took a long breath and shook my entire body, like a dog after a bath. "I'm okay. What are you doing here?"

"I am guardian of the falls." He glanced at Megan's body, then nodded past my shoulder. "A shockwave in the magical fabric drew me here."

"A what?" I scuffled in a half circle, until I realized what he'd seen. The two bodies next to the bush. The flames had died out, but the branches smoldered.

"Who has done this?" Brennus asked.

"He calls himself a sorcerer." I swallowed, but my throat remained tight and dry. "Can the vortex resurrect them? We should find Tris and—"

"No, my lady." Brennus gave a single, sad shake of his head. "The magic that caused their deaths is poison. It cannot be reversed."

"How do you know? We have to try."

"I can taste the poison in it."

Though I had no reason to doubt his word, I couldn't shake the realization I'd had earlier. One of my allies had betrayed me. Was the traitor Brennus?

"You have powerful magics," he said. "If you try, you may taste the vile energy that has suffused their flesh."

When I'd asked Tris to heal Megan, he'd told me he could taste the dark magics in her. His words rang in my mind, harsh and final. *Ain't no coming back from this kinda sickness.*

I holstered the derringer and wrapped my arms around myself. "Do you know where Nevan is?"

"With the tribunal."

"Still?" I scrubbed my arms, uneasy at the thought of asking. "Could you check on him?"

Brennus blinked out, then blinked back a second later.

"I do not know," he said, "where the king is. I cannot detect him, but if he is with the tribunal that would be the case."

Dammit. I needed to talk to Nevan.

"It's okay," I said, waving a hand at Brennus. "You can leave. I'm fine. But if you see Nevan, tell him I'll be waiting for him at work or at my apartment."

His gaze flicked to the bodies and back to me, a question on his forbidding face.

"Don't worry," I said, "I'll call the sheriff and make sure these poor girls are taken care of."

The shapeshifter relaxed a bit, as if he'd been anxious about the fate of the deceased women.

Despite the fact he made me uneasy, thanks to our unfortunate past history, I'd come to realize of late that he had a softer side. His insistence on calling me "my lady" and his voluntary commitment to serving Nevan, those spoke to his innate honor. But his concern for the murdered girls told me he had compassion too.

"We'll find their families," I assured him, "and make sure they get home."

He didn't move, but glanced at the bodies again.

"Tell you what," I said, "why don't you stay here to watch over the bodies until the sheriff gets here. That way, nobody will stumble onto them by accident."

Brennus nodded once. "As you wish, my lady."

It continued to baffle me how a shapeshifting raven-man could project the aura of a medieval knight.

With a guard in place to protect the scene, I trudged back to the shop. Along the way, I called Travis to report the bodies in the woods.

How I made it through the rest of the day, I had no idea. Travis came and went without talking to me. An ambulance came and went, carrying away the remains of the young women who'd died because they resembled me. Images of the dead girls plagued me, and in between, worry for Nevan gnawed at my heart. Like a zombie, I ground through the day without any consciousness of what I was doing, performing tasks by rote until Stan told me he'd close up and I should go home.

I arrived at my apartment as the sun sank below the horizon—loosing fiery tendrils of pink, purple, and gold across the heavens—and made my way to my second-floor apartment.

A sorcerer whose name started with N claimed Nevan wouldn't choose me when some kind of battle began. The same anonymous sorcerer expected me to trust him with my powers after he murdered three young women who happened to look like me. He claimed I'd willingly join forces with him.

Yeah, right. I was *that* gullible.

Inside my apartment, I sank onto the sofa, letting my head fall back against the thick cushions. The air conditioning hummed in the background. The lamp on the endtable bathed the sofa and me in warm, pinkish light. The hum and the soothing glow lulled me into a dreamless sleep, and when I woke, for a minute I couldn't remember where I was. Oh right, my apartment. Alone.

Where was Nevan?

Sitting up, I yawned and rolled my head left and right to iron out the kinks in my neck. The clock on the wall read 11:03. I'd slept for about three hours. And still no Nevan? He'd said he'd find me right after his three a.m. meeting with the tribunal. An entire day had gone by without a hint of him anywhere around.

The sorcerer must've known Nevan would be detained, and he would be free to impersonate my lover in his attempt to freak me out. Much as I loathed admitting it, the sorcerer's tactics had worked. I was balanced on the head of a pin, teetering on the verge of tumbling off into an abyss of fear and doubt.

Stay strong, don't give him what he wants.

I pulled the soul stone out of my pocket, turning it over and over between my thumb and forefinger. Energy zinged over my skin, faint yet distinctive. It was the unmistakable essence of Nevan. Unfortunately, the bit of his soul infused into the stone gave me no clue to his whereabouts or his well-being, so I stuffed it back into my jeans pocket.

The hairs on my arms and the back of my neck lifted, as awareness sizzled over my skin. *Nevan.* I jumped to my feet in the instant he poofed into the room right in front of me, with no more than a couple inches separating our bodies. His heat radiated over my skin, and the tension inside me unwound at the sight of him. I threw my arms around his neck and hugged him tight.

"Where have you been?" I asked, unwilling to relinquish my hold yet. "I was afraid something went wrong at your meeting."

"I am unharmed."

The weariness in his voice made me pull back enough to see his face, though I kept my arms around his neck. His hair looked messy, tangled. Dark circles bruised the skin under his eyes, which themselves seemed duller, more like the slow swirl of cream in a coffee cup than the blazing whirlpool of his supernatural irises.

I cupped his face in my hands. "You may be uninjured, but you're not okay."

The only other time I'd witnessed him appearing so exhausted had been right after Skeiron almost killed him. Then, a gaping sword wound in his chest had bled the life out of him. Tonight, I had no explanation for his state of utter exhaustion.

But I felt it. Inside me. A cold undercurrent trickling through the radiant heat of his body into my flesh, my heart, my soul.

Nevan shut his eyes, leaning into my touch, and exhaled a long sigh. "I'm in need of sleep, love. That's all."

"We can go back to your place."

He cracked his lids open and gave a weak shake of his head. "It will have to be here. No energy left for...traveling."

No energy? Nevan? He was a living nuclear reactor, pumping out a life force more vital and alive than anyone I'd ever known. Now he couldn't zip back to the Unseen?

I clasped his hand and ushered him into the bedroom, pulling back the covers when we reached the bed. He collapsed onto the mattress, and it bounced under his sudden weight. His eyes slid shut. His breathing grew shallower.

He was asleep. Just like that.

This was bad. Very bad.

Without bothering to undress, I crawled into bed with him and tucked my body close against his, with my back against his front. Though he remained asleep, he unconsciously slipped an arm around my waist. His breaths fluttered my hair, tickling my ear. I drew the covers up over us, disturbed by a deep, though nebulous, unease. Twice he had gone off to meet the tribunal and not returned for an unnaturally long time. His long absence when he retrieved my endued gun and ammo seemed explained, but now I had to wonder. This time, he'd been MIA for twenty hours, his longest absence yet.

I shouldn't have slept, not with a maelstrom of worries whipping around in my brain. But the warmth and solidity of his body cocooning mine soothed me into slumber. I dreamed of a dark, faceless figure haunting the woods, snatching away innocent girls no matter how hard I tried to stop it. The girls were whisked away into the abyssal blackness of the forest, their tortured screams echoing after them. The sorcerer's demonic voice rasped in my ear.

Accept your fate or we will consume your power and your soul.

Coming awake with a jerk, my heart racing, I held still until I felt sure no one had sneaked into the room. Nevan hadn't moved even a millimeter. The burnished glow of sunrise filtered through the lacy curtains that hung closed over the window. I slipped out of Nevan's arms, out of the bed, and he never stirred. His face seemed peaceful in sleep, no longer shadowed by dark circles and fatigue.

I brushed a wisp of hair from his eyes, then bent to feather a kiss over his forehead. I couldn't lose him. I wouldn't allow it.

Megan had said forces were allying against me. The sorcerer had said "we." Did he mean Ceara was on his side? Or did he have more evil masterminds as his allies?

No matter who rallied against us, Nevan and I would fight them together.

He won't choose you.

Screw what a damn anonymous sorcerer claimed. Nevan would always choose me, like I would always choose him. We'd been through too much together to let anyone jam a wedge between us. They'd separate us only one way—by prying my dead body away from his.

Realization shivered through me, warm instead of frigid, exciting rather than unsettling. I knew what I wanted. What I'd always wanted. What I'd been afraid of because my last serious relationship ended so horribly. No more would I let fears rooted in the past taint my relationship with Nevan.

I sprinted out of the apartment, set on a mission.

I LAY ON THE BED, ON MY BACK, FULLY CLOTHED AND WITH MY TOES TAPping a drum tattoo in the air while I waited for Nevan to wake up. Given his exhaustion last night, I hadn't wanted to disturb his sleep. But I needed to know he was okay and to talk to him about my encounter with the sorcerer, as well as the murdered girls.

And to share my news with him. Maybe my decision should've seemed unimportant in light of recent events, but instead it seemed even more important than ever. With imminent death once again looming, I needed him to understand the depth of my commitment to him.

Sighing, I drummed my fingers on my belly.

"Impatient as always," Nevan murmured, snaking an arm over my waist, beneath my hands. He wriggled closer and nuzzled my neck. "What vexes you this morning?"

"Are you serious? What vexes me?" I flipped onto my side to face him. "You disappear for twenty hours, then you come back looking like a vampire sucked the life out of you and literally fall into bed—but not to ravish me, to lapse into a coma."

He caressed my cheek with his fingertips, a gentle smile on his lips. "I apologize, Lindsey, I had no intention of causing you distress. But you're mistaken, I could not have been away for such an extended time. It was only a few hours at most."

"Like hell it was. I can tell time, Nevan." I studied his face, hunting for a clue to whatever was going on with him. "Maybe you're the one having trouble counting the hours."

He pushed up onto one straight arm, frowning. "Time can move differently in the Unseen."

"Only when funky magic interferes with it. You told me that." I sat up too and fixed my attention on him, willing him to recognize the truth. "Why would your magic be funky? I've only noticed time passing differently over there when I'm the one crossing the veil."

"Perhaps your magic…" He scratched his head, his features cinched up in confusion.

"You can't seriously be claiming my Janusite magic traveled all the way from here into the Unseen to screw up time for you."

"I've no idea what caused it."

I ran a hand over his forehead, trying to smooth out the lines. "We'll figure it out together."

He relaxed a bit, nodding.

"But first," I said, skimming my fingertips over his lips, "I need to tell you what happened while you were gone."

I relayed the entire sequence of events, from Lilia's disappearance from the hospital to the sorcerer's final words to me. Nevan listened without comment, without expression save for the lines etching into his forehead once again.

"What do you think?" I asked.

"I don't know." His mouth twisted into a frown, then relaxed as he pressed his lips to mine. "We will figure this out together as well. I should speak with Brennus. Perhaps he and I can—"

"You are not leaving me again, not after the coma incident."

He fell silent, his fingers absently tracing the curve of my collarbone.

I debated whether to tell him my good news, but if I'd learned one thing since meeting him, it was that I shouldn't waste any opportunity for happiness. Besides, solving our problems required plenty of thought and plenty of dangerous endeavors, no doubt.

"We could both use a bit of good news," I said. "Don't you think? I mean, before we traipse off to get poisoned by death magic or whatever."

"You have happy news to share, I gather."

Hopping off the bed to stand beside it, I straightened my clothes. "I have a surprise for you."

His dark brows hiked up, as did the corners of his mouth. "What is it?"

"Me."

"You?" He slid off the bed with feline grace, rising up before me, taking my upper arms in his muscular hands. "I already have ye, darlin'."

"True," I said, skating my palms up his chest. "But not the way you really want."

His eyes narrowed.

I swept my hands over his pecs, drawing invisible circles on his flesh, delighting in the firmness of his muscles contrasted with the silky smoothness of his skin. "I want to move in with you. I've already told my landlord he should look for a new tenant and I started packing—"

Nevan sealed my lips with two fingers. He didn't blink, but his lips seemed to tremble the tiniest bit. "Did you say..."

"I'm moving in with you."

He scooped me up and twirled us both around and around, whooping and laughing. I couldn't keep from giggling and kicking my feet out, letting them fly through the air as the floor receded from us. Nevan had levitated us halfway to the ceiling before he ceased spinning and just grinned at me, his face lit up with pure joy. He was stunning this way, glowing from within, from a wonderful melee of emotions. The same joy rushed through me as well, and I peppered his face with kisses between my giggles.

My boots dangled several feet above the floor.

I glanced down, at last catching my breath. "You can come in for a landing anytime now."

"Why?" He claimed my mouth with his own, thrusting his tongue deep, pausing only to say, "Shall we head for a cloud?"

My body flashed back to a full-sensory memory of the one and only time he'd whisked me away to a cloud, to make love to me in the stratosphere. No experience on earth could compare with Nevan's aerial prowess.

I tore my lips from his but had to shove a hand between our mouths to keep him from diving in once more—and to keep myself from letting him. "On the floor, please. I'm still not used to this flying stuff."

In the blink of an eye, we went from floating in midair to lying on the floor with me flat on my back and him on top. And we were naked.

"Nevan," I chastised halfheartedly, "this isn't what I meant."

"You should be more specific in your requests."

Oh yeah, I should've learned that lesson by now. "Wouldn't you rather get me moved into your place first?"

We winked out and winked back in, both of us on our feet and fully clothed. Well, he was as clothed as he ever got, the loincloth in position around his hips.

Nevan flicked his wrist, gave a decisive nod, and said, "There. You are moved in."

"Huh?" I glanced around and realized my belongings had vanished. Shaking my head, I tried to suppress a smile, but failed. "Did you poof my stuff into your underground lair?"

"I did."

"Thank you." I hooked my arms around his waist, my chin on his chest, and gazed up at him with unabashed adoration. "You sure are convenient to have around."

"Convenient?" Amusement glittered in his eyes, like golden stars plucked from the sky. "Perhaps I should demonstrate precisely how *convenient* sharing a home with me will be."

"Oh yes, please do." I snuggled into him, inhaling his unique and delicious scent.

"We should discuss—"

"After." I wriggled my hips and raked my tongue across the scar over his heart, earning a sharp intake of breath from him. "Take me home and make love to me."

He whisked us to the ledge beside the waterfall, launched us through the cascade, and before I had time to gasp at the sudden onslaught of cold water, he threw open the portal and flew through it. We emerged into the Unseen realm dry—well, I was dry on the outside. Another part of me had grown very wet from the way he spirited me away. So masculine. So authoritative. So damn bossy and yet totally hot.

After a brief few seconds of adjustment, he transported us straight into our home. The underground lair glowed with a mellow light from the mysterious source that emanated from everywhere and nowhere. The air, attuned to my temperature, caressed my suddenly naked skin. He'd popped us in on the bed, me on my back and him on top. The weight of him pressed me into the fur blanket. His rigid shaft stretched across my belly, pinned there by our joined bodies.

"It's been days," he rumbled against my lips, "since I felt your heat around me."

"Promise me one thing." I spread my legs, bending my knees to bracket him. "If the damn tribunal summons you, ignore it."

"Fuck the tribunal."

I'd never heard him use the F-word before. Oddly, hearing him say it now gave me a warm, glowy feeling. He meant it.

Nevan collected my hands, securing them above my head with one of his hands around my wrists. His other hand drifted down my side, skimming my flesh, making my pulse accelerate and my breaths quicken. He slid his hand between our bodies, into the cleft where I was drenched and aching for him. Strong, sure fingers worked my nub and rubbed my folds until I arched into him and gasped from the sheer bliss of his touch.

I struggled to free my hands, desperate to grope him everywhere I could reach, but he held my wrists fast. "Please, Nevan, please."

"Shouldn't speak that word here."

"Don't care, I want you inside me." When he mercilessly ground his thumb into my nub, a sweet arc of pleasure shot through me and I writhed beneath him. It felt so good, but I still hadn't reached the climax, though I strained to get there, driven ever nearer little by little while his fingers tortured me. "Oh God, Nevan, I'll do anything you want if you take me *now*."

He chuckled, low and husky. "I need no magic to entice you to do anything I want."

It was true, and maybe I should've been embarrassed by that fact, but with his body on top of mine I couldn't feel anything but so damn good.

"Thunder and hail," he cursed, his voice an erotic rasp, "you are so wet for me."

"Always," I moaned. "Hurry it up, I—"

My voice choked off on a cry of pleasure when he surged downward and latched his mouth onto my nub, lapping at it and scraping his teeth over the tender flesh. My release exploded through me, scorching me from the inside out with a stunning ecstasy.

Nevan raised his head to gaze at me over my mound. His lips tightened in a smile of pure masculine satisfaction, with a hefty dose of carnal hunger. Those dazzling irises flared in bright, molten shades of red, purple, and bronze. The colors of his passion.

He dragged his tongue across his glistening lips, sampling my wet-ness.

Speechless, my sex throbbing with a new and far more intense need, I could nothing except gaze, enraptured, at the man I loved.

Rising onto his knees, he towered above me with his erection waving in the air.

A drop of moisture beaded on the rosy tip. Any inhibitions I might've had left crumbled away at the sight of his gloriously nude body. I pushed up into a sitting position, my face in front of his cock, and daubed the liquid from its tip with my tongue.

He hissed in a breath, his chest heaving.

I fell back onto the bed and hit him with my sauciest grin. "You're right. Without any magical compulsion, I will do anything to satisfy you."

Letting out a long groan that resonated in his chest, he dropped onto all fours, his hands at either side of my shoulders, one knee between my thighs. He urged my legs wider apart and filled me in one powerful thrust. The sensation of his hard shaft inside me, stretching my body, never failed to thrill me. Goose bumps tingled over my skin, activating every fine hair. I craved him with a lust like none I'd ever known before Nevan—and like I'd never experience with any other man. I recognized this fact without an ounce of fear or doubt. I belonged to him, and he belonged to me.

Nevan began to move inside me, gliding in and out, his rhythm slow and steady, stoking the fire in me with deliberate tenderness. He let his elbows buckle, his head lowering until his lips touched my forehead. I grasped his upper arms and held on tight for the ride, rocking my hips into his gentle strokes, moaning and gasping. He shifted position, bowing his back to bring our mouths into alignment, and then he crushed his lips to mine, plunging his tongue deep and demanding my response. I wrapped my legs around him, flung my arms around his shoulders and clung to him, answered his kiss with frenzied lashes of my tongue, starved for the flavor of him.

The connection between us, the bond engendered by love and passion and commitment, flared inside me, bright and warm and unquenchable. Pleasure and magic swirled together, coalesced into a power beyond comprehension, rising within me and expanding to suffuse my entire being and spread into Nevan. His eyes flew wide, his focus snapping to me, but his movements stayed smooth and fluid, his shaft gliding out and diving back inside me as if our bodies had merged. A wave of glittering magic, ice blue and heartbreak-ingly beautiful, flowed out of me to envelop us both. It tingled through our bodies, enhancing the physical pleasure, infusing it with a depth derived from more than lust, from a bond no one and nothing could sever.

Nevan's pace quickened, his thrusts harder and deeper. An expression of shocked joy overtook his features, fueled by the spectacular blue magic that shimmered all around us.

Tears streamed down my cheeks, tears of completeness and a kind of happiness I'd never dreamed possible. Oh God, this connection, it was… eternal.

I buried my face in his neck, desperate noises bursting from my lips. A new excitement, sexual and emotional, propelled me through the atmosphere and rocketed me higher and higher toward the weightless bliss of release. Nevan's thrusts grew frantic, his grunts and groans as desperate as my noises. Higher. Higher. Couldn't breathe, couldn't move except to cling to him.

My orgasm convulsed through me and hurled me into outer space, spinning, flying, screaming from the earth-shattering ecstasy. Nevan froze for a heartbeat, his breaths ragged and hoarse, then his release pulsated inside me. He threw his head back and roared his pleasure, as I floated back down to earth.

The glittering magic fizzled out, tiny blue sparks the only remnant. They faded too, leaving no sign of the incredible event.

Nevan collapsed beside me, drawing me in to tuck me close against his sweat-slicked body. I enjoyed the afterglow for a moment, while my heartbeat and my breathing returned to normal. Sex with Nevan was like a wickedly naughty ride in an adults-only theme park, and I didn't even have to worry about birth control. The first time we'd made love, he'd assured me he couldn't get me pregnant without a conscious effort to make it happen.

With my power of speech restored, I shimmied away from him far enough to see his face. "Did you see that? Did you feel it?"

"Yes." He touched my face with his fingertips, his eyes shining with… tears. "I saw and felt it."

"What was that?"

"Lindsey, my love, you know what it was." He kissed the tip of my nose. "That was your magic."

Nevan hadn't witnessed the only other time I'd tapped into my Janusite powers on purpose. When Brennus had abducted me and was about to cut out my heart, I'd summoned the same kind of glittering blue energy. "Yeah, I know it was me doing it. But I don't understand why it happened. I wasn't trying to use magic."

"You agreed to share a home with me, to share a life with me. I know you wrestled with the decision for weeks." He took my hand and laid it over his heart. "Perhaps the heightened emotions of finally reaching a decision activated your powers."

"How did it feel to you? I mean, did I hurt you?"

Shaking his head, he laughed. "No, darlin', I felt nothing close to pain. Only the ecstasy of worshiping you, intensified by whatever unconscious magic you employed. It was as if our souls had merged, for a few moments."

"That's what I felt too. But I have no control over my powers, don't understand them at all, so I want to make sure you don't feel any side effects."

He pulled me snug against him, roving his hands up and down my back. "I have noticed one aftereffect. I feel energized, fully free of whatever had robbed me of energy last night."

Energized? Free? Wow, I'd done that. And I had no clue how.

I wiggled to get a small distance between us while staying on my side. "We need to talk about your prolonged absences."

"I was with the tribunal."

"For twenty hours?"

He shrugged one shoulder. "I must have been."

"You're not sure?" I sat up, braced with one arm, my palm flat on the bed. "Tell me everything you remember about visiting the tribunal last night."

Nevan rolled onto his back, one arm bent above his head, and frowned as he struggled to recall the event. "I remember taking you to the portal. I waited until you had crossed the veil, then I went to the tribunal's chambers and I was admitted inside. They had many complaints. I listened to their irritating demands for as long as I could stand—a length of seconds that could likely have been counted on one hand—and then I informed them I am king. They may bring their grievances to me, but I will do as I see fit, not as they desire."

"What happened next?"

"I—" He gazed at the ceiling, his face blank, for long enough I began to wonder if he'd gone catatonic. At last, he swiveled his head toward me and blinked slowly. "I've no idea. At that precise point, things grow…hazy. The next thing I recall is appearing in your apartment, feeling drained and confused."

"Hazy? Drained? That's not good, Nevan."

"No, it is not."

I folded my legs under me, hands on my thighs. "Have you, um, seen Ceara again?"

He shook his head. "Not that I recall."

Not that he recalled. Hardly comforting. "We need to find out what happened during your missing time incidents."

"You speak as if it's occurred more than once."

"It has." I shifted to sit cross-legged, turned to the side so I could look at his face. "Two days ago, when you moved me to my apartment while I was asleep, you were gone until afternoon, but you said you only met with the tribunal. Then you left for hours when you supposedly visited the fae witch and nothing else. Then there's the last time." I bit down on my lower lip, remembering the entire day of waiting, worrying, not knowing. "You were gone for twenty hours and you don't know why. I count three incidents, but the last one was the worst by far. Your missing time has to be related to the sorcerer."

Not because he is the sorcerer, I assured myself.

Unless somebody bamboozled him into a bargain that gave them total control over him.

My instincts told me that wasn't the case, and I'd learned to trust my intuition.

Nevan swung his legs off the bed, rising, now seated on the mattress's edge, with his back to me. "I had not realized…You are right, Lindsey. I have no explanation for why each of those absences took so long. However, I was not exhausted after the first two."

"Something was different this time." I slid to the bed's edge and let my feet dangle off it. Taking Nevan's hand, I folded both of mine around it. "We need to retrace your steps. Start with the fae witch and work forward from there. Are you sure the witch didn't curse you or whatever?"

"I cannot believe Ennea would do anything of the sort."

"One way to find out." I jumped off the bed. "Let's go interrogate the witch."

"Ah…" Nevan rubbed the back of his neck, wincing, avoiding my gaze. "I'm not certain you want to meet her."

"Why?" Hands on hips, I waited for him to answer. When he didn't, but simply kept grimacing and looking everywhere but at me, I cleared my throat in the most obvious way. "Nevan."

"She is Tris's sister." He made a face, somewhere between annoyance and embarrassment. "The one I, ah…became involved with."

"Oh, I get it. This Ennea chick is the sister you slept with, and when Tris found out, he stopped talking to you."

"Yes."

I marched up to Nevan, grasped his chin, and angled his face up so he had no choice but to meet my gaze. "Do you really think I'm so sensitive I can't handle meeting one of your ex-lovers? Hell, I just met your dead wife who isn't dead and wants you back. I think I'll survive an introduction to Tris's sister."

He shut his eyes, his shoulders slumping. "Perhaps it's I who cannot handle you meeting another of my former lovers."

"You're embarrassed?"

One massive shoulder hunched in a half shrug, and still he would not look at me. "I've endeavored to keep my past away from our present. Whatever came before you matters not one bit. However, if you're confronted with the reality of my previous behavior…"

Now I got it, and I was mildly offended that he thought I might disapprove. But then I realized with a heady rush why he worried about it. He loved me so much he couldn't stand to risk alienating me with a parade of his ex-bedmates. When we first met, I had been jealous of the women he kissed in the commission of his duty, hunting for the Janusite. A lot had changed since then—me, in particular.

I knelt before him, pushing between his thighs to fold my arms around his waist and hug him close. His face was still averted, but I felt his body stirring from my proximity, the way my body inevitably awakened when he pulled me close.

"Listen," I said in a gentle voice, "I'm not jealous, not anymore. What we have is real and powerful and forever. I don't care how many women from your past flounce up to throw me haughty looks and announce you belong to them. I know the truth."

His eyes moved only his eyes to consider me.

"You're mine," I said, sliding my arms up to encircle his neck. "Nobody's taking you away from me because you want me and only me, just like I want you and only you. There's no need for jealousy or insecurity. And that goes for you too, my scorching-hot sylph king. Got it?"

At last, he turned his face to me and his expression softened. "Yes, I've got it."

He smirked when he spoke the last two words. His arms came around me, crushing me to him as he mashed his mouth to mine, thrusting his tongue inside to tease the roof of my mouth. I opened to him fully, surrendering to the demands of his lips and tongue, loving every second of the kiss.

Before I knew what had happened, we were on our feet and no longer kissing.

"Let's talk with Ennea," he said, "and try to discover what occurred during my missing hours. It may well hold clues to the sorcerer's identity."

With my arms around his neck and his around my waist, I held on for the journey ahead.

And for whatever might come next.

Chapter Eight

Inside the gloomily lit cavern, the flames from several oil lanterns flittered their light across the coarse rock walls and floor, but my eyes needed time to adjust to the new environment. The space housed tables of various sizes, and on each table sat sundry tools and bowls that looked straight out of a movie about witches, complete with a small cauldron bubbling and steaming atop the nearest table.

Behind the waist-high table, a young woman bent over the cauldron with a slight smile on her lips, her gaze directed at the cauldron's contents. She stirred the boiling liquid with a large ladle as she hummed a lovely yet eerie tune. Though she appeared young, I'd learned better over the past weeks than to assume she was young. Her red hair and creamy, freckled face mirrored her brother's coloring, but she had an elven cuteness to her that the other leprechaun lacked.

Nevan led me toward the table and the woman.

"Ennea," he said, inclining his head in greeting.

The witch glanced up at him and a knowing smile spread across her face, making her eyes glint with what I could describe only as amused knowledge. Ennea set her ladle down on the wooden tabletop, placed her hands on the surface, and swept her gaze from Nevan to me and back again. Her brows hopped up and down twice.

"Well, lookie here," she said in an accent much like her brother's, somewhere between Chicago and the Bronx. "It's the king of the sylphs, gracing a lowly witch with his presence."

Her tone conveyed teasing rather than disdain. This woman had slept with Nevan, who knew how many times, and I was getting the impression she still held a certain fondness for him. It seemed more like friendly familiarity than sexual desire or romantic attachment.

Ennea turned her sly gaze on me again. "And you must be the king's mortal plaything."

I bristled at the mention of my unwanted moniker. Tried not to, but I couldn't help it. "My name is Lindsey."

"Easy, girl." The fae witch grinned. "I like anybody who ticks off the sylph tribunal, seeing as they're a bunch of stick-up-the-ass know-it-alls. The fae council isn't much better. Why do you think I live in a cave? To get away from all those arrogant cheese-heads who think the universe revolves around their egos."

I flashed a grin at Nevan. "I like her."

He rolled his eyes and tilted his head back in a melodramatic gesture of resignation. "Spare me from female bonding."

Ennea tapped her long, black nails on the tabletop. "You guys didn't come here to gab about the elitist asses who run the worlds. What's up?"

"We need your help," Nevan said, his hand tightening around mine. "I seem to have, ah…a sort of problem with, uh…"

Oh for heaven's sake. We'd never get anywhere if he kept hemming and hawing.

I barged right into the conversation. "Nevan has missing time. He was gone for twenty hours, but he only remembers coming here, then coming home to me, and a little while later going to meet the tribunal. We think something happened to him during or right after the tribunal meeting, because his memory goes hazy at that point. He came home totally exhausted."

Ennea's brows knit together over her button nose. The humor vacated her features. "That is a conundrum."

"Can you help us find out what happened to him?" I asked. "Unless, of course, you're the one who did it to him. Are you?"

She folded her arms over her chest and eyed me with appreciative respect. "Nevan's got himself a feisty one, huh? But to answer your question, no, I didn't do a frigging thing to him except endue that weapon he brought me. Took awhile, and he got grumpy about the wait, but I wouldn't screw with his memory just because he annoyed me."

To Nevan, I said, "I believe her."

"As do I," he confirmed. He asked Ennea, "Can you help?"

"Sure can do." The witch leaned her hip against the table, pulling in a deep breath of the steam wafting out of the cauldron, and smiled with blissful contentment. Focusing on us, she tapped a finger on her chin. "If I'm going to cast a spell for you, Nevan, I need to know if there's anything I need to know first. Magic's a delicate and dangerous craft, the slightest unknown variable might throw the whole thing off. And next thing you know, you're a toad hopping around at my feet. I think you catch my drift, Your Majesty."

"I do," Nevan said. He angled toward me and I looked into his eyes, struck by the gravity of his expression. "She needs to know."

He was right, of course, but I didn't relish exposing my secret to someone I'd met a minute ago. One of my allies might've betrayed my secret to the enemy, but I had to trust somebody sometime. Her brother, Tris, knew I was the Janusite. If I trusted him, surely I could trust Ennea. Besides, my powers did have a tendency to muck up magic. The spell might be for Nevan, but we were connected in ways I didn't understand one hundred percent. My Janusite powers had affected his magic before.

I nodded. "Tell her."

Nevan faced Ennea again, though he maintained his hold on my hand, his fingers intertwined with mine, his thumb rubbing my skin. "Lindsey is the Janusite."

Ennea gave a low whistle. "Leave it to you to hook up with the prophesied gatekeeper of the worlds. Does the tribunal know?"

"Of course not," he snapped, then took a breath and regained his composure. "You mustn't tell anyone. Lindsey will be in grave danger if the truth is revealed."

The witch raised her hands. "This bird won't sing."

"Good."

"You think Lindsey's powers might knock my spell out of whack?"

"They have interacted with my magic on previous occasions," he said, "as well as affecting other types of magic. The first time I brought her to the Unseen, her powers caused time to pass more slowly on this side of the veil."

"Good to know. I'll need to work a little something-something into the spell to account for it."

I stepped into the discussion when Nevan fell silent. "How will this spell work?"

"This kind of memory spell taps into the Oversoul to bypass whatever mojo your unknown baddie worked on Nevan." Ennea rubbed her chin with her thumb and forefinger. "It'll rewind his recollection to the last moment he remembers clearly and let him relive it from there, in his mind."

Nevan fidgeted beside me, his fingers flexing and curling around mine.

I must've looked baffled, which I absolutely was, because Ennea gave me a patient smile. "See, it's kind of like retroactive astral projection. Your mind experiences the event as it happens, and you feel like you're actually there, but you're invisible to the participants and can't interact with the environment."

Sure, that made perfect sense.

Nevan grasped my other hand and turned us toward each other. He stared down at me with a tension-darkened expression, his full mouth squashed into a slash. "Without knowing what was done to me, the magics involved may cause a severe reaction with the spell implanted within me. I need you to do this for me, love. Will you?"

"Experience your memories?" I glanced at Ennea. "Is that possible? Can I do it for him?"

"You can," she said. "If your bond with him is strong enough, you can act as his proxy during the spell."

"It's strong enough," Nevan said. "Will you do this?"

The silent "please" at the end of his question tugged at my heart. He was asking me because he worried about magical interactions, yes, but also because he was afraid of what he might see.

As if he'd read my mind, he said, "We need an objective party to witness whatever occurred. I trust you to handle this."

"You could handle it too." I extricated one of my hands from his to caress his cheek. "You're the strongest man I've ever known. But if you need me to do stand in for you, I'll do it."

He nodded, his gratitude evident on his face.

"But for the record," I said, "where you're concerned, I am in no way objective."

Ennea smiled and shook her head at us. "New love is so adorable. But if we're going to do this thing, I need a magical assist."

"From whom?" Nevan asked.

She held up one finger in the universal gesture for patient silence. Then she opened her mouth and hollered, "Triskaideka!"

Ennea canted her head as if listening.

Nevan screwed up one corner of his mouth. "Perhaps he doesn't care to respond, since you are helping me."

My gaze flicked back and forth between him and the witch. "He who?"

Ennea rolled back her shoulders. "Oh, you bet your rock-hard ass he'll respond. Triskaideka, get your sorry butt in here before I call Ma and tell her what you did last night!"

A figure blipped into view alongside Ennea. Tris rolled his bright blue eyes at his sister, who narrowed her bright green eyes at him.

"Ya don't gotta scream," Tris said. "I heard you the first time, but I was trying to have a piss in the woods."

I couldn't help asking. "What did he do last night?"

Ennea smirked. "Went drinking with a busty little undine. Our ma hates those slippery water sprites. She wants Tris to settle down with a nice fae girl, preferably a copper fae."

"Copper fae?" I repeated, lost in this conversation. "Undine?"

Tris aimed his most condescending look at me. "Don't Nev teach you nothing about our world? Undines are water elementals. Copper fae is what leprechauns are, on account of we're tied to the element copper."

"I thought elemental referred to air, water, earth, and fire."

"You think that's all there is? Sure, we got the basal elemental beings— sylphs for air, undines for water, salamanders for fire, gnomes for earth. But the fae are tied to more specific chemical elements."

I stood mute as comprehension dawned little by little. "You mean chemical as in the periodic table of elements?"

"Yep." He scratched his head. "Though we ain't got no charts or tables. That's a mortal thing."

"How many kinds of fae are there?"

"As many as there are elements." He puffed out his chest, his chin raised. "The fae are the largest race of elementals in the Unseen, comprised of one hundred and eighteen tribes."

Nevan groaned. "Enough. Lindsey doesn't need the unabridged history of the magnificent fae."

"He's right," I said. "We have a mystery to solve."

Ennea led me behind a deck of shelves to a wooden chaise upholstered with dark fabric and plenty of cushioning. She waved a hand toward it. "Lie down, get comfy."

I settled onto the chaise, fidgeting until I found a comfortable position, my legs stretched out along the length of the backless sofa. The elevated end held my head and torso at an angle.

Nevan perched on the chaise's edge, concern dulling his eyes.

"Don't worry," I said, "everything'll be fine."

He gave a weak nod, but seemed less than convinced. Hell, I would've been freaked out too, if somebody was messing with my brain, so I couldn't blame him.

Ennea took a position at the foot of the chaise, her back straight and shoulders square. "Nevan, you'll need to hold her hand to keep her grounded to you. Lindsey, remember you can't interact with anyone or anything, and no one can see or hear you. Tris, let's get ready."

I heard rustling behind me, followed by the noises of Tris knocking around in search of whatever they needed for the spell.

"Careful with that," Ennea chastised in the kind of tone used only by mothers and bossy sisters. "That's all the potion I've got. You know how long it takes to chant up another batch?"

Tris grumbled. A moment later, he emerged from behind me to approach his sister. With one hand, he offered her a gilded ceramic mug.

Ennea nodded toward me. "Give it to the one who's drinking it."

"Drinking what?" I asked, levering up into a sitting position. Tris held the mug out to me. I studied it with trepidation, my stomach churning at the thought of imbibing an unknown magical substance. "What is it?"

Nevan's eyes crinkled at the corners with restrained laughter. "Relax, my suspicious love. It's not poison."

"How do you know?" I said with a touch of sarcasm in my voice and a teasing lift of my brows.

Tris bristled, but Ennea looked amused. "It's a potion to ease you into the memory spell. I could explain the magical mechanics of it—"

"Unnecessary," Nevan said. He enfolded my hands in his, rubbing his palm across the back of my hand. "Trust me."

I understood what he was asking. He trusted Ennea, and I trusted him, so therefore I should trust her.

Accepting the mug from Tris, my other hand still enclosed in both of

Nevan's, I swigged the contents. Tart and viscous liquid rushed over my tongue, making me splutter as it washed down my throat. I coughed a few times, waving a dismissive hand when Nevan leaned toward me with wide, worried eyes.

"Nothing wrong," I said. "Take it easy, honey."

Tris smirked at that, barely choking back a derisive snort. "Honey? Man, you are domesticated."

"Shush," Ennea hissed, her expression going stern. "It's our turn, Triskaideka."

He made a face. "Stop calling me that."

I started to smile, but froze as a bizarre sensation spread through my body, sprouting in my chest and expanding outward into every nook and cranny of my being. It began as a cool tingling behind my breastbone, then mushroomed into a hard, hot tingle that scorched through me. I gasped, my eyes flew wide, my back bowed and my head was thrown back into the cushion.

Nevan gripped my hand, while with his other palm he grasped my face.

"Stop fighting," Ennea said, and though her tone was forceful, it was tempered with an underlying calmness. Her face exhibited the determined serenity of one used to toying with unnatural forces. She bent close to my face, as I struggled to drag in breaths. "Listen to me, Lindsey. The magic will try to push you out. This kind of memory spell fights back, so you need to fight even harder. Focus on Nevan. Let your bond with him soothe and guide you. *Focus.*"

When she straightened and took Tris's hand, moving out of my direct line of sight, my gaze shot to Nevan. The tightness and anxiety smoothed out of his features. He held my hand between his again, and I let myself spiral down into the vortex of his eyes, carrying me ever downward toward the depths of his soul. I felt him, like a warm and sultry breeze caressing my skin, delving beneath the surface of my being to embrace me in a way no one else could.

Peace. Completion. Belonging.

My eyes drifted shut. My body relaxed into the upholstery, its softness cradling my limbs. An odd lightness overcame me as my mind disconnected from my body, and yet the heat and solidity of Nevan's hands tethered me to him. A sweet, wonderful binding. The safety of our connection quieted my nerves.

I floated through an abyss, nowhere and everywhere at once.

"Hear me," Ennea intoned. "Empty your thoughts. Hold to the bond and let it take you where you need to go."

An energy tugged at me. I resisted the urge to struggle against it. My mind moved through nothingness toward a destination I could neither see nor sense.

The tingling erupted in my chest again. Hot. Hard. Hungry. This time, the nasty thing came with tiny, razor-sharp teeth that clawed at me from the inside, tearing, shredding, devouring.

A strong and soothing wave crested over me, sweeping away the pain.

Nevan. I clung to him in the darkness, shoving the evil thing out of me with all the strength in my soul. But another power intensified mine—the essential strength of Nevan's soul fused with mine.

Blinding whiteness exploded around me.

I burst out into an underground chamber lit by a fire burning within a single, large, metallic bowl situated atop a wide dais. It must've been four feet in diameter, with flames leaping up from its confines to lick at the air. Five beings, cloaked in flowing robes of gold with hoods shielding their faces, had assembled in a semicircle around the fire on the dais.

Nevan stood before the group, with the fire between them. He wore a white, toga-style garment that hooked over one shoulder, held in place with a bronze clasp.

His expression was thunderous.

I edged closer, tiptoeing despite the fact I knew none of them could see or hear me. Somehow, sneaking just seemed prudent. I stopped alongside Nevan, angled so I could see both him and the tribunal.

"My answer remains the same," he said, grating the words through his clenched teeth. "I am king, you will accept my decree."

"Decree?" said one of the cloaked figures, the voice male and raspy. "We are the oversight for the king. If we determine your actions are against the welfare of the sylph kingdom—"

"Shut up." Nevan barked the command, his shoulders bunched so tightly he seemed ready to explode. "I have told you. There is no discussion, and my decision has no bearing on the welfare of my people, which I have worked diligently to assure. Only the five of you seem to have a grievance with my ruling techniques."

"Your Majesty," said another of the beings, raising a placating hand. "You cannot truly mean to install a mortal as queen."

Ohhhh, of course they were talking about me. The mortal plaything.

Nevan clenched his fists, his jaw tight as steel, and he seemed to grow taller and larger, his eyes glinting with bright red fire. "Lindsey is my mate. She will rule at my side, and you will accept and obey her—and swear your fealty to your new queen."

Obey me? Swear fealty to me? Aw, he really did say the sweetest things.

"You leave us no choice, then," the tribunal member said, lowering his hand.

Nevan narrowed his eyes to slits. "You have no say in this."

He assumed the position I'd come to recognize as his pre-vanishing posture. He flinched the tiniest bit, his eyes darting.

"You may not leave," the raspy-voiced being said. "We have activated the wards and tuned them to prevent your departure."

The tribunal chamber had wards protecting it. I should've guessed. But holding their own king hostage? Unease slithered through me. This could not be good.

Nevan's nostrils flared. "How dare you attempt to—"

Feminine laughter echoed through the chamber, light and mocking. Ceara emerged from the shadows behind the tribunal, the epitome of ethereal beauty, her gray dress swishing as she sashayed across the chamber. The pendant suspended from her belt swayed with every motion of her hips.

Her silvery eyes took in Nevan, and her lips curled in an arrogant smile.

The raspy-voiced being, who seemed to be in charge, stepped forward and spread his arms wide. "We have chosen your queen."

"No one," Nevan growled, "chooses my queen for me."

"She is your wife. And she is of the Unseen."

"Do you know what she is? Of what elemental race?" Nevan squinted at Ceara, his gaze assessing and austere. "What are you, wife?"

He spat the last word.

She sashayed toward him, halting alongside the fire. "I am your wife, Tuathal. The rest is immaterial."

"Why," Nevan said, "have I not seen or heard of you for five thousand years?"

Ceara shrugged one elegant shoulder. "Perhaps you were too busy fornicating with every female you encountered. This mortal child is merely the last in a line of meaningless flings, and you will come to realize that once you cease resisting me."

Nevan ground his teeth hard enough for me to hear the noise. He scanned his furious gaze over each of the tribunal members in turn. "Never will I accept this creature as my wife, much less my queen. Never."

Mr. Raspy clapped his hands together and the fire flared high and blindingly bright for a heartbeat. As the flames settled down again, he jabbed an accusing finger at Nevan. "So be it. If the king refuses to concede, we must take dire action against you."

I glanced at Nevan's face, my pulse racing, but he'd gone stony. Was I about to discover what they'd done to him? Did I want to know?

Yes. I did. I had no choice, because no way in hell would I stand by while they manipulated him.

The air in the chamber quivered. The walls groaned and rippled, like a living thing awakening.

Ceara's eyes were wild, her hair fluttered on a phantom breeze. An eerie glow surrounded her, silvery and sparkling. When she spoke, her voice became imbued with an echo-like quality. "Let my master's will be done."

Nevan spluttered, gasped, his eyes bulging.

I jerked, stopping myself from running to him at the last second. I couldn't do anything about this. Couldn't stop whatever was happening. *Powerless.*

He froze for an instant, then his entire body slackened, though he remained on his feet. His eyes had gone flat, his gaze distant. My vibrant, vital sylph had been transformed into a zombie.

"This will require much time," Ceara told the tribunal as she strolled up to Nevan. "I must take him to my master, but I can begin the process here."

I watched, helpless to intervene, while she bracketed his face with her pale hands.

"Tuathal," she cooed, bringing her lips near to his. "You may not have loved me before, but soon I will become the center of your existence. Without me, you will be an empty shell devoid of purpose. Only I possess the power to enliven you."

She pressed her mouth to his.

Tendrils of silver energy snaked out from her fingertips and her lips to burrow under his skin, pulsating as they entered him.

Bile leeched into my mouth, searing and sour.

Nevan began to kiss Ceara. Claiming her mouth. Plunging his tongue inside. His arms crushed her slender body to him, and their kissing escalated into a more heated and frantic encounter, as if they couldn't get enough of each other.

My gorge surged high in my throat. Cold sweat broke out on my brow, and I gulped down the nausea. He couldn't really want her. He couldn't really be enjoying her as much as it seemed like he was. She'd done something to him, I saw it.

Nevan loved me. She might force him to respond to her touch, but she could never—never in all eternity, never in any world—make him love her.

But could she coerce him into leaving me? Or...killing me?

Ceara separated from Nevan, taking a step back, her smile rife with disdain. Nevan seemed paralyzed, his expression vacant.

The evil bitch rotated her gaze toward me.

My heart thudded. No, it couldn't be. She couldn't—

"Little mortal," she said, her lips twisting into a nasty grin, "you see how he wants me. How I can make him want me. Nothing will prevent me from taking my place at his side, as queen of the sylph kingdom. Nothing—not even your pathetic love."

A bolt of soul-shattering power slammed into me. Agony ripped through my astral body, wrenching a scream from me.

I was yanked back through the abyss, through the frigid cold of emptiness, and hurled into my physical form. A gasp exploded out of me as my eyes flew open, and violent shudders racked my body. Sweat streamed down my face, mingling with hot tears that flowed like salty rivers down my cheeks.

Nevan hauled me into his arms. He rocked me and stroked my hair, murmuring soothing sounds.

The agony and terror seeped out of me gradually. I went limp in his embrace, my head on his shoulder, exhausted beyond anything I'd experienced in my life.

Drained.

After several minutes, I managed to lift my head and look at Nevan. The grief on his face stabbed a pang into my chest.

I raised a trembling hand to his cheek. "I'm okay."

"You don't look it." He brushed a hand over my forehead, then down my face, and swept his palm over my shoulder and down my back. "You seem… drained."

I couldn't deny it, and besides, I 'd vowed to keep no secrets from him. "Yeah, but I'll get over it."

Ennea peeked at me over Nevan's shoulder. "Did you see?"

"Oh-ho yeah. Did I ever see."

"We can discuss this later, when you're well again."

"There's no time," I said. "It was Ceara."

Surprise flickered on his face. "Why?"

"Not sure yet, but she's turning you into some kind of zombie." I pulled in a deep breath and let it out slowly. "Her sorcerer friend is helping her. She took you to him, and they did God knows what to you."

"You didn't follow?" Ennea asked.

"Couldn't." I looked straight at her. "Ceara saw me."

CHAPTER NINE

"THAT IS IMPOSSIBLE," ENNEA SAID, HER VOICE AND HER FACE TAINTED with a potent mixture of shock and wonder. She shook her head weakly. "The spell is like a recording, not a live event."

"I don't know much about magic," I said, "but I know Ceara saw me. She looked right at me. Spoke to me. Told me my pathetic love couldn't save Nevan from her evil plan to become queen of the sylphs. And yeah, I'm paraphrasing. Not about the pathetic love part, though."

"What else went down?" Tris asked. He scuffled closer, a pained look on his face, seeming for all the worlds to care about the answer to his question.

I glanced at my proud sylph, who kept his arms around me. "Maybe I should tell Nevan in private first."

"Your discretion is appreciated," he said, "but unnecessary. It's clear you and I alone cannot defeat this unidentified enemy. Ennea and Tris are powerful elementals, ones we can trust."

Had he admitted to trusting Tris? Next, he'd confess to liking the leprechaun. They had been friends once, but for as long as I'd known the two of them they'd been less than friendly to each other. A lot had changed since then, though. Like Tris helping me save Nevan's life when Skeiron drove an endued sword through Nevan's chest.

And somehow, that event had begun to pale in comparison with the threat we now faced. This was different, worse, more insidious. I had no evidence to support my assertions. Nothing more than a deep, icy wriggling in my gut.

I related everything I'd seen and heard during my astral journey into Nevan's memories, concluding with Ceara's zombie-fication of him, their super creepy kiss, and the way she'd ejected me from the spell.

"Kicked me to the curb," I said, swinging my legs around Nevan's body to clamber off the chaise. He rose as well, twining his fingers with mine, and I looked to the leprechaun on the other side of the chaise. "If that was really the past, a recorded memory, then how on earth could Ceara interact with me?"

Ennea scrunched her lips and her brows. Her delicate nose crinkled, and her striking emerald eyes sharpened on me. "This is far outside the scope of my powers and knowledge. Seems like Ceara's nothing but a minion. The sorcerer must've installed some kind of alarm in Nevan's memories, to alert him if anyone tried a spell like we did. I'm good, but this is insanely advanced magic."

Nevan's fingers tightened around mine. "What are you saying?"

"You need somebody way more powerful than me."

Tris nodded, his expression grave. "Yeah, you need an oracle."

"Exactly," Ennea said.

Back when we'd first learned I might be the Janusite, Nevan had planned on taking me to the oracle who issued the prophecy about me, but we'd never made it to his hideaway. Skeiron had ambushed us.

"Where do we find an oracle?" I asked.

"Tris can take you," Ennea offered. "He knows where to find one."

I turned my attention to Tris, who'd lost all his snarky attitude since the spell-casting.

"Yeah," he said, "I'll take you to one. Never talked to this oracle myself, but I went to his pad a few times to request an audience. He turned me down."

Ennea snorted. "Because you wanted the oracle's help in finding a wife. That's not in his job description."

My exhausted mind couldn't quite wrap itself around the concept of Tris volunteering to help Nevan. I probably gaped at him when I asked, "You're going to take us to the oracle? No griping or bargaining?"

Tris rolled his eyes. "I know you think I'm an obnoxious little twerp, but I ain't a villain."

He was quoting the words I'd screeched in order to summon him when I needed his aid in healing Nevan. I would've screamed anything to get the leprechaun's attention. "I don't think that anymore. But you are prickly at times."

"Yeah, Ennie's always telling me that."

"Off to the oracle, then?"

Nevan rubbed his neck. "Perhaps you should stay behind, Lindsey."

"Why?"

"You are the Janusite," he said, "and I'd be more comfortable keeping that secret amongst a small, select group of allies."

"Then we won't tell the oracle."

Ennea cleared her throat. "It won't be so simple. Oracles can sense what you are, even if you try to hide it with a glamour or another type of spell. They have the power of foresight, yes, but also insight. As soon as he looks at you, the oracle will know."

Terrific.

I tugged Nevan's hand, and he followed me to a corner of the room out of earshot of our hostess and her brother.

"Take me with you," I said. "I can wait outside the oracle's underground lair."

"What makes you believe he has an underground lair?"

"Don't all of you live inside mountains or hills or whatever?" I raised one finger, swirling it in the air to indicate our surroundings. "This is underground, right?"

He almost smiled. "Indeed it is. But you cannot come with us to the oracle's abode. I will not risk anyone else discovering what you are. The Janusite's power has been coveted for over a century, and there are those who would go to any lengths to possess you." He bent to stare into my eyes. "You may recall Skeiron."

Yeah, I had a vague memory of that bastard. "Vague" as in completely clear and as vivid as the day it all went down.

I stared right back at Nevan. "Told you before, I am not leaving you alone. Ceara might find you, or worse, her sorcerer pal."

"Tris will be there to—" He grimaced. "Protect me."

"I thought he ate copper and fueled the healing vortex."

"As you've seen tonight, he has great power. He does far more than manage the vortex, he also oversees and guards the portal."

"I thought Brennus was the guardian of the portal, since you quit to become king."

"He is guardian of the falls, protecting the portal from the mortal side. Tris handles the Unseen side."

Every new fact I learned about the supernatural made me realize how many more I had yet to discover. No wonder elementals were immortal. They needed eternity to comprehend the full scope of their own world.

"Guess that explains," I said, "how Tris pulled a little of the Unseen into the mortal world when he healed you."

"It does," Nevan said. "I will take you home and return here so Tris and I might travel to the oracle."

"No." I all but snarled the word, overcome by a stab of panic. "I mean, I don't want you to be alone at any time, not with a brain-sucking sorcerer after you. Tris can come with us to our place."

"As you wish."

I wasn't getting what I wished because I wished his previously dead wife hadn't teamed up with a sorcerer to scour out my lover's brain and murder three women. Oh if wishes were candy, I'd be on a major sugar high right about now.

"Wait," I said. "Take me to the portal, not home. I have to tell Stan I need some time off, and I need to talk to Travis."

About the dead girls. Nevan understood that without asking, and he also realized I didn't want to talk about it in front of Tris and Ennea.

"One more thing," I said, guiding Nevan back to the leprechauns. "Ceara wears a green pendant around her waist. It looks like a round sword with a dull point and a flared top. There are chevron lines on the cap. Anybody know what that is? It feels important, but I can't explain why."

Three elementals exchanged thoughtful glances.

And then they all shrugged.

"Without seeing it," Ennea said, "it's hard to say."

"Do you have a pen and paper?" I asked.

Nevan lifted his open hand, and poof, a pen and paper appeared in his palm.

I took the items and quickly sketched the pendant, then held up the drawing for all to see. I was no artist, but my rather crude depiction illustrated the basics.

Nevan took hold of the paper's edge, his gaze trained on the image. "I cannot say for certain, but this appears ancient Egyptian. A symbol I can't quite recall."

Egyptian. That gave me a starting point for uncovering more about the symbol.

"I'll check it out later," I said, and folded up the paper to stuff it into my back pocket. I hopped up on my toes to kiss Nevan's cheek. "What would I do without you?"

"Get into a great deal of trouble."

I pinched his arm. "Smart-aleck sylph."

Tris made an irritated noise. "We going to the oracle's pad or what?"

"We are," Nevan said, and waved to Tris. "Come. We will stop off at the portal to deposit Lindsey there and then journey on to the oracle."

The icy wriggling started up again in my gut. The tiny, slippery worms of doubt and dread coiled around my soul. If the oracle couldn't help us...

God save us all.

NEVAN CLEAVED ME TO HIS BODY FOR THE TRIP TO THE PORTAL. HE dropped me off there, kissed me goodbye, and vanished without speaking one syllable. I'd felt the tension in his body and seen it in the tight lines of his expression, as well as in the roiling, cool colors of his eyes. The sorcerer, and his apparent hold over Nevan, bothered my honey more than he cared to admit.

Men, even immortal ones, disliked feeling powerless. Hell, they hated it with a burning intensity. They'd resort to almost anything to avoid it.

I got myself through the portal and back to the rock shop without incident. When I informed Stan I needed a few days off, he responded by saying, "Sure, fine. Do what you gotta do."

Once a grumpy, confirmed skeptic of the paranormal, my boss had seen his illusions shattered on that day six weeks ago when the sylph army invaded the mortal realm. These days, Stan Lagorio adopted a "don't look, don't ask" attitude. He'd listen if I told him about the supernatural among us, but he never asked about it and worked really, really hard to avoid seeing anything unusual. Steering clear of the vortex and the waterfall kept him safely ensconced in his comfort bubble—most of the time.

Before I had the chance to call Travis, he walked through the shop's open front doors.

I hurried out from behind the counter to meet him halfway. Though he was in full cop mode, stoic and erect, the look in his eyes betrayed his true mood. Something was up.

"What is it?" I asked.

He blew out a breath and scratched the back of his hand. "It's about Megan."

I fiddled with the neckline of my shirt, trying to pull it a little higher.

"The doctors got the final test results," he said. "They'd been giving her tons of fluids, but it's like her body was rejecting it. They couldn't get her rehydrated."

"What does that matter? The sorcerer cut her throat."

"Lindsey, it wasn't your fault." He reached out to grasp my hand. "Even if you'd saved her from him, she would've died anyway."

Dark magics made her sick, that's what Tris had said. Brennus told me he smelled the poisonous magic on all the dead girls. Nothing, not even a vortex, had the power to bring them back. Slitting Megan's throat in front of me had been, what? A show of power?

No. The sorcerer had meant to torment me. Drive a searing blade of guilt into my heart. Make me doubt myself. Make me doubt everything and everyone.

"Dammit," I hissed. "He got exactly what he wanted."

Travis squeezed my hand. "Who?"

I'd forgotten he was holding my hand. Maybe I should've pulled away, but in this moment I needed human contact. He was my friend, after all.

"The sorcerer," I said. When I called to report the deaths, I'd given Travis a summary of my encounter with the man in the black robe, so he'd understand the context of the murders. Not that he could do anything about it. Arrest a sorcerer? No cop received training in how to handle a supernatural perpetrator.

"How'd he get what he wanted?" Travis asked, his fingers warm around my cold hand.

"I let him unsettle me. Let him get inside my head and make me suspicious of everyone. But worst of all, I let him convince me I can't stop him."

"You can do it, Lindsey." He gave my hand another squeeze. "But you don't have to do it alone. Me, Nevan, Stan, even that weird Tris kid, we're all here for you."

"I know." Wriggling my hand out of his, I stuffed my hands in my pockets. "What about the other girls? Have you identified them?"

"Not yet." He hesitated, shuffling his feet. "Seems like they had the same severe dehydration as Megan, though, which means they would've died even without being murdered."

"They were murdered either way. The sorcerer used dark magics to poison them."

His face went slack. "Uh-huh."

I patted his arm. "Don't worry, you'll get used to this stuff eventually."

We said goodbye, and Travis headed back to the sheriff's department.

I trudged down the path to the falls, intent on examining the crime scene. Travis had done so earlier, but I needed to investigate on my own. At the wooden railing, I paused to study the gushing water that careened over the cliff and pummeled the pool below. Sometimes when I studied the falls, I got an odd feeling of…discontinuity. I couldn't describe it any other way. This was where the mortal world collided with the elemental realm, like a breach in the space-time continuum. I could almost feel the energies of both worlds merging and dividing like solar systems crashing into each other.

Who controlled the collisions between the mortal and elemental worlds? Elementals would say they did, for sure. Humans were not slaves to the desires of immortals, though. We could fight them. We had fought them. If the worlds ever went to war, for real, could we win? Was this why the boundaries existed? To keep the Unseen realm at bay and prevent an apocalypse?

A sensation of awareness prickled over my skin, as if another presence hovered nearby.

I stepped away from the railing and turned in a circle, scrutinizing every shadow, every tree, every bush and blade of grass. Nothing. I was alone.

My intuition warned me otherwise.

The breeze delivered a familiar odor to my nostrils. The stench of ammonia faded away within seconds.

I froze, touching my fingers to my lips. That smell, I recognized it. Yes, I'd smelled it two days ago when Megan staggered out of the woods and again today just before the sorcerer appeared. That wasn't the reason for my déjà vu. I recognized the ammonia-like stench from six weeks ago. Back then, a shapeshifter had produced the odor, thanks to the monkey-like traits he inherited from the curse that spawned the kerkopes.

That shapeshifter had been Calder Blackwell.

But he had been destroyed. Nevan snapped his neck and drove an endued sword through his heart. No coming back from that, right?

Anything is possible, Nevan had said.

I swung my head left and right but saw nothing.

"Calder?" I shouted. "Are you there?"

Silence.

This was crazy, right? But hadn't I commented to Nevan how recent events reminded me of Calder's campaign to push me over the edge?

A black-robed figure separated from the shadows, shuffling out into the sunlight filtering down through the trees. That preternatural hush had come over the earth again. It seemed to surround him like a bubble, spreading outward wherever he moved. The sorcerer halted halfway across the clearing from me.

"Why do you call for a dead man?" he asked.

"Are you Calder Blackwell?"

His head tipped left and then right. "We are many things."

My hands wanted to wring each other, but I flattened them on my thighs, wiping away the clamminess. "What does that mean?"

"We can be whatever, whomever, you most desire."

His image quivered, the colors morphing as his shape altered.

The sorcerer assumed the likeness of Nevan, complete with the loincloth and the face of the sylph king.

I laid a hand on my chest, pressing it flat. This was not Nevan. The glamour was excellent—perfect, in fact—but the being facing me was not my lover.

"Nice try," I said. "I didn't fall for it the first time, and I'm not falling for it this go-round. You are not Nevan."

The sorcerer ambled closer, hips undulating with each step, the loincloth tightening and loosening as muscles worked. "Are ye certain of that?"

His Irish brogue hit the bull's eye, even better than his first attempt.

My throat went thick, my blood chilled. He lingered an arm's length away, too close for my comfort, but I refused to give this being the satisfaction of making me retreat. I lifted a hand to my hip, reassured by the hard outline of my holstered derringer.

"Don't I look like Nevan?" the sorcerer asked in a casual, slightly amused tone. "Don't I sound like him? Don't I smell like him?"

He inched forward, so close I could scent him. He smelled of earth and thunderstorms, like Nevan, but underneath another odor gave away the game. The stench of something acrid and sour, almost sulfurous. Like spoiled meat or...death.

I slipped my hand inside my waistband, taking hold of the gun's grip. "Oh, you've done a bang-up job of impersonating Nevan. The scent was a nice touch, but you can't cover up what you really are. You stink of rotten things."

He chuckled, grinning, and his eyes crinkled the way Nevan's did. The colors inside his eyes, however, had a sickly green undertone. "You are as clever as I'd hoped. Perhaps you prefer this?"

The image of Nevan went fuzzy, morphing into the likeness of Travis in his sheriff's uniform.

I took one step backward. "Since you glamoured right in front of me both times, why would believe I'd fall for this trick? What's the point?"

He shrugged, and in Travis's Texas drawl, he said, "Don't listen, do ya? We can be whatever you want. Once you've reached the pinnacle of your powers, and you accept you can't defeat us, all you gotta do is say the word. Sweet thing, we can replace what you're going to lose."

More head games. *Just like Calder.* Except Calder hadn't glamoured to impersonate people I knew. He'd lurked in the shadows until the moment he had me at my weakest, when he was positive I'd give in to his plan to make me his monkey-mate.

The sorcerer was doing the same thing, except he coveted my Janusite powers. Calder hadn't cared about that.

Fake Travis smiled. "You'll see."

He vanished.

I'd see what? Maybe I didn't want to know, but I realized I had to know the answers to every question raised by my encounters with the sorcerer.

Travis, the real one, had been right. I needed my allies with me in this battle.

I climbed over the railing and up onto the rock ledge alongside the falls, sidling up to the thundering cascade. Dozens of times, I'd leaped through the curtain of water, going to or coming from the portal within the cave behind the falls. My encounter with the not-Nevan and not-Travis glamours seemed to have infected me with a lingering uncertainty about everything. What if I stumbled when I jumped through the waterfall? What I hit my head and tumbled into the pool below to drown in its depths?

Oh for heaven's sake. What kind of wuss had I turned into if one measly old supernatural encounter with a creepy sorcerer had me quaking in my hiking boots?

"May I be of assistance, my lady?"

I squawked at the sudden appearance of Brennus right in front of me, his bare feet planted on the rock ledge.

Suddenly breathing hard, I slapped a palm on the red sandstone of the cliff. "You scared the bejesus out of me."

He bowed his head in apology, then offered me his hand. "May I?"

"Sure, why not."

Brennus grasped me around the waist, hefted me off the ledge, and spun toward the falls. His long arms pushed me through the water into the cave, where he set me down on the solid, if pockmarked, stone floor without the shapeshifter ever stepping off the ledge outside.

"Thank you," I hollered through the waterfall.

I hadn't expected him to respond, since he probably couldn't hear me, but my innate politeness compelled me to say it anyway. Nevan would've winced at my expression of gratitude, but I was still on the mortal side of the veil.

Water drenched me and streamed off my body onto the floor. My dripping hair hung limp around my face, locks of it pasted to my skin. I swiped them away.

The wall to my left caught my eye, and a memory barreled through my mind. Nevan backing me up to that wall, both of us naked. The slap of my back meeting the rock. Nevan hitching my legs over his shoulders as he set his mouth to my sex and pleasured me. His voice echoed in my mind, his words as fresh as that night, when he'd stripped away the last threads of my inhibitions with two syllables—*trust me.*

In that moment, I'd relinquished all my trust to him. My faith in him had only increased since that night, because of everything we'd survived together. No goddamn sorcerer or formerly dead shrew of a wife would destroy my trust in Nevan.

Squeezing my eyes shut, squeezing my fingers into my palms, I sent out a silent invocation. *I believe in you, Nevan.*

I opened my eyes, shook off the remnants of fear and uncertainty, and willed the portal to admit me. The swirling, inky blackness telescoped open in front of me, the tendrils of purple and blue thrashing within it. I marched through the portal and out into the Unseen.

Chapter Ten

I TRAVERSED THE LITTLE CLEARING THE PORTAL OPENED INTO, HEADING for the dirt path through the trees. At the edge of the woods, I stopped. Where was I going?

Glancing around, I realized I had no idea. Nevan had always accompanied me and whisked me straight from the portal to his—our—home. On my own, I'd have to take the long way there. I had no idea which way to go. Nevan hadn't given me directions or a map, and I hadn't thought to ask. At least he had the excuse of someone screwing with his brain. I should've remembered to ask the question. *So, honey, how do I get home?*

Of course, I'd been distracted by his predicament. And by the weirdness of the Nevan impostor and the murders of three innocent women. Still, how could I have been so stupid? I got myself stranded.

Letting out a little growl of frustration, I turned to stomp back to the portal and go back to the mortal world until I figured out a solution.

Something tiny and red leaped out of the grass to land at my feet.

I yelped. My heart thudded and my hand flew to my chest.

The little lizard gazed up at me with shiny black eyes, its fiery red skin glistening in the sunlight. Glints of iridescent orange flashed on its flesh as the breeze rustled the moss-like foliage of the trees, causing the sun to glint brighter and flash darker with each flap of the branches. The creature—with its long and slender body, stubby legs, and tapering tail—resembled lizards I'd seen in the mortal realm.

Listing its head to the side, the creature blinked once.

I crouched to get closer to the little guy—for some reason, I thought of it as male—and reached a finger out to touch it.

Flames erupted around the lizard in a miniature conflagration, only to snuff out a split second later.

The lizard was gone.

I stared at the spot where it had been. A red critter that vanished in a puff of flames. This world kept getting weirder and weirder.

A burst of itty-bitty fire caught my eye peripherally. Leaping up, I spun toward the flash.

The tiny creature squatted there, no longer aflame, its dark eyes gazing at me with what I swore was curiosity. It tilted its head to the side again, blinked, and scuttled toward me.

I scuttled away from it, not at all certain I wanted to attract this little guy, no matter how cute he was. Things in the Unseen could appear innocuous, then spin around to bite you in the ass in the most literal way. But this was the first animal life I'd encountered here, and I couldn't help feeling as curious about the alien lizard as it seemed to be about me.

The creature halted, blinking up at me with wide, gleaming eyes. Its little mouth opened and closed.

I had the oddest sensation the lizard was trying to communicate. My intuition assured me this creature meant me no harm. I bit my lip, studying the tiny beastie. What harm could come from interacting with a teeny-weeny thing like this lizard?

Kneeling, I lowered my hand to ground level and turned my palm up.

The lizard toddled to me and climbed onto my palm.

Its miniature feet felt strangely warm. Its tail flicked, tickling my skin. Thanks to its tail that measured longer than its body, the creature occupied the entire length of my hand from the heel to the tip of my middle finger. I touched a fingertip to the top of its head. The skin was warmer there, almost hot, with a slick, smooth texture. Giving in to an inexplicable impulse, I began to pet the lizard's tiny head.

The creature purred softly, and I swore its almost nonexistent lips curled into a smile.

I couldn't keep from smiling too. This had to be the most adorable denizen of the ooky and dangerous Unseen realm I'd met so far.

The lizard pushed his head up into my finger as I petted him, like a cat would've done. Filaments of flame, red and orange and yellow, flitted through his black eyes. His skin grew hotter, almost too hot.

What was I doing? Petting a lizard? Nevan was in trouble, and I paused to befriend a cute critter I came upon in the woods? *Cut it out, Lindsey. Get back on task.*

I set the lizard on the grass, gave him one more pat with my finger, and said, "Nice meeting you, little guy, but I have to go."

Rising, I wheeled toward the portal.

The lizard chirped.

I half turned, eying the creature.

He sat back on his hind feet, lifting his front legs in the air like a dog sitting up to beg for treats. His throat quivered on another chirp.

"I really have to leave," I said. "Go on home, little guy."

The lizard slowly blinked his big, dark eyes.

Crouching, I spoke to the beastie. "Look, my boyfriend is in a load of trouble and I need to get back to our house, but I can't find my way. It's a long story, okay? I have to go back to my world and…Hell, I don't know what I'm going to do. You're really cute, and I'd love to hang out with you, but I just can't. Understand?"

No idea why I told the lizard all of this, but in normal life I'd talked to dogs and cats and even cows. Why not an otherworldly lizard?

The flame-colored creature raced to me, skittered up my leg, and grabbed onto the pocket of my jeans with his tiny front feet. He tugged on the fabric, looking up at me with unblinking eyes.

"What are you doing?" I asked, as if a lizard could respond. But he did seem to be…I don't know, trying to tell me something.

Like what?

The lizard tugged at my pocket again.

What in my pocket could attract the interest of a creature like this one?

A chill shimmied down my spine, raising the hairs all over my body as I realized the answer. The pocket where the salamander perched held the soul stone.

I took the little red guy in my hand, holding him gently, and rose. I dug the soul stone out of my pocket. Taking it between my thumb and forefinger, I lifted it to the eye level of the lizard.

"This what you wanted?" I asked.

The salamander nodded. Swear to God, it nodded.

"Why?"

His onyx eyes blinked.

No idea what that meant. I didn't speak salamander.

Groaning out a sigh, I bent to deposit the lizard on the ground and patted his head. "I don't know what you're trying to tell me, and I don't have time to figure it out. I'm going home. Bye-bye, little cutie-pie."

I took one step toward the portal.

The salamander chirped and raced toward the dirt path that led into the woods. There, he stopped to gaze back at me. The creature jerked its head, beckoning me to follow the way a person might.

My mouth open but unable to speak, I gaped at the beastie. Could a lizard know how to find Nevan's underground lair? The salamander had drawn my attention to the soul stone right before he scampered over to the woods trail. Maybe he meant the stone would guide me.

I rolled the stone in my palm, the awareness of Nevan it engendered rippling through me in warm, calming waves. If I followed the salamander's advice, such as it was, I might wander in the woods for days, lost and alone. But if I went back to the mortal world, I might never come up with a better plan.

Better than taking advice from a lizard? *Ugh.* My life had become totally surreal.

Closing my hand around the stone, I marched to the salamander.

He skittered up my leg, hopped onto my arm, and scampered up to my shoulder. Stationed there, he nodded toward the stone in my hand.

"Got any idea how I make this work?" I asked.

The lizard sat up on his hind legs and shrugged his little shoulders.

Ohhh-kay. Guess I was doing this. Taking advice from a red lizard.

I shut my eyes and focused on the sensations from the soul stone. Warmth tingled through me, emanating from my hand and spreading throughout my entire body. The familiar, arousing energy of Nevan infused my being, as if he'd wrapped his arms around my very essence. The thrilling intimacy of it triggered sense memories of making love with Nevan, of our magics twirling around each other while our bodies merged and the pleasure mounted.

Nevan. I needed to help him. Needed to find our home. Right now.

My eyes flew open in the instant the world shifted. I zipped through the dark tunnel that had once clawed at my flesh, before I'd come to terms with my Janusite-ness, but that now whisked me away in a fraction of a heartbeat. I barely glimpsed the void around me before I popped out at the base of the mountain that concealed our home.

And the salamander still sat on my shoulder, on all fours, his tiny fingers clutching at me. His eyes had gone wide and I could've sworn his red skin had paled a shade.

"Wow," I said, swaying the tiniest bit. "That was a rush."

My new friend grinned, exposing tiny little teeth lined up in rows on his upper and lower gums.

I stroked his head. "Guess you liked it too, eh? I had no idea I could do that. Thanks for pointing me to the soul stone. Hell of a lot easier than tromping through the woods for who knows how long hoping to stumble onto this place."

The salamander closed his mouth and banked his head to the side.

"I live here," I said. "So I'm afraid this is where we say goodbye."

He made a soft, whimpery noise and scampered up my neck to perch atop the shell of my ear. My hair fell over his tiny body, even as his tail tickled the skin behind my ear.

Laughing, I plucked him off my ear to hold him in my palm. "Ah, little guy, I can't take you with me."

Well, since I'd brought him along on my interdimensional journey here, I supposed I probably could take him inside the house with me. But should I? Nevan and Tris might return at any moment or they might be gone for hours and hours. I had no idea how long it might take to track down an oracle, or what kinds of hoops that oracle might force them to jump through to gain his help. That left me alone with nothing much to do.

My new friend had assisted me. Maybe I could find a way to communicate with him better and learn something from this odd little critter.

Some individuals, not all of them human, would've called me an odd little critter.

What the heck.

Cradling the salamander in one hand, I raised the soul stone in the other and commanded the entrance to open. The solid rock wall, with its overhanging weeds and moss, telescoped out until a large, oval hole appeared in the mountain. The doorway extended from the ground up to about eight feet in height, just the right size for my tall and hunky significant other.

A sliver of worry wormed its way into my heart. Nevan was in danger, and I had to do something—anything—to help him. Trouble was, I had no idea what I could do.

I crossed the threshold with my red friend. The door telescoped shut behind us. I stood in the vacant living room, bathed in the omnipresent golden light, inside the home I shared with the only man, of any world, I'd ever loved. My gaze wandered to the bed, the mussed sheets, and my brain conjured a memory of the musky scent of sex permeating the room as Nevan and I expressed our passion and devotion to each other in the most carnal and intimate ways.

The salamander danced in my hand.

"Oh no," I said, glancing down at him, "am I squishing you? Let me set you down."

I dropped to my knees, lowered my hand to the floor, and opened my fingers.

My new friend dashed away, darting this way and that, his tiny head bobbing as he examined his surroundings. How odd that I called a lizard my friend. How sad that I did. Of course, I had other friends of the bipedal variety, but they were all busy. Travis had murders to investigate. Stan had a business to run. Tris was off babysitting Nevan on his oracle quest.

At the very least, I had a pet to keep me company.

I sat back on my butt, my legs outstretched, hands limp on my thighs.

The salamander halted at the bed, his little neck craned to stare up at it. He rose onto his hind legs and grimaced.

No, I must've imagined that.

Then again, he'd grinned at me earlier. Why couldn't he grimace as well?

"What's the matter?" I asked, leaning forward a bit. "You want up on the bed?"

My new pet spun around, raced toward me, and stopped a few feet from my boots. He went stone-still, eyes unblinking.

A gigantic mass of flames shot up from him to lick at the ceiling.

The heat roasted me, and I scrambled backward on my ass using hands and feet like a crab.

The flames snuffed out.

In their place lounged a man as tall as Nevan, with a physique as broad and muscular as the sylph's. The stranger's skin, tanned and tinged with a coppery sheen, glimmered with tiny gold flecks as if dusted with glitter. His dark brown hair, shot through with maroon streaks, cascaded down to his shoulders in wavy locks. But the aspect of him that captured my focus resided lower than his shoulders, much lower.

The guy was stark naked. And his long, thick penis hung slack between his massive thighs.

With a long-suffering sigh, he stretched his enormous body and said, "My, it's good to be in human form again."

"I—wha—" My legs splayed before me, still flat on my ass, I gaped at him. "Who are you?"

"Max." He said it as if I should've known this fact.

Sitting forward, I surveyed the being in front of me. "What are you?"

He grinned and chuckled. "I've been assigned to you. I'm your new familiar, which means I'll lend a hand in your efforts to understand and control your newfound magics."

This creature, Max, spoke with an English accent.

"Uh-huh, sure." I pushed up onto my knees, staring up his naked body to his face. "What kind of elemental are you?"

"An incubus, naturally."

CHAPTER ELEVEN

"AN INCUBUS?" I SCRAMBLED TO MY FEET, BACKING AWAY FROM him. "You say 'naturally' like I should've expected an incubus to show up and announce he's my familiar. And I thought witches had familiars. I'm not a witch."

He laid a hand on his abdomen, his lips pursed but curled upward at the corners and his eyes crinkled with amusement. "Familiars are for any magical beings in need of a helping hand."

"Hmph. Isn't an incubus a sex demon?"

"Not a demon." He tsked. "Mortal mythology can be bloody annoying and inaccurate. An incubus feeds off sexual energy, but I don't steal into women's bedrooms at night to ravage them."

"If you say so."

He looked to the ceiling, perhaps hoping for divine intervention, and then his shoulders wilted. "I'd heard you were quite difficult. The rumors are spot on."

"Seriously? I'm the bad one? You tricked me." I stabbed a finger in the air in his direction. "Pretended to be a cute little salamander so I'd bring you into my home."

"I am a salamander." He roved his gaze up and down my body, and one corner of his mouth ticked up. "Glad to hear you think I'm cute, though. Means you're up for it."

"Up for what?"

"Getting a leg over."

Maybe I was dense, but only then did I realize he was talking about sex. And only because I'd watched a lot of British TV.

"Oh please," I said. "Calling a tiny lizard cute does not mean I'm going to sleep with you. And you're avoiding the real issue here, which is that you tricked me."

"Tosh," he said with a dismissive toss of his head, then strode closer to tower over me. "Since you clearly weren't listening the first time, let me repeat it. I am a salamander."

I threw my hands in the air. "Salamanders are little lizards. Not giant, manlike whatevers."

"Whatevers?" He stared at me like a mushroom had sprouted from my ear. "I am not a whatever. I am a salamander." When I started to protest, he held up a hand. "Wait. Salamanders are incubi. The term incubus is more of a general description, since we're shapeshifters who can take human form whenever we like. In fact, we spend more time as humanoids than as salamanders."

"Of course. I should've known."

"Yes, you should have." He gave me a closed-mouth smile, his dark eyes lit up with unwinding ribbons of bright red and yellow. "Has your lover taught you nothing about this world? The various species of elementals? How we interact? What a bloody familiar is?"

"Nevan's been kind of busy lately."

Max's smile deepened, dimpling his cheeks. "I'll teach you. As your familiar, it's my duty."

"I don't recall ordering a familiar. Afraid I'll have to return you to the magic shop."

His brow scrunched, wrinkling his forehead. "I am not returnable. I was sent to help you."

"Sent?" I clasped my hands in front of me. "Who sent you?"

"Can't say."

"Naturally," I said, mocking the way he'd spoken the word earlier. I walked around Max in a circle, surveying him from head to toe and front to back. Though he had a hot body and a gorgeous face—were there any ugly people in this realm?—his good looks did nothing for me. Since I'd met Nevan, no other male of any realm could compete. I wanted him and no one else.

"Do you mean," I said, stopping in front of him again, "you feel it's your duty to help me, or that someone magically compelled you to be my familiar?"

"Ahhh," he said with appreciation. "I see you've learned about debts and bargains. That's a relief. You're much less likely to get yourself in trouble when you understand the stakes."

"You haven't answered my question."

"Because I can't."

I lodged my hands in my pockets. "I get it. You're stuck in a bad bargain that prevents you from speaking the words. Was it the sorcerer who did this to you?"

"That," Max said, "I can tell you. The sorcerer wants you to know I'm his gift to the Janusite. Use me as you see fit."

"Hmm." I rocked back on my heels, tapping my tongue on my front teeth. "Why should I trust you? I mean, you're the sorcerer's puppet. No offense."

"None taken. You're right, I am his puppet."

"Which means anything I tell you, anything you see me do, you'll go back and tattle to your master."

"No." He turned away, ambling toward the bed, then turned around again and stopped. His face was pinched as he threw a sidelong glance at the bed. "The sorcerer wants me to help you, and he knows you won't accept my help unless it's confidential. I'm forbidden to share with him anything I learn, see, hear, smell, or whatnot while I'm with you."

"And I'm supposed to take your word for that."

Max shrugged. "I have nothing else to offer. This is a show of good faith on his part."

Show of good faith, my ass. This was all part of the sorcerer's plans, though I couldn't puzzle out the purpose yet. He wanted me at full power so he could steal my magic. But giving me Max and ordering him to respect my privacy? Weird.

"Okay, fine." I moved to one of the chairs and settled onto it, hands on my knees. The Nevan-size chair all but swallowed me. "Don't suppose you can tell me who the sorcerer is. Or what his plans are."

"Afraid not."

"Or if Calder Blackwell is involved."

He shook his head.

"Maybe you can answer one question." I hesitated, part of me balking at the idea of asking, but I squared my shoulders and did it anyway. "When an elemental is destroyed, can they be resurrected?"

His brows lowered as he gazed down at the floor as if considering his answer. His tone uncertain, he said, "I haven't heard of it happening, but then, if someone did pull off the feat they might not want to spread the news. The threat of destruction is the best deterrent for bad behavior."

"What happens to the soul when somebody's destroyed?"

"It moves on, I guess. Unfortunately, I can't be more informative."

"Don't worry about it. I'll ask Nevan later."

Max glanced at the bed again and grimaced.

I leaned back in the chair. "What's your problem with the bed?"

He sauntered to the other chair, situated alongside mine but separated from it by a little table, and sat down. The chair fit him just right. He relaxed into it, his arms on the chair's arms. "The bed smells of sex, a fragrance I'd normally fancy. But it also smells of…him."

"Him?" I tucked my legs under me, angling slightly toward Max. "You mean Nevan."

"Yes." Max's mouth twisted into a partial frown. "I don't fancy smelling him, knowing you've shagged a sylph."

I laughed, but it came out as a snort. "You're prejudiced against sylphs?"

"They prance around like they own the forest. In fact, they're air elementals." He lifted his chin, puffing out his chest. "The tossers have no claim on the ground. They sniff their haughty noses at salamanders, but we have domain over the true power—fire."

Oh great. I'd not only acquired a familiar who was some kind of sex demon, but I'd also been dropped smack in the middle of the Unseen realm's socio-political shenanigans. I hated mortal politics and snobbery. Sure as hell didn't need the immortal variety.

"I love Nevan," I told Max in a firm tone. "I live here with him. If that bothers you, then toddle on back to the salamander cave."

He harrumphed.

"Besides," I continued, "sylphs are made of air and earth. They have as much right to walk on the ground as you do."

"You would defend the sylph king. He protects you. Though I can't fathom why a beautiful woman like you would fall for a—"

"Before you finish that sentence," I said, nailing him with a hard look, "you should think carefully about what you want to happen here. We could be friends, maybe, if you stop dissing my boyfriend. Or I could destroy you."

He barked out a laugh. "You? Destroy me?"

"Don't scoff. I took out Skeiron."

"Did you now?" He ginned, slapping his hands on the chair's arms. "Brilliant! That wanker deserved to be shredded into atomic bits 'n bobs."

"You're very strange, Max."

"Same to you, Lindsey."

As I considered my new familiar, my thoughts gravitated back to Nevan and the fact he'd been forged rather than born an elemental. I asked Max, "Were you a mortal once upon time?"

"Yes, during the heyday of the Roman empire."

"Did you ever forge anybody?"

He moved his hands onto his lap, staring down at his restless fingers. "Once. I will never repeat the mistake."

My curiosity pestered me to question him about it, but his limp posture and his gloomy expression dissuaded me. I didn't know him well enough to press him for details.

I settled into my chair, chewing on the larger situation for a moment. "You mentioned you're not returnable, but I could kick you out of my house anytime. Right?"

"Why do you call this your house? It belongs to the sylph, doesn't it?"

Of course he would assume that. I hadn't gotten around to adding my feminine flair to the place. "I live here too. That's my girlie stuff over there."

I jabbed a finger toward the boxes of my still-not-unpacked possessions stowed against the wall. One box was open, and a flowery scarf dangled half out of it. Some of the boxes contained books, most of them related to mythology and ancient history.

"Ah yes," Max said in a condescendingly patient tone. "How could I have overlooked it."

"What is your problem? You've been Mr. Prickly Pear ever since you smelled the bed."

He arched one brunet brow. "Prickly pear?"

"Missing the point, Sherlock."

The incubus stared at me for a moment before leaning back in his chair again. "I can't help it. I am an incubus, and the urge to mate with fertile females is both innate and virtually irresistible. To be in the presence of a sensual woman and then to scent that another bloke has mated with her, it's maddening. Your passion rolls off you in enticing waves, so much so I can almost taste you."

"Get this through your innately urged head. Only one male is allowed to taste me or mate with me or any other dirty things you're thinking of."

A lazy grin spiced up his demeanor. "I can think of well over a thousand things to do to you. And that's what I've dreamed up in the past few minutes."

"Forget it all. Not interested." And I wasn't. If Nevan had spoken the exact same words to me, I would've melted into a puddle of lust at his feet. Max's statement left me unaffected.

Well, mildly annoyed. But unaffected in any sexual way.

He scrutinized me with narrowed eyes, his gaze drifting down to my breasts. But then he sighed and faced forward. "I can see you aren't in the least aroused by me. It's bloody humiliating. The incubus power of seduction is legendary, but you look at me like I'm a genuine lizard."

"Sor—" *Crap.* I'd almost apologized, something I couldn't risk in the Unseen. I jiggled in my seat, wishing to hell Nevan would come home. "Don't take it as an affront to your mojo. Nevan and I have a connection even I don't understand, but it is unbreakable."

"I'm beginning to understand that."

I slumped back against my chair. "There's also the weirdness of me to consider. Magic tends to go wonky around me."

He leaned forward to squint at me. "Wonky?"

"Means it messes up other magic." I drummed my fingers on the chair's arm. "You never answered my question. Why do you think I can't send you packing?"

"I'm bound to serve you until one of us dies."

"Can't I zip away and leave you in my magical dust?"

His brows furrowed as his eyes glazed over. He shook his head, as if shaking off the confusion. "Now that we've met, and I've declared my intention to serve as your familiar, I can't leave you or be left. Should you 'zip away,' as you put it, I'd pop in wherever you landed."

Just what I needed. A salamander-slash-incubus I couldn't shake off my tail.

I cringed inwardly. Nevan would freak when he found out I'd brought home a pet sex demon.

Where was Nevan? How long did a trip to the oracle take?

"I'm going to trust you," I said, "and accept your help. If you promise to stop insulting Nevan."

"No promises. Not in this world."

"Right. Almost forgot."

He slouched in his chair. "I will voluntarily refrain from disparaging him. Though I still can't understand the appeal of King Nevan of the Air Fairies."

Max was soooo lucky Nevan wasn't around to hear him insult sylphs. Nevan had once tossed Travis into tree for calling him a jungle fairy.

I fidgeted in my too-big chair but couldn't quite get comfy. "Man, I wish this place had a sofa."

Max waved a hand, and a sofa appeared in the corner adjacent to the doorway to the kitchen. No, not a sofa. A red velvet chaise lounge, of the sort a decadent queen might sprawl herself across to entice a lover.

I glanced at Max. "Thought you were supposed to help me with magic, not indulge my every whim."

"Can't I do both?"

"Rather you didn't. Just because I say I wish for this or that doesn't mean I actually want it. I have a bad habit of voicing my passing thoughts out loud."

"I'll take that into consideration."

"How about you ask me if I really want something before you make it appear?"

The incubus screwed up one side of his mouth. "If you insist."

"I really do."

Max let his head fall back onto the chair, his gaze unfocused though his eyes pointed at the ceiling. His face went slack, as if he were lost in thought.

"Lindsey."

The stern voice from behind us made my pet incubus jerk forward and twist around to peer over the back of his chair. His eyes widened briefly, but he regained his cavalier bearing as he unfurled his body from the chair.

I stayed curled up in my chair, gazing at the sexy hunk of sylph standing behind Max's chair. The two men stared at each other—Max with a neutral expression, Nevan with flinty eyes and squared jaw.

"Hi, honey," I said brightly. "You're home."

Nevan swiveled his gaze to me. "Who, may I ask, is our visitor?"

"Oh, this is Max. My familiar."

"Your what?" His entire body bolted straight and taut. He tucked his chin, his eyes locked on me. Those swirling pools of brilliant color shimmered and sparked with white, a sign of anxiety. Nodding toward Max, Nevan said, "He is an incubus."

"I know, Max told me." I clambered out of the chair. "Maybe we should talk privately, huh?"

Max smiled with territorial glee. "Yes, I'd love to have a private discussion with my mistress."

"Not you," I told the incubus. I pointed a finger at Nevan. "You."

The white still shimmering in his eyes made my stomach knot up and an invisible hand clamp around my heart. It wasn't my new friend unsettling him. It had to be what he'd learned from his visit to the oracle.

"You," I said to Max, "over there."

I gestured toward the chaise lounge.

Grumbling, shoulders slumped, he shuffled toward the backless sofa and flung his body onto it lengthwise. With one arm draped down his thigh, he propped his head up with the other arm.

Nevan came up behind me, curving a hand over each of my upper arms. "Where did that thing come from?"

"The incubus or the sofa?"

"Both."

"Well, you see, I kind of wished out loud for a sofa and Max sort of poofed one into the room for me."

He laid a hand on his forehead, head down. "Lindsey, you must be more careful around magical beings."

"I didn't know he'd do that."

Nevan caught my hand and led me toward the bed on the opposite side of the room from the nude incubus, who had begun to smirk. Nevan gestured for me to sit on the bed. I perched on its edge, my feet suspended several inches above the floor, and Nevan lowered his big body onto the fur blanket beside me.

"Tell me," he said quietly, "how you acquired a familiar. An incubus, no less."

"Well..." I hunched my shoulders and peeked up at him through my lashes. "You see, I wanted to come home, but you forgot to tell me how to get here...I should start at the beginning."

I relayed the whole story to him, from the revelation about the dehydrated girls to my latest encounter with the sorcerer, and finally to my befriending of the harmless little salamander and Max's big reveal in the living room. Nevan listened without expression, his gaze on me, his eyes calming to a bronze-and-gold whirlpool that spun in gentle circles. By the time I finished explaining, he'd slipped his hand into mine and laced our fingers.

"So that's it," I said. "Totally unintentional acquisition of a familiar. If I'd known what Max is, I wouldn't have brought him into our home."

"Mm." Nevan raised our joined hands to fold his other hand around them. "Lindsey, my love, you are far too intelligent and suspicious to do such a thing. Whatever possessed you?"

Yeah, I'd wondered that too. I gave him the best explanation I could offer. "I was worried about you, and I wanted to do something to help, but I couldn't think of anything. I was feeling, um..."

"Powerless."

"Kind of."

"And uneasy, because you fear the sorcerer is Calder."

"That too." I hadn't stated my fear in explicit terms, but as usual, Nevan had no trouble reading between my lines.

He released my hand, pulling me into his arms. With my cheek to his chest, he combed his fingers through my hair. "Neglecting to tell you how to find your way home was inexcusable. Did you truly employ the soul stone to get here?"

"Uh-huh." I snuggled into him, grateful to have him here again, alive and well. But his skin felt a touch cool again, almost clammy. "Are you feeling okay?"

He sighed, his chest deflating. "Quite tired, to be honest."

Beneath the bronzed surface, his skin evidenced a faint pallor. I noted shadows under his eyes too.

Placing a hand on his cheek, I searched those beautiful eyes, now dulled by a deep exhaustion. "How did the meeting with the oracle go?"

His face blanked. "The oracle?"

"Yeah, the—" I glanced around, suddenly aware of one fact. "Where's Tris?"

"Tris?"

I grasped Nevan's face in both hands. "Your friend, the leprechaun. Snarky redheaded kid in ripped jeans."

He scowled. "I know who Tris is."

"Then where is he? Tris promised he'd stay with you every second until he brought you back to me."

Nevan opened his mouth, then shut it. His eyes went cloudy, his gaze distant.

He had no idea what I was talking about.

With my hands still bracketing his face, I gave his head a little shake. "Wake up, Nevan. What's the last thing you remember?"

His focus reeled back to me. "Our visit with Ennea."

"But not our discussion about the oracle, or visiting the oracle with Tris."

"No." He shut his eyes. "It's happened again."

"Looks like. But where the hell is Tris?" I jumped up and snagged Nevan's hand. "Come on, we have to find him. I need to know the sorcerer hasn't gotten his mitts on Tris."

Nevan heaved his body off the bed, seeming more wiped out with every passing moment. He trudged toward the wall that concealed the doorway. I trailed behind him, suffering an ever-increasing sense of impending doom.

He flourished his hand. The doorway telescoped open.

There, inches beyond the opening, hunched one very irritated leprechaun. Tris had his hands on his hips, one foot tapping the ground. His mouth was compressed into a tight line.

"About damn time," Tris said. "Where have you been?"

"Get him inside," I told Nevan, who plodded over the threshold to grasp Tris's shoulder and usher him through the doorway, then shut it again.

Tris held up his hands to me, palms out. "Don't blame me, sister. I was sticking right beside him, like you told me to, but then—" He snapped his fingers. "Just like that, the dude was gone."

"Did you try to find him?"

"Searched everywhere I could think, but found zilch." The leprechaun rubbed his jaw. "Even went to Ennea, but she couldn't catch the tiniest magical whiff of him. Like the sylph just ceased to exist."

"Ceased to exist?"

"For a while, yeah," he said, his tone uncertain. "Ennea finally got a hit on her locater spell, and I hightailed it over here." Tris swept his gaze over Nevan. "Man, you look like roadkill."

I could think of a solitary explanation for Nevan's disappearance. The sorcerer had summoned him.

"We need to talk to an oracle," I said. "But we can't let Nevan out of this house. So far, he's been taken only when he's out in the world. Right?"

"It would seem so," Nevan said. He squinted at me. "I know what you're thinking, and the answer is no."

I marched up to him, bent my head back, and fixed my hardest stare on him. "The answer is no? Since when are you the boss of me?"

He ran a hand over his eyes. "Never have I succeeded at reining you in."

"Exactly." I rose onto my tiptoes, spreading my palms over his bare chest. "Here's my plan. Uh-uh, stop right there. Before you get all snooty on me, remember I came up with the plan that got rid of Skeiron."

"Indeed you did." He laid his palms on my back, over my shoulder blades. "Let us hear your grand plan, my clever love."

Couldn't keep from smiling. Every time he complimented me, I went all gooey inside, even in the face of unknown peril.

He hugged me to him, his hands holding me up on my toes.

"Tris will stay here with you," I said, "while Max and I track down the oracle."

"No," barked Nevan, Tris, and Max.

The one time all three men could agree was when they wanted to thwart my plan. Figured.

Max piped up first. "I have no idea how to find an oracle."

"I do," Tris offered, "which means it's me who needs to go with Lindsey, not the man-whore over there."

He threw a derisive look at Max, whose self-satisfied smile deepened.

Nevan touched his nose to mine. "I still have considerable reservations about letting you out in the world when an unidentified sorcerer is after you.

One who has, it seems, contacted you directly and sent you—" He scowled at Max. "—a gift incubus."

"I prefer salamander," Max said, still sprawled across the sofa. He let one foot hang off the chaise, his toes swishing, and I got the impression he argued about designations strictly for the sake of being contrary.

Nevan scowled harder, but his features softened when he focused on me. "I must go with you."

"Every time you venture outside," I said, "you vanish and come back exhausted, like somebody vacuumed the life out of you. The part of my plan where you stay here is nonnegotiable. I love you too much to risk it happening again."

Out the corner of my eye, I noticed Max rolling his eyes. Tris simply stared at the floor, hands in his jeans pockets.

Nevan kissed the tip of my nose. "I love you equally as much. Which is why I cannot let you leave here with only an inc—a salamander for protection. Tris would suffice."

"Suffice?" Tris said, insult evident in his tone.

Ignoring him, I slid a hand up to Nevan's cheek. "And I'm not leaving you alone."

"Then we are at an impasse."

"Maybe not." I chewed on my lip, chewing on the problem in a physical way. The answer came to me, and I smiled. "Tris will go through the falls and bring Travis here. Then, Max and Tris and I will find the oracle."

Max sat up, suddenly attentive. "Who is Travis?"

"The sheriff," Nevan said, "of the region on the mortal side of the falls. He despises me."

I patted Nevan's cheek. "Not anymore. Travis puts up with you these days, like you put up with him. And he knows how important you are to me, which means he will guard your life for my sake."

"Because he's smitten with you," Nevan muttered under his breath.

Winding my arms around his neck, I molded my lips to his, rewarded by the rush of heat along his skin that spread into me, kindling a matching warmth. The heat didn't last, though, snuffed out by the clammy coolness of his body.

A hard pit congealed in my gut. I couldn't do nothing while his very life force seemed to be trickling out of him. I knew of a single technique that might work, because it had worked once before.

My mouth to his ear, I whispered, "Maybe we should have sex. It reinvigorated you before."

"Not with an audience," he murmured in my ear. "Besides, I have a feeling I would be unable to, ah...perform."

I dropped down onto my soles. "Really? It's that bad?"

He nodded slowly.

"Then we have to go with my plan."

"I suppose we do." He bent to rest his forehead on mine. "I'll be relying on you to save me—again."

"You've saved me plenty." I twisted my head around to speak to Tris, who was watching us. "Go get Travis. He'll be at the sheriff station, which is outside the boundary. Stan will let you use the shop phone to call him. Be sure to tell Travis this is an emergency and a favor to me."

"Will do."

Nevan opened the doorway and escorted Tris outside. The leprechaun blinked away. Nevan strode back inside, shutting the door.

He glanced at Max, and his lip curled for a brief moment. "Darlin', would ye mind instructing your servant to cover himself?"

I poked a finger into his chest. "You walk around naked, or almost naked, all the time."

"This is different."

"Are you jealous?" I fanned my hand over his chest, moving it in a slow circle. "You know I don't want anyone but you."

"He is an incubus. They possess powers of seduction."

"There's nothing to worry about." I glided my hand up to his shoulder, massaging with my fingertips. "I've spent awhile with Max today, and I haven't felt the slightest inkling of and inclination to ravish him. But the second you got home, I was ready to jump you."

His lips stretched into a gratified smile.

I dragged a finger down his bicep. "I'm yours and only yours."

"And I am yours." His hands drifted down to my buttocks. "But…"

"If it'll make you feel better." I craned my neck to see around Nevan's big arm. "Max, put some clothes on, hey?"

"How much clothing?" he asked, sounding a tad petulant.

I looked at Nevan, whose smile had turned down. "A shirt and pants. Shoes, if you want."

When I glanced at Max again, he'd donned a pair of gray slacks and a black, skintight T-shirt. His feet remained bare.

"Good enough?" I asked Nevan.

"I suppose it will do."

"You don't like him, I get it, but Max has already helped me. I didn't know the soul stone could bring me home." A thought occurred to me and I asked, "How will we know when Tris comes back with Travis?"

Nevan stepped back. "I hadn't thought of that."

"Why not leave the door open? It couldn't take that long."

He opened the doorway with his usual hand gesture.

The three of us stood there in silence, the awkward variety, for several minutes. I swung my hands, clapping them together in front of me on each pass, while Nevan leaned one hand on the wall beside the doorway. Max paced the width of the living room.

At last, Tris and Travis popped up outside the doorway.

"Little help?" Tris said, waving at the invisible barrier of the wards.

Nevan shambled outside, clapped a hand on each man's shoulder, and ushered them inside. He left the door open.

Travis caught sight of Max, and his brows shot up. "Who the blazes is that?"

"My pet incubus," I said. "Travis, meet Max. He's my familiar. Max, this is Travis Blackwell."

Max halted his pacing, eying the newcomer with strange interest.

"Let me get this straight," Travis said. "You're asking me to babysit your boyfriend?"

"Yep. Nevan, give him your endued sword."

Nevan opened his mouth, then clapped it shut. After brief pause, he asked, "Why?"

"To guard you with. If anybody shows up to nab you, at least Travis will have a shot at stopping them."

"I suppose," he said cautiously.

"Come on, honey, give it to him."

Nevan conjured his sword and handed it to Travis. The sheriff accepted the weapon, but his arm wavered a little under its considerable weight.

"Can you handle it?" I asked.

Travis hefted the sword, giving it a cautious swipe through the air. "You bet your ass I can."

Nevan pinched the bridge of his nose with his thumb and forefinger.

I kissed him on the cheek. "Be nice. He's doing us a favor."

My honey grunted, but he escorted me, Max, and Tris outside before retreating back into our lair. Neither I nor Nevan moved, our gazes glued to each other, as the doorway telescoped shut and severed us from each other.

I pulled in a shaky breath, exhaled it with more confidence, and faced my companions. "Let's go find us an oracle."

CHAPTER TWELVE

WE MEANDERED THROUGH THE NIGHT-SHROUDED FOREST, THE ALIEN stars above concealed by a canopy of stringy foliage and vines. Despite the fact it was daylight beyond the confines of this precinct, we'd plunged into full night on crossing into the woods. Max assured me this was part of the safeguards established to protect the oracle. *Creepy magic at work here*, my paranoid subconscious warned.

The girths of the tree trunks measured in yards, most far too big for me to wrap my arms around, if I'd been so inclined. I wasn't. The bark, even masked in gloom, looked gnarled and slippery with a dark, viscous liquid. The scent of ammonia crept over me, faint yet distinct.

Calder? The sorcerer? Both?

Max and Tris, my ersatz guardians, had taken up positions at either side of me. They meant well, and I appreciated their support, but I would've felt much safer with Nevan.

"What is this place?" I asked.

"The dark woods," Max said.

"Of course. And why does it smell like disinfectant, and why do the trees look like they're oozing something I don't want to touch under any circumstances?"

"This place is connected to the source of all magic. It looks forbidding on purpose, to deter passersby from trespassing here."

"Well, it's working. I feel plenty deterred."

I let my arms drop to my sides but then snaked one hand into my pocket to feel the soul stone. The warmth of Nevan's essence surrounded my skin, as if he'd wound both his hands around mine in my pocket. I swore I could hear his voice rumbling in my ear, assuring me, "You are far too obstinate to let the oracle's theatrics stop you."

And I was. For Nevan, I had to be.

I withdrew my hand from my pocket with reluctance, and said, "Shouldn't we go faster? We need to find this oracle guy—person, creature, whatever—in a hurry. Nevan's getting weaker by the minute. Can't we blip there?"

"Blip?" Max asked.

"She talks funny," Tris said. "You'll get used to it. And no, lady, we can't travel that way through this forest. The whole place is warded to prevent it."

I slung an irritated glance his way. "But we can walk faster."

"Yeah-yeah."

Tris sped up his pace, forcing me and Max to hurry to catch up with him. The leprechaun led us down a narrow trail partly overgrown with grass and weeds that, if there'd been more light, I was pretty sure would've still looked black and glossy. The moons must've glowed in the false night sky, but their light filtered down through the forest ceiling to trickle over us and the ground in a wan, greenish glow. In the odd lighting, Max's elegant face took on an otherworldly quality. In daylight, he resembled a human in many ways. In the gloom of the forest, he exemplified this world. Strange, powerful, beyond my comprehension.

Tris looked pretty much the same in the eerie glow of the dark forest.

I kept scratching my arms, infected with an itch I couldn't dispel. The creepy forest was affecting me, that was all. A distraction might make this never-ending journey more bearable, I decided, and opted for my usual backup plan. When in doubt, or when creeped out, ask annoying questions.

"Since we have nothing else to do at the moment," I said, "maybe one of you will answer a question for me."

The leprechaun and the salamander both groaned.

"I'll take that as a yes." Jamming my hands in my pockets, the fingers of my right hand brushing the soul stone, I waited out the wave of Nevan-flavored energy and then asked my question. "Are there boundaries on this side of the falls? Like the ones in the mortal world, I mean."

"Nah," Tris said. "We don't need 'em over here."

"Why not?"

Max replied this time. "The Great Bargain made provisions for barriers only in the mortal realm. Some wanted boundaries here as well, but to convince all elemental species to sign on to the Bargain, the elders had to make concessions."

"Great Bargain?" I glanced at him, but he kept his focus squarely ahead of us. "I don't understand."

Tris grumbled. "Humans don't know crap, do ya? The Great Bargain was a deal hammered out a way long time ago by the elders of all the elemental races. It's kinda our code of laws, but with magic to enforce it."

"But why—"

"The Bargain," Max said, "came about for practical reasons. Eons ago, elementals used magic whenever and however they pleased. The bad among us perverted white magics into black magics, manipulating and controlling anyone who stood against them. The mortal realm became a playground for denizens of the Unseen. A wicked playground I very much doubt mortals enjoyed."

"Okay. So this Great Bargain cleaned things up."

"Yes." He tipped his head left and right, his lips scrunched. "For the most part."

"And the boundaries?"

"It was a concession. To stop evil magic from spreading and consuming both worlds, the elders had to give up the notion of closing the portals." Max ducked as we passed under a low-hanging branch. "The boundaries were a compromise. Elementals can visit the other side, but they can't go more than one mile from a portal. The Bargain also created the healing vortexes as an extra layer of protection for mortals. That's why there are no vortexes in the Unseen."

"Does this world have one leader? A king or something?"

"Each elemental kingdom has a ruler, but there is no ruler of the world." He eyed me sideways. "Would you want that? I seem to recall humans fight against a single ruler having so much control."

"Yeah, we don't like dictators."

"Neither do we. That's why Skeiron had to die, isn't it? At any rate, the only being with omnipotence is the Oversoul."

"The what now?"

He gave me a patient smile. "An ethereal, unknowable, and benevolent presence that governs all of existence, in all worlds."

"You mean a god."

"Oh no. We have gods, not all of them benevolent."

Through the trees up ahead, a gurgling sound emanated from a small stream. We halted about a dozen feet from it. The waters flowed and burbled, skipping over stones embedded in the glistening earth, and steam wafted up from the water. The odor of sulfur choked my nose, making me gag.

Max waved a white cloth in front of my face. Cool, fresh air seemed to emerge from the cloth, and I gulped it in, cleansing my lungs and my sense of smell. He held his hand there, keeping up the flow of sweet, clean air from the strange fabric.

"What is that?" I asked.

"A little something I conjured. Cloth made of air, which I stole from a sylph."

I snatched the cloth from his hand. "Did you steal this from Nevan?"

"He won't miss it."

Holding the fabric over my mouth and nose, I shook a finger at him. "No more stealing from my boyfriend. Got it?"

"Fine. I won't take from him again."

"We gotta cross the stream," Tris said. "No 'blipping' over it."

The hint of trepidation in his tone awakened butterflies in my stomach. Butterflies with steel-tipped, razor-sharp wings.

I glanced at the steaming water, which began to churn and spit. The stream was too wide to jump over, at least twenty feet across. "You mean we have to wade through it?"

"Absolutely not," Max declared, straightening and squaring his shoulders. "I can jump it. You'll need to lock your legs around my waist and tightly hold your arms around my neck. Otherwise, you'll risk falling into the waters. It's pure acid."

Of course it was.

I had to cling to an incubus? Good thing Nevan wasn't here to see this.

My chest ached. If Nevan were here, I would've clung to him for the ride.

"You can't let go of me, Lindsey, no matter what happens." Max glanced at the stream. A glint of cold, white fear sliced through the red-hot lava in his eyes. "There are things in the trees, things that wait for a weak moment and pounce on it."

Of course there were. "I assume leaping over this obstacle counts as a weak moment."

"It does. We will be vulnerable." Max turned toward me, his expression grave. "You can still give up and go back."

"No way. I need to do this, and I trust you and Tris to keep me safe."

"Are you sure about that? I'm enslaved to your enemy."

"But you're my familiar. You serve me, right?" When he gave a curt nod, I stuffed the air cloth in my pocket. "I trust you. Take me over the stream."

Max averted his eyes for heartbeat, then met my gaze. "You do realize getting the truth from the oracle might cost you more than you want to give."

"Oh, I figured as much. But I've got no other options."

Circumstances left me a single path. Charge ahead, or Nevan would die.

Max moved closer, but stopped a couple feet away. He gestured at me with one finger. "I'll need to take hold of you."

"Go ahead."

He sidled up to me, lowered his hands to grasp my buttocks, and hefted me off my feet. I locked my legs around him, ankles tight as a padlock, horrible visions flashing in my mind of being incinerated by acid water. As he shifted his arms to my back, firming up his grip, I hooked my arms around his neck.

My cheek flush with his, I said, "Ready."

In a blur of motion, he spun toward the stream and launched us into the air. Tree branches whizzed past. Air buffeted my face and arms, brittle and cold as the vacuum of space. My eyes burned. I held my breath, unable to summon the courage to inhale whatever those bizarre trees exuded. Our momentum shifted downward, the gale instigated by our flight gusting up at me instead of down.

A clawed hand latched onto my leg. The sharp talons dug into me through my jeans, and without thinking, I kicked out at the attacker.

"Stop!" Max's voice hollered in my ear.

The talons dug in deeper. One pierced my jeans, and the razor edge sliced my flesh with searing agony that overwhelmed reason. I knew I shouldn't move, but my body had taken control of itself, shutting out my brain. I flailed my leg. The thing attached to the talons lost its grip, freeing my leg.

I glimpsed a dark, monkey-like shape sailing downward away from us.

An inhuman shriek rang out below us.

We veered sideways. I padlocked my legs around Max again, but it was too late. The momentum of my battle with the monkey-thing had thrown us off balance. We spun out into a wild tumble, aimed straight toward the ground. I held onto Max, helpless to do anything to spare us from a bone-crushing impact with the ground.

He lurched. The movement flipped us over and halted our free-fall with his back to the ground. He shoved me away, hurling me up instead of down while he slammed into the earth with a sickening thud.

I sailed down, about to strike him.

He reached up to pluck me from the air and curb my descent. My body balanced on his palms, he lowered me to the ground beside him, easy as a leaf. My body met slippery earth. I sprang to my knees, scrubbing at my face and arms and chest, desperate to cleanse myself of the greasy, foul-smelling mud.

Max lay motionless beside me.

I scrambled to my knees. He'd smacked into the ground at full speed. I threw a hand out, intent on jabbing my finger into his neck to check for a pulse.

His strong fingers clinched my wrist.

"You're alive," I gasped.

Max sat up, letting go of my wrist. "Didn't I explain, in explicit terms, you shouldn't let go of me under any circumstances?"

His anger hit me like a slap. I deserved it, yeah, but his warning had been a tad vague. "If you'd said watch out for the crazy monkey-things with razor claws, I might've suggested we find another way around the acid river. Hey, why is my familiar getting testy with me? I'm your mistress."

"There's no other way across the bloody river. And yes, you are my mistress. But I'm allowed to point out when you bollocks up the plan and nearly kill yourself." He flung his arms around my waist and leaped to his feet, hoisting me up with him, then ripped his hands away and stumbled backward a step. He stared at the ground for several seconds before his head slowly lifted. "Did you say a creature attacked you?"

"Uh-huh. Looked like one of those damn kerkopes things." I gave an exaggerated shudder. "I had to shake the monster off. I know you said not to let go, but what else could I do? Its claws—"

"Are you hurt?" His unblinking gaze searched my body.

"It scratched my leg a little, but I'm okay."

Max dropped to a crouch. With one hand he seized my ankle, while with the other he yanked up the leg of my torn jeans. He muttered in another language, different from Nevan's sylph tongue, but I was pretty sure it was a curse. With a swish of his hand, he conjured a bandage. After securing the adhesive bandage over my wound, he uncoiled his body before me and ducked his head to fix me with a chastising glare.

"Don't give me that look," I said. "If Nevan can't cow me with it, you sure can't. What did you expect me to do? Let the monkey-beast shred my leg?"

He growled out a sigh, his tension easing a bit. "I realize you acted on instinct, but you could've told me one of the kerkopes was attacking you."

"What would you have done about it?"

"I don't know. Shot flames at it, for a start." He rubbed his neck. "How do you know about kerkopes? You seem ignorant of most everything about this world."

"Way to brown nose with your mistress, lizard boy." I rubbed my arms, not cold but still itchy from the weirdness around me. "I met one. He was my ex-fiancé, forged into a monkey-man monster."

"I see."

"Didn't think, and I caused a problem that got you—" *Slammed into the ground like a meteorite.* If he'd been hurt, it would've been my fault. "You hit the ground so hard. Are you okay?"

"Yes." He whirled around to confront the path that led away from the acid river. "We should go."

We marched onward through the forest, as its bows thickened into an impenetrable roof. No light leaked in from above, yet the pale green glow suffused the environment. It seemed to originate from nowhere and everywhere, its light enough to guide us but too faint to reveal any details. We trudged through a landscape of shadows and silhouettes, Max and Tris at my sides, Max's bare feet slapping on the greasy earth. My boots squished into the ground, the earth giving just enough to slither unease through me.

My stupid imagination kicked into overdrive, assailing me with vile visions. Me stepping into a hidden sinkhole, the slimy dirt gobbling me up whole. Monkey-things plummeting out of the trees to slash me to ribbons. A hooded figure popping out of the blackness to abduct me and suck my brain.

The sorcerer. He couldn't know where we were, could he?

I stopped dead and grabbed Max's arm to halt him.

He gave me a questioning look.

"The sorcerer." I glanced up at the sky, or where the sky should've been. "Can he find us here? Do the kerkopes work for him?"

Max's jaw clenched, a muscle jumped there.

I threw my head back and moaned. "You can't tell me."

"Try rephrasing your question."

I contemplated the options. How to phrase it so he could answer without violating his deal with the sorcerer? "Will the wards in this forest keep anyone and everyone from whisking in? Does everybody have to travel the old-fashioned way?"

"Yes and yes."

I gazed up into the darkness. "What about the monkey-things?"

"They guard the river," Max said. "I doubt they'll hunt us anymore."

"If you say so."

Setting out again, we followed Tris down a narrowing trail. No more monkey-things leaped out at us. I wondered whether the kerkopes attack had anything to do with Calder. He might've been the beast that assaulted me, but since I'd never seen him in his monkey form, I had no way to figure that out.

After a time, the length of which I couldn't gauge, the forest spread its arms out to reveal a small clearing and a gigantic boulder seated at its center. The rock was taller than Max, though not by much. He escorted me to the giant rock and knocked on it. A portion of the stone rippled, thinned into a semi-transparent barrier, and dissolved. Its absence exposed a doorway and a pitch-dark passage beyond it.

Tris entered first, and Max shepherded me inside. The passage was narrow, so I walked behind Tris with Max behind me. I clenched the soul stone in my pocket, grateful for the connection to Nevan as we penetrated deeper into the blackness.

The passage curved left. When we rounded the corner, a faint yellow glow became visible in the distance. Max moved in front of me, and I peeked around his massive shoulder to spy the source of the light. Up ahead, the passage dead-ended at a doorway shorter than the corridor ceiling, shorter than Max but taller than Tris. Inside the doorway, a fire burned within some kind of large container.

Tris entered the room.

Max stepped sideways, blocking my view, then hunched over to cross the threshold.

Inside the room, he stopped. I hurried up beside him, suddenly aware of the surroundings. We'd entered a chamber hewn from solid rock, but the dark walls were gilded with a semi-translucent coating of pale gold.

A solitary object occupied the space. The fire I'd glimpsed burned inside a metal bowl about five feet wide, perched atop curving legs that terminated in cat-like feet. The bronze bowl had a rough texture to it, catching and releasing the light in glimmers and glints. The flames stretched upward several feet, their amber color intensely beautiful.

The fire reminded me of Nevan's eyes.

I sidled closer to Max, though not so close we touched. "Is the oracle some kind of elemental?"

"No," a strange voice replied, echoing from elsewhere. "Not anymore."

A figure traipsed out of the shadows at the room's periphery.

The oracle was a man. His tailored, navy-blue suit conformed to his slender body as he moseyed up to the fire, a few yards away from us. The flickering light shimmered on his short, slicked-back gray hair.

The oracle smiled, his copious wrinkles deepening. "Not that I've got anything against elemental kind, mind you." He wandered closer, stopping a few yards away. His voice bore a strange accent, unlike any I'd heard before. "I've got nothing against anybody. I've moved beyond those designations is all. Understand?"

His bright green eyes fixed on me and sparkled—not from the firelight, but with an internal brilliance. His irises exuded a light so similar to the eerie illumination in the woods that I knew the two must be connected. I sensed it on a visceral level.

"Do you understand?" the oracle demanded.

"Yes, I get it." Didn't really, but telling this being I was confused seemed like a bad idea.

"No need to apologize, dearie." He ambled to the fire, waving a hand into the oily flames, fluttering his fingers with indolent interest. "You came to ask a question. Get to it, then. I'm a busy man."

"Are you really the oracle?" I think my mouth flapped a couple times, as I took in his appearance one more time. "You look like you might negotiate a corporate merger, not foretell the future."

"Were you expecting flowing white robes?"

Yeah, I had been. Another preconception dashed on the invincible rocks of reality.

"Guess I was," I said.

A soft laugh accompanied his brief smile. He shook his head and let out a melodramatic sigh. "You humans and your mythology." All business again, he fixed me with a stare so laser-sharp it cut down to my soul. "Your question, please."

"I, uh, well—"

"Spit it out, mortal."

His tone sharpened the word mortal into a threat and an insult.

Max's shoulders arched in high tension, and the air around him buzzed with it. I settled a hand on his arm, amazed by the granite hardness of his muscles, and grumbled under my breath, "Take a chill pill. I'll handle this."

His mouth opened, a protest on the verge of erupting, but he heeded my command.

The oracle shoved one hand inside his waistband, one hip cocked. The fingers of his other hand curled and uncurled within the flames. His eyes drilled into mine, the power of his attention searing. "This matter concerns the sylph king, yet you bring a leprechaun and a salamander instead."

"Nevan isn't feeling well. Besides, somebody's after him and he has to stay inside our warded home for his own safety."

"You speak for the king, Janusite?"

Everything inside me went ice cold, freezing me in place. Ennea's warning that the oracle recognize my true nature had done nothing to cushion the impact of his statement.

"Relax," the oracle said. "I'm a seer. Did you really think I wouldn't know what you are? But rest assured, I have no interest in spreading the news. Only those who make it here receive my counsel, and I don't share with anyone who has an evil heart." He gaze flicked to Max, but his expression did not change. "The fact this one was admitted to my sanctum should tell you something."

"Are you saying Max won't betray me?"

Wrinkles deepened on the oracle's face as he smiled with genial fatherliness. "You know the answer. You feel it in your heart. And you, dearie, have the truest heart and strongest soul of any I've met."

Two forbidden words rose in my throat. I gulped them down. Thanking this man—or whatever he was—seemed even more ill-advised than my gratitude to Tris had been all those weeks ago. "Mr. Oracle—um, your highness—er…"

"Call me Bob."

"Seriously?"

He chuckled, sounding very much like Santa Claus. The unsettling green glow of his eyes dimmed to a twinkling emerald. "You could invoke my full name, Bobanzhistilanovitz, but most people find it easier to call me Bob."

"I can see why." I took three halting steps toward him and proffered my unsteady hand. "I'm Lindsey Porter, puny and inconsequential mortal from the other side of the falls."

"And I thought my appellation was a mouthful."

Bob clasped my hand, his cool against my palm, the grip firm and powered by taut sinews. As he bent toward me, his pecs flexed against the thin fabric of his dress shirt.

No Santa Claus after all.

He slid his other hand beneath mine, pancaking my palm between both of his. "Pleasure to meet you, Lindsey. But you should know one thing before we continue."

"What's that?"

"The sylph will be your undoing."

Chapter Thirteen

WHICH SYLPH?" I ASKED, THOUGH THE SICK FEELING IN MY STOMACH told me I knew the answer. It had to be a load of crap. Someone was messing with Nevan's head, though, and I had to wonder whether the oracle's claim held any truth.

"You know the answer," Bob said. "The sylph king, Nevan. Your lover."

"Nevan wouldn't hurt me."

"That's true. And yet, he will destroy you. Leave him now, before—"

"No." I barred my arms over my chest. "I'm not abandoning Nevan because a weirdo in a cave claims to have mystical insight."

"Listen to me, mortal." Bob's voice resounded through the cavern, loud and clear and tinged with empathy. "You are the most important being ever to be born in any realm. The power of the Janusite must not fall into the wrong hands. If you stay with the sylph king, he will lead you to your destruction."

I squinted at Bob, desperate to debunk his claims. Really, how did I know he was an oracle and not an impostor? The sorcerer had impersonated Nevan, after all.

"Your turn to listen, bucko," I said. "I need some proof you are who you say you are. All the immortals I've met have the ability to glamour into any disguise they want. You're the oracle, huh? Prove it."

His lips formed a tiny smile, without mirth. "You're a canny one, aren't you? And rightly suspicious. Someone has been impersonating your lover, someone with immense power and a grudge to settle."

Okay, so he knew about something I'd told no one but Nevan. If Bob was the sorcerer, he would know about the fake Nevan because he was the one inside the black robes.

"I need more proof than that," I told the oracle. "For all I know, you are the one who's been pretending to be Nevan."

"There is something else I could reveal," Bob said, "but you might not want your friends to hear it."

Max glanced at me sideways, a question in his eyes. Tris shuffled forward to stand at my other side.

"Your decision," Tris said. "But we won't tattle. Will we, salamander?"

"Never," Max agreed.

Did I trust these two? Tris had been through an apocalyptic battle with me, besides performing the magics that saved Nevan's life. Max I'd just met, but my instincts assured me I could trust him. He was my familiar, after all.

Oh hell, it wasn't like I had a choice.

"It's okay," I told Bob. "You can say it in front of them, whatever it is."

"If that's what you want." He strolled around the fiery cauldron to stand directly in front of me. "The last time you had sexual relations with Nevan, you invoked your magic to restore his vigor. Blue energy surrounded you both." He smiled with his lips closed, yet it wrinkled his eyes and dimpled his cheeks. "And it was the best sex either of you has ever had. Nevan theorized your magic was activated by the heightened emotions that came from your decision to move in with him."

I opened my mouth but couldn't form words. Bob had quoted Nevan almost verbatim. No one but Nevan and I knew what had gone on in our home this morning.

Tris snickered. "Feeling a little tired myself. Can I get some of that magic?"

Max glared at him. "Show respect to the Janusite."

"Zip it, both of you," I said. "My magic is for Nevan and nobody else."

Bob tilted his head left and right, as if sizing me up. "Now that you know I'm the real deal, maybe you'll take my words to heart. You are the most powerful—"

"Yeah-yeah, I get it." I yearned for Nevan's arms around, for his presence filling me with a depth of solace the soul stone couldn't replicate. "How does being a supernatural taxi service make me so damn important, anyway?"

"Has anyone told you the whole prophecy?"

"No."

"You should hear it." Bob scratched his chin, then squared his shoulders and lifted his chin. In a resonant and powerful voice worthy of a deity, he said, "In the twentieth era of the mortal calendar, a girl child shall be born into an enlightened clan. She will possess the power of Janus, god of the doorways and of transitions, and like him she will face both ways, belonging to neither but bound to everything. Boundaries fall in her presence. The veil shall open to her, she who holds the power to converge the worlds, she whose power is beyond any seen before in any realm. She is the bearer of the key and the staff, the child of the god, she is the Janusite."

I tried to speak, but managed only a squeak too soft for anyone to hear.

Max spoke to the oracle. "You told this to Skeiron."

Bob made a raspberry and flapped a dismissive hand. "I'm not dumb. I told Skeiron the Janusite would be born in the twentieth century of the mortal calendar, and she will have the power to escort immortals across the portal boundaries."

"That's it?" I demanded. "You didn't slip up and tell him I'm the most important thing ever to be born?"

His eyes locked onto mine, sending a faint shiver through me, pure cold and certainty transmitted from him into me. I hated the way he could do that. My connection with Nevan seemed rooted in our sensual bond, and thus, it gave me a pleasurable shiver. But the oracle's gaze made the hairs at my nape quiver.

"I don't slip up," he said. "Skeiron wanted you because he was dead-set on taking over the mortal realm."

"What about the sorcerer? I'm assuming you know about him. You said he has a grudge to settle."

"I know of him, but I haven't had the displeasure of meeting him." Bob jammed his thumbs inside the waistband of his slacks. "I imagine he wants you for the same reason Skeiron did."

"Dominating one world isn't good enough for these creeps? They have to trample my world too?" Before he could respond to my rhetorical questions, I charged ahead with a real one. "Who is the sorcerer? What's his grudge? And does it have anything to do with what you said about me being the bearer of the key and the staff?"

Bob rocked back on the heels of his shiny leather loafers. "The sorcerer's grudge is hard to pinpoint, though I can sense the seething nature of it. I can't see his identity, which is odd. Whatever magic he's tapped into is blocking my foresight, but I can sniff the odor of stolen power on it. The girls he killed, they all had a touch of the Unseen in them. He depleted them of whatever magic was inside them and extracted the innate magic of their souls."

That explained so much, more than I could comprehend at the moment. "Can't you give me any information about the sorcerer himself?"

"What I can tell you is—"

A *thwack* reverberated through the small space.

Bob twitched, his eyes bulging.

The blade of a sword burst out of his chest, blood dripping from its tip.

He tumbled to the floor. His eyes remained wide, the vitality leeching out of them as his body crumpled into a heap on the stone floor.

The oracle was dead.

Paralyzed, I couldn't move so much as my eyes—and for a moment, I couldn't process the sight before me. At the back of the cavern, behind where Bob lay lifeless on the floor, the sorcerer's minion wielded a blood-soaked black sword.

Skeiron's sword.

Ceara smiled, like a snake opening her jaws to consume her prey.

"You lose again," she said. "Stop fighting and come to the sorcerer. Only then might your friends and loved ones be spared a horrific death."

A rage burning with a cold fire erupted inside me. I yanked out my endued derringer, aimed it straight at her head, and fired.

She vanished.

The bullet slammed into the rock wall.

Max laid a hand on my arm, the one still raised to brandish my gun. "She's gone."

I whirled on my so-called familiar, shoving my gun into his chest. "Did you lead her here? You both work for the sorcerer."

"I haven't knowingly led his consort here. A familiar serves his mistress above all others and cannot knowingly endanger her safety or betray her confidence."

"You said knowingly twice. I'm guessing that means you're not sure you didn't accidentally lead Ceara here."

Max made a pained face but did not look away from me. "I can't be sure. I wish I could, because I don't want to betray you, even without my knowledge."

Damn if I didn't believe him. A matter of weeks ago, I'd scoffed at the idea of intuition—until I met Nevan and had no choice but to trust my gut about him. That instinct had proved right. Today, my intuition whispered I could trust Max. Once again, I had no choice but to rely on my inner voice.

"I believe you," I told Max. "But these woods are supposed to be protected. I'm guessing this chamber is too. How did Ceara get inside?"

Tris, who'd been stiff and immobile since the villainess attacked, turned his haunted gaze toward me. "Bob said the sorcerer has immense power, and he's somehow able to cloak himself. If even an oracle can't divine the creep's identity…"

"We're in deep shit." I curled my fingers into my palms. "The sorcerer and his minions can break through the forest wards, which means we can't get away from them."

My pulse accelerated, my mouth went dry, and the room seemed to tilt around me. I must've swayed, because Max grasped my upper arms to steady me.

"What is it?" he asked.

"Nevan. The wards." I wrenched free of Max's grip, shoved the gun into its holster, and sprinted for the doorway. "I have to get home. *Now.*"

Tris and Max raced up behind me, the narrowness of the passage keeping them from coming up beside me. Our footfalls thudded on the dusty rock floor, echoing down the passage.

"Lindsey," Max began.

I cut him off with a flap of my hand. "No time."

Bursting out of the passage into the coal-dark woods, I exploded into a dead run.

Max leaped in front of me, forcing me to halt.

"Out of my way," I spat. "I have to get home."

"Why? You said something about Nevan."

Through clenched teeth, I said, "Our home is protected by wards. The sorcerer can get through wards. You do the math, genius."

His eyes widened, his lips parted.

Tris sidled around me to stand beside Max. "There's the river and a gang of kerkopes in our way."

I shoved my hand in my pocket to stroke the soul stone. It sizzled with Nevan's energy, with his life force, and tears stung my eyes at the sensation of it pouring through me. *Hold on, Nevan, fight it. For me. For us.*

"We have to hurry," I said, and dashed down the trail through the murky woods with an incubus and a leprechaun hot on my heels.

Running. Running. Shoes slapping on slimy earth. Lungs burning. Muscles cramping. On and on and on I ran without any thought for my companions, my mind consumed with visions of Nevan being abducted, or worse, all because I hadn't considered the sorcerer's incredible power and that he might be able to infiltrate the wards. If anything happened to Nevan, it would be my fault.

I barreled onward, heedless of my surroundings.

Max's arms locked around my midsection, and he snatched up me mid-step as he hopped backward away from the river. My heart thumped against my ribs. I hadn't noticed the acid-spitting flow in front of me. Max didn't have to tell me what to do this time. I spun around, flung my arms around his neck, and locked my legs around him. He clenched me tightly, on the verge of cutting off my air, as he bounded up and over the river.

We struck the ground with a jarring thud. Tris landed right beside us, already breathing hard, his cheeks flushed.

Max released me, and I took off.

Chattering broke out overhead, in the treetops.

Recognition zinged through me. I glanced back to see Max and Tris sprinting after me, edging closer with each stride but still a good fifteen feet behind.

"That noise," I called to them. "What is it?"

"Kerkopes," Max shouted. "Stop and I'll—"

A black shape hurtled down from the treetops. It smacked into Max, bowling him over, and he whumped onto the ground face-down. Another monkey-thing collided with Tris and sent him careening into a glistening black bush.

A weight smashed into me from above and behind my head. I stumbled forward. Lost my footing. Tumbled toward the ground. Talons snagged the back of my shirt, jerking me back but then shoving me forward. Fabric ripped. I crashed into the ground face-first, oily mud thrust into my nostrils and open mouth, gagging me with its acrid stench and revolting taste. Those talons latched onto my waist at either side, sinking into my flesh.

The monkey-monster hefted me up and propelled us into the treetops.

I screamed Nevan's name.

Somewhere in the back of my crazed mind, I realized he wasn't here. And down there, in the murk far below, I spied two limp figures.

My captor let out a gleeful cackle. We rocketed straight out of the trees into the vacant, blinding sky.

CHAPTER FOURTEEN

M Y LEGS DANGLED FREE, FLAILED BY THE WILD CURRENT OF OUR MO-
tion. I held my arms up to shield my face from the gale. The monkey-thing soared so high over the forest, I knew if I shook free of the beast
I'd plummet to my death, crushed by my own velocity. The beast's talons
pierced my skin. The pain stung, but not as hotly as the knowledge I was
being flown Air Sorcerer, right into the clutches of the one being I did not
want to meet again.

Max excelled at jumping, but he couldn't jump into the stratosphere. If
he could have, he'd be killing this flying monster right now. So what, I'd
just wait to be dumped in the sorcerer's lap?

Like hell. I'd rather die.

I wrestled with the talons, but the monkey-thing gripped them harder,
puncturing deeper. A warm liquid trickled over my skin, and pain shot out
across my back and abdomen. A wave of nausea pushed my gorge high in
my throat. I choked it back and swung my fists up to pummel the beast in
the face. My fist connected with a crack.

My captor cackled.

Dammit. I couldn't get a good position to attack while restrained by black
talons. I felt my flesh ripping within the wounds, those talons shredding deep.

Darkness speckled my vision.

I could not go down like this, no way. I struggled, but succeeded only in
unleashing a torrent of agony that racked my whole body. My ears rang. The
darkness encroached more and more into my vision. The wind of our travel
lashed my arm into my body, and my hand slapped into the holster hidden
beneath my shirt.

The gun. Of course, the gun.

I floundered for the holster and missed it, my body thrown side to side
by the flapping of the beast's wings and its zigzagging flight path. At last,

my fingers latched onto the gun's grip. I closed my hand around it, tearing the weapon free. I'd fired one shot at Ceara, which meant I had one round left in the chamber. One shot to save myself.

My finger poised over the trigger, I jammed the muzzle into the monkey-thing's chest and fired.

Its body convulsed. We swooped lower, my feet grazing the treetops. Pitch-black leaves erupted up around us. We flew onward, even as crimson blood streamed from the wound in the creature's chest, spraying over my head, into my hair and onto my face.

I flipped the derringer over to pound the butt into the creature's wound.

The monkey-thing wobbled. Its talons popped open.

I sailed downward, straight into the trees. Branches scraped my skin and thwacked into me. I grunted with each blow. The gun slipped out of my hand, and I shielded my head with both arms.

The ground. It was coming. Fast.

I would die. It would be more agony than I could imagine but at least, I prayed, it would be quick.

Something caught me.

Arms cinched me tight against a hard body. I kicked at my new captor.

"Stop, it's me. It's Max."

I stopped struggling and cracked my lids open to peek at the being holding me in his arms. It looked like Max, but that was no comfort anymore.

As if sensing my paranoia, he set me down on my feet.

Tris galloped up behind him, doubled over and fighting for breath. "Jeez Louise, I didn't know salamanders could run like that."

"Powered by fire, we can."

That was when I noticed it. Tiny, flickering flames of yellow and white. They flowed over his skin, dying out here only to pop up there, like a second skin made of fire.

And then I noticed his hand, the one he cradled in the opposite palm.

I grabbed at his wrist. "Are you hurt?"

"Take it easy," he said, dropping his uninjured hand to show me the damaged one. "It will grow back."

His middle finger was gone. Snapped off. No blood poured from the wound, because there was no wound. The skin had sealed shut over the stump.

"Grow back?" I asked.

"Yes," he said, eying me with concern. "Salamanders can regrow many of our body parts."

I remembered reading that once, long ago, in a magazine article or something. The mundane salamanders in the mortal world could regrow limbs.

Max scanned his gaze up and down my body, assessing me without even the tiniest hint of sexual interest. Instead, he seemed...worried. Very, very worried.

"You're injured," he said, his tone gruff. "Let me see the wounds."

"Most of the blood isn't mine."

"I can tell. It's kerkopes blood." He gently lifted the hem of my shirt, exposing my side, and swallowed a gasp. "These wounds…"

Blackness licked at the edges of my vision. The pain in my sides had dulled, overtaken by a growing chill. Part of me recognized this was bad news, but my mind was clouded, my body energized by a burst of adrenaline I knew wouldn't last long.

Max's brow furrowed as he studied my wounds. He lifted my shirt higher to expose the other side of my abdomen.

"Lindsey." The shock in his voice barely penetrated my brain, as numbness swept through me. He shifted his hands to my upper back, his gaze zeroed in on mine. "You're seriously wounded."

"Duh." It came out as a frail murmur.

I swayed against him. The world gyrated around me, but I was sinking ever downward. "I'm going to pass out. Promise you'll get to Nevan first, worry about me later."

Max scooped me into his arms. "I have to obey, but my friend doesn't."

He passed me to Tris.

The last thing I saw was Max's face, darkened by grim determination, right before he blazed into the woods moving faster than any being I'd seen and dragging a wake of fire behind him.

My eyelids, too heavy to stay open, drifted shut and the world slipped away.

***

I WOKE WITH A JOLT, MY HEART POUNDING. LIGHT ENVELOPED ME, COMING from nowhere and everywhere. Blinking rapidly, I tried to sort out what my eyes revealed to me. I was lying on the red velvet chaise, cushioned by its plushness, with my head elevated. Pushing up into a sitting position, my legs splayed before me, I rotated my head left and right to take in the scene around me.

This was home. Mine and Nevan's.

Tris hunched several yards away near the doorway to the kitchen fiddling with his fingers. He nodded as if listening to something or someone. Gradually, the sounds penetrated the fog around my mind and I recognized Max's voice. I couldn't understand his words, though, because he spoke in a hushed tone.

The open doorway caught my attention. The door to the outside. The sun shined out there, and despite knowing the oracle's forest had existed in a false night, my brain tripped up in its efforts to comprehend the presence of daylight.

Out the corner of my eye, I spied a shape on the bed maybe ten feet from where I huddled on the floor. I glanced at the bed—and the breath caught in my throat.

Scrambling to my feet, I rushed to the bed and perched on its edge.

Nevan lay limp atop the fur blanket, eyes shut, face ashen. His chest seemed not to move, and even when I settled a palm on his torso, I couldn't feel his lungs inflating. I mashed my ear to his chest, my arms going weak when I heard the steady, if slow, beating of his heart. I held my ear to his face and felt the faintest whisper of his breaths on my skin.

With my hands at either side of his head, I bowed mine in silent thanks to whatever power kept him alive. *Thank God. Thank the Oversoul. Thank every divine being in the heavens.*

"You're awake," announced a male voice tinged with a Texas twang.

I startled, lurching upright, and half turned toward the man who'd slunk to the head of the bed a few feet away from me.

Travis looked sick, like he might throw up any second, but he kept his posture straight and taut. "You okay?"

"Yeah." I knew without checking my wounds had healed. "Tris fixed me up?"

"He did. Couldn't heal Nevan, though. Something about putrid magic." Travis ducked his head, bunching his shoulders. "I fucked it up big time."

I slipped my hand around one of Nevan's, grateful for the contact but disturbed by the chill of his skin. "The sorcerer was here."

"No, his girlfriend."

"Ceara." I shut my eyes for a moment, struggling to hold back the anger and terror swelling inside me. Time to rein it all in and make this right, somehow. "She must've zipped over here right after she killed the oracle."

"Seems like. Max filled me in on your little adventure."

I ran my hand up to Nevan's cheek. Cold, so cold.

"Tell me," I said, "what happened here."

"She came, she attacked, I tried to fight her off." Though my focus remained on Nevan's pallid face, the way Travis cleared his throat told me he dreaded sharing the rest. "I tried to use the sword, swear to God I did, but she was so freaking fast. And he was helping her."

My gaze shot to Travis. "Nevan? He helped Ceara fight you off?"

"Yeah." His attention shot to something past my shoulder, and I glanced there to see Nevan's sword leaning against the wall. A long, thin, dark-red splotch stained its blade. Travis gripped the back of his neck. "I got in one good poke, but all I did was wing her. Nevan threw me into the wall, and I was too stunned to think for a minute. That's when she, uh…"

One hand on Nevan's chest, I fixed Travis with my hardest glare. "She what?"

He cleared his throat again, shoving his hands in the pants pockets of his sheriff's uniform. To his credit, he met my gaze head-on. "She kissed him. A full-on, all-tongues-in kiss. And he stood there, not moving, like he was—"

"In a trance." I smoothed my fingers over Nevan's forehead. "I've seen it before."

"After that, she skedaddled." Travis sighed and crouched beside me. "I let you down, Lindsey, big time. You left me here to protect him and I—"

"Did the best you could." I clutched my hands on my lap, feeling my lower lip tremble as I said, "This was my fault. I should never have left him here, should've guessed the sorcerer would have a way to get past the wards. He's got loads of power, and I'm—" I held my breath for a moment, refusing to cry. "I am nothing compared to him. What chance have I got to stop this and save Nevan?"

Travis settled a hand on mine, the touch tentative. "You can't blame yourself. This ain't nobody's fault but that bitch and her boyfriend."

Boyfriend. The word rang in my mind, stirring a memory of what Max had said about Ceara. *I have not knowingly led his consort here.* At the time, I'd focused on the "knowingly" part of his statement. Another fragment of it became so much more important right now.

I stalked across the room to where Max and Tris loitered. "Max, you called Ceara the sorcerer's consort. Are you saying she's his lover? His mate?"

"Lover, yes," he answered, bracing his body against the kitchen doorway. "Mate? Can't say for sure. The term implies a bond, and I can't speak to that. He does impart some of his power into her when they join."

"You mean when they screw."

He gave a bitter laugh. "Yes, I do mean that. An apt description for the bloody disturbing things they do to each other."

"You've watched?"

Max averted his gaze, his head bent downward. "They would order me to revert to salamander form, then lock me in a cage. It was kept near their bed."

Yech. I couldn't imagine being forced to witness whatever depraved acts two evil sickos performed on each other.

Tris made a disgusted face. "How does knowing they do the nasty help us?"

"Not sure yet," I said, "but every scrap of information we can get has to be of use sooner or later. If they're lovers then maybe, just maybe, one or both of them has gotten attached to the other. We may be able to use that."

Travis had joined our little confab, coming up beside me. "What now?"

"Nevan doesn't look so good," Tris said. "Anybody got an idea what they're doing to him?"

Travis raised his hand, like a kid in a classroom. "Almost forgot, Ceara said to give you a message."

"What message?"

"Said when she's done with him, Nevan will be as hollow as a the trunk of a dead tree, the perfect vessel, and you will have surrendered willingly."

"Hollow…" I struggled to comprehend the meaning, but couldn't. "No idea what that means. I failed Nevan. I can't save him, can't save anyone, can't do a damn thing to stop the sorcerer."

"Bullshit," Travis said, with a conviction that gave his voice a raspy edge. "You're the Janusite."

"Which means I can ferry immortals across the boundaries in the mortal world. I can open portals on my own. Big fucking whoop. When I'm confronted with real power, I crumble. Being the Janusite means diddly-squat."

Max grabbed my shoulders and shook me. "Stop this, Lindsey. You are not powerless, not against this Ceara and not against the sorcerer. You heard what the oracle said. You are the most powerful being ever to be born in either world."

His eyes glowed with swirling torrents of flame. Red, white, blue, orange, yellow. All the colors of fire whipped through his irises while feathery, translucent flames licked upward from his skin.

"I am your familiar," he said, with a forcefulness that captured my attention, "to use as you see fit. I can help you harness and strengthen your magics, to understand where your power stems from." He pulled me a smidgen closer, near enough the scorching heat of him seared my skin. "So use me, Lindsey."

Travis edged away from us, studying the Janusite and her familiar with furtive glances.

Alongside Max, Tris leaned back against the wall. "Can I watch?"

Max threw him an annoyed glance. "There will be no sex involved, perverse little leprechaun."

"I wasn't talking about that. Never seen a familiar and his mistress at work, though. Might be kinda cool."

Max stared into my eyes. "Use me."

"Okay, fine." I wrestled out his grasp, turning to look at Nevan's unconscious form. "But I need Tris and Travis to do something else in the meantime. And I will not leave this house."

Max inclined his head. "Of course."

"The wards are down, I assume. Since you and Tris got inside."

"Yes, they're gone." Max gave me a considering look. "Maybe you and I can get them up again—and give them a power boost."

"Think we could sorcerer-proof the wards?"

"Worth a try." He arched a brow at me. "If you're willing to fully embrace your magics."

I glanced at Nevan again, and my heart constricted. "I'm ready. Time to use my familiar."

Which didn't sound at all weird. These days, weirdness had become my new normal.

"Tris," I said, "go to Ennea and see if there's anything she can offer."

"Like what?" he asked.

"Anything," I repeated, over-enunciating each syllable. Then I looked to Travis. "You go home and find out everything you can about the murders. I know they're connected. I'm counting on your cop skills to ferret out as much information as possible."

"You got it," Travis said.

He and Tris headed out the still-open doorway.

I pointed at the door. "Was that open when we got here?"

"Yes," Max said. "Your friend the sheriff told me Ceara blasted it open. Apparently, the whole mountain shook."

"Terrific. That doesn't sound at all impossible to stop."

"Not impossible," a weak voice said from behind us.

Max and I both swung our gazes toward the bed, where Nevan slouched in a semi-upright position with his legs hanging over the edge, his feet on the floor. He pushed up with both arms, clearly trying to stand, but his limbs gave out. He dropped back onto the bed, still half sitting.

I hurried to him, kneeling in front of him with my hands on his knees. He looked so exhausted, so tapped out. I lifted a hand to his cheek. "You shouldn't get up. Lie back down and rest."

Despite the pallor of his skin and the redness of his eyes, he gazed at me with the same certainty and determination as always. "Not until I convince you all is not lost. Not for you."

"I'm not worried about myself. I'm worried about you."

"You can defeat the sorcerer, I know this with every fiber of my immortal being." He laid his cool hand over mine on his cheek. "Listen to the incubus. Let him assist you in harnessing your magics. You are the only one who can stop the sorcerer from enacting whatever plan he has in mind, and you can be certain it's nothing benign."

"Kill all mortals, probably." I sat on the bed next to him, considering everything I'd learned so far. "Then again, the oracle said the sorcerer has a grudge to settle. Maybe he wants to punish other elementals."

"Perhaps," Nevan said, his eyes half closed, shoulders slumped.

I took his hand and guided his arm to rest across my shoulders, supporting him with my own body.

"What else did the oracle say?" Nevan asked.

As I recounted my talk with Bob, Max retreated into the kitchen. Giving us privacy. Had to admit my familiar had shown nothing but respect for me. Good to know, since I was about to let him teach me how to use magic.

I told Nevan what he himself had done when Ceara arrived, since once again he had no memory of his fugue state. Finished with my tale, I let my head rest on Nevan's shoulder.

He kissed my forehead, his lips cool and dry. "There's no time to waste. You must stay here with Max, reestablish the wards, and practice your powers."

"You mean we have to stay here with Max."

Nevan said nothing, his breaths soft but unsteady against my forehead. "I mean you, Lindsey. I must leave this place, go far from you and make certain no one can employ me as a weapon again."

"Make certain how?"

Ice crystallized around my heart as the things he'd said replayed in my mind. He'd said all was not lost—for me. I was the only one who could stop the sorcerer. I must stay here with Max, while Nevan made certain no one could...

"No," I said, shrugging off his arm so I could face him. "Nevan, you are not killing yourself to save the world."

"For the world? No." He straightened with an effort that made his face warp with pain. "I will do this for you."

"Absolutely not. I forbid it."

"Lindsey."

I jumped up to stand in front of him, determined to dissuade him by any means necessary.

He managed to lift one eyebrow, though just a little.

My hands on my hips, I declared, "You're way too weak to leave here without help, and I will not help you. In fact, I'll order my familiar to hold you down until you pass out from exhaustion. Give up on this stupid idea right this instant."

Nevan sighed, sounding wearier than I'd imagined anyone could. "Lindsey..."

"Uh-uh." I grasped his face in both hands. "I would never force you into a bargain to make you stay here, but I need you to do it voluntarily. For me. Please don't give up, Nevan."

He grumbled, making a face. "You've said that word again. I thought you'd given up saying it with gleeful abandon."

"I'm serious, Nevan. I will get Max to restrain you if necessary." When he maintained his mulish expression, I turned my head to shout, "Max, get in here—"

"Fine," Nevan growled. "I will refrain from ending my existence."

His self-sacrificing side had shown itself before, when he tried to make me stay home in the mortal realm while he confronted Skeiron. This time was different, though, and it terrified me. I could not let him commit suicide to protect me. We would find another way, we had to.

Looking miserable, he slumped even further.

I turned his face toward me and pressed my mouth to his, unsettled by the coldness of his skin, and lingered there a moment with our lips barely touching. We gazed into each other's eyes, like two souls bound by a silent and unbreakable promise. He'd given me his word, and he would never renege on it.

Brushing my fingers over his temple, I murmured, "You know what I want to say."

Thank you. But I couldn't say it. Nevan would hate to have me indebted to him, even an itty-bitty bit.

"I do know," he said. "It's unnecessary."

Max ambled out of the kitchen then, munching on what looked like an oddly shaped apple. "Were you summoning me, mistress?"

Yep, I detected a bit of sarcasm in the question.

And he'd shed his clothes.

"Clothing, Max," I said. "And give me a minute."

His outfit materialized on his body.

I took a seat beside Nevan again, our shoulders nudging each other. "Killing yourself was a dumb-ass idea. There's another way, and we will find it."

"A moment ago you believed you're powerless to change our fates."

"I realized I have to do it." I covered his hand with mine. "You know I'll do anything to save you. Anything. If that means fighting Ceara and her master, I will do whatever it takes."

"Even if it's the death of you."

"No one on my team is dying."

His mouth formed the barest of smiles. "Your team?"

"All my allies. Travis, Max, Tris, Ennea." I pecked a kiss on his cheek. "And you, my soul mate."

Max approached us. "This is terribly touching, but we need to start your training. The situation is somewhat dire, wouldn't you say?"

"Yes." I stroked my palm over Nevan's cheek. "Rest, honey. Max and I have work to do."

I rose, and Nevan stretched out on the bed with his hand over his abdomen. Yesterday, I would've fantasized about those sculpted muscles. Today, the sight of his gorgeous bod couldn't stir any desire in me. Things had gotten so much worse and so much more pressing since this morning, when Nevan had made love to me in this very bed.

"Okay, Max," I said. "Let's crack open my magic."

Chapter Fifteen

ACE TO FACE, THE INCUBUS AND I RAISED OUR HANDS BETWEEN US. MAX held his hands palms up, while I hovered mine palms down above his with a space of millimeters between our skin. Within the gap, currents of magic crackled and pulsed over my flesh. They seeped under my skin to permeate my flesh, radiating out from my hands into the whole of my body. The magic burned strongest in my palms, instigating a stinging sensation that was both frightening and exhilarating.

Magic suffused me. Infused me. Charged me like a high-voltage cable plugged straight into my soul. My pulse raced, my mouth went dry, and I had trouble drawing in enough oxygen. The tingling that swept over my scalp and face had nothing to do with the supernatural energy coursing through me. It was a sign of hyperventilation.

I recognized this, and yet I couldn't force my lungs to work.

The incubus stationed immobile and impassive before me coughed. "Breathe, Lindsey. Or you'll pass out and this will all be for naught."

We'd have to start again. Max had warned me about this heady and disconcerting sensation, and that I'd need to call on my strength of will to control the power. It was difficult, though, when so much energy coursed through my nerves, my blood, down to the core of my being.

Maybe a mortal wasn't supposed to carry this kind of power. Maybe I couldn't handle it, but I had to try. Marshal every iota of willpower I had in me and make this work.

I inhaled, my breaths ragged at first, dragging in as much air as I could in spite of my muscles resisting the effort. My breathing grew steadier, stronger. I exhaled and hauled in another long, deep breath. Sweet, clean air flooded into my lungs and energized my mind and body for the battle ahead.

The battle for my own power.

"It's your magic," Max said, his tone even and assuring. "Do not let it control you. The Janusite owns her power and molds it to her needs. Take the reins, Lindsey."

Once upon a time, in another age that had been six weeks ago, I'd admonished myself to "rein it in." Then, I'd meant my emotions and especially my passions—anger, joy, lust, anything that put me at risk of getting hurt. Nevan had shown me holding back had kept me from experiencing the full spectrum of life and that embracing strong emotions and sexual desires could set me free, make me stronger.

I closed my eyes, let the magic rush through me for a moment, and reveled in the sheer power and intensity of it. My magic. My power. *Serve me, you wild energy, serve the Janusite.*

The magic balked at my command with a tiny jolt. I gritted my teeth, envisioning the power as an unruly stallion and imagining a bridle in my hands. First, I had to calm the magics. I summoned the memory of my most placid moments, all of which had taken place in Nevan's arms. When he held me after we made love. When he consoled me during tough times. When he gaze gazed at me with pure love.

My magic calmed enough I could slip my imaginary bridle over it, jump onto its back, and rein in the power.

An intoxicating sense of victory surged through me, but I resisted the impulse to celebrate. I hadn't gotten what I needed yet. The tingling had dissipated, and the energy coursing down my nerves had quieted into a gentle current, but I still couldn't direct the power. *Use the reins*, I reminded myself, and gave them a light tug in the direction I wanted.

I aimed the magic at the wards—or where the wards had been.

Tendrils of power spiraled out in visible blue streams that twirled and whipped in the air in every direction as they crept toward the walls of the underground lair. The tendrils diverted around Max, curling around his body as if tasting him. They flowed over Nevan, where he lay on the bed with his eyes closed and his body slack. I fed more fuel into the magic, commanding it with my thoughts instead of spoken words.

My magic, my desires, they melded into a swirling mass of glowing, sparkling streams emitted from my skin. The feel of energy unleashing from within me was empowering, exciting…arousing.

The vacuum left behind by the shattered wards began to fill in, as I crafted a web of magic to protect my new home. The web in turn filled in with more solid, stronger power. The wards became a blue wall of shimmering power erected like a second skin over the earthen walls, the body of the mountain. When I sensed the completion of the barrier, like a lock thunking into place, I reeled my power back inside myself.

The walls became solid earth again, the wards once more invisible.

I understood, in a way I couldn't explain, that the barrier was stronger than before and impenetrable even to the sorcerer's efforts. I had become connected to the wards, and they in turn had become an extension of me.

"Well?" Max asked, his arms hanging loose at his sides.

"It worked." I listened to the soft buzzing of the wards as the sound faded away. "Didn't you feel it? When the wards clicked into place?"

"A familiar can't experience his mistress's magic. He provides an anchor, not a conduit for power."

"I'm still kind of confused about the familiar thing, but it doesn't really matter. I control my own magic now." Glancing toward the bed, I squared my shoulders and lifted my chin. "Which means I can recharge Nevan. All the way this time."

Max touched my arm. "Is that wise? The sorcerer might bleed him dry again, and you can't keep recharging his magic indefinitely."

"Won't have to. We're going to stop this damn sorcerer coward."

"How?"

"Not sure yet, but I know we can do it. With my power under better control, I can do a lot more than shoot the bastard with my endued gun."

I hurried to the bed and settled on the blanket beside Nevan. My heart hurt when I took in his appearance, his skin so pale it was nearing white, his lips almost blue and his breaths deathly shallow. At least I could energize him, for a time, and alleviate his suffering. He would be virile enough to fight at my side.

The aftereffects of harnessing my power rippled sexual desire through me, a warm and stimulating energy. My body hummed with it, and my nipples grew hard.

Over my shoulder, I called out to Max. "Maybe you should go in the kitchen again. I need to recharge Nevan the only way I know how."

Not sex. Nevan was too weak for that. But I needed physical contact and a connection fueled by passion. A bone-melting kiss ought to do the trick.

And I didn't particularly want an incubus watching.

Without a word, Max retreated into the kitchen.

I smoothed hair from Nevan's forehead, running my fingers over his temples and down his jawline. His skin was cold and clammy.

Not for long.

Leaning over him, I set my hands at either side of his head and invited the magic to vibrate through me again, hot and electric. The hairs on the back of my neck lifted, then the hairs on my arms. Goose bumps pebbled my skin beginning at my wrists and sweeping up my arms. My breaths grew labored, my breasts tightened, my lips burned for what was to come.

I laid a thumb on his chin, easing his mouth open.

He stirred, mumbling wordlessly, his eyes still shut.

My head seemed to float above my body, weightless and disconnected. But the second I crushed my mouth to his, everything inside me reconnected and awakened. I licked at his lips, relishing the distinctive flavor of him, even as my lips imparted magic into him. *Not enough*. I delved my tongue into his mouth, coiling it around his again and again, desperate for a response, thrilled by the way his flesh heated up and his breaths grew heavier. I plastered my chest to his, my breasts mounded against his firm muscles.

The magic whirled around us, penetrated into us, swelled and spread and enlivened every inch of our bodies as if we were one being.

His arms came around me, his hands groping my back.

I braced my forearms at either side of his head, thrusting my fingers into his hair in the same instant I thrust my tongue deeper into his mouth. He groaned, his hands shifting to my ass, and plunged his tongue into my waiting mouth. Our tongues tangled and danced, wound around each other and separated, while the heat of our kiss saturated his entire body.

My scorching sylph was back.

Without severing our lip-lock, he flipped us over so I lay trapped beneath his massive body, a willing prisoner. I hooked one leg around his, arched my hips into him, tunneled my fingers through his hair to hold him against me and prolong the kiss. I moaned into his mouth, and he grasped my hip in one big hand to pull me snugly into him.

His erection began to blossom between us.

Nevan tore his lips away from mine. Panting, eyes glossy and lips swollen, he gazed down at me with his familiar sexy smirk. "We must stop, for the moment. Though I have to admit, darlin', I do love the way you save me."

"Wish we could do the hot sex kind of saving." I nodded toward the kitchen doorway. "But my familiar is waiting."

His lips kinked downward, though only for a second. "He has helped you, then."

"Max is an invaluable assistant."

"Glad to hear it." Nevan rocked his hips, grinding his rigid shaft into me. "Your magic has grown powerful—and powerfully arousing."

I scrunched up my face. "Hope I don't have to use sex to defeat the sorcerer. I might let the worlds be annihilated if that's the price for saving them."

"Have faith. You control your power, which means you may channel it however you wish."

"Mm, I wish to channel it into a steamy kiss with you."

A grin lit up his face, making him seem younger and less burdened by current circumstances. "As long as it's only with me, I have no objection to your method."

"Probably need to come up with an alternate method, though."

He rolled off the bed and sprang to his feet, then grasped me around the waist and lifted me onto my feet.

I flattened my palms on his chest. "Sure are spry for a man who was almost a goner a few minutes ago."

"You must have used a great deal of magic to reinvigorate me." He scowled, though I knew he was frightened rather than angry. "Don't do it again, Lindsey. I will not have you depleting your magics in an effort to keep me alive. It's far too dangerous for you."

"A minute ago, you said you loved the way I save you. All of a sudden it's dangerous?"

He laid his hands over mine on his chest. "I do love your method, but I fear for your health if you continue to resurrect me after each attack by Ceara and the sorcerer."

"I won't stand by and let you wither away into nothing."

"You must, for your own sake." He crushed my palms to his chest. "Please consider the consequences. This may be the sorcerer's plan, to siphon away your power using me as a sort of battery to store the energy of your magics. He then has Ceara retrieve the energy from me."

"Nevan, you said the P-word."

"Your bad verbal habits are infecting me. And I am desperate to keep you from harm."

His theory almost made sense, except for one thing. "If the sorcerer can siphon anyone's power, why wouldn't he kidnap me and suck me dry? Why use you as a go-between?"

I watched him struggling to compose an answer, his lips contorting and his eyes flashing.

After a moment, he said, "I cannot explain it."

"Care to hear my theory?"

"I'm listening."

"The oracle said the sorcerer has a grudge to settle." I wrested my hands free of his, leaning in to garner his full attention. "He's teamed up with your formerly dead wife. He keeps having her suck the life out of you. The answer seems pretty obvious to me. You're part of his grudge."

"But he covets your magic."

"Sure, but he's definitely punishing you for something. He sent Max to me, to get my powers in tiptop shape before he does whatever he plans to do to me." I rose onto my toes, leveling our gazes. "He won't take my magical energy until I've increased it as much as possible. Until it's worth stealing. But you...This guy has a serious jones for torturing you, destroying you bit by bit. That's not using you as a tool. That's revenge, Nevan."

His mouth opened, but he said nothing.

"I'm right, and you know it." Dropping back onto my heels, I let my hands rest on his shoulders. "So tell me, sweetie. Who hates you with an eternal, blistering vengeance?"

"Besides Skeiron, who is gone, only one individual meets your criteria." He scrubbed a hand over his mouth. "Notus. The one who forged me."

Chapter Sixteen

"Notus?" I felt my brows crinkle at the mention of the former king of the sylphs, the one who'd ruled before Skeiron, the one Skeiron had defeated to become king. "You told me once Skeiron beat Notus in a long and bloody war for the kingship. What exactly did Skeiron do to stop Notus? I thought elementals destroyed each other, like I destroyed Skeiron."

Nevan pursed his lips, his gaze going distant as if he were peering into the past. "I've also explained that immortals, such as the elemental races, cannot die in any conventional sense."

"It takes something supernatural, like an endued weapon or an enchanted poison."

He focused on me again, his eyes simmering with molten shades of bronze and silver. "A dark spell can also achieve the desired result. That is what Skeiron employed."

"Dark spell?" I moved my hands to his chest, relieved to feel his hot skin, obliged to whatever power had allowed me to restore his natural heat. My power had done it. The magic I'd somehow acquired from a long-gone god, Janus. "Is that how Janus was taken out too?"

"Not precisely the same. The gods, not elementals, destroyed Janus."

"Right, I remember you said they combined their magics to get rid of him because they feared how much power he'd amassed." I let my hands fall to my sides and rocked back on my heels. "I don't understand. The gods aren't elementals? They live in the elemental realm."

"They exist in the Unseen realm."

"Which is different how?"

"Ah…" Nevan scratched his head. "It's difficult to explain. The gods are not strictly elemental in nature, but neither are they not elemental. They exist apart from all other beings in the Unseen and might be viewed as one level below the Oversoul."

"You mean God."

"I mean the unknowable force that created the universe."

The same vague thing Max had said. The first pang of a headache sprouted behind my eyes, and I rubbed my forehead. Understanding the big picture of the Unseen realm seemed out of my grasp and, for now, unimportant. "Let's forget the philosophical stuff for the moment and get back to Skeiron and Notus. Tell me what Skeiron did to get rid of his competition."

Nevan exhaled a long and weary sigh. "I was not present when Skeiron annihilated Notus. I know only what Skeiron told his followers after the battle. He claimed he had undergone an arcane and arduous ritual to acquire greater power, darker power, with the intention of using it to end Notus's existence. The magics he gained allowed him to destroy the one-time king and scatter his essence to the Four Winds."

"The same way the gods scattered Janus to the Four Winds."

"Yes, though by a different method."

Just when my headache had waned, it threatened to return. "What's the difference between an essence and a soul, or an essence and powers?"

"None that I'm aware of. They might be the same, or they might be different, depending on the circumstances."

"In other words, you don't know." I threw my head back on a gusty sigh. "Does this mean I might have Janus's soul inside me?"

"Doubtful. His essence was scattered, but the Four Winds captured his powers and held them until you were born. Then, they imbued them into you."

"Hmm." I rocked forward on the balls of my feet, considering what he'd told me, but I didn't have time to wonder about Janus's essence. "Let me see if I get this. The gods scattered Janus to the Four Winds, Skeiron scattered Notus to the Four Winds, I scattered Skeiron to the Four Winds, and Brennus planned on scattering my power to the Four Winds—at the command of my ex-fiancé. There's kind of an epidemic of scattering, hey?"

Nevan hooked a finger under my chin, lifting my face to him. "You killed Skeiron in self-defense. Skeiron acted out of a lust for power."

"My point, which I admittedly am not making too well, is that I have magical abilities because I inherited Janus's powers after they were scattered." I walked around Nevan, stuffing my hands in my jeans pockets, absorbed with the thoughts bouncing around in my mind. Making sense of all this craziness could tax a human brain. "Scattering doesn't eradicate a being's power—or the soul?"

"No, it eradicates the being's physical form. The soul generally moves on, but the power is redistributed to the Four Winds."

"Which are avatars and guardians of energy and magic," I said, quoting what Nevan had told me six weeks ago. "I still don't quite get that. What do they do with the powers they receive?"

"Guard them," Nevan replied, turning to watch me pace the length of the room. "They protect the orphaned magic so it will not fall into the wrong hands, and in the right circumstances, they might gift another being with all or a portion of the magical energy."

"Could someone steal the power of a destroyed elemental from the Four Winds?"

"Perhaps, though I've never heard of such a feat being accomplished."

I stared down at the floor as I paced back and forth, my shoulders caving in toward my chest. An inkling of an idea had formed in my mind, but I couldn't quite express it in words yet.

Nevan stepped in front of me, halting my nervous movement, and took my upper arms in his hands. When I looked up at him, he gave me a patient, if small, smile. "What are you thinking?"

We gazed into each other's eyes for a moment, comfortable in the silence between us, until I at last formulated a coherent idea.

"If a being's power survives," I said, "could someone steal that power from the Four Winds and use it to resurrect the destroyed elemental?"

He studied me, his brow furrowed and his eyes squinted. "I don't know. With enough magic, nearly anything is possible. But a being is made of more than power, and what is re-created may not be the same as the original being."

"Is there any way to resurrect the physical body of an elemental?"

Nevan opened his mouth, but quickly closed it again.

"I believe there is a way," said a voice from the kitchen.

Max emerged from the kitchen in human form, dressed in his conjured clothing, and strode up to me and Nevan.

"How do you know this?" Nevan asked.

The incubus shrugged. "Because of Ceara's pet name for the sorcerer."

I turned to Max. "Which is?"

"My undead inamorata."

"Undead? Please don't tell me he's a vampire."

Sylph and incubus alike scoffed. They exchanged a look that implied I was being ridiculous, but really, zombies didn't seem any more outrageous than shapeshifters—at least, to a mortal like me. Nevan had said ghosts were real, so how should I know if other supposedly mythical creatures existed? *No vampires, check.*

I believed that for about three seconds, until Nevan wrecked my limited peace of mind.

He shook his head, still making a huffy scoffing sound. "Vampires have only the most limited of magics."

"Weaklings," Max concurred.

My shoulders caved in a little further. I pulled my hands out of my pockets to clamp them around my head. "Oh dear lord. Vampires are real? What about zombies?"

"Those can exist," Max said, "only if a powerful mage creates them from scratch."

Head. About to explode. My brains, all over the floor.

Nevan wrapped an arm around my shoulders and hugged me to him. "Take it easy, love. You still have much to learn about this world."

"No kidding." I leaned my head against him, in need of his solid and comforting presence. To Max, I said, "I know you can't tell me who the sorcerer is, but you must've seen his face."

"I have, but I don't know what Notus looks like. I was born and forged long after the former king's demise."

"Can't confirm or deny, then."

"With or without a bargain restricting me, I'm afraid I can't identify the sorcerer."

"Not your fault." A portion of what he'd said rang a bell in my mind. He'd mentioned earlier today that he was born during the age of the Roman empire. Interesting, but not relevant at the moment.

Wait a second. Maybe it was relevant.

Extricating a piece of paper from the back pocket of my jeans, I unfolded it and offered the sheet to Max.

He took the paper and squinted at my drawing of Ceara's pendant. "What is this?"

"A pendant Ceara wears around her waist. Nevan thinks it might be Egyptian, and I was hoping you might recognize it. The Romans conquered Egypt, after all."

"That they did, and I spent some time in Alexandria." He pursed his lips, his eyes darting as he studied the image. "I didn't notice the pendant when I saw Ceara, but it was rather a kerfuffle then."

"Do you recognize the symbol?"

"It looks like a papyrus column." He turned the paper left and then right. "Can't recall what it means."

I blew out a breath between my lips. "Back to square one, eh?"

"Not quite," Nevan said. "Thanks to your wonderful mind and your bravery in seeking out the oracle, we now have reason to suspect Notus has been resurrected. Or, at the least, his powers have been transferred into another being determined to enact vengeance for the king's destruction."

"What does that have to do with you?"

"I was Skeiron's right hand during the war for control of the sylph kingdom." He tucked me against him, seeming to need the soothing contact while he revisited the past. "I believed Notus had strayed too far into the darkness, and Skeiron would be our salvation. When Skeiron bade me to lead our army against Notus's as a distraction, so he might confront the king alone, I agreed without hesitation. I had believed, until recently, Skeiron became depraved because of the power he inherited from Notus. Only after Skeiron's death did I learn he'd employed the darkest of magics to win the war with Notus, and it set in motion his own descent into madness."

I propped my chin on his chest. "How did you find that out?"

"When I became king, the tribunal told me. They presented the information in the form of a warning that I should not attempt to use dark magics, else they would depose me by any means necessary."

"But they're working with Ceara and the sorcerer. I doubt those two are using sweet, fluffy spells."

Nevan smiled with an affection that sparkled in his eyes. "You do say the most bizarrely charming things. To address your concern, I suspect the tribunal thinks the sorcerer is their only hope of dethroning me."

"Or controlling you. But why would they want to do either? You're way better than that skeezy bastard Skeiron."

Max chuckled softly behind me. "Skeezy bastard? His Highness is right. My mistress says the most unusual things."

Had my familiar called Nevan by a kingly appellation for the first time since they'd met? Why yes, he had. *Interesting.*

"You should talk," I said to Max. "I bet you've never been to England, but you spout all the Brit-speak."

"Can't argue with that," said the incubus. "It's instinct, though, picking up modern language from my descendants."

"Whatever you say." I addressed Nevan next. "Any more thoughts on why the tribunal hates you?"

Nevan threaded his fingers through my hair. "I have no idea why the tribunal despises me. Within days of crowning me king, they became wary of me—and they've become decidedly hostile."

"And I'd bet all my Janusite power the sorcerer convinced them you're a threat."

"I do wish you'd refrain from betting. Far too close to bargaining for my liking."

"Yeah, I know." I gave him a sheepish smile. "My mouth tends to run off on its own when I'm distracted and totally freaked out."

"I am well aware of that."

My gaze bounced around the room, while thoughts bounced around in my brain. I saw the chairs, the bed, the boxes of my stuff pushed up against the wall.

I snapped my gaze back to the boxes. My stuff. I had books about ancient mythology, a topic I'd become a bit obsessed with since learning I was the Janusite. Max had identified Ceara's pendant as a papyrus column, an ancient Egyptian symbol.

Racing to the boxes, I rifled through them one by one, tossing unbreakable items aside in my hunt for the right book.

"What are you doing?" Max asked.

"Gimme a sec." I found it at last, and flipped the book open to a section about ancient Egyptian symbols. Skimming my finger down the list of symbols, I located the papyrus column. "Ah-ha. Ceara's amulet, the papyrus column, was believed to grant the wearer vitality and the power of regeneration."

The clanging of an alarm bell resounded through the underground house.

Max flinched, his gaze swerving back and forth. "What the bloody hell is that?"

"Whoops, I did that," I said. "When you helped me reestablish the wards, I installed a security system so we'd know when somebody's out there."

"Do we have any way of knowing," Nevan said, "who it is out there?"

"Open the door and see. The wards will stay up, so there's no risk." I hesitated, then added, "Well, very minimal risk."

Nevan pulled away from me to approach the section of rock wall where the door was hidden and activate it with a swift motion of his hand.

Travis waited outside in his uniform, one hip cocked, his hand on the Sig Sauer holstered on his belt.

"Gonna let me in or what?" he said.

Nevan glanced back at me with a questioning look.

I waved my hand toward the open door. "The wards should work like before, letting you and me bring people inside."

He still seemed uncertain, but he walked out the doorway in spite of his less-than-complete trust in my magical aptitude.

I couldn't blame him. Until today, I'd done little more than ferry him over the boundary in the mortal realm and open the portal to the Unseen. Well, that and destroy Skeiron. But the boundary had done all the work for me there.

Having survived crossing through my new wards, Nevan clapped a hand on Travis's shoulder and gestured for him to proceed into the house. The two men strode inside, and Nevan closed the door.

Neither of them burst into flames or started screaming in agony. *Nonlethal magical wards, check.*

"You got the whatchamacallits back up and running," Travis said as he came toward me. "Nice job, Lindsey."

"Th—" *Oops.* Almost thanked him. "I appreciate the vote of confidence. What did you find out about the dead women?"

"Found out who they are, for starters." He adjusted his belt, his lips twisting into an odd expression. "The bodies may have been dumped in Mandan County, but only the last girl was in the area at the time of her disappearance. One was from Israel, the other from Australia. Megan was a tourist, but the other two had never been to America. All three somehow wound up on the outskirts of Lutin Falls, in the woods behind the rock shop."

Three young women had died near the town where I'd lived for the past three years, in the woods behind the shop where I worked.

"All of them have got two things in common," Travis said. "First, they've got a resemblance to you. Not like you're twins, but enough similarity to be suspicious."

"We knew that already. What's the other thing?"

"They were all born on the same day. Your birthday."

CHAPTER SEVENTEEN

EVERYTHING INSIDE ME FROZE, AS IF I'D BEEN INJECTED WITH LIQUID nitrogen that penetrated every single cell of my body. All the dead women shared my birthday. I'd suspected the women had some connection to me, besides our resemblance to each other, but this confirmation hit me hard. I couldn't speak or move, and even breathing became difficult. A phantom weight bore down on my chest, making it hard to pull in enough air.

My birthday.

One of my allies had betrayed me. That's what I'd thought yesterday, because the sorcerer knew about my powers—and my birth date, it seemed. The more time I spent with my allies, including the newcomers Max and Ennea, the less I could believe any of them might betray me.

Who else could have done it?

Nevan took my face in his hands, the heat of him chasing away the chill in my cheeks but failing to eradicate the coldness in the rest of my body. I let his mesmeric eyes capture my focus, but for once, their swirling couldn't distract me from the fear seizing control of me.

No. I would not give in to the fear. Not this time.

The old me would have, but I'd changed in the past six weeks. I wasn't a coward repressing my feelings anymore.

I placed my hands over Nevan's. "It's okay. I'm okay."

He searched my face—for a sign I was reining it in like I used to, no doubt—but then nodded and lowered his hands to my shoulders. "The connection to you is no longer a hypothesis. The sorcerer killed these women because they resemble you. Perhaps in an attempt to find you, based on appearance and birth date."

"But he knew who I was when he killed Megan. He said the girls were an offering to prove his devotion to me."

The sorcerer had vowed to "whittle away" at me until I had nothing left but fear and regret. He swore I'd want to go with him in the end. Why did he want me? It was more than my powers, of that I was certain. The sorcerer had told me he could become whomever I wanted, offering to glamour into Nevan or Travis. Nevan, I could understand, but why did he choose to glamour into Travis?

He'd called me "sweetness" and "sweet thing." Only one person had ever called me either of those things.

"The sorcerer is Calder Blackwell," I said. "He has to be, it's the only way this makes any sense."

Everyone looked dubious, so I laid out the evidence supporting my claim.

Nevan spoke first. "It does make a certain sense, though your theory fails to account for the sorcerer's vendetta against me. Calder wanted me out of the way, so he could have you."

"And the sorcerer is spending a ton of time and energy on torturing you," I said. "That seems more Notus-ish. But murdering girls as an offering, and trying to wear me down so I'll join him, that seems more Calder-ish. I still don't understand the burning bush thing either."

Max coughed, garnering everyone's attention. "That would be me."

"You set the bush on fire?" I asked. "And the sorcerer doesn't mind you telling me?"

"Apparently not."

"What was the burning bush supposed to mean?"

"Nothing. I was supposed to get your attention by igniting the bush, to lure you to the bodies."

"Well, at least we solved one mystery," I said. "But I still think the sorcerer is Calder, somehow brought back to life. He would know I'm the Janusite, and he'd know my birthday. Notus couldn't know any of that."

"He could," Nevan said, "if someone told him. The entire sylph army witnessed you destroying Skeiron. I erased their memories of the battle, but the sorcerer might have restored their recollections using his dark magics."

Travis cleared his throat, making a pained face. "You're ignoring the obvious, Lindsey. There's somebody who could've told them and might not even remember doing it."

Cold sluiced through me anew, and every hair on my body stiffened.

No, it couldn't be true. I refused to believe it.

And the sorcerer might be counting on exactly that reaction.

I looked steadily into Nevan's eyes. "It could've been you."

The alarm clanged.

Nevan and I kept our gazes glued to each other, each of us praying it wasn't true but unable to refute the idea. I knew him well enough to realize he was thinking the same thing I was. And I knew what he'd believe he needed to do to protect me.

He wanted to sacrifice himself—and somehow, some way, take out the sorcerer at the same time.

The alarm clanged again.

Nevan stalked to the doorway, commanding it to open.

Tris and Ennea smiled at us from the other side of the wards. Well, Ennea smiled. Her brother had his mouth contorted into a hybrid of a frown and a smirk.

Passing through the invisible wards, Nevan guided the leprechauns into our home. He moved his wrist as if to shut the door, then dropped his hand. "I will leave it open for the moment. I suspect we will be leaving soon, on separate missions."

"Fine," I said. "Come back over here, though. We're having our little mission briefing on this side of the room."

He returned to my side, his expression unreadable.

My intuition shivered a warning through me. Nevan had promised not to take his own life, but that left so many other options open to him if he resolved to act on my behalf. He knew how I felt about such recklessness, but his damn honor might override his promise if he decided I was in too much danger and only he could rectify the situation.

I slipped my hand into his, twining our fingers. His hand closed around mine, warm and strong, but the comfort of his touch failed to melt the icy spike lodged in my heart.

Travis spoke first. "What do we do? If Nevan can be controlled, any of us could be under the sorcerer's....whatever you call it."

"His thrall," Max offered.

"Under his thrall, then," Travis said, looking miserable at the idea. "How do we handle this? We can't have the bad guys finding out our plans."

"We got plans?" Tris said. "Nobody told me."

Max raised his hand. "Don't forget about me. I'm already influenced by the sorcerer, thanks to our bargain. I might've exposed Lindsey's identity and had my memory wiped clean."

"I appreciate your honesty," I said, "but this game of 'who's the traitor' will get us nowhere. We need one person we can trust, someone who has the means to figure out which, if any, of us is enthralled by the sorcerer."

The six of us lapsed into silence, our expressions running the gamut from extreme unease to befuddlement. The problem seemed insurmountable, but I had to believe we could find a solution.

"Come on," I said. "Look at us. A sylph, a salamander, a law enforcement professional, two leprechauns—one of whom is a fae witch—and the Janusite. We're like a team of superheroes, and we can't figure it out? Baloney. We can do this."

Travis arched his eyebrows. "I'm not a superhero, Lindsey. Just a cop. A mortal one. I'm the one who doesn't belong in this group."

"You're smart and tough as nails. You belong here."

"He can be our Batman," Tris said. "You know, the guy with no super-powers who fights evil."

"You read comic books?" I asked.

"Uh, no. I watch TV sometimes." He hooked a thumb at his sister. "Ennea created a spell to catch satellite signals from the mortal realm. She's addicted to home improvement shows."

Maybe it was a nervous response, but I couldn't keep from laughing. An image had flashed in my mind, of Ennea and Tris gathered around a TV in a cave somewhere eating popcorn and heckling the shows for their inaccurate portrayals of the fae.

"The point is," I said, having gotten my inappropriate laughter under control, "we can find a way to do this. To determine if any of us is being used by our enemies."

Ennea's face brightened, as if a proverbial light bulb had powered up in her brain. "You, Lindsey. You're the one who can do it. Of all of us, you are the only one we can be sure isn't under the sorcerer's influence."

"How do you figure that?" I asked.

"Girl, you told me yourself the first time we met. Magic goes a little woo-woo in your presence."

"Yeah, but I don't know for sure that means I'm immune to the sorcerer's control."

"Think about it," she said. "If he could exert any power over you, he'd have you already. Instead, he's torturing Nevan and sending his nasty girl-friend to wreak havoc."

"Someone told him my birthday."

Max's gaze ping-ponged around the room, like he was trying really hard not to meet anyone's eyes.

I squinted at him. "You know something, but you can't tell me."

He coughed into his fist.

"I'll take that as a yes." Hands on my hips, I drummed my fingers and ran-sacked my brain for a way around his restrictions. He'd managed to convey the fact he knew something without violating his bargain with the sorcerer. Maybe grunts and coughs didn't count as telling me. Worth a shot. "Maybe the sor-cerer mentioned how he found out my birthday."

Max coughed.

"Okay." *Eureka*. I'd found a chink in the armor of Max's deal with the sorcerer. "Maybe he talked to another elemental, or some other being who lives in the Unseen, and they told him."

Another cough.

Nevan curled his hand around my forearm. "An oracle."

Silence.

Time for the life-altering question. "Was it Calder?"

Max shrugged.

"Notus?" Nevan asked.

Another shrug. The incubus didn't know the answer.

I thought for a moment, then said, "The tribunal must be working with the sorcerer. He must have a hold on them."

Max coughed twice.

"They're forced to do it against their will."

Silence.

I canted my head at Max. "They allowed the sorcerer to enchant them or whatever, because he offered them something they want."

A short cough.

Nevan huffed. "They want to dethrone me, because they fear I'll lose my mind as the previous kings did. The sorcerer convinced them of this."

Max cleared his throat.

"But they don't know," I said, "I'm the Janusite. The sorcerer's keeping that to himself."

One loud, harsh throat clearing.

"Ceara killed the oracle because he was going to give us vital information about the sorcerer."

Max cleared his throat so forcefully he almost choked.

Tris waved toward Max. "That's all super cool to know, but how do we know we can trust the incubus?"

"Lindsey needs to do a spell," Ennea said. "One that will show her who's lying, even if they don't realize they're lying."

"Me?" I pointed at myself. "I don't know how to work a spell."

Nevan clasped my hand. "Of course you do. The spell you crafted to reestablish the wards is stronger even than the one Ennea created for me."

"Ennea created the original wards? You didn't mention that before, only that a fae made them."

"It didn't occur to me to tell you her name."

"Have your tiff later," Ennea said. "Lindsey needs to do a spell now."

The fae witch took my arm and guided me away from the group, motioning for Max to accompany us. When Nevan moved to follow, Ennea shook her head. He gritted his teeth, a muscle in his jaw ticking, but stayed put. Ennea led Max and me across the living room, to a doorway on the opposite side from the kitchen.

She leaned across the threshold, craning her neck to peer inside the room beyond. With a decisive nod, she motioned for us to trail her into the room.

"What is this?" she asked, turning in a circle to admire the surroundings.

"The bathroom," I said, though the word fell short of describing the amazing space Nevan had created.

A cascade splashed out of a crevice high on the eight-foot walls, raining down in a perpetual shower. The water flowed into an ankle-deep pool that spilled out a hole in the floor opposite the miniature waterfall. Green plants and colorful flowers sprouted out of cracks in the rock walls, their long limbs tumbling down toward the water.

"Amazing," Ennea said. "I've never seen a bathroom like this one, and I've been to a lot of elemental homes."

Most sylphs, Nevan had told me, leaped into the nearest natural pool or lake to cleanse their bodies. He, however, enjoyed having his own private waterfall. When I'd asked him how many women he'd bathed with under the cascade, he'd declared, "I have brought only one woman to my home."

A delicious glow warmed me at the memory of those words. No one else had reveled in the sensual delight of showering with Nevan in the privacy of this beautiful space.

"Wake up, Lindsey."

Ennea's voice yanked me back to the here and now. I must've zoned out, lost in the memory of happy times. It felt like an eternity had elapsed since the last time I'd showered with Nevan in this room, but only a few days had gone by.

"How do I do this?" I asked.

"Have to figure that out on your own," the witch said.

"But you're the expert on spells."

"I'm not the Janusite, I'm a witch. Your magic is clearly different." She closed her eyes, rubbing her finger up and down the bridge of her nose. When she looked at me again, she said, "You created a security system for the house, as part of the wards. How did you do it?"

"Commanded it, and it happened."

"Will-based magic. Interesting." She studied me with a thoughtful expression. "Do that again. Access your power and command it to show you who's honest and who's lying."

No, it couldn't be that easy. But I had no better ideas.

I held my hands out to Max with my palms down, and he hovered his hands below mine with his palms up. The small gap between our hands crackled with unseen energy as my magic reflected off him, strengthened and enhanced by the presence of my familiar. It felt different this time, because I no longer worried about what might happen when I accessed my power. I knew what it would feel like.

The first time, magic had flooded through me and overpowered my intentions. With experience under my belt, I could funnel and direct the flow of power so it enlivened my magic without steamrolling me. Blue energy glittered on the surface of my skin, and my scalp tingled as the same energy lifted my hair like static electricity.

I focused all my will on one task. *Show me truth versus lies.*

Nothing happened.

Squeezing my eyes shut, I gritted my teeth and commanded the magic to obey. A wave of stronger energy rushed through my body, hot and crackling with power, stunning a gasp from me.

Click. The spell powered on.

At least I thought it powered on. Time for a test.

I opened my eyes and, with my hands still hovering above Max's, I said, "Tell me a lie. Need to test the spell."

He hesitated, then told me, "I am a mortal man."

A red ball of light flashed once on his forehead, then vanished.

"The truth now," I said.

"I'm an immortal incubus."

A white ball flashed on his forehead this time, then winked out.

I clapped my hands together. "Seems to work."

Ennea took my shoulders and turned me toward her. She squinted, scrutinizing me with her lips compressed and her hands grasping me stiffly. After several seconds she let go of me, and the tension smoothed out of her features. "You seem fine. Time for the big test."

She gestured for us to exit the bathroom.

As we crossed the threshold, I murmured to Ennea, "Did you see the balls of light?"

"What lights?"

"The ones my supernatural lie detector made. A red one for lie, a white one for truth."

"Only you saw them," she said, making a beeline for the three males awaiting our return in the center of the living room. "Makes sense, though. You wouldn't want a traitor to know you know they're lying."

"Do you think it'll work if the person doesn't realize they're lying?"

"Beats me." She cast me a thoughtful sideways glance. "But remember, it's magic. You control it, and it has no limits. Elementals can control their physiological responses, but they can't stop a spell from sniffing out the truth. If you make proper use of your spell, that is."

Not the comforting answer I was hoping for, but I'd have to accept it. Whether this worked depended on the strength of my will and my belief in my own magic.

When we reached the others, Ennea instructed all of them to line up for me to assess their honesty. She took her place at the end of the line, beside Tris.

I wedged my clasped hands under my chin as I pondered what I must do. Determine who betrayed me. Could I deal with the answer?

What if I learned Nevan was the traitor?

I scanned the row of potential traitors—my friends, my cohorts, and my lover. Ennea wore a pleasant expression, and when she saw me looking at her, she smiled and nodded her encouragement. Tris had his thumbs hooked in the pockets of his ratty jeans and a rueful half smile on his lips. Next to him, Travis stood tall and straight with his arms at his sides and a stoic look on his face. Max came next in line, his posture relaxed but his eyes a duller red than usual and his mouth tight at the corners.

And then there was Nevan. He resembled a bronze statue in a museum, unmoving, giving away nothing in his expression.

I longed to run to him, fling my arms around his neck, and kiss him until we both forgot about the current circumstances and the world outside our little underground haven. I couldn't do it. Despite dreading what I'd learn, I had to test each and every one of them.

Starting with Ennea, I asked each of my friends the same question. "Did you tell the sorcerer details about me, including my birth date and that I'm the Janusite?"

Ennea answered, "No."

The white light flashed.

Tris answered, "No way."

A white light flashed.

Travis met my gaze head-on when he answered, "No, never."

Another white light. Another honest ally.

Nodding, I moved to Max. He lifted his chin slightly and said, "I have not."

The white light flashed.

Nevan was next. The only one left to test.

I couldn't move, my feet seemed cemented to the floor in front of Max.

Nevan aimed a sad smile in my direction. "It's all right. Do what you must."

Taking a deep breath, I stepped in front of Nevan. Our eyes met, the connection between us as strong as ever, a warm current of love and commitment and trust. Yet my pulse thundered in my ears, and ice trickled down my veins.

"Ask," he said.

"Did you tell the sorcerer details about me, including my birth date and that I'm the Janusite?"

"No."

A white light pulsed on his forehead.

Relief gushed through me, weakening my knees. I locked my knees to stay upright. "It's not you either. None of my allies is the traitor."

"It makes no difference," Nevan said, finality in his tone. "I may not have exposed your secrets to the sorcerer, but I remain susceptible to his control. As long as the sorcerer lives, as long as I live, I pose a grave threat to you. You know what must be done."

Dammit, he was right. I recognized the truth of it in my soul, but I couldn't condemn the only man I'd ever loved without even trying to save him. I wouldn't do that to any of my allies.

Skeiron had tried to take Nevan away from me. I'd scattered that scumbag to the Four Winds. The sorcerer had somehow gotten a hold over Nevan, without his knowledge, and would use my lover in his plot to steal my powers.

Like hell he would.

Nevan eyes widened the tiniest bit. "No, Lindsey."

I stalked up to him, grasped his face in both hands, and kissed him hard. "Stop telling me to give up on you." When he opened his mouth to speak, I cut him off. "Not. Going. To. Happen."

He closed his eyes, exhaling a sigh that deflated his shoulders.

Backing up a few steps, I addressed my friends. "We need to figure out how the sorcerer is controlling Nevan, how he's draining the life out of him. Any ideas?"

Ennea, Tris, Max, and Travis gathered around me to hash out ideas, but none of us could think of anything feasible. There had to be a way. I was too new to magic to know how to handle a situation like this.

Nevan lingered several feet away from the group, his head still bowed.

I stared at the top of his head, at the wavy locks falling over his forehead, and I longed to brush them away and murmur comforting words to him.

His head lifted, his eyes locked onto me.

Not giving up on you. I prayed my silent vow showed on my face, prayed he would give up his self-sacrifice plan.

His lips curved up in a small, melancholy smile.

An odd sensation wriggled in my gut, a kind of unease I couldn't decipher.

Tris tapped my arm to regain my attention. I turned back to the group, listening as Ennea explained the difficulties with attempting to free Nevan from the sorcerer. We had no conception of what type of spell bound Nevan, no clue how much magic would be required to break it, no frigging idea about much of anything, and on and on.

"If the tribunal's involved," Ennea said, "maybe we can get them to talk."

"Good luck with that," Tris said.

"Squeeze them hard enough and maybe they'll pop."

"I'd love a crack at 'em," Travis said, his hand resting on his Sig.

The conversation prattled on, but words began to smear into noise in my brain. Meaningless, incomprehensible noise.

An awareness rattled through me, sharp and unforgiving.

Max's lips moved as he focused his worried gaze on me, though I heard nothing he said. My gaze swung past my friends, beyond their shoulders, to the front door still wide open.

Nevan was marching toward it, shoulders back, head held high, every bit the strong and decisive king of the sylphs. In one hand, he grasped the endued sword.

Determined. Armed. *Enacting his plan.*

"No!"

My cry reverberated off the stone walls as I bolted for Nevan, shoving my friends aside on my way to him.

He strode across the threshold and through the wards, glanced back at me, and vanished.

Chapter Eighteen

I BROKE THROUGH THE WARDS, SPINNING IN A CIRCLE WITH MY HEAD thrown back, as if I might glimpse Nevan flying away. A patch of empty, eerily blue sky glared down at me, and the moss dripping from the trees swayed in a light breeze.

He'd abandoned me—in the name of protecting me.

"Lindsey?" Ennea's voice called to me from inside the wards. "Where's Nevan?"

I tilted my head down and found Ennea watching me, her eyes large as saucers.

"Gone," I said. "Grabbed his sword and took off. He still thinks he needs to sacrifice himself to save me."

Cursing, I kicked the ground but only managed to send a sharp pain shooting up my ankle.

Travis appeared in doorway, inches from the wards. "What do we do?"

I shoved my hands in my pockets, shoulders hunched. The fingers of my left hand contacted the smooth, warm surface of the soul stone, and a delicious energy rushed up my arm. A piece of Nevan, with me always.

The soul stone had brought me to our home.

Yanking the stone out of my pocket, I held it between my thumb and forefinger. The sunlight shimmered on the disk-shaped chunk of cream-colored rock. I swept the pad of my thumb over the surface, and a taste of Nevan whispered through me, the taste of strength and power and determination.

Something else rippled beneath the surface emotions. Something far more powerful than any magic. The unending strength of our love.

The soul stone had empowered me to whisk from the portal straight to my new home. Could it take me to Nevan?

I closed my hand around the stone. "I'm going after him."

"How?" Ennea asked. "You have no idea where he went."

"Don't need to know." I clamped my hand tighter around the little rock. "Nevan gave me a soul stone. Max showed me I could use it to transport myself here. I'm sure I can get it to take me to Nevan, wherever he is."

"You're sure?" She toyed with her ear, her expression hesitant, but then seemed to shrug off her doubts. "You are the Janusite, so who am I to question what you can do."

Max stepped into view behind Travis and Ennea. "Take me with you, mistress."

No sarcasm in his voice this time when he called me his mistress.

"You can't come with me this time," I told Max. "Have to do this on my own."

"I'm meant to stay at your side and—"

"Not this time." I held up the soul stone for everyone to see. "I'm sorry, Max, I need you to stay here with the others and brainstorm plans."

I could tell he wasn't happy about my orders, but he nodded his agreement.

The worrier in me reared her head, compelling me to ask, "Max, would you ever tell the sorcerer or any of his cohorts what you, me, and the rest of my gang talk about? Would you ever share our plans?"

"No. Absolutely not."

A white light flared on his forehead.

One less thing for me to worry about, assuming my lie detector spell was accurate. I had to believe it was. I needed to believe in my powers, in myself, or I'd never get through this ordeal.

Nevan had always believed in me, even when we had no idea I was the Janusite. I would not let him down.

"Hold down the fort," I told my friends. "This might take awhile."

"Good luck," Travis said.

I faced the woods. Faced the sky. Head thrown back, eyes closed, absorbing the fiery power of the Unseen realm's twin suns. Nevan had been forged from the earth and the sky, from the elemental power of the air and everything contained within it—particles of water and dirt, even fire in the form of electricity. I clutched the soul stone between both of my hands, and the distinctive scent of Nevan enveloped me.

Male spiciness. Damp, virgin earth. And the sweetness of ozone, evocative of thunderstorms.

Energy hummed through the soul stone and spread outward into the whole of my body, and deeper into core of my being. I concentrated all my willpower on Nevan, on reaching him, saving him. The world shifted, faster than the first time I'd done this, and the momentum pushed against my back.

I peeled my eyelids apart, squinting into the gloom around me. Though I'd emerged inside a shadowy corridor carved out of solid rock, up ahead I glimpsed the inconstant light of a fire. It lay beyond a doorway, out of my direct line of sight.

No Nevan.

Without knowing where I'd wound up, I couldn't risk calling out his name. I sensed him near, in a visceral way I couldn't describe. The way I always sensed his approach. My bond with him remained intact, for now.

No, not for now. Forever.

I tiptoed down the rough-hewn corridor toward the doorway, sidling up to the wall so I could peek around the threshold into the chamber beyond.

A fire burned within a single, large metallic bowl perched atop a wide dais. Flames lashed upward from the depths of the bowl, striving to reach the ceiling. This was the tribunal's chamber. I'd seen it when Ennea's spell let me tap into Nevan's memory of the last time he'd come to this place.

The five members of the tribunal gathered in a semicircle around the fire, atop the dais, like they had in Nevan's memory. The hoods of their flowing gold robes masked their faces.

Nevan stood before the tribunal, tall and stiff, the sword in his grip with the point aimed at the earthen floor.

"Why have you summoned us?" one of the tribunal asked in a raspy voice.

Oh yeah, I remembered this jackass from before. Mr. Raspy, the one who'd ordered Nevan to take Ceara as his queen.

"I am king," Nevan said, his voice sure and authoritative. "I summon you at my pleasure."

"We are not your subjects."

My lover sneered at Mr. Raspy. "Every citizen of the sylph kingdom is my subject. I serve their interests and welfare, but I also must know when to take decisive action against those who would endanger my kingdom."

"The tribunal no longer recognizes your authority." Mr. Raspy raised a long, skinny finger at Nevan. "You will serve our master, or you will be destroyed."

Nevan adjusted his grip on the sword, probably itching to plunge it into Mr. Raspy. I would've loved to do it myself.

"I serve no one," Nevan said. "And my subjects do not serve me. I am their leader, not their master. Anyone who volunteers to become a slave to another's whims is a fool at best and a traitor at worst."

"You threaten us?" another tribunal member said.

"Only if you threaten my kingdom."

Mr. Raspy took a shuffling step forward. "By your kingdom, you mean your mortal whore."

The muscles in Nevan's shoulders bunched, and he growled his words through gritted teeth. "I mean every innocent being under my aegis."

"This is your last chance," Mr. Raspy said. "Take a proper queen or suffer the consequences."

"Ceara will never be my queen."

Nevan raised his sword, widening his stance. The firelight glanced off the blade.

I pulled the derringer out of my waist holster, flicked the safety off, and stepped through the doorway.

An invisible force flung me backward.

Flat on my back, I slammed into the solid rock floor of the corridor, the thin covering of dirt no cushion against the bone-rattling force of the impact. My head smacked down last, and bright white lights exploded in my vision. Pain erupted in my head, my shoulders, my hips, scorching through my entire body.

The derringer skittered across the rock floor.

I must've screamed, because some kind of horrible keening reverberated off the stone walls and ceiling.

Dazed, I lay there for what seemed like an eternity but had probably been a matter of seconds. As the pains in my body ebbed to a dull ache in more places than I could count, my mind recovered from the shock. The world around me came back into focus, ushering in an awareness of what had happened. An awareness of two facts.

One, a ward had deflected my attempt to enter the tribunal's chamber.

Two, the keening hadn't been me. It had been Nevan.

He towered in the doorway, breathing hard and flirting with the ward that must've been millimeters from his skin. The sword he held at his side, tip down. He bared his teeth, his eyes wide and aflame with shades of crimson fury.

I pushed up into a sitting position. My head swam for a couple seconds but then settled down. "I'm okay."

"You should not be here."

"Neither should you." I tried not to wince as I scrambled to my feet, but the pains in my body overrode my wishes. "You promised."

"I will not harm myself." He narrowed his eyes to slits, the breath blustering out his flaring nostrils. "I will harm them."

"Nevan, please calm down before you do something—"

He whirled toward the tribunal, and Mr. Raspy stumbled backward.

Nevan swung his sword up and, roaring so loud it hurt my ears, stormed at the tribunal.

Dammit, I had to get through the ward.

A few feet from Mr. Raspy, Nevan froze. Sword raised. Mouth open on a bellow that died on his lips. He seemed to be bound in place by an invisible force.

Ceara winked into view right in front of him.

The fucking wards. My heart pounded, my head throbbed, but I summoned all the will I had inside me to harness my power. Blue energy shimmered in my palms. The power grew inside me, wild and hot, surging in my veins and waiting for my command.

I hurled it at the ward.

And the magic ricocheted off it, slamming into me.

Wham. I hit the floor on my backside, lights bursting in my vision, pain coruscating through my bones. Dizziness rocked my senses, but I scrambled to my feet and confronted the ward, my body swaying.

Inside the chamber, Nevan was paralyzed. Only his eyes moved to glimpse me, and in them I spied a miserable desperation. He couldn't protect me, and it tore at his heart the way my inability to reach him tore at mine.

Ceara smiled at me, the kind of smile that oozed menace and wicked glee. She ran her hands up Nevan's bare chest, fondling and stroking him as if she owned his body.

Maybe she did, for the moment. Fueled by the sorcerer's magic, the power he'd stolen from others, she controlled Nevan's movements but could never control his mind or his heart.

"It is time, Tuathal," she said to Nevan, but with her silvery eyes fixed on me. "Time to complete your humiliation and destroy your soul."

Her dress billowed around her legs, and her long hair fluttered around her face. The papyrus column amulet hung from the chain around her waist, its shiny, bluish green surface reflecting the flickering firelight. The same eerie glow I'd seen in Nevan's memory glittered like shards of silver around Ceara, and even her voice had taken on an eerie quality.

I pounded my fists on the ward. It hurled me backward, but I twisted to the left and struck the floor on my side. The impact reverberated through my hip and shoulder, though I'd spared my skull. I could do nothing but watch as Ceara enacted her master's plan.

Powerless again.

The evil shrew grasped his face in her hands, and with a triumphant glance at me, she mashed her mouth to his. He didn't move or react, his eyes open and haunted. Then his whole body slackened, his gaze turned remote and lifeless. Thin, silvery threads of magic snaked out from her fingertips, whipping and coiling around Nevan's face, slithering over his shoulders and down his arms.

Heaving my body off the ground, I kept my arms down and rotated my hands to direct my palms at the doorway. My magic had failed before. Not this time. Fear had ruled my heart when I lashed out at the ward the first time. For this go-round, I summoned every iota of searing hatred within me.

In the chamber, the serpents of Ceara's energy squirmed their way down Nevan's chest and back, converging around his hips to bleed down both legs. Soon, the visible evidence of the spell sheathed his body in its tentacles.

My hands grew hot, burning with the power I'd marshaled.

Ceara's magic pierced Nevan's skin, the tentacles burrowing in one by one with startling swiftness.

Blue energy exploded from my hands and rammed into the ward.

Nevan's body jerked. White sparked in his eyes, then sputtered out.

The magic shielding the doorway shattered with a boom that echoed in the corridor and the tribunal chamber.

Shaking all over, my head pounding as hard as my heart, I snatched my derringer from the floor and stormed into the chamber, straight to Ceara and Nevan.

Every member of the sylph tribunal backed away, retreating into a shadowed corner of the room.

Ceara curled her lips in a victorious smile.

"Tuathal," she said, and gestured toward me with a sweep of her arm, "show the Janusite the true nature of what you feel for her."

Nevan swiveled toward me, stretched out one thickly muscled arm, and clamped his hand around my throat. His long and powerful fingers encircled my neck, squeezing just enough to make me fight for breath. He lifted me off my feet as if I weighed no more than a feather, my feet suspended a foot off the floor. I lost my hold on the derringer, and it clattered to the ground.

Clutching at his wrist with both hands, I peered into those dead eyes but recognized nothing in them, no fragment of the man I knew and loved. Not the sweet and passionate lover or the fierce and noble warrior, not the former mortal afflicted with guilt from his past or the sylph liberated from magical enslavement. Nothing of Nevan remained in the body that gripped me with steel-reinforced efficiency.

I couldn't feel him either. The warm and vital connection between us had disintegrated. This was not Nevan anymore, but a hollow shell bearing his likeness.

He was hollowed out, exactly how Ceara had predicted.

Tears stung my eyes, threatening to flow, but if I let them come I might never be able to stem the tide. I'd been too late to save Nevan.

"Ahhhh," Ceara purred, moving closer to brush the back of one hand down my cheek, "you begin to understand. Would you like to know what I've done to him?"

I couldn't respond, what with Nevan's hand around my throat. No, not Nevan. I had to think of this shell as separate from him, or else I'd never have the resolve to do what must be done. This wasn't Tuathal either, because Nevan had carried a piece of his former, mortal self within him. This creature was the Anti-Nevan.

"Oh, you poor thing," Ceara cooed, stroking my cheek again. "Can't speak, can you? I shall assume you want me to tell you what I did to your beloved."

I gathered enough saliva in my mouth to spit in her face.

Chuckling, she wiped away the saliva. "My master was right, you are a feisty little mortal. It won't save you, though. Not your or your friends. You are powerless to stop what is coming." She pressed her lips to the Anti-Nevan's, then patted my cheek. "You see, pitiful human, I have stolen his power and channeled it into my master. Nevan's magic will add to that which the sorcerer has already amassed, making him more powerful than any other being in the universe—excepting the sorcerer, of course."

I kicked out with one foot and punted the bitch in her knee.

She winced but then sneered at me.

"That's not all I've done to him," Ceara said, backing away. "Release her, Tuathal."

The Anti-Nevan opened his fist, and I tumbled to the floor.

In a heap on the cold stone, I levered up into a sitting position and massaged my throat. "Tell me what the hell you did and get it over with. All your dramatic pauses make me want to rip your shriveled, slimy heart out. Oh wait, I already wanted to do that."

Ceara squatted before me, her silver eyes glowing. "I've stripped out his soul. It's gone, forever, lost in the abyss of time and space."

"Bullshit." I knew she'd turned him into a hollow shell, but to annihilate his soul…No, I refused to believe it. His essence was out there, somewhere, and I would find it.

"It's true," Ceara said. "And now Tuathal—or rather, his vacant body—will become the weapon of your destruction. You and every other mortal."

A shape moved among the shadows in the farthest corner of the room.

The damn tribunal. While Ceara had carved out Nevan's soul and tormented me, the spineless tribunal had cowered in a dark corner. They'd allowed this vile woman to destroy their king. They had betrayed him.

My Nevan. Lost. Adrift in an eternal abyss.

I would get him back, whatever the cost.

The Anti-Nevan stood motionless and vacant, its eyes unfocused.

My derringer lay near the Anti-Nevan's feet. I snagged the gun and leaped up, swerving my arm to target the derringer on Ceara's forehead.

She wagged a finger at me as she clucked her tongue. "Silly mortal, your weapon cannot harm me."

"Never heard of an endued firearm, eh?" I curled my finger over the trigger. "Let me enlighten you."

I fired the gun. The blast reverberated inside the chamber.

Ceara blipped out.

The noise of the gunfire should have been deafening, but something in this chamber dampened it. The cave behind the waterfall, the one concealing a portal between worlds, featured a similar noise-dampening spell. The waterfall where Nevan had taken me after Skeiron almost killed him. The place where he'd taught me how to let go of my fears.

Do this for Nevan. No fear, no doubt.

The shot had missed Ceara's head, but a robed figured stumbled out of the darkness pawing at his chest. Blood spread across the fabric of his robe, bright red against the gold. The sylph staggered another two steps, then collapsed to the cold, hard floor.

Ceara reappeared beside the fallen tribunal member. She touched a slender finger to the blood pooling around the sylph's body and sniggered.

I fired the gun straight at her.

With her attention on the fallen sylph, Ceara responded to the shot too slowly. The .357 round slammed into her side in the instant before she ducked out again.

Fortified by a determination I'd never known before, I glared at the spot where she had been. Had I killed her? Doubtful. She could run back to her master-slash-lover and, most likely, get patched up by his pilfered magic.

I dug two more rounds of .357 ammo out of my pocket and fumbled to get them into the derringer's barrels. My fingers trembled as I dumped out the spent cartridges. I dropped the new rounds, snatched them up, and stuffed them into the barrels.

Ceara winked back into view inches in front of me. Sweat beaded on her brow. Her chest heaved with each breath, her pale face had gone a shade whiter, and red blood poured from the wound on her side, dribbling out between the fingers of the hand she'd pressed to the wound.

"You," she snarled, teeth bared, spittle flying from her lips. "You will pay for this. The storm-bringer shall consume your powers and lay waste to your world. No mortal will survive his wrath, for it is the apocalypse."

"I've heard this spiel before," I said. "Didn't go well for the last creep who threatened to raze the mortal world. He's in the wind these days, as in annihilated."

"That is what you think?"

My nemesis pitched her head back and cackled. When her wicked laughter subsided, she angled her head up to peer down at me over her nose upturned. "Silly child, you think you know so much and yet know nothing at all."

I clacked the derringer's barrel shut. "I know I'm going to kill you."

Ceara disappeared.

Shit. I knew better than to chat before shooting.

The other woman's voice resounded in the chamber. "I would kill you now, but my master requires you alive, for the moment. Come, Tuathal, we have much to do."

The Anti-Nevan disappeared.

Alone in the hollow silence of the chamber, I trembled not from fear or anguish. I trembled with a deep, dark fury unlike anything I'd experienced in my life. I hated Ceara. *Hated* her. This was no mere dislike. I burned to tear the heart out of her chest and ditch her body into a well of acid. The rage had fueled my powers, letting me crack the ward around this chamber. I sensed it could fuel anything I wanted to do, any dark spell I wished for, any evil deed I could imagine. Was this what I had to become to defeat my enemies? A heartless monster willing to use any magic, no matter how evil, to achieve my goal?

I stuffed the derringer into its holster. No, dammit, this wasn't me. I was not a monster.

A warmth burgeoned inside the left pocket of my jeans. It seeped into me, sweet and gentle, infused with an inherent goodness beyond explanation. I shoved a hand into the pocket, and my skin slid over the stone disk hidden there.

The soul stone.

I shut my eyes, inviting the stone's essence into me. A piece of Nevan's soul lived on within the simple chunk of smooth, round rock.

Awareness rushed over my skin, penetrating beneath it to suffuse me with the wonderful, unmistakable essence of the only man I'd ever loved. He wasn't dead. His soul persisted, if only in the smallest way.

Nevan wouldn't want me to give in to darkness. It would've been a betrayal of everything he'd shown me and taught me and inspired in me. And I had a sick feeling it was exactly what the sorcerer—the storm-bringer, as Ceara had called him—wanted from me. If he pushed me into staining my soul with darkness, that might make it all the easier for him to gobble up my power.

I pulled the soul stone out of my pocket and touched my lips to the warm and oddly soft rock. Something pulsed through me, spreading from my lips throughout the rest of my body. Tender, sweet, passionate, resolute, and strong.

Nevan. Dear God, he'd kissed me back.

Which made no sense whatsoever, and yet I knew with total conviction he had touched me. He was out there, waiting for me to bring him back.

I felt enlivened, awakened, and…purified. His soul had cleansed mine.

Shutting my eyes, I closed my fingers around the stone. *Thank you, Nevan.*

Footsteps shuffled.

I slipped the soul stone back in my pocket and leveled my gaze at the tribunal. The four surviving members had gathered before me in a loose grouping, their postures slumped and their wary eyes on me.

"You are the Janusite," Mr. Raspy said, his tone cautious and almost fearful. "This is why the king defended you with such passion. He has been protecting the Janusite. You."

"Nevan defended me because he loves me, and I love him."

Mr. Raspy pushed his hood back, and it settled around his shoulders to reveal the face of an elderly man with gold-sheened skin. "You speak as if he lives. The sorcerer's consort has taken him, body and soul."

"He's alive and I'm going to bring him back."

"What of us?" He nearly cringed, as if he expected me to lash out with my power.

I'd done just that moments ago, so I couldn't blame him for fearing me.

"Listen," I said, "I didn't mean to shoot your friend. I was aiming for Ceara."

"We know," Mr. Raspy said. "Understand we had no knowledge of what the sorcerer intended for the king. Stripping his soul…If we had known, we would never have dealt with the sorcerer. We wish we could aid you, but our bargain with him prevents it."

My lie detector spell seemed to have fizzled out after the enormous amount of magic I'd expended to shatter the ward around this chamber. I didn't need a spell this time. My instincts told me the man was telling the truth, and my instincts had never led me astray.

"I believe you," I said, "and I'm not going to hurt you. Even though you tried to force Nevan to dump me and take the sorcerer's evil slut as his queen. Even though you let Ceara hollow him out like a discarded Halloween pumpkin. Even though you betrayed your own king."

Mr. Raspy had the decency to look ashamed.

I sighed, weary of wasting time on these worms. "Can you at least tell me what the sorcerer promised you in exchange for your help?"

"He promised to ensure Nevan would no longer be king, and that we would rule over the sylph kingdom in his stead."

"You accepted the deal without bothering to ask how Nevan would be dethroned."

Another tribunal member plodded forward and flipped back his hood. His copper-tinged face was youthful and fringed with red hair. "We could not have guessed the sorcerer meant to destroy Nevan's soul."

"What you mean is, you didn't give a shit how it was done as long as you got the power you've been lusting for." I shook my head, eying each tribunal member in turn, even the ones who still hid inside their hoods. "A bunch of cowards, that's what you are. The lot of you should be grateful for the chance to kiss Nevan's feet. He's a thousand times the man any of you could hope to be."

The other two tribunal members lowered their heads, and as one the entire group fell to their knees.

"Forgive us," Mr. Raspy said. "If we had known the king wished to make the Janusite his queen—"

"You would've sucked up to us both because you're afraid of my power." Oh, I really didn't have time for their sniveling. I waved my hands in a get-up-off-your-sorry-asses gesture. "Stop genuflecting. I'm not going to hurt you unless you hurt me or the people I care about. By the way, that includes every single person in the mortal realm."

The tribunal rose but kept their heads down.

"You slimy little toadies," I said, "aren't worth my time. I am going to stop the sorcerer and save you gutless backstabbers, even though you don't deserve it. You can thank me later."

I yanked the soul stone out of my pocket and tapped into its energies, whisking myself out of the chamber and straight home.

Chapter Nineteen

My ragtag band of allies had gathered around me in the living room to listen as I recounted the events in the tribunal chamber. Max had sprawled over the red sofa, but the tension on his face belied his nonchalant posture. Ennea and Tris occupied the two chairs, while Travis leaned against the wall in the threshold to the kitchen.

I slouched on the bed, my back against the wall, with my legs stretched across the bed's width and my feet barely reaching past the other side. I kept petting the fur blanket without any conscious intention, as if I might draw strength from the silky feel of it or from the memory of being with Nevan in this bed. In our bed. In our home.

Travis cleared his throat. "I know you want to save Nevan, but should that really be our priority?"

"He's my priority, not yours." I yawned for the umpteenth time, exhausted from the expenditure of magic required to break into the tribunal chamber. "I asked you guys to brainstorm ideas for a plan. Haven't you got anything?"

Four sets of eyes zeroed in on me, surprise evident in them.

Okay, maybe I had sounded a tad bitchy. Finding out your boyfriend had his soul ripped out of him and his formerly dead wife had control of his body did not ease a girl's anxiety. And this girl needed some serious easing.

I sneaked my hand into my pocket, sighing as the soul stone imparted a fragment of Nevan to me, but then withdrew my hand. As much as I needed the connection, the reminder he wasn't completely lost to me, I could not keep relying on the soul stone for comfort. What I needed was a plan for rescuing Nevan, but I shouldered the responsibility for that task, not my friends. Stopping an apocalypse had to be their number one priority.

Even if we saved the world, living in it without Nevan…That was unacceptable.

"We do have an idea," Ennea said.

Tris snorted. "A crap-ass one."

"You got a better one, big mouth?"

"Nothing's better than something that'll get us all shredded into confetti."

Ennea slapped her hands on her chair's arms. "Nothing is what we've been doing, and in case you haven't noticed, the bad guys are winning. They got Nevan."

All gazes veered toward me, rife with apology and sympathy. I didn't want them to feel bad for me. I wanted us to do something.

"It's okay," I said. "You can mention his name. I won't fall into a heap on the floor, weeping and wailing over my lost love. He's not gone forever, and I will get him back."

The only word to describe their expressions was doubtful.

My friends believed I couldn't get Nevan back.

Let them believe what they wanted, I knew I'd find him. No force in the universe, not even a sorcerer and his whackjob consort, would stop me from rescuing Nevan.

Everyone else in the room continued to look at me like I'd morphed into a pathetic little abused puppy.

I clambered off the bed to stand straight and resolute before them. "Everyone stop looking at me like I'll fall apart if you breathe in my direction. I'm not hopeless or helpless. But I do need my team to stand with me in defeating the sorcerer."

"Team?" Travis said, his brows hiking up.

"Yes. We are a team." I surveyed my allies, once again struck by the strangeness of this group. We were all so different and yet united in a cause. United by friendship. "We can do this, guys, I know we can. I need you to believe it too."

As for that twinge of uncertainty in my gut, they didn't need to hear about it. My team needed bolstering, and apparently, I had become the de facto leader. If Nevan were here, he'd know what to say. He wasn't here, so I had to do this on my own.

I'd never led anything. Not so much as an online chat.

The sylph will be your undoing, the oracle had warned.

Bob had told me his foresight was hindered by the sorcerer's magic. Since Bob hadn't foreseen his own death at Ceara's hands, I wondered how accurate his predictions were. Maybe I prayed they were faulty. I could've gotten mired in denial, refusing to see the potential consequences of attempting to save Nevan. I'd given in to my darkest impulses back in the tribunal chamber. Would I succumb to it again in my desperate attempt to get Nevan back? Would the sorcerer win because I darkened my own soul?

A figure moved in front of me.

I struggled to focus on the world me around again after getting mired in my thoughts.

Travis watched me from a couple feet away, concern tightening his features.

"What's going on?" he asked in a hushed voice. "I can tell you're freaking out on the inside, but you're trying to hide it from the rest of us."

Sometimes I forgot how well Travis knew me. Not as well as Nevan did, but pretty damn well. Travis and I had been friends for years before I met his brother and everything went to hell. No point in lying to him.

"I..." My voice trailed off as I struggled to find a way to explain. "I had a weird experience in the tribunal chamber."

He examined me for a moment, then faced the rest of the group. "Lindsey and me need to have a private talk. You guys hash out your plan or come up with a new one. We'll be back in a minute."

Our friends said nothing, though they looked uncomfortable.

Travis took hold of my elbow and guided me across the living room toward the bathroom doorway. The soothing rush and patter of water cascading into the pool emanated from the space beyond. As we entered the bathroom, I glanced back to find our friends staring after us. When they noticed me looking at them, they quickly averted their gazes.

Inside the bathroom, Travis led me to the farthest corner from the doorway. The pool frothed beside us, and the wall behind penned me between its smooth stone and Travis's bulk.

He grasped my shoulders, bending down to peer into my eyes. "Tell me what's going on, Lindsey."

I sagged into the wall, my arms crossed over my belly. "Ceara was about to rip the soul of Nevan. I couldn't get to him because the tribunal chamber has a ward protecting it. To get past the ward, I had to summon a hell of a lot of magical energy."

"You've done that before."

"This was different." I hugged myself, rubbing my arms, chilled despite the temperate weather inside this little sanctuary. "I had to channel a lot of rage in order to power up my magic enough to blast through the ward. A lot of rage. It was...disturbing."

"Getting mad is understandable."

I shook my head. "You don't get it. This wasn't normal anger, it was pure hatred. I gave in to the darkness and let it feed my power. What if I'm evil?"

He sighed, laying his hands over mine on my upper arms. "Lindsey, you are not evil."

"But—"

"I know a thing or two about evil." One corner of his mouth kinked in a sardonic expression. "My brother turned into a monster—an actual monster, straight outta Greek mythology. You're nothing like him. Even when Calder was trying to turn you into a kerko-whatsit like him, you would've rather died than give in to it. You're one tough chick, Lindsey Porter."

Travis hadn't been there when his brother tried to kill me in hopes of making me into a monkey-thing. Nevan had told him about it while I lay unconscious after Tris healed my wounds. The story had impressed Travis, who had begun calling me a tough chick—his way of showing respect for my fortitude, I guessed.

"Listen to me," Travis said. "You went through hell to get over your troubles. Don't let one wacko sorcerer and his hag of a girlfriend make you doubt yourself again."

He was right, of course. I'd almost died multiple times on my journey to realizing my true potential, not only as the Janusite but as a mere mortal too. The sorcerer wanted my powers at full strength, yes. But he also wanted me weak, wanted me doubting everything, so he could steal my power. If I cowered in a corner worrying about turning evil, I would give him exactly what he wanted.

"You're getting it, aren't ya?" Travis said, his warped mouth smoothing out into a closed-lip smile.

Pushing away from the wall, I opened my mouth to speak. The words "thank you" wanted to come out, but I cut them off. Could I indebt myself to another human? Travis wouldn't abuse the debt, but I preferred not to test the boundaries of our resurrected friendship.

"I appreciate the pep talk," I said. "You're right. I let myself wallow in self-pity for a while, but that's over."

"You would've gotten out of the funk on your own, but I was glad to lend a hand." He patted my arm. "That's what friends do, ain't it?"

I smiled, amazed I could under the circumstances. "Yeah, I think it is."

Someone whistled from the other room.

"We got a half-assed plan," Tris hollered. "Come and hear it, ya mooks, or we'll sign you up for the crummiest jobs."

Travis rolled his eyes. "Never thought I'd be teaming up with a snotty leprechaun."

I slapped his arm. "Welcome to my world, sheriff."

He sighed with dramatic heaviness. "Better get out there. Team Lindsey is having a mission briefing."

I LOITERED IN THE CENTER OF THE ROOM, SURROUNDED BY MY ALLIES, digesting the plan they'd laid out for me. The name Team Lindsey sounded ridiculous to me. When I'd voiced my objection to the team being named after me, Max had replied, "You are the fearless leader of this micro-army. Of course, it bears your name."

"Fearless?" I'd said. "I'm not a superheroine."

"You confront your fears and break through them to achieve great things." Max had sat up on his sofa then, elbows on his knees. "You're the bravest of us, and not because you're the Janusite."

To my total shock, Tris had piped up to add, "Yeah, you could've gotten massacred when you gutted Skeiron with a sword. And you almost drowned coming to get me so we could heal Nevan." He'd looked at me with genuine admiration. "You're a rock star, lady."

At that point, I'd grown uncomfortable with the "Lindsey is awesome" festival and steered the conversation back to their plan. Ten minutes later, I remained skeptical.

"I want this to work," I said, sneaking my hand into my pocket. The soul stone feathered a trace of Nevan over my skin. The sensation was beautiful, but very distracting. I hooked my thumbs inside the waistband of my jeans. "I'm still not clear on how we pull this off."

Ennea, slouched in one of the chairs, propped her head up with one hand. "We capture Ceara, that's how."

"Uh-huh, I got the what part of the plan. It's the how part I'm fuzzy on."

Max heaved his body off the red sofa and traversed the room to me. "You lure her, mistress."

"I'd really appreciate if you could stop calling me mistress. Makes me sound like a brothel-keeper. Lindsey will do."

"If you insist—Lindsey."

"Much better." I tapped the toe of one boot on the floor. "Nobody has explained how I'm going to lure Ceara anywhere."

"She despises you," Max said. "You shot her, and she wants vengeance. Anger can be a powerful tool, but it can also lead a person astray. Play on her hatred of you."

"How, exactly?"

"That's up to you, our courageous leader."

"Flattery will not make me love this plan."

Their plan, as outlined to me over the past twenty minutes, involved using Ceara as bait to draw out the sorcerer. I'd once mentioned we might be able to use his feelings for Ceara against him, if he had feelings for her. Max had told me the sorcerer and Ceara were lovers, which might indicate a bond deeper than lust. "Might" was the keyword.

"Your whole cockamamie scheme," I said, "revolves around the assumption the sorcerer gives a damn about Ceara. They might be sleeping together, but we have no idea if he cares about her as anything but a tool for achieving his goals." When Tris started to speak, I silenced him with a raised hand. "And may I point out, we still don't know our enemy's endgame."

"The crazy broad told you," Tris said. "Apocalypse."

"A bit vague for my comfort." I scratched the top of my head, mussing my hair with random movements of my fingers. Combing my hands through my hair to smooth it out, I began to pace the length of the room. Pacing had become my go-to action when I needed to think, particularly pacing inside this house. My new home.

If I didn't iron out the mountain-size kinks in this plan, I'd wind up living alone in the home Nevan had built, with nothing but the soul stone to keep me warm at night.

"Even if we capture Ceara," I said, halting near the bed and turning to face everyone, "the sorcerer still has the Anti-Nevan, and the Anti-Nevan still has sylph powers."

"Anti-Nevan?" Travis said.

"What they have is not Nevan, it's a shell that used to be his body. I will not think of that thing as Nevan, so I call it the Anti-Nevan. It's the opposite of everything he is."

"Kind of like the Antichrist?"

Was that a smirk he was trying to quash?

"Get snarky with me if you want," I said, "but pay attention to the important point I made. Even if we get Ceara, the sorcerer still has a powerful weapon in the Anti-Nevan."

Tris levered his body out of the chair where he'd reclined throughout our discussion. He moseyed up to me, shoulders hunched, hands in his pockets. Despite his discomfited posture, he met my gaze with a sharp clarity in his bright blue eyes. "That's where your plan comes in. It's up to you to restore Nevan's soul and take away the sorcerer's new toy."

Max touched my upper arm. "Are you sure you can do it?"

"Yes."

"Then I'm with you, Lindsey. Until the end."

"We all are," Tris said. He glanced over his shoulder at Travis and Ennea. "Aren't we?"

"Absolutely," Ennea said.

"Damn straight," Travis added. "Though I'd like to know how you're planning to get to Nev—the Anti-Nevan."

"How else?" I smiled. "Magic."

"All right, but you gotta find Nevan's soul first."

"Don't need to find it." I dug the soul stone out of my pocket and held it up for everyone to see. "I have it right here."

Max's mouth slid into a knowing smile. "The soul stone. That's brilliant."

Travis frowned at the stone. "A soul what?"

"Nevan gave me this," I said, tossing the stone and catching it in my palm. "It's a soul stone, a special rock from the Unseen realm that can hold a piece of someone's soul. He intended it to help me get through the wards around our house, since they were attuned to him. Max showed me I can use the stone to access Nevan's poofing ability."

"Poofing?" Travis looked so flummoxed, I had the urge to give him a hug.

"Yes," I said. "Poofing, or whisking, is what I call teleportation. The point is, I have Nevan's soul right here in my hand."

"A piece of his soul," Ennea said. "Where's the rest of it?"

"Still connected to the soul stone, I can feel it." At the skeptical looks I received, I reminded them, "I have a connection with Nevan. Anyone doubt that?"

Four people muttered, "No."

"I believe his soul couldn't be scattered or destroyed or whatever," I told them, "because of our connection. Because of the soul stone. I'm going to use it to return his soul to his body."

Travis grasped the back of his neck. "The shell you call the Anti-Nevan."

"Yep."

"Sounds good, but you have to get him here."

"Not here. I need a secluded place to do this." The rest of my plan I'd kept to myself, because I had no proof of what I believed. The Anti-Nevan may have been a shell, but magic gave it life. The shell being was alive. Its hot skin and audible breaths told me as much. If it lived, even without a soul, it must have some kind of emotions. I planned on tapping into them to get him riled up, get him incensed. No one knew better than I did the destructive power of out-of-control emotions.

Yep, that was my plan. Crazy, for sure. But our physical connection had provided a fertile conduit for my magic and allowed me to restore Nevan's vitality, which I theorized had meant reinvigorating his soul. Getting the Anti-Nevan worked up, without risking my safety, should provide a suitable conduit for me to use the soul stone to get Nevan back into his body.

I might have gone insane. Totally, irreversibly insane.

Didn't care, as long as I got Nevan back.

Boom.

The mountain shook from a massive concussion. Another boom made the furniture jump and my friends stagger to stay upright. Bits of rock sheared off the walls, crumbling to the floor.

"What the—" Travis cut off his question as another boom rocked the house.

"Is it Ceara again?" Tris asked.

"No," I said, overcome by a grim certainty of what was assaulting my home. "It's not her this time."

"Then who?"

I approached the hidden doorway and willed it to open. The stone wall shimmered and telescoped open to reveal the being standing just beyond the wards.

The Anti-Nevan's gaze snapped to mine.

A horrible dread coiled around my heart, cinching tight until my chest felt as if it might implode from the pressure.

The Anti-Nevan held out his hand to me and smiled. "Come, love, and I will spare your friends."

He'd called me love. He sounded like Nevan, looked like Nevan, but he was not Nevan. This was a new ploy from the sorcerer, one I should've expected. Use the shell that once contained my lover to confuse me. Something was different this time. Back in the tribunal chamber, the Anti-Nevan had acted like an empty shell, devoid of feeling or awareness. Now, he seemed like a real, living being—though not like the real Nevan.

What had Travis said Ceara told him? Nevan would become a hollowed-out shell. But there had been more. A corollary to the hollowed-out statement. She'd said...

The perfect vessel.

Ah, of course. A vacant statue wouldn't make me throw down my derringer and surrender. The sorcerer had filled in the shell with something else, something dark and bound to his will, something that looked and sounded like Nevan. The sorcerer hoped to confuse me, make me reticent to harm the Anti-Nevan. He thought Nevan was my weakness, but he was wrong. Nevan gave me strength.

I had the soul stone in my palm, protected by my fingers closed over it. The real Nevan was with me.

A hand on one hip, forcing my body to relax, I cast a haughty gaze on the Anti-Nevan. "Nice try, but no. I'm comfy here."

"Your wards are puny." He leaned forward, looming over me despite the five feet of space between us. "I will breach them and take you anyway. But that is what you like, is it not? For me to take you."

I resisted the urge to back away, unwilling to expose the fact I was disconcerted. Did this creature know what I'd told Nevan the night we first made love? *Take me, Nevan,* I'd said. But this thing couldn't know about that.

Unless he retained some or all of Nevan's memories. A cheap photocopy of our life together.

A weapon I could use.

"You?" I scoffed. "I enjoy sex with Nevan, but I don't screw hollow shells being controlled by an evil scumbag. The nasty crud he filled you with would leave a bad taste in my mouth."

"Nevertheless, I will take you from here." Lips parted, he darted his tongue out to moisten them. "He has promised me your body, after he strips away your powers. As a powerless mortal, you will be helpless to stop me from enjoying you. Whether or not you enjoy me."

Oh, that sneaky sorcerer. He had no intention of handing me over to anyone else, but he lied to the Anti-Nevan to gain his loyalty. Maybe the sorcerer sensed what I did, that the Anti-Nevan suffered from uncontrollable passions. Either way, I decided to keep the truth to myself for now. Might come in handy later.

As for me being powerless...The Anti-Nevan would learn a hard lesson about that too.

I let my arms fall slack at my sides and shrugged one shoulder. "Go ahead. Bang your head against the wards as long as you like. You'll get a migraine, but you will never breach my magic."

The Anti-Nevan slammed his fist into the wards. The recoil sent him flying backward into a tree. He struck it with a *thwack*, slumping down onto the grassy earth.

I folded my arms under my breasts, producing the unintended effect of pushing them up so they mounded against the V-neck of my shirt. "See? I'm stronger than you, puny shell-man."

His face twisted into a mask of raw fury, redness blooming beneath his bronzed skin. He sprang to his feet and rushed at the wards, moving so fast he became a blur. A hair's breadth from the wards, he stopped.

"You," he spat. "Soon, you will need to leave this place. I will be waiting for you."

Anti-Nevan vanished.

I glanced back at my friends. "That's how I'll get to him."

Travis glared out the doorway. "I don't get it. How does what just happened give you a way to get to this Anti-Nevan? He's waiting for you to go out there so he can grab you."

"He has Nevan's memories, or at least some of them." I leaned against the wall beside the doorway. "And he wants me. I can use all of that against him and get close enough to put my plan into action."

Four people stared at me, confused, but it was Travis who asked, "What plan?"

"Saving the real Nevan."

"But that thing out there will come and get you the second you leave the wards."

My gaze wandered back to the view beyond the wards. The Anti-Nevan was out there, somewhere. When I left this house, he would find me. "I'm counting on it."

Travis shook his head once, his brows lowered. "This is nuts."

Ennea waved a hand to get my attention. "How can you be sure the soul stone will work?"

"It's simple." I tossed the stone in the air and caught it in my palm. "Intuition."

"If you're wrong," Max said, "you might die in the effort."

"A risk I'm willing to take." I pushed away from the wall, looking through the doorway into the darkening woods beyond. Sunset had arrived in the Unseen realm. I couldn't see the Anti-Nevan, but I knew he waited for me out there.

I faced my friends, rolling my shoulders back. "I'm getting Nevan back tonight. And once that's done, we are going to destroy the sorcerer."

Chapter Twenty

"SO THAT'S OUR PLAN?" TRIS ASKED, SEEMING EVEN MORE DUBIOUS than he had when I explained my idea for getting Nevan back. "Don't you think it's way too simple?"

My allies had collected in a haphazard grouping in front of me. Ennea lingered near her brother, while Max had sidled closer to me, and Travis hung back behind the others. He kept his gaze trained on me, like a cop monitoring a suspect. Actually, it was more like a cop protecting an endangered witness.

I planted a hand on the edge of the open doorway to the outside. "Complexity is a recipe for disaster. If we each do our part, this will work."

"You're awful confident about that," Travis said. "Overconfident, maybe."

"Believe me," I said, "I am fully aware of how this could turn into a cataclysmic disaster. We have no other choice, though, do we? Unless somebody thought up a new plan in the last ten minutes."

No one spoke up.

I gazed out into the deceptively still night. "Then we go with what we've got. But may I remind you negative thinking could get us all killed. If you walk out there screaming 'oh shit, we're all gonna die,' then we all will die."

Tris quirked a brow. "We should be thinking sunshine and rainbows?"

"Be smart. Be strong. Think positive, but be vigilant."

Travis saluted me. "Yes, ma'am."

"We're ready," Ennea said.

Max nodded. "We are."

An army of misfits. That seemed the best description of us. But we were all that stood between two worlds and total devastation. What else could an apocalypse mean?

It wouldn't happen on our watch.

"Everyone gather 'round," I said, waving them closer. "Once I get us through the wards, all hell might break loose. Remember, the Anti-Nevan is out there waiting for us—for me. Don't get distracted by whatever happens, stick to your assigned tasks."

My allies, my friends, gathered close around me. Each of them offered a single hand to me, and I took two in one of my hands and two in the other. Thus linked, we were ready to exit the wards.

I glanced at Tris and Ennea. "The second we're outside, you two hightail it out of here. Max, you get Travis to the designated rendezvous point."

Travis had taken up a position right next to me, his shoulder and arm pressed to mine and his free hand on his Sig. Since his weapon wasn't endued, and we had no time for Ennea to undertake the long and arduous spell to endue it, he would have to aim for the head and hope any attackers were stunned by a .40-caliber slug to the brain. It might give him enough time to escape.

My derringer rested snugly in its holster, inside my waistband. I'd reloaded it and stuffed additional rounds in my pocket. If it came to a choice between the Anti-Nevan and me—or Travis or Max—I would do what Nevan would want.

I'd shoot him straight between the eyes.

My chest ached at the idea of killing his body. I could do it. I would do it.

But only if I had no other recourse.

I surveyed my friends. "On three. One, two—"

We stepped over the threshold, through the wards, to halt inches past it.

Nothing chirped or croaked or howled. No breeze stirred the leaves. Stars glimmered in the oval of sky we could glimpse above us, but trees penned us and blotted out the rest of heavens. The only light came from inside the underground lair and from the full moon overhead. I recognized it as the smaller of this world's two moons. The larger one must've been in its new moon phase. The smaller one bathed the world in a glow slightly brighter than a full moon in the mortal realm.

"Go," I whispered.

Ennea and Tris blinked out.

Travis threw me a worried look as Max zipped him away.

Rather than pulling out my derringer, I withdrew the six-inch knife Max had conjured for me. Mystical symbols decorated the wooden hilt and curled down the center of its curved, double-edged blade. The knife was not endued, as I had requested. I needed a nonlethal weapon this time. Besides, I had the derringer in case of emergency.

With the knife gripped in my hand, I walked into the center of the clearing, scanning the darkness for some sign of the Anti-Nevan. A sign of anything. The world seemed to have frozen, as if time had stopped. Though time could move slower in the presence of my magics, I doubted time had actually stopped for me. The sensation of unnatural stillness disconcerted me nonetheless.

A pair of iron-hard arms seized me around my waist, dragging me backward and belting me to an equally hard body.

I flinched at the hot skin mashed into my backside, searing me through my clothes. Hotter than Nevan. Filling his body up with evil crud must've overheated it.

The Anti-Nevan bent his head to growl in my ear, "I have you."

I'd figured there was a fifty-fifty chance he'd pop up behind me, but I'd hoped for the other option. It was the hard way, then.

"You sure about that?" I said.

His arms strapped me tighter to him. "I am certain."

"Arrogance is a nasty habit. Might get you killed."

Though I held the knife in front of my thigh, he clearly hadn't noticed it. Adrenaline electrified my body, heightening my senses, and I realized I had one shot at this. No room for screw-ups. No room for doubt. All in or nothing.

I swung the knife up and drove it into his leg.

He bellowed and staggered backward, releasing me so he could use his hands to staunch the flow of blood from his thigh wound. Blood streamed from the wound anyway, dribbling out between his fingers. His lips peeled back from his clenched teeth. "You will suffer for this."

I brandished my knife in the air, twirling it to let the ambient light glint off its silvery blade and glisten on the streaks of blood there. "Why don't you bad guys ever get a new line? Just one. I mean, 'you will suffer' and 'I will decimate the world' are getting pretty stale."

Crouching, I drove the blade into the soft earth and withdrew it. The dirt had cleansed the knife, leaving behind only scraps of earth. I wiped them off on my jeans, then rose to watch the Anti-Nevan struggle to stand up straight.

The agony on his face crumbled away.

I hadn't expected the wound to stop him for good. A few seconds had been all I needed.

"Since you like tired phrases," I said. "Here's one for you. Catch me if you can. I'm headed for the spot where Nevan and I steamed for each other."

A spark of something in his eyes gave me hope he retained that memory too.

Shoving my hand into my pocket, I touched the soul stone and teleported out of the clearing. I caught a glimpse of the Anti-Nevan's face contorting with rage but then the abyssal tunnel swept me away toward my destination.

I materialized at the portal, in front of the boulder that housed it. With a Nevan-like flick of my wrist, I spun the portal open and leaped through it into the cave behind the waterfall on the mortal side. The rock shop was not far from here, but I had a different destination in mind. Leaving the portal open—wouldn't want to make it too hard for the Anti-Nevan to follow me—I marched through the falls onto the ledge outside and whisked myself to the predetermined location.

Woods surrounded me. The branches of the trees—aspen, maple, pine, and fir—curved over the small clearing, almost forming a canopy overhead. Through the small, circular opening above, the bright light of Earth's full moon shined down on me.

I turned in a circle to canvas the area. A smile pulled at my lips, a smile tainted with heartache but underpinned by the sweetest memories of the night my entire life had transformed. I'd been here once before, six weeks ago, on the night Nevan had enticed me to let go of my iron grip on my desires by asking me to steam for him. The night we became lovers. The night he'd come far too close to dying. I'd risked my life to find Tris and get him to heal Nevan via the unmarked healing vortex in this clearing. This location held great significance for me and for Nevan, and I needed to give Nevan a powerful anchor to draw him back to his rightful place in the universe. What held more meaning for either us than the night a metaphor about pots and kettles had become an erotic reality?

Yes, I'd once been a pot who locked up her strong emotions under a tight lid. Nevan had coaxed me into becoming a kettle and releasing all that pent-up steam. Right here, in this clearing.

Tris had provided invaluable aid the last time I'd come here, but he couldn't help me tonight. No one could. The sole burden of saving Nevan weighed on my shoulders, a massive boulder of responsibility and risk.

Nevan had told me vortexes could enhance our bond and our pleasure. Tonight, I was counting on this vortex to strengthen our connection.

I advanced toward the trees at the clearing's edge. "You guys there?"

Two figures separated from the shadows of the forest, moving toward me. The moonlight glinted off the badge on Travis's chest as he and Tris halted an arm's length from me, sneaking out from behind a screen of bushes and saplings.

"The creepy dude ain't here yet," Tris said. "Started a magical trail at the portal's edge, like we planned, but you're the only one who's come through."

"Yeah, he might need a few minutes," I said. "The gaping knife wound will slow him down a little, but it's probably healing as we speak."

"The trail should lead the shell guy right to you."

"Your trip go according to plan?"

"We hopped around so much," Tris said, "the tough guy here almost hurled. The overlapping boundaries got us here, though. Eventually."

Travis watched me, stoic as ever. "Are you sure about this, Lindsey? Your plan is pretty damn dangerous."

"I know. But we need Nevan if we're going to beat our enemies." I needed him, but that was rather irrelevant to anyone else.

Travis took another step toward me, the intensity of his stare making me uneasy. "I don't want anything to happen to you."

"Neither do I." My tone came out a bit too breezy, like I was trying too hard to minimize the danger. In a more sober tone, I added, "I'm counting on you and Tris to barge in if things go pear-shaped."

Tris lifted his right hand, wielding a wickedly sharp and curved sword. "Got me an awesome weapon. Take him awhile to get over being stuck with this bad boy."

"I got one too," Travis said, hefting a bigger, badder sword reminiscent of Viking weapons I'd seen on TV. The lowly human sheriff held it as if the massive thing weighed next to nothing, his biceps bulging and straining the fabric of his uniform. Yet his arm was steady, he seemed comfortable with the weapon. "One of us'll get him if he lays a finger on you."

"Uh-uh," I said, shaking my head. "He has to lay a finger on me for this plan to work, and I'll have to let him. You don't attack unless I'm in imminent danger of death. Understand?"

He ground his teeth. "Yeah. I get it."

The leprechaun raised his free hand. "Question. How are we gonna know if you get Nevan's soul back where it belongs?"

"You'll know, trust me." I glanced back at the clearing, then to my allies. "I don't know exactly what will happen, but I'm positive it will be unmistakable. At that point, you two will want to leave."

"Hell no," Travis said. "Ain't leaving without you."

"You don't want to see the rest. When I use my magic on Nevan, it has… um…unusual side effects."

"Unusual? Like what?"

"Well…" Oh hell, what was the point in being coy about this? They'd figure it out once things got moving. "We'll both be highly aroused."

Travis scrunched up his entire face in disgust, diverting his attention to the ground. When he looked at me again, I swore I noticed a faint blush on his cheeks. "Yeah, I get the picture."

"Maybe Tris should keep watch, and you should turn your back."

"No." Travis shot ramrod straight, shoulders back and chin lifted. "I'm a goddamn officer of the law. I've seen worse than you and him getting it on."

"Fine, watch if you want." I waved them away. "But for now, shoo. I need stealth guards, not obvious targets for the Anti-Nevan to mow down with a flick of his finger."

Travis winced, and I suspected he was remembering when Nevan had tossed him into a tree. Of course, Travis had been threatening to arrest me at the time. *Bygones.*

Tris's eyes flared wide. "He's through the portal."

"Good," I said. "Let's hope he understood my hint."

"Be careful," Travis said, his voice low and intense.

"You too." I gave Tris's arm a quick squeeze. "Both of you."

Generating almost no noise, the two men retreated behind the screening vegetation.

Everything depended on the fact Nevan could cross the boundaries as long as I was somewhere in the mortal world. If the trick didn't work on Anti-Nevan, I'd lose the real Nevan forever.

One deep breath. I exhaled it slowly, turned, and walked to the exact spot where everything had begun the last time I'd visited this place. My gaze fell on the patch of grassy earth where, mere weeks ago, Nevan lay dying from a wound inflicted by an endued sword. The fingers of my right hand crooked into my palm, my throat went tight and dry. *I can do this, I will do this.*

With the knife in my left hand, I slipped the derringer out of its holster with my right hand. Shooting was my last resort.

A chilly breeze rustled the leaves in the trees. Goose bumps cropped up on my arms, not solely from the cool air whispering over my skin.

The Anti-Nevan materialized in the center of the clearing, a dozen feet from where I waited. We faced each other, his hand brandishing Nevan's endued sword, my hands gripping the knife and my endued derringer.

He sneered at me. "I caught you."

Overconfidence. Excellent, my plan was on track.

He sauntered toward me with long, leisurely strides. His hips swayed, his muscles flexed and slackened with each step, the loincloth stretched taut over his groin. That unearthly gaze locked onto me, a glowing, sizzling whirlpool of molten metal. Bronze, gold, silver—and an undercurrent of bright, hot red.

I couldn't hide the shiver that rippled through me. No going back now.

He stopped an arm's length away, dipping his head to the side to examine me with detached interest. "Why did you permit me through the boundary?"

"Figured it was time we meet and discuss the situation."

"The situation is simple." He crept closer, silhouetted by the full moon behind him. "I have you, Janusite. Attempt to run, and I will seize you. Attempt to stab me again, and I will strike you down. You will remain alive, though you may wish you were not."

Raising the knife, I turned it side to side so the moonlight gleamed on its blade.

He bristled the tiniest bit, his jaw tensing.

"Try to leave," I said, "and the boundary will disintegrate you."

Anti-Nevan growled through clenched teeth. "I can kill you where you stand."

"But your boss wouldn't like that, would he? You have to deliver me alive and well enough to keep my powers at full strength. Correct?"

The way a muscle jumped in his jaw answered my question.

"I thought so." A lump hardened in my throat at the realization of what I must do next. The biggest gamble of all. I resisted the urge to glance into the trees, to where Tris and Travis hid, and instead focused on Anti-Nevan. "The sorcerer lied to you."

He moved closer, forcing me to bend my head back to keep our gazes aligned. "You are the one lying—to yourself."

"The sorcerer promised you could have me after he steals my powers." Pulse racing. Skin prickling. No way but forward, plunging into the unknown, bolstered by faith. "He's never going to give me to you. He wants me for himself. Told me as much, when he murdered an innocent girl right in front of me."

Anti-Nevan gave a derisive little laugh.

Before he could speak, I said, "The sorcerer offered to become whomever I want him to be. You, Travis—"

"Not him." Spittle sprayed from Anti-Nevan's lips, while his face flushed crimson.

Jealousy. I could work with that.

"Why not?" I said. "Travis is a big, strong man. And hot? Whoa, mama, is he ever."

Anti-Nevan pitched toward me, narrowing the gap between our bodies to scant inches. Menace rolled off him in waves of psychic energy that gnashed at the edges of my magic.

We both occupied the precise spot where not so long ago Nevan had sprawled in a pool of his own blood. The potency of the memory, of the location, shivered through all my senses and roused the Janusite within me.

"Maybe," I said, "I'd rather be with a human male, not a freak from another dimension."

Anti-Nevan glowered at me for a long moment, so long I feared I'd pushed him too far in the direction of anger. His physical strength alone gave him the power to smite me. I could've tried to craft a personal ward around me, but he'd sense the energy of my spell for sure.

His gaze wandered down to my cleavage. His features softened, his lips parting and his breaths quickening. He touched a finger to the neckline of my shirt, skating the tip down to the slope of my breast. "No mortal can bring you to climax as swiftly or as powerfully as I can."

The empty shell chock-full of evil was trying to seduce me. *Ick.*

Anti-Nevan licked his lips as his hooded eyes blazed with the scorching colors of fire.

He reached out to touch me.

I whipped the knife out, slicing it across the back of his hand.

Fury blackened his expression and seethed in his eyes. His nostrils flared on a blistering exhalation.

He grabbed for me.

I slashed his arm, drawing a thin line of blood. "No touchy, no feely. I'm not that kind of a girl."

Shouting through his gritted teeth, he swung the sword up as if to strike me down with it. His arm froze in mid swing. Frustration warped his features. He bellowed, mouth open wide, and hurled the sword to ground. It landed point down, wedged into the earth with only the hilt and a few inches of the blade protruding.

Score one for the puny mortal.

He flung his hands up, bellowing again, his face crimson and his eyes wild.

I started to shuffle backward, the instinct to flee an efficient motivator, but I stayed my movement with my heel elevated off the ground. Setting it back on the earth, I steadied myself for the most terrifying part. I'd known I might need to adjust my plan midway, and the time had come for a new tactic. To restore Nevan's soul, I would risk everything.

Raising the knife, I flipped it tip down and let it fall to the ground.

Anti-Nevan's gaze tracked the knife's nosedive, then veered up to my face. His brows knit together and his mouth fell open a crack.

I dumped my gun. The derringer hit the grass with a soft thud.

He angled his head to the left and then to the right.

Back when we first met, I'd confounded Nevan quite often. I could still confound him one in a while. And clearly, my talent for befuddling elemental males extended to this magically created entity.

Score two for the puny mortal.

"What," he said, his confusion tinging his voice, "are you attempting to accomplish? I could have you whenever I wish."

"Go on, then. Try it." I summoned an eensy bit of magic, just enough to make my palms glow a faint, shimmering blue. "I've got more in my arsenal than mortal weapons."

"As do I."

Squelching the magic, I slipped my hands into my jeans pockets. My left hand found the soul stone, and the essence of Nevan heated my skin. "Bet you can't take me."

Anti-Nevan rushed at me.

I forced myself to hold still, to accept his hands clamping around my upper arms and yanking me into him. When he crushed his mouth to mine, I nearly choked on the vile, ice-cold energy that roiled out of him. I refused to open my mouth, though, and he snarled deep in his throat, like a wild and deranged animal.

Clutching the soul stone, I wrenched my left arm free of his grasp. Before he could react, I slammed my palm onto his, the stone trapped between our flesh, and locked my fingers around his hand to bind us.

Energy pulsated through me, a crackling power that surged along my nerves and veins, shooting straight down my arm and into the soul stone.

Anti-Nevan flailed his head back, gasping for breath.

I seized his head with my other hand.

His eyes bulged, the whites shining in the moonlight.

The magic had hit a barrier where our hands met, exerting pressure against my palm. I bore down on the barrier with everything inside me, every scintilla of Janusite power, every ounce of my love for Nevan, shaping it all into a magical battering ram.

I bludgeoned the barrier.

It fractured with explosive force, bucking us both.

Anti-Nevan gurgled and choked.

Energy poured through our hands into the body possessed by the invading force of the Anti-Nevan. A black, sticky energy assaulted me in response, encasing me with its tendrils. The dark power writhed beneath Anti-Nevan's skin as a visible force, caught in a desperate battle to fend off the strength of my magic, magnified by the soul stone. I propelled the energy deeper and deeper into the vacant region where Nevan's soul belonged.

The darkness shattered.

A black cloud whooshed out of Nevan's body, dissipating as a wave of blue magic sparkled all around him and a bolt of pure goodness rocketed through us both.

We gaped at each other, breathing hard, our hands still coupled.

My other hand skidded down his neck to his shoulder.

I gazed into the eyes of the man I loved. The swirling, burning eyes of Nevan.

Blue energy pulsed inside us, rushing into him only to rush back into me in a never-ending loop that united our bodies, our hearts, our souls. The power grew warm, liquid, a sensuous flow of magic that shivered over my skin and awakened every fine hair on my body. Desire throbbed within me, setting off a heated torrent of wetness between my thighs.

A flash of movement diverted my attention for heartbeat, just long enough for me to spy Tris and Travis hustling away. Tris slapped a hand on Travis's shoulder, and the pair vanished.

"Lindsey?"

Nevan's voice, rough and yet bewildered, pulled me back to him.

"You're here," I said, between panting breaths. "I did it."

He peeled his palm away from mine, took hold of the soul stone, and stared blankly at it. "This…"

"I saved you with the soul stone. Brought you back from…wherever."

Nevan ran a finger over the stone. "I recall darkness, emptiness, nothingness. And then a bright, warm light embraced me. I felt it was you." The inferno of lust in his eyes stole my breath. "You saved my life, my indomitable love. Thank you."

His gratitude lashed a magical tether between us, cementing a life debt, the strongest kind.

Neither of his gave a damn about that. We couldn't sever our gazes. His loincloth had grown tighter, with a distinct lump swelling beneath it. My nipples shot rigid, my breasts ached for his touch, all of me ached for him. The intensity of the hunger swept everything else aside, encasing us in a bubble of our own making, molded out of love and passion and all-consuming need.

Nevan dragged me into his arms, devouring me with his kiss. I hooked my arms around his neck and sagged into his hard, hot body. He thrust his tongue deep inside my mouth, spurring me to plunder his slick and velvety flesh with my tongue. He tasted sweet and spicy, earthy and unearthly, so good I moaned and plunged deeper into his mouth. His hands raked down my back to grasp my ass and hoist me up.

I flung my legs around him. He groaned, growled, shoved my groin against his engorged shaft. The pressure of it rubbing against my sex through my clothes impelled me to nip at his tongue, at the inside of his lips, frantic for more of him.

Just like the first time, here on this spot, when passion had overtaken us both. We couldn't resist it now any more than we had then.

He staggered forward with me wrapped around him, until my back slapped into a tree. His tongue rolled around mine once more, a possessive stroke that made me whimper into his mouth.

Nevan broke away, his nose brushing mine, our eyes riveted to each other.

"I need you," he said, his voice hoarse and hungry.

"Yes." I rocked my hips into him, loving the feel of his hardness against my soft and wet core. "Get rid of our clothes."

"Lindsey, I—" He snared my bottom lip with his teeth, scraped his tongue across it, and let it slide out of his mouth. "Can't be gentle, barely in control as it is. If I take you—"

"I can handle it."

His mouth dropped open, his sultry breaths blustered over my face.

"Nevan, please." I dove my hands into his hair, hauling him closer until our lips grazed each other as I spoke. "I trust you with my life, with my soul. I need you inside me *now*."

Our clothes vanished.

And he whisked us away.

Chapter Twenty-One

Cool night air flooded over us the second we materialized, and goose bumps prickled my naked skin. The heat scorching me from the inside, the searing and desperate need for Nevan, erased my awareness of everything except him. His mouth claimed mine while his fiercely aroused body shackled me to a wall of cold rock. A delicate curtain of water spilled down the rock, trickling over my shoulders and down to my breasts, hardening my nipples, dribbling down between our bodies and exciting every inch of my skin. With our bodies plastered together, the water dribbled off my skin and onto his. The gentle cascade murmured a soft sound behind our passionate moans and cries.

To experience the satiny texture of his skin, the silken glide of his tongue, the firm nudging of his erection…These things reminded me of what we'd nearly lost today. His soul might've been extinguished, the glorious light of Nevan gone forever. We might still die, if the plan I'd hashed out with my friends failed us. We should've stopped this and hurried to meet our friends, to finish the battle tonight.

I couldn't make myself pull away from this ravishing kiss and forsake the bliss of making love with Nevan. Passion propelled us like a runaway train barreling toward a cliff.

His tongue toyed with mine, and his fingers kneaded my ass as he rocked my hips forward, angling my body for penetration.

If this was our last night together, I'd hurtle over the edge with him one more time.

Frantic with lust, I bucked my hips into his erection, chafing my swollen flesh along the length of his cock, up and down, up and down. I shoved a hand between our bodies to fasten my fingers around the base of his shaft.

He tore his lips from mine, gasping for air, then sealed his mouth over the pulse point on my throat. With one hand on my lower back, he urged me to arch my spine, boosting my breasts up. With a feral noise, he latched onto my right nipple with his open mouth.

I threw my head back on a loud, throaty moan and tunneled my fingers into his hair. His tongue teased my nipple with light licks until I ground my sex into his erection and cried out for more, then he nipped my taut peak and began to suckle it with a fervor that shot arcs of pleasure straight down to my core.

"Please, yes," I begged, scraping my nails on his scalp.

He froze, his mouth still covering my nipple.

"Nevan," I gasped, "don't stop."

The air chilled my damp nipple as he unhooked my legs from around him and set me on my feet, leaving me confused and thrumming with need. Struggling to catch my breath, I couldn't summon my voice to complain. The spillover from the delicate waterfall lapped around my feet, just deep enough to tease my sensitive arches and tickle my toes. The gentle streams of water rolled down my body, tormenting my rigid nipples and drizzling over the hairs at the juncture of my thighs.

Nevan backed away a couple steps. His shaft bobbed in front of his body, but he either didn't notice or didn't care. His voice came out rough and strained. "We must talk."

"Huh?" My body burned, my sex throbbed. A haze of lust clouded my thoughts, and all I could focus on was his rock-hard arousal and its glistening, red tip.

"Lindsey."

His stern tone should've snapped me out of it, but I'd completely lost my hold on reality. I craved. My body felt empty and starved, and I knew only one thing could satisfy this want.

Nevan let out a sharp groan. "You said pl—that word. Far too close to gratitude for this side of the falls."

Dazed, I gaped at him for a moment before my brain powered up again and my thoughts cleared. "You can't seriously be upset I said the P-word. After you thanked me and triggered a life debt."

"I shouldn't have."

Though my legs trembled, I pushed away from the wall to lay my palms on his chest, where droplets of water still beaded on his hot skin. "What's really bothering you?"

"You shouldn't have done this."

"Done what? You kissed me, which means you started this."

"Not...that." He shrugged away from my touch. "Restoring my soul. You wasted precious time bringing me back, when you should have been searching for a way to stop the sorcerer."

"I—" A tightness gripped my chest as I flashed back to the moment when Ceara had banished his soul from his body. "Wasted time? Nevan, I could not leave you stranded in limbo, or wherever you went. If the situation had been reversed, you would've done the exact same thing for me."

"Lindsey."

"Don't." I stabbed a finger in the air at him. "You know you can't *Lindsey* me into shutting up. I don't regret what I did, and I'd do it again. Rescuing the soul of the only man I've ever loved is not a waste of time." When he started to protest, I slapped a hand over his mouth. "Shut up. I need you with me if we're going to defeat the sorcerer. I need you, period, so quit telling me I made a mistake. We're stronger together."

I lowered my hand.

His entire body had gone as rigid as his waving penis. He fisted his hands at his sides, his jaw tight enough to pulverize diamonds to powder.

Christ, if he got any more tense, he'd snap in two. I couldn't watch him suffer like this. His anxiety I could deal with later, but his physical needs I could handle right here, right now.

I splayed my hands on his smooth chest and let my breasts brush against him. The lines etched across his forehead softened the tiniest bit. I caught his earlobe between my teeth, nibbling and licking it. The tension drained out of him little by little, and his hands drifted up to span the small of my back.

"We can't have a reasonable conversation," I whispered into his ear, "when we're both high on lust and desperate to have each other."

"There's no time for it. We must talk about the sor—"

I snared one of his hands and shoved it between my thighs, mashing his fingers into my drenched cleft. "Talk later. Take me now, you stubborn sylph."

He yanked his hand away. I fastened my hand around his shaft, pumping his length in long, firm strokes. He made a strangled noise and hoisted me off my feet with both his hands on my ass. A thrill of anticipation raced through me. He hauled me into him as I strapped my legs around his hips.

"Yes," I moaned, mindlessly writhing against him.

"This is a terrible idea," he hissed, even as he backed us up to the rock wall, my backside flush with the cool, wet stone and pinioned there by his body.

"You need this," I said. "I need this. Forget the rest of the world and give us both what we want."

"Indulging our desires is a luxury we do not have at the moment. Our enemies are hunting for us as we speak."

"So what's new? We're always being stalked by evil bastards."

Maybe the mention of imminent danger and probable death should've doused my passion, but my thirst for Nevan obliterated everything else. I sank my teeth into his shoulder, earning a deep groan from him that resonated in his chest.

"We'll face the danger together," I said. "But first, let's come together."

He collared both my wrists in one big hand, effectively handcuffing me to the rock wall and stunning a gasp from me. "You have no idea what you're asking."

"Yes I do." I struggled with halfhearted effort, more on principle than anything else. I had no desire to be free of him. His grip was unyielding, though not painful. He seemed to know the exact amount of pressure to exert to keep me bound without hurting me.

He slanted his head down, and with his free hand cupped my chin and tipped my face up to his. Those luscious lips swept across mine. His entire body quivered with a need so contained it threatened to erupt out of him.

"You convinced me to let go," I reminded him, "and embrace my passions. It's your turn. Quit holding back and show me how you feel, all of it, no holds barred."

"I can't, don't make me—" He squeezed his eyes shut, lips flattened. "I am in no state to make love to you. Not the way you deserve."

"You're scared of letting me see all of you, I get it. But I can handle it, Nevan. I can handle you. Any way you need me, I'm yours."

He switched his hand to my behind and kneaded it with fierce ardor, his strong fingers branding me even as he rested his forehead on mine. "Careful, darlin', or I'll take ye up on that offer. And it won't be like anything I've shown ye before."

No, with so much dark tension coiled up tight inside him, it wouldn't be like any other time with him. My need for him deluged me, sultry and thick, like heated oil poured over my skin. I was dying to know how he'd take me this time, with fear and lust warring inside him, his need a living thing clawing to get out.

"I will not risk hurting you," he said, "no matter how great my need for you."

"Honestly, Nevan." I rolled my eyes to the heavens, letting out a frustrated growl. "I love you, but sometimes you are such an overprotective idiot. I trust you. I know you will never hurt me, I don't care how racked with lust you are. I'm not afraid of you, and I never will be."

"A mistake. You have yet to experience the full force of my passion."

"Suddenly I'm a wilting flower?" I leaned back against the wall, hissing in a breath at the sensation of water cascading over me. "What are you really afraid of?"

"You risked your life for me, again." He braced his forehead on the wet stone beside my ear. "I should walk away from you, to spare you from the necessity of saving me in the future. But I lack the will to leave you. I've developed a crushing need to both protect you and bury myself inside you as often as possible."

A crushing need. I experienced the same passion every time he touched me, and the need to protect him, to save him, had overwhelmed me after Ceara stole his body and expelled his soul. "I get it, I really do. But avoiding me, avoiding having sex with me, won't fix a damn thing."

"If I cannot protect you from the sorcerer," he said, "at least I might protect you from me. You have no conception of what it will be like if I unleash all of my desire for you. In my current state, I would lose every last fragment of control."

"Good."

He raised his head, the fiery shades in his eyes a spellbinding spectacle.

With his body restraining me against the cliff and his hand shackling me there, I found my breaths quickening and my heart pounding.

Nevan dipped his head to sniff my hair, my neck, my cheek. The moonlight glistened on his damp skin, accentuating his straining muscles, transforming him into the embodiment of unstoppable hunger.

"You smell of honeysuckle and sunshine," he purred. "And sex."

My skin tightened from his proximity, from the delicious heat radiating off him and soaking into me. Since the day I'd met him, the heat of his body had taken on an erotic significance, no simple fact of his biology but a means to stoke me into higher arousal. I reveled in the intensity of it, in the nearness of him, in the response from my body as it readied for him.

With a low growl, he freed my hands only to reposition them and cuff my wrists to the wall with both of his hands, gliding them up to my palms to interlace our fingers. "Are ye certain?"

The gruffness of his tone belied the tenderness of his hold on my hands, but the combination of his command and his body molding every inch of me into the wall left me breathless and lightheaded. Latched around him, I couldn't move except to nuzzle my face into his neck and absorb the exotic, heady scent of him.

"Do it, Nevan. I want you to."

He rasped his tongue up my throat, then nipped at the hollow where jaw met neck.

I shuddered, every inch of me sensitized to his touch.

A ragged breath escaped him. He rolled his hips back, nailed his gaze to mine, and plowed into me so deep he filled me to the hilt. I cried out, clenching my fingers around his hand. His hips thrust in a relentless rhythm, driving his length impossibly deep, exciting every nerve and hitting sensitive spots I'd never known I had.

With a primal roar, he punched his fist into the rock wall. Bits of stone showered the pool, and the cliff trembled.

His cock throbbed, scorching me with each thrust, and his body scraped against my clit, pushing my arousal higher and higher, so high my head spun. Robbed of breath, of sense, of the ability to feel or hear or smell anything except him, I clutched him tighter with my legs and hoisted my hips up as he lunged into me again and again, harder and faster, until the pace became frantic and almost violent.

"Nevan!" I screamed, my spine arching, my head falling back.

The orgasm wrenched my entire body, my sex pulsating around him, gripping and releasing his shaft, as out of control as we were. He kept on pumping into me, even as my screams echoed off the trees and the rock wall until I went hoarse with the last spasms of my climax.

Nevan plowed into me again, roaring, ramming my body into the wall hard enough to force an explosive gasp from me. A hot jet exploded through my womb, penetrating me further than his body could, claiming the deepest and most secret parts of me. It must've been an extension of his magic, the way the rush of it consumed me with its power. Another punishing thrust shot more of his searing energy into me, and with a third and final plunge, he collapsed against me and let his head drop to my shoulder. His hands slid down my arms, across the coarse and wet rock, to fall slack at his sides.

With him still buried inside me, his magic warming me from the inside, I cradled his head in my arms. The waterfall washed away the sweat of our passion and pasted my hair to my cheeks.

"Wow," I said. "When you let go, it's a genuine earth-shattering experience."

His face in my hair, he released a miserable groan. "I shouldn't have done that."

"No complaints here." I rubbed my cheek against his head, his hair silky soft and damp on my skin. "It was even better than this morning."

"But I—" He raised his head to stare at me, wide eyed, his expression almost panicked. "I've taken away your choice."

"My choice?" I searched his gaze but found no answers there. "I don't understand."

He urged my legs away from his hips, depositing me on my feet.

My body felt empty without him inside me, and the vestiges of my monumental orgasm still buzzed through me. Sex with Nevan was always spectacular, but this…I had no words to describe it.

He shuffled backward a couple steps, into the shadows of the trees. "Do you recall what I told you about birth control?"

"Sure. You can't get me pregnant unless you consciously decide to."

"That's how it has always been." He swiped a hand over his mouth. "Never before I have lost control completely."

"What are you trying to tell me?"

"You must've felt it. At the end, when I—Did you not feel it?"

He lifted his head to aim those beautiful, otherworldly eyes at me. They glowed with cool colors, white and pale blue, the shades I knew represented fear.

I walked up to him and took his hands in mine. "I felt it. Your magic, right?"

"No." He shut his eyes briefly. "I released my seed into your womb."

My hand flew to my belly, right over the womb in question. "Are you saying…"

He fisted his hands at his sides. "I may have impregnated you."

"Would that be so horrible?" My mind still reeled from his revelation and what it might mean for us—for me. A half-sylph baby? How would I raise a supernatural child? The kid would part human, but also part Janusite. What did that mean for our baby? I wasn't sure I wanted to burden a child with my powers and their associated problems.

On the other hand, our child would be half Nevan. Half wonderful, strong, compassionate, loving, protective Nevan.

"It would not be horrible," he said, "in terms of having a child with you. I would love nothing more than to start a new family with the woman I adore. But a hybrid pregnancy can be perilous for a human mother."

"Perilous? How?"

My clothes reappeared on my body amid a blast of heated air that dried my skin. He'd dried himself as well and regained his loincloth. "The human body is not designed to contain the magics inherent in a part-elemental child. I've witnessed the trauma such a pregnancy can bring about."

I squinted up at him. "You're being awfully vague about it. Exactly what might happen to me?"

"Of the fourteen hybrid pregnancies I know of…" He swerved his gaze to the sky. "The human mothers perished in every instance, within the first three months."

Cold poured over me, as if someone had dumped a bucket of ice water on my head. All of them died? Jesus. But the deed was already done, and neither of us could change it.

"I'm the Janusite," I said, knowing it was probably a lame response. "Maybe I can handle the pregnancy magics. I mean, I've handled my Janusite powers pretty well."

"Perhaps you would be different." He fingered a lock of my hair, admiring it much the way he'd done the first time we met, as if he'd never seen such a thing before. "I cannot lose you."

"I don't want to lose me either." I smiled but received no reciprocation from him. "Look, the odds are I'm not pregnant anyway. Don't know how it is with elementals, but mortal women don't automatically get knocked up whenever a guy, um, releases his seed. We might be worrying about nothing."

"You are not angry? For what I've done to you?"

"Oh, you mean for rudely unleashing your sperm?" I rose onto my tiptoes to peck a kiss on his nose. "Relax, honey. I ordered you to lose control, so I can't possibly be mad that you did. Besides, it was the most incredible experience of my life."

I secured my arms around his neck and kissed him full on the mouth. He folded his arms around me, and his lips yielded little by little, softening and opening to welcome me inside his mouth. We explored each other with slow, tender strokes of our tongues, savoring the intimacy of this moment—not simply the kiss, but the realization we might've created a baby.

When we separated our lips, I brushed a lock of hair from his face. "Whatever happens, with our potential baby or with our enemies, we'll deal with it together. Agreed?"

"Agreed."

"No more running off either, no matter how noble you think your mission is."

"I will never abandon you again. I vow it." He feathered a kiss over my lips while tracing a line down my jaw with one fingertip. "In my entire existence, I have loved but one woman."

"Who might that be?"

He tapped my chin, the old twinkle in his eyes again. "A maiden I met in Peru."

"Well, maybe I've got a hottie on the side too."

"You don't." Both his hands rushed down my body to grasp my behind. "You belong with me, and I belong with you. We need no one else."

Feeling suddenly weak, in a good way, I leaned into him. "You're the only man I've ever loved. Can't imagine ever feeling this way about anyone else. We do belong together, but more than that, we gain strength from being together."

"We do."

"And it's more than magical strength."

"It is." He slid his hands up my back. "We have other, more urgent matters to deal with. Ceara and the sorcerer—"

"Oh, we've got a plan for that." I smiled at his obvious disbelief. "Chill out, Nevan. Team Lindsey's got it covered."

"How?"

"While you were in limbo, we came up with a plan to trap Ceara. Then we'll use her to draw out the sorcerer." I bit my lip, considering another dilemma. "I wish we could go into this knowing for sure who the sorcerer is and what he wants."

Nevan let go of me and stripped my arms away from his neck. "He must be Notus. Only the former king would want to punish me in this manner."

"Yeah, but something's hinky about the whole thing." I glanced around absently, taking in the entirety of my surroundings for the first time. The rock wall behind us scaled up about ten feet, half the height of the falls behind the rock shop. The trees seemed different. The waterfall had scoured out a flat, shallow pool on the ground composed of rock that matched the short cliff. Though the moonlight provided good illumination, it couldn't dispel the shadows that concealed the top of the cliff.

"Are we in the mortal realm?" I asked.

"We are."

"You sure? We didn't go through a waterfall, but this clearly isn't the Keweenaw and—"

Nevan sealed my lips with his fingers. "Chill out, Lindsey."

He over-enunciated the words, clearly pleased he'd gotten the chance to tease me with my own slang.

I smacked his chest with the back of my hand. "Explain, please. This does not look like Michigan."

"Because it is not." His expression changed, becoming softer and rather wistful. "This is Ireland. Five thousand years ago, I was born and lived in this region, and I frequented these woods. When the Fomorians attacked, I fell for the last time here."

I couldn't speak, too stunned by the revelation to have any idea what to say. The mortal version of him, Tuathal, had died right here on this spot.

He nodded at the waterfall. "This is where I was forged."

Chapter Twenty-Two

"In this puddle?" Positioned inches away from the small and shallow pool, I couldn't mesh the sight before me with what I'd envisioned as the site of Nevan's forging. "The way you described it before, I was picturing something more like the waterfall behind the rock shop."

He wandered closer to the pool, his pensive gaze gravitating to its waters. "This was larger thousands of years ago, and the precipice was taller. Time wears away the mightiest structures."

I longed to pull him into my arms, because he looked so sad, but I had the feeling he needed to keep a distance while we talked about this moment from his remote past, from another lifetime.

Lifetime. Life. I froze. Life debt. We were in the mortal realm, though.

"How did you seal a life debt to me," I asked, "when we're in the mortal world?"

"We are standing atop a portal," Nevan said without glancing at me. "Perhaps your Janusite powers allowed you to pull in a bit of the Unseen, as the fae do if they need to utilize a healing vortex from this side of the veil. Remember, debts incurred in the Unseen hold sway here."

Pulled in the Unseen. Like Tris had done back when he healed Nevan after his battle with Skeiron. This was interesting, but I cared more about other matters at the moment.

"Why did you bring me here?" I asked.

He knelt by the pool, swishing his fingers in its cool waters. "I did not bring us here intentionally. My need to get you away, to a secluded place far from our friends and our enemies, drove me to transport us."

"Your subconscious led you here." When he nodded, I said, "Why do you think that is?"

He withdrew his fingers from the water and shook them dry. "I do not know. Perhaps because I believe Notus is the sorcerer."

"Yeah, I know you think so, but something doesn't add up here."

He swiveled his head to look at me. "You believe he is Calder."

"Not sure. I can see Notus wanting to punish you." Kneeling beside him, I laid a hand on his arm. "But the sorcerer wants more. He banished your soul, then filled up your body with evil muck and tried to use it to torment me. My powers are super strong, I've embraced them completely, so why not grab me and suck me dry? From everything he's said to me, and based on his actions, his plans are similar to what Calder had intended to do. Push me to the breaking point and make me wish for death, so I'd volunteer to be forged. But you're right, parts of this point to Notus..."

My voice trailed off as an impossible realization occurred to me. *Totally impossible.*

Nothing was impossible. I'd learned that lesson weeks ago.

"What is it?" Nevan asked.

I looked into his eyes, baffled by what seemed to be. "I'd swear we're dealing with two or three different bad guys. The sorcerer wants to punish you, like Notus would want to do. He also wants to steal my powers, like Skeiron planned on doing. And he's tormenting me, seemingly in hopes of making me want to die."

Nevan's muscles tensed under my hand. "You've seen but one sorcerer. Though we've all seen Ceara, no other associates have shown themselves."

"The sorcerer often refers to himself in the third person. 'We' will consume your powers. 'We' can do this or that. Only when he was glamouring to look like you and Travis did he speak in the first person."

"He is insane. Nothing he says can be taken at face value."

"Maybe—I don't know." I let the spinning waters of the pool take hold of my focus, easing me into a semi-trance that freed my mind to explore the possibilities. "Ceara said something to me, something I didn't understand at the time. She told me 'you think you know so much and yet know nothing at all.' I had just mentioned Skeiron being gone, scattered into the wind. I've also smelled that weird monkey-man smell, like I did back when Calder was stalking me. And the kerkopes attacked me. I assumed the sorcerer sent them, but it's a weird thing to do when he has Ceara to do his bidding. Though he might use the kerkopes if he's one of them."

Nevan rose and urged me up with him. "What are you suggesting?"

"Think about it. Ceara represents a past you'd rather forget, and Calder does the same for me." I took in the falls and the pool, the place he had died and been reborn all those eons ago. "Our pasts are being used to torment us, to weaken us. We talked about someone possibly having resurrected Notus. What if that person resurrected Skeiron and Calder too?"

Nevan's gaze bored into me with such penetrating intensity it seemed to pierce straight into my soul. "I killed Calder. Ran him through with Skeiron's endued sword after I severed his spine."

"Okay, but if Notus could be brought back..."

Nevan cursed under his breath. "So could the others."

"We should assume they're all back." I frowned at the ground, because so much still made no sense. "It's weird, though. I've only seen the sorcerer and Ceara. Even if one of our previously knocked-off baddies is the sorcerer, why haven't the other two shown themselves? I guess the better to torment us, but it feels off somehow."

"We have no time to determine the answers to these questions."

"I know, we have to take out Ceara and her boyfriend." I bracketed his head with my hands and compelled him to look down at me. "Ceara has power over you only if you let her. Whatever might've happened to her is not your fault. I need you in warrior mode, not wallowing in guilt over things that happened in the Stone Age. Got it?"

His lips tightened, ticking up at the corners. "You're quite fetching when you issue commands."

"Right back atcha, sweetie." I skimmed my hands down to his neck. "And you're wicked hot when you smite the bad guys with your big, manly sword."

"Am I now." He laid his hands over mine, removing them from his throat to clasp them to his chest, right over the scar that slashed across his heart. "Best be on our way, before we forget the hammer of imminent death hovering over our heads and forgo our mission in favor of tearing each other's clothes off."

"Oh, we wouldn't do that." I smiled brightly. "You'd make our clothes disappear."

"Nevertheless…" He enfolded me in his arms, hugging me to his body. "We should be going. You can tell me our final destination en route."

Chapter Twenty-Three

The six of us gathered inside a clearing, surrounded by the moss-laden trees with their black bark, beneath a sky lit by a moon three times the size of Earth's companion. The milky glow of the moon illuminated the area with an eerie pseudo-daylight. A thick carpet of grass silenced our footsteps.

Ennea and Tris loitered near the periphery of the clearing, while Travis had taken up a position to my left with the Sig in his grip. Both he and Tris had given up their swords for the sake of mobility, since they weren't used to handling the hefty weapons.

On my right, Nevan grasped his endued sword, legs spread to strengthen his stance, shoulders back and his face a mask of absolute resolve. I would've preferred he conjure his armor, but he'd rightly pointed out Ceara would become suspicious the instant she saw him dressed for battle. He'd offered to conjure armor for me, but I declined for a similar reason. Ceara would realize Nevan must've whipped up the protection for me. He groused about my refusal of armor because, according to him, I had a tendency to get in trouble.

Nah, not me.

Well…maybe.

Nevan's gaze rotated in my direction, as if he'd sensed me studying him.

"Perhaps you should leave," he said. "You seem distracted, and distractions herald danger to come."

"You know better than to tell me to go away." I nudged his upper arm with my shoulder. "Stubborn, annoying mortal here, remember?"

"Stubborn, yes. Never annoying." His mouth twitched in a half smirk he struggled to repress. "I've grown rather fond of your relentless determination. In all facets of our shared life."

"You don't complain about my stubborn streak when it benefits you."

His lips curved into his trademark devastating smile, the one that melted me in the most intimate and wonderful ways. "I don't mind at all, darlin', in certain contexts."

We both knew what he meant. In bed, he loved my determination to give him as much pleasure as he gave me.

Apparently grasping our meaning, Travis let out an irritated sigh. "Can we focus on the mission?"

"Absolutely," I said. "We're good to go, right?"

Four heads nodded, with Nevan abstaining.

I touched his arm. "This will work."

He flung an arm around me and hauled me in for quick, hard kiss. "I love you, Lindsey."

"I love you too."

Releasing me, he stood tall and strong and ready for a fight. "Let us begin."

I glanced at Travis.

He gave a sharp nod and retreated to the clearing's edge, behind a thick tree.

Tris and Ennea linked their hands and ducked behind a large bush.

Each of us had our jobs to do in this crazy plan. Crazy had worked for me, for all of us, before. If Team Lindsey could defeat a sylph army, we could sure as hell capture one evil shrew.

Please, God, let this work.

"You're up," I said to Nevan.

He threw his head back and bellowed, "Ceara!"

The roar of his voice thundered in the clearing, resounded off the trees, and left the rest of us wincing at the unbelievable power of his voice. I'd heard Skeiron bellow, but Nevan's call boomed like nothing else.

"Better manhandle me," I said.

Nevan grasped my upper arm.

I gave him my best exasperated look. "Be more convincing, honey."

He gave me *his* best exasperated look, huffed out a breath, and dragged me backward into his body. One of his arms clamped around my midsection, leaving his other hand free to wield the sword. He raised its tip to my throat, careful not to nick me.

My derringer was holstered inside my waistband, concealed by my shirt. Ceara wouldn't notice, with any luck.

Squashed against Nevan, I muttered out the corner of my mouth, "Much better."

He grumbled his displeasure.

"You're not hurting me," I assured him. "Did you do your thing?"

"The confusion spell is active," he said.

When we'd first met, he'd used the spell—one he acquired from a fae, though not from Ennea—to confuse Travis and his deputies when they sought me, believing I'd killed a man. The spell made them think I'd gone in the opposite direction from where I'd actually ended up. The confusion wouldn't last long, but it ought to give us enough time to nab Ceara.

The minion in question materialized in front of us.

"Tuathal," she said, her silver eyes luminous in the moonglow. "What are you doing? You were to bring her to us, not hold her here."

She surveyed the clearing with a suspicious gaze and blinked as if trying to clear her vision.

Nevan stiffened. "Her magic interferes with mine. She has cast a spell of some sort to prevent me from taking her with me."

"Hmm." Ceara sauntered closer, her gaze wary even as she turned her nose up to gaze down it at me. "The little mortal is resilient. I must admit to a certain admiration for her."

"Do not admire her," he hissed, his act awfully convincing as he prodded me with the sword's blade. The sharp tip pressed in enough to put pressure on my skin without hurting me. "The filthy human stabbed me with her pathetic little blade."

My turn. I struggled against Nevan's grip, but he held firm. "This filthy human is right here, you know, listening to your stupid conversation. Maybe you should address me directly."

Ceara sniffed, waving a dismissive hand in the air. "I have no further to need to speak with you, the chattel of my master."

I barked out a laugh. "Oh man, you are so in for it."

The other woman lifted one slender brow. "You are mistaken. My master will—"

"Torture me endlessly, bend me to his will, make me wish I was dead. Blah, blah, blah, I've heard it all before." I jammed my elbow into Nevan and, understanding my request, he moved the blade to lay it across my throat. The sharp edge didn't pierce my skin, but I couldn't help the frisson of anxiety that whispered through me like the chill breath of a ghost. "Listen up, evil assholes. If you don't release me, I will unleash my wrath on you."

Ceara laughed, the brittle melody of it echoing off the trees. "You puny—"

Unseen energy electrified the air as the wards slammed down around us, sealing off the clearing inside a dome of magic.

Ceara whipped her head left and right, her eyes large.

"How's it feel to be caught?" I said. "Like a puny animal snookered by a hunter's trap."

Her face flushing crimson, Ceara screamed her frustration. She jabbed a finger toward Nevan. "Kill her!"

Nevan dropped his sword arm and hugged me with the other arm in an embrace no one would mistake for hostility. "Why would I murder the only woman I have ever loved to save the pale shadow of my deceased wife?"

Ceara, her eyes so wide the whites shone in the moonlight, thrust out one hand with her palm to the sky. She screamed again, swatting the air with her hand as if some foul substance had become glued to her skin.

"You cannot conjure," Nevan said, stepping sideways to stand alongside me. "The wards block any attempt to use magic within their confines."

"Except by me," I said, "and Nevan and our friends."

Ceara hurled her entire body at mine, tackling me amid a flurry of scratching nails and gnashing teeth, spittle flying from her lips with every enraged cry. Her hands seized my throat to throttle me.

I kicked her, punched her, bit her—but the woman held on like a demon.

Until she was ripped off of me.

Ceara shrieked. Though she thrashed and scratched at him, Nevan gripped her by the back of her neck with one of his hands.

He pitched her to the ground.

She smacked down with a thud and a crack, flat on her face. Stunned, she lay there panting and shaking.

Nevan took my hands and helped me to my feet. He touched his fingertips to my throat.

"I'm fine," I said. "She's damn strong, but I'm damn stubborn."

Ennea and Tris hurried to us, while Travis jogged to the dazed woman on the ground. Ceara blinked up at him, her silver eyes bleary, as the sheriff pulled her hands behind her back and slapped cuffs around them. The shiny gray metal of the handcuffs glimmered with a faint blue sheen, thanks to the spell Ennea, Tris, and I had cast on them. Our collaboration imbued the cuffs with enough power to hold back a god, according to Ennea.

The fae witch fixed her blue eyes on me, and I sensed the question there. She wasn't worried about the cuffs. Though Ceara struggled against them, the metal bound her with solid magic. Ennea worried, I knew, about the wards. I had helped with that spell too. Since the wards I'd constructed around the underground lair had repelled the Anti-Nevan, we figured a dash of my magic would prevent Ceara or the sorcerer from penetrating the wards around the clearing. Nothing was for certain, though.

Not with a sorcerer who'd acquired immense power.

Travis bent over Ceara with one foot on her back, confining her to the ground. He glanced at me and mouthed, "Too easy?"

I shrugged. Maybe it had been, maybe not. We'd expended a lot of magic on setting the scene and confusing Ceara long enough to trap her. The toughest part lay ahead of us, though, and we all knew it.

Pulling the derringer out of its holster, I squared my shoulders. "Time to get the sorcerer. Nevan, will he feel her distress?"

"If he has true feelings for her, yes. He should."

I turned toward Travis and his prisoner. "Let's get her up."

Travis moved his foot off Ceara's back, rolled her over, and gestured for her to get up. She thrashed a bit, hampered by the cuffs, but clambered to her feet. Her long hair fell wild over her face.

She blew a blustery breath out the side of her mouth to disperse the hair away from her face. "You will be destroyed, every last one of you. In the most pain—"

"Zip it," I said, shooting a pointed look at her bound hands. "Nobody wants to hear the sorcerer's little puppet mouthing off."

The puppet's eyes narrowed to slits and she hissed a breath out her nose.

I glanced at Nevan, but didn't need to tell him what to do.

He jammed the tip of his sword into Ceara's chest, right over her breastbone, pushing until he drew a bead of blood. It trickled down her alabaster skin.

"If I pierce your chest," he said, his voice low and menacing, "you will not die immediately, but you will suffer excruciating pain. Call for your lover, and I will slice your head from your body for a clean and relatively painless death."

She spat at him.

"As you wish." He grasped the sword's hilt in both hands, as if preparing to drive it into her chest with painstaking slowness.

Ceara's mouth dropped open on a gasp, her eyes went wide and pure white. Only two small disks of black indicated her pupils. Whatever kind of elemental she was, her eyes were like nothing I'd ever seen.

Was she an elemental? The pendant she wore around her waist signified vitality and regeneration. Might the sorcerer have rejuvenated her body with a spell, not the forging?

Nevan hesitated, his features tense and rife with a dark anger. "This your final chance, Ceara. Call your lover."

"I cannot," she said, her lips quivering despite her haughty stance. "He forbade me to do so, to dissuade our enemies from attempting what you are."

Nevan glanced at me, a grim resignation on his face.

We had no choice but to test the theory her lover would sense her fear and come running to her aid.

"Step away," Nevan told Travis.

The other man hustled backward away from Ceara, and away from Nevan and me. I backed up a few steps too. Nevan and I had discussed the options, and I realized what he must do.

With the sword held to Ceara's chest, Nevan did not look away from her fear-whitened eyes. He made no motion at all, giving no hint of what he was attempting.

A wind whipped to life inside the dome of the wards, whirling around and around all of us, concentrating itself until it narrowed into a dervish that revolved around Ceara's body. Her hair lashed her face and shoulders. Grass and bits of earth spun up from the ground, caught within the whirlwind, and the kinetic energy of it ripped clumps of mossy stuff off the trees, incorporating the debris into the chaotic mini-tornado that imprisoned Ceara.

She thrashed, desperate to escape the whirlwind, but it formed a gale-force wall around her. Dirt and grass stained her skin. She ducked to avoid debris and, finally, squatted inside the tempest with her head between her knees.

The mini-tornado howled, its racket bouncing off the wards in a frenetic feedback loop.

I covered my ears, and the others did the same—everyone except Nevan. He'd retracted his sword, focused on the tempest with a deadly intensity.

Ceara screamed. Her voice conveyed not anger or frustration, as before, but a wrenching terror.

We had succeeded in terrifying her. How long would the sorcerer take to respond? Would he respond? Getting naked with Ceara didn't necessarily mean he cared about her. Max had thought the sorcerer did care, though he admitted he couldn't be sure.

Nevan gripped the sword in one hand, and with the other he crooked his fingers into his palm. The whirlwind answered his command, constricting around Ceara. Not much, an inch or two at most. Enough to make her scream and wail and curl up in the fetal position.

A pained look squinted Nevan's face.

I laid a hand on his arm, squeezing gently. He hated this, I knew. Hated tormenting anyone this way, even if she had purged his soul from his body. Nevan had not one ounce of cruelty within him, and I loved him all the more for it.

Our friends had averted their eyes, their faces displaying varying levels of discomfort. Despite the impulse to shut my eyes, I had to bear witness to Ceara's suffering. I would not leave Nevan to watch it alone.

An explosion rocked the earth with a deafening boom.

The wards flashed blue, undulating from the force of the blast. The epicenter of it mutated a circular section of the ward, perhaps four feet wide, into a blood-red splash. Power as black and frigid as the depths of space walloped into me and rebounded away. I choked on a gasp, doubling over as if someone had slugged me.

Nevan's attention swerved to me, and the whirlwind around Ceara faltered.

I gave him a tight smile.

He reinforced the spinning gale that bound Ceara.

Another explosion rocked the wards, the earth, and ricocheted off me. I glimpsed Ennea and Tris, but the attack seemed not to have affected them. My blue magic formed the foundation of the wards. I was connected to the spell far more than either of them.

Or they were more accustomed to this kind of assault.

I braced myself against the onslaught of dark magic, weaving my blue energies into a kind of suit around me. And then I prayed the protection would work.

Another deafening boom. Another flash of blue as the wards quavered and the center of the attack spilled blood-red over the dome's side. The darkness pummeled my suit of magical armor, but it couldn't breach my protections.

"Let her go," I told Nevan. "He's here."

The tempest evaporated. Bits of dirt and grass rained onto the ground, some of it landing on Ceara. Panting and whimpering, she lay motionless for a few seconds before she opened her eyes and realized the tornado had gone away.

Another blast crashed into the wards.

I waved for Travis to come closer.

He took up his position beside Ceara.

Nevan and I approached the epicenter of the assaults on the wards. The moonlight petered out within the forest, the darkness there deep enough to shelter anyone hiding beyond the protective dome. A shadow moved, seeming to ripple as it swelled bigger and bigger.

It wasn't growing, though. It was coming toward us.

The shadow solidified the closer it approached, resolving into the tall and slender figure of a robe-cloaked individual.

I resisted the urge to grab Nevan's hand. We had to portray a strong front, no weakness allowed. Though I didn't consider holding Nevan's hand to be a weak gesture, the sorcerer might. Instead, I let my arms hang loose at my sides.

As the figure neared the wards, it slowed and finally stopped a few feet away. Pale hands protruded from the baggy sleeves of the billowing black robe. The hood concealed the sorcerer's face, though the moonglow shimmered off glimpses of pallid skin.

Nevan took the lead, stepping forward to confront the sorcerer. "If you wish to save your lover—"

The sorcerer laughed. It was a harsh, crackling sound. Far from weak, though, he sounded frighteningly self-assured. "I have no special fondness for my creation. Kill her, and I will make another."

Creation? Make another?

The pendant. Vitality and regeneration. The meaning of the clues dangled so close my mind could almost touch it, but not quite.

Nevan gave voice to my own confusion. "Of what do you speak?"

"My *shabti*, of course." The sorcerer aimed one pale finger at Ceara. "She has served me well, but I can vivify another."

I opened my mouth to speak, but hesitated. *Shabti*. I recognized the term, but couldn't quite summon the information from my brain. *Shabti* was ancient Egyptian, I remembered that much. Something to do with tombs.

Ah-hah. I remembered. *Shabti* became servants to the deceased in the afterlife, an army of slaves to do all the menial labor.

Nevan glowered at the sorcerer. "You gave new life to Ceara in the forging."

The sorcerer sniggered. "No, Your Exalted Majesty, he who assumes he knows all but understands nothing. That is not what I have done. Haven't you wondered why she resembles no known elemental race?"

"You have imbued her with your dark magic. It altered her makeup."

"In a sense, you are correct." The sorcerer sighed, the breath rattling in his chest. "I carved her body from solid alabaster, then vivified it with the power of elemental fire combined with the magic of the papyrus column amulet." The sorcerer pointed at me. "If you don't believe me, ask your familiar. His fire animated her."

Max helped create Ceara? I refused to glance at Max, unwilling to expose my surprise to the sorcerer. I shouldn't have been surprised, though. Max had been enslaved by this being, this purveyor of the blackest magics. My familiar though he may have been, Max couldn't tell me everything the sorcerer had forced him to do—even if he wanted to tell me.

Nevan clenched his fists. "Why create a being fashioned after my wife?"

"Oh, you misunderstand," the sorcerer said. "She is not merely fashioned in the image of your wife. She contains the soul of Ceara. Rather than forging her, at the moment of death I trapped her soul within a *pithos* and then carved a stone form for her, modeled after her former body. This took a great deal of time and effort, but not nearly so long as I required to find the appropriate conduit to vivify my creation. At last, I came upon a forlorn salamander willing to bargain away his freedom, and with his help I vivified this woman."

He raised an arm, sweeping it in Ceara's direction.

"You distorted her soul," Nevan said, "into a reflection of your twisted darkness."

"What I did," the sorcerer said, "merely gave voice and form to the secret recesses of her soul she hid from you."

"My wife was a kind and good woman, not a vicious creature like the one you have created."

More crackling laughter, rife with derision. "You mean she was meek, always deferring to your wishes. You truly understand nothing at all."

"You are blind, Tuathal." Ceara spoke from behind us, causing Nevan and me to both swivel our heads in her direction, to where she hunkered on her knees beside Travis, seated on her heels. "I was meek because it was my duty to please and obey my husband. I did not choose to marry you, it was imposed upon me. Throughout my life, duty to one's husband was hammered into every girl child."

Nevan shook his head, baffled. "We shared, if not love, at the least a friendship."

"Friendship?" She let out a harsh laugh. "You fool, Tuathal. I despised you from the moment we married. I despised your self-righteous insistence upon doing right by your people, marching off to battle the enemy but leaving your wife and child defenseless. Most of all, I despised you for impregnating me, forcing me to endure childbirth and take responsibility for a child I did not want. I would have slaughtered you in your sleep, if not for the surety of my execution for such a crime."

I glared at the other woman. "If you could've gotten away with it, you would've had the courage to murder him in his sleep. You are a slimy little coward."

"Perhaps." Ceara wriggled until she rose up off her heels. "But I am allied with the true power in this world. You lay claim to a band of weak and useless beings."

"Says the woman caught in my trap."

Ceara scuffled forward on her knees until she could glimpse her lover behind us. "Free me, storm-bringer. Free your most faithful servant, your one love."

He spread his hands. "Why should I waste my power on you? I can fashion another bedmate."

"But—" Tears streamed down her cheeks. "You vowed to protect me."

Enough of this crap. It was time for the next stage in our plan. We had the sorcerer, now we needed to trap him inside the wards.

And it was all on me.

Nevan flashed me a look assurance, conferring his strength of spirit into me without speaking a word or touching me. Not a magical transference, but an emotional one.

I concentrated on the wards, on the threads of glittering magic invisible to the naked eye that comprised its walls. Feeding energy into the spell, I commanded the wards to expand. The spell responded, pulsing as it inched outward, still unseen. *Faster.* I needed the barrier to move faster. My whole body tensed as I funneled more energy into the wards, pushing and pushing and pushing, my head pounding from the effort, sweat dribbling down my temples. Pushing, pushing, pushing.

The ward ballooned outward to encompass the sorcerer. He was trapped inside my dome.

With us.

Oh God, I prayed the magic-dampening effect of the wards worked on him.

The sorcerer lifted one hand, scrawny fingers outstretched toward Ceara. "You have indeed served me well and pleased me greatly. Thus, I grant you a swift end."

He jerked his fingers closed.

Ceara's head snapped back. Her mouth popped open, her eyes went lifeless.

She collapsed into a heap on the ground, dead.

Oh shit. A vicious shiver rattled my bones. The sorcerer's magic still worked.

He waved his hand, and everyone except Nevan and me flew backward across the clearing to slam into the wards.

Nevan whipped up a tempest around the sorcerer, working so hard to surround the lunatic with hurricane-force winds that veins in his neck and temples throbbed.

The sorcerer waved a single finger.

Nevan sailed backward through the air and hit the ground with a sickening crack.

I hurled every ounce of my magic at the sorcerer, expending my physical energy and my powers in a frantic attempt to demolish my enemy.

The sorcerer flinched but remained standing.

I staggered backward, swerved my derringer up, and fired.

The bullets bounced off him, hitting a nearby tree.

He moved his fingers, and I flew into his arms.

Shackling me with both arms, he whispered in a hoarse voice, "You cannot defeat me, Janusite. No one is more powerful than I am."

He swept a hand in an arc over his head.

The wards tumbled down.

We vanished, hurtling away through the abyss.

Chapter Twenty-Four

OUT OF THE TUNNEL WE PLUMMETED, INTO A GLOOMY AND DANK space where a draft prickled my skin. My eyes needed time to adjust, spoiled by the bright moonlight in the clearing. While I blinked and struggled to discern my surroundings, the sorcerer placed a hand on my back and shoved me forward. I stumbled over a threshold of some sort, into a colder and darker space.

A door banged shut behind me.

Flickering lights appeared around me, small and not bright, but enough to let my eyes separate out the shapes around me. The lights were oil lamps that seemed to grow out of the jagged rock walls, their flames an odd, sallow shade. I inched forward, tripped over a depression in the floor, and glanced down to note an array of pockmarks in the stone beneath my feet. Water had collected in many of the holes, and it had splashed onto my boot to darken the leather.

The windowless room was small, no more than ten foot by ten foot. Behind me, the black door stood shut. Shackles affixed to the back wall hung open, awaiting a new prisoner.

I had wound up inside the sorcerer's dungeon.

Would I become the next victim, chained to the wall and drained of magic and life?

Screw that. I would only become a victim if I did nothing. Unlike those poor women the sorcerer had murdered, I had multiple weapons at my disposal. My derringer for one. I raised the gun I still held in my hand. He hadn't confiscated it, which made me suspect he didn't know it was endued and viewed it as no threat to him. I also had magic, the full powers of the Janusite.

My confrontation with the sorcerer had weakened me, physically and magically. How much time would I need to regain my strength? Even when I regained it, what could I do to stop the evil bastard?

Think, Lindsey. Janusite powers, Janusite…means you've got the essence of a god inside you. Use it.

Self-inflicted pep talks were great, but I needed information. Since finding out I was the Janusite, I'd delved into the mythology about the god in hopes of learning more about what I'd become. I needed that information tonight.

If I could remember it any of it.

Why was it when you most needed to remember a thing, the knowledge flew out your ears?

The lock clanked, and the door crept inward. Its metal grated across the floor.

Brighter light from outside the room leaked through the doorway. His robed figure revealed in the backlight, the sorcerer stepped onto the threshold.

"Are you prepared to cooperate?" he asked. "You cannot overpower me, so there is no benefit in fighting."

I'd rather die than give in to you. Keeping that thought to myself, I replied, "Sounds like there's not much point in making a fuss."

Sounded like. I hadn't lied but rather obfuscated. Before I rifled my brain for answers, I might as well glean as much from this creep as possible. Play along, that was my strategy—for the moment.

"Come," he said, and shepherded me out into the chamber beyond.

Yellowish-white light poured down from unseen sources in the ceiling, maybe eight feet above us, much like the everywhere lighting in the home I shared with Nevan. In our home, though, the light soothed and warmed. Here, it cast a wan illumination that stained my skin with a jaundiced color and seemed to enhance the damp chill in the chamber, a space roughly carved from the same dark rock as the cell where he'd stashed me.

No furniture in the room. Not one speck of decoration, or any sign anyone lived or worked here. Ennea's spell lab had tables and potion bottles and myriad other items to aid in her magical endeavors. Her lab was a living space. This place was…dead.

Max had mentioned a bedroom. This must not be where the sorcerer lived. Either that, or he used magic to conceal his living spaces.

I made a show of surveying the chamber, swinging my head left and right, up and down. "Not big on creature comforts, are you?"

He turned toward me, but his face remained hidden in the shadows of his hood. "This is a prison, not a palace."

"No duh."

His head tilted to the side. "You speak nonsense."

And he sounded as baffled by me as Nevan had when we'd first met. Nice to know I could confound anyone, even a supposedly all-powerful sorcerer.

"I speak mortal," I said. Stuffing my hands in my jeans pockets, I rocked back on my heels. "Seeing as you're going to suck me dry and chuck me out with garbage anyway, how about you answer a few questions? You know, satisfy my curiosity before I bite the big one."

"Death need not be your end. The forging awaits you."

My first instinct was to shout *hell no*. Instead, I told him, "Not sure about that yet."

He said nothing, moved not one muscle.

The draft raised goose bumps on my arms, making me wonder where the draft came from, since I saw no windows or doors—except the door to the windowless cell. I couldn't detect any cracks or ventilation shafts either.

A rattling sigh gusted out of him. "It is no mystery why Nevan has become weak and confused, unable to defeat a mouse, much less one as powerful as I. Dealing with an insane mortal has destroyed him."

"Your ignorance of human culture doesn't make me insane."

This jackass might drive me batty, though, if he kept prattling on about how powerful he was.

"Nevertheless," he said, "I will answer your questions. Since you will join me or die shortly, nothing I tell you matters. Your acquiescence will give me your loyalty, and your rotting corpse cannot damage my plans."

"Awesome," I said with sarcasm, as I gave him a matching sarcastic thumbs-up. "First question. Who the hell are you?"

He chuckled, low and harsh and dripping with dark pleasure. "Nevan has not guessed, then? Ah, more proof he is nothing but a demi-mortal."

Demi-mortal? Nevan was all strength and masculine power, with or without magic. More than a mortal, more than an elemental, he was...my Nevan. No one held a candle to him.

"You said you'd answer my questions," I reminded my captor.

"And I shall."

He reached up to take hold of his hood, drawing it back and away from his face. The shadows retreated inch by inch to expose the face of...

I jerked my head back, staring at the sight before me. What was I looking at? Not Skeiron. Not Calder. Not really Notus either, I suspected.

The iris of one of his eyes was onyx, seething with metallic ribbons of vile green and orange. The other eye featured a golden brown iris, with no white at all, and a black pupil dilated by the dim lighting in the chamber. Fiery red hair covered his head, the shaggy locks curled and frizzy. His skin shimmered with a faint silvery sheen.

He lifted one scrawny hand and flexed his fingers.

Black claws shot out from the tips.

The sorcerer twitched one finger, and a wind tore through the chamber. It whipped my hair in my face, then died as swiftly as it had begun.

A show of power? No, more like a clue he intended for me to interpret.

I scrutinized his face, chilled by the familiarity of his features. They reminded me not of one individual, but of two. His left eye, that belonged to Skeiron. His right eye and the clawed fingers, that came from Calder. The rest of him was different, from someone I'd never met before.

He couldn't be three people. Could he?

Oh hell, after everything I'd witnessed and experienced I no longer had the option to deny anything was possible.

"Ah," he said, almost purring the word, "I see you are coming to a realization."

"I am, but it makes no sense." I leaned toward him, peering into his eyes. When I focused on the left one, I had the eerie sensation of staring into Skeiron's eyes. When I focused on the other, a shiver of recognition told me I was eye to eye with my ex-fiancé, Calder. I pulled back, doing my damnedest to suppress my revulsion. "You seem to be part Skeiron, part Calder, and part somebody else. Notus, maybe. Never met him, so I can't say for sure."

I really, really wanted him to say I was imagining the similarities.

But he smiled, exposing yellow teeth, and said, "Perhaps you aren't as unintelligent as I'd first assumed."

Rock. In my throat. Cold, hard, and stuck.

He stretched out one long, bony finger to stroke his claw down my cheek with a bizarre and disturbing tenderness. "You are correct, though I gather you have no conception of how this is possible."

"So explain it to me." I swallowed, but my mouth had gone dry and the rock refused to budge from my throat. "How did you even know Calder? How did he get to be a part of you? Are you really Notus?"

"I am what remains of him." He withdrew his claws. "When Skeiron defeated me, I was scattered—but not to the Four Winds. A powerful sorcerer intercepted the remnants and attempted to resurrect me. However, the spell went awry. Instead of being born anew, my previous body regenerated, I possessed the sorcerer's body."

"But your appearance. If you're in the sorcerer's body…"

"My essence was too much for his body to contain." He made a slicing motion with one finger. "Our essences were disassembled and combined into one being. The sorcerer's soul is gone, but I retain his memories, knowledge, and skills—combined with my own, of course."

"Okay, that explains how Notus—how you came back." Sort of, kind of, not really. Maybe Nevan would understand it, but I had trouble with the idea of essences versus souls versus…*Gah*. I was getting a headache thinking about it. "How did Skeiron and Calder get in there with you?"

"The sorcerer had the ability to sense when an elemental has been destroyed, as well as the magic to capture the essence of that being before it reaches the Four Winds." He scratched the bridge of his narrow, bumpy nose. "I despised Skeiron, but he was incredibly strong, thanks to the magics he'd stolen from others. I absorbed his essence and took his purloined power into me."

Stolen power. Stolen essences. A gear clicked into place in my mind.

"That's what you wanted to do to Nevan," I said. "Steal his power. But you didn't want his essence, did you?"

The sorcerer frowned. "Why would I want to take a part of him into me? He aided Skeiron in my destruction, and his power pales in comparison with the former king's. Besides, once I'd absorbed Skeiron's essence, I acquired more than his memories. I acquired his hatred of Nevan." The sorcerer's voice mutated into a growl. "Torturing him, tearing the very soul from his body and corrupting the mortal he loves, it seems an appropriate punishment for the one who assisted in dethroning two kings."

Well, at least that explained why the sorcerer appeared so soon after Skeiron's demise. Infused with Skeiron's memories and power, the Notus-Skeiron-sorcerer being inherited the former king's anger and hatred of Nevan as well. Nevan had, after all, been instrumental in thwarting Skeiron's plan to steal my power and conquer the mortal world.

I couldn't keep calling him the Notus-Skeiron-sorcerer being.

"What do you call yourself?" I asked. "You must have a name, everyone does."

"You may refer to me as Notus. I am predominantly the storm-bringer."

Ceara had used the term storm-bringer. It must've been Notus's moniker, as a wind god.

"I'd really like to know," I said, "how and why you incorporated Calder into your…self. He wasn't destroyed and scattered."

"Your former beloved?" He skimmed his gaze up and down my body, licking his lips when his attention stalled on my breasts. "He wasn't destroyed, no. But he was killed, by an endued weapon. When your new lover and the raven spirited you away for healing, I sneaked into the cave to draw Calder's essence from his lifeless body before it could be snatched away by the soul-taker. Your kind call him Charon."

The Greek myth about the underworld ferryman was true too. Huh. Since it didn't help me at the moment, I set the information aside in my mind.

I screwed up my mouth. "Don't get it. Why would you want the soul of my dead ex-fiancé? He wasn't particularly powerful."

"But he has a connection to the Janusite, to you." Notus lifted a finger, hooking the claw under my chin. "He knows you. And as they say, knowledge is power."

If he believed Calder had ever really known me, Notus was way more deluded than I'd imagined. Nevan knew me on a deeper level than anyone else, especially Calder. My ex-fiancé had believed I'd want to become one of the kerkopes, a monster chained to the eons-old curse that created the first pair of shapeshifting monkey-men.

Let Notus believe that. His misconception might give me an edge, somehow.

"Strictly for curiosity's sake," I said, "what do you plan on doing with all this power once you've collected it? You want to steal mine, but then what?"

His smile evinced pure self-satisfaction. "I will become the most power-ful being in the universe. I will conquer the mortal realm first, to acquire slaves and concubines. Then, I will conquer the Unseen. Worlds will fall at my feet, every being in my domain will clamor to appease me. Not even the Oversoul can stop me."

"What then? You'll have two worlds at your mercy. Okay, that's super cool. But what then?"

"I rule. Forever."

A mere mortal like me simply couldn't grasp the appeal of multi-world domination, I supposed. Living forever as the ruler of two subjugated worlds, forcing everyone to kiss your feet, it seemed to me that would get old pretty fast. What then?

He'd need more worlds to conquer.

My shoulders fell. "Let me guess. There are other realms of existence you could access, what with all your new-and-improved magical prowess. You'd keep on enslaving worlds to your heart's content."

Someone like him would never be content, though.

"Yes," he said, "precisely. There are unknown numbers of worlds, which are currently inaccessible. I will have the power of the Janusite, the power to thrust open any doorway to any world I desire."

And there it was. The endgame.

My powers would bring about the destruction of every world, countless souls subjugated or murdered to service the insatiable hunger of one dement-ed being. Three demented beings, actually, crammed into one body.

Oh, this would not do. Not at all. No way would I become the instru-ment for universal domination.

Time to make use of the tools at my disposal.

I shambled closer to Notus and bent my head back to look at his face. The monkey smell he'd inherited from Calder infiltrated my nostrils. Tapping into all my strength of will, I kept from wrinkling my nose at the stench.

He gazed down at me with crinkled brows, his Skeiron eyes swirling faster, his Calder eye dilating further. It was the creepiest thing I'd ever seen, but I didn't have the luxury of cringing.

"If you really have a part of Calder inside you, then you know what he meant to me." I'd told Calder I loved him, only later realizing it hadn't been love after all. Nevan had shown me the true meaning of the word. "I can feel he's in there, and that's why you haven't killed me yet. Why you insist I'll join you. A part of you doesn't want to let me go."

Calder had believed, until his last breath, he was my true love. Notus had those memories, otherwise he wouldn't have sought to take Nevan away from me. I was banking everything on the strength of his need to possess me.

Notus's lips parted, his breathing grew labored.

"Tell me the truth," I said, floating my arms up to settle my hands on his bony shoulders. "You want me, don't you? More than you wanted Ceara."

His gaze fevered, he sloped his body closer. "She was a creation. It took thousands of years to carve and vivify her body, and yet she meant nothing to me."

"But I do." I zeroed in on the Calder eye, holding his focus. "Haven't you thought I chose Nevan over you, Calder, because his magic was stronger? But now you are the strongest of all. You have the power to protect me. We can be together again."

A ragged breath inflated his chest. The pupil of his Calder eye had blown, while his Skeiron eye churned wildly.

Gotcha.

I slid my hands to his neck. "The question is, what do you want?"

Breathing so hard he was almost wheezing, he slapped his hands over mine. "I will harvest your power and take you as my consort."

Never, ever if I lived to be a thousand would I submit to him.

"First, Calder, I'd like you to bring me a gift. Bring me—" I couldn't say Nevan, as badly as I wanted to. Might tip my hand. "Travis Blackwell. He was your brother once upon a time, and you know he always had a thing for me. Fetch him so he can serve as a sacrifice, to prove your devotion to me. Then I will gift you with my power."

Excitement invigorated his face. "Yes. Punish my brother."

Oh God, I prayed this would work. Getting Notus out of this chamber would give me time to come up with a plan. When Travis arrived, he could distract Notus while I enacted said plan. Nevan would've been better, but I couldn't risk alerting Notus to the fact I was faking my desire for him.

"Find him," I said. "Bring me Travis."

Notus poofed out.

I stumbled, since I'd been leaning against him. Righting myself, I tugged my shirt down and brushed hair from my face. All I needed now was a plan.

Where could I find one?

Chapter Twenty-Five

WITH NO CLOCK TO SHOW ME THE TIME, I HAD NO IDEA HOW LONG I waited in the damp and musty prison. The cell door hung ajar behind me, the shackles visible in the deeper shadows within the cell. I started to pace, then decided to preserve my energy for the fight to come.

And it would be a fight. A big old nasty one.

I slouched against the wall, my hands linked over my belly. Maybe Notus would observe, invisible and undetected, but I had no time to waste on worrying about it. Let him watch, if he wanted. As long as he brought me Travis, I didn't give a damn about a peeping sorcerer. Sylph. Monkey-thing. Whatever.

My powers were the key, I felt it in my soul. The Four Winds had, presumably, granted me the magical essence of the god Janus. Why? I had no clue, but why didn't matter. I needed to understand what I might do with these powers.

I needed to understand Janus.

Bob had told me a bit about what being the Janusite meant, Nevan had told a bit too, and I'd learned a lot about the mythology of Janus on my own. Mythology wasn't the best source of information, but often legends held at least a kernel of truth. Based on my experiences with the Unseen, myths had a great deal to tell me about this world.

Resting my head on the wall, I shut my eyes and tried to recall everything I'd read about Janus.

He was the god of doorways and transitions, as well as beginnings and endings. Nevan had told me that much. The mythology about Janus elaborated on his nature and his power. He was a doorkeeper, yes, but he also had a connection to time. Though most often shown as a being with two faces, he could also have four faces to signify his dominion over all lands. All worlds?

A god with dominion over every world, every doorway and gate, every beginning and ending, and even time itself. His temporal association connected him to past, present, and future—though nothing I'd read explained exactly what that meant. One article had mentioned the god Jupiter could travel through time thanks to Janus. From what I'd gathered, it was his dominion over time that gave Janus power over transitions, doorways, and everything else he over which he held sway. Time affected the flow of our lives, and thus the flow of history and the future.

Time was the ultimate doorway. It linked everything else.

Could the doorway go both ways? Janus's dual faces implied it did.

What about his four faces? Maybe that implied time moved in four directions, not merely backward and forward, but also laterally.

Right. Lateral time. What the hell did that mean?

I pushed away from the wall. Lateral movement through time. What would that look like? I began to walk the length of the wall, skating my hand over its rough surface as I traveled. Well, if I dodged sideways I could avoid an obstacle. What, then, constituted an obstacle to time?

To freeze time would create an obstacle. Anyone wanting to travel through a frozen moment would need to sidestep it.

I halted, flattening my palm on the cold wall. The idea made a certain kind of screwy sense, but then, everything about me being the Janusite was screwy. A human with the powers of a Roman god. One woman in all the universe who could open the doorways between worlds and ferry elementals across the boundaries in the mortal realm. One woman with dominion over transitions and…time.

What had Bob said in his prophecy? I pressed a hand to my forehead, willing the memory to return to me. I'd sworn I could never forget the strange and spooky prophecy.

Time to break it down, line by line.

In the twentieth era of the mortal calendar, a girl child shall be born into an enlightened clan.

That part fit me. I came from a family of New Age believers.

She will possess the power of Janus, god of the doorways and of transitions, and like him she will face both ways, belonging to neither but bound to everything.

Okay, I had the powers. How did I face both ways? I'd assumed that meant backward and forward, as in entering and exiting the portals. It might also mean traveling through time.

Boundaries fall in her presence.

I'd assumed that part referred to the boundaries in the mortal realm, the ones that kept elementals from invading our world. Other types of boundaries existed, however—like those delineating past, present, and future.

The veil shall open to her, she who holds the power to converge the worlds, she whose power is beyond any seen before, in any realm.

Converge worlds? Not sure I wanted to do anything of the sort. The veil Bob mentioned had, at the time, seemed obvious. It was the veil between worlds. Maybe time had a veil too, an invisible and intangible barrier preventing anyone from breaching it. Anyone except Janus.

Or the Janusite?

The prophecy ended with *she is the bearer of the key and the staff, the child of the god, she is the Janusite.* In mythology, the Janus key had symbolized "I come in peace." Travelers would use a key symbol to let everyone know they meant no harm. The staff represented Janus's dominion over all lands, all doorways and roadways.

And time?

If I had more time I could've tested my theory. Tried to bend the universal clock to my will, played around with the power if it worked, learned how to control it. Max might've helped me with that. I had no time to spare, ironically.

Two people materialized in front of me.

Notus, his hood still pushed back, gripped Travis's arm.

"Your sacrifice," Notus rasped.

Travis went dead still. "Sacrifice?"

I shrugged.

Notus released Travis, and his mismatched eyes homed in on me. "May I kill him?"

"Why don't we play with him a little first?"

Travis gaped at me, the whites of his eyes seeming brighter in the inconstant light.

I looked straight into his eyes and said, "You better not try anything, sheriff. Your brother never liked you lusting after me."

"Brother?" Travis did a genuine double take, then glanced sideways at our captor. "What the blazes are you talking about?"

Notus turned toward Travis, his stance imperious as he glared down his lifted nose at his ex-brother. "I am Calder Blackwell."

Travis snorted, though he still appeared baffled. "You ain't my brother. I know what he looked like, even as a beast-man whatsit."

"He's telling the truth," I said. "The original sorcerer merged with Notus, who forced out the sorcerer's soul. Later, Notus merged with Skeiron and Calder to absorb their powers and knowledge."

Travis staggered backward, shaking his head slowly. "That ain't right. Three guys inside this…thing? Calder may've been screwed up, but he'd never have gone for this."

"He had no choice. His essence was dispersed, and Notus captured it. The being you see is not just Calder, but an amalgamation of three beings."

Travis rubbed his jaw. "Sure, that makes shitloads of sense."

I'd have to explain it better after we saved the world. For now, I needed to make sure he understood what I wanted him to do. "Remember what I said, sheriff. No funny business, or we'll bump up your sacrifice."

The confusion and shock on Travis's face metamorphosed into a clear understanding.

God, I hoped I was reading him right. If he didn't get my meaning, we were both in big, big, gigantic trouble.

Notus moved closer to me, his lustful gaze devouring me. "What punishment shall we mete out upon him first? I've dreamed of making my proud brother fall to his knees before me and beg for mercy."

Jesus, I could not believe the real Calder felt that way. He might've been weak, giving in to the siren song of power and immortality when it was offered to him, but he'd always seemed like such a decent guy before this craziness started. Nevan had told me the forging was a horrific process and only the strongest souls could survive it intact. Calder's weakness had broken him.

My thoughts backtracked, to the part about immortality being offered to Calder. I'd wondered, more than once or twice, who had forged him. I'd assumed another of the kerkopes had done it. Yet during the ordeal in the cave, when Calder had tried to kill me and make me into his monkey-mate, he'd said a man offered him a new life. A man. The kerkopes looked manlike, but they retained much of their monkey-ness even in human form because, as Nevan said, the curse Zeus had placed on the kerkopes to create them prevented them from shifting fully back into human form.

Calder wouldn't have called his so-called savior a man. He would've called him a being or a creature or…something.

Once I destroyed Notus for good, I'd give up any chance of ever knowing the truth about Calder's transformation.

I gazed up into Notus's eyes, focusing on the golden brown one—the Calder eye. "I'm curious. You must know who forged you, and I've always wondered."

A serpentine smile crept across his face. "Notus did."

Referring to himself in as a separate entity? Hmm. Maybe I'd succeeded in drawing out the Calder part of him, and it had taken precedence.

I laid a hand on his cheek. "I assumed the kerkopes would be the only ones who could make more of their kind."

"One with our level of power knows no limits."

He'd slipped back into the royal "we" mode.

Travis stomped his foot. "Hey! The sacrificial human has something to say."

Notus—Calder—cast a scathing glance over his shoulder at his ex-brother. "Perhaps we should tear out his tongue first."

"Like hell you will," Travis said.

"I will do whatever pleases me."

"You never could best me, Calder." Travis scratched his cheek and smirked. "Bet ya never knew I kissed Lindsey."

Technically true. In the midst of the Skeiron melee, while he was still reeling from revelations about the existence of magic, Travis had gotten drunk and given me a sloppy, awkward kiss.

Notus stalked toward Travis, stabbing a de-clawed finger into his chest. "She would never have let you."

"She did." Travis smirked some more, hands on his hips. "And she liked it."

Outright lie, but so what. If it pissed off Notus enough to distract him…

Time for my lateral move. Time for a miracle.

Notus seized Travis's shirt and hefted him off his feet. "She hates you."

"Does she?" Travis laughed with a derisive edge to it, his feet dangling six inches above the floor. "Then why'd she kiss me back? With tongue?"

Notus roared, shaking Travis hard.

I summoned my power, gritting my teeth against a resisting force. It fired a scorching tingle over my skin that plunged deep beneath the surface to sear my veins and nerves. The force hungered for my power, its phantom claws hard and hot as they tore at my psyche, shredding and consuming me.

Dear God. I recognized this pain, this ravenous energy.

The same thing had occurred when Ennea helped me tap into Nevan's memories. This vile force, it came from the sorcerer. From Notus, Skeiron, Calder. All of them at once, crammed inside a single body and recombined into a new and dark entity. Maybe he didn't realize he was giving off the consuming energy, but I had to shake it off either way.

Thrusting with all my energy, physical and magical, I bore down on the invading power. It slashed and thrashed and burned, frantic to stop me. I gathered my Janusite power, the blue magic crackling and glittering on my skin, and hurled the invader out of my way.

The physical form of the sorcerer convulsed. His hold on Travis broke, and Travis tumbled to the floor. Notus stumbled backward until he hit the wall, his eyes wide and unseeing.

Now, I commanded myself. Summoning every scrap of power within me, reaching out to gather in more of it from recesses I hadn't known existed inside me, I pictured the energy coalescing and condensing into a tight ball of brilliant blue light, it surface shimmering with a mottled white gleam. I grasped the ball in both hands and tossed it into the air.

The globe of glittering magic hovered above my head for the briefest moment, then burst. Sparkling sapphire energy rained down, expanding outward.

I spread my arms wide, directing the power to stretch out its billions of microscopic fingers. The energy suffused the room, the walls, and I sensed it mushrooming out into the world and the universe to fill in every crack in every structure and every infinitesimally tiny gap between the atoms in things and creatures and people.

Everything froze. Everything except me.

I glanced around, hardly able to conceive I'd succeeded. Travis sat frozen on the floor, his mouth open, caught in the middle of pushing up with one arm to raise his body off the floor. Notus hung slumped in the air, in the act of collapsing to his knees, his face rent with fury and agony.

No whisper of a draft. No sound save for my own breathing and the thumping of my heart.

Holy shit. I had stopped time.

Chapter Twenty-Six

The pause in time didn't affect me, until I tried to walk. It felt like wading through mud. The absolute silence and stillness around me made for a creepy atmosphere, and it seemed as if everything had taken on a grayish tinge. How long the freeze would last, I had no clue. This was my first time halting the procession of time.

Halting time. Just thinking the phrase gave me the creeps.

I moved in front of Notus, kneeling so I could look him in the eye—not that he saw me, or so I hoped. Given the mind-boggling amount of power he'd amassed, nothing seemed impossible. Maybe he'd leap at me any second, having only pretended to freeze.

Oh great. Now I'd keep picturing that.

No, he was frozen. He had to be.

I stretched out a hand to wave it in his face. No reaction. I shouted at him. Nothing. I almost touched him, but pulled my hand away. Since teleportation worked on others when I touched them, I didn't care to find out if laying hands on Notus might liberate him from the frozen timeline.

This creature before me, composed of fragments of four beings, seemed evil at his core. But was he? Staring into the monkey-like eye of Calder, I flashed back to those months with him. He'd loved to surprise me at work by turning up with a bouquet of flowers and whisking me off to a lunch at our favorite restaurant. He'd taken me to museums, even though he hated art and history. I went to Dallas Cowboys games with him, even though I hated football. We'd laughed together, cuddled up to watch movies together, talked about the future together. When he'd proposed, I'd said yes without hesitation.

Neither of us ever could've envisioned our true futures. Him, metamorphosed into one of the kerkopes. Me, gifted with the ancient powers of a god. Christ, we'd planned on buying a little house and raising kids.

My hand flew to my womb. I might be carrying a baby right this moment. A half human, half sylph child. Definitely not the life I'd imagined.

I pictured Nevan, and the truth rushed through me like a sweet, sultry breeze coming off a tropical ocean. This life was better, so much better. I must save the life, the happiness, I'd found.

Yet gazing at Notus, I began to see Calder. His features were different, of course. Somewhere beneath the unfamiliar exterior, though, I sensed the man I'd known—before his forging, before everything imploded and our lives were reassembled into a new and unforeseen present.

Could I really destroy Calder? I'd done it to Skeiron, but Nevan had killed my ex-fiancé. I'd thought I killed Calder three years ago, when he'd attacked me, but even then I'd realized the person assaulting me was not the man I'd promised to marry. I'd never actually faced this dilemma, destroying the soul and essence of Calder. Could I do it? Should I do it? He'd been a human once, a decent guy. According to Nevan, Skeiron and Notus had started out as good kings, corrupted the power they amassed because they believed it was the only way to secure their positions and the safety of their kingdoms.

I covered my face with my hands, letting the breath flood out of me, drooping my shoulders. I was getting damn tired of being the instrument of men's destruction.

Maybe I could save Calder. Maybe I could save them all.

Staying on my knees, I shuffled around to face Travis and placed a hand on his chest.

He flinched, sucking in a wheezing breath. His eyes darted, then stalled on Notus. "What the—"

"I froze time."

"You—huh?"

While I kept my hand on his chest, unsure what might happen if I removed it, I tried for a sympathetic expression. "I know it sounds insane, but I really did freeze time."

"Okay," he said slowly. Still propped up on the arm he'd been using to push himself off the floor before I froze everything, he sat up. "Why am I...thawed?"

"Because I'm touching you. I figured time-freezing might work like teleporting, so I tried putting a hand on you and, voila, you unfroze."

"Uh-huh." His gaze shifted past my shoulder to Notus. "You sure he's frozen?"

"Pretty sure."

Travis flattened his palms on his thighs, his face pinched. "This was your plan? I distract him while you stop time."

"My plan was for you to distract him, yes." I made a sheepish face. "The rest I made up on the fly."

"Now what?"

I moved my hand to his shoulder and glanced back at Notus. "I was going to kill him, but…"

"What?" His gaze searched mine for a few seconds, then he dropped his head and sighed. When he looked at me again, empathy shone in his eyes. "Lindsey, that ain't Calder."

"A part of Notus is Calder."

"Yeah, the monkey-beast part." Travis settled a hand over mine on his shoulder. "The Calder we knew died three years ago."

"But his soul is inside Notus."

"How do you reckon that?"

My jaw began to quiver as I spoke, my voice too. "The forging doesn't create a different being. Nevan became a sylph, but he kept his personality, his memories, his soul. Calder would have too. He wasn't as strong as Nevan, so the forging warped him into a tortured, angry monster. But the essence of Calder, his soul, remained intact."

Travis slumped, though his hand stayed on mine. "Lindsey, I—What are you saying? You don't want to kill him? The sorcerer killed three women, he stripped out Nevan's soul, and he murdered his own girlfriend. He doesn't deserve to live."

"I know. He has to die." Tears streamed down my cheeks, hot on my skin, dribbling their salty tang into my mouth. "Destruction of an elemental banishes the soul to hell, Travis. I can't condemn Calder for all eternity."

Travis's face blanched, his eyes went dull.

Gripping his shoulder, my nails digging into his flesh, I said, "Can you honestly tell me you'd be okay with sending your brother to hell?"

He squeezed his eyes shut, his mouth crushed into a hard line. "Fuck."

If ever there had been an appropriate time for cursing, this was it. As long as I'd believed the Calder we'd known had vanished years ago, I could plot the sorcerer's demise without any guilt. Now that I'd proved to myself something of Calder survived inside Notus, I couldn't blithely riddle him with endued bullets.

"Are you sure," Travis said, nailing me with his cop stare, "Calder's soul is in that thing you're calling Notus?"

"Positive." I swiped my eyes dry with the back of my free hand. "Everyone keeps saying that to scatter an elemental means his essence and powers are sent to the Four Winds. Notus himself told me when the sorcerer absorbed his essence, the sorcerer's soul got displaced by Notus's essence. That means the essence is the soul."

Travis opened his mouth, and from his expression I knew he was about to object.

I silenced him with a shake of my head. "Listen to me. Destruction of an elemental doesn't always eliminate the soul. Your brother's soul might be stranded, or worse, if we destroy Notus."

"Jesus H. Christ. What do we do? Can't let Notus run around with all his superpowers while we try to save Calder's soul."

No, we couldn't do that. Neither could I keep time frozen for as long as we needed to figure out a plan. At least, I assumed I couldn't hold this time freeze for much longer. The magic buzzing on my skin had grown hotter, sharper, almost a stinging pain. My physical energy was siphoning away too, a sure sign I was approaching the limits of this spell.

A solitary idea sprouted in my mind, so I told Travis.

"If I could sap Notus's power," I said, "we'd have a better chance of containing him until we come up with a plan for Calder. I wouldn't have to pump him dry, which I'm not sure I could do. Just bring him back down to the level of an average elemental."

Travis made a face that said he wasn't quite convinced. "What makes you think you can do that? You ever tried it before?"

"No, but I'm confident I can handle the task." Semi-confident. Edging toward confident. "No choice, I have to try."

He lifted my hand off his shoulder to clasp it in both of his. "Lindsey, don't go killing yourself to save Calder."

"I don't want to die, trust me."

"Maybe you should get Nevan. He could help, right?"

"Not sure if—" I swore I saw a light bulb pop on above my head, but I probably imagined that. Probably. "The one whose help I really need is Max."

"The—incubus?" Travis's lip curled. "Don't tell me you're dumping Nevan for that weirdo."

"You used to call Nevan a weirdo. My how times have changed." I patted his hand, which still encompassed mine. "Relax, I'm not interested in Max that way. He's my familiar, remember? I think he can help more than Nevan could."

"Right, your familiar."

Travis's eyes had glazed over, a sign I recognized all too well. I had felt the way he looked on more than one occasion since discovering the hidden world parallel to our own.

"Problem is," I said, gnawing on my lip, "I have no idea what will happen if I whisk away to get Max. For all I know, time will start up again. I could try whisking Notus away with me, but again, I have no idea if my teleporting will break the time-freezing spell."

His brow pinched, Travis regarded the corner of the room and made a clucking noise with his tongue. After a moment, he swung his attention back to me, the tension of deep thought ironing out of his features. "You got your endived gun?"

I stifled a laugh. "Endued, not endived. It's not a salad, Travis."

"Fine, whatever. You got your gun, right? And it can kill anybody, even this Notus guy?"

"Yes. But we can't kill him until we save Calder."

"I know how to shoot a bad guy someplace that'll hurt like hell but won't kill him." Straightening, he reset his expression to cop mode. Determined, confident, sexy. "Give me your derringer. That way you can concentrate on getting Max here."

"Got a better idea. I'll whisk all three of us—you, me, and Notus—straight to the rest of the gang. That way, I can get all the help I might need."

A fae witch, a surly leprechaun, my roguish familiar, and my super-hot sylph boyfriend. We were a dream team, for sure.

The team included Travis.

"I'll have to let go of you for a minute," I said, "so I can get my gun out and reload. You'll probably freeze again."

"Let's get this done."

The instant I withdrew my hand, he turned into a statue again. His hands hovered where he'd held mine.

I pulled out my derringer, flipped the barrel down to expose the twin chambers, and dumped the empty shells. Switching the gun to my other hand, I dug in my pocket for two fresh rounds and dropped them into the chambers, then snapped the barrel shut.

Scrambling to my feet, I touched Travis's shoulder.

He woke up, and without a word, got to his feet.

"Ready?" I asked, offering him the derringer.

Travis accepted the gun, holding it barrel down with his finger on the barrel just above the trigger. "Ready."

We stepped closer to Notus. I placed my other hand on his shoulder.

And I zipped us away in the instant Notus came back to life, roaring his fury.

Chapter Twenty-Seven

BACK IN THE CLEARING WHERE WE'D LEFT THE REST OF THE GANG, the second we touched down Notus leaped at Travis.

And froze in midair.

Travis froze in the act of ducking out of Notus's path.

In the clearing around us, the others were paused in various poses. Tris and Ennea seemed to have been arguing at the moment I stopped time, his arms raised and his mouth open on what must've been a snarky complaint, her hands on her hips and her mouth puckered. Max and Nevan were about twenty feet away from me, engaged in a serious conversation, by the looks of it. Nevan wore his stern king face, while Max listened with a strained expression.

My first impulse? To run over there and throw my arms around Nevan.

Second impulse? The right one. To grab Max and siphon enough power out of Notus to make him no stronger than any other elemental.

I sprinted to Max, slapping a hand on his arm.

He looked confused for heartbeat, then grinned at me. "You have temporal powers."

"Yeah, I do. Big whoop."

"It's an enormous whoop, my mistress."

He executed an exaggerated bow, and somehow I kept my hold on him through the whole, silly display.

"Temporal powers mean nothing," I said, "unless I can weaken Notus."

I quickly outlined the plan Travis and I had devised.

Max scrubbed his hands on his conjured pants. "You need Nevan. He can—"

"Both of you would be ideal," I said, "but I can't unfreeze you both and hold onto the time-freeze spell. I feel it slipping already. You're my familiar, and I need your help. Okay?"

"Here to serve, mistress."

"I keep telling you to call me Lindsey."

"Of course, Mistress Lindsey." The twinkle in his eye gave away the fact he was teasing me, the smart-ass familiar.

We approached Travis and Notus, my hand on his arm the whole time. I laid a hand on Travis just long enough to urge him aside, and as he struggled to comprehend the situation, I sent him back into the frozen timeline. No time to explain. No time to waste.

Max and I took up positions in front of Notus. I had to keep one hand on his arm, leaving me only one hand to link with his, maintaining a slight gap between our hands as we'd done before. Energy began to sizzle and glitter within the gap, but he couldn't give me more power. His assistance grounded my power so it wouldn't run out of control, providing—as he'd told me the first time—an anchor for me in the stormy sea of magic.

I had no idea how to drain an elemental's power. With my previous spells, I'd imposed my will on my power, commanding it to perform a task. No words spoken, nothing more than intention and resolve. I did the same now, concentrating on the idea of reducing Notus's power, of stealing the magic he'd stolen from others, and of funneling it into...

A container. I needed a container for the magic, to ensure no one else could snare it out of the ether as the sorcerer had done.

Max's expression evidenced a dawning understanding and an unflinching commitment to the mission.

"Whatever you need," he said, "I will do it."

Christ. How could I ask him to be the container for dark magic? What would that do to him?

"I am your servant," he said.

"No you are not." The magic bridging our hands unified us in a strange and not unpleasant manner—not sexual or romantic, but a strong bond nonetheless. "You are my friend, Max. What I need to do...It requires a container for the power we pull out of Notus."

"Then I will be the container."

"What will that do to you? Can you stay yourself with all that crud inside you?"

"I am stronger than you realize. Perhaps not in terms of magic, but in the ways that count."

"I know you're strong," I said, "but I don't want to lose a friend today."

"You won't." He took a breath, exhaling it in a rush. "I'm ready."

"Max—"

"Lindsey," he said, his tone gentle yet firm, "this is my purpose. To serve you, as your familiar and as your friend. I'll fight the dark magics and survive this, you have my word." He winked. "Why should everyone else get the chance to be selfless and brave, but not me?"

I tried to smile, but faltered. "You are brave, Max. But you're also an amazing friend and an amazing familiar."

"That sounded like goodbye. We're not parting ways."

"No. You're coming back from this, if I have to rip that scuzzy magic out of you with my bare hands and hand deliver it to the Four Winds."

He turned thoughtful. "You will need to deliver me to the Temple of the Four Winds and summon them to remove dark the magics from me. Nevan can lend a hand with that."

"We will fix you. And you have *my* word on that."

I focused on the blue magic simmering between our hands, rising into a rolling boil of power tempered by the anchoring magic of my familiar. Max shut his eyes, his expression strained as if waiting for and dreading the transfer to come. I let the power tingle over my skin, lifting every hair and awakening the Janusite within. Tendrils of sapphire energy snaked out from between our hands, whipping through the air as they sought out the target.

The tendrils latched onto Notus. They coiled around his limbs, crawling over his torso and over his head, engulfing him in a mesh of pure power. It shimmered as sparks erupted all along the tendrils.

Darkness fought back. It clawed and scorched and screamed down the lines of magic connecting Notus to me and to Max. I clenched my teeth, battling for breath, the strain of the spell like a steel corset ratcheting tighter and tighter around my torso. The dark power scrabbled for a foothold, a way to get inside me, but I fought back with every ounce of energy within my body.

A blue fireball raced down one of the tendrils, straight into the grounding space between my hand and Max's. Oily blackness writhed within the ball, searing my skin.

No turning back.

I funneled the darkness into Max and felt it scour down the lines of power connecting us, shy away from me, and dive straight into him.

Max's body convulsed. His eyes shot wide as black threads whipped through the swirling colors of his irises. His chest inflated on a breath that roared like a hurricane wind.

I pushed a wave of my blue energy into him, desperate to bolster his own power with mine, the instant before our connection shattered. The force of the disconnect sent me reeling backward, but Max did not freeze.

He went stone-still, but his chest heaved with each hollow breath.

While I staggered and caught my balance, time resumed its forward motion. The rest of my friends, and Nevan, spun toward the weird sound emitted by Max.

Notus came to life screaming like a sinner pitched into the fires of Hell. His gaze landed on me, and he lashed out one bony hand as if to strike me down with his magic. His power, what remained of it, hit me like a light slap in the face but nothing more. He stumbled, lost his balance, and smacked onto the ground on his butt, breathless from the exertion of magical energy. And likely from having his stolen power ripped out of him.

Travis clapped his boot on Notus's chest and shoved him down on his back, the amalgamated being too weak to fight.

Victory.

Not quite yet. We had to save Calder.

I caught sight of Nevan. He smiled, lips closed, eyes crinkled at the corners, and my heart melted.

The smile disintegrated. He swung his sword up, the moonlight glancing off its blade and shouted, "Lindsey!"

I spun around.

Travis went flying past me, limbs akimbo, a strangled cry bursting out of him. He crashed to the ground a dozen feet away.

Notus threw his body at me, and we tumbled to the grass with him on top. One of his elbows rammed into my gut. His clawed fingers clinched around my throat, but I fired a burst of power into his chest, hurling him off me. He collided with a tree, dazed but no less infuriated.

I shoved up onto hands and knees, winded from the attack.

A feral roar split the air from behind me as Nevan sprang through the air headed for Notus. His massive body sailed down toward the sorcerer, but Notus thrust one foot up to kick Nevan in the chest, punting him backward. The sword popped out of Nevan's hand and wheeled through the air.

Nevan careened to the ground at my left, grunting from the impact.

His sword punched into the ground inches from my right hip.

Notus clambered to his hands and knees. He raised one hand with the fingers curled, as if holding an object though nothing was there.

A thin, curved sword materialized in his grasp.

Everything unfolded in a heartbeat, so fast even Nevan couldn't get to me in time. Notus lunged at me, slashing the sword down toward my neck. I reached for my holster, but the derringer wasn't there because I'd given it to Travis. With no time to think, I grasped the hilt of Nevan's sword, levered myself up, and vaulted over the sword an instant before Notus's blade lanced the air where my throat had been.

He bounded to his feet, hunched but with a firm grip on his curved weapon.

On my knees, I took hold of Nevan's sword with both hands, yanking it out of the earth, imbued with a new strength fueled by adrenaline. I knew the boost wouldn't last, and I'd have one shot at this.

Notus raised his sword with both hands, wielding it high above his head in preparation for a death blow. With a banshee-like scream, he drove the blade down toward my chest.

I propelled Nevan's sword upward.

The blade punctured Notus's stomach, plunging deep, all the way to the hilt. His sword tumbled from his hands.

I teetered backward, about to fall over from the weight of him skewered on the sword.

Nevan appeared beside us. He grabbed Notus's shoulders and tore him off the sword, flinging him aside.

Bent backward at an awkward angle, the sword in my grip, I couldn't move. My body had begun to tremble, as the adrenaline rush flooded out of me and my overtaxed muscles wailed for relief.

Falling to his knees beside me, Nevan snatched the sword away and tossed it onto the ground. He lifted me onto my knees again and hugged me to him for a brief moment before he took my face in his hands and scrutinized me.

"Are you harmed?" he asked, anxiety tightening his features.

"I'm fine." Turning my face into his hand, I kissed his palm.

He touched his forehead to mine. "I will dispatch him."

Nevan rose.

"No." I grabbed his hand, scrambling to get up. "Nevan, we can't kill him yet. I have to save Calder first."

Nevan's brows knit together. "Save him?"

"Calder's soul is trapped inside the sorcerer's body. I have to set him free."

A rustling erupted to our left, from where Notus had wound up crumpled on the ground. He'd pushed up off the ground, blood oozing from his mouth and pouring from his gut wound, his fevered gaze locked on me.

A gunshot detonated.

Notus crumpled.

Halfway across the clearing, Travis held the derringer pointed at where Notus had stood a second ago. A faint wisp of smoke curled up from the gun's barrel.

An endued bullet had felled Notus. What if he was dead? For real?

Travis must've noticed the panic on my face, because he lowered the gun and strode up to me and Nevan. "Don't worry, Lindsey. I told you I know how to shoot somebody where it hurts like hell but won't kill 'em."

Notus lay crumpled on the ground, his legs bent, but his eyes were open and he was breathing, though his breaths were labored. He clutched one hand over a wound on his shoulder. Blood stained his fingers, but the wound didn't seem life threatening. He was weak from the previous attack and from getting a good deal of his magic siphoned out of him.

Travis squinted at a sight past my shoulder. "Is he okay?"

I tracked his line of sight past Nevan, to a figure crouched near the clearing's perimeter.

Max lifted his head to fix his gaze on me.

Unease crawled along my skin and shivered through my veins.

His eyes had become a maelstrom of molten metal shades, with bright red flames licking at the pupils. Tiny flames on his skin burned orange and red. His mouth was open slightly, his expression savage and dark. His hands rested on the ground, the palms flattening the grass. The fire on his skin erupted, flaring high enough to set his hair ablaze and singe the trees behind him. Smoke drifted up from the grass as it blackened beneath him.

"Max?" I said, taking a few tentative steps toward him, until Nevan grasped my arm to halt me.

The salamander's skin had gone crimson, and white flames sparked within the fire engulfing him. He sank his fingers into the earth, gritting his teeth with his lips peeled back.

Oh God. He must've been fighting the dark magics with all his power, all his strength of will. How much longer could he hold out?

I looked to Nevan, who still grasped my arm, but he was staring intently at a spot on the other side of the clearing.

"We have to fix Max," I said. "Get him to the Temple of the Four Winds before that evil crud wrecks him. Can they save Calder too?"

Nevan remained silent, his gaze glued to the empty swathe of earth across the clearing. I turned toward him, and his hand fell away from my arm.

"Hey," I said, pushing on his upper arm in a vain attempt to shake him. His superior strength made him immovable. I waved a hand in his face. "What are you staring at? We have pressing issues to deal with."

"Yes," he said, finally looking at me, "we have extremely pressing concerns. Such as where Ceara's body has gone."

"What do you m—" I flashed back to the sight of Ceara's lifeless body on the ground, in the exact spot Nevan was staring at now. The empty spot. "Maybe Notus took it."

Nevan's jaw worked, as if he were literally chewing on the idea. Then he stomped over to Notus, still prone on the ground, and dropped into crouch straddling the defunct sorcerer.

Notus cringed.

All-powerful no more, eh, Mr. Baddest of the Bad?

Nevan closed one hand around Notus's throat without squeezing. His voice was menacing, but deceptively soft. "What have you done with Ceara's body?"

"I did not take it," Notus rasped, his speech halting.

"Someone did." Nevan shook his captive's neck. "You must have witnessed the taking of her body."

Notus spat blood. "She simply vanished."

I moved up beside Nevan and spoke to Notus. "Was she really dead?"

"Difficult to say." He glanced past Nevan to the vacant spot where Ceara had died by his magic. "She was a vivified statue, after all."

"You killed her with magic," Nevan said. "It takes an endued weapon or a magically enhanced poison to destroy an elemental. Simple telekinetic magic does not kill, unless it's polluted with dark energies. I did not detect the odor of fouled magic." Nevan shot me a chagrined look. "I should have considered this at the time."

I settled a hand on his shoulder, bending over to say, "It's not your fault. We all had a lot on our minds." To Notus, I said, "Did you know you weren't actually killing her? If simple magic can't do the trick, you must have known."

Notus sniffed. "My magic is not simple."

Straightening, I considered the winded and wounded creature slumped at my feet, and a thought occurred to me. "Ah, I get it. You believed you were the most powerful badass ever in the history of badassery. Naturally, your spectacular magic would destroy another elemental where regular magic fails to get the job done."

Nevan sprang to his feet. "Arrogant fool."

"This means Ceara might still be alive."

"The least of our concerns at the moment." Nevan pointed toward the conflagration that was my familiar. "We must take care of that problem first. And then find out if this one can be saved."

He nodded at our prisoner.

Travis held the derringer out to me. "You might need this where you're going. Who knows if these wind people are friendly or not."

Nevan shook his head. "If she arrives at the temple carrying a weapon, she will be ejected from it."

I waved away the gun but dug the rest of my endued ammo out of my pocket. "Travis, you'd better take these. Might need them if Ceara comes back."

Nevan proffered his sword to Travis. "Take this as well. I cannot bring it with me to the temple."

With a small nod, Travis accepted the sword. He held out his hand, and I dumped the ammo into his palm.

"Good luck," he said, stuffing the bullets into his pocket.

Ennea and Tris reached us then, offering their own statements of support and wishes for luck. Tris assured that such wishes "coming from a frigging awesome leprechaun" like himself meant a great deal more than a similar statement coming from an average elemental.

I believed him.

Nevan kissed me, a quick and sweet meeting of our lips, and said, "I will transport Max, as I'm far more fireproof than you."

He assumed I could transport Notus. The silent vote of confidence made my heart swell.

"I've got this guy," I said, kneeling to clap a hand on Notus's shoulder. "You lead the way."

Nevan zipped across the clearing to Max, bending to touch the salamander's shoulder. The pair vanished.

I followed Nevan's warm and brilliant trail of magic.

Chapter Twenty-Eight

A GALE BLUSTERED AROUND ME. I THREW AN ARM UP TO SHIELD MY eyes from the onslaught, but the roar of the wind made it hard to hear anything. I knelt on rocky ground, that much I could tell. The fog that somehow shrouded the landscape in spite of the wind obscured my view of anything further away than the man slumped at my feet.

Notus groaned, sounding as miserable as anyone I'd ever heard.

Keeping my arm up to protect my eyes, I cupped my other hand into a makeshift megaphone and shouted, "Nevan!"

I sensed him nearby but couldn't see a damn thing.

The air around me began to clear within a bubble of calmness, expanding outward to form a protected dome perhaps ten feet in diameter. Beyond the bubble, the wind raged and the fog obscured everything.

Nevan stood before me, his expression grim.

Though his body blocked most of my view ahead, I saw the flames raging behind him. Leaning to the side, I peered around him at the man-size mass of flames. Max's skin and face had vanished into the conflagration.

"We have to hurry," I said to Nevan. "He doesn't have much time."

"I know." Nevan grasped my upper arms. "Listen to me, Lindsey. I may not be able to accompany you into the temple."

"What? Why?"

"I've been here once before, shortly after Skeiron and I defeated Notus. To enter the temple, one must be deemed deserving by the Four Winds. They ejected me."

Nevan always said what he meant, which told me he'd been tossed out of this place—ejected, rather than simply rejected.

"Why would they do that?" I asked.

"I aided in destroying the king of the sylphs. The Winds deemed me a traitor and therefore unworthy of their assistance."

We had so little time, but I had to know. "What did you want from them?"

He avoided my gaze, his darting everywhere except to my face. "It does not matter. You must hurry to save these two."

"What if I'm not deserving?"

Nevan looked at me then, his grip tightening on my arms. "You are."

My throat had grown tight, thick with emotion. I gulped, but couldn't quite shake the disturbing sensation of weight bearing down on me. The weight of responsibility. The weight of so many lives riding on my success or failure. If the Winds denied me entry, I had no idea how to save Max or Calder.

If Max lost his inner battle, the darkest powers would consume him and turn their voracious eyes on the rest of the universe.

"Summon them," Nevan said.

"How?"

"Request an audience. In not words, but intention."

I rolled my eyes. "Thanks for the unambiguous instructions."

"Close your eyes and concentrate on your desire to meet with the Four Winds." He squeezed my arms, his expression turning gentled. "You will be admitted. Because you, my love, are the most worthy being in any world."

He loved me, so of course he'd have to say that. But I believed him. I believed he meant it.

I shut my eyes and let his grounding presence, the calming effect of his touch, draw me into a kind of trance. The noise of the wind outside our bubble faded into silence.

The ground rumbled and shuddered beneath my feet.

If not for Nevan holding me steady, I would've toppled onto my ass on the hard rock ground. As I scanned our surroundings, I realized the wind hadn't faded because I'd been in a trance. It had just...stopped. The fog retreated away from us as if sucked up by a gigantic vacuum cleaner, sweeping up and up and up the rocky slope ahead of us. The sun emerged from the retreating fog, and the sky cleared in its wake.

Soon the earthbound clouds had gathered above us, at the top of the now-exposed mountain. The fog condensed into a vaguely rectangular shape, rotating around a central point.

We had landed on the side of a mountain, a barren peak amid a field of barren, craggy peaks with steep slopes and only a smattering of grass and the occasional bush to interrupt the pockmarked rock surfaces. The mountain range extended to the horizon in all directions. Above us, the sky shimmered such a deep blue it was almost purple, with nary a cloud to mar it.

"You are worthy," Nevan said.

I tapped his chest. "So are you. Otherwise, you'd be tumbling down this mountainside, wouldn't you?"

His brows lowered and crinkled. Then, with all the brilliance of the sun dawning after a month of storms, he smiled.

Motion above us attracted my gaze, and I discovered the condensed fog bank had begun to rotate with more vigor. Nevan followed my gaze, turning toward the mountain peak some hundred feet or so away.

A burst of wind dispersed the fog.

In its place, perched atop the summit, hunkered an imposing structure with Corinthian columns and enormous wooden doors. A steep set of steps carved out of the mountain led up to the structure's portico, where a shallower series of steps approached the doors. The entire building appeared to be fashioned from white stone that glimmered in the sunlight as if dusted with the essence of stars.

Nevan stared at the huge building, starstruck. "The Temple of the Four Winds."

I slipped my hand into his, lacing our fingers. A sense of awe, mixed with fear, overtook me at the reality of what was to come. The Four Winds, those avatars and guardians of power more immense than anything I could imagine, awaited us inside the temple. My gaze shifted to Max, his body aflame with wicked power, and I wondered. We had been deemed worthy of entry, but would the Winds help us?

Max disappeared.

"Nevan—" Before I could finish my exclamation, Notus poofed out too. I latched onto Nevan's arm with my free hand, the other still clutching his hand. "Where'd they go?"

He patted the hand I'd clamped onto his arm. "Easy, love."

A horrendous grinding noise made us both look to the summit.

The doors of the temple crept open.

"Our invitation," Nevan said. "Or the closest we'll come to receiving one."

He tucked my arm under his and guided me to the steep steps embedded in the slope.

I let my gaze skim up the narrow steps. "Can't we zip up there?"

"Unfortunately, they have wards around this peak. I cannot zip us anywhere."

But the Winds could poof Max and Notus away to wherever. *Not fair at all.*

I sighed. "Trudging up these steps is probably a test of our commitment, or some baloney like that."

Nevan threw me a sideways glance. "Perhaps you shouldn't think of it as baloney when you seek their aid."

"Point taken." I shouted up the mountainside, "Excuse me, your eminent windinesses. It's not baloney, it's a perfectly reasonable test."

Nevan groaned.

We ascended the steps side by side, mounting step after step until my legs started to ache, soon joined by my stomach muscles. I couldn't quite catch my breath, probably because the air was thinner up here. Five times, Nevan paused to breathe clean air into my lungs—and that wasn't a metaphor. He sealed his open mouth over mine and exhaled, feeding me oxygen-rich air that tasted like him.

At last, we made it to the top, to the base of white stone stairs that accessed the temple doors. I bent over, panting, my hands on my thighs and my knees bent.

"Need a sec," I huffed.

Brawny arms lifted me off my feet. Nevan cradled me to his body, and his mouth descended on mine for another life-giving lip-lock. As the sweet, clean air filled my lungs, I wrapped my arms around his neck.

"Better?" he asked.

"Yes."

Nevan carried me through the massive wooden doors. They dwarfed us both, their ornately carved panels towering at least five times as tall as Nevan. He halted just inside the temple and set me on my feet.

The room was vacant—of life, of furnishings, of decoration. A smooth floor made of marble-like rock stretched away from us in three directions. I estimated the building measured about a thousand feet in breadth and half that in width, though I had minimal confidence in my ability to gauge the size of such a vast and empty space. It was huge, period.

High up on the walls, sixty feet overhead, intricate friezes depicted winged beings dressed in flowing robes.

A delicate, tepid breeze wafted around us. It seemed to investigate us, brushing over my skin, ruffling my hair, touching me with the sensation of soft fingertips. From Nevan's look of mild surprise, I knew he was experiencing the same exploration.

Four beings materialized before us.

They wore white robes that dragged on the floor, their arms and heads exposed. Two were women, two men. At least, they appeared to be male and female. Since they served as avatars of magical power, who knew if their current appearances bore any resemblance to their actual forms. If they had real forms.

All of them had white hair and pale skin, but their eyes shone glossy black.

I sidled closer to Nevan.

They watched us, unmoving, expressionless.

Unnerved, I gave a curt wave of my hand. "Hello there."

Nevan tensed. He was probably cringing inside at my silly greeting.

Well honestly, I'd never met an avatar of power before. How did one introduce oneself to such a being?

You didn't. *Duh.* You waited for them to say howdy.

One of the females glided toward us. She halted a foot away from me, her body bobbing the tiniest bit, as if she floated barely above the floor. Her black eyes drilled into me, and she canted her head.

"Lindsey Astrid Porter," she said, her voice as ethereal as the wind and as alien as her appearance. "We have received your request."

"I—I didn't make one yet."

She flourished one slender hand.

Max and Notus winked into view behind her—Max a pillar of man-shaped fire, and Notus sprawled on the floor. The erstwhile sorcerer moaned, his head lolling.

The wind-being in front of me reached out one pale finger to touch my jaw. "You wish us to save these two. Of what benefit is it to us?"

"Isn't it your job to collect scattered powers and guard them?" Despite the knot in my stomach, I looked directly into her spooky eyes. "You're supposed to keep a destroyed being's power from being misused, right?"

She drew her head back, as if surprised or maybe annoyed.

Not sure which option would've been worse for me.

Her nose lifted, and she sniffed. "You dare question us?"

I glanced at Max, his body covered in fire thanks to the evil crud stuffed into him. His brave and selfless willingness to take in the discarded powers had put his very soul in danger. And he'd done it for me.

Separating from Nevan, I confronted the wind-being. "Yes, I question you. It's your job to pick up scattered powers, but a sorcerer got his hands on the essences of three elemental beings. He became so powerful, he might've destroyed two worlds."

"Yet he did not." She looked way too smug about that statement.

"Because my team—two fae, a salamander, a sylph, and two humans—risked our lives and our eternal souls to take him down." I flapped a hand toward her ethereal buddies. "You guys screwed up big time. Dark power got stolen, and you don't seem to have done a damn thing to get it back."

She stared at me, her eyes wide, her nostrils flaring. The black in her eyes pulsated.

Nevan tugged my hand.

I glanced at him, expecting to see his dismayed look. Instead, he smiled with his lips closed, his eyes gleaming with pride.

The wind-being narrowed her gaze on me. "We gifted you with great power, Janusite. Are you not grateful?"

"Honestly, I'm not sure yet."

The black in of her eyes shrank into a dark pupil, rimmed by a wide iris of shimmering emerald green. "You are forthright and courageous, but without arrogance. We admire this, especially from a mortal imbued with the essence of a god. Power of that magnitude can and often does corrupt the bearer."

Was that a compliment?

She curled a lock of my hair around her elegant finger. "You remain pure of heart, despite the sorcerer's attempts to blacken your soul."

"I—" Lying to this being seemed like a very bad idea. "I gave in to the darkness, for a little while. I'm not pure."

Her pale mouth curved into a smile. "You never succumbed to darkness, child. You gave in to anger in a time of desperation, but that is not the same."

"Um…How do you know what I did?"

"We are one with the Oversoul. The connection grants us far-reaching knowledge." She let go of my hair, settling her hand on my cheek, the touch barely perceptible. "You are worthy of our intervention. We will remove the unwanted power from the salamander."

The other three wind-beings nodded in unison.

I could've hugged her, but I restrained myself. "Thank you."

Nevan made a strangled noise somewhere between a groan and gasp.

Oops. I'd said the T word—to a hugely powerful being, at that.

"Be at ease, sylph," the female said. "Your soul mate owes us nothing in return. We owe her a unpayable debt for retrieving the lost magics."

She'd called me Nevan's soul mate. I wanted to ask why, what that term meant to someone like her, but I had other concerns.

"What about Calder?" I asked. "Can you save him and send his soul to a good place?"

"I am afraid saving him is beyond our purview." She stepped back, sweeping an arm in the direction of Notus. "Only you can liberate his soul."

"Me?" I shook my head. "I wouldn't know how. Not very adept with my magic yet."

"No magic is required. Make use of your humanity."

Sure, that sounded way easier than magic. "I don't suppose you could explain what that means."

"The answer lies in your heart." She glided toward Max, and her three companions floated up to encircle the incubus. "We shall render aid to this one, while you consider the other."

As the Four Winds raised their spread arms, a wind erupted around Max. It spun around him in wild torrents of air that doused the flames on his body. The wind mutated into a whirling fog so dense it obliterated my view of Max, and even the Four Winds became indistinct figures at the periphery of the cloudy tempest. A pillar of glittering black energy punched through the fog, shooting straight up to the ceiling. An opposing current of pure white power coalesced out of the roof, seeming to emanate from the stone itself, and wound its tendrils around the blackness, swallowing it whole.

The white energy receded. The fog dispersed.

Max huddled on his knees, doubled over with his forehead on the floor.

I rushed to him, laying a hand on his shoulder. His skin was hot, though not scorching.

He raised his head to look at me. "Lindsey. It is…gone."

The female Wind who had addressed me before moved closer to us. "Yes, the darkness has been stripped from your being. It is now quarantined."

I bit my lip, contemplating the wind-being. "Shouldn't dangerous magic be destroyed?"

She gave me an empathetic smile. "Magical energy cannot be destroyed, only contained. This is the reason we exist, the purpose of the Four Winds."

Max pushed up onto his knees, facing the female. "You have saved me. I owe—"

"You owe us nothing," she said. "We removed the dark magics from you, but we could not have done, if your mistress were not the Janusite."

I leaned toward her. "What does that have to do with anything?"

"Your power protected him." She must've noticed my confusion, because she gave me another empathetic smile and explained. "Janus had dominion over transitions, and this includes changes in condition. When you transferred the dark magics into your familiar, your Janusite power protected him from the brunt of the intrusion. You maintained his condition, defending his innate magic. He needed to fight the invading energy, but he could not have survived without the shield of your magic and your desire to protect him."

Max swerved his gaze to me, his expression one of utter astonishment. "You saved my life, Lindsey. Thank you."

I was astonished too, by the revelation I'd shielded him from the dark energy and by his gratitude. A tether of magic snapped taut between us, cementing the debt.

Shit. I hadn't wanted anyone owing me, but now two men had sealed a life debt.

"Aw, Max," I moaned, "why did you go and do that?"

"Because you saved me." He rose to his full height, his skin coppery skin seeming brighter compared to the white of our surroundings. "I accept debts when I owe them. And I know you will never misuse the debt."

"Still wish you hadn't done it."

"You can always absolve me later."

The wind-being swept an arm toward Notus. "To save this one, Janusite, you must demonstrate his worthiness."

"Me?" I stared at the prone figure in black robes and his ashen complexion. "How on earth do I do that?"

"You are not on Earth," she said with a hint of annoyance. Then she paused, as if to regain her composure, and continued in her serene tone. "You knew the mortal whose soul you wish to spare. Only you understand how to do this."

Great. Vague instructions for something I had no idea how to accomplish.

Nevan turned toward me, splaying a palm over my cheek. "You cared for Calder once, and he cared for you. Speak to him. You do not need magic, only your strong and good soul. If the man you knew is truly there, he will respond."

"I'll try."

"You will succeed."

"Because I'm the Janusite."

"No." He smiled, stroking my cheek with his thumb. "Because you are Lindsey Astrid Porter."

"I really love you, Nevan."

"And I love you." He stepped back. "Now save that man's soul, as only you can."

Only I could do it. He meant it as encouragement, that I would this my way, but I felt the burden of salvation for Calder's soul bearing down on my shoulders. The wind-being had told me only I could do this. If I failed, it was all on me.

"His weakness condemned him," Nevan said. "If he can be redeemed, you will succeed. If he cannot, you bear no responsibility."

Sometimes I swore he could read my mind.

But he was right. And I had to try.

To the wind-being, I said, "Will he be destroyed if I can't help him? The bullet was endued, but he was shot in the shoulder."

"Endued weapons always kill." She eyed Nevan, then returned her attention to me. "Unless there is extreme intervention, that is. Depending upon the location of the injury, death may come slowly or quickly, but it will come. And his body was already weak from the strain of housing three essences."

The body would perish. The soul might be saved.

Approaching Notus, I knelt beside him.

His bleary, mismatched eyes rolled up to look at me. Sweat dampened his gray skin, and blood stained his hands from his attempts to staunch the bleeding. His face was slack, and his arms had slid down to the floor.

I picked up one of his blood-stained hands. "Calder, I know you're in there."

His brows twitched faintly, as if he couldn't quite draw them together.

"You're dying," I said. "Nothing can stop it. You have a choice to make, between condemning your soul or saving it. I want to help you, but you have to help me do that."

His mouth opened, then closed. He pulled in a slow, rattling breath and tried once more to speak. "We are doomed."

"Cut the 'we' crap." Keeping his hand in mine, I leaned down to gaze into the Calder eye. "I know you can speak as individuals. You've done it before, when you took me prisoner and Calder came out to talk to me. Please, I need you to come out. This is your last chance."

"We…" He coughed, the sound wet and crackly. "Cannot."

"Yes you can." I grasped his face in both hands, staring hard into the eyes of this being, possessed by a powerful certainty I could find the man I'd once vowed to marry buried somewhere inside this creature. "I know you cared for me, Calder. I know you're a good man at heart. The forging brought out your weaknesses and messed with your head, turning you into a tortured, confused soul. That part of you is gone. You can become yourself again. Please try, please."

His mouth opened, his jaw quivered.

What more could I do to convince him? I glanced back at Nevan, and in his eyes I saw the answer.

"Please, Calder," I said, "give everyone who cares about you the peace of knowing you died with salvation. Travis loves you, he wants you to be safe. I care about you, and I can't stand to watch you die this way. Fight for you salvation, Calder. Do it for me."

I pressed my lips to his cold and clammy mouth. I held the kiss, willing him to see the truth and fight. The change was impossible to describe, impossible to pinpoint, but I sensed it happening. Something deep within him shifted.

Pulling back, I searched signs of the change.

The Calder eye, once the golden color of a monkey, roiled and altered. The pupil shrank, and the iris turned a very human shade of lustrous brown.

Tears stung my eyes. My throat grew thick, almost choked with the emotion surging up inside me. I recognized that eye. It belonged to the man I'd once wanted to share my life with, the man who'd made me laugh and made me feel wanted. The monkey-man had crumbled away, and the human had reasserted himself. Calder Blackwell had come home.

"Lindsey?" he said, his voice weak but familiar. His face might've looked like someone else, but I was hearing Calder's voice, complete with the Texas twang. He coughed and tried to lift his hand, but it dropped back to the floor. "Why are you here?"

"Don't you remember? You're dying."

"Meant why are you trying to save me." His cast his eyes downward. "After what I did to you…I killed a man, and I tried to kill you."

"You weren't yourself, I understand that now." I swiped away the tears that escaped my eyes, rolling down my cheeks. "The forging made you crazy. I'm not excusing what you did, but I believe you can redeem yourself."

Again, he struggled to lift his hand.

I clasped it in mine, holding our hands on his chest, over his heart.

"God, Lindsey." His own eyes teared up, the whites reddening. "I'm so sorry. What I did I can never take back, but it's almost like it was a dream. A nightmare. Can't believe I did those things."

"I know."

He grimaced, summoning enough strength to raise his other hand and brush his fingers over my cheek. "I love you, and I always will. I know you don't love me, but we had a good thing and I trashed it. Don't expect you to forgive me, won't ask for it. I just need you to know I'm sorry."

Tears streamed down my cheeks, my throat burned with a sharp pain, and I had trouble speaking at all. I bowed my head, and the tears dripped onto his face.

Despite everything he'd done after his forging, I believed him. Maybe it was crazy. Maybe I should've hated him. I couldn't, not anymore. His behavior after becoming an elemental shapeshifter had made me question whether our relationship had ever been real, and at last I knew the truth. He had cared for me.

Calder glanced at Nevan and managed a rueful laugh. "Hey, I'm glad you broke my neck. I deserved it."

"Yes," Nevan said, tall and stiff, his face unreadable, "at the time, you did."

"Take care of her," Calder said. "She deserves to be happy—and loved."

Nevan T's gaze veered to me, branding me with its intensity, and then he returned his focus to Calder. "As long as I live, Lindsey will never want for love."

Calder let his hand fall away from my cheek and settle atop our linked hands on his chest. "Tell Travis I'm sorry. I may not have shown it, but I was always grateful to have him for a big brother."

"I'll tell him."

"One more thing before I…go." He hesitated. "Don't feel sorry for me. Doesn't matter what happens to me now, all I care about is that you stop blaming yourself for what happened to me. I did this to myself. I wanted you, and that need turned into an obsession, to the point I was willing to kill you to keep you."

"The forging changed you, I know."

He sighed, his eyes closing briefly. "The seed was there before I died and turned into something else. Travis knows what I mean. He probably thinks he'll become like me, but tell him not to worry. He's stronger than I ever was, and a better man."

I couldn't speak. Had no idea what to say.

"Be happy, Lindsey," Calder said, "and have a good life. That's the only salvation I need."

I squeezed my eyes shut, but the tears leaked out anyway. My heart hurt for what we'd once had, but I'd done my grieving years ago. This was closure, for both of us.

His chest stopped rising and falling under our hands. His hands went limp around mine.

My eyes popped open, and I stared at the lifeless face of a dead man.

"Look," Max said.

I followed his gaze to a spot behind the group of wind-beings.

There, Calder stood tall and straight, wearing jeans and a T-shirt with cowboy boots covering his feet. His mouth spread into the boyish grin I remembered so well.

And then he was gone.

I jumped up. "Does that mean he's okay? His soul moved on to a good place?"

The female wind-being smiled with beatific grace. "You succeeded. The soul of Calder Blackwell has been redeemed and welcomed into eternal peace."

"Oh thank God." I slumped, swaying a little.

Nevan rushed to bolster me with his body, one strong arm around my shoulders.

The body on the floor twitched.

I startled, sidling closer to Nevan. "What was that?"

The wind-being floated closer to the body, regarding it with detached interest. "The other essences will attempt to revive the body."

Maybe saving Calder had made me mushy, but I had the sudden to impulse redeem a couple more souls. "Can I save them too? Nevan said Skeiron and Notus used to be good men."

"Indeed they were," the wind-being said, her spooky eyes zeroing in on me. "But they squandered that goodness of their own volition. They sought power in order to subjugate others, to enforce their own wills rather than serving their people justly. Calder Blackwell became corrupted by his forging, which amplified preexisting weakness. These two—" She gestured at the body. "—were not forged, but born as elementals. They had no excuse for their greed and lust for power."

I tilted my head up to meet Nevan's gaze. "I'm sorry."

"Don't be, love." His gaze darted to the body. "They sealed their own fates."

To the wind-being, I said, "Do what you have to do. Their powers should be locked up forever, where they can't do any harm to anyone."

"They shall be." She clasped her hands before her and lowered her head. "Let it be done."

Her airy friends gathered around the body, all bowing their hands and clasping their hands as she had done. Wind whipped around them, growing and roiling, lashing the women's hair around their faces and tearing at the dead sorcerer's clothing.

As the gale picked up speed, Nevan and I backed away to the doorway, and Max joined us there.

The sorcerer's robe billowed and flapped. The wind latched onto the fabric, ripping it asunder, but a dense fog rushed in to conceal the sight of his exposed flesh. Soon, the gale and the fog encompassed the wind-beings.

A gust ripped through the entire temple.

The wind snuffed out in a puff of fog, the clouds dissipating swiftly.

Both the body and the wind-beings were gone.

We lingered in the temple for a moment, silent and awestruck. What we'd experienced here seemed like a weird dream, but none of us could awaken from it. Finally, we exchanged uncertain glances and turned to leave.

The female wind-being popped up in front of us.

She looked at Nevan. "You wish to know why you were turned away the first time you came to us."

Nevan didn't move or blink, but arm around me tightened a fraction.

"You were worthy then," the wind-being said. "Shortly before you came to this temple, an oracle visited us. He foresaw your visit to the temple, as well as your bond with the Janusite and that you would need your powers to aid and protect her. We rejected your request for this reason and this reason alone. You have never been deemed unworthy in our eyes."

Though I wanted to know more about Nevan's previous visit to the temple, I had the feeling the wind-being wouldn't stick around much longer. So I asked the question that had plagued me for weeks.

"Why was I chosen to be the Janusite?"

Her lips formed a faint smile. "You must ask Janus."

She blinked out amid a puff of air.

I laid a hand on Nevan's chest. "What was she talking about? Why did you come here the first time?"

"When I visited this place before," he said, "I had already realized Skeiron would become a tyrant like Notus. And I saw but one way to be free of the madness."

My fingers crooked against his skin. "What way?"

"To be stripped of my powers and made human."

"Oh." I bit my lip. "You don't want that anymore?"

He tugged me closer, dipping his head to nuzzle my nose. "I don't care if I'm human or elemental, as long as I can be with you."

"I don't care which you are either. I want you, not your powers."

"And I want you, Lindsey, not your powers." He smirked, his eyes glittering with humor. "Though perhaps it's best I keep my powers for the time being, considering how much trouble you get into."

Max chuckled. "She is a challenging mistress."

I glanced at the spot where the sorcerer had died, and where Calder had been freed from damnation. "Ceara might still be out there."

"Better get home, then," Max said, "and make sure the bloody woman is gone for good."

We marched out the temple doors, headed back to our friends.

Chapter Twenty-Nine

T HE CLEARING STOOD EMPTY AND DARK, THE MOON HAVING SET IN preparation for sunrise. The first rays of dawn cast a meager light on the vicinity. I disengaged from Nevan, and the loss of his heat enhanced the chill of the predawn air, triggering a flurry of goose bumps. The chill stemmed from more than the air temperature, though. It came from deep inside me too, from a primal part of me that recognized the inherent wrongness of the scene around me.

"Where are they?" I asked, turning in a circle, squinting into the gloom.

Nevan scanned the area in full warrior mode, his body taut, his gaze narrowed and sharp, his mouth compressed.

Max, his body as taut and ready for battle as Nevan's, flexed his fingers and released a small burst of flames from the tips.

Kind of like cocking a gun, I supposed. I'd never seen him do that before, but then, I'd known him for barely a day. It felt like so much longer.

Nevan's gaze locked onto something on the ground, near the clearing's edge. He stalked toward the object, and I trailed behind him with unease shivering down my nerves.

This was wrong, all wrong.

He bent to nab the object. The sword glistened in the ever-increasing glow of sunrise, its blade cast in the pink and yellow shades of the burgeoning dawn.

"You gave that to Travis for safekeeping," I said. "He wouldn't ditch it."

"Here!" Max called from our left.

We hurried to him, arriving as Max rose and showed us the object seated in his palm.

He held my derringer.

Max ducked down to dive his hand into the grass. When he straightened, his fingers were damp with a dark liquid. With a shake of his hand and a puff of fire, he cleansed the stain from his skin.

"Blood," he said.

Nevan latched a protective arm around my waist. "Someone has attacked our friends. We must find them at once."

I snatched the gun from Max's hand. "It's Ceara, it has to be."

"I agree," Nevan said.

A storm of cracking and rustling erupted in the forest ahead of us.

Nevan removed his arm from my waist and gripped his sword in both hands, raised before him.

Max flexed his fingers again and emitted tiny flames, each like the pilot light on a gas stove, from their tips.

I checked the derringer's chambers, finding a fresh round snug inside each barrel. As the racket drew nearer and nearer, louder and louder, I raised the gun and sighted in on the vicinity of the noises.

Tris and Ennea barreled out of the forest, stumbling to a halt a few feet from us. Ennea grasped her belly with both hands and struggled to catch her breath, her face flushed from exertion. Tris, his cheeks just as red, bent to slap his palms on his thighs as he gasped for air and held up one finger in the universal gesture for *wait a damn minute, please.*

Nevan couldn't wait, evidently. He demanded, "Where is Travis?"

Hold up. Why were they breathless from running?

"Why didn't you zip here?" I asked. "Didn't think elementals ever sprinted."

"More like stampeding," Tris said, still breathing hard. He rose from his bent posture, though his shoulders stayed slumped. "Couldn't travel the usual way. She did something to us."

"She?" A shiver raced down my spine. "Ceara found you."

"Yeah, and that broad is pissed." Tris shoved a shaking hand through his red hair. "She hit us with some kinda spell, and wham, we couldn't do any magic. Had to skedaddle the mortal way. Totally humiliating."

"But how…" I looked to Nevan. "Her powers came from the sorcerer. Shouldn't they have gone bye-bye when he bit the dust?"

"Yes, they should have." Nevan lowered his sword to his side, the blade horizontal to the ground. "Ceara should be no more dangerous than a mortal."

"Then how—" A realization rushed through me. "The pendant she wears. The papyrus column amulet."

Nevan arched one brow. "Notus must have instilled his own magics within it, to enliven her stone body. The pendant connects them, which allowed her to absorb enough of his power to continue on and make use of his powers. We must vanquish her with an endued weapon."

Tris snorted. "Good luck, pal. The broad's wacko, threatened to wipe out all life in both worlds one by one to get back at Lindsey."

"Me?" I lodged one hand on my hip. "What'd I do that nobody else did?"

Nevan canted his head at me. "The sorcerer snapped her neck and took you away with him. He made it clear to her he always wanted you, above all others."

"Oh great. This is a supernatural cat fight." I bent my arm, the derringer aimed at the sky. "Fine. She wants to throw down with me, she'll get her wish."

Tris flapped his head wildly. "You can't do that. She'll take away your powers too."

Nevan puffed up, but not out of self-pride. He moved a touch closer to me and said, "Lindsey is the most powerful being in either world. More than that, she is the most intelligent and resourceful being I've ever met."

Wow. I loved it when he waxed complimentary about me.

"Thanks, honey," I said, patting the bulging bicep of his sword arm. I asked Tris, "Where did you guys go? And why?"

Both leprechauns looked sheepish, but Ennea spoke. "That broad tricked us. We heard you shouting for us, and we ran to help. Turned out it was Ceara doing a bang-up imitation."

Tris gave a sour laugh. "She oughta be doing Vegas, with impersonation skills like that."

"I'm sorry, Lindsey," Ennea said, her shoulders deflating and caving in toward her chest. "Ceara took Travis."

"Took him?" I said. "Where?"

She shrugged.

The five of us exchanged glances, none of us sure what to do next.

We got our answer anyway.

"Help me!" a male voice cried from further into the woods. "Lindsey! Help me, please, she's crazy."

The voice mimicked Travis's drawl and twang.

Ennea made a bewildered face. "Does the broad think we're so stupid we'll fall for the same trick again?"

"No," I said. "She doesn't care. She's taunting me."

Tris threw his hands up. "What the hell do we do?"

Nevan's watchful gaze, trained on me during this whole conversation, flared wide and then narrowed into slits. "No, Lindsey."

"Yes, Nevan." I closed my hand around his, the one gripping the sword. "It's the only way and you know it."

He sighed, his body deflating for a moment before he went taut and erect again, ever the ancient warrior.

"Uh, excuse me," Tris said. "What did we just decide?"

I answered. "We're sneaking up on the evil bitch, with me as bait."

Chapter Thirty

I TRACKED THE FALSE TRAVIS VOICE THROUGH THE WOODS UNTIL I reached a small waterfall that poured its waters into a small—but deep, judging from its color—pool at its base. The trees closed in around the pool and the cliff that formed the waterfall, leaving a narrow path around the periphery.

Nevan and Max prowled the forest behind me, somewhere, though I could neither see nor hear them. Ennea and Tris had gone back to her magic lab, against their complaints they didn't want to leave us. Without magic, they were too vulnerable.

Despite having two stealthy and powerful men as backup, I felt nothing close to secure. Ceara could've been hiding anywhere.

"Here I am," I called out. "Come and get me, you lifeless hunk of rock. I brought my hammer and chisel."

"Your attempts to goad me are wasted."

Ceara's smooth voice sounded behind me.

I turned around, poising my finger over the derringer's trigger, though I kept the gun aimed at the ground.

She stood a few feet away, at the pool's edge—with Travis.

He was on his knees, clothes and hair unkempt, dirt smudged on his face. Blood dribbled down from his scalp. He seemed unable to move, as if an invisible force bound him.

"Do not worry," Ceara said in her saccharine voice, "he will survive his current wounds. Whether he survives beyond this depends on you."

"What do you want, Ceara?"

She smiled with feral hunger. "Your powers, of course."

"Can't give them to you even if I wanted to. No idea how to do it."

"You will discover a way, given the proper motivation." She conjured a knife in her hand, turning it this way and that so its wide and long blade glinted in the light of the newly woken sun. "Do it, or I will end this mortal's life."

She held the blade to Travis's throat.

He made a disgusted face. "Don't do it, Lindsey."

I couldn't move, my thoughts a tangle of conflicting needs. I had to stop Ceara. I had to protect the people I cared about. I needed to end this now, with Ceara's destruction. But I couldn't let Travis die because of me.

"Do you bother to think," Ceara said, caressing Travis's throat with the blade, "how many have died in your name? Three young women, whose only crime was their resemblance to you. The man you were to wed, who became a monster because he longed to be with you forever. Two kings. And how many sylph soldiers, in the battle to dethrone Skeiron?"

I realized what she was doing, but that didn't lessen the blow of hearing the death toll recounted aloud.

Ceara smiled again, with a vicious edge to it. "Nevan almost lost his eternal soul because of you."

No, he'd almost died because her magical mashup of a boyfriend thought it would be fun to torture Nevan. And Ceara had helped the sorcerer do it. She wanted to shame me into giving up, but I'd had enough of this bullshit.

"Nice try," I said, "but I'm canceling my reservation at the guilt trip hotel."

I swung the derringer up and pulled the trigger.

The shot bounced off her.

Dammit. She had a personal ward, like the sorcerer.

And I had one bullet left.

Ceara's smile twisted into a nasty grin. She yanked Travis's head back and slashed the knife across his throat. Blood streamed from the wound as she let go of him, and his body crumpled, his head slumping over the pool's edge, his hair touching the water.

"No!"

I barreled toward Ceara, slamming into the wards that encased her, throwing both of us to the ground. The wards shoved me away, but I sprang forward to pin her to the ground. I pounded my fists on the barrier, and shockwaves of white magic erupted through the wards. Blue sparks exploded from my hands, punching into the wards like glittering steel spikes.

Ceara screamed, thrashing to get me off her.

I punched and punched and punched, hitting the wards over her chest, her stomach, and landing a wicked hit directly in her face.

The wards fractured.

Ceara shrieked, part anger and part terror. She lashed out with one foot, punting me in the knee. She slugged me in the shoulder, and the derringer popped out of my hand, flying through the air to splash down in the pool, sinking into the dark depths.

I punched her in the gut. "You fucking bitch!"

The breath exploded out of her.

"Lindsey!" Nevan's voice roared from the edge of the woods.

He was banging his fist and his sword on the solid wall of another ward.

Ceara hauled in a wheezing breath.

No time to think. I flung up one hand and conjured Nevan's sword.

My arm shook from the weight of it, but adrenaline gave me more strength than I'd known I could summon. I rose onto my knees, aimed the sword straight down, and drove it into Ceara's chest.

Blood coated her chest and soaked through her clothing. She let out a choked gasp and went limp, her eyes staring up but seeing nothing. She would never see anything again.

I wrenched the sword free of her flesh, wedged its tip on the ground, and heaved myself to my feet.

Her body hardened, her skin growing paler and smoother, her posture locked in the final moment of horrific awareness that she was dying.

My legs weak, I braced my body with the sword.

Ceara's body metamorphosed into stone, then crumbled into dust.

The wards crashed down, and Nevan and Max bolted toward me.

I dropped the sword and ran to Travis, falling to my knees beside him. His eyes were closed, his body limp. One hand dangled over the pool's edge, and the blood accumulated under his head oozed over the edge to drip onto the water. The droplets spread out in the water, carried away by the spinning current. I laid a hand on his back but detected no sign of life.

My eyes stung. I sucked in a breath through my nose, not wanting to cry. Not here, not now. We'd won the battle, saved the worlds. We couldn't lose one of our own. Dammit, this shouldn't have been happening.

Nevan knelt beside me, his arm coming around me.

"We have to save him," I said. "Must be a vortex around here somewhere, we have to find Tris—"

"No, love, it's too late." Nevan pulled me close, burying my face against his neck. "There are no healing vortexes on this side of the falls."

Over his shoulder, I glimpsed Max a few feet away. He watched us, lines tightening at the corners of his mouth and eyes. The flames at his fingertips had snuffed out.

Tris and Ennea appeared just behind him, at either side.

When their eyes fell on Travis, Ennea bit down on her lip and Tris scrunched his mouth.

"But we can take him through the portal," I said, my voice hitching and rising to a higher pitch. "Tris can heal him."

Nevan cradled the back of my head with his hand, murmuring to me with his cheek against mine. "He is gone, it's too late."

"But—"

"Shh." He kissed my temple. "You can't feel it, but the rest of us can. Ceara coated the blade that cut his throat with poisoned magic. Nothing can bring him back. I'm sorry, my love, I would do anything to spare you pain but there is nothing I can do. Nothing anyone can do."

Max cleared his throat. "Not entirely true."

I jerked my head up. "What? There's a way?"

The incubus aimed his steady gaze at the sylph, but spoke to me. "There is one way."

Nevan's jaw hardened, a muscle ticking there. "No."

I glanced from Nevan to Max and back again. "You have to tell me."

"Travis wouldn't want it," Nevan said gently. "He saw what became of his brother."

A shiver of understanding whispered over my skin. I scuttled backward on my knees, never taking my eyes off of Nevan. "You're talking about the forging."

"Yes." He ran a hand over his mouth. "But we cannot put him through it. I have never and will never forge another, you know this and you know why."

"But you and Max came through it fine."

Nevan stared at the swirling pool for a moment, his eyes half closed. When he faced me again, his eyes had taken on a haunted look. "I survived the forging with my sanity intact, but only by a hair. This is nothing I would inflict on another, no matter the situation."

"You wouldn't do it to save me."

His features hardened into a steely resolve. "No."

Though his answer should've warned me off this path, I couldn't accept it. Refused to believe it. Desperation obliterated reason, and all I could see was Travis lying dead on the ground in a pool of his own blood, murdered by an evil mirror image of my lover's dead wife.

If Max and Nevan could survive the forging intact...

My familiar told me he'd forged somebody once before.

He'd also sworn he would never do it again.

If I ordered him to do it...

Nevan grabbed my hands. "Do not do this, Lindsey."

"Calder was weak, Travis is strong. He can come through it okay."

"You can't know what will happen. The risk is too great. I will not do it."

Max strode toward us, crouching alongside me. "I will do it."

Nevan squinted at Max, forcing words out between his gritted teeth. "Don't encourage her. She is grieving and has no conception of what she asks."

"I know what's involved," Max said, his voice calm but his face pinched. "And I understand the consequences. If Lindsey wants this, I will do it."

"You would forge another without his consent?" Nevan sat back on his heels, his hands slipping free of mine. "I will not allow it."

My gaze wandered over the pool, the falls cascading into it, the foaming water that swirled in eddies. Nevan had lain beside a pool once, ages ago, dying and desperate to live. Notus had offered him a new life, but left out the details of becoming an immortal and an elemental. This world, the Unseen, was harsh and strange and unforgiving. Magic lurked in every nook and cranny of this realm, some of it benign, some deadly. How difficult would it be for Travis to learn the ins and outs of the Unseen?

I'd had six weeks to adjust, and I still didn't understand everything. Travis would be hindered by the forging, by a kind of change I couldn't fathom, a change that would alter him from the inside out and mold him into a different man.

Not a man. A salamander. An incubus.

Tears flowed down my cheeks, searing my eyes and moistening my skin. They dripped off my chin onto my hands. Could I really do this to another person? Without his permission? What gave me the right? Nevan swore he wouldn't even do it to spare my life, yet I was willing to force it on Travis, my oldest friend, my ally in these crazy supernatural battles, a hero in his own right. And I would destroy him, in hopes he'd be reconstituted into something I might recognize.

Oh God, what was I doing?

Sobs burst out of me, wracking my body. I flung my arms around myself, rocking as I wept and wept.

Nevan dragged me into his arms, frisking his hands up and down my back, murmuring wordlessly.

"Time is short," Max said. "If he's dead too long, even the forging won't bring him back."

My head on Nevan's shoulder, I waited a few more seconds until the sobbing faded. Then I swallowed, sniffed, and told Max, "We can't do this. It isn't right. We may have won the battle, but Ceara gets her revenge on me. She took away someone I care about."

Nevan stroked my hair, combing his fingers through the locks. "She has not won. Travis died for a good cause, for the safety of two worlds."

"I wish that were true." Pushing away from Nevan, I mopped my eyes dry with my shirt. "But he was held captive, couldn't move or fight. She tried to convince me all the deaths that have happened since we met are my fault. I denied it, but in this case she was right. Travis got lured into Ceara's trap because of me, and he died because of me. The blame for this death is squarely on my conscience."

"It was not your doing."

"Doesn't matter." I got to my feet, every muscle aching, my heart aching. "Travis would never have gotten involved in any of this insanity if he hadn't followed me. He was always trying to protect me. His death is my fault, and I have to live with that."

Nevan rose but didn't touch me.

Max stood too, glancing at Nevan. "You should take her away from here."

I balked. "We can't leave Travis lying there."

"Of course not," Max said. "I'll bring him back to the mortal world. You have my word."

"Thank you." Considering he owed me a life debt, my gratitude couldn't enact any kind of debt on my part. It only scratched the surface of the monumental debt he owed me. To Tris and Ennea, I said, "I appreciate your help. You're my allies and my friends, so if you need anything, all you have to do is ask. Okay?"

"Goes both ways," Tris said. "Like you said, we're friends."

Ennea nodded. "We're Team Lindsey."

I couldn't muster a smile. "See you later. Be safe."

They left in a blink.

At the instant Nevan whisked me away, my eyes met Max's and something flickered on his face. Regret? Determination? Dread? I had no time to puzzle it out before Nevan took me away.

We landed at our usual portal, the small pond in front of a burbling boulder. He moved his hand toward the water splashing up out of the rock, about to open the portal for us.

He froze, an odd look on his face.

"What is it?" I asked.

Muttering a curse in his ancient language, he threw an arm around me and teleported us back to the falls where we'd left Max. We wound up on the other side of the water from Max, where he stood beside Travis's body.

Max chanted in a language I'd never heard before, his voice infused with a rumbling intensity, and the sound of it skittered a cold prickling down my spine. This was a forbidden language, something inside me whispered. Where the idea had come from, I had no clue, yet I recognized the truth of it. No mere mortal was meant to hear the tongue Max spoke.

He raised his hands, palms out. Glowing, shimmering orbs sparked to life inside the forest—fairy lights, I recognized—and swarmed out to surround Max and Travis, sheathing them both in a cloak of glittering brilliance. The illumination intensified into a blinding whiteness.

I flung up an arm to shield my eyes. Energy crackled over my skin, the backwash of whatever Max was doing.

Nevan zipped to the other side of the pool. He tried to approach the mass of energy that engulfed Max and Travis, but every time he got close he flinched away. Nevan gave up and returned to my side.

"We should go," he said. "You do not want to see this."

"He's forging Travis, isn't he?"

"Yes."

When he reached for me, to take me away again, I shrugged away from his hands. "I'm staying. This is my fault, I have to see it through."

"Max decided to do this. You told him not to, which means it is not your fault."

"Don't you get it?" I twisted the hem of my shirt in my hands. "Max owes me his life. He thinks this is how he can repay me."

Someone screamed.

Not Max, I sensed that much. No, someone else. I shut my eyes, afraid to breathe or move.

Travis was screaming, from an agony I could never comprehend, as the forging tore him apart and remade him.

I forced my eyes open, focusing on Nevan and only Nevan. "Tell me what it's like, the forging."

He covered his face with his hands as the screaming went on and on.

"Tell me," I said, seizing his hands to tear them away from his face. I felt sick, I didn't want to know, but I had to know. "Please, Nevan."

His eyes shut, he told me. "The forging will rend his limbs, his mind, every particle of his body and soul, crushing and melting them. A power beyond imagining will reshape his form, and he will be born anew through the scalding agony. He might wish for death with his last coherent thought, before the pain and fire consume everything that made him human."

"Everything?"

"Only his soul and his memories will remain."

I collapsed to my knees, unable to process the information, unable to look at anything except the boiling, amorphous mass of supernatural energy on the other side of the pool.

The screaming cut off.

Nevan hauled me to my feet, one arm around me, ready to spirit me away.

The cloud of energy dissipated, revealing Max hunched beside a naked man who lay facedown in the dirt. Smoke, or maybe steam, wisped up from the coppery-skinned figure.

I gulped but couldn't dislodge the lump in my throat. My heart raced, my pulse thundering in my ears.

Travis lifted his head. His gaze zeroed in on me.

A soul-deep anguish wrenched my gut. His eyes had become burning red coals.

Max bent to lay a hand on Travis's shoulder, and they vanished.

CHAPTER THIRTY-ONE

IN THE DAYS FOLLOWING THE LONGEST DAY OF MY LIFE, THE DAY WE defeated the sorcerer, we did our best to tighten up the loose threads dangling in the wake of the sorcerer's vendetta. Three young women had died. Their families needed answers and closure, but we couldn't exactly tell them a sorcerer with multiple personalities had murdered their loved ones in order to torment me. With the sheriff missing, the undersheriff took over the investigation—and he knew nothing about the Unseen.

Although Nevan and I both hated it, we'd agreed he must enchant the acting sheriff and the medical examiner to convince them only one woman's body had been found behind the rock shop. Since Travis had kept the other two bodies under wraps, no one questioned the story the American girl had died of dehydration after getting lost in the woods.

Nevan had taken the other bodies back to the women's respective home countries. No one knew they'd wound up in Michigan, and their deaths were ruled accidental, due to dehydration.

We needed to explain Travis's disappearance too. Nevan and Max worked together to concoct a car accident that killed him and, thanks to a fiery explosion courtesy of Max, his body had been burned to ash. There had been a funeral, and I had cried as if Travis was actually dead.

Not dead, but gone. I hadn't seen him since his forging, though Max turned up at least twice a day every day to reassure me Travis was doing okay. The transition took time. That's what both Max and Nevan kept telling me.

We'd covered up everything. What a victory.

I felt sick every time I thought about it, but I understood we'd had no choice.

Seven days after the thwarted apocalypse, Tris waylaid me when I was getting out of my car in the shop's parking lot.

"You gotta take me over the boundary," he said. "Come on, Lindsey, I helped save the worlds twice. Don't I deserve a break?"

"We've been over this." I shut the car door, bracing my butt against it. "I have no idea if I can take anyone other than Nevan over the boundaries. I won't be responsible for your destruction."

"Your powers are way stronger now. Please?" His tone had turned wheedling. "If you're worried I'll rat on you about being the Janusite, I won't. You got my word."

"That's not what concerns me."

He raised his hands, palms together. "Please? I wanna meet a hot mortal chick, like Nevan did."

"A hot mortal chick?" I caught my lips between my teeth to stave off a laugh. "That's why you're so dead-set on crossing the boundary. To meet girls."

He shrugged.

"Tris, you're risking annihilation. You know, getting ripped apart molecule by molecule until nothing of you is left, except a thin cloud of atoms." I clapped my hands on his shoulders. "Why don't you find a nice elemental girl?"

The leprechaun made a whiny, groaning noise. "They're so boring. Even the busty little undine."

What could I say to that? The Unseen was far from boring in my estimation, but then I hadn't grown up over there. Maybe a compromise was the ticket.

"Tell you what," I said. "Let me practice my powers some more, and when I'm confident I can control them, I promise to take you over the boundary. Deal?"

"Awesome. It's a deal."

I could rest easy knowing I wasn't bound by magic to keep my word. When and if I felt confident in taking him over the boundary, I would do as I'd promised.

Tris left then, satisfied one day he might meet a hot mortal chick.

Although I'd absolved Nevan of his life debt to me, Max absolutely refused to me do the same for him. Three times I tried to do it anyway, and three times he absconded before I could finish. The next time I saw him, I ordered Max to stay put and tell me what his problem was. After grousing a bit, he sank into one of the chairs in the underground home I shared with Nevan and finally told me the truth.

"You may remember," he said, "I mentioned I forged someone once."

"Before Travis. Yeah, I remember."

He squirmed in the chair. "Her name was Aurelia. We had fallen in love before my forging, as humans, and a decade after my change I found her again. She was ill, dying from an incurable disease. I couldn't find a fae to heal her through a vortex, but I told her everything about me, about what I am. On her deathbed, she begged me to forge her so we could be together."

"What happened?" I asked.

"The forging was not kind to her." He leaned forward, elbows on his knees, and clutched his head in his hands. "It happened gradually, over many centuries. She went insane little by little, became a wild thing addicted to the sexual energies of any male she encountered. Many of her lovers were not willing. She used her powers to force them into wanting her, and many of them died from her attentions. She took more than she needed to survive, more than any being could give."

Jesus. I wanted to comfort him, but I had the feeling he wouldn't have accepted it. Instead, I asked, "What happened to her?"

He looked up at me through his spread fingers. "I bargained with the sorcerer to end her life. I became his slave to stop her. Three young women have died, and I am partly to blame for that."

"Max…" Nothing I might say seemed appropriate, so I let my words trail off.

"Don't you see?" he said. "I deserve to be enslaved. At least you're a compassionate mistress. Please let me keep this debt to you."

I relented then, unable to force him to relinquish something that made him feel he'd atoned in some measure for the sins he believed he'd committed. Later, when I understood him better, I could convince him to give up the debt. The fact he'd said "please," here in the Unseen realm, proved to me this was the right course.

"The debt stands," I said. "For the time being."

He rose shakily and teleported away.

On the tenth day, I was lounging in the home Nevan and I shared on my day off. With Ennea's help, Nevan had installed a TV that somehow received satellite signals from the mortal realm, letting me watch all my favorite shows in the secluded comfort of our underground lair. Nevan was spending a lot of time with the tribunal, this time around trying to mend the badly torn fences between king and traitorous tribunal. The old members had resigned, replaced by new members chosen for their diverse backgrounds. One was a high-ranking soldier in Nevan's army, another was a metalsmith, a third was an elder of the kingdom, and the fourth hailed from a family of sylph witches.

Yep, the sylphs had witches too.

Today I reclined on the red sofa Max had given me, my gaze aimed at the TV but not really seeing anything on the screen. When I glanced at the two clocks on the wall—an addition I'd brought to our home, with one clock for mortal time and a second for elemental time—they told me Nevan had left his latest tribunal meeting nearly three hours ago. Nevan had balked at the presence of clocks, but he'd finally accepted I'd never be cool with not knowing the time. The dual faces ensured I wouldn't be late to work.

And I'd know exactly how long Nevan had been gone.

The aftermath of the sorcerer's plot had lasting effects. I couldn't help getting a little anxious whenever Nevan met with the tribunal, even knowing it was a new and improved group. Every day, I worried a little less—but I didn't know if I'd ever stop worrying. About Nevan. About being the Janusite. About Travis.

The last time I'd seen him, seconds after the forging, he'd looked so...alien.

Why wouldn't Max give me details about Travis's condition? I deserved to know. For that matter, why wouldn't Nevan? He'd seen Travis since the forging.

I shut off the TV. No relaxation for me.

Pushing up off the cushy sofa, I began to pace the room with my hands linked behind my back and my gaze directed at the floor. Thoughts bounced around in my mind, a mishmash of fears that set acid to churning in my stomach.

"You're ruining my hard work again."

I yelped at the sound of Nevan's voice.

He'd materialized no more than an arm's length away, watching me with an amused little smile.

I poked him in the chest. "You scared the crap out of me."

"How could I do that," he said, moving closer, "when you can sense my approach?"

"Kind of distracted at the moment. Not sensing much of anything."

"Mm, yes, I can see how tense you are." He slid his hands down my arms, following them to my hands behind my back. Those large, muscular hands of his settled over mine, and he drew me snug against his body. "And you are ruining my hard work. I spent so much time convincing you to relax and stop restraining your emotions. But you've reverted."

"Not totally." I looped my arms around his neck, and his hands draped over my buttocks. "I won't be anxious if you vanish our clothes."

"Ah, darlin', I'd love to but not yet." He lifted me with his palms on my ass, raising me until our eyes were level. "What are you worrying about today?"

"You were gone an awfully long time."

"I had an errand to run after the tribunal meeting."

"Errand? Since when do you run errands?"

He skimmed one hand up my back and around to my breast, cupping it in his hot palm. "I'll explain later. What else are you fretting over?"

"The old tribunal aided and abetted the sorcerer."

"The newly convened tribunal has no connection to the old one. From now on, the tribunal will be restricted to its original function of mediating disputes and will stay out of the business of ruling the kingdom."

"Sure you can trust them?"

"Positive." He pecked a kiss on forehead. "You, my love, should know better than anyone how trustworthy the new tribunal is. You employed your lie detection spell on them, after all."

"Hmph." I threaded my fingers through his hair absently. "Just means they didn't lie when I interviewed them."

"Your paranoia is endearing but unnecessary." He scrutinized me for a moment, then asked, "What else?"

Even if I could've lied convincingly to him, I didn't want to deceive Nevan. "Can't stop thinking about Travis."

"He is doing well. As well as can be expected."

"Not super comforting." I wriggled out of his arms. "I want to see Travis."

Nevan groaned, a sound of frustration I knew all too well.

I planted my hands on my hips. "You really want to *Lindsey* me, don't you?"

"But I've learned it will do no good." Nevan scratched his jaw. "You are the most stubborn being I've ever met."

"And you're the king of evasion." I nailed him with my hardest stare. "What aren't you telling me?"

He placed his hands on my arms, frisking them up and down. "Leave it alone, please."

"You said the P-word. This must be really bad news you're trying your damnedest not to tell me."

Nevan glided his hands up to my shoulders. "You cannot see Travis, because he has expressly forbidden it."

Taken aback, I could do nothing except make huffy, gasping sounds. When I found my voice again, I managed only to stammer. "I—wha—that—no."

"It's true."

"He wouldn't say that."

"You must understand." Nevan squeezed my shoulders gently, his eyes full of love and understanding. "The forging is a brutal process that doesn't end with the physical transformation. One must adjust to a new existence with new powers."

"I get that, but—"

"Lindsey, he has become an incubus." Nevan slanted his head to bring our gazes nearer to each other, and his voice took on a grave tone. "Travis is experiencing urges he cannot yet control. Max will teach him how to cope, but the adjustment will take time. For now, he must stay away from females—especially you."

When Max had told me what he was, I'd called him a sex demon. He'd scoffed at the demon part, but then he'd been born an incubus. Travis underwent a massive and agonizing transformation to become a completely different kind of being. The human version of him died, and he was reborn a salamander. An incubus. A being who thrived on sexual energy.

A being who needed sex to survive.

Max had flirted with me in the beginning, even making a minor attempt to seduce me away from Nevan. When I'd called him on it, he'd said seduction was an innate instinct for him. He couldn't help it. If he hadn't learned to control his urges...

My scalp prickled. Did I really want to find out what uncontrolled incubus urges looked like?

Nevan brushed hair from my face, tucking it behind my ear. "You understand, I can see it in your eyes."

"You said he can't see women, but especially not me."

"He is in love with you," Nevan said. "Travis admits he has not yet moved past his feelings for you, though he understands you don't love him in that way. But his incubus urges will have enhanced his physical reaction to you, and they might drive him to, ah..."

"You think he'd attack me?"

Nevan cradled my face in one hand. "That is his greatest fear at the moment. Give him time, and he will want to see you again."

I nodded, clamping my bottom lip between my teeth.

He pulled me into his arms.

After a moment of blissful intimacy, I propped my chin on his chest to gaze up at him. "You haven't told me about your errand."

"Later, when the time is right."

I let him lead me to the bed, knowing he would make love to me and banish all my worries with the exquisite pleasure of our joining. Afterward, my fears would resurface—but for this precious time with him, I would enjoy the bliss of forgetfulness.

He settled me onto the plush bed, our clothes suddenly gone, and pressed his warm, soft lips to my throat. I sighed my pleasure, my body melting. He kissed his way down my throat, tracing my collarbone to my ribs, dragging his mouth lower and lower until his hair tickled my breasts. Just as he shifted his head, opening his mouth to seal it over one nipple, I laid a staying hand on his cheek.

"What is it?" he asked, his brows adorably crinkled.

"I love you, with all of my heart and soul, and I never want to be without you."

His dark brows cinched tight, rising over the bridge of his nose. "I love you, Lindsey, you know this. What is it you truly want to say?"

"Do you remember the conversation we had right after Ceara showed up, before we knew she was working with the sorcerer? I wondered if you were tempted to go with her, to have an immortal queen."

Nevan levered up on straight arms, appraising me with a tight expression. "I told you, I have no wish to be with anyone but you."

"I'm not sure you've really thought about the consequences." I folded my arms over my breasts, oddly self-conscious all of a sudden. "You love me as much as I love you, and I know from experience how devastated

I'd be if something happened to you. I don't want to be the cause of your suffering."

He bent his arms, dipping his head to feather a kiss on my lips. "Nothing will happen to you. I will not allow it."

"But one day I will die. I'm a mortal, Nevan. You can't stop the natural course of life and death."

"We've had this discussion before." He dropped onto his side next to me, one hand spread over my belly. "I will take whatever time I have with you and be grateful for it. Believe me when I say I have watched many I cared for die, even immortals. We have no guarantees. I want my life to be with you, for as long as the fates allow."

I diverted my gaze to the ceiling, following the lines in the grain of the stone.

Nevan placed a hand on my cheek and turned my face toward him. "Do you believe me, love?"

"Yes. I believe you." Of course I did. He wouldn't lie about this, and he was right. An immortal could die. Death wasn't the exclusive domain of humans. "I'll take you for as long as I can have you."

His hand on my belly drifted lower, moving in circles over my womb. "There is a chance we've created a child."

Oh damn. With all the chaos surrounding the murders and Travis's disappearance, I'd forgotten to tell Nevan. "I'm not pregnant. I had my period last week, which means no little sylph on the way."

"You're certain?"

"Uh-huh." I slapped my fingers lightly on his chest. "I explained the menstrual cycle to you weeks ago, when you wanted to have sex and I said 'not tonight, I've got cramps.' You were going to pout all night if I hadn't explained."

He focused on his own hand drawing patterns on my belly.

I tapped his chin. "Are you disappointed?"

Though he stilled his hand, he kept gazing at my lower abdomen. "It's for the best, given the dangers involved in a mortal bearing a hybrid child. But I must admit, I looked forward to creating a new life with you."

"Me too."

His head came up, his swirling eyes incandescent in the gentle glow of the house lighting. "You wished to have a child with me?"

"Yes, you silly boots. I love you, and I would love to make a family with you."

For the first time since I'd known him—and, I suspected, the first time ever in his millennia-long existence—Nevan got choked up. Not the way I would, of course. Being a manly sylph-man, he pinched the bridge of his nose and squeezed his eyes shut, determined to stave off the tears glistening in them. He took a few stuttering breaths, his head down, then rubbed his eyes with the heel of his hand.

"Wow," I said, ruffling his hair. "Never seen you so emotional before."

His clear eyes met mine. "Never before have I envisioned a future of true happiness."

"I'm happy too." Laying a hand over his on my belly, I couldn't tear my gaze away from his, away from the depth of emotion sparkling in his eyes. I also couldn't stop myself from saying, "About this errand of yours…"

A glorious smile enlivened his face, lending him a younger and more innocent air, sweeping away the pain of past losses. "Perhaps this is the right time."

"For what?"

"You shall see." In the actual blink of an eye, he repositioned us with him on his back and me seated astride him. "Close your eyes."

"Why?"

"Because you adore and trust me."

I grinned. "Do I?"

"Yes." He gave my rump a playful slap. "Eyes closed, or I'll make you wait another day or two to find out what my errand entailed."

"Playing on my impatience. That's a dirty trick."

"You know full well how many dirty tricks I have at my disposal."

I closed my eyes, hands on my thighs.

He skated a hand up my inner thigh. "You may look."

My lids fluttered open, and I giggled. Seriously, I giggled. It was all his fault, because he held up a small jewelry box with its lid flipped up to reveal the diamond ring seated within the velvet interior.

He took hold of my left hand, raising it between us. "Lindsey Astrid Porter, my sweet and precious love, will you marry me?"

"Yes." I lunged down to shower kisses over his face. "Yes, yes, yes."

Nevan laughed. "I've never heard you say yes with such fervor except when I'm inside you."

Hands flat on his chest, I grinned down at him. "You will be in a minute."

"Indeed I will." He wagged the box at me. "Your finger, if you will."

Proffering my hand, the appropriate finger extended, I giggled some more as he slid the ring into place. He tossed the box aside. It hit the floor with a soft thunk.

A hard object prodded my belly.

I glanced down at his erection. "Ready to go, eh?"

"For you, always." He thrust a hand between my thighs, feeling the slickness there. "You seem ready as well, in record time."

"I got wet the second you asked me to close my eyes. I was expecting a sexy surprise, though." I rocked my hips as he stroked my sex, setting off a wave of liquid heat and burning need. "Oh, Nevan…oh yes."

His eyes had gone hooded, his breaths heavy. "Your sexy surprise is still to come. As are you."

I let my head fall back, riding his hand, gasping when his thumb found my rigid nub and rubbed it in vigorous strokes. One of his long fingers plunged inside me. I rose up on my knees, moaning and pumping my hips to make his finger thrust in and out of my depths. The pleasure of my climax hit me hard and fast, my body milking his finger like it never wanted to let him go, even as his thumb get rubbing. I doubled over, my hands on his chest and my fingers digging into his flesh as the spasms of my orgasm subsided.

Nevan withdrew his hand and gave me his most devilish smile. "Your move, my love."

"Which of my moves do you want this time?"

He opened his mouth, but I silenced him with a finger on his lips. "Never mind. I'll surprise you."

I took hold of his shaft, positioning it with the head at my opening, and impaled myself on his engorged length. He hissed out a breath and secured my hips with his hands. I clapped my palms on his chest, bent forward with my breasts dangling above him, and began to move. The delicious sensation of his hardness gliding through my slick, inflamed sex had me moaning again and grinding my body into his, craving the deepest connection imaginable.

He surged his head up to capture my nipple and suckle it.

Pure ecstasy. Hot and molten and firing down every nerve.

"Oh, Nevan." I bent lower to grant him better access to my breast and moaned yet again as he took the entire areola and nipple into his greedy mouth. His tongue laved the rigid tip, his teeth nipped at my flesh. "Oh God, yes. I love the way you feel inside me, I love you so much."

Poof. I lay on my back with Nevan stretched atop my body, his weight a wonderful pressure as he thrust deep and slow, over and over, his shaft gliding out and driving back inside me until I was writhing under him, shoving my fingers into his hair, ravishing his mouth with a kiss of mind-altering passion. Our tongues lashed each other, our bodies moved together, our souls merged.

I locked my legs around him.

"Lindsey," he growled into my ear, thrusting harder and faster, "I love you more than life."

He pounded into me, bouncing us both on the bed, his knees wedged into the mattress to give him incredible leverage. I came again, screaming with the abandon of a woman being loved by the only man I ever wanted to love. My fiancé. My soul mate. My Nevan.

With a feral cry, he succumbed to his own release, his shaft pulsing inside me. After two more powerful thrusts, he collapsed on top of me, spent.

I laced my fingers through his hair, his head on my chest. "No rude unleashing of sperm this time, hey?"

"Did you want me to?"

"Not right now. We need to understand what an elemental-human pregnancy means for us before we go that route." I kissed the top of his head. "We'll find a way, though. After all, we are two pigheaded people."

"That we are." He rolled off me, tucking me against his side with one arm around my shoulders. "We've earned a good night's sleep."

"Mm, yes." I cuddled into him, one arm across his body. "I'd love to sleep with my fiancé."

There, ensconced in his arms, I realized a truth I'd doubted since the moment I met Nevan. We belonged together. Not as the Janusite and her protector, but as Lindsey and Nevan. I belonged with him, and he belonged with me.

I couldn't wait to marry him.

Chapter Thirty-Two

A FEW DAYS LATER, NEVAN STOPPED BY THE SHOP DURING MY SHIFT. HE was dressed in his human-friendly attire and had altered his appearance into a mortalesque version of his true self, as he always did when consorting with humans in the mortal realm. Despite his toned-down body and his human eyes, he took my breath away.

I trotted out from behind the counter, seized his hands, and bobbed up on my tiptoes to kiss him. "Hi, honey."

He smiled. "Hello, darlin'."

We strolled hand in hand down the nearest row of wooden bins, each filled to the brim with various types of rocks. At the bin of moonstone, Nevan stopped us.

He picked up a polished rock. "Do you recall what this stone signifies?"

During our early acquaintance, he'd told me the answer. "Love and passion."

"I should make you a necklace of these," he said, rotating the stone in his palm, "to remind you of how much I adore and desire you."

"Don't need a rock for that. Speaking of rocks…" I dug in my pocket, pulling out the soul stone. "Been meaning to ask you. This thing seems to have stopped working."

He plucked it from my fingers. "Because you purged it when you restored my soul. I can recharge the stone, if you like."

"Not necessary." I leaned into his side, nestling my head against his shoulder. "Got my own way into our house, and I don't need a stone to remind me we belong together."

Nevan hooked his arm around my waist. "Neither do I."

We lingered there, relishing the comfort of each other, for several minutes. Tourists wandered by, ignoring us. Stan caught sight of us, but he only smiled and rolled his eyes. We'd told everyone about our engagement, and the planning had begun for our wedding. Yep, we were going to have a real, mortal-style wedding. My mom insisted on it.

She'd threatened to shoot us, actually, if we denied her the privilege of harassing her only daughter and her future son-in-law about cakes and napkins and table settings.

The guest list would be limited, since Nevan wanted to recite his vows while in his native form. I concurred with that decision. I'd met and fallen in love with him as a sylph, and I was proud to marry my half-naked, bronze-skinned, swirling-eyed king from the Unseen realm.

"I talked to my mom this morning," I said. "There's a bit of a hitch in your let's-get-married-quick plan. My mom really wants to spend the week before the wedding with us, getting the final prep done. But Ash can't get off school until Thanksgiving break."

"And that would be when?"

"Late November." I tilted my head back to peek up at him. "Can you wait two months?"

"Your brother must be here, and I wouldn't wish to disappoint your mother. Of course we will wait." He gave me a quick squeeze and winked. "As long as I don't have to wait until our wedding night to make love to you again."

"Oh God no. I couldn't possibly wait that long."

"Glad to hear it." The playful gleam faded from his eyes, and he stepped back to face me, holding my hands in his. "I did interrupt your work day for a reason."

"What's that?"

"Travis wants to see you."

Something like eager dread rippled through me. I wanted to see him, but it had been only a couple weeks since his forging. "Are you sure he's ready?"

"Max assures me Travis can handle a brief meeting." Nevan stroked his hand over mine, warming my skin. "Both I and your familiar will be present in case of…mishaps. You can deliver your message from Calder without undue risk."

A sylph and a salamander as my guardians. No girl could've asked for more.

I glanced at the clock on the wall, above the checkout counter. "It's almost my lunch break. Let's see if Stan minds me leaving a little early."

Nevan trailed me back to the counter, waiting there while I ducked into Stan's office to inform him of my early departure for lunch. He grunted and shrugged, his way of saying it was A-okay with him.

When I returned to Nevan, the shop was vacant. He wrapped an arm around me and whisked us away to the falls, carried me through the water, and ushered me through the portal into the Unseen. He spared a moment to dry our clothes with a flick of his wrist, then zipped us to our destination.

I took in the surroundings—a short waterfall cascading into a deep, if small, pool hemmed in by the forest.

Stumbling backward a step, I grabbed for Nevan's hand. "Is this…"

"The place where he died and was reborn."

My gaze flew to the spot where I'd driven an endued sword into Ceara's chest. A dark stain on the earth snagged my attention. The blood stain. Where Travis had died.

"Easy," Nevan said. "You must be calm when he arrives."

I nodded, taking a deep breath to cleanse my psyche of the memories. Concentrating on Nevan helped, and I took several more long breaths.

"Are you prepared?" he asked.

"Yes. I'm ready." Was I? How could I answer the question with any certainty? I'd never met a newly forged…anything.

Nevan whistled.

Max appeared first, naked as he preferred. He muttered something I couldn't make out, and another figure materialized beside him.

I choked back a gasp, determined not to expose my shock.

Travis…Well, he resembled the man I'd known, but his hair had darkened to a glistening ebony and his skin bore the same coloring as Max's, tanned but tinged with a coppery sheen. His muscular physique had expanded, and he'd grown several inches taller. The forging had remade him into a mountain of masculine power rivaling both Max and Nevan. Unlike those two, however, Travis wore a pair of jeans that fit his new body like a glove. Max or Nevan must've conjured those for him, or else he'd learned that trick already.

But his eyes. Christ, those eyes. They flamed bright red, with yellow and orange tentacles spinning within the fiery color.

Travis's gaze snapped to me, and his eyes erupted with pure white fireworks. Lips parted, he stared at me with the intensity of a starved man presented with a steak dinner he couldn't quite reach.

I fought the urge to back up closer to Nevan. Strength and calmness, that's what I needed to portray for my friend, the man who'd died in defense of me.

Rolling my shoulders back, I managed a smile. "Hi, Travis."

He flinched, averting his gaze. "Lindsey."

His voice was gravelly, as if his throat was parched.

I clasped my hands in front of me, trying for a nonchalant pose. "It's good to see you. Max says you've been doing okay with the, uh, adjustment. Are you feeling better?"

He nodded once.

What was I supposed say now? I had no idea.

Travis's gaze reeled back to me. His lips worked, as if he struggled to form the right words. "I—am sorry."

"For what?"

"Everything. I—harassed you for—three years."

Like I cared about that anymore. He'd believed I killed his brother, but he'd followed me from Texas to Michigan in a misguided effort to protect me.

"All in the past," I assured him. "Forget it. Besides, you've proved what kind of man you really are, fighting alongside the rest of us and—" I'd almost said *giving your life for me.* Not the way to maintain a calm atmosphere. "Well, the point is you've made up for any past transgressions."

His attention zeroed in on left hand, and his eyes widened.

I covered the ring with my other hand.

"Married?" he asked.

"Not yet. Engaged."

His lips twitched into a near smile. "Congratulations."

Not awkward at all, no sir. "Uh, I appreciate that."

Travis glanced at the blood stain on the ground and his lips flattened. "Should've died."

"I'm really glad you didn't."

"But Calder." Travis covered his eyes with his hand. "He turned into—a monster."

"You won't."

"Don't know that."

The pain in his voice made my chest ache. Oh, to hell with this standing idly by nonsense. I couldn't watch my friend agonizing over what he'd become without doing something.

I took a step.

Nevan laid a hand on my arm.

Glancing back, I said, "I have to do this. Trust me."

He withdrew his hand.

I walked straight up to Travis and took his face in my hands.

Travis went rigid, his eye unblinking.

"You are not Calder," I said. "He was weak and gave in to the lure of power. Still, in the end he realized what he'd done and he atoned for it."

Travis shook his head—or tried to, but my hands stayed him.

"Calder gave me a message for you." I boosted myself up on my toes. "He said to tell you he's sorry, and he's grateful he got to have you for a brother. He also said not to worry, because you're stronger than he ever was and you're a better man too. You will never become like him."

Travis swallowed visibly, his face wrenched with a myriad of emotions.

I felt for him, more than I could ever have explained. Turned into an incubus, forced to deal with powers and instincts he didn't understand and couldn't control. I could relate to having uncontrolled powers.

"You are my friend," I told him, "and I will never give up on you."

He closed his eyes, struggling to control his erratic breathing.

I let my hands fall to my sides as I backed away a little. "You'll be fine. I believe in you."

Max cleared his throat to gain my attention. "We should go."

He indicated Travis's pants with a motion of his eyes.

That's when I noticed the growing bulge inside Travis's jeans. *Oh lord.* He couldn't control it, but this seemed like the appropriate time to split.

I returned to Nevan's side.

Max told me, "There will be more visits in future. It's good for him to test his willpower. A salamander needs a great deal of it."

Travis and Max disappeared.

Nevan took me back to the mortal world, but not back to the shop just yet. I had more than forty minutes of my lunch break left. We ambled past the healing vortex, with its stone benches, and veered off the path to head for my favorite secluded spot. I used to eat lunch here every day to avoid other people, and I'd had my first real conversation with Nevan here, under the bows of a maple tree.

We sat down beneath that same tree, side by side, nestled against each other with my head on his shoulder and his arm around me.

A man appeared before us.

Nevan and I both jumped.

I gaped at the visitor, speechless at the sight of him. "Bob?"

The oracle I'd thought was dead grasped the lapels of his navy blue suit, the one that appeared tailored exclusively for him. The sun made his gray hair seem lighter and glinted off his bright green eyes. They once again glowed with an eerie light, the same shade as the illumination in the creepy dark forest.

I scrambled to my feet, kneeing Nevan in the gut in the process. He didn't seem to feel it, or maybe he was too shocked by our visitor.

"How are you alive?" I asked, my wonder evident in my voice. "I watched Ceara plunge a sword through you. Why aren't you dead?"

"Told you before, I've moved beyond all designations." He moseyed over to a tree to lean against it. "The sword wound took me out of commission for a while, but I'm back."

Nevan sprang to his feet. "Why have you sought us?"

"Got a couple messages for you two."

I sidled up to Nevan, and he looped an arm around my waist. What messages could be so important the oracle would set foot in the mortal world to deliver them? I flattened a hand over my stomach, suddenly queasy.

Bob smiled up at the sun. "First, you can stop fretting about whether you and Nevan will ever conceive a child. You'll have several."

"How? A hybrid pregnancy is dangerous."

The oracle chuckled, his smile broadening. "Have faith, Lindsey. A way will present itself."

He'd called me by name. Back in his lair, he'd called me "Janusite" or "mortal." Might he have decided he liked me? What would it mean if he had?

"Oh dearie," Bob said, giving me an empathetic look, "you worry about everything, don't you?"

Nevan piped up. "She does."

I elbowed him gently in the side.

He smirked.

"Yes," Bob said, "I like you, child. You have spirit and courage."

Though I appreciated the words, I restrained myself from thanking him. We might've been in the mortal world, but for all I knew he carried the magic of the Unseen with him wherever he went. Better not to risk it.

"What's the other message?" I asked.

"Trust in Janus."

"Um…Not to sound ungrateful, but what the heck does that mean?"

Bob smiled, tapped his head, and vanished.

I stared at the place where he'd stood, flummoxed like never before. "Ohhh-kay. I'm clearly not enlightened enough to understand that one."

"Neither am I," Nevan said. "But we'll concern ourselves with that later."

He scooped me up and poofed us back to where we'd been sitting before the oracle arrived. This time around, I perched on his lap with my legs outstretched and my arms around his neck.

"Hungry?" Nevan asked.

"Well, it is my lunch break. So yes, I'm hungry."

"Since I had no time to cook you a sumptuous meal, I'll conjure one instead." He held out his free hand, palm up, fingers spread.

A takeout pizza box poofed into his hand.

I laughed. "You could conjure anything you want, and you chose pizza?"

He set the box across my lap. "You enjoy pizza. This one has extra cheese, the way you like it."

"You are hands down the awesomest fiancé ever." I kissed his cheek. "I love living with you, and I can't wait to marry you."

"But you'll have to wait." He flipped the pizza box open and extracted one gooey slice, the cheese stretching beneath it. "Can you survive two months until we wed?"

I opened my mouth as he held the slice of pizza for me to bite. My teeth sank through the crispy crust, and I tore off a mouthful. "Maybe I can talk my mom into a shorter prep time and less planning. We don't need a big-deal wedding. Just you and me—and our friends and my family."

"That's all we ever need."

As usual, he was right. I couldn't have done better than to find a man who loved me and my incessant questions, who adored my stubbornness and my family, a man who taught me to embrace my passions and find my courage.

Let the future unfold as it would. I had everything I needed right here.

After the Fires

Nevan and I strolled hand in hand along the shores of Lake Superior, admiring each other a lot more than the scenery. Gentle waves lapped at the sand, and a soft breeze tickled our skin. After two weeks of being engaged, we hadn't quite adjusted yet. We kept gazing dreamily at each other or ripping each other's clothes off to "celebrate." Though it was now October in Michigan and the weather had turned brisk, the air around us remained temperate. Nevan had created a bubble of summer that enveloped only us.

The sunshine was all natural.

I couldn't stop looking at my engagement ring. Every time I lifted my hand to study it, the sun glinted on the facets and my heartbeat sped up. Sure, I'd been engaged once before—to a man who clicked the opt-in button for becoming a creepy monkey-thing. This time, I'd said yes to the right guy. My hot sylph. My Nevan.

Life was perfect.

Nevan brought us to a halt and moved to face me. He clasped both my hands in his larger, hotter ones. "Lindsey, there is something I must ask you."

"Uh-oh. Is another bad guy we vanquished coming back for more?"

"No." He smiled a teeny bit, just enough to crinkle the skin around his eyes. "This is a far more serious question."

"Shoot."

"What does a mortal wedding entail?"

I laughed. "That's your urgent question? Jeez, I thought you were about to tell me you still have some of that ooky Anti-Nevan crap inside you."

"The ook is completely gone." He pulled me closer, folding our hands on his chest. "I want you to have the wedding you deserve, the one you've dreamed of. But you'll need to explain to me what that involves. I was married once, literal lifetimes ago, and the ceremony consisted of Ceara and I standing inside a tent and nodding our heads in agreement when the priest asked if we consented to the marriage."

"Wow, so romantic."

"The marriage was arranged, not borne out of love." He wrapped his arms around me, bending his head to bump my nose with his. "This time, I am wedding the only woman I have ever loved. I want this to be done right. Please help me."

"You're lucky we're in my world or you would've just indebted yourself to me."

"I would gladly owe you anything, but all I need is for you to explain mortal weddings to me."

"Okay, but it's not like I'm an expert." I glanced at the diamond glittering on my left hand. "You got the ring part right."

"Your mother assisted me with that. I need your help for the rest. Please."

"Stop begging. You know how hot it gets me."

He stepped back, robbing me of his arms and his body and the delicious scent of him. "I am listening."

Oh great, I was supposed to explain weddings to a man who had lived in another world for thousands of years. He'd assured me elementals did marry, but they had something called handfasting rather than a formal ceremony. Since I'd never had a wedding, never even got to the planning phase before, I wondered how I was supposed to instruct Nevan in the ins and outs of marriage ceremonies.

I crossed my arms over my chest and tapped my chin. "Well, I know there's a dress. That's very important."

"Why must I wear a dress?"

A poorly repressed laugh snorted out of me. "Not you, silly. Me. I have to buy a fabulous dress that will knock your socks off."

"I don't wear socks."

"Why are you teasing me? You're the one who insisted you had to know all the details of a mortal wedding." When he opened his mouth to speak, I held up a hand. "Never mind, moving on. Oh, you will not see the dress until I walk down the aisle on our wedding day."

"I see. What else?"

What else indeed. I racked my brain for an answer, but all I came up with was things I'd seen in romantic movies. Oh well, that would have to do.

"Flowers," I said. "That's a biggie, I guess. Not that I care about schlepping down the aisle with a clump of roses in my hands. Anyway, there must be bridesmaids and groomsmen too."

Nevan tipped his head to the side, his brows squished together. "You need women to clean this aisle down which you must walk? What do stable boys have to do with a wedding? Will there be horses involved?"

He wasn't teasing this time. The genuine confusion on his face was unbelievably cute.

"No, honey, you're being too literal," I said. "Bridesmaids are women who stand by me at the altar, kind of like backup in case you try to bolt. They'll tackle you and chain you to the altar so you can't get away from me."

"Chain me?" He jerked his head up and snapped his shoulders back. "I will not bolt, Lindsey. Bridesmaids are not necessary."

I snickered. Couldn't help it. "You are so easy to mess with. I'm kidding about what bridesmaids do. They stand there and look pretty, that's all."

Nevan relaxed. "You've had your revenge for my teasing. I deserved it."

"You know I don't do revenge, but you should also know better than to expect I won't tease you right back."

"Indeed I do." He moved closer, slipping an arm around my waist. "Continue your explanation of weddings."

"First of all, groomsmen are not stable boys. They're like bridesmaids, but they're men."

"They stand about looking pretty?"

"Yep." I tapped his chest. "You'll need a best man too. That means one groomsman who is your closest friend."

Nevan started us walking again. "You are my closest friend."

"I can't be your best man and your bride. You'll have to pick somebody else to be your second-closest friend."

"Ah, I see."

After several minutes of quiet walking, while we enjoyed the pleasure of simply being together, Nevan asked, "Do you believe Bob is correct about a way presenting itself?"

"Sure. He's an oracle after all."

"What do you think the way will be?"

"Not a clue." I rested my head in the hollow of his shoulder, sliding my arm around him. "I believe we will have a family someday."

"As do I." He kissed the top of my head. "We love each other far too much for this union not to result in children."

I cuddled up to him even more, loving the firmness and heat of his body and the safety of his arm around me.

"Continue," he said. "Tell me more about mortal weddings. I know of dresses and flowers, as well as groomsmen and bridesmaids."

What else was there? Tucked up against Nevan, I found my body and mind both relaxing to the point I couldn't focus on anything. "Um, there's the bachelor party and bachelorette party, I guess."

"Parties? I believe I can handle that mortal tradition."

"The bachelor party is for the groom and his male friends only, and the bachelorette party is strictly for the bride and her lady friends." I lifted my head to aim a teasing smile at him. "There are usually strippers involved. You know, dancers who remove their clothes. So if you're going to have stripper, then I should get one too. I could have Max do it."

He pulled us up short and grasped my shoulders. "You will not have your familiar perform a dance during which he removes clothing."

"Max walks around naked all the time."

Nevan's jaw tensed, making a muscle jump. "I am aware of that."

I prodded his chest with my fist. "Relax, I don't want to see any man other than you strip for me."

He sighed out his irritation, his body slackening. "I do not wish to observe the disrobing of any woman other than you."

"Good. No bachelor or bachelorette parties." I skimmed my hands up and down his chest. "Never liked that tradition, anyway."

Nevan took my hand and led me down the beach.

"There's one more thing," I said. "We won't be having sex the night before the wedding. We will sleep in separate places."

His mouth contorted in irritation. "Are you certain that's necessary?"

"Positive." I hooked my arm under his. "You wanted to give me a traditional mortal wedding. No sex the night before is a must."

Nevan groaned. "I truly will do anything for you."

FOUR WEEKS AFTER

"Come on," Tris whined. "You promised. I almost died helping you and Nevan stop his wacko ex-wife and that mook she hooked up with. Don't I deserve a reward? Besides, eighteen days ago you promised you'd do it if I stopped razzing Nev about the wedding. I stopped, didn't I?"

"Yeah, sure you did." Standing behind the sales counter in the shop, I paused in the middle of sorting through the summer's sales receipts. The shop had closed for the season a month ago, but Stan insisted I double check all receipts and compare them with what was in the accounting software. After that, we would both conduct an inventory check. Joy of joys. "Look, Tris, I'm kind of busy today."

"It won't take long."

Despite his complaints, I couldn't be annoyed with Tris. The leprechaun and his sister had proved vital to the downfall of Ceara and the sorcerer. And yes, I had promised to give him what he wanted. Of course, I hadn't really believed he would stop haranguing Nevan. Tris loved making jibes about the things Nevan still didn't quite get about mortal weddings. My mom had mentioned "something old, something new, something borrowed, something blue," and my husband-to-be had been completely flummoxed. Though I'd assured him we could forget that silly tradition, he remained harried by the whole process.

And Tris took advantage of that, ribbing Nevan as often as possible. "Better paint your face blue," he'd told my sylph, "cuz that's what they mean by something blue. I think ultramarine is your color."

I gave up on the receipts. "You're right. I did promise. But I do have work, so I can't take off with you today. Maybe tomorrow."

Nevan poofed in right beside me. "I can assist your employer."

"You want me to go off with Tris?"

The king of the sylphs shrugged one shoulder. "He may be irritating, but you made him a promise. I know you dislike breaking any vow, even with no magic to bind it."

I grabbed a fistful of receipts and held them up. "You know nothing about accounting."

"Your employer says it merely involves comparing results. I can do it, and besides, Stan has offered to assist me."

Nevan, the monarch of an entire kingdom of elementals, wanted to help my boss reconcile the books with the receipts. What would his subjects think of that? Ascending the throne had not made him uppity at all.

"Okay," I said, pushing the receipts into a pile. "Have at it."

Tris brightened and actually smiled, with no sarcasm. "You mean it? We're going?"

"Yep." I kissed Nevan's cheek and marched out from behind the counter. "Let's do this."

We blipped to the mile marker on US 41.

"You do realize," I said, "we'll have to hold hands the entire time. I can take Nevan over the boundary without touching him, but I don't love you the way I love him. Better safe than disintegrated."

"Sure, whatever." He thrust out his hand. "Take me to the hot mortal chicks."

I rolled my eyes and grasped his hand, leading him over the invisible line beyond which no elemental could travel without my help. We stopped a couple yards past the boundary.

Tris glanced around, his mouth twisting. "Where are the hot mortal chicks?"

"Did you think they would magically appear when we stepped over the boundary?"

He hunched his shoulders, sheepishly avoiding my gaze. "Well, yeah. Kinda."

I supposed I couldn't blame him for that. He lived in a world where people and things did magically poof into view.

Tris straightened, his attention squarely on the woods, and jabbed a finger in the direction of the trees. "What's that?"

Following his line of sight, I spotted a flash of white. "It's a deer."

Before I got the whole sentence out, Tris took off toward the woods, dragging me after him. I tripped in a pothole.

And my hand was torn from his.

We both froze, gaping at each other.

Tris did not disintegrate.

Seconds ticked by, becoming minutes.

"How do you feel?" I asked.

"Fine." He patted his chest and belly. "All in one piece."

Relief gushed through me, sagging my shoulders. "Thank heavens for that."

Tris smirked. "Guess you do love me."

"You're my friend, and we've been through a lot together. Guess that's all it takes." I laid a hand on his shoulder. "Don't get cocky about it. Better stick close to me just in case."

He swept his gaze over the landscape—the empty road, the dark woods, the blue sky dotted with gray-edged white clouds. "If this is what all the mortal realm is like, I gotta say it's kinda disappointing."

"This isn't all of it." With my hand still on his shoulder, I whisked us to the location I'd read about in a magazine. Since I had no experience with the singles scene, I'd needed a bit of inspiration. I made sure we appeared in a dark corner where no one would notice us. "Here we are. Welcome to Dance Ardor, the number-one underground club in Chicago, Illinois, USA."

"Whoa," Tris said, drawing out the word. "This is wicked cool."

Strobe lights in shades of violet, crimson, and sapphire streaked across the interior of the darkened night club while couples on the dance floor writhed and thrashed their bodies in time to the loud electronic music. More clubgoers loitered near the bar or huddled around the tables arrayed in a semicircle around the dance floor.

Most of the women wore skimpy outfits.

"This hot enough for you?" I asked Tris, nudging him in the side.

He grinned at me. "This is awesome, Lindsey. You're the best."

I waved toward the club proper. "All yours."

The leprechaun took off.

Leaning against the wall, I kept an eye on his shenanigans. Tris had more luck with the ladies than I'd expected, but then, he was a leprechaun after all. Didn't they have natural good luck or something? I watched him dance with lovely, scantily clad females while I rebuffed several men who offered to buy me a drink and one who asked, "Wanna go into a private booth with me?" *Uh, no.* I was a soon-to-be-married woman. Even if I'd been single, this kind of club was not my style.

Tris had a blast.

I'd finished off my third virgin strawberry daiquiri when Tris finally returned to me.

He held up a handful of napkins. "Got their numbers, whatever that means."

"They want you to call them, that's what it means."

"Maybe I will." He stuffed his napkin collection in the pocket of his trendily ripped jeans and puffed up his chest. "I'm a stud muffin. That's what Delilah told me, and her friend Ariana agreed."

"You sure are a hit with the ladies."

"Don't gotta look so shocked by that."

"I'm not. Already knew you're sweeter than you want everybody to think." I held out my hand. "Ready to go home?"

"Yeah." He glanced back and waved at a buxom blonde. "Whew. it's exhausting being a ladies' man."

"Uh-huh." I slapped my hand on his shoulder and took us back to the boundary at the mile marker on US 41. We walked across it.

Tris shoved his hands in his pockets and sighed. "That was great. When can we do it again? I got all these numbers and all…"

"Let's take it one step at a time, Romeo."

"Sure, yeah. Gotta play it cool with the ladies." He assumed the about-to-poof pose. "I really appreciate you taking me to meet those hot mortal chicks. See ya."

Tris vanished.

I returned to the shop and Nevan, and we went home so I could show him the dance moves I learned at the club. I turned it into a striptease. He loved that. I mean, he *really* loved it. We didn't get much sleep, but we had a blast of our own.

Yep, I stood by my assessment from two weeks ago. Life was perfect.

THE MORTAL TEMPEST

Prologue

"LINNNNZEEEE," THE WIND WHISPERS AS IT TOUSLES MY HAIR AND TICKLES my skin. The wind has a voice and, I sense, a body that could rip me to shreds if it wanted. And it does want. Everything. The air stirred by unseen forces possesses a sentient energy. It sees. It hears. It knows, and it schemes.

The wind escalates, no longer a tepid breeze but a hot and seething mass of rippling, gnashing gusts. It speaks my name, transforming Lindsey into a snarling epithet.

A gust slams into me.

I stagger backward, my white dress trips me up, and I flail my arms out to buffer my fall. I just stop my head from cracking into a boulder.

A figure materializes in front of me where I lie prone on the ground.

The manlike being towers over me, a living statue hewn of copper, his eyes swirling with sickening shades of green. This is Skeiron, Greek god of the northwest wind, former king of the sylphs, an elemental being of immense power and dark intentions.

I destroyed him. He came back. I destroyed him again.

And he has come back again.

"Janusite," he growls, "your power will be mine. The wind assures it."

I scramble to my feet, whirl away from him, and try to run.

He seizes me around the waist, hoisting me off the ground. With his mouth pressed to my ear, he hisses, "You will be undone."

Another figure appears before me.

This is Notus, Greek god of the north wind, king of the sylphs before Skeiron, as dark and powerful as his successor.

He stalks up to me, grasps my chin, and forces me to look into his roiling eyes.

"You," he says, "have done your last deed. Let it all be undone."

Notus conjures a sword. His mouth twists into a sneer.
He thrusts the blade straight into my heart.
And I am…undone.

Chapter One

I STUDIED MYSELF IN THE FULL-LENGTH MIRROR, TURNING SIDE TO SIDE TO get the whole picture of my wedding dress, from the lace that covered the bodice and short sleeves and billowed over the flowing skirt to the pearl-like beads that dotted the lace. Shimmering green-and-gold earrings imbued with good-luck magic dangled from my ears. The teardrop earrings not only shimmered, the colors swirled faintly too.

Here in the confines of my old bedroom inside the Porter family motor home, I appraised my reflection in the mirror once again. The glass revealed my mom and Ennea observing me from behind. My dad and my ten-year-old brother waited in the main area near the front of the motor home.

Today I, Lindsey Astrid Porter, would marry an elemental being.

My mouth gaped on a big, noisy yawn.

"Didn't sleep well again?" my mother asked, eying me with concern. "Nightmares again?"

"Yeah, but it's no big deal. Wedding jitters, I'm sure." I gave a phony laugh, the best I could muster. "After everything I've seen and almost died for, bad dreams are to be expected."

Mom rubbed my arm. "You sure, sweetie?"

"Absolutely. I'm about to marry the love of my life, what's to worry about? This is a happy day, so let's forget about my stupid nightmares."

So what if a cold, viscous unease had been slithering through me all morning. It meant nothing. Every bride got nervous on her wedding day. Besides, I probably felt a chill due to the November weather. My groom had promised to use his sylph magic to warm things up in the vicinity of our ceremony, but I wasn't there yet.

I turned to the fae witch responsible for my accessories, holding up my wrist to show off the diamond-like bracelet that twinkled even in the dark.

"The jewelry is amazing," I told Ennea, the redheaded fae with creamy, freckled skin and a sweet, lovely face. She may have looked young, but the leprechauns, her tribe of fae, always turned out to be much older than they seemed. In the few months I'd known Ennea, I'd never asked her true age. Learning my fiancé, Nevan, was over five thousand years old had been all the shock I needed for a good while. To Ennea, I said, "Thank you for the earrings and the bracelet. They're gorgeous, and I need all the luck I can get."

"Enh, it's simple fortune magic," Ennea said in her Bronx-like accent. "Child's play."

She waved a dismissive hand and slapped my mother's arm by accident.

Mom grasped her arm like it really, really hurt, though her smirk gave away the game.

The witch's eyes flew wide. "Oh Cindy, did I hurt you?"

"No, sweetie, I'm joshing. You elemental beings need the occasional reminder we mortals aren't invincible."

I sighed. "Mom, could we skip the culture-clash lessons for today? I'm walking down the aisle in five minutes."

And my stomach was churning. My shoulders had bunched of their own accord, and my pulse quickened at the mere thought of what I'd be doing in a few minutes. Marrying an ancient warrior, a former human forged into an immortal sylph. As my thoughts drifted to Nevan, the anxiety trickled out of me and my shoulders relaxed. Marrying Nevan. Tall, impossibly muscular, bronze-skinned Nevan with the swirling, mesmeric eyes. His wild ebony hair. His lips. His smile. That loincloth. Mmm, and everything hidden beneath the scrap of tawny fabric.

"Cut that out," Ennea said, slapping *my* arm on purpose. "No mooning over your gorgeous sylph before the ceremony. Save it for after, when he whisks you away for an exotic honeymoon."

Ah yes, the honeymoon. Nevan wouldn't tell me where we were going, only that it was somewhere in the mortal realm. I would have plenty of time to drool over my new husband then.

Drool. Lick. Devour.

Ennea clipped me with the back of her hand again. "Focus, Lindsey. You look beautiful."

She fluffed the waves of my chestnut hair, which she had coiffed for me. The locks fell over my shoulders and framed my face. The makeup my mom had applied accentuated my pale-blue eyes. Nevan would love this. He'd never seen me spiffed up before.

In the mirror, I caught my mom dabbing at her eyes with a tissue. She sniffled. "Oh Lindsey, you're as pretty as an angel."

"Thanks, Mom." I got a little choked up too. "Don't make me cry, it'll smear my makeup."

Cindy Porter sucked in a breath and swiped at her eyes. "No more tears. It's time for smiles."

"Yes, it is." I straightened, smoothed my dress, and nodded. "I'm ready."

I whirled around, skirts flouncing, to face the door.

Ennea swung it open, and she and my mom stepped aside—as much as they could in the tin-can space.

Chin up, shoulders back, I marched out into the short, narrow hallway and straight through the living area past my dad and my brother. Ken Porter sprang up from the breakfast nook, banging into the table. My father, who loved to *ohmm* and take the lotus position, was gaping at me like he'd never seen me before. My ten-year-old brother, Ash, hopped up to stand on the curved bench seat of the nook. He clapped and cheered.

I winked at both of them.

My entourage trailed me out of the motor home, Mom and Ennea right behind me with Dad and Ash behind them. The rest of the wedding party awaited us at the ceremony site. We traipsed past the rock shop where I'd once been a lowly hourly employee and now served as a salaried assistant manager. The barn-red, corrugated-metal building squatted amid the woods of the Keweenaw Peninsula, the northernmost part of Michigan that housed many secret doorways to the Unseen realm. I led my little procession across the gravel parking lot, behind the shop, and through the garden populated with concrete statues of fantastical creatures like unicorns and trolls. The gravel path turned to dirt as we exited the garden and headed through the woods toward the waterfall.

Even from this distance, the waters rumbled.

We reached the healing vortex, marked by a not-so-subtle sign with white-painted letters proclaiming this the "HEALING VORTEX." Natural stone benches encircled the space. This spot did indeed possess regenerative magics, and it held sentimental value for me and Nevan, but this was not our destination. The further we traveled, the more the air warmed around us until it became as temperate as a Florida beach, thanks to Nevan's air-elemental powers. We stayed on the path until we reached the clearing beside the falls.

I froze, immobilized by the sight before me.

All the people who mattered most to me in the world gathered in this clearing, but I couldn't see Nevan yet. Maybe he'd hung back until I showed up. I glanced at each member of the wedding party in turn. Tris, Ennea's brother, stood alongside Brennus, the raven shapeshifter who now wore his humanoid form as a dark-skinned behemoth of a man with blue-tinged, shimmering skin and biceps the size of locomotives. Okay, that might've been a slight exaggeration. Tris seemed tiny next to Brennus. The leprechaun resembled a human teenager, with his rangy build and youthful face, but like his sister he was older than he seemed. With his peaches-and-cream skin and buzz-cut brown hair, he was a stark contrast to the shapeshifter. Brennus wore skintight shorts while Tris sported his usual ripped blue jeans, flannel shirt, and beat-up sneakers.

The leprechaun swiveled his bright-blue eyes to me and made the thumbs-up sign.

My mom and my brother joined Tris and Brennus.

A shadow among the trees shifted, and I glimpsed a familiar figure hiding there. A pang pierced my heart. The being formerly known as Travis Blackwell, sheriff of Mandan County, lingered in the shadows wanting to join the wedding party but afraid to do it. Travis had been my friend for years until he was forged into an elemental being—into a salamander, a type of incubus. Even two months after his transformation, he struggled to adjust to his new life.

It was my fault. All my fault.

"Wake up, Lindsey."

The voice of Ennea, my maid of honor, snapped me out of my jaunt down guilt-ridden memory lane. My boss, Stan Lagorio, hovered near the others. Though he'd come to terms with the existence of another world where magic reigned, he still preferred to avoid contact with that world and its denizens.

I looked toward the wooden railing that bounded the falls and the frothing pool beneath it. There, on the adjacent path, stood my friend and magical familiar, the incubus Max. He moved aside, and I saw Nevan.

My heart stuttered at the sight of him, like I hadn't seen him just yesterday and every day for the past three months. Tall and ripped, dressed in only his loincloth, he looked like the hottest Tarzan ever to grace the silver screen, except for his bronze-sheened skin and the molten ribbons of bronze, gold, and silver whorling in his amber eyes. When he caught sight of me, he smiled—a broad, ebullient smile that made me shiver with delight.

I was about to marry that sizzling-hot man.

My dad cupped my elbow in his hand and guided me toward Nevan and Max, his best man for the ceremony. Beside Nevan, our officiant waited. Bob, full name Bobanzhistilanovitz, was an oracle and a sort-of friend. He liked me and Nevan and had volunteered to conduct the ceremony when he heard we were tying the knot. The oracle wore his favorite attire—a finely tailored, navy-blue suit that hugged his slender body and went well with his short gray hair, which he always kept slicked back.

I took my position alongside Nevan with Ennea on the other side of me. Nevan and I faced each other, and he clasped my hands. His broad smile had softened into a gentler expression, loving and adoring. Tears stung my eyes again, threatening to flow, but I blinked them away. A dizzying mix of emotions swelled in my chest, and I focused on Nevan's face, on his warm hands holding mine.

"Welcome," Bob said in his odd accent, and his green eyes glittered with an internal fire. "We have gathered here for the handfasting ceremony of Nevan, king of the sylphs, and Lindsey Astrid Porter, the Janusite."

Why did he have to mention that? Sheesh, it wasn't very romantic to be called the Janusite at my wedding. I hoped he wouldn't recite the whole Janusite prophecy. So I had the powers of the Roman god Janus. Today, I was just a woman pledging her devotion and fidelity to the man she loved.

"These two individuals," Bob continued, "have expressed their heartfelt desire to join their lives and their souls, to become one in the most elemental sense. Can anyone give a reason why they should not be joined in this way?"

No one spoke.

A trace of a chill whispered through me, but I pushed aside the disquieting sensation and focused on Nevan, gazing into his whirlpool eyes. My breaths grew heavier as if the air had become thicker. I hadn't expected to feel this much, to be affected so deeply by a simple ceremony. Then again, we'd survived a hell of a lot to get here. I'd almost died, he'd almost died twice, and two worlds had nearly been destroyed.

My breaths grew more labored. I struggled to suck in air.

Nevan fought for breath too, his eyes widening.

This was more than excitement over the wedding. I glanced around and saw everyone, even Bob, gasping for air. My ears began to ring, and darkness encroached on my vision. My heart pounded as cold sweat broke out on my brow.

The ground trembled.

Nevan gripped my hands tighter.

A crack of thunder split the air, and the ground beneath us erupted.

Chapter Two

THE EARTH HEAVED UPWARD, CARRYING ME WITH IT. NEVAN'S HANDS were ripped from mine. The world became a blur of motion and dust clouds as the ground under my feet plummeted away from me and I sailed downward through empty space into a black abyss.

Hands seized my wrists.

I hung suspended in the blackness, choking on dust, my eyes squeezed shut to shield them from the debris raining down around me. The hands holding me hefted my body upward, out of the darkness. Weak light penetrated my closed lids.

A burst of sweet-smelling air gusted over me, dispelling the dust cloud. Only a sylph could summon clean air for me.

Without opening my eyes, I flung my arms around Nevan. "Thanks for the oxygen, honey."

He clutched me tight for a moment, then pushed me away to pat me down from head to toe. "Are you injured?"

His Irish brogue soothed me better than a swig of booze.

At last, I peeled my lids apart to gaze at him through a blur of grit-induced tears. "I'm fine. What about you?"

"Immortal, love. An earthquake can't hurt me."

Right. Only a weapon or poison endued with magic could take down an elemental. Since I'd just been attacked by the earth itself, I didn't feel stupid for forgetting the rules of the Unseen realm for a minute.

Nevan opened his palm. A wet washcloth appeared there.

Not as romantic as the day we'd met, on this very spot, when he'd conjured a perfect daylily for me. Not even as romantic as when he'd had my Bond Arms Mini derringer pistol endued for me. But as romantic gestures went, conjuring a washcloth to wipe me off after I nearly fell into the center of the earth ranked in the top ten.

He wiped my face, my neck, and the parts of my shoulders and chest exposed by my dress. The washcloth was filthy after that. He flicked the cloth, and it became moist and clean once more. While he cleansed my arms, I took stock of the devastation around us.

My parents and Ash looked dirty but otherwise okay. When I shouted to them, they replied they were unharmed. I shouted to Ennea and Tris too, even Brennus. All responded with affirmations they were all right. Stan stared into space, unblinking, his face ashen. When I called to him, he swung his gaze toward me.

"Somebody help Stan," I said. "He's in shock."

Max strode up to my boss and conferred with him in hushed tones.

Tris and Ennea meandered across the clearing, inspecting the damage.

Bob stood serenely in the same spot as before, his clothes spotless and his hair shipshape.

I waved my hand to snare his attention and asked, "You have any idea what that was?"

"The earth moved."

"Gee, Bob, thanks for the insight."

Nevan thrust a hand through my hair, his palm emitting a burst of air, and all the grime vanished. My hair was as shiny and bouncy as before the earthquake.

Earth buckling. Earth upthrust. Whatever.

"It felt like an attack," I said to no one in particular.

Nevan, his hand in my hair, went stiff. "Why would you say that?"

"Because we don't have earthquakes in the Keweenaw." I sighed and shook my head. "I mean, there's a fault that runs through the spine of the Keweenaw, but the earth doesn't suddenly shoot up under our feet. Until today. Our wedding day."

Nevan glanced down, scrutinizing the ground, then jerked his head up. "The earth shot up under *your* feet."

I sagged my shoulders and groaned. "Please tell me this is not the work of another lunatic bent on stealing my Janusite powers. That shtick is getting really old." I glanced at the hole in the ground that had almost swallowed me. "This isn't what my nightmares looked like."

Nevan went rigid and stopped blinking. "You had another bad dream?"

"Yes, but I'm sure it was wedding jitters. It couldn't have anything to do with this. I dreamed Skeiron and Notus came back to life and wanted to undo me, whatever that means."

"It cannot be a coincidence." He picked a tiny leaf off my dress and tossed it away. "You have suffered from terrible dreams for several days, and now a terrible event has occurred. There must be a connection."

"You're probably right, but I'd rather hug my denial a little longer."

"Lindsey, you are the one who called it an attack."

"I'm vacillating, okay? Stress does that to me."

Brennus lumbered up to us. "My lady, you should be escorted to a safer location."

"No dice," I said. "I'm not running away because of an itty-bitty earthquake."

"Itty-bitty?" Nevan said, a muscle jumping in his jaw. "A canyon opened up beneath your feet. Brennus is correct, you should be taken—"

"Not running away. You know me better than that."

He grumbled out a sigh. "Yes, I do."

"Yo, peeps!"

Tris's voice echoed through the woods.

I searched the area with my gaze but couldn't locate Tris or Ennea.

The snarky leprechaun trotted out of the trees and flapped his hand, urging us to follow him. "Hurry up! We found something…interesting."

"Why are you running instead of poofing?" I asked. Teleportation would've been faster.

"In case ya didn't notice, the landscape's kinda changed. Might accidentally 'poof' into a big hole. Besides, sometimes it's safer to do the legwork. Get the lay of the land, so to speak." He flapped his hand again. "Hurry it up, will ya?"

Nevan grasped my hand and led me toward Tris. We followed him down a narrow deer trail until he abruptly stopped. Ennea emerged from the trees, her face paler than usual.

Tris pointed to his right. "It's over there."

Brennus pushed past us, marching straight in the direction Tris had pointed.

I tried to follow, but Nevan pulled me against him, capturing me with his arm around my waist.

"Wait," he said. "Please, love, let Brennus survey the area first."

Nevan worried about me, and I loved him for that. But I suffered from a curiosity that often made me take off after strange beings or odd noises. This time, I let Nevan restrain me. To be restrained by his strong arm and his sexy body wasn't much of a sacrifice.

Brennus returned a moment later and announced, "There is a being. He is asking for you, my lady."

"Me?" I said like the dumbest person on the planet. Shock would do that to a girl. "This being is asking for me by name?"

The shapeshifter nodded.

"Did this creature," Nevan said, "seem threatening?"

"No," Brennus told him, "he is calm."

Nevan took my hand again, and we followed Brennus through the trees to a small clearing. The earth had cracked open here too as it had beneath my feet. We approached the chasm with caution, leaning forward to peer down into its depths. From six feet below, a man observed us.

A naked man.

He tilted his head back to eye us. When his focus landed on me, he snapped his spine straight. "Lindsey Astrid Porter."

I bit my lip. "Um…yes. Who are you?"

The man puffed up his chest, chin held high. "I am Janus. And I want my powers back."

Chapter Three

"Excuse me?" Like I would believe a naked man who appeared in a chasm ripped open by an earthquake just because he said he was the Roman god Janus. I wasn't that dumb. Sure, he had freaky gold eyes and golden-blond hair, but that didn't prove anything. He also boasted big muscles, another unhelpful observation. Hands on my hips, I squinted down at the man. "Janus was destroyed a long, long time ago. His powers got scattered to the Four Winds. Why on earth would I believe you are Janus? I don't suppose you've got some identification."

"Identification?" the naked man said, his brows scrunched.

Nevan hooked his arm around my waist. "Gods don't have driver's licenses."

Lips pinched, I looked up at him. "Don't tell me you're buying this 'I'm the god Janus' crap."

"Perhaps not." He grimaced. "Or perhaps yes."

"Thanks for the ever-so-helpful wishy-washiness." I flapped a hand toward the chasm and the being standing within it. "How do we find out if he's legit?"

Nevan shrugged.

To the stranger, I said, "Do something godlike."

He scowled at me. "Since my powers currently reside in you, I cannot do anything remotely godlike."

"Don't get snippy with the woman you're trying to convince to buy your story." I gnawed my lip, considering the problem for a moment. "There must be some way to figure this out. Where did you come from, anyway? And if you don't have powers, how did you cause an earthquake?"

"I did not," he said snippily, ignoring my advice. "Even as a god with all my powers intact, I could not control the earth. Gnomes are the only elementals tied to the earth in such a manner."

Nevan grudgingly nodded. "He is correct. Gnomes have the power, but they haven't left their home territory in ages. They have no interest in the mortal world or in conquering the elemental realm. After the sylph army defeated them roundly several thousand years ago, they retreated into their domain and have stayed there ever since. It's a bit of a mystery why they attacked us at all. Gnomes have never been militaristic before or since that solitary battle."

"We can't blame the gnomes. Check." I set my hands on my hips and drummed my fingers as I returned my attention to the man in the chasm. "So, you're claiming it's a coincidence the ground ripped apart right when you turned up—in the middle of a hole made by that earthquake."

"Perhaps it is a coincidence, or perhaps not." The supposed god huffed out a breath, screwing up his mouth. "Apparently, I will need your assistance to determine the answer."

"Where did you come from? How did you get here?"

"I have been imprisoned within the Temple of the Four Winds for many thousands of years." He glanced around, frowning at his surroundings. "I do not know how I came to be in this place, but I assume the Winds released me for a purpose." His gold eyes zeroed in on me, and he canted his head. "They sent me to you."

"Gimme a break." My heart stuttered despite my dismissive words. If he was Janus, he must've been released by the Four Winds, those guardians and avatars of power who had helped me and Nevan a couple months ago. I'd asked one of the Winds why I'd been chosen to receive Janus's powers. She had told me to ask Janus.

Well, here was my chance. Assuming I believed this guy's story.

Nevan piped up before I could. "Why do you believe Lindsey has your powers?"

His Godly Snippiness hissed a breath out his nostrils. "She is the Janusite, the prophesied mortal female who serves as the vessel for my powers until I can reclaim what is rightfully mine."

My turn to get snippy. "Vessel? I am not a bucket for you to dump your stupid powers into. And since the Four Winds gave me these magics, they are rightfully mine."

"You are the vessel. I will not leave what is mine within you, subject to the whims of a mortal who does not deserve to command such power."

"Maybe you're the one who needs to prove you deserve it." I narrowed my gaze on him. "Gee, didn't the other gods destroy you? Probably did it because you're such an arrogant twit."

Janus opened his mouth to speak, but a throat-clearing behind me stopped him. Both Nevan and I twisted our heads around to glance at Brennus.

The shapeshifter said, "My liege, may I suggest consulting the oracle."

Duh. I'd forgotten about Bob. He must've been here. Somewhere.

I threw my head back and hollered, "Bob! Get your butt over here."

The suit-clad oracle materialized beside me. "There's no need to shout for me. Only the leprechauns are too stubborn to pay attention to a subtler call."

"Sorry, but we have an urgent problem and need your insight." I pointed down at the naked stranger. "This guy claims to be the god Janus."

Bob gingerly stepped closer to the chasm's rim, leaning forward to peer down at our new friend. He squinted, turned his head this way and that, then straightened and backed up to stand beside me again. "He claims it because he is Janus."

"You're positive?"

He gave me a fatherly smile. "I'm an oracle, child. I don't lie about such things."

"But have you ever been wrong?"

Nevan's arm tensed around me. He was probably worried I would offend the super-powerful oracle, but I trusted Bob not to smite me just because I opted for a blunt approach.

"Hmm," Bob began, rubbing his beard, "I don't believe I've ever been wrong. There is a first time for everything, though."

"That's the best you've got."

"Nothing is a certainty, not even death. You should know that better than most."

Yeah, I'd been healed by a mystical vortex when my formerly dead ex-fiancé tried to murder me. Nevan had almost died twice and been resurrected twice, once by a vortex and once by me. Anyone who submitted to the forging, the supernatural transformation from human to elemental, must die for the process to begin. Even Bob had been run through with an endued sword, the only type of weapon that could kill an elemental, and he came back too.

Death wasn't a one-hundred-percent certainty.

Oh, sometimes I missed the days when I had been free to scoff at the supernatural. At least then I'd known anyone who died would stay dead.

I opened my mouth to ask Bob another question, but he poofed away.

Bob's assessment that this was Janus relied on his statement that he didn't "believe" he'd ever been wrong. He had also implied he could be wrong in the future. Or today. Right now. About the naked man scowling up at me from the bottom of a deep crack in the earth.

"There is another possibility," the man calling himself Janus said, seeming to have tempered his, uh, temper. "The Winds might have sent me to you because they sensed a great, dark power emerging. That power may have caused the earthquake."

Which probably meant the quake had been aimed at me. *Fabulous.*

"Okay, fine," I said, throwing my hands up in defeat. "For the time being, I will accept you might be the god Janus."

Nevan arched one brow at me.

"Yeah-yeah," I muttered to him. "I know, this could be a huge mistake. What if he's right about the earthquake? Some tips from the god whose powers I have could be helpful."

My almost-husband growled under his breath. "Ye do attract naked men, don't ye?"

"Not my fault naked men keep getting sent to me as gifts."

An evil sorcerer had sent me Max to serve as my familiar, and the salamander had arrived buck naked, his preferred state. Now, the Four Winds had apparently sent me Janus. What was the return policy on supernatural gifts?

Max I would never send packing. The cranky god in the chasm was another story.

I bowed my head and sighed. "Would somebody please conjure clothes for this guy?"

Nevan withdrew his arm from around me and flicked his wrist toward the chasm.

Janus jerked as a fluffy pink robe and pink bunny slippers materialized on his body. He glowered up at Nevan.

"Honey," I said, patting Nevan's chest. "Let's not tick off the god, 'kay?"

"If you insist." Nevan flicked his wrist again. "Will this do?"

Janus now sported a plain white toga. No footwear this time.

The god waved a hand toward Nevan but looked at me. "Would you mind ordering your servant to assist me in climbing out of this hole?"

"Servant?" Nevan said with an indignation that hiked up his chin and roiled in his eyes. "I am the king of the sylphs, you impotent god."

Well, at least Janus didn't have any powers with which to smack down Nevan.

I hollered over my shoulder, "Brennus, help the impotent god out of the hole in the ground. Pretty please."

Nevan flinched at my use of the dreaded P-word, but we were in the mortal realm. I could be as polite as I wanted without incurring any magical debts. I should be more careful, though, since I didn't want to wind up owing any nasty types. Max owed me his life, and that debt bound him to me even two months after it was incurred. It would bind us forever unless I absolved him. The stubborn incubus wouldn't let me free him, for reasons I didn't yet fully understand.

Brennus sauntered up to the chasm, knelt, and offered his hand to Janus. The god stretched his arm above his head to grasp Brennus's hand. Once he'd hoisted Janus out of the hole, Brennus retreated behind me and Nevan.

I smiled brightly at the shapeshifter. "Thank you."

He bowed from the waist. "As you command, my lady."

Nevan frowned at me. "Lindsey, you know better than to speak those words."

A flap of my hand dismissed his concerns. "Mortal world, sweetie. Chill out."

"Someone with immense power may have instigated an earthquake." He leaned in to nail me with a hard look. "How do you know the perpetrator didn't summon a bit of the Unseen realm into the mortal world to accomplish the task?"

Oh. He had a point. When I'd dragged Tris over to this side to heal Nevan, the leprechaun had needed to pull a smidgen of the Unseen into the mortal realm to do it. I might have possibly incurred an itty-bitty debt to Tris in the process, since pulling a sliver of the Unseen into the mortal world had the same effect as crossing the veil into the land of elementals where magic reigned. I'd learned a lot since then, but clearly not quite enough. In my defense, a god had appeared and demanded his powers back. I had some stress to deal with here.

"My bad," I said to Nevan. "Won't happen again."

Janus, who now loitered six feet in front of us, chuckled. "I had thought you commanded him, but it seems the sylph has ultimate control over his consort."

"Not a consort," I said, hands on my hips once again. "We were about to get married before you so rudely interrupted. And what do you mean you want your powers back? Nobody told me these things were returnable."

"There must be a way. Ask your oracle."

My oracle? I wasn't sure Bob would appreciate that assumption.

Nevan took hold of my arm. "I will speak to the Janusite alone."

The god folded his arms over his broad, incredibly muscular chest. "What am I to do? Hang about in this forest?"

"Yes."

And with that, Nevan towed me away from the god and into the trees. We could see Janus and Brennus from here, but they most likely couldn't hear our conversation. I leaned back against a tree.

Nevan bracketed me with his hands on the trunk. "You're believing what that…creature tells you?"

"Of course not. I'm suspicious and paranoid, remember?"

"Suspicious, yes, but not paranoid. We have good reason to be distrustful of what that being tells us. And how does he know your name?"

"I would've asked him, but you dragged me over here."

Keeping one hand on the tree, he lifted the other to cup my cheek. "I worry for you, love. Twice before we've battled beings determined to appropriate your powers. This creature may have the same goal in mind."

"You've told me before you trust my instincts."

"And I do."

I laid my hand over his on my cheek. "I think he might be Janus. Bob said it too, and I have a gut feeling about this."

Nevan's head sagged, and he groaned miserably. "I suppose I have no choice but to defer to your instincts." He raised his head, mouth crimped. "For the record, I do not like this situation one bit."

"I'm with you on that."

He lowered his body to the ground like he'd suddenly aged a million years, his legs stretched out in front of him. "The wedding must be delayed."

"Oh hell no." I dropped to my knees beside him. "We are not putting our lives on hold because another nebulous baddie decides to wreak havoc. I'm sure Bob is hanging around, my family is here, our friends are here, and we are not canceling the wedding."

"Lindsey—"

"No, you cannot *Lindsey* your way out of it." I plopped my tush onto his lap and linked my hands at his nape. "We are getting hitched. Today. No griping, no grumpy mumbling, no excuses."

Nevan smirked. "I know better than to argue with you when you've made a decision. You are extremely stubborn."

"So are you."

He wrapped his arms around my waist and tugged me closer. "The wedding does lead to the wedding night. I'm looking forward to stripping this dress from your body, my sweet mortal morsel, and nibbling on your delicious flesh all night long."

I slanted in, my mind set on kissing those luscious lips of his.

Brennus cleared his throat.

We both looked at the shapeshifter.

"The god grows anxious," Brennus said. He fixed his coal-dark eyes on me. "He insists upon speaking to you."

Nevan rose, taking me with him and setting me down on my feet.

"The god can bloody well wait," Nevan declared. "We have a wedding to finish."

"What shall I do with Janus?" Brennus asked.

"Keep him here. I do not want him disrupting the ceremony."

"Yes, my liege."

Brennus marched back into the clearing, planted his massive body in front of Janus, and barred his arms over his chest. He towered over the powerless god.

"What is this?" Janus said. "I demand to speak with the mortal vessel."

"My name is Lindsey, which you damn well know." I pointed a finger at him. "Stay there. I'll speak to you after we get married. If you cause any trouble, I will use your own frigging powers to knock you back on your ass. Got it?"

He compressed his lips, nostrils flaring.

"Do you understand?" I said sternly.

Janus huffed out a breath and spoke through clenched teeth. "I will remain here."

Nevan and I, hands joined, turned our backs on the god.

And that was how, ten minutes later, we wound up standing inside the healing vortex ten feet from the crack in the earth that had almost swallowed me while Bob performed the handfasting ceremony. I paid little attention to the oracle's words as he explained the meaning of the tradition and how it represented our love and the binding together of our hearts and lives. Nevan made an impatient noise, spurring Bob to pick up the pace. We had an irritated god waiting for us, and neither I nor Nevan wanted to risk another earthquake or who-knew-what disrupting the ceremony.

We exchanged rings, a nod to the traditions of my world, and then paid homage to the elemental world.

"It's time," Bob said, "for Lindsey and Nevan to bind their hearts, minds, and lives in eternal devotion."

Facing each other, Nevan and I crossed our hands—my right hand in his right hand, my left hand in his left hand. We gazed into each other's eyes, and suddenly, the weight of this moment struck me. My throat constricted. Tears pricked at my eyes. My chest tightened, and my lips trembled the tiniest bit. I was marrying Nevan. After a lifetime of feeling out of place in the world, in any world, I'd found my home with him.

Bob hovered his hand over ours and intoned words in another language.

Energy zinged through me, soft and gentle. I felt it echo between me and Nevan, looping from me into him and back again three times.

"It is done," Bob said, withdrawing his hand. He smiled at the crowd behind us. "Congratulations to the happy couple. You may kiss the bride, Your Majesty."

Nevan pulled me into his arms and kissed me.

Cheers erupted. Hands clapped. Someone whistled.

As our kiss ended, I caught Max's gaze just as he lowered his fingers from his mouth, his piercing whistle completed. He grinned and shrugged.

Everyone surged toward us. I got hugged by every single being in attendance, even Bob and Tris. My mom and Ennea hugged Nevan, but the guys all slapped him on the back.

A figure amid the trees snared my attention. My gut told me the identity of the lurker, and I trusted my instincts.

Nevan was surrounded by well-wishers.

I snared his gaze and mouthed, "Be right back." Then I sneaked away from the group and into the trees.

Travis hunched behind a wide pine tree peeking around it toward the clearing that housed the vortex. When he saw me approaching, he ducked behind the tree.

"It's okay," I said, stopping a dozen feet away. "You don't have to hide."

He swung around so half of his body became visible and peered out at me. "Shouldn't have come. Sorry. I just had to, uh…Never mind, I oughta go."

"Wait, please." I took a step toward him. "How are you?"

"Fine, I guess."

His Texas accent had lightened since the last time I'd seen him two months ago. Max had warned me Travis would change now that he'd become an elemental, an incubus like Max. The transformation happened gradually, though, and Travis might lose his twang altogether. His body had changed, for sure. Like Max, he sported deeply tanned skin glistening with copper. He'd gotten taller and far more muscular, and his hair had darkened from dirty blond into a rich ebony. His eyes flamed red with ribbons of yellow and orange lashing within the irises.

Unlike Max, Travis preferred to wear clothes. Today, he'd donned faded blue jeans and a white cotton shirt with all the buttons undone.

"Congratulations," Travis said. "I saw the ceremony. You and Nevan deserve to have a good life."

"Thanks." *What the hell should I say to him?* A few months ago, before his transformation, Travis had admitted he was in love with me. After the forging, his attraction to me had proved much harder to fight, which was why I hadn't seen him in so long. *Glad you're feeling better and please don't assault me* seemed like an inappropriate response, but I couldn't summon anything more useful.

Instead, I clutched the skirt of my dress in my hands.

He noticed and flinched. "Shouldn't be here. You're afraid of me, and you got every reason to be. I just wanted to…I don't know. Be here for the big moment, I guess."

"Max says you shouldn't cling to your old life."

Travis slithered out from behind the tree, keeping one side of his body glued to it. "I'm real sorry, Lindsey, about everything."

He was sorry? Max had forged him because I'd been grief stricken by his death at the hands of an evil shrew with endued weapons.

"I'm the one who should apologize. This happened to you because of me." I wrung my hands in the skirt of my dress, making the fabric swish and crinkle. "You died protecting me, and Max forged you for my sake. I'm so sorry, Travis."

"Don't do that. This ain't nobody's fault." He scratched his bare chest, exposed by his shirt. "I've realized most things are out of our control. We do the best we can, but sometimes it's not enough. I have to accept there's a higher power overseeing it all, and things will work out for the best in the end."

Higher power. The elementals talked about the Oversoul, the equivalent of God in the mortal realm. Maybe Max had introduced Travis to the concept.

"You really do seem better," I said. "I'm proud of you. The forging can twist a weak person into something awful, like what happened to Calder. You're strong and good, stronger than your brother was, and you will get through this. I believe that."

He shifted his hips like his groin pained him. "Maybe I am better, but I probably should stay away from you."

And of course, my gaze unconsciously snapped to his groin and the bulge growing and hardening in his pants. The sight of me got him way too excited.

"I think it's the dress," he said, understanding that I'd grasped his dilemma. "You look real pretty in it."

His voice had gone rough and deep, and his gaze had zeroed in on my bosom. The neckline of my dress revealed a hint of the inner slopes of my breasts.

I crossed my arms over them, my hands on my shoulders. "Well, I guess I should get back to the festivities."

And the impotent god currently fuming while a shapeshifter guarded him.

"Yeah, sure," Travis said.

His focus moved past me, and his eyes widened.

Travis stumbled backward to hide behind the tree again, leaning sideways to peek around it while keeping the lower half of his body hidden.

"Yes," Nevan said from behind me, "you should return to the festivities, Lindsey."

I whirled to face my husband. "Hi, sweetie."

He shook his head, his lips kinked in a sardonic smile. "Can't leave ye alone for a moment, can I? You sneak off to speak with an incubus."

"At least Travis wears clothes."

"Yes, I'm exceedingly grateful for that."

I glanced back at Travis. "See you later."

He nodded and vanished.

Nevan backed me up to a tree, his body molded to mine, and murmured in a sultry voice, "I need to give my wife a proper kiss."

CHAPTER FOUR

"W E DON'T HAVE TIME—" I MOANED AND MELTED WHEN HE TOOK POSSES-sion of my mouth, sweeping his lips across mine, nipping and licking, teasing me until I moaned again and opened my mouth in a silent plea for more. He mashed his lips to mine, thrusting his tongue deep. Every swipe of his flesh against mine pushed me to respond, heightened my desire, set my whole body on fire. I lashed my arms around him and bent one knee, tipping it to the side to spread my thighs in blatant invitation.

While he ravaged my mouth, Nevan struggled to lift my skirts. The voluminous layers of lace and satin hindered him. With a growl, he tore his mouth from mine to glare down at my dress. "I can't get under your bloody skirts."

"Sorry." I skated my hands up his naked back. "We don't have time for sex, anyway."

"Perhaps not." He gave up on my skirts and twined a lock of my hair around his finger, then let it unfurl. "The first time I saw you, I had the strangest sensation I'd seen you before. Known you before."

I gave him a teasing smile. "Was the first time you saw me in the shop, when you disguised yourself with a glamour? Or the first time you saw me when I actually saw you too?"

"The former." He curled that lock around his finger again, studying it. "I could not explain why I felt I'd known you before. Perhaps it was merely fate nudging me in the right direction, leading me to my soul mate." He released my hair and touched my nose with one fingertip. "To you, my sweet mortal angel."

"You called me that after the first time you made love to me."

"Because you are an angel. The savior who resurrected my heart by showing me Skeiron had lied about cursing me to have no feelings."

"You would've figured it out eventually." I took hold of a lock of his hair, coiling it around my finger the way he'd done with my hair. "You saved me too. You encouraged me to stop holding back my passions and let go of my fears."

Nevan leaned in closer and gazed into my eyes so deeply my heart sped up from the intensity of emotion in his whirlpool eyes. "After my forging, I swore…My memories of that time are hazy, but I have vague recollections of an angelic being who tended to me."

"You never mentioned that before."

"I had long assumed it was a hallucination brought on by the trauma of the forging. There are several periods in my existence of which I have only hazy recollections. Even an immortal's mind cannot hold on to every memory." His eyes began to shimmer and swirl faster, their colors brightening. "When I called you my sweet mortal angel, on our first night together, I used those words because you saved me much the way that other angel had done so long ago. And just now, when we bound our souls with the handfasting, I had the oddest feeling I owe everything I have with you to that other angel."

"Why didn't you ever tell me about this other angel?"

"I seem to always forget about my first savior until something reminds me." He stared past my shoulder into a distance only he could see. "It's as if someone or something prevents me from regaining my memories of the time after my forging."

"We'd better shelve that mystery for the moment. A god is waiting for us."

Nevan palmed my breast through my dress. "I want to be alone with you. Let us deal with the other troublesome supernatural being in a swift manner."

I knew he was referring to Travis when he called Janus the "other troublesome supernatural being." Nevan might have developed a non-hostile relationship with the formerly human former sheriff, but he and Travis would never become besties.

Nevan moved back half a step.

"Don't worry," I said, skimming my hands over his chest. "We can quiz the god some more, then stash him in a motel for the night."

Laughter rumbled deep in Nevan's chest. "Stash a god in a motel? In the mortal realm?"

"Got a better idea? He has no powers, which means he can't do any real damage other than annoying the hell out of anybody he meets."

"A motel it is." Nevan smirked. "I shall enjoy this."

"Is it Janus you don't like or gods in general?"

He sniffed, his nose lifting. "Gods are, as a rule, arrogant and dismissive of any being they consider to be of lesser stature. And they believe everyone who is not a god is a lesser being."

"Well then, let's get this over with." I slung my arms around him. "Blip us to the clearing."

One corner of his mouth kicked up because he always thought my various terms for his preferred mode of travel were silly, but he did blip us away. I could've teleported myself, tapping into his powers like I had many times before, but I liked traveling with Nevan. He always wrapped his arms around me even though it wasn't strictly necessary. Holding my hand would've done the trick.

Janus sat on the ground near the big hole, knees bent, arms draped over them.

Brennus hulked near the god's feet, his arms locked over his chest and his stance wide.

"Finally," Janus snapped, springing to his feet.

Behind us, footfalls pounded and crunched on dead leaves. Nevan and I half turned toward the sound and spotted Max emerging from the woods.

"Couldn't miss this," the incubus said in his usual English accent. "I heard there's a god out here who claims to be Janus. As Lindsey's familiar, it's my job to be at her side during any exciting events."

"Right," I said, "you're doing your duty. Your appearance has nothing to do with the excitement you mentioned."

Max grinned and shrugged. "I do love a good ruckus."

Shaking my head, I sighed with affectionate exasperation. Max was a good friend and a powerful ally, but he could be goofy sometimes. His life debt to me might also have encouraged him to join the party. I didn't yet grasp all the implications of another being owing me a magically enforced debt. God, I wished he would let me absolve him.

Max's mouth tightened, and he shook his head minutely as if he knew what I'd been thinking. Well, I had developed a problem with my emotions showing on my face. The days of locking up my feelings inside a steel-reinforced mental vault had ended months ago when Nevan taught me to embrace all my passions.

I faced Janus. "Okay, Mr. God Not Almighty. I want to know how you know my n—"

A hurricane-force gale tore through the clearing.

My hair whipped my face, and I stumbled backward. I couldn't see through my own hair.

Beneath my feet, the earth shuddered.

I staggered sideways, off balance as the ground undulated faintly. As the earth settled down and the wind died, a current shot through me. Magic? I had no clue because I'd never felt anything like it before. Sharp like a blade. Diffuse like a toxic cloud. Electric, searing energy. I tried to blow the hair out of my face, but it kept lashing me. With both hands, I peeled my hair away so I could see again.

Nevan was gone. Brennus too.

I spun in a circle. "Nevan!"

Max and Janus were here, but my husband had vanished. Nevan would not have left me alone.

Cold realization tingled through me. I couldn't explain how or why, but I understood on a visceral level something had changed. The world had changed. The woods seemed darker, denser, and the chasm from which Janus had emerged was gone.

I bolted for the healing vortex, tearing through the woods with reckless speed, my heart pounding and my skin tingling with that bizarre energy I'd sensed a moment ago. Max raced after me, shouting for me to stop. I could not stop or slow down.

Everything felt *wrong*.

Gasping for breath, I broke through the trees into the clearing around the vortex.

The stone benches had disappeared.

Everyone—my family, my friends, Nevan, and even Bob—had vanished too.

A flaming blur rocketed toward me. Max slowed his speed as he caught up to me, his skin alive with rippling fire. The flames dwindled and snuffed out. He seized my arm. "What happened? I felt something."

"Me too."

Janus trotted out of the woods.

I whirled on him. "What the hell was that? Where is everyone?"

He lifted one shoulder. "The timeline has shifted. If you are worthy of my powers, you should have sensed it."

"Seriously? You're getting uppity with me right now?" Fueled by a panic-driven rage, I rushed at him and pounded my fists on his chest. "The timeline shifted? What the hell does that mean?"

"Someone has altered the past, and everyone you know has changed as a result."

No, no, no, it couldn't be.

I barreled down the deer trail that had somehow replaced the dirt path to the rock garden. My skirts flapped around my legs, tripping me up a couple times, but I flew through the woods without any clue about what the hell I thought I'd do if Janus was right. He couldn't be. I had to cling to that denial because the alternative was terrifying. I ran and ran, breaking out of the woods into the rock garden—or where it had been.

The rock garden was gone.

Stumbling over a tree root, I flailed my arms out to break my fall.

Max caught me around the waist and steadied me. He kept his hold on me while I surveyed the new reality. Weeds covered the area that had once held concrete statues of whimsical creatures. My mouth fell open as my focus tracked further ahead, beyond the missing rock garden to the vacant field where the rock shop had once hunkered.

A vacant field. Weeds. Saplings. No shop.

The highway remained, but it cut through empty land.

"Oh God," I gasped, shaking my head so hard my hair flapped. "No, it can't be…"

"It is," said the voice of the powerless god.

Max would not let go of me even when I shuffled around to face Janus. Maybe he was afraid I would disappear too or that he would. I had no doubts plastering himself to me would not stop whatever was happening if the force behind it wanted one or both of us gone.

The god stood stiff and stone-faced a dozen feet away.

My bottom lip quivered, but I managed to snarl, "Explain."

Janus raised his brows.

"Don't act like you have no clue what I'm talking about." I stabbed a finger toward him. "You said somebody changed the past. I demand you explain yourself. Did you do this?"

"No. Since my powers currently reside in you, I have no capacity to influence time." He tilted his head, studying me. "Perhaps you did this inadvertently."

"Me?" Sure, I'd once frozen time, but this…I couldn't be responsible. "Why would I want everyone to disappear?"

"Why would I?" Janus rubbed his jaw. "This must be related to the earthquake."

"I thought that was connected to your return."

"The Four Winds cannot cause earthquakes, and neither can I."

Panic made clear thinking difficult. I had to calm down, despite the fact my husband was gone and my family was gone and the shop was gone. What else had vanished? Were my loved ones dead? Erased from history? Christ, I couldn't think like that or I'd lose it.

What little of "it" I had left.

Max's arm around my waist steadied me in more ways than one. Knowing at least one person in my life hadn't vanished helped to calm me. I drew in deep, slow breaths until the shrieking panic settled into a background hum of unease.

Pushing away from Max, I stalked up to the god. "You said the Four Winds must've released you for a reason and that they must've sent you to me."

"For what reason, I have no conception."

"I thought gods knew everything."

"You are confusing gods with the Oversoul. I am not and have never been omniscient. Nor am I an oracle gifted with prescience."

His mention of an oracle gave me an idea.

"Bob!" I screamed.

He appeared right in front of me.

I started to speak, but he cut me off with a raised hand.

"Yes," he said, "the timeline has been altered. No, your loved ones are not dead or gone, though they may not be as they were the last time you saw them. Afraid I can't help with the what, who, or why of the time shift."

A single fact smacked me in the face, and I had no clue how I'd overlooked its glaring obviousness for so long. Being completely freaked out by time shifting around me had messed with my head.

I glanced around at the three beings who had not vanished. "Why do we remember everything? Time hasn't changed for us."

Janus stepped closer, almost parallel to Bob. "You and I are immune to timeline changes. My powers bind me to time itself, which means you are bound to it as well."

"You don't have your powers. How are you bound to time?"

He gave me a look that said I was a puny-minded mortal and he would deign to explain these concepts that clearly were above my mental capacity. "I have shared a connection with you from the moment you were born. The connection became stronger once you came into your powers—my powers. That is how I know your name, and that is how I remain immune to timeline alterations."

Connection? I wasn't sure I liked that idea, but I had bigger problems.

"What about Max?" I asked. "How is he immune?"

Janus shrugged.

Bob cleared his throat. "I can answer that one. The incubus owes you a life debt. I can sense these things, and his debt to you is powerful. More than owing you his life, he feels indebted in a far-reaching way that goes beyond you. The power of that guilt has become entangled with the life debt, making it immensely strong and binding him to you in a much deeper way than any life debt should. That's how he has stayed immune to the time shift."

I looked at Max, but he'd bowed his head, refusing to meet my gaze. Did he feel that way? Indebted to…who? What? I knew about the woman he'd loved during his mortal life in ancient Rome, and how he had chosen the forging rather than death. Later, he'd forged Aurelia instead of letting her die a natural death the way she'd wanted. She became a succubus and went insane. Max had to destroy her. Could that be the far-reaching debt Max believed he owed?

Later, I'd quiz him about that. After we settled this time-shift insanity.

"And you, Bob?" I asked. "How are you immune?"

He smiled, his eyes blazing with an eerie green fire. "I am an oracle, child. As I've told you before, I'm beyond all designations, even time itself."

Yeah, he'd mentioned that "beyond all designations" thing. He'd been run through with an endued sword and survived it. But sidestepping time? I couldn't comprehend how any of us had accomplished that feat.

Magic, Lindsey, remember?

Would I ever get used to this stuff? I'd accepted being the Janusite. I'd accepted that my formerly dead ex-fiancé—Calder Blackwell, whom I had shot seven times at close range—had come back as a monkey-thing from another realm of reality. Hell, I'd accepted that Nevan's formerly dead wife from his mortal life had been resurrected by a sorcerer. And oh, I couldn't forget the fact the sorcerer had been an amalgamation of the essences of the sylph kings Notus and Skeiron jumbled up with the essence of Calder Blackwell.

Yeah, suddenly time shifts didn't seem all that crazy.

Bob rubbed his temples. "I may be immune to the time shift, but it's giving me a monster of a headache. All those timelines twisting and snapping and merging...I need to head back to my lair. The magics will shield me."

"You can't leave yet," I said. "How do I fix this time-shift thing?"

"The Janusite is one with time."

I threw my hands up. "That's your great wisdom? I'm one with time? Jeez, Bob, couldn't you be less cryptic this one time?"

He laid a hand on my arm, his eyes quieting to a subdued green and filled with empathy. "I know you're worried about your husband. But remember one thing." He leaned in. "Whenever you are, it's always him."

Seriously? That's all he had to say. Jeez, I hated oracles.

No, I didn't really hate Bob. He must have rules he had to abide by, like everybody did, and I needed to accept that he was doing the best he could to help me.

Bob squeezed my arm. "I know it's not what you want to hear. My foresight is like a picture book, not an encyclopedia. I see images of the past, present, and future, but I cannot control what I see or how detailed it is or is not." He rubbed his forehead, wincing slightly. "The Janusite prophecy is the only foresight I've experienced that came to me in words and pictures. It was like a Hollywood epic from the golden days, but with you and Nevan instead of Elizabeth Taylor and Richard Burton."

"I hope that epic wasn't *Cleopatra*. They both died in the end."

"Have a little faith, child. Remember what I told you after the sorcerer incident." He glanced over his shoulder at Janus, then released my arm. "When he asks, tell him."

Bob poofed away.

I didn't get a chance to ask what he'd meant. When who asked what? Guessed I'd find out eventually.

What he'd told me after the sorcerer incident. Bob had instructed me to remember it. I hadn't seen Bob after his running-through by the nasty piece of work once known as Nevan's wife, not until after we'd dealt with the sorcerer. Bob had approached me and Nevan, telling us two things. First, that we would have children someday despite the fact a human-elemental pregnancy could kill me. Bob had assured us "a way would present itself." Second, Bob had said, "Trust in Janus."

Oh crap. He wanted me to work with the powerless god.

Bob popped back in right in front of me.

I yelped.

He held out his hands, palms up. "I almost forgot to give you my wedding gift. Lay your palms on mine."

"Why?"

"Trust me, Lindsey."

I laid my palms on his.

Energy jolted into me through my hands, spiraling out into my entire body, settling in my womb. What on earth?

Bob withdrew his hands. His mouth tightened in a self-satisfied smile. "That ought to do it."

"Do what?" I asked.

"I gave you a magical prophylactic." He glanced down at my lower belly. "You can do what you need to do without worrying about a dangerous hybrid pregnancy."

"What exactly do you think I'll need to be doing that involves sex?"

He chuckled. "Remember, child. Whenever you are, it's always him."

Bob winked out.

I was so goddamn sick of vague bullshit and unhelpful advice that made no sense.

Janus watched me with a curious expression.

Max stared at the ground, peeking up at me every few seconds.

Enough of this. I needed someone who didn't feel weirdly indebted to me and the universe and who hadn't demanded *his* powers back,

I threw my head back and screamed, "Nevan!"

Nothing.

"Ah," Max began, fidgeting and glancing at me sideways, "he must've been affected by the time shift. What makes you think he'll come when you call?"

"We have a connection, one nothing and nobody can break." I spun in a circle, shouting to the trees and the heavens. "Nevan! Get your half-naked self over here right this minute!"

Nevan poofed in at the edge of the grassy area behind Janus.

I bolted for Nevan, flung my arms around him, and with my feet off the ground, crushed my mouth to his.

He stayed motionless, not reacting to my kiss.

My pulse roared in my ears, my heart pounding like a crazed drummer.

Nevan latched his arms around me and ravished my mouth.

The kiss was ravenous, wild, full of tangling tongues and groping hands. I shoved my fingers into his hair. He dragged one hand down to my bottom and the other up to grasp my breast. Even while we devoured each other, I sensed something off about our kiss. Nevan was always passionate, but this seemed not quite right. Too rough. Too…impersonal.

I pushed away from his mouth, though his hands pinned me to his body. Scrutinizing his face, I found no answers there. "Nevan?"

"Yes. And you are?"

My heart plummeted straight through the earth and out into the vacuum of space. "It's me. Lindsey."

Nevan set me down, his hands lingering on my hips. "Pleasure to meet you, Lindsey."

Chapter Five

"WHY WOULD YOU KISS ME IF YOU HAVE NO IDEA WHO I AM?" I ASKED, my mind reeling from his reaction. Sure, I should've expected it given the time shift. Though my brain understood this, my heart refused to accept Nevan could ever forget me. I felt a little queasy, my skin growing colder every second and the chill seeping inside to freeze my blood. He didn't know me. My husband didn't know me.

My gaze flicked to his left hand. His wedding ring had disappeared along with his memories of us. I swallowed three times, but the constriction in my throat would not abate.

Nevan slid his hands up to my waist, his mouth curving into a seductive smile. "I never turn down a kiss from a beautiful, sensual woman."

"I'm your wife."

He chuckled. "I think you're barmy."

My husband thought I was crazy. My throat ached. Tears stung my eyes.

I staggered backward out of Nevan's reach and spun around to face away from him, swiping at the tears gathering in my eyes. Looking at him shot stabbing pains into my heart. But the heat of his body, his unique scent, the timbre of his voice, the weight of his hands on my hips…

Those things would undo me.

Even with my back to him, I could feel Nevan watching me.

Max grabbed my arm and hauled me further away from Janus and Nevan. He turned me toward him, searching my face. "Are you all right? I know that's a rubbish question, but—"

"I'll be fine. Well, as fine as possible under the circumstances." The only way I could get through this was if I believed we could reverse the time shift, so I held on to the idea with all the strength of a shipwrecked man who had only a half-deflated life raft to keep him afloat during a hurricane.

The sympathy on Max's face made my gut twist. "You hoped he would remember because of your connection with him."

"If you and Janus kept your memories, why shouldn't Nevan?" I made a disgusted noise at my own pathetic hopes. "He thinks I'm some crazy chick who threw herself at him."

Max gazed past me, his lips puckering as if he were expending a great deal of mental power on puzzling out a mystery.

The brainpower I had access to at the moment wasn't enough to let me figure out what had caught his attention—or to care about it. Minutes ago, I'd been married to the love of my life, getting ready for my honeymoon, happier than ever before. Suddenly, everything had been ripped away from me. The tears I'd fought so far threatened to break free and trickle down my cheeks.

I sniffled, determined to keep them at bay.

Cut that out, I admonished myself. *No crying, no giving up, keep fighting.*

Max threw his arms around me, crushing me to his body, and began moving his hands in circles on my back while murmuring soothing sounds. I tried to pull my head back, but he slapped a palm on the back of my head and mashed my face into his naked chest.

"What on earth are you doing?" I mumbled into his flesh.

He shoved me away, smirked, and gestured past my shoulder. "Have a look."

"You suck at consoling me. I almost suffocated."

The incubus grasped my shoulders and whirled me around to face Nevan. "Look at him."

Christ, that was the last thing I wanted to do. Since Max seemed oddly determined to make me look at Nevan, I did it.

My husband-not-husband was glaring at Max, his gaze narrowed. A muscle pulsed in his jaw as he ground his teeth. He had shot ramrod straight, every muscle bulging, the picture of sheer power and boiling anger.

I blinked rapidly, sure I must've been hallucinating.

"See?" Max hissed into my ear. "He's jealous because I had my hands all over you."

"There's got to be another reason for his behavior. He has no clue who I am, so why would he get jealous?"

"Have you considered the possibility he might remember? On some level deep down in his unconscious mind. You and Nevan have a bond like nothing I've ever seen. If anyone could overcome a time shift, it's you two."

Oh God, how I longed to believe that.

I shook my head weakly and muttered, "False hope won't do me any good."

With a huff, Max slung his arms around my waist, dragged me backward into his hard body, and nuzzled my throat.

Nevan lunged at us. He ducked around me to seize Max by the neck and fling him thirty feet across the vacant field.

Max whumped down with a grunt.

I should have been concerned with his well-being, but instead, I slowly turned to face Nevan.

His chest heaved with breaths that gusted out of him. His shoulders rose and fell too, in time with his exhalations. An expression of total confusion tightened his features.

"I'm all right," Max called. "Don't worry about me."

The sarcastic tone of his statement indicated he actually was okay, and a quick sideways glance assured me of it. On his feet again, he dusted himself off and strode toward us.

Nevan bowed his head, grasping the back of his neck.

I couldn't stop myself. I moved toward him, laying my hands on his bare chest. "Why did you do that?"

He dropped his hands but kept his head down. "I've no bloody idea. When that creature touched you in such an intimate way…" He shook his head. "I could not tolerate it."

A dangerous hope flickered inside me, weak but undeniable. This was what Max had intended to happen. Make Nevan jealous. Insanely jealous. Somehow that would prove his memories of me, of us, lurked somewhere deep inside him.

Max came up beside me. "I was right, wasn't I?"

I twisted my mouth into a peeved expression. "Maybe."

Nevan lifted his head. His focus landed on me but then swerved away. He swallowed hard enough to make his Adam's apple bounce.

He vanished.

"Wha—" I spun in a circle, my heart thrashing in my chest. "No, no, not another time shift."

"It was not a time shift," Janus said.

Max and I turned toward the god in unison.

He leaned back against a tree, arms crossed over his chest. "You would have felt another shift. He simply left the vicinity."

Relief flooded through me, sagging my shoulders, weakening my knees. I sucked in a deep breath to calm myself. Janus was right. I hadn't noticed any change in the time-space continuum as I had when the shift occurred. Nevan's reaction to me, to Max's feigned sexual interest in me, had disturbed him so much he fled. Maybe that indicated what Max had suggested, that Nevan's real memories hid somewhere in the recesses of his mind. I had no frigging clue. Max and Janus retained their memories because of their connections to me.

What else had changed?

I seized Max's arm. "My family."

"You can find them if you concentrate and take us to them."

"What if I don't share Nevan's powers anymore? It was our emotional bond that made it possible."

Max laid his hand over mine on his arm. "You still have a connection, Lindsey. His jealousy proves it. Trust in that bond."

I nodded, but another problem occurred to me. I spread my arms and pointed my fingers at my body and the wedding dress. "I can't go out in the world like this. Could you conjure me something more appropriate?"

"Thought you hated conjured clothing. You told me so." He switched to a high-pitched voice that was apparently supposed to represent the way I talked, complete with a half-assed attempt at an American accent. "Oh please, Max, don't give me clothes you snatched away from who-knows-where, it's ooky."

"Very funny," I said. "This is a special circumstance. I've been living with Nevan, so I'm guessing all my belongings have disappeared thanks to the time shift. I give you permission to conjure me appropriate clothing."

He executed an exaggerated bow. "As you wish, mistress."

My dress vanished at the instant new clothing materialized around me. At least he hadn't gotten rid of my dress and waited a few seconds before giving me new stuff just so he could get a peek at my nakedness.

I appreciated that for about a second—until I took in my new appearance.

A leather bustier hoisted up my full breasts, which did not need hoisting. A matching leather miniskirt barely covered my rump, and thigh-high leather boots with black fishnet stockings completed the ensemble. For accessories, I had a leather choker with silver studs, leather wrist cuffs with silver studs, and black nail polish. When I shook my head, something moved up there. I raised a hand tentatively to touch my hairdo. Max had whipped it into a messy bun secured with—what else—a silver stake. Seriously. It felt like the metal version of the wooden stakes vampire hunters used.

"Honestly, Max," I said. "I need to blend in, not frighten children while I get arrested for solicitation. What should I call myself? Lindsey the Mistress of Pain?"

Max shrugged one shoulder, struggling not to smile. "It seemed appropriate to me."

Janus, propped against the same tree as before, observed us with a fascinated expression. With arms crossed over his chest, he lifted one finger to wave it toward me. "If this is how mortal women attire themselves these days, I shall enjoy spending time in your world."

I stomped my foot, which made my overly hoisted boobs jiggle. "Shush. No one asked for your opinion." To Max, I said, "Conjure me normal clothes."

Sighing, Max flicked his wrist.

The tension eased out of me when I took in my new outfit. He had given me leather pants, snug but not too tight and with a flare at the bottom to accommodate the sturdy black ankle boots that covered my feet. The bustier had been replaced with a short-sleeve, pale-blue shirt the color of my eyes. The choker and wrist bands were gone. And my hair, thank heavens, had lost the silver stake. It hung loose around my shoulders.

"Thank you," I told Max.

Both he and Janus winced.

I rolled my eyes again. "We're in the mortal world. I can say 'thank you' if I want."

Max examined my attire, tapping his chin. After a moment, his face lit up. "I forgot the most important accessory."

Something prodded my hip.

I glanced down. A holster tucked inside my waistband housed my Bond Arms Mini derringer. My gun could hold two rounds, and Nevan had gotten both it and the ammo endued. I had no idea if the time shift had stamped out that magic, but at least I had a modicum of protection. Two .357 rounds slamming into an elemental's forehead would slow the villain down and give me a fighting chance.

"The ammunition has remained endued," Max said. "I can feel the magic. Not sure how it's possible, but I was able to conjure this even though your world has changed."

"It's magic. Let's not overanalyze it."

"Good point." He glanced at my waist where the gun was concealed. "I conjured your weapon because I knew you would feel more at ease with it on your hip."

"Aw," I said, pinching Max's cheeks, "you got my gun for me. That's so sweet."

Max scrunched up his face. "Lindsey, I've asked you not to say things like that when others are around."

I patted his cheeks. "Don't be so uptight. You're a total sweetie-pie, and anybody who's met you knows it."

The incubus groaned, utterly defeated.

Janus laughed. "You are far more entertaining than the mortals I met last time I was corporeal."

"Gee, I'm so flattered." I flashed Janus a sharp look and turned back to Max. "Time to track down my family."

"May I assist?" Max held out his hands, palms up.

"Sure."

I held out my hands, palms down, hovering them a hair's breadth from his skin.

Currents of magic crackled between my skin and his where our hands almost touched. He was gifting me with magical energy to amp up my powers in the hopes our united strength would prove enough to enhance whatever latent connection I might share with the new version of Nevan. With any luck, it would allow me to tap into his powers to poof and whatnot. The energy permeated my skin, traveling down every nerve and blood vessel, penetrating through the physical to the heart of my being. My skin tingled, from my scalp down to my toes. The magic energized me, physically, emotionally, supernaturally.

I sucked in a breath, let it out gradually, and shut my eyes to concentrate on the image of my parents and my baby brother.

We whisked through the abysmal tunnel so fast I hardly felt the stinging pain of traveling the elemental way. I kept my eyes shut as we popped out into the real world. Sunlight radiated through my eyelids. I peeled them apart, squinting at the brightness of the world around us.

Max released my hand and moved away from me.

I surveyed the surroundings. A lawn of brown grass encompassed a small brick house with a detached garage. Beyond the lawn lay woods populated with leafless trees much shorter and thinner than the ones in Michigan. My parents lived in Kentucky, which also had tall trees.

This was not Kentucky.

"Where are we?" Max asked.

"Not sure."

I walked toward the house, suffering a weird sensation of wrongness that prickled the hairs on my arms.

The front door swung open, and my mom rushed outside. She sprinted for me, flinging her arms around me to haul me into a bear hug.

"Lindsey, honey," she said, "we were so worried. Where have you been? You weren't in your bed this morning when I came to wake you for breakfast."

My bed? Here? Where the heck was here, anyway?

"I…" Had no idea what to say to my mother. She let me go, and I mumbled, "Sorry I worried you."

Mom squinted at my clothing. "What are you wearing?"

"Uh…something new I picked up recently."

Her gaze drifted past me, her brows knitting together. "Who's your friend?"

I twisted my head around and noted Max had assumed his semi-human glamour. He wore gray slacks and a white shirt as well as black loafers. His swirling, glowing eyes had dimmed and calmed to a reasonable facsimile of human eyes, and his skin had a deep tan but no coppery sheen.

"Um, this is Max." They had met before, many times, but she had no memory of it. "Are Dad and Ash okay?"

"Sure. Why wouldn't they be?"

"No reason."

Mom lodged her hands on her hips. "Where have you been, Lindsey?"

"Uh…"

"It's my fault," Max said. "My car broke down, and I needed a lift. Lindsey was kind enough to pick me up."

My mother glanced around, her eyes going squinty. "Where's your car, Lindsey? The garage door is shut, but it seems like you came from the other direction. Almost like you walked out of the woods."

I was spared from floundering for an explanation when someone else raced out of the house to halt near me and my mother. A cold as deep as the vacuum of space froze my blood. I couldn't blink, couldn't speak, couldn't comprehend what I saw. Who I saw.

The man before me ran a hand through his sandy hair, his lustrous brown eyes searching my face. "Where you been, sweetness? We were worried sick."

I tried to summon words, but my voice emerged as a reedy croak.

Calder Blackwell pulled me into his arms.

Chapter Six

M Y ARMS HUNG SLACK AT MY SIDES. MY BODY STAYED STIFF. THE
only sounds I could make were little choked gasps. My ex-fiancé—the
man I'd shot seven times and thought I'd killed, the man who'd been transformed into one of the monkey-men known as kerkopes—was currently hugging me. He looked like he had before all the madness started. He looked like
the man I'd agreed to marry, the man I'd thought I loved.

Calder let go and grasped my shoulders. "Lindsey, what's the matter?"

"N-nothing." *So convincing.*

His gaze roved my body, his forehead crinkled. "What are ya wearing, sweetness? Never seen this outfit before."

"Well, I, uh, thought I'd try something different."

"You don't seem like yourself." He picked up my left hand, caressing
my knuckles, and his fingertips bumped the dual bands around my third
finger. His mouth popped open as he stared at my diamond ring and gold
wedding band. "What the—This ain't the engagement ring I gave you last
month."

Last month? In the timeline I remembered, we'd gotten engaged more
than three years ago.

Calder shuffled backward, baffled.

Another man rushed out of the house toward us.

Travis Blackwell stopped beside his brother. "What's going on? And what
in tarnation are you wearing, Lindsey?"

In my timeline, Travis had been a cop in Texas before he followed me to
Michigan after Calder's apparent demise. Travis had become sheriff of Mandan
County, died protecting me, and had been transformed into an incubus.

Just when I'd gotten used to the new Travis, I was confronted with the old
one. Or the newer one. Or…whatever.

My dad and Ash tumbled out of the house.

I did not have time to sort this out. My family was okay, that was enough for the moment. I ran to Max, grabbed his hand, and whisked us back to the field where we'd left Janus.

He hadn't moved one inch. "Was your family not what you expected?"

"You could say that." I rubbed my forehead. "This is giving me a headache. We need to reverse the time shift."

"And find out who did it and why," Max said.

"First, we fix it. Then, we take down the villain." I rounded on Janus. "How do we fix this?"

"With my powers, which you have."

"I don't have time for your bruised ego. I repeat, how do we fix this?"

He pushed away from the tree, pacing a ten-foot span of earth. "First, we must ascertain at what point in the past the timeline was altered."

"And we do that how?"

"You must do it. I do not have the power." He held up a hand before I could grouse. "This is not a complaint brought on by my bruised ego. It is a statement of fact."

"Okay. How do I do that?"

He stopped pacing, studying me with an unsettling intensity. "You seem to operate under the assumption you and time are separate entities."

"Time isn't an entity." I drew my head back. "Is it?"

"Not precisely, but it does behave as a living thing might. Wound it, and it will protect itself from further injuries. If the party responsible for the shift attempts another one, it will be more difficult to enact. This gives you a window of opportunity."

"To do what?"

"Connect with time."

I couldn't help the panicked laugh that snorted out of me. "That's crazy. Even if I could do that, what if I go back in time to fix things and run into myself? Physicists say that's a bad thing. A paradox."

He sighed heavily. "Mortals have limited understanding of such matters. You are not *in* the timeline, Lindsey. You are *of* the timeline."

Sure, that made perfect sense—in the world of total insanity.

I felt my lips tighten into a pucker. "Thought I was the mortal vessel, just a place to stash your powers until you, the imperious god, returned to claim them."

Janus flitted his gaze around the area, from the trees to the sky and down to the ground, then cleared his throat and looked at me. "It does not matter what I think. You command the powers, and only you can undo what has been done."

With all my heart and soul, I wished Nevan was here. My Nevan. The one who loved and cherished me and would do anything for me, as I would for him. The Nevan in this timeline had run away. I had no choice but to trust in Janus like Bob had suggested.

But that cold, slithery sensation inside me would not go away. I glanced at Max, who shrugged.

I scrunched my lips, zeroing in on Janus. "When you first showed up, you demanded your powers back. Now you're advising me on how to use them. How do I know you're not tricking me into giving back your powers?"

"Because I am not." He walked straight up to me, forcing me to bend my head back to meet his gaze. "Listen to me. I do want my powers back, but whatever is transpiring here overrides our personal desires. We must work together to prevent irreparable damage to the timeline. Temporal shifts are delicate and dangerous magics. Even I have enacted only one shift, and that was at the command of Jupiter. I had no choice but to obey my king."

"You have power over time, but you've never used it?"

"I have used it to travel into the past and future strictly to observe. Toying with the natural progression of events could wreak unspeakable consequences." He paused as if considering the issue. "This shift was relatively minor. We have a chance to undo it and prevent irreparable damage, but we must act swiftly. You must act swiftly."

Janus shambled to the nearest tree and leaned his side against it like he had the weight of a thousand worlds bearing down on him.

And I couldn't help wondering what consequences his one and only attempt at time manipulation had wrought. That was a question for after we undid this shift.

"I don't know how to do this," I said. "Connect with time? Sheesh. I froze time once, but that might've been a fluke."

Janus jerked away from the tree. "You froze time?"

"Uh, yeah." I shrugged. "There was a wacko sorcerer who absorbed the essences of Skeiron, Notus, and my ex-fiancé, Calder. Anyway, he had so much power none of us, not even my elemental friends, could stop him. I had to trick him into doing what I wanted. I figured the only way I could get the upper hand was if I sort of moved laterally instead of blipping from place to place. That's how I froze time. And my plan worked. The sorcerer is gone."

"I see." Janus stared at me like I'd grown a forest of red, spiky horns on my head. "I am beginning to understand you are no ordinary mortal."

Max chuckled. "You're just now figuring that out? Some god you are."

"You, salamander, should be grateful I am not one of the vengeful gods who easily takes offense."

"You have no powers. Maybe you, tosser, ought to be grateful I don't crush you to bits for disrespecting the Janusite."

"Ugh," I said. "Enough machismo. How do I connect with time?"

Janus stared hard at Max for a moment, but the incubus remained unperturbed. At last, the god spoke to me. "You must feel the connection. If you had a familiar—"

"She does," Max snapped.

The god gave Max an assessing glance, then sniffed his lifted nose. "A salamander as your familiar? I would have expected more from the mortal imbued with my powers."

At least he'd stopped calling me "the mortal vessel."

Max flattened his lips and tensed his whole body as if preparing to attack.

I shook my head at him, holding up a warning finger.

He growled softly but stopped preparing for battle with the god.

"Get over here, Max," I said. "I need my familiar's help."

My familiar trudged to me and held out his hands, palms up. I hovered mine over them with a minute space between our palms. We took a simultaneous breath and exhaled it slowly, our gazes locked. The magic crackled between our hands, sweeping up my arms in a tingling wave of energy, branching out into the rest of me until I felt like my whole body had fallen asleep and woken up with an electrical surge.

I shut my eyes and let all thoughts vacate my mind, focusing on the sensation of the tingling magic, blocking out everything else. The sounds of the woods dwindled into a silence. The whispers of Max's breaths and my own receded into silence. Everything receded from my consciousness, and I floated in a nothingness so vast I couldn't comprehend its dimensions. It had none, I supposed. This vacant space knew no bounds.

Time, time, where are you?

My single thought became a sing-song litany I repeated in my mind over and over, letting the emptiness take me wherever it wanted. For this was a river, the slow-moving and incomprehensible flow of…time.

I'd made it. I had connected with time.

The current of it propelled me forward, but I needed to go against the flow. Where was the event that had rewritten the entire timeline? When was it?

Show me the wound. Let me heal it.

The flow shifted course, curving and arching backward until it connected with itself again somewhere upriver from where I'd started. This place had no light, no landmarks, nothing to guide me except the sensation of movement, always movement. How could I find the time-altering event? I needed to jump into the point where the change had occurred and reverse it. Somehow.

That part I hadn't figured out yet.

I dived toward the point where the river merged with itself at the closing point in the loop. My fingers, not really fingers except in my mind, stretched out to touch the intersection. Almost there. A little further. *Stretch, stretch, reach for it, almost there.*

Just as I latched onto it, a massive burst of power slammed into me.

I careened out of the void, my eyes popped open, and I tumbled backward to land with my feet above my head and my butt in the air.

"Shit!" I rolled onto my side and accepted Max's help in getting up. I shook my whole body, needing to shed the remnants of whatever had ejected me from the time stream. I glared at Janus. "Connect with time. No problem. Thanks for the brilliant advice."

He lifted one brow. "What happened? Did you undo the change?"

"No. I tried, but something shoved me out with one swift kick of its ginormous, steel-toed, ethereal boot."

Max's lips kinked in a slight smile, but Janus simply stared at me.

Nice to know I could confound a god. It gave me a little glow inside.

"If I am of the timeline," I said, "why couldn't I get in there to fix things? Everything seemed okay, but then the cosmic boot punted me out."

Janus canted his head. "What were you doing when you were ejected?"

"Trying to connect with time. I sensed where, or rather when, the change had happened, and I was heading straight for that moment when—whack!"

I smacked my palms together to emphasize the point.

Janus's lips parted as if he meant to speak, but he sealed them again.

Max waved a hand toward the god. "I don't think he understands your terminology. Try speaking to him like he was a child." Max sidled up to Janus and spoke in a baby-talk voice. "Lindsey tried to make friends with time, but it got mad and wouldn't play with her."

I threw my head back and groaned. "Max, honestly. You are not helping."

Janus shot a haughty glare at Max before smoothing out his expression when he looked at me. "Your familiar is very protective of you. It is highly unusual, in my vast experience, and could become a problem."

Naturally, he emphasized the word vast to make sure we lesser beings understood our place.

Oh, I was getting really tired of his imperious attitude.

I jabbed a finger in the air in Max's direction. "I command you to stop harassing Janus. Understood?"

"Yes, mistress." Max sighed and scratched his neck. "If you insist."

"I do." His life debt to me ensured he would obey. I hated using magic in this way, but I couldn't have Max and Janus bickering while I tried to fix whatever some crazy-ass weirdo had done to the timeline.

Nevan, I really need you now.

A big, strong body materialized behind me, flush with my backside. Arms encircled my waist, tugging me more firmly into the hard muscles pressed against me. The heat and scent of him surrounded me.

"Nevan," I breathed, and leaned into his body.

Way, way in the back of my mind I realized this was the altered version of him, not my husband. Rationality insisted I move away from him. *Screw rationality.* I relaxed into him, resting my palms on his forearms, loving the feel of his hands clasped over my belly.

He dipped his head to murmur in my ear, "I tried to stay away, but something inexplicable draws me back to you."

Inexplicable. Because he had no idea who I was.

Oh, but he felt so good around me.

"I wanted you all to myself," he rumbled into my ear. "Do ye mind, darlin'?"

Mind what? That's when I realized I had my eyes closed. I opened them.

We weren't in the field near where the rock shop had once stood. Max and Janus were nowhere in sight. Nevan had whisked me away to a clearing in the woods. Where, I had no clue.

He nuzzled my throat. "Well, darlin', do ye mind?"

"That you brought me here? No." I should've pushed away from him, but I really, really did not want to do it. My body ached all over from whatever force had kicked me out of the time stream, and his presence soothed me. "Why did you come back?"

"I couldn't stay away. You intrigue me." His hands drifted up my belly. "I suffer from an intense need to claim your body."

He'd come back for sex. I should've been offended by that, I supposed, but I'd sunk too deep into the bliss of his presence to give a fig about anything. Maybe I should have sex with him. Forget the world, forget the wounded timeline, forget everything except the pleasure he could give me.

Those big hands of his drifted higher to cup my breasts, and he whispered to me in the sultry voice that always melted me. "I may not know you, but that's never stopped me before."

Suddenly, the wrongness of this hit me.

I smacked his thigh. "Hey! Get your hands off my tits. Do you fondle every strange woman you meet?"

"No, only the ones who claim to be my wife."

Wriggling out of his embrace, I rounded on him. "That happens a lot more often than you might think."

Yeah, I remembered the moment when his formerly dead wife had flounced out of the woods to proclaim she wanted her husband back. Like I'd ever lie down for that one.

I couldn't lie down for this battle either. I had to get back to Janus and Max and figure out how to repair the timeline.

Nevan snared me with one brawny arm and hauled me into his body. "I have no idea what you want, why you claim to know me, but as long as you're here…" He caught my bottom lip with his teeth, releasing it slowly. "Might as well enjoy the pleasure of each other's company."

My body responded like it always did—softening, warming, tingling in all the right places.

"I can't have sex with you," I said. "Not until you can tell me my name. My full name. First, middle, and last."

He palmed my ass with one hand. "Tell me your name, then, and I'll gladly repeat it."

"That's cheating." I wrestled free of him. "I'm sorry, Nevan. I cannot have sex with you until you say my name."

This time, I didn't need Max's help. I zipped myself back to the field, tapping into Nevan's powers much more easily than before. And yeah, I longed to believe that meant our bond endured and was growing stronger. Because maybe, just maybe, that would mean his memories were trying to resurface. I could not afford to cling to such a slender thread of hope. It would distract me, and distractions could be fatal.

Max gave me a closed-mouth, knowing smile. "Nevan swept you away for a quickie?"

"No." Well, that had been his intention, but I'd rebuffed him. Eventually. "Getting back to the matter at hand, do we have any idea what pushed me out of the time stream?"

Two supernatural beings shrugged and shook their heads.

"Come on," I said. "That's all you've got? Zippo?"

Janus cleared his throat. "I do not know what or who is behind the time shift, but to create one would require immense power the likes of which none have seen. The perpetrator would need to tap into the darkest magics."

"Oh jeez, I'm so tired of villains who tap into the darkest magics. Why can't you people destroy the world with giant bombs like normal lunatics do?"

Janus gave me that confounded look again.

"Forget it," I said. "How do I get past this immense magic that's locked me out of the time stream?"

"I do not know," the god said.

Max raised a hand like a kid in school. "Anyone care to hear my idea?"

"Go on," I said.

"When you're in there, freeze time."

I stared blankly at him for a couple seconds until I grasped his meaning. "When I'm reaching for that moment when time was altered, I should freeze time to stop that immense force from attacking me."

"Exactly."

"Max, you are so smart."

He puffed up a little. "Just doing my job as your familiar."

"It's a brilliant idea." I bit my lip. "Though I suspect I could get seriously hurt if this doesn't work."

Janus spoke up. "You must weigh the risks and benefits and decide which is more worthwhile."

I didn't need to think about it. "It's worth the risk."

"Then do it."

Without waiting for Max to assist me, I shut my eyes and soared out of myself into the sightless abyss of the time stream. Why didn't I need Max's magic to enhance mine, a small part of me wondered. I knew the answer without mulling the question.

Nevan. Somehow, my encounter with him had bolstered my spirits and my magics.

I followed the stream as it looped back around to the moment where I needed to be. That mysterious dark force stretched out its tendrils toward me, but I concentrated all my energy on the task I'd set for myself.

The flowing river of time stopped moving.

And the dark force froze too. I couldn't see it or feel it, but I sensed the change. Everything in the domain of time had ground to a halt.

Except me. Because I was *of* time, not in it.

I dived for that one point in time where everything had shifted. My body caught up to me with a whoosh that left me breathless for a few precious seconds. Smells and sounds of the woods tantalized my senses, and I dared to open my eyes.

Ten feet in front of me, frozen in time, Calder Blackwell lay prone on the ground at the edge of a small pool inside a clearing in the woods. A natural spring burbled up at its center. Deep scratches marred his face, his jacket was torn, and his hand had fallen into the water. The blood dripping from his fingertips hung suspended in the instant before it would have dropped into the water.

A cougar hunkered nearby, seeming on the verge of pouncing for the kill.

This was the moment when Calder had lain dying, and out of desperation, accepted an elemental's offer to be forged into an immortal creature. This was where everything had shifted.

I had to know why.

CHAPTER SEVEN

I WANDERED AROUND THE SCENE, TAKING IN EVERY DETAIL I COULD see. Calder had told me a cougar attacked him and it was the precipitating event that spurred him to accept an elemental's offer to make him immortal. Knowing the truth and witnessing it...two very different things. If I released my hold on time and let events unfold, I would watch Calder get ripped apart by a wild animal, then watch as he underwent the far more agonizing experience of the forging. It ripped apart the human body, transforming it into something new.

A memory barreled through me. Travis lying in a puddle of blood, dying. Me begging Nevan to forge Travis. Nevan had talked me through my grief, showing me it was selfish to do that to Travis without his consent. I was prepared to let my friend go, but Max had taken matters into his own hands. Linked to me by a powerful life debt, caring for me because we had become friends, Max did the one thing he'd sworn never to do again. He forged a mortal. He forged Travis.

But he'd done it for me.

Travis's forging had happened because I left my friends to fight alone while I took out the sorcerer. While I was gone, Ceara—Nevan's first wife and the sorcerer's accomplice, not to mention his lover—had attacked my friends. By the time I returned to them, it was too late. Ceara had slit Travis's throat right in front of me. Travis hadn't chosen his fate, but Calder had. He wanted the power and immortality granted to an elemental, and he hadn't cared if he became a monster in the process.

I tiptoed up to Calder where he lay facedown in the mud at the pool's edge. His eyes were open, evincing life. The cougar had been about to deal the final blow, the one that would end Calder's life, when I froze time. Could I watch this happen? I had no choice. I had to let him die and be transformed in order to repair the timeline. Something or someone had spared his life, triggering the time shift.

Calder Blackwell must die.

My gut twisted. I swallowed hard, my throat dry as sandpaper. Watch him die? Christ, why did the universe keep forcing me to be a spectator to death and destruction?

Tears stung in my eyes. I squeezed them shut, willing the tears to stop.

Rein it in, Lindsey. Do what you have to do.

I hadn't issued that mental command in months, not since Nevan stormed into my life and changed everything, changed me, changed the fates of two worlds with me. Rein it in? I hated resorting to my old ways, but I would never get through this unless I did just that.

Eyes wide open, I rose and marched to the edge of the trees, peering into the twilight shadows for any sign of the person or creature responsible for the time shift. Something had changed here, now, and Calder had not died. I walked the perimeter of the clearing, determined to spot the perpetrator, but I found nothing.

Wait. What was that?

I backtracked a few feet, squinting into the trees.

Between two closely spaced trees, something hovered. It looked like...a blur. A vaguely human-shaped blur in shades of beige and white. Everything else around me was as sharp as the best high-definition television, but the thing ten feet in front of me, suspended between two trees, seemed to have been moving so fast it froze as a blur. What on earth could move that fast?

Nothing of this earth could. Something or someone from another world might. I'd seen Max run as fast as any comic-book superhero, becoming a blur of flames.

A blur.

Could the hazy figure in the trees be an elemental?

Energy scraped at my psyche, and the world around me twitched. I couldn't describe it any other way. Everything moved slightly, then returned to its original position so swiftly I experienced it as a twitch of the world.

An instinct warned me of what was happening. The blur-being was fighting my time freeze.

I marshaled all the power I could but initiating the time freeze had consumed most of my magical energy. I took everything I had access to, every ounce of magic left inside me, and funneled it into strengthening the freeze. My head throbbed. My body ached like I'd done a three-hour workout at the gym. Not that I'd ever visited a gym. Cold sweat dribbled down my temples and the back of my neck. I squinted and gritted my teeth, concentrating everything I had on the task.

Blue energy sparkled around me.

The world jerked one way, then the other, and settled back into position.

Pain tore through my entire body. I gnashed my teeth, and an agonized sound burst out of me.

Time unfroze.

I staggered backward, gasping for air, phantom lights sparking in my vision.

The blur-being raced past me, bowling me over with a gust of hurricane strength.

Flat on my back, I struggled to catch my breath and gain my bearings. Everything spun around me, but it wasn't the world twitching again. Dizziness had seized me, and I could not summon the energy to get up. My muscles had turned to jelly.

"Linnnzeeee."

The raspy, breathy word originated to my right where I knew Calder lay dying. My hair had fallen over my face, though, blown there by the wind. I couldn't see a thing. With an effort that shot pains through my every nerve, I rolled onto my side.

The blur-being hovered beside Calder. Both he and the cougar remained frozen.

"Why are you doing this?" I asked, my voice strained.

The being blasted out another gale.

Calder and the cougar unfroze.

A skeletal finger stretched out from within the blur to point at the cougar.

The animal yelped and galloped away.

"Janusite," the blur-being said in that bizarre voice, part sigh, part growl. The "S" in Janusite became a drawn-out hiss. "You cannot stop me. Vengeance shall be mine."

The skeletal finger stabbed in my direction.

I careened across the clearing, rolling and rolling, rocks and twigs and other things I couldn't identify scraping and slashing at me. I shut my eyes and covered my head with my arms to shield my face. When at last I stopped spinning like a glass tube tossed down an oil-slicked incline, I realized I'd ended up on my back. Prying my lids apart, I saw the blue sky above me, darkening with every second it slid toward the impending night.

Scrambling to my feet, I bolted for the clearing.

Only to slam into a magical barrier.

I bounced off it, stumbling into a tree. When I regained my balance, I peered into the clearing.

The blur-being was nowhere in sight. Calder lay where he had before. His hand twitched. He moaned. With an agonized noise, rolled onto his back.

Movement drew my attention to the woods opposite where I stood. The blur-being hung suspended there.

Calder, hands shaking, dug his cell phone out of his pants pocket. He struggled to dial a number, succeeding after some nasty swearing. He held the phone to his ear, waiting for someone to pick up at the other end of the call.

"Yeah," he said, his voice quavering, "I need help. A cougar attacked me. Don't know where I am exactly." He listened intently. "GPS? Thank God, I don't know if I can walk."

Every cell phone had GPS built into it for just such a circumstance. First responders would track him down.

I had needed to stop this, to let Calder die in order to undo the time shift. Instead, I'd gotten blown away by a blurry creature with skeletal fingers.

My gaze flicked to the blur-being. It poofed away.

The magical barrier disintegrated.

Calder lifted his head, bleary-eyed and blood-stained. "Somebody there?"

I had no choice. To avoid any further damage to the timeline, I had to get out of here.

So I returned to the present, to Max and Janus.

And to Nevan, who was glowering at the other two like he itched to pummel them. He had his fists clenched at his sides and his every muscle tensed. His eyes burned and whorled with shades of black and crimson.

He was more than mad. He was infuriated.

"What is going on here?" I asked.

Max nodded toward Nevan. "The sylph is accusing us of keeping him away from you on purpose."

Jealousy again? My heart did a dopey flip-flop at the idea, but mostly I wanted to defuse the situation before Nevan did something rash like hurling Max or Janus across the nearest boundary. No elemental aside from Nevan could cross the invisible, magical boundaries around natural water features in the mortal world. Nevan got around the rule because of me, because of our deep connection and my Janusite powers, giving him the ability to go anywhere he wanted so long as I was somewhere in the mortal world at the time. For any other elementals, violating the boundary rule would result in their destruction, a process that disassembled their bodies molecule by molecule. I assumed Nevan had his immunity despite the changes in him, but I didn't care to test that theory.

The last thing I needed today was another display of misplaced machismo.

Nevan raised a fist, shaking it at Max.

I stomped up to Nevan. "Cut that out this instant."

He lowered his fist and turned toward me. "You vanished. Only an elemental being may travel that way, which means one of those two snatched you away from me."

"No, I did it myself."

"A mortal can't—"

"This one can."

He flashed a scowl at Max and Janus, but a tinge of desperation weakened its effect. "That is not possible."

"I tapped into your powers. You must've felt it."

Nevan's brows crinkled, and he grasped his head in both hands. "I felt…something. I do not understand any of this. No mortal could access my powers."

Max, of course, chose that moment to get snarky. "Bloody irritating, isn't it? You can commiserate with our friend the impotent god."

"Shush, Max," I said. "Could you and our new friend give me a minute alone with Nevan? Go over there or something."

I waved vaguely toward the other end of the field.

Janus balked. "I will not obey the commands of a mortal."

Max gave a melodramatic sigh, slapped his hand on Janus's shoulder, and said, "You'll want to obey this one. She's going to make out with Nevan, and trust me, that's not something you want to watch."

The god grunted, contorting his mouth, but then followed Max to the far end of the field.

I splayed my palms on Nevan's chest. "Take it easy, no one is taking me away from you. I'm yours. Even if you never remember what we had together, I will never leave you."

He relaxed visibly, exhaling a long breath. "If they did not take you, why did you abandon me?"

God, I wanted to throw my arms around him. Instead, I moved closer to gaze up at him with our bodies inches apart and my hands lingering on his chest. "I didn't abandon you. I had something to do, that's all. Didn't work out the way I'd hoped, but I had to try."

"What did you do?"

"I tried to undo the time shift."

His hands lighted on my hips, and his expression softened. "What went wrong?"

"Somebody else was there, some kind of blurry being with skeletal fingers. It knows what I can do, and somehow, it prevented me from correcting the timeline. That thing was outrageously powerful." I shivered a little thinking about it. "And that being said it wants revenge."

"Revenge for what?"

"I don't know."

Well, maybe I did if I could piece together the clues. The blur-being had rewritten the timeline by stopping Calder's forging. Of all the things the being could've done, why did it choose that event? As far as I knew, Calder hadn't done much of anything as an elemental other than trick Brennus the raven shifter into a bargain that enslaved him. Everything Calder had done after his forging served one purpose.

To get me back.

I'd refused the forging even when he had slashed my throat, prepared to die rather than become a monkey-thing like him. His so-called love had been nothing more than a need to control me.

Okay, but what did any of that have to do with altering time? I couldn't believe the blur-being wanted to spare Calder the pain of his transformation or spare me from the things Calder had done in an attempt to make me so desperate I'd choose the forging. Even his efforts to frame me for murder had not convinced me to become like him.

No, the blur-being had another agenda, but it must center on me.

Or maybe I was becoming narcissistic and thought every villain had it in for me. No, I'd been right those other times to believe somebody was out to get me. I trusted my instincts, and they warned the blur-being had a beef with me.

Great. What had I ever done to that hazy, crazy creature?

Think, Lindsey.

Something about the way my windy friend had called my name twanged a memory. I'd heard that voice before.

In my nightmares.

"Linnnnzeeee," the wind had called in my dreams. The last nightmare had involved Skeiron and Notus, but previous ones had been too vague and confusing for me to puzzle out their meaning. Maybe the blur-being had some connection to the sylphs. Nevan had control of the air and could even create thunderstorms. Of course, every sylph I'd ever met looked humanoid and had a solid, unblurry body. Besides, Notus and Skeiron were gone for good. The Four Winds had sent their essences packing and assured me no one and nothing could ever bring them back.

Okay, I'd stash the sylph connection in the mental box labeled "consider later, more evidence required."

Back to the me connection, then. What ripple effect had saving Calder effected? He was alive and human, apparently happy. So was Travis. Based on what I'd seen when I visited my family, my life had changed too. If I weren't immune to the time shift, I would've been living in Texas with my fiancé Calder, my good buddy Travis, and my family. What else, though? I never would've come to Michigan since I never would've needed to flee from Texas after Calder's disappearance and apparent death.

I would never have met Nevan, which meant I wasn't the Janusite—or at least, I would have no clue I was. The blur-being might have hoped to eradicate the Janusite.

There had to be more to it.

What about Nevan? The shift had altered him too.

My hands lingered on his chest, on his hot skin.

"You seem to be deep in thought," he said.

I chewed the inside of my bottom lip. "Who is the king of the sylphs?"

"Notus, of course. He has ruled over us for a very long time."

Another change. Skeiron had usurped Notus, and Nevan had ascended the throne after I took out Skeiron.

"What about Skeiron?" I asked.

"Notus destroyed him during the violent battle for the kingship three thousand years ago."

"So, um…" I tapped my fingers on his chest. "You have never been king."

He laughed softly. "Me? No, darlin', I have never been king of anything. After Skeiron's demise, I became the leader of the sylph army."

"If you're a general or whatever, why do you prance around in a loincloth?"

"Because I resigned from the army and requested to become the guardian of the falls." He nodded over his shoulder. "The waterfall here."

Requested? In my reality, Skeiron had forced Nevan into a bad bargain. Nevan had become bound to the falls, coerced into searching for the Janusite, all because he'd enjoyed a few rolls in the hay with Skeiron's daughter.

"Did you sleep with Skeiron's daughter?" I asked.

"Well, yes." Nevan smirked but then the expression melted away. "Skeiron never knew of it. How did you?"

"I know you, that's how. In my reality, you are king and both Skeiron and Notus are dead."

"That would be preferable. Notus has become quite depraved."

"Did you ask to be guardian of the falls to get away from him?"

"Partly." Nevan's gaze went distant. "I also had an overpowering urge to come here. I do not understand it." He nailed his gaze to me. "The need I felt then is similar to the need I feel now."

"What need?"

"To protect you and care for you." Though he kept his hands on my hips, he shifted uncomfortably. "To be with you, always. I did not like it when you vanished."

"I'm sorry about that." I glided my hands up to his neck. "I got scared, and I ran. That will never happen again."

"What frightened you?"

"You don't recognize me. After everything we've been through together, all the pain we've both endured to get to this day, our wedding day...I'm scared you'll never remember me, remember us."

He slid his hands up my back. "I may not recall the things you remember, but I can't stay away from you. Something pulls me back to you no matter how far I travel. I heard your call, but that shouldn't be. No mortal has the power to summon an elemental."

I'd screamed for Tris once upon a time, and he had come. But then, I'd already known him. He must've liked me even though he wouldn't admit it. He came when I called because he sensed I'd needed help to save Nevan's life.

Nevan came to me a little while ago because of our bond.

Maybe he didn't recognize it yet, maybe it was submerged under layers of time-shift confusion, but it had to be the truth.

"You came when I called," I said, "because we have a connection deeper and stronger than any magic, stronger even than time."

He stared at me for a moment, then nodded slowly. "Perhaps we do."

I'd settle for "perhaps." It meant he didn't think I was crazy, and that was a very good thing.

"Gah!"

The shout from across the field made both Nevan and me swing our attention in that direction. Janus was swatting at his shoulders and chest, twisting this way and that, spouting a slew of words in another language. Given his tone of voice, it sounded like he was swearing a blue streak.

I grabbed Nevan's hand. We rushed to the god.

Just as we reached him, a bright-red salamander leaped off Janus's shoulder and onto mine. The critter gazed up at me with large, dark eyes.

I pointed a finger at him. "Max, what did you do to Janus?"

He shrugged his tiny red shoulders. If a salamander had shoulders.

Max sprang off my shoulder onto the ground. In a burst of flames, he assumed his usual humanoid form, stark naked. Shaking himself like a dog, he said, "The impotent god was being imperious and bloody aggravating. A real wanker, that one. What else could I do?"

"Not tick off the god, that's what."

He grunted.

Janus clenched his jaw but said nothing.

"Still want your powers back?" I said. "Considering what happened to me in the time stream, I'm thinking I should hand over these powers and let you fix the time shift. You're the expert, right?"

I got a strange queasy feeling when I thought about relinquishing my magic, but then, it wasn't really mine. Never had been. I'd grown kind of attached to these powers I had never wanted.

Janus frowned. "I have no conception of how to transfer the powers back to me."

"Seriously? The first thing you said after popping up in an earthquake rift was 'give me back my powers,' but you have no clue how to do it."

"That is correct." His frown deepened. "I had assumed the Four Winds would enact the transfer upon my resurrection. They did not. Apparently, I am meant to assist you in some way before reacquiring my powers."

"Hmm." I wondered if maybe the Winds wanted him to learn a little humility first but decided to keep that theory to myself. "Anybody got another idea for how to reverse the time shift and stop the blur-being from creating any more of them?"

The group response came in the form of shrugs and noncommittal noises.

"Great," I said, throwing my arms up and letting them fall again, my hands slapping on my thighs. "I've got a god and two powerful elementals on my side, but nobody has a frigging clue how to handle this situation."

"You are the most powerful among us," Max said. "We're here to serve you."

"But I have to come up with a plan. Fantastic." I groaned out a sigh. "Last time we fought a big baddie, you guys helped with the planning. Besides, I doubt Mr. Prickly Godlike Being over there is here to serve me."

Janus sniffed. "I serve no one but Jupiter. And I am not a god*like* being, I am a god."

"Whatever." I rubbed my temples, head bowed, and tried to focus on the problem at hand. The blur-being was too powerful for me to fight alone. I jerked my head up. "I'll take Max and Nevan with me into the time stream. They can help fight the mystery villain, and together, we'll have enough power to undo the time shift."

"No," Janus said, looking at me like I was a total idiot. "You cannot take another entity into the time stream with you. Weapons are permitted, as long as they reside on your person."

"On my person? Jeez, I hope you don't mean it has to be surgically attached to my body."

"It does not. A sword in a scabbard attached to your belt will suffice."

Lifting my shirt a touch to expose my derringer in its holster, I said, "What about this weapon? I didn't have a chance to use it against the blur-being, too weirded out by seeing Calder in the moment before his forging."

Janus squinted at the handgun. "I am unfamiliar with that sort of weaponry, but it does reside on your person. So yes, it would survive the journey into the time stream."

"What if I wrap my body around Nevan's good and tight? Could he survive the journey then?"

Nevan perked up at the suggestion.

But Janus looked irritated at my ignorance. "He would remain a separate entity, not contained on your person."

I took another minute or so to mull what he'd said and how I might transport something useful into the time stream with me. I couldn't take Nevan or Max with me. They weren't "on my person" no matter how sluttily I pasted myself to one of them. Unless…

"What about this," I said. "Max can turn into a teeny-tiny lizard. If I tuck him in my pocket, would that qualify as on my person?"

Janus's brows cinched tight over his nose, and his mouth opened a smidge. He stayed like that for several seconds before he literally shrugged off his confusion and said, "I imagine it would qualify. Your familiar is bonded to you as a servant, a sort of weapon or implement. In his smaller form, if he were concealed in your pocket, he likely would survive the journey. However, having never attempted such a thing, I cannot guarantee it."

"Good enough."

Max's jaw went slack. "Excuse me? I'm to crawl into your pocket and pray the time stream doesn't annihilate me?"

Janus made an impatient noise. "It wouldn't annihilate you, tiny salamander. You would be forcibly ejected and might suffer physical injuries, which would heal."

"Oh." Max's expression brightened. "In that case, I'd love to tag along. But not in your pocket, Lindsey. I'll suffocate."

His smile mutated into a smirk as he zeroed in on my bosom.

I laid a hand between my breasts. "You want to ride in my bra?"

"There's no better way to travel than tucked between a woman's breasts."

Nevan bristled, snapping straight and stiff. "He will not."

"Cool down, Nevan," I said. "This is strictly business. Right, Max?"

"Of course," the incubus replied with a twinkle in his eyes.

Nevan narrowed his gaze on Max.

I laid a hand on Nevan's arm. "Relax. Max is an incubus. That means he's a big-time flirt, but it's just his nature. He has no interest in me except as a friend."

"Sad but true," Max agreed. "I spend a large amount of my time with a beautiful woman but never feel inclined to seduce her. It's bloody depressing."

Though he spoke the words in a light tone as if he were joking, I sensed something else beneath the surface. Max needed to feed on sexual energy to survive, which meant he needed to have sex on a regular basis to stay healthy and strong. Since he hung out with either Travis or me and Nevan most of the time, I wondered when he got a chance to get some.

He did have the faintest dark circles under his eyes.

Max squirmed under my scrutiny.

I waved for him to approach. "Shift into salamander form, and I'll slip you inside my bra."

Amid a flash of flames, Max shrank into his salamander form. I knelt to lay my hand, palm up, on the ground. He scampered onto my palm.

Rising, I took hold of my shirt's neckline and lifted it out, then let Max scamper off my hand and into the space created by my bra. He smiled up at me, his tiny lizard teeth exposed, and blinked his tiny lizard eyes once, slowly.

I let go of my shirt. Max was as "on my person" as anyone could get.

His long tail twitched, tickling my skin.

Shivering, I laughed.

Nevan glared at my bosom.

"Cut that out," I said to my bra where the roguish salamander resided. "Behave, Max."

I swore I heard an adorable, teeny-tiny sigh.

He settled down in his odd little nest.

"Okay," I said. "Here goes."

I shut my eyes and jumped into the time stream.

Chapter Eight

I EMERGED IN THE SAME MOMENT AS BEFORE, EVERYTHING FROZEN with Calder lying wounded at the pool's edge. A quick glance around showed me the blur-being hiding among the trees like the first time I'd been here.

Max skittered out of my bra, up to my shoulder, and leaped to the ground. At the instant he touched down, flames erupted. He resumed his humanlike form.

"Let's do this," I said, grabbing his hand. "We need more power."

The energy sizzled through his hand into mine, spiraling out into my entire body. The blue energy of my powers crackled and snapped around us both in a curtain of magic. With time frozen, would the blur-being remain immobilized? The being had enough power to travel through time and alter the past. Since she'd fought off my time freeze before, I couldn't count on it affecting the creature this time. We needed to hurry.

Max seemed to understand this without words. He funneled more energy into me, more than he ever had before, and the blue curtain shimmered and thickened into a semi-opaque haze alight with snapping sparks.

Now or never.

I raised my free hand and hurled magic at the blur-being.

The blast flung the entity backward, and it smacked into a tree with a wet cracking sound. The blurry cloud around the being dissipated in a puff, revealing the being that had hidden within it, but the entity was too far away for me to see anything more than dirty white robes.

No time to waste. I had to let Calder die.

I kept my one hand raised, spewing magic at the creature slumped on the ground, while Max channeled more and more energy into me. Somehow—I couldn't explain how, only that I sensed Max driving it—we became invisible. All of us. Me, Max, and the being currently prone on the ground across the clearing, further into the trees.

My gaze fell on Calder. Injured. Bleeding. Suffering. My stomach wrenched into tight knots, and I couldn't breathe.

He must die. I must watch it happen.

Oh God, Calder, I'm so sorry. I resisted the impulse to shut my eyes. If I had to do this, I must bear witness to it.

Holding on to Max's hand, surrounded by my blue magics, I released the time freeze.

A figure rose up out of the murky depths of the natural spring, water sluicing off its monkey-like, humanoid body. The being crouched over Calder. The creature—one of the kerkopes based on its wiry black hair and large, golden eyes—chanted in an alien language I had heard once before.

On the night Max forged Travis.

As Max had then, the monkey-thing chanted while he raised his hands, palms out, and shimmering orbs of bluish-white light popped up throughout the clearing, swarming around the elemental being and Calder. The lights flared brighter and brighter until I had to shield my eyes from the blinding brilliance.

Energy seared my skin, the backwash of the forging process.

Calder screamed with an agony and terror like nothing on earth.

On the night Max transformed Travis, I'd begged Nevan to tell me what the forging felt like. His words echoed in my mind now.

The forging will rend his limbs, his mind, every particle of his body and soul, crushing and melting them. A power beyond imagining will reshape his form, and he will be born anew through the scalding agony. He might wish for death with his last coherent thought before the pain and fire consume everything that made him human. Only his soul and his memories will remain.

Helpless to spare Calder, I covered my ears and squeezed my eyes shut. His screams penetrated into me anyway. Silence. I stood there for a moment, immobilized, my pulse racing. Somehow, I had held onto the magics keeping us invisible through the whole horrible event, but now, they crumbled away.

I opened my eyes and gazed into the clearing.

Calder and the monkey-thing were gone.

An inhuman shriek rattled my eardrums.

The formerly blurry being flew off the ground, through the trees, and straight across the clearing toward me. A burst of wind knocked me sideways into Max. He stumbled too, but just as we found our footing, the creature landed smack in front of me.

She landed.

And the earth shivered.

The female being stood half a foot taller than me, her waist-length, ghost-white hair tumbling over her shoulders in a tangled mess. Her skin was pale as death, her lips purple. Her fathomless black eyes glittered with red sparks. Perky little breasts seemed out of place on her emaciated body, covered by tattered and filthy robes that must've started out white. And those skeletal fingers…

The being raised one finger to point at me. The long, curved, and sharp-looking nail was black and resembled a bird's talon.

"Linnnzeeee," she said, her voice breathy and raspy like a roaring wind. "Lindsey Astrid Porter, Janusite and lover of the sylph king, hear this. You may have won this battle, but only because I had not expected your familiar to make it through the time stream. Next time, I will be prepared."

"What do you want?" I asked. "Why are you doing all of this?"

"Vengeance, my pretty," she said, stretching out that finger to slash the wickedly long nail in front of my nose. "Never again shall I suffer betrayal. You took them from me, and I will have them back whatever the cost. I shall avenge what you have done before it was done."

I tore the derringer out of my waistband and fired both rounds straight into her forehead.

Singed holes appeared where the rounds had struck her. She flinched, but no blood poured from the wounds. The creature jerked her head side to side with sharp cracking noises. The .357 slugs popped out of her forehead to plop onto the ground.

Endued bullets had no effect on her? How could I defeat an unkillable foe?

A gust of wind barreled into me. I tumbled into Max, we both got bowled over, and we wound up tangled on the ground. Max hissed in a breath, choking back a cry.

The woman-thing had vanished.

Chapter Nine

MAX AND I RETURNED TO THE FIELD MOMENTS AFTER THE WINDY Witch had smacked us down. With Calder's life path restored, his forging completed, everything should have gone back to normal. Well, as normal as my life had ever been. Maybe "back to the original timeline" was a better way to phrase it.

Except neither had happened.

We came back to the same empty, overgrown field. The rock shop had not reappeared. Before anyone could speak to me, I zipped away to the house in Texas where I'd found my family earlier—and found them there again. With Max's help, I'd figured out how to glamour myself invisible during Encounter Two with the Windy Witch. I stayed out of sight while I quickly reconnoitered the area around my parents' house. Peeking through the picture window in the living room, I spied my parents and Ash in the midst of a boisterous discussion with Travis. They were smiling and laughing, clearly exchanging jokes. I peered through every other window but saw no sign of Calder.

How could nothing have changed except for Calder? It made no sense. The Windy Witch had stopped Calder's forging in order to rewrite history, and his survival had set off a chain reaction that altered everything. Letting him die and undergo the forging should've reset the timeline.

Yet it hadn't.

I rushed back to the field. Janus and Nevan both gave me irritated looks.

Max slumped on the ground, propped against a tree with his legs outstretched. His coppery skin had taken on an ashen pallor beneath the supernatural coloring. Half-moon shadows darkened the skin under his eyes. He had his lids closed, his mouth open.

"Lindsey," Nevan began, but I cut him off with a flap of my hand.

I raced to my familiar, falling to my knees beside him. "Max?"

He peeled his lids open, revealing bloodshot eyes. "Not dead, if that's what you were thinking. I'm tired, but I will survive."

Biting down on my lip, I scanned his body but found no visible wounds. "You sure you're not injured? We got knocked on our asses back there."

"Used a lot of power too, more than I've used in centuries."'

He held one hand around the fingers of the other hand as if hiding something.

I pried his hands apart.

The middle finger on his left hand was missing, broken off at the first knuckle, the flesh already sealed over the wound though a hint of blood stuck to the skin.

"What happened to your finger?" I demanded. "And why were you hiding it from me?"

He groaned. "It was crushed under my body when we got blown over. I tore off the damaged part."

"You what?" I couldn't help the shock in my voice. Who ripped off their own finger?

Max rubbed his eyes. "It will grow back faster than the broken bones would heal. I'm a salamander, Lindsey. You've seen me regrow body parts before."

Sure I had, but I'd never known him to snap off a damaged part. *Ech.*

His head lolled against the tree, though his eyes stayed mostly open.

I hadn't considered the toll our little escapade must've taken on him. I felt okay, but then, he'd been the one to bolster my magics with his own, giving more even than he had on the day we fought the sorcerer and Ceara. Plus, he had torn off his finger and needed more energy to regrow it.

I laid a hand on his forehead like I had any clue how to tell if he had a fever. Most elementals ran hotter than humans. I hadn't noticed it with Tris or Ennea, but Max and Nevan definitely had the hot-blooded thing going on in more ways than one.

"Max, I'm so sorry," I said. "Didn't think…It never occurred to me you'd be hurt by using so much magic. What can I do to help?"

"Nothing. Time is all I need."

"What about, um…" I didn't think I would ever get comfortable discussing this with Max, but I forced myself to do it anyway. "Do you need to feed?"

His lids had drifted shut again, but he cracked one open to peek at me. "Lindsey."

Great, now my familiar was Lindsey-ing me the way Nevan liked to do. Like he used to do.

I glanced over my shoulder at Nevan.

He watched me from a short distance away, his expression unreadable.

The back of my throat hurt. Somehow, without speaking to him, I recognized he had stayed the new Nevan rather than reverting to the man I'd vowed to share my life with earlier today.

I turned back to Max. "There's no reason to be embarrassed. When did you last feed?"

He screwed up his mouth and squirmed, avoiding eye contact. He opened his mouth as if to speak but shut it.

Yeah, he probably wanted to *Lindsey* me again.

A throat-clearing behind me drew my attention to Janus. The god loitered a few feet behind me, much closer than the discreet distance Nevan had chosen. Janus didn't seem to understand discretion or common courtesy. I supposed being a god could make a person arrogant after a while, assuming he hadn't started out that way.

Janus gave me a tight-lipped, squinty-eyed look. The message was clear: *Hurry the hell up and get back to paying attention to me.*

Oh yeah, he had definitely been born arrogant. Or created. Or however gods came into existence.

I flapped a hand in Janus's direction. "Shoo. I need a private moment with my familiar."

The god rolled his eyes and huffed, but finally backed away to stand near Nevan.

Focusing on Max again, I said, "When did you last—"

"It's been a while." He fidgeted some more and refused to meet my gaze. "Not since before I met you."

Before he met me? That had been over two months ago.

"How long can you last without feeding?" I asked.

"Once, I went six months without it. That was far too long." With his hands on the ground, he pushed up to sit straighter. "Being tired like this is a sign of malnutrition, but I'll recover without feeding. If I use up too much magical energy, or if I go too long without nourishment, things will...deteriorate rather swiftly."

"Deteriorate how?"

Face pinched, he finally looked at me. "The hunger will take over, and all my inhibitions will disintegrate. I'll have some control for a time, enough to keep from raping anyone, but if I don't feed within a few days of the hunger seizing me..."

He didn't need to finish that sentence. I could imagine. Witnessing Travis's struggles with his incubus urges had shown me a glimpse of what might happen. And Travis wasn't starving. He had his wits and his inhibitions intact. Without those things to keep him in check...

"The last time," Max said, "was after I had to destroy Aurelia. I—I couldn't stand to live with what I'd done to her. I wanted to die. As a newly forged elemental, I hadn't yet become aware of the full import of immortality. I'd gotten a handle on my urges, but I stupidly believed if I refused to feed, I would die." He gave a harsh, bitter laugh. "What a bleeding moron I was. I'd stayed in my lair for most of those months, waiting to die. When the hunger seized me, I went out to hunt for...prey. I attacked a sweet little leprechaun, but I managed to stop myself before I violated her. Word of my condition soon found its way into the Unseen realm's grapevine."

"Elementals gossip?"

"We're more like humans than you might think." He rubbed his jaw. "Thanks to the gossip, a certain goddess became aware of my plight. She sent two of her warriors to capture me and bring me to her temple. I was in no condition to hold back in any way, so I told her about Aurelia. She was sympathetic, or pretended to be, and she offered me something I couldn't refuse, particularly in the state I was in."

I wanted to ask questions but realized I needed to let him tell me in his own way. So, for the second time today, I ordered myself to rein it in.

"We became lovers," he said, his voice quieter, shame evident on his face. "The sexual energy she provided was intense and almost addictive. She has powers you can't even imagine, powers to seduce and give pleasure and make you never want to leave her. You don't want to know everything she talked me into doing, believe me. After a century or so, she finally went too far, and I found the willpower to leave her. She was not pleased to lose her favorite toy, and as it turns out, she has a tendency toward obsession. I've been hiding from her ever since."

My mouth refused to stay shut any longer. "Who was she?"

"Please, Lindsey, don't ask any more questions."

For him to use the P-word proved to me how much shame his time with the goddess had instilled in him. Whatever they'd gotten up to, he didn't want to tell me.

And I didn't need to know.

I flattened my palms on my thighs. "On a scale of 'just tired' to 'shacking up with a wacko goddess,' how bad off are you?"

"Midway between the two."

"Earlier you said you were just tired."

He scratched his arm, evading my gaze again. "This isn't something I ever wanted to discuss with you."

"I get that, but it's important. I need to know whether you'll be up to helping me or if I should send you home."

"Not going home. As long as you need me, I'll be here with you."

"That's sweet, Max, but I won't let you drain yourself to the point of, um, doing bad things without meaning to."

"I'll be right as rain after a little lie-down."

"Okay," I said, not believing him even a tiny bit, "you take a nap while I chat with Janus and Nevan."

Max's eyes slid shut. Within two seconds, he was snoring softly.

Jeez, I wished I could relax like that.

Had he relaxed in an instant, or had he passed out from exhaustion?

I considered taking his pulse, but I had no idea what normal was for a salamander. I had no clue about the vital signs of elementals in general. Even

Nevan's body, which I'd explored in every way imaginable, remained somewhat of a mystery to me. Besides, Max was snoring. He must be okay.

Reluctantly, I left Max to his "lie-down" and marched over to Janus and Nevan. I related what had gone down in the past, from the moment we'd entered the time stream until we'd reemerged in this field.

Nevan slipped an arm around my shoulders. "It must have been heartbreaking to allow your former lover to die and be transformed in such a way."

Even with weird timeline amnesia, Nevan's first impulse was to comfort me.

Janus, on the other hand, squinted at me with pursed lips.

I made a somewhat rude noise. "What's your problem now, Your Godly Snippiness?"

He arched one brow. "I am merely considering the facts you have related."

"And?"

"Describe this being to me in greater detail."

Seriously? I'd spent several minutes going through this in plenty-sufficient detail.

With sarcastic hand gestures to illustrate my words, I said, "She had wild, long hair that whipped around when she made the air go whoooosh. Her eyes were black. Her body was emaciated, her skin was pale, and her fingernails were long and curved like talons, sharp too. She wore white robes that looked like they'd gone through a meat grinder, and her voice was like a raspy wind. Endued bullets can't kill her. She kicked our asses. That enough detail for you this time?"

He rubbed his chin, staring at the ground. "And she wanted vengeance?"

"Yes, yes, and 'dammit, if you ask me again I'll bust your jaw' yes."

This god guy was driving me bonkers.

Nevan gave me a gentle squeeze. "You are concerned for your familiar, aren't you? That's why you have become…testy."

I glanced at Max, but he was still asleep. "Yeah, I guess so."

Maybe I should've apologized to Janus, but he'd done plenty to annoy me today. I didn't feel terribly inclined to say "sorry."

Janus at last lifted his gaze to me. "I believe you have met a harpy."

Chapter Ten

"A WHAT?" I ASKED. "YOU MEAN THOSE NASTY WOMEN WHO PUNISH men?"

"No," he said in a remarkably patient tone. "That is a mortal myth. The harpies are wind spirits."

"Well, that would explain her penchant for huffing and puffing. What else can you tell me about them?"

"Nothing. The harpies had only recently emerged when I was imprisoned in the Temple of the Four Winds."

After his buddies, the other gods, banded together to destroy him. I supposed his imprisonment would've hampered his knowledge of the Unseen realm, or any realm.

He made a pained face. "I am utterly ignorant of anything that transpired after my imprisonment."

I looked up at Nevan, who kept his arm around me. "Do you know anything about the harpies?"

"Nothing concrete, I'm afraid. I have never encountered a harpy." He gave a resigned sigh. "All I can offer is legends, little more than hearsay."

"I'll take it. Gossip away."

He ran his hand up and down my arm while he spoke. "They say the harpies started out as beautiful women, the female embodiments of the cardinal winds. As the counterparts of the male wind gods, the harpies inevitably became their lovers. All was well for a time, but eventually, jealousy took root. Their hatred for each other escalated into an all-out war. For centuries, they seemed content to fight with each other, always seeking vengeance for slights real or imagined out of blind envy. They stole each other's lovers. They plotted against each other. Some even obtained endued weapons in an effort to destroy their sisters."

"Did any of them die?"

"It's rumored a few did. They continued to procreate, though, spawning more wind spirits who took after their mothers, becoming depraved and fixated on vengeance for slights none of them could remember anymore."

"Awesome," I said, making a thumbs-up sign. "No wonder the Windy Witch I met was such a sweetie-pie. She's got a jones for vengeance, that's for sure. But I have no freaking clue what she thinks I've done to her."

"She claims you took someone from her. Correct?"

"Uh-huh. She said I took 'them,' but she didn't elaborate."

"Your familiar explained to me that you've 'taken out' several elementals."

I turned sideways to him, his arm staying around me, and let myself enjoy the heat of his body. This whole conversation, this whole day, had embedded a permanent chill in my bones. "I took down Skeiron. And the sorcerer. And Ceara."

Nevan stiffened. "Ceara?"

Oops. I'd forgotten he had no memory of his first wife's resurrection and the evil things she'd done.

"How do you know of my mortal wife?" he asked, clearly baffled.

"It's a really long story. The abridged version is a sorcerer brought her back from the dead, they became lovers and plotted to destroy you and me, they got nixed. The end."

He gaped at me like I'd spoken Japanese with a German accent.

"Never mind," I said, patting his chest. "What else can you tell me about the harpies?"

"Very little. The harpies are rarely seen, though any vicious storm is usually blamed on their actions."

"Harpies are the boogeymen of the Unseen realm."

"They are females, but in essence, your assessment is accurate."

I replayed my encounters with the Windy Witch in my mind. "Do harpies have earth powers? First, we had the big quake that split the ground open. Since then, whenever I see this witch the earth moves but less each time. It's like she's finding her footing, in terms of altering time."

Nevan regarded me for a few seconds as if considering what I'd said. "Harpies do not inherently possess that kind of power. If she has indeed acquired dark magics, perhaps those energies shake the earth whenever she attempts to use them. As she adjusts to her new powers, the earthquakes might indeed lessen in intensity, perhaps even stop completely."

Janus turned toward us, his expression grim. "If a harpy is responsible for the time shift, she must have acquired an immense amount of power, magics the likes—"

"The likes of which none have ever seen," I said. "Heard you the first time you gave me your vague explanation."

His nostrils flared on a huffing exhalation. "The point is that you and your familiar barely survived an encounter with the harpy. Even your combined magics were not enough."

"What can we do? How do we find and stop her?"

Janus's shoulders slumped. He gave a faint shake of his head.

"Okay," I said, "answer this for me. I undid the time shift. Why hasn't anything changed other than Calder dying? Everything should've gone back to the way it was before the shift."

He shook his head again, even more slowly.

A clueless god. Go figure.

"Lindsey," Nevan said, "are you certain nothing else changed?"

"Well, I took a peek at my family. Other than Calder not being there, things seemed like they were before Max and I fought the Windy Witch."

"Perhaps you should take a closer look."

"You want me to blip over to my parents' house."

The corner of his mouth kicked up. "Blip? What a charmingly unusual term for it. Yes, I believe you should do that."

"Will you come with me?"

He pulled his head back, chin tucked, and tipped his head to the side. "If you wish it."

"I do." Gesturing at his lack of clothing, save for the loincloth, I added, "But you'll need to glamour into a more mortal-friendly style."

Without letting go of me, Nevan effected a glamour pretty darn close to human, complete with jeans, a T-shirt, and sneakers.

I whisked us to my parents' house in Texas and shrugged out of his embrace. "Better act casual, like we're just friends. I don't want to freak them out."

"As you wish."

I knocked on the front door.

A moment later, the door swung open and my mom said, "Sweetie, why are you knocking? You live here." She squinted at Nevan. "Who's he?"

"My friend, Nevan."

The first time my mom had met Nevan, in the original timeline, she'd instantly adored him. Today, she studied him with suspicion.

Another person pushed past my mom.

Travis dragged me into his arms. "Lindsey, where ya been? Baby, I was worried sick when I woke up and you weren't beside me."

Beside him? In bed?

Shock paralyzed me, so much that I couldn't react when Travis kissed me like we were…a couple. In love. Married? *Oh no, please don't let that be.* I mean, I cared about Travis as a friend. But this was waaaaay too much.

He broke the kiss, keeping his hold on me, and turned his flinty gaze on Nevan. "Who the hell are you?"

"Nevan," the sylph said through clenched teeth.

His jealousy was back, and I knew I'd better get us out of here quick.

Travis lifted my left hand, fingering the engagement and wedding rings. "What the—We ain't even engaged yet. Where'd you get these rings?"

Christ, twice in one day I'd been asked the same question.

And for the second time, I dodged it. Squirming out of Travis's grasp, I snagged Nevan's hand and zipped us back to the field where Janus and Max waited. Janus was pacing while Max hadn't moved from his position slumped against the tree. Little snorts punctuated his whistling snores.

"Well?" Janus said.

"You were right, something changed." I rubbed my temples in a vain attempt to ward off a sprouting headache. "It makes no sense whatsoever. If Calder died and was forged like before, why am I married to his brother and living in Texas? I should've wound up fleeing the state after Travis accused me of murdering Calder." I grasped my head in my hands. "I should've wound up here, met Nevan, and…Gah! But the shop hasn't come back and Nevan doesn't remember me. I haven't felt another time shift, so what gives?"

My brain had begun to hurt. I needed a concrete explanation, but it seemed unlikely I'd get one. Both Nevan and Janus watched me like they expected answers to appear as a flashing neon sign on my forehead.

I asked Nevan, "Out of curiosity, who is the sylph king?"

"Notus, of course."

Okay, no change there.

Right then, Max roused from his nap. He yawned, stretched, and jumped to his feet. When he caught sight of me, frazzled beyond belief, he said, "What did I miss?"

"That was an awfully short nap," I said. "Are you sure you're rested up?"

"In rude health." He winked. "As always."

I explained what had gone on while he slept, then glanced at each male in turn. "Anybody got a clue here?"

Noncommittal noises and shrugs ensued.

Grr. I was getting awfully sick of that reaction. Elementals loved to think they were superior to mortals, and one of these guys was a freaking god, but they had no insight. Not even a half-assed guess.

"The earthquake started it all," I said. "Janus swears he didn't cause it and neither did the Four Winds. That leaves our gusty friend, the time-shifting harpy. Maybe when she made her first attempt, it failed—with earth-shattering results. She tried again, and it worked. Then Max and I reversed the shift, so she did something else."

Nevan cocked one hip and braced a hand on it. "Such as?"

Not a clue. I had to come up with something, so I took a few seconds to ponder the day's events. "Janus, you said time will protect itself if it's injured, like by a time shift."

"Yes," the god replied.

"The Windy Witch changed the past, stopping Calder from being forged. Max and I undid the change. What might happen if the harpy tried to make the same change a second time? Would time defend itself from another wound?"

"Perhaps." He angled his head left and right, examining me. "Are you suggesting that when she attempted to effect the same change again, time would not permit it? But you reported some circumstances had been altered."

"Yeah, but in a different way. Did you sense another shift?"

"No."

"Maybe trying to repeat the same change triggered a timeline defense mechanism, and things came out a little different. The shift wasn't complete, so we couldn't sense it."

Janus remained impassive for a moment, his gaze glued to me. When I was about ready to slap his face to snap him out of his standing coma, he finally spoke. "Your idea has a certain logic."

"Gee, thanks." I stuffed my hands in my pockets but changed my mind and folded my arms under my breasts instead. "We need to brainstorm ways to take down the Windy Witch."

"That is not her name," Janus said.

"Unless you know her name, I'm going to keep calling her the Windy Witch."

Janus stared at me blankly. "What is a brainstorm?"

"It's when we all think really hard and come up with ideas, then decide which ones are good and which totally suck."

He kept staring.

Nevan looped an arm around my waist, smiling at Janus. "Modern mortals have odd ways of speaking, and Lindsey enjoys inventing unusual terms for everything. You'll become accustomed to it."

Was he saying that because he remembered or because I'd called his favorite mode of travel "blipping"? I gazed up at him, admiring his profile and the confidence and sensuality he exuded without even trying.

He glanced down at me and winked.

Just like the old Nevan. My throat hurt for the umpteenth time today, and I swallowed. Every time he showed me a glimmer of the old Nevan, I got choked up. No wonder I hadn't come up with a solid plan for stopping the Windy Witch. The time shift and the changes it had instigated were keeping me on edge.

Exactly what the harpy wanted.

Max flapped a hand to gain my attention. Once he had it, he waved for me to approach.

I pulled away from Nevan, telling him, "Excuse me for a minute."

When I reached Max, he said, "You're distracted by the changes in Nevan."

Our Janusite-familiar connection seemed to give him insights about me I didn't want him to have. Then again, my distraction was probably plain for everyone to see.

"That's true," I admitted. "Can't help it."

"You need to help it. You need to get Nevan back to the way he should be so you can focus."

"I tried that. You were there, you know how it went down."

Max placed a hand on my arm. "I don't mean by undoing the time shift. You need to get Nevan back the Janusite way."

"If I could do that, don't you think I would have already?"

"Maybe I'm not being clear enough." He bent forward to level our gazes. "The good old rumpy-pumpy ought to do the trick."

"And that's supposed to be more clear?"

He bent even closer, our noses almost touching. "Shag him, Lindsey. It worked last time."

Well, at least I understood that term for sex. "Last time? Nevan has never before developed time-shift amnesia."

"But he did have his soul ripped from his body and tossed out in the cosmic bin. You saved him by having a good hump."

"Honestly, Max, stop throwing the dictionary of sex slang at me. My brain is already wiped out." I growled out a sigh and massaged my temples. "Besides, we didn't have sex until after I restored his soul. It was the soul stone that made it possible, and I don't have that anymore."

Oh, I had loved that little soul stone. The small, smooth rock imbued with a fragment of Nevan's soul had produced some unusual and titillating effects, besides fulfilling its purpose by letting me feel Nevan was alive and okay at any time as well as helping me to tap into his powers. Since I'd developed the ability to do that without the stone's assistance, and restoring his soul had drained the thing, I'd given up the soul stone. It lay in a drawer in my dresser in the underground home I shared with Nevan in the Unseen realm.

The soul stone was currently nothing more than a pretty rock.

Max straightened. "Sorry, I forgot about that."

"It's easy to get confused when we're constantly fighting supernatural baddies."

He patted my arm. "Couldn't hurt to try it. Give him a quick shag and see if it helps."

"Sure, I'll take him behind that bush over there."

"Yes, brilliant. Do that."

I wasn't about to take Max's advice and "shag" Nevan, but he did make a valid point. Unless I stopped fretting over Nevan, I wouldn't have the brainpower or the magical power to defeat the Windy Witch. I was always stronger with my husband beside me, but we needed our emotional bond intact for that to happen.

"All right," I said. "I'm going to try to jog his memory, but not with sex."

"Keep that option in your pocket. Trust me, an incubus knows the power of bloody great sex."

"Uh-huh." *Not going there—yet.* "Keep the nosy god out here, okay? Don't need an audience."

Max saluted. "Yes, mistress."

I marched up to Nevan, grabbed his hand, and towed him into the trees where neither Max nor Janus could see or hear us. Nevan seemed more amused than baffled by this turn of events, and he followed me without question. Once we'd traveled far enough to have some privacy but not so far I couldn't shout for help, I leaned back against a tree.

Nevan positioned himself in front of me, edging closer until he could brace one hand on the tree beside my head.

As always, his proximity made my skin tighten and tingle.

"You wanted me alone," he said, his voice a sultry purr. "What will you do with me now?"

He'd spoken those exact words on the night we'd first made love. After Skeiron had attacked us and I risked my life to get Nevan healed, I had needed to see all of him to make sure no wounds remained. Nevan had tossed fairy lights into the air where they hovered like supernatural versions of the sparklers kids played with on the Fourth of July. Then, he'd spoken those words.

Here I am, love. What will you do with me now?

I pulled in a shaky breath. Desire and anxiety shot currents of adrenaline through my veins, each vying for control of me. I had no time for an inner struggle, but my heart had other ideas.

Nevan fingered a lock of my hair, examining it while he twisted the lock around his finger, his head down. Without raising his head, without relinquishing my hair, he looked up at me through those dark, thick lashes. "You want me to be the man you knew."

I couldn't speak, couldn't move. Yes, I longed to have my husband back, but did I have the right to wipe away the man he was now? I'd brought him here so I could jog his memories of the original timeline, but that stupid anxiety kept haunting me.

He released my hair and bent his arm, bringing his face closer, his cheek alongside mine, almost touching me. He whispered in my ear, "Am I anything like the man you loved?"

Get a grip, Lindsey. Speak.

"Yes," I said, my voice breathless. "You are so much like him."

"Do you truly believe I can remember the previous timeline?"

"I do."

He nuzzled my neck and kissed his way up my throat to my ear. "I want to remember. I want to love you again."

A rock solidified in my throat. I gulped but couldn't get rid of it. My breaths came shallow and fast, my body melted against the tree, and without conscious thought I tipped my head back to arch my neck.

Nevan dragged his tongue up my throat to my jaw.

I shivered, overcome by the need to touch him, kiss him, hold him, make him remember everything we'd felt for each other and everything we'd done together.

He feathered soft little kisses over my skin, making his way from my jaw to the corner of my mouth. "Show me what we mean to each other."

Powerless to resist, I locked my arms around him and pulled his body into mine. Our mouths gravitated to each other, questing, craving, melding in a kiss of passion and desperation, our tongues lapping and scraping and delving deep. I moaned, and he wrapped his arms around me to haul me away from the tree, stumbling and grunting as he guided me down to grassy earth but never once severing our lip-lock. His hands roved my body, fondling, kneading, cupping my breasts and my ass.

I'd sworn I wouldn't have sex with Nevan until he spoke my full name, but in this moment…

Shagging him sounded like the way to go.

His hands whisked under my shirt. The sensation of his skin on mine drew a long, throaty moan out of me. Eyes closed, reveling in the kiss and his touch, I surrendered to the desperate need to feel him—on top of me, around me, inside me.

Right now.

The ground shuddered beneath us, but even an earthquake couldn't tear us away from each other or break through the blind hunger. He pushed up my bra. My breasts popped free into his waiting hands. The heat of his skin shot pleasure through me, but when he flicked his thumbs over my nipples, I whimpered into his mouth and latched my leg around his hip.

Another, stronger quake rattled the earth.

Even the crack of a tree breaking couldn't penetrate the haze of lust.

The weight of his body vanished. His mouth had abandoned mine, and his hands no longer explored my body.

My lids fluttered open. The brightness of the sun made me squint for a minute. While I waited for my vision to clear, I pushed up into a sitting position.

Nevan was gone.

An emptiness gaped inside me, a yawning hole where my connection with Nevan had once warmed and soothed me. Our bond was gone.

I scrambled to my feet. "Nevan!"

My cry echoed off the trees, as vacant as the void inside me.

"Nevan!" I screamed his name over and over, but every cry reverberated back to me through a giant nothingness. I spun in a circle, barely able to breathe, hands clenched into fists. The truth stabbed through me like a sword slicing out half of my soul.

Nevan had been erased from history.

I threw my head back and roared.

CHAPTER ELEVEN

A COLDNESS DEEPER THAN ANYTHING ON EARTH CONSUMED ME from the inside out. I began to tremble, my teeth chattering. This wasn't possible. No, it couldn't be true. Nevan must've had his memory altered again, and he wouldn't come when I called because the new time shift had further hampered our connection.

Dimly, I noted three facts. One, a large crack had split the ground ten feet from where I stood. Two, a large aspen had broken off and was lodged against neighboring trees, teetering on the verge of dragging the smaller ones to the ground. And three, a blur of flames was racing toward me through the woods. Though I noted these facts, I couldn't decipher their meaning.

The flames snuffed out as Max skidded to a halt in front of me, breathing hard. He grasped my upper arms. "Lindsey, are you all right?"

I shook my head weakly and spoke without knowing what I was saying. "Why didn't you poof here?"

"Too risky with the downed trees and such." Max glanced around, his jaw tightened, and he bent to meet my gaze. "Where's Nevan?"

I managed only one whispered word. "Gone."

"He's been erased," Max said.

Whether our bond had given him insight, or he simply saw the truth on my face, I didn't know. I nodded. He pulled me into his arms, holding me until I stopped shaking.

I stepped back and noticed Janus loitering behind Max. The god seemed strangely empathetic.

"Ah…" Max began, gesturing at my shirt. "You might want to…"

Glancing down, I realized though my shirt had fallen down to cover my breasts, my bra had stayed lodged above them. I turned my back to the men, fixed my bra, and faced them again. My heartbeat thudded in my ears as the deep-freeze inside me evaporated on a wave of hot, simmering anger. I balled my hands into fists, my shoulders bunching.

"I'm going to find that windy bitch," I said, "and rip her apart molecule by molecule with my bare hands."

Max scratched his neck. "I know you're angry and grieving but—"

"Not grieving. I'm going to undo this goddamn time shift and save him."

"Lindsey…" Max winced as if in anticipation of an outburst from me. "You couldn't fix the timeline before. Why do you think you can do it now?"

"The first time, I didn't have the right motivation." Despite Max's obvious fear I would freak out, I remained calm. My fists had relaxed, my shoulders too, and the simmering anger had cooled into an eerie composure that probably should've unnerved me. I didn't care. Let me be freaky-calm Lindsey. It was better than falling apart. "This time, I have the strongest motivation of all. She ripped my husband away from me, and that bitch is going to pay."

Janus sidled around Max to confront me. "Have you considered that this may be precisely what the harpy wanted? She claimed you took someone from her, and she has taken someone from you. She must have known this would anger you. Perhaps she wants you to strike out at her, so she might destroy you."

"I am not lashing out." I squared my shoulders, suffused with a grim resolve. "First, I undo whatever she did to the timeline. Second, I'll kick her bony ass back to the Big Bang."

"Your grief makes you irrational."

"This is not grief because Nevan is not dead." I aimed my steady gaze at the god. "Do I seem unhinged?"

"No," Max replied, "you're so bloody calm it's making my skin itch."

"You can help me, or you can wait here while I take care of this. Which is it?"

Max scrutinized me for a moment, scanning me up and down, his mouth tight. "If you're going into the time stream again, I'm going with you."

Janus sighed. "This is a mistake. In her condition—"

I surged forward to jab a finger into his chest. "You know nothing about my condition. Unless you have something constructive to say, keep your mouth shut."

Maybe I was a teeny bit irrational. My heart was overriding my common sense—like I'd ever had an abundance of that—and all I could think about was getting Nevan back.

Janus raised his hands in surrender and stepped back.

The fact I was scaring a god should have clued me in to the fallacy of this mission. I didn't care. I couldn't care. That blustery beast had stolen the only man I'd ever loved from me. If she wanted vengeance, I'd cram a potful of it down her raspy throat.

With a poof of flames, Max shrank into salamander form.

I tucked him inside my bra. He didn't even twitch his tail.

Janus gave me a strange look, something like fear. "I beg you to reconsider this action. Wait until you have calmed yourself before raging into a battle with a being who has defeated you twice."

A god was begging me?

Stop and think, Lindsey, before you screw up big time.

"Yes," Janus said, taking a tentative step toward me. "You see the danger. You realize this is not a wise path to take, and if you venture down it, you will lose more of the ones for whom you care so deeply. You risk losing yourself as well. Love between a mortal and an immortal leads to only pain and tragedy."

The rough tone of his voice implied deep emotion. I should have stopped to consider why he seemed so invested in convincing me not to do this. I should have stopped to think, period.

I couldn't.

"What are you saying?" I demanded. "Nevan and I are doomed anyway, so why bother saving him from the harpy's machinations? That's bullshit."

"This course of action is unwise." He paused, his face pinched. "I do not wish for you to die, Lindsey."

How bizarre that the man, the god, who had been nothing but a pain in the neck all day had suddenly become concerned for my safety. Had I misjudged him? Underneath all the godly arrogance, did he have an actual heart?

If Janus thought I was walking into a disaster…

Nevan wouldn't want me to do this.

The thought stopped me. My chest ached. I clutched my hands over my belly, feeling the rings on my left hand. "You're right. This isn't such a good idea."

A gale ripped through the woods.

The broken aspen, balanced against much slimmer trees, shifted.

Wind roared around us, swirling like a tornado.

And the aspen toppled straight toward me, dragging its brethren with it.

I staggered backward, tripped over the crack in the earth, and whumped down on my ass. The trees kept coming as if in slow motion, looming nearer and nearer. I scrambled backward like a crab. Max skittered up my chest, trying to climb out of my shirt, but my frantic movements sent him tumbling down into my bra.

Janus tumbled head over heels backward into the woods.

The aspen crashed down a dozen feet to my right. The tangle of skinnier trees smashed down on my legs. Agony tore through my left leg, and my hoarse cry reverberated through the woods.

The Windy Witch raced toward me, a blur of tattered robes and flying hair, surrounded by a mini tornado. She slowed when she reached the pile of trees that pinned my legs to the ground and stepped onto it. Even the weight of her emaciated body proved too much.

A new agony shot through me, and I let out a strangled scream.

Max scurried around inside my shirt, but he couldn't get past the slender branch that had landed at a diagonal across my chest.

The harpy grinned at me, exposing jagged teeth. She pointed at me with one taloned finger. "You took from me, so I took from you. How does it feel, Janusite?"

In spite of the pain, I mustered a nonchalant tone. "Fantastic. I couldn't wait to get rid of that annoying sylph. You did me a favor."

She hopped off the tangled trees to hunch beside me.

The shifting weight of the aspens had me choking back a cry.

"You lie," she hissed. "Your pain is great, though not as great as that which you inflicted on me."

"Who are you? Or should I just call you Windbag?"

"Perhaps you should know the name of the one who will destroy everything you care for and then destroy you." She tapped one talon on my nose. "I am Aello."

"Who is it you think I've taken from you?"

"*Daimones.*" She raked her talon down my throat, drawing a trickle of hot blood. "*Anemoi Thuellai.*"

Was she speaking Greek? I recognized the word *daimones*, though I couldn't remember what it meant.

Max scampered up my chest again, determined to get free.

The movement snared Aello's attention. She slipped her talon inside my shirt and tore it open.

With a tiny hiss, Max sprang off my chest.

Aello caught him in her hand, his little red head peeking out between her talons. She canted her head side to side, scrutinizing the creature in her grasp. "This is your familiar, a salamander. He was in human form when last I saw him."

Dread coiled in my gut, its tendrils snaking up into my chest.

The harpy turned her hand so I could see Max's tiny face. "You care for this one too, do you not? The bond between a magical being and her familiar is formidable."

Why didn't Max poof into human form?

As if she'd read my mind, Aello said, "Oh, he cannot shift while in my grasp. My magic prevents it."

"You're not the only one with powers."

"Perhaps not, but you are weak in comparison." She opened her hand, holding Max by the throat between two of her fingertips. Her talons curved under his small body, and his tail whipped against them. "I shall take another from you."

She slashed one of her talons.

Max's leg was severed from his body. It dropped to the ground.

He let out a squeal of pain and thrashed in her grip.

"I will take him limb by limb," Aello said. "Until nothing remains."

My pulse beat so fast it almost fluttered. Max could regrow limbs. I'd seen it before. He could do it again, he had to.

Aello moved her talon into position, preparing to slice off Max's other leg.

I ground my teeth, pouring all my energy into a single task—gathering enough power to stop this creature from hurting my friend. Blue magic exploded around me, sparkling, snapping, spreading outward toward the harpy. When it contacted her skin, she shrieked like a storm wind. Her fingers shot open, and Max tumbled to the ground.

A gale corkscrewed around us, shuddering the trees piled atop me.

I gritted my teeth against the pain, fighting for every breath.

Aello vanished.

Chapter Twelve

I GRIMACED AND GROUND MY TEETH WHILE JANUS HEFTED THE TREES OFF of me enough that I could roll out from under them. Pain stabbed through my left leg, but I kept rolling until I was clear of the trees. Gasping for breath, hurting in more places than I wanted to count, I lay sprawled on my back and struggled to understand…anything.

With a sharp bellow, Janus released the trees. They whumped down again.

He had no powers, and apparently, he had no super strength either.

A flash of red in my peripheral vision made me glance to my right.

Max, stuck in salamander form, lay motionless on the ground.

I sprang to a sitting position, determined to get up and run to him, but the pain in my leg seized my entire body. I cried out, my head spinning.

Janus crouched beside me, dead leaves clinging to his hair and his toga smeared with dirt. He examined my leg, probing gently with his fingers. Even his cautious examination hurt like hell and had me grinding my teeth again as breaths gusted out of my nostrils.

"I believe it is broken," he said. "In multiple places."

Wonderful. "Check on Max, please. He's not moving."

Janus nodded and scurried over to the tiny red form lying in the grass. He touched a fingertip to Max's little chest. "He is breathing. Perhaps you can force the shift and return him to human form. That will make it easier to deal with his injuries."

"Don't have the energy, magical or physical, to force anything." I glanced down at my leg. Something stuck out from it, poking into the fabric of my jeans. Something? I had a sick feeling I knew what it was. A broken bone. Nausea swelled in my gut, and my gorge rose into my throat, but I managed to croak, "The vortex."

Janus stared dumbly at me.

"The healing vortex," I squeezed out between my clenched teeth. "There was one behind the shop, when it existed. I have to assume the vortex hasn't gone away. Max and I need healing, fast, and that's the closest option. You'll need to carry me, I can't walk or teleport. And bring me Max."

For once, the god did not balk. He scooped Max into his palm and hurried back to me, then transferred the limp body of my familiar into my cupped hands.

Janus glanced around, clearly searching for something.

"What is it?" I asked, my voice scratchy.

"I will need to bind your broken bones with something sturdy to prevent further damage."

"No time. Get me to the vortex." I held my breath, wincing through a wave of dizzying pain. "Please."

He studied me with a tense expression, his Adam's apple jouncing as he swallowed hard. After a couple seconds, he slid his arms under me and lifted.

Agony. Searing. Wrenching. I cried out, battling against the impulse to clench my fingers because that would crush Max. "Hurry."

Janus raced through the woods, following my instructions for where to go. Sweat dribbled down his temples, and his breaths came fast and shallow. Sweat dribbled down my temples too, though I hadn't exerted myself the way he was doing. Mine was a cold sweat.

We reached the vortex, now nothing more than a patch of weeds, after a few excruciatingly long minutes. I fought to stay conscious despite the agony slicing through me with every step Janus took.

He carefully set me down in the weeds. "What should I do?"

"Wait and pray. That's all we can do."

I collapsed onto my back, Max cradled in my hands. *Please work, please.*

Nothing happened.

When Tris had healed me and Nevan, on separate occasions, he had needed to consume a lot of copper to power up the vortex for the task. Nevan and I had been on the verge of death, though. I prayed the vortex had enough energy on its own to do this. I doubted Tris would answer my call if I screamed for him, since he would have no idea who I was.

A trickle of magic tickled my skin and fizzled out.

"Dammit," I whimpered.

Janus knelt beside me. "What is it?"

"I don't think the vortex is strong enough. We need a leprechaun."

"Call for one."

"Nobody knows me anymore. Would an elemental answer the call of an unknown mortal?"

"Try, Lindsey," he said with an intensity I hadn't heard from him before. "You are the Janusite. Infuse the call with your magic. It is a risk, letting a stranger know you have power. If you do not do this, you may die. Your leg may not heal properly and could become infected." He glanced at my hands. "And your friend is severely wounded."

I could do this. I had to—for Max, if not for myself.

Summoning all the magic left in me, which wasn't a hell of a lot, I screamed, "Triskaideka! Get your scrawny, obnoxious butt over her right this minute."

Nothing.

"Triskaideka!" I screamed so loud it mutated into a coughing fit.

I was about to holler again when the leprechaun appeared at my feet. His bright-blue eyes darted this way and that as he took in the scene, then he roved his gaze up and down my body. His lip curled. "Jeez, lady, you're a mess."

"Need your help."

"I don't do favors for no mortals."

"You sensed my magic. You had to. I'm no mere mortal." I tenderly shifted Max so he rested in my left palm and pushed up with my right hand, elevating my head and shoulders. "I have power, you want to know why, and the only way that happens is if you heal me and my familiar."

I spread my fingers to reveal the salamander in my hand.

Tris tucked his chin, staring at Max with his lip curled even more. "That's a frigging incubus, lady. I don't heal their kind."

I slammed my hand down on the dirt, gritting my teeth against the pain it triggered. "You will heal this one. There's a harpy screwing with the timeline. She's erased a powerful sylph from existence with a time shift. You could be next."

"Why should I believe you? Time shifts? Come on, that's crazy."

Janus surged to his feet and stalked up to Tris. "I am the god Janus. What Lindsey says is true, and you will do as she asks." He leaned in to tower over the much-smaller leprechaun, causing Tris to shrink back a smidgen. "Or you will suffer my wrath."

As much as I appreciated Janus's effort, I knew this was not the way to gain Tris's help.

The leprechaun rolled his eyes.

"How did I know your full name?" I said.

Tris darted his gaze to me, not blinking, lips parted.

"If I'm nothing but a worthless mortal," I said, "how do I know your name?"

"Well…" He focused on my feet. "I don't know."

"Because you and I have met, that's how." Another wave of pain and nausea hit me, and I collapsed onto my back. "In the original timeline, we're friends. Even though you're sometimes an annoying brat. I've gotten used to it. I know your sister, Ennea, too."

Tris's mouth fell open. For a moment, he said nothing. At last, he squared his shoulders, lifted his chin, and said, "What the hell. I'll power up the vortex for ya, but I need copper."

How on earth was I going to get that? The rock shop no longer existed.

"Lucky for you," Tris said, "I got a stash at home. Gimme a minute."

The leprechaun poofed away.

I set Max on the grass, suddenly too exhausted to hold him any longer. Seconds ticked by in my mind, loud as hammer blows, timed with my slowing heartbeat. I'd grown numb too, and a strange floaty feeling enveloped me. Part of me recognized this was a bad sign, but the numbness kept spreading, infecting my mind. I fell back onto the ground.

Tris blipped back into view at my feet. Copper dust crusted his lips and chin. He swiped at his mouth with the sleeve of his flannel shirt. "You ready? Considering your injuries, this is gonna hurt like a son of a bitch."

"Do it," I mumbled.

Warmth poured over my skin, seeping under the surface, blossoming through my whole body. I relaxed into the sensation, sighing with relief. The warmth transformed into a sizzling energy that tingled inside me, faintly at first, intensifying into a harder and hotter tingle with every second that elapsed. I gasped. The energy crackled and bit into my flesh from the inside, a million tiny teeth burrowing down to the source of the damage.

Bones cracked, resetting themselves.

A strangled scream burst out of me as my body convulsed.

Crack. Snap. Rip.

The scorching heat of the healing energies set my body on fire. I clawed at the weeds, sank my nails into the earth, clenched my teeth so hard I heard enamel breaking, but the vortex healed those wounds too with a ferocity that transformed my entire skull into a mass of misery. Desperate, agonized noises echoed around me, and with a jolt, I realized I was making those sounds.

The energy dwindled, sluicing out of me, washing away the pain along with it.

"It's done," Tris said, and vanished.

I lay sprawled on the grass for a moment, not because of exhaustion or pain, but because of a shock that paralyzed my every muscle. I was healed. I knew this without so much as glancing at my body. Tris had cooperated, and the vortex had worked. I lifted my left leg, bent the knee, swung my foot side to side.

No pain. No shattered bones. Even my torn shirt had been repaired.

Sitting up, I hauled in a deep breath and let it out little by little. The vortex had done more than heal my injuries. It had reinvigorated me. I glanced down at my hands, turning them upside down, revealing my empty palms.

Max.

I jumped to my knees and scanned the area.

A tiny red form lay in the weeds a few feet away, one leg missing.

"That lousy leprechaun," I growled. "He didn't heal Max."

I screamed Tris's name until he showed up.

"What's your problem, lady?" he asked. "I got other things to do besides help you."

"Max is not healed." I pointed at the salamander. "His leg is still gone."

"Can't do nothing about that. The vortex can't regrow parts that got lopped off." The leprechaun peered over my shoulder at Max. "He'll be fine. Those weirdos can regrow anything."

Tris winked out.

I touched Max with my fingertip, wiggling him slightly in an attempt to rouse him. "Wake up, Max. Come on, wake up."

His tiny eyelids fluttered open. He raised one itty-bitty hand—or foot, or whatever—and motioned for me to move away. It was the cutest thing I'd ever seen, but I couldn't appreciate the adorableness at the moment. I scuffled backward in a crouch.

With a burst of flames, Max shifted into human form. He remained prone on the ground, missing one leg.

"Are you okay?" I asked. "Aside from the, uh, missing limb."

He yawned loudly and sat up, propped up with both hands on the ground. "Feel better, but regrowing the leg will take time."

"Don't worry. I'll deal with Aello on my own."

"The hell you will." He fixed me with a mulish look. "I am your familiar, Lindsey, and I won't abandon you."

"No offense, sweetie, but you've only got one leg. Speed tends to be important in confrontations with crazy elementals."

Max frowned at me.

I gave him my best stubborn look.

He grumbled and raised one hand. A thick branch, stripped of its bark, appeared in his grasp. Next, he conjured some leather strips and strapped the branch to the stump where his leg had been, creating a kind of peg leg and securing it with another strap around his hip. With a self-satisfied smile, he poofed himself into a standing position. His peg leg wobbled a bit, but he found his equilibrium. Taking cautious steps, he figured out how to walk with his new appendage.

Max stopped in front of me, where I was kneeling, and spread his arms wide. "See? Good to go."

"Uh-huh," I said, dubious to say the least.

He rubbed his hands together. "What's the plan this time?"

Janus made a dismissive noise. "There is no plan unless we discern what Aello wants. We have no conception of her final goal or her true motivations."

"Maybe you have no clue," I said, "but I get it. She thinks I took someone from her, so she wants to take away the people I care about." My near-death experience and the excruciating pain of the healing had granted me a crystal clarity about a few things. "Why would she care about messing with Calder's fate? In the first shift, she stopped his forging. After Max and I undid that, she tried again, with a slightly different outcome. In both cases, if I weren't immune to the shifts, I would've wound up with someone other than Nevan. Aello wanted to keep me from ever meeting him."

Janus regarded me with an expression reminiscent of appreciation. "When the second shift did not take Nevan away from you, she resorted to a direct assault in addition to a third shift."

"Exactly."

Max cleared his throat. "Ah, Lindsey…"

"What is it, Max?"

"She won. Nevan is gone."

I rose, resisting the urge to fist my hands, resolved to stay calm and rational this time. "We are going to undo this shift too."

"That was a right mess when we tried it before."

"Are you suggesting I let her keep screwing with time? Maybe you'll disappear next."

"I'm not suggesting we give up." He hobbled toward me. "We need to defeat Aello on our own terms, here in the present, before we reverse the latest shift."

"We've had so much luck fighting her face to face."

Max touched my shoulder. "You're feeling hopeless because Nevan is gone, I understand that. You will get him back. If you think about what I've said, I know you'll realize I'm right."

"What if Aello creates another shift while we're plotting to take her down? I can't lose anyone else. All I've got is you and—" I flapped a hand in Janus's direction. "Him."

Janus flashed me an annoyed look.

I let my head fall back and gazed up at the blue sky. Max was right, of course. Running after Aello whenever she altered time had not worked. She seemed to get stronger while Max and I got weaker. Endued bullets couldn't kill her. How was I supposed to destroy her?

The answer hit me with the suddenness of a rock dropped on my head. *Duh.* How could I have forgotten?

I looked Max straight in the eyes. "I need to drag that whackjob across the nearest boundary."

"Yes, good luck with that," Max said, his voice dripping with sarcasm. "I'm sure she'll follow you to the boundary and happily traipse across it."

"Got a better idea? Endued weapons don't work on her."

Janus approached us. "Aello is immensely powerful, more powerful than any elemental should be. Until you discover the source of her power, you will have little chance of defeating her by any method."

I smacked his godly chest with the back of my hand. "Told you to shut up unless you've got something useful to say. 'She's unstoppable, oh shit, we're all going to die' is not constructive criticism."

The incubus and the god both watched me warily.

Had I cowed these two powerful beings?

Another idea struck me. "I need to go back in time to find out when and how Aello acquired so much power."

"Fabulous idea," Max said. He tried to bow from the waist, but the strap of his peg leg hindered him. "How may I serve you in this endeavor, my mistress?"

"Cut the sarcasm, that's how. I get that you think I've gone insane, but unless either of you two has a better idea, this is the plan."

Max and Janus exchanged a look, shrugged, and focused on me.

"We will follow you," Janus said.

"Thank you."

Both males winced at my use of the dreaded T-word.

I looked to Janus. "Since you can't go with us into the time stream, I need you to stay here and keep an eye out for Aello while we're gone. Don't want her sneaking up on us when we come back." I tapped a finger on Max's chest. "Could you conjure the endued shotgun shells for my derringer? And the barrel that fits them?"

"Well, I could try." He went motionless for a second, his gaze distant. Then he held out a hand, and the shotgun shells and barrel materialized in his palm. "There."

He offered the items to me.

I pulled out the derringer, dumped the spent .357 shells, and removed the barrel, replacing it with the one that fit the shotgun rounds. Plucking the rounds from Max's palm, I slid them into the barrel and snapped it shut.

"You'll have two shots," I told Janus, handing him the gun. "Endued ammo doesn't kill the Windy Witch, but shotgun shells ought to slow her down. Use them wisely. You've only got two."

"I could conjure more," Max said.

"But I would have to teach Janus how to reload. I've got an ooky feeling in my gut that tells me we don't have time for a lesson in loading ammo." I pointed at the derringer's trigger. "Aim at her forehead and pull that."

He took the gun in his hand, the grip firmly in his palm, and curled his finger over the trigger. The gun looked tiny in his big hand.

"Not yet," I warned. "Don't touch the trigger until you're ready to fire."

"I understand." He hefted the gun as if testing its weight and aimed the muzzle at the ground.

"You seem awfully comfortable with a firearm," I said. "Considering you've been locked up in limbo since the Stone Age."

He gave me a long-suffering look. "As I have said before, you and I are connected. I've sensed things about you over the years, particularly since you came into your powers." He glanced down at the pistol in his hand. "This gun is a vital appendage for you, as your arms and legs are. I've absorbed a bit of knowledge about it from you."

Yeah, I didn't know how to feel about a god having some kind of telepathic link to me. No time to worry about that, though.

"Remember," Janus said, "the time stream is your ally and your servant. Treat it with respect, and it will do as you command."

My ally and my servant. I would've thought that was dumb, because how could anything or anyone be both, but I knew better these days. Max had become my ally, my friend, and—thanks to the life debt—my servant, in a way. The contradictions felt strange but no longer impossible.

"Injure the timeline," Janus continued, "and it will defend itself."

"Yeah, I know." I gestured at Max's wooden appendage. "Will that shrink with you? Or are you going to be hopping around on one leg when we get to wherever we're going?"

He thumped a hand on his peg leg. "You can take me into the time stream as long as I'm on your person, and I can shapeshift this with me because it's attached to me."

To prove his point, he shifted into salamander form amid a burst of flames.

I couldn't help grinning at the sight of the small, red lizard with a tiny wooden leg fashioned from a minuscule twig. Tucking Max in my bra, I stifled a laugh when his peg leg tickled my skin.

"*Bonam fortunam*," Janus said. I must've looked confused, because he added, "It means good luck, Lindsey."

I nodded and jumped into the time stream.

Hovering above the twisting, diverging tributaries of the temporal river, I concentrated on the task I'd set for myself. Find the moment when Aello first acquired dark power. The river curved back in on itself, forming the same kind of loop I'd seen before. This time, I knew the loop would guide me to the critical moment.

Sailing down toward the intersection where the loop closed in on itself, I focused all my energy, boosted by Max's power, on diving into that single moment. Closer, closer. I sailed downward faster, plummeting toward my goal. Closer, closer.

An unseen force plowed into me.

I tumbled backward away from my destination, my mind spinning, dizziness whirling through me. I fumbled for a connection to the time stream, but something immensely powerful hurled me away from it. My mind slammed back into my body with so much force my feet flipped out from under me. Max flew out of my shirt to hit the ground with a sharp squeak. I shouted wordlessly, my head reeling, flat on my back in the grass. Above me, the sky seemed to twirl, dragging the treetops in its wake.

Max assumed human form with the usual burst of flames.

A gust of wind ripped through the clearing, dousing his fire.

I lay there dazed and motionless, observing events as if from a great distance, as if I peered through a spyglass.

Aello emerged out of a small tornado that snuffed out to reveal her. She aimed a taloned finger at me. "Foolish mortal. Did you not think I would learn your methods? I knew you would attempt to swim the waters of time once more, and I set a trap for you. My magics created a false beacon which you dutifully followed—to your destruction."

"Destruction?" Max said with a forced laugh. "We aren't destroyed."

The harpy grinned, her jagged yellow teeth exposed. "I have not finished yet."

She raised one hand, palm up, fingers writhing.

A gunshot detonated.

Blood spurted from a wound in Aello's forehead.

Another shot boomed, striking her forehead an inch to the left of the first round.

Janus held the derringer, aimed at her though he had no ammo left. The shotgun rounds had penetrated Aello's skull but caused far less damage than they should have. Yes, blood poured from the wounds. But her head should've exploded like a watermelon.

She swiped a hand across her forehead, and the wounds vanished.

I pushed up with my arms, but my head kept spinning. Christ, the force she'd used to kick me out of the time stream, it had been…something the likes of which none had seen.

Until today. Lucky us.

Aello lowered the hand she had swiped over her forehead. She fanned out her fingers to reveal the objects in her palm.

The shotgun shells. She had somehow reconstituted them.

Raising her hand, she blew a foggy breath at the shells.

One of them shot at me like an invisible gun had fired it.

Max dove toward me.

The shotgun round slammed into his side intact, a thick projectile punching straight into his flesh. He landed sideways across my lap, blood pouring from his wound.

Aello blew on the other shell.

Max bellowed and flung his hand up as if to catch the shell. It bored right through his hand, ripping it apart. He bellowed again, from pain instead of anger.

Aello curled her taloned fingers and snapped them straight.

The intact shotgun shell popped out of Max's side and flew back into Aello's hand like she'd reeled it in with a fishing pole. She raised it in her palm, her lips puckering in preparation for another wind-blown shot.

Aimed at Janus.

I howled with fury and swung my hand up. Blue energy burst forth from my palm, shooting across the distance to Aello in a concentrated stream that barreled into her chest at the instant she blew the shotgun shell at Janus. Her shot veered a hair off course and sideswiped Janus's shoulder. Aello was hurled backward a good thirty feet where she landed with a cracking thud.

Janus collapsed to his knees, one hand pressed to his shoulder, his face strained. Blood oozed out between his fingers.

Aello shrieked with the voice of an enraged tempest.

She vanished amid a gust that swept up earth and grass, flinging them in a spinning dervish.

Breathing hard, I glanced down at Max where he lay sprawled over my legs, bleeding but conscious. That bitch had shot him twice with endued shotgun shells. He couldn't heal from that on his own. He needed help, from a vortex or some other magical method.

I glared at the space where Aello had hunched seconds earlier.

She would pay for this. Whatever I had to do to stop her, I would do it.

Chapter Thirteen

Janus waddled toward us on his knees, clutching his injured shoulder as he made his way around the debris field Aello had left behind. His face had turned a touch ashen, most likely from shock rather than his not-life-threatening wound. "How is your familiar?"

"Not dead yet," Max muttered, "if that's what you were hoping for."

"Shush," I told Max, brushing hair from his eyes. "Janus is being nice for once. And I want to know the same thing. Those were endued shotgun shells, Max. You can't heal naturally from that."

"I know." He shifted position and winced, hissing in a breath. "Had to save you."

My throat went thick, my eyes burned, and my vision blurred. I brushed hair away from his eyes. "Don't you die on me, Max. I won't allow it."

"If the Janusite commands it, I have no choice, do I?"

"Better believe it."

When I sniffled, Max turned his head to gaze up at me with bleary eyes. "A healing vortex won't be enough this time, not with my leg working to regrow itself and the effects of an endued weapon on top of it."

"There has to be something. The Unseen is a world of magic, for heaven's sake."

He made a pained face, not entirely from physical discomfort. "There is one way."

Based on his expression and the resignation in his voice, I had a feeling I knew what way he meant. "The goddess."

Max nodded weakly.

"Well, go to her already."

He crimped his lips. "Lindsey, if I go to her, I may never get free of her influence. It was bloody difficult the first time round."

I swallowed, but the constriction in my throat wouldn't loosen. How could I ask him to go to an obsessed goddess who had the power to enthrall him? If he didn't go to her, he would die. If he did, I might never see him again.

At least he would be alive.

Our bond, cemented by his life debt to me, had kept him immune to the time shifts. Maybe it could give him the strength to resist the goddess's pull.

I bent closer to his face. "Listen to me. If you don't do this, you are going to die. You have something you didn't have the first time you went to this crazy goddess. You have me. Your life debt combined with the familiar's bond has made you immune to the time shifts. It will keep you free of her influence too."

"You can't know that."

"Maybe not logically, but Logical Lindsey gave up the ghost months ago." I laid a palm on his cheek and bored my gaze into his. "I trust my instincts these days and my intuition. Whatever that goddess does, you can always tap into our bond to break free of it. I believe it, and you need to believe it too."

I hadn't lied. I did believe it. Speaking the words had convinced me. But had I convinced him?

He said nothing for a moment, his face tight with pain. "All right."

"You'll do it?"

"I will."

Max slapped his hands on the ground and, with an agonized groan, heaved his body off of mine. Janus hopped up to assist Max in getting to his feet. Despite his peg leg and the bleeding wounds on his side and his hand, he stood up straight.

Janus stepped back.

I leaped up to grab Max's arm. "Wait. Before you go, at least tell me the goddess's name. If I need to go whup her ass to get you back, I will. It would help to know who she is."

Max's mouth ticked up at one corner. "Always the feisty heroine, eh?"

"Hiding under my bed got old pretty fast. It's dusty under there."

"I can't picture you hiding under anyone's bed." He sighed, then leaned in to whisper in my ear, "Hathor."

He poofed away.

Janus looked at me like he expected I'd share the information with him. Max had entrusted me with his secret, and I would not violate that trust merely to satisfy a prickly, powerless god's curiosity.

"Forget it," I said. "The goddess's identity is need to know, and you do not need to know it."

He harrumphed.

"Instead of being grumpy," I said, "you could try being helpful. With Max and Nevan gone, I have only one ally left. You." I eyed his wounded shoulder. "And you need a healing vortex."

"No. I will be fine. The endued ammunition seems not to affect me as badly as it would if I had powers. You should not waste energy on summoning a leprechaun." Janus scratched his head. "I have little to offer. This enemy, this harpy, I know nothing about her. My knowledge is limited to the time before I was destroyed and confined to the Temple of the Four Winds. You need someone who has a deep understanding of the Unseen realm as it is today, as it has been for the previous several millennia."

"Maybe I could get Tris to help."

"You need someone who will fight by your side, who will protect you, who will die for you if necessary."

I squeezed my eyes shut, clamping my lips between my teeth. I knew what he was getting at, and the idea tore a new gash in my heart. I pulled in a long breath and let it out slowly, opening my eyes. "I need Nevan."

"Precisely."

My surprise at Janus suggesting this without a hint of sarcasm evaporated in a heartbeat as the gravity of the situation settled on my shoulders, the weight of two worlds resting on me once again. I'd always had Nevan to shoulder the burden with me.

Aello had stolen him from me forever.

Or had she?

"Do you think," I said, voicing my thoughts without really expecting an answer, "that I could get Nevan back? He remembered me, on some level, even with the time shifts. What if I could bring him back from being erased?"

"You do have a powerful bond. I have never seen anything like it. Can you feel him?"

I hadn't tried to because the loss of him had shredded me inside. Our immediate connection might have been severed, but could a latent link persist?

"Try to sense him," Janus said, his tone gentle.

Even if I had to do this alone, I could. If Aello eradicated Janus, if she wiped away everyone else in both worlds, I would find a way to defeat her. With Nevan by my side, though, I'd have the shared power of our bond, of our love, to win the battle faster.

I closed my eyes and focused on the image of Nevan. His whirlpool eyes, the way they glowed and changed color with his emotions. Those lips, the ones that curved into a sensual smile whenever he wanted me. Nevan, the strong and virile warrior. Nevan, the sweet and generous lover. Nevan, my husband, my soul mate.

Something tickled at my ethereal senses.

Nevan, please, hold on to me. Come back to me.

The tickle intensified into a tingling shiver.

A thread whipped around me. I latched onto it, pulling with all my psychic strength, reeling it in closer, closer, closer. The connection strengthened, thickening into a rope instead of a slender thread. I dragged it toward me, feeling a physical sensation of muscles straining with the effort, though I knew this was a phantom sensation.

My eyes flew open.

Nevan stood in front of me, wearing only the loincloth. His gaze darted, his lips were parted, and his chest heaved as if he'd run a very long distance. Beads of sweat on his chest glistened in the sunshine.

That's when I realized sweat was trickling down my skin too, and I was breathing as hard he was. My body trembled a little. Nevan, on the other hand, appeared rock steady.

Christ, getting him back had taken a lot of energy.

"Are you okay?" I asked.

"Where have I been? It feels as if I went away for an eternity, which for an elemental is no mere figure of speech."

Eternity? I couldn't fathom how empty and frightening that must've been, and I realized I shouldn't try to understand it.

"Are you unwell, Lindsey?" Nevan asked.

Hearing him say my name, even just my first name, rushed a tide of relief through me. My knees buckled.

Nevan caught me in his brawny arms, hugging me to his body. "Lindsey?"

"I'm okay. Bringing you back took a lot out of me is all." I let my forehead fall against his chest, let his strong body support me. He'd called me Lindsey twice, which meant he remembered that much about me. Was it possible…I jerked my head up. "What do you remember?"

"About what?"

That idiotic hope sparked to life inside me. "About me. Us."

"You are Lindsey," he said, "I recall that much. But if you're hoping I've turned back into the man you married, I'm afraid you will be disappointed."

I couldn't move any part of myself, not even my eyelids.

He cupped my cheek and brushed his thumb over my lips. "I also recall wanting you, feeling connected to you in ways I cannot explain. And I remember growing quite jealous whenever another man touches you or approaches within ten feet of you."

At least he hadn't been altered any further. He seemed to have remained the version of Nevan he'd been before Aello expunged him from history, or at least from the version of it everyone else knew. Even the Windy Witch didn't have the power to erase him from my history.

Holy mackerel. I'd brought him back.

Movement to my left drew my attention to Janus. He looked shell-shocked, gaping at me like I'd turned into a unicorn. Did they have those in the Unseen? I'd never asked.

"What's wrong with you?" I said to the god.

He angled his head this way and that, his eyes unblinking. "You brought someone back from oblivion."

"Yeah, it was your idea. Did you think I couldn't really do it?"

"I believed you needed to, but…" He blinked once in slow motion. "Even I could never accomplish such a feat. I tried once, but I failed."

Wow. I had done something a god couldn't do.

His shocked expression softened into appreciation. "This is why the Four Winds chose you to wield my powers. They sensed your strength."

"I thought they chose me when I was born. I didn't have powers then."

"Not your magical strength." He rolled his shoulders back and lifted his chin, assuming his all-knowing-god pose. "Your strength of character, your determination, your unwillingness to accept defeat. Even when gifted with immense power, you refrain from abusing it. I suspect it has never occurred to you to misuse these gifts."

Did unleashing my magic during sex count as abusing my powers? I wouldn't ask Janus that. Frankly, I didn't care. He was right, though. Not once had I thought about using my magic to get what I wanted, like maybe conjuring a red Mustang convertible. My old Chevy Malibu did fine.

Since Janus had mentioned the possibility…

Oh no, I was not going there. Way too dangerous.

"He is right," Nevan said. "Even with my limited knowledge of you, I can tell you're the sort of woman who never misuses magic."

"Thank you, honey."

Neither man flinched, not even a teeny bit. They'd gotten used to my politeness.

Janus frowned. "You did not thank me."

"I appreciate your confidence in me too."

He actually seemed pleased that I'd thanked him. How strange.

A breeze tickled my skin, ushering in a chill that penetrated to the core of my being.

That was no mere breeze.

I grabbed Nevan's biceps. "She's coming."

"Who?" he asked.

Janus looked up to the sky. "Aello."

I tracked his gaze to the heavens, and my blood froze.

A storm cloud as black as the harpy's soul consumed the blue sky, roiling and spreading with unnatural speed. Part of the cloud stretched downward, a finger of black snaking toward the ground, writhing and expanding into a whirling funnel.

What was it with these wind gods and tornadoes? Skeiron had dispatched one to annihilate my family and friends during our final battle with the sylph king. Aello employed the same tactic.

A bell chimed inside me, an idea struggling to form, but I had no chance to examine it.

The tornado lunged downward. A huge pine tree was torn out of the earth and flung aside like a toy. One after another, trees were ripped free of the soil and cast aside as the funnel gouged its way through the woods toward us.

"We must go," Nevan shouted to be heard above the din.

Even while he kept his arm around me, he clamped a hand on Janus's uninjured shoulder.

The three of us stood there, exchanging confused looks.

"Whisk us away already," I shouted.

Lips parted, Nevan shook his head. "I cannot."

I tried to whisk us away. Nothing happened.

The tornado lifted into the sky, hovering a hair's breadth above the tops of the remaining trees. A shape emerged from the funnel, twirling on its way down to the ground.

Aello touched down with a nasty grin on her face.

I thrust up a hand, intending to hurl magic at her.

Nothing. I had nothing.

The harpy cackled. "I grow more powerful whilst you grow weaker. The Anemoi shall be avenged on you."

She stretched out one bony finger to waggle her talon at me.

"Are you done boasting?" I said. "We've got more important things to do than chat with a lonely old crone."

"Lonely?" She cackled again, the sound infused with the wind. "I have driven your familiar away from you, wounding him so grievously he shall not recover. And I—"

Aello froze, her black eyes swiveling to Nevan.

Had she really not noticed he was here until now? Maybe her thirst for vengeance left her vulnerable to tunnel vision. She saw only what she wanted to see.

Maybe I could exploit that weakness.

Her face seemed to grow even paler as she stared at Nevan.

"Yeah," I said, "Nevan's back. I plucked him out of wherever you sent him. Guess you thought you'd gotten rid of him for good, huh? Bad luck for you."

Aello spread her arms wide, and Janus flew forward into them. She locked an arm around Janus's neck and ground her elbow into his wounded shoulder. He cried out, gritting his teeth.

"You shall not win," the harpy snarled. "You may have saved your lover, but I have your mentor. Without this one—" She jabbed her elbow into his wound. "—you will have no one to advise you on how to manipulate time."

I started to move toward them, but Nevan clutched me tighter to his body. What could I do, anyway? Somehow, she had dampened our powers or canceled them out.

"Do not worry," Aello said with mock sympathy, "I will not harm your favorite god unless you attempt to enter the time stream again. Stay out, Janusite."

"You won't win. I will find another way to take you down."

"Oh, you will try." Aello smiled. "But you will fail. I have taken away another of your allies. What have you left? A sylph who does not know you and powers you cannot fully control." She tsked. "Poor little mortal, all alone with nowhere to hide."

She vanished, taking Janus with her.

CHAPTER FOURTEEN

A WEIGHT BORE DOWN ON MY CHEST, MAKING IT HARD TO BREATHE. I fought for air, my ears ringing, while I stared at the place where Janus and Aello had been seconds ago. She'd taken him, and I'd been helpless to stop her. How the hell had she gained the power to stifle ours? How was I supposed to fight that?

"Dammit!" I shouted, then I roared out my frustration.

Nevan enfolded me in his arms, my cheek to his chest. "I am sorry. You must've cared for Janus deeply."

"I barely knew him. But I'm sick of that witch winning every battle." I raised my head to meet his gaze. "How does she keep getting more powerful? I knock her down, and she rises up again stronger than ever. Endued weapons don't hurt her, and now she can cancel out our powers. How am I supposed to fight that?"

"Dark magics empower her. She must be ingesting a great deal of the blackest energies to accomplish these feats."

"Fantastic. I can't enter the time stream or she'll kill Janus. She took you away, and she nearly killed Max."

"Where is the incubus?"

"He had to go somewhere else to heal." I shut my eyes, doing my damnedest not to panic. "What if I don't have the power to stop her?"

"You brought me back, and you will find a way to defeat the harpy." He crooked a finger under my chin, rubbing his thumb over it until I looked at him. "We will find a way. Together."

He sounded so much like the old Nevan that it made my heart hurt. I may have returned him to the timeline, but I hadn't restored his memory.

My gaze wandered around the clearing. Trees lay uprooted and overturned, their roots dangling, the earth torn asunder with giant wounds from the harpy's rampage. Why had she summoned a tornado? I'd expected she might use it to mow us down, but she hadn't. Maybe she had simply wanted to make a big entrance. A voice in the back of my mind urged me to study her actions more closely, to figure out her motivations. It seemed vital, but I couldn't concentrate.

I buried my face in my hands.

Nevan peeled my hands away and kissed my forehead. "This place is rife with bad memories of losing your friends. I will take you somewhere less fraught with anguish."

He zipped us away.

We landed in a clearing beside a small stream. Its waters burbled softly, the sound calming me more than I would've imagined possible. Or maybe it was the hot sylph wrapped around me that made my muscles slacken and my thoughts spiral away into the ether.

I shuffled away from Nevan, leaning back against a tree. As much as I craved him and everything he made me feel, I couldn't take what I wanted, what I needed, from him. He was so much like my husband and yet he had no memories of our life together. How could I accept comfort from a man who viewed me as a virtual stranger? He knew my first name because I'd told him, and I doubted he would ever accept we were married.

Speaking more to myself than to him, I muttered, "Why can't you remember me? I rescued you from oblivion, but I couldn't save your memories of us. I'm your wife, but..."

My words died, because I had no clue what I'd been about to say. There was nothing more to say. I was powerless to restore his recollections of us.

"You claim to be my wife," he said, "and I wish it to be true. But it cannot be."

"Doesn't matter anymore."

"It matters to me." Nevan braced his hands on the tree's wide trunk at either side of my head. His eyes burned a brilliant bronze with ribbons of fiery red whipping through his swirling irises. His voice took on a darker, smokier tone when he leaned in close and said, "If we had been lovers, I would remember that. To have a woman like you beneath me, wet and wanting, begging for me to take ye...I'd remember."

"Aello messed with the timeline repeatedly. Everything is screwed up, and I can't fix it."

"Stop trying to." He brushed his nose against mine. "You're tense and frightened and weary. Everything seems hopeless when you feel this way."

"No kidding. Thanks for the revelation."

"Your sarcasm enchants me. I suppose that means we must've been lovers, otherwise I'd be irritated with you."

"Nice twisty logic, but it doesn't help either of us."

"You would feel better if I could remember you."

"Duh. If you're going to keep stating the obvious—"

"Hush, love." His breaths teased my skin, and the earthy scent of him surrounded me. He dipped his head to sniff my hair and inhaled a deep breath filled with the aroma of it. Groaning out a long sigh, he turned his head enough to bring his cheek into contact with mine. "Perhaps if ye stripped for me, the sight of your luscious, nude body would stir my memories."

Stir his memories? Well, this discussion was definitely stirring his penis to swell. I guessed my sarcasm really did enchant him, or least it enchanted his manly bits. As for me…My body had begun to ache and tingle in the most intimate ways. I wanted him. Of course I did. This version of Nevan possessed all the seductive allure of the man I'd married, and I couldn't stop my body from responding to his proximity, the radiant heat of him, and the sense memories of every time we'd made love. But he wasn't my husband. In his world, we had never met.

Whenever you are, it's always him.

Back when Bob had spoken those words to me, I hadn't understood what he meant. Part of me had figured he misspoke. He must've meant "wherever," not "whenever." That was before the timeline mutated. Post-shift, I had to wonder if Bob said exactly what he'd meant. And what was that, exactly?

Whenever you are, it's always him.

I gazed into the swirling eyes of the sylph penning me to the tree. Despite the fact he had no memories of me, despite the fact his past differed from what I knew of my husband's experiences, this man was Nevan. I felt it in ways I couldn't explain or quantify. I still shared his powers, and he still felt drawn to me. I'd been able to retrieve him even after Aello obliterated him. Our connection had weakened, but it had not disintegrated. A bond lingered between us, a connection even the shifting sands of time itself could not eradicate.

And that must've been what Bob had meant.

No matter what timeline or what time in the past I found myself in, Nevan would always be Nevan. The man I loved. My husband. Fragments of our life together must remain inside him, if only I knew how to revive them.

I'd shied away from intimacy with him because it seemed like cheating. I'd sworn to this Nevan I wouldn't have sex with him until he could speak my full name. Yet if he was *my* Nevan, dressed up in different memories but him at the core…

He rocked his hips forward, rubbing his erection against my belly. "What shall we do, darlin'?"

I longed to kiss him, touch him, beg him to vanish my clothes and ravish me all night long. I couldn't. I mean, he didn't know me. Maybe I was misinterpreting what Bob had said. The oracle did have a tendency toward vagueness.

Clearing my throat, I said, "We should keep this professional. You're helping me search for the crazy woman who wants revenge on me. That's all."

"Professional?" Nevan chuckled darkly. "When I first saw ye, darlin', ye threw yourself at me and kissed me like a wanton."

"I thought you were the same Nevan I married. I was wrong." Despite the fluttering in my tummy, I added, "We should brainstorm a plan to stop Aello."

"Mm, we could do that." He nuzzled my throat and dragged his tongue up to my jaw near my ear, flicking it out to tease my lobe. "But I can think of other, more interesting things we might do together."

Every hair on my body, from my scalp down to my nape and through my arms straight down to my toes, shivered and stiffened. Nevan had spoken those exact words to me months ago, not long after we'd met. I had been asking him questions he didn't want to answer, so he'd made an alternate suggestion: *Let's not start with the questions again. I can think of other, more interesting things we might do together.* The sylph currently licking my earlobe seemed to have no memories of me, but he had spoken the precise phrase the original Nevan had said to me.

Oh God, could it be true? Was this man really my Nevan?

Nevan had always trusted my instincts and my intuition. I trusted my gut because he believed in me. The changes to the timeline, and the changes they brought about in Nevan, had thrown me for a loop. Maybe that's what Bob had been trying to tell me, that I needed to trust my instincts no matter what things seemed to be on the surface.

This was Nevan. My husband. If he remembered one thing about us, he could remember the rest.

With a little jump start.

Max had half-jokingly suggested I have sex with Nevan to trigger his memories because it had worked before when I restored his soul. I'd assured Max the soul stone had done it, not my kiss or my body. Maybe I'd been too quick to dismiss the idea. Our deep, immutable bond had begun as an instant attraction beyond anything I'd ever experienced with another man. Maybe the physical connection could serve as a catalyst.

Then again, maybe I'd lost all my wits because I was insanely horny thanks to the hot, seductive sylph rubbing himself all over me.

Stop doubting yourself. Go for it.

What was the worst that could happen? I'd have awesome sex with Nevan, and he wouldn't regain his memories of me. Nothing gained, but nothing lost either. It wasn't like I'd never done the deed with him before.

He raised his head in front of mine, his eyes blazing with need. And that was no metaphor. "I want ye more than seems rational."

"Screw rational." I grasped his face, my pulse quickening and my breaths shortening. "Nothing about us has ever been rational."

I crushed my mouth to his.

He went stiff, in the sense of his body tensing. Another part of him had gone stiff several minutes ago. He sucked in a breath through his nostrils.

My pulse thundered in my ears.

Nevan shoved an arm behind me, fastening it around my back, and hauled me against him, our bodies plastered together.

I opened my mouth, doing exactly what he'd said—begging him to take me.

He thrust his tongue into my mouth, possessing and devouring me with every lash of his tongue. I coiled mine around his, moaning with intense pleasure, reveling in the flavor and feel of him, hungry for so much more than a kiss, more than his lips and tongue. I hungered for his body merging with mine. He plunged deeper into my mouth, groaning and whisking his hand down to my ass to clutch it with his strong fingers, kneading fiercely.

A desperate noise escaped me, part moan, part whimper. My body pulsated with a need so powerful it consumed my thoughts and my inhibitions, like I'd ever had any of those with Nevan, while he consumed my mouth.

He tore his lips away from mine, breathing hard, and latched both hands onto my bottom. "You are the most desirable woman in any realm."

Despite the fire raging inside me, the start of tears stung my eyes. He had spoken those words to me once before, on the night when I gave myself to him for the first time.

I hooked one ankle around his, flung my arms around his neck, and spoke the same words I'd said to him that night. "Take me, Nevan."

He stared at me, eyes aflame, chest heaving.

After a heart-stopping moment of frozen anticipation, he slid his hand down to clasp my thigh, the one raised slightly so I could lock my ankle around his. "I hope ye mean that, love."

"I do. My body is yours, I'm yours. In every way."

He hoisted me up, and with his hands, he encouraged me to lock my ankles behind his ass. His palms cupped my bottom, and his erection was nestled against my cleft with only my jeans and his loincloth separating our flesh.

Nevan kissed me like he'd never kissed me before, wild and demanding, almost brutal in his need. I met him thrust for thrust, lash for lash, our teeth clashing and our lips glued to each other, the lust inside us seeming to erupt from our pores in a spray of sparkling blue light.

No, that blue glow beyond my eyelids wasn't my imagination.

I opened my eyes even while we kept kissing. The sparkling energy of my powers activating enveloped us in a cloud of blue. It clung to our bodies, drizzling down our skin like droplets of water.

Nevan pulled his head back and glanced around the clearing. "This won't do at all."

We rocketed through the tunnel so fast I had no time to process the journey. Before I realized what he'd done, we rematerialized inside a house.

I blinked several times, struggling to catch my breath. No, we weren't inside a house. Nevan had brought me to a place I knew well, a place where we had spent countless hours together.

"This is my old apartment," I said. "Why did you bring us here?"

"I…don't know. I wanted to take you somewhere private."

"I used to live here, but I gave up this apartment when I moved in with you a couple months ago. You remembered my old apartment."

"No, I—" He glanced around, seeming panicked. "I must've chosen this location at random, unconsciously, because I sought a vacant premises."

A quick survey of the living room around us proved to me someone lived here. Personal items and furniture occupied the space, and the occupant had left a floor lamp on.

"Nevan, we need to talk about this," I said, "but I think we'd better go somewhere else first."

He didn't move, didn't even blink, his hands trembling the tiniest bit against my bottom.

Someone screamed.

Nevan and I jerked at the same instant. He yanked his hands away and sent me tumbling to the floor. I landed with a squeak, my feet in the air and my hair in my face. I blew the hair away from my eyes.

The young woman who had just stepped out of the bedroom screamed again.

I opened my mouth to speak but realized I had no frigging clue what to say. *Gee, sorry we scared the bejesus out of you, please don't call the cops on us. This home invasion was an accident, I swear.*

Footsteps thudded on the concrete walkway outside the front door.

A fist pounded on the door, and a male voice shouted, "Shelly, what's going on? You okay?"

Shelly screamed.

Nevan scooped me up and whisked us away.

Chapter Fifteen

W E EMERGED IN A CLEARING ALONGSIDE A TWENTY-FOOT-HIGH WA-terfall. Though the wooden railing that used to protect the falls and the pool below was no longer there and the path was gone, I recognized this place. I would've known that waterfall blindfolded. The sound of it, the scent of damp earth, the sensation of cool water misting over my skin. This was the falls behind the shop, if the shop had existed in this reality. The cascade tumbled down the cliff, pummeling the pool below and churning up foam.

Nevan kept his arms around me, though his face had paled beneath its bronzed surface. His gaze flitted everywhere. He licked his lips, though not in a sexy way, more in the manner of someone struggling to comprehend the incomprehensible.

He'd brought us to the spot where we had first met.

Nevan let go of me, stumbled backward a few steps, and shoved a hand into his hair. "What the bloody hell is happening?"

I held up my hands in a conciliatory gesture. "Take it easy. I know this is confusing, but you need to listen to me. You took me to my old apartment, and now you've brought us to the place where we first met." I dared to move one step closer. "Like I told you before, the timeline has been altered. Someone is messing with it, with you, with everyone except me and Janus and Max. What you're feeling, it's your real memories trying to come out. You need to stop fighting it."

"Why?" He squinted at me, streaks of ice blue unfurling in his irises. His tone turned darker, almost angry. "Perhaps you are the one attempting to rewrite my memories, to make me believe we have a relationship."

"No, Nevan." I lowered my hands and walked up to him, tilting my head back to meet his gaze head-on. A few minutes ago, he'd said he wished we really were married, but popping up inside my old apartment had freaked him out. Maybe his memories struggling to resurface had knocked him off kilter too. "I have no reason to trick you. Trust your instincts, trust what you feel, and stop trying to make sense out of something that's not logical. It's emotion and magic and destiny."

He made a derisive noise.

"You're the one who taught me," I said, "how to trust in things I couldn't quantify, to trust my gut and believe in the magic all around us. Most of my life I refused to believe in things I couldn't see and touch and explain. Until I met you."

I rested my palms on his chest, praying he would believe me. How could the man who'd introduced me to a world of magic doubt what I'd told him was possible? I believed because of him, yet I couldn't make him believe what I'd told him, what he'd experienced himself. Maybe I was expecting too much. After all, his memories had been wiped away and rewritten. How could he accept what I claimed to be true? He might've brought me to the place where I'd met him three months ago by coincidence, since he was the guardian of the falls here.

No, his memories weren't rewritten. He'd taken me to my former apartment. Why would he do that if he had zero knowledge of me? The timeline had shifted, but rather than wiping out his memories, it must have overwritten them. Remnants lingered. Did all of his recollections of me, of us, hide somewhere inside him?

One way to find out.

I glided my hands up to his neck, around to his nape where I linked them. Leaning in, I pressed my body against his. "Whether you believe me or not, I know you want me. You could've run off to find any number of attractive elemental women to satisfy your urges, but you didn't. You came back to me. You got jealous of other men talking to me. Why is that?"

The colors in his whirlpool eyes morphed from white and ice blue, the colors of fear, into shades of fiery red and molten bronze. His lips parted slightly. His breaths quickened.

"Go on," I said, toying with the hair that fell over his nape. "Tell me why your attention has been focused exclusively on me. Say it, Nevan."

I shimmied my hips, rubbing myself on him.

His hands came around my waist, though he seemed to do it unconsciously, and his head tipped toward mine.

"I want you," I told him. "It's okay. Say it, Nevan."

The molten colors in his eyes sparked with bright gold, and he grasped my hips to tug me into his rejuvenated erection. "I want you, Lindsey, only you. Got no bloody idea why, but I cannot resist you one moment longer."

He slung his arms around me, pulling me into him and devouring my mouth in a kiss of raw, primal possession. I moaned into his mouth, sagging against him, lost to the thrill of his tongue ravaging me and the heat of his body soaking into my skin. He kissed me like he'd spent a thousand years in the desert and I was the only oasis.

Take me home, I wanted to say, but I couldn't speak, couldn't tear myself away from him.

I felt the world melt away, sensed we rocketed through the abysmal tunnel, but we traveled so fast I had no time to think about it. If I'd been able to think. Nevan's tongue scraped over mine, hot and demanding, obliterating thought and reason and intention. I clutched my arms tighter around his neck and flung my legs up to latch them around his hips. Oh God, the hunger, the heat, the desperate need to forget everything and succumb to the bliss of our bodies entangled…

Light glowed beyond my closed lids.

The air temperature had changed, becoming a perfect balance between warm and cool. With an enormous effort, I detached my mouth from Nevan's. My lids fluttered open, and the space around us came into focus. Smooth rock walls. Light that emanated from everywhere and nowhere. Chairs. A table. And a sylph-size bed covered with a fur blanket. All my stuff had vanished, of course, but I recognized this place.

We had come home.

"How did you do this?" Nevan asked, eying me with a cross between suspicion and wonder. "A mortal cannot cross the veil without assistance. Crossing it without opening a portal…It's impossible."

Yeah, that was weird. I couldn't explain it, but in this moment, I didn't care about anything except getting naked with Nevan.

"I'm the Janusite," I said. "I can open portals all by my itty-bitty self."

"You're the what?"

Maybe there was no Janusite, no destruction of the god and no prophecy, in this version of the two worlds. I didn't care about that either. Not now. Not until after I'd felt him inside me.

"But you did not open a portal," he insisted. "I would have sensed it opening for us, but I did not. And we aren't wet from piercing the falls."

I glanced down at my dry clothes and fingered my dry hair. How…

Nevan answered the question I could not voice. "You transported us here without the use of a portal."

Expanding powers? *Think about it later*, my aroused body urged.

I raked my lips across his, sneaking my tongue out to sample his skin.

Though his breath hitched, and he took hold of my bottom with both his hands, his expression blanked. "How could we cross the veil without a portal?"

His hands supported me, but I adjusted my hold on him to make sure I wouldn't tumble out of his embrace. "I don't know how I did it. All that matters is I did. I've given up trying to understand this stuff. What is, is."

If he'd retained all his memories, he would've found that statement highly amusing. I, the once pragmatic mortal who got into heaps of trouble on a regular basis, had given in to the mysteries of magic and the supernatural. He would never understand unless he *remembered.*

"Nevan," I said, tunneling my fingers into his silky hair, "let's not talk anymore. I need to be naked with you. I need to feel you inside me, and I can't wait another second."

I didn't even have to ask him to vanish our clothes. They disappeared the instant I said I needed him inside me.

Faster than I could process the change, we lay on the bed—me on my back, Nevan lying on top with his body covering mine. He pushed a hand between our bodies to palm my mound, then dived his fingers between my folds, already slick and swollen with desire. I moaned at his touch. He slithered down my body, kissing and licking and nibbling my flesh as he moved. When he reached my breasts, he skated his tongue around one taut peak, teasing me until I gripped his shoulders and made an impatient noise. His mouth sealed around my nipple, suckling with fervid hunger, his tongue raking over the tip.

"Oh Nevan," I breathed, and spread my thighs, my movement and my words pleading with him to take me.

A growl resonated low in his throat. He released my nipple only to catch the other one in his teeth and tug it. When I gasped, he released the stiff peak. "The scent of your lust is maddening. It fills my senses and makes me want to fuck ye like a wild thing."

"Yes, do it." I dug my nails into his shoulders. "Please."

That word invoked a slender tether of magic, creating a minor debt between us, snapping taut and binding us. I knew better than to speak the P-word in the Unseen, but I was beyond caring. Owing Nevan could not be dangerous, not ever, not if we both lived to the see the universe collapse in on itself and explode in a new Big Bang.

He slithered further down my body, between my legs, until his face hovered above my groin.

"Nevan," I moaned. "Do it. Hurry."

With a growl, he ducked his head between my thighs and latched his mouth onto my rigid nub, suckling and nipping and licking it until I was thrashing under him. The pleasure mounted with such force and speed that I felt sure I'd explode like a star going supernova. He shoved a finger inside me, thrusting it wildly even as his mouth tormented my bud with the same reckless ferocity. My release struck with the suddenness of a star detonating, convulsing my entire body, the ecstasy so intense it was almost unbearable, and I screamed.

Before I could come down from the climax, Nevan rose to his knees, hoisted my knees up onto his shoulders, and plunged inside me. He thrust hard and deep and fast, grunting every time he plowed inside me, blustering in a breath with every withdrawal. My body bounced on the bed, and I fisted my hands in the fur blanket. The decadence of its silken texture rubbing on my skin heightened my arousal. I whimpered and cried out, certain of one fact.

I would come again, and the orgasm would devastate me with its power.

Nevan slapped his hands onto the bed at either side of my head, his arms straight and rigid, punching into me again and again, the bed creaking and thumping on the floor, my breasts bouncing. His face had pinched into a pained expression, but he never took his gaze off of mine. Our gazed were riveted to each other even while our bodies merged with a frantic, almost crazed intensity. With my legs over his shoulders, bent close to my body, his every thrust drove him deeper than ever before.

Blue sparks erupted on my skin, dribbling down like water. While Nevan kept up his brutal pace and energy, the sparks crackled and expanded. I couldn't concentrate on them or what their presence meant, too consumed by the outrageous passion of our love-making. As our need escalated, so did the blue energy. It blanketed us in a cloud of sparkling, topaz-blue light, and it danced over our skin eliciting tiny shocks of electrical magic that only enhanced the intensity of our joining.

Our climaxes seized us at the same instant.

I screamed again, my cries echoing off the stone walls. He threw his head back and bellowed as the scorching jet of his release pulsed deep inside me.

Nevan collapsed onto the bed beside me, breathing hard, almost gasping for air.

Limp as a wet noodle, I lay there with my legs splayed where they'd fallen off his shoulders. Stunned, I could do nothing more than gape at the ceiling and wait for my breathing to return to normal. Even then, I couldn't speak. Nevan and I always had sizzling-hot sex, but this…

He rolled onto his side to peer down at me, his cheeks ruddy and his eyes ablaze. "That was like nothing I've ever experienced before."

"Likewise."

"Was that your magic?" He fanned a palm over my belly. "The energy that surrounded us, it came from you, did it not?"

"It did." I shivered at his touch, my skin sensitized by our passion. "We always have great sex, but this was a whole new level of wow."

"Mm, indeed." He swirled his palm over my belly, focused on the task with an adorable concentration. He froze, his hand over my womb. "I released my seed. If you become pregnant—"

"Relax, an oracle gave me a supernatural prophylactic." Our wedding gift from Bob, a spell to prevent pregnancy. It was the magical equivalent of handing us a box of condoms.

"I see," Nevan said, sounding like he didn't get it at all. He stared into my eyes for a long moment, so long I was about to say something when he finally spoke. "Lindsey."

"Yep, that's me." I smiled and tapped his nose. "And you are Nevan, the sexiest sylph in any realm."

He rose to hands and knees, swinging his right arm and leg over my body to straddle me. Poised over me, he held completely motionless and studied me with an unnerving intensity, not blinking, not breathing.

At last, he sucked in a shaky breath and fixed his tender gaze on me. "Lindsey Astrid Porter."

It was my turn to freeze, unable to move or speak or breathe. Though I'd told him my first name, I had never said my last name and definitely not my middle name. This version of him had no way of knowing my full name. Unless…I didn't dare think it.

Tears shimmered in his eyes. He choked on a breath, almost a sob.

I pushed up onto my elbows. "Nevan? What's wrong?"

He swiped a hand across his mouth. "I remember."

Chapter Sixteen

My heart thudded so hard my head spun for a second. "What do you remember?"

"You." He hauled in a long breath that seemed to steady him. "We met near the falls when you were kneeling beside a dead man. You tripped, and I caught you before you cracked your lovely head on a large rock."

The entire room spun. My pulse raced, and I made a choked noise.

Nevan lowered his body onto mine, our faces aligned. He stroked my cheek with his fingers, his gaze so tender it made my chest ache. "We made love for the first time in this bed when you gave me your virginity. We married by the falls earlier today. You are my wife, my sweet Lindsey, the half of my soul I cannot live without. How could I have forgotten you?"

The question rang with anguish and guilt.

I bit my lip, tears blurring my vision. "Time was altered. The whole world, two worlds, changed fundamentally. Only Janus, Max, and I weren't affected by it. For you to remember me at all proves we have a connection nothing can erase. Nothing." I grasped his face and touched my lips to his. "This is a miracle, Nevan. Don't feel guilty, be grateful."

He claimed my mouth in a sweet, slow kiss that dissolved all my worries. Nevan was back. My Nevan. My husband, my lover, my best friend, my soul mate.

When we broke the kiss, he smirked at me. "This time, I needed less than a day to get you in my bed, in spite of your vow you wouldn't have sex with me until I spoke your full name."

"I was predisposed to give in." I swept my thumb over his kiss-swollen lips. "But in point of fact, I seduced you this time. Which means you're the one who's easy."

He sucked my thumb into his mouth, releasing it slowly. "For you, always."

"Even without your memories of me, you had no interest in other women."

"What we have transcends magic and time itself. How could I want anyone else? You own my heart and soul, Lindsey."

"Goes both ways."

He rolled off of me to lie on his back, and his expression turned serious. "What will we do about Aello?"

"I haven't got a clue."

"You are the Janusite, which means you have the power to stop her." He clasped my hand, holding it to his heart where his scar had once been before the time shifts. "You were able to cross the veil without opening a portal. I believe you can do anything you set your mind to."

"I appreciate the vote of confidence, but every time I've gone up against Aello, I have failed spectacularly." I made an explosion noise accompanied by a matching hand gesture. "Whatever I try, it explodes in my face. Max nearly died. You were obliterated from the timeline. Janus got kidnapped, for heaven's sake."

"You now have something you did not have during your previous attempts."

"What's that? A ticking time bomb strapped to my chest?"

"No." He flipped onto his side to face me, holding on to my hand. "You have me. My powers combined with your expanding magics may prove more powerful than the time-traveling harpy."

"May prove more powerful? I need something more than maybe." Despite my dismissal, his words had sent a surge of hope through me. Could he be right? I longed to believe it, but I'd gotten smacked down too many times today.

Nevan rose up on one elbow to gaze down on me, the force of his focus like a palpable energy between us. "We can do this together, Lindsey. If you can't trust yourself, trust me."

"I always trust you, Nevan. But this catastrophe is epically worse than the other times we've almost died and almost lost two worlds." I swallowed, my throat and mouth suddenly dry. "Aello can manipulate time, and I can't even try to undo the shifts. If I go into the time stream, she will kill Janus. He might be annoying on occasion, but he doesn't deserve to die."

"You always want to save everyone, even a sorcerer who tried to destroy you."

"The sorcerer had a piece of Calder inside him. That's who I had to save."

"But you also asked the Four Winds to spare Notus and Skeiron, despite all their depraved acts."

"I'm a sap. A weak, foolish sap."

"No." He draped an arm across my waist to grasp my hip. "You are a kind and compassionate woman. It's one of the many qualities I admire and adore in you."

"That's really sweet, honey, but it doesn't tell me how to destroy Aello." I scratched my arms, recalling my encounters with the Windy Witch. "Next time, she could kill me. I'm not immortal like Max and Janus. And you."

"I will be by your side to protect you."

"And possibly die doing it, like Travis did." I hugged myself as goosebumps cropped up on my arms thanks to a sudden chill. "If I were an elemental, that harpy would have a much harder time trying to off me. And maybe I'd have enough power to take her down."

Nevan pulled the fur blanket over me. "We will find a way, and I will not allow anything to happen to you."

"I know you mean that, but I don't want anyone else getting critically injured or dying while trying to protect me." Even with the blanket over me, the cold penetrated my skin. "You have to forge me."

"No." He glowered at me, but his eyes churned with the colors of fear. "I will never forge you or anyone."

"Max swore he'd never do it, but he forged Travis."

"Because you were distraught over losing your friend. Max forged him to spare you pain." Nevan sat up and rubbed his neck. "You're asking me to do this simply to give you more power."

"Not only that." I sneaked a hand out from under the blanket to touch his arm. "If you do this, we could have children. We could be together forever. Do you really want to watch me get old and die?"

"We've had this discussion before. I will love you no matter what, even when you grow old."

"I know, but this way—"

"No, Lindsey."

Shoving off the blanket, I sat up to confront him. "You'd rather let Aello murder me."

"Of course not." He flashed me an irritated look, but it quickly softened even has he rapped his knuckles on the fur blanket. "We don't know if you can be forged. Your Janusite powers cause magic to work differently around you. I could not enchant you to determine if you had a touch of the Unseen realm. You have acquired the ability to cross the veil without a portal, and you restored me to the timeline from which I had been erased."

"I'll take the chance. Forge me, please."

Another slender thread of magic snapped taut between us.

Nevan winced. "Cease using that word."

"Forge me."

He dropped his face into his hands, exhaled a long sigh, and raised his face to me. "If you can't be forged, you will die."

"I'm willing to risk it."

"But I am not." He clutched both my hands between his. "You've seen what the forging does to a mortal. How can you ask me to do that to you, not knowing if it will work?"

My mind flashed back to Calder and the cougar and the elemental monkey-thing. Calder had screamed with a soul-crushing agony.

A shiver raced through me. Did I really want that? Could I survive it?

"If I ever lost you," Nevan murmured, "I would pray to be destroyed."

"Don't say that. If anything happens to me, you have to go on living." I wriggled my hands free of his. "Okay, no forging. But promise me you will not destroy yourself or purposely let anyone else destroy you after I'm gone. Promise me, Nevan."

He flattened his lips.

"Promise," I insisted.

With a growl, he sighed and slumped his shoulders. "I vow to do as you ask."

A thicker thread of magic sealed the vow, shivering through me.

I kissed him. "Good."

"Never again ask me to forge you."

Drawing a cross over my heart, I said, "You have my word. No more forging talk."

He nodded wearily.

I kissed him again. "Somehow, arguing with you gave me the boost I needed to stop feeling powerless. I've got a plan."

"Do I want to know?"

"Would you rather I blip away and do this on my own?"

"Absolutely not."

I couldn't help laughing softly at his indignation. "You don't really think I'd go fight a crazy harpy by myself, do you?"

Nevan pulled his knees up in front of him and rubbed his eyes. "I know you would not do that, but our previous conversation disturbed me."

"I promise I will never ask you to forge me again, and I will never try to get anyone else to forge me." The newest magical tether canceled out the ones Nevan had sealed with me, our debts equal to each other. I patted his knee. "Let's talk about my plan."

He made a go-on gesture.

"Actually, it's the plan I already had but couldn't implement. I need your help figuring out how to do this without Aello noticing."

"You will need to tell me your plan before I can assist."

"Right." I squared my shoulders, planted my hands on my thighs, and told him. "I am going into the time stream to find the moment when Aello first tapped into dark magics. And I'm going to destroy her."

"First, you must devise a plan for doing that without the harpy noticing."

"I already said I need your help with that part. You're the king of the sylphs, a smart and determined man, surely you can come up with an idea."

He gave me an exasperated look. "Flattery won't make the answer appear to us. Besides, I am not the king in this version of reality. Notus is."

"Don't confuse me with facts. Especially when the facts keep shifting."

Nevan reached out to touch the corner of my mouth. "You're frowning, love."

"It's called hopelessness."

He pulled me into his embrace, combing his fingers through my hair. "Think back on what Aello has said to you in your previous encounters with her. She may have given you clues to her true motivations."

I ransacked my memories, squinting my eyes and my mouth in the effort.

Nevan began to paint circles on my back with one hand while the other combed through my hair. The soothing sensations relaxed me, and I let my mind drift.

Aello. The earthquake. The tornadoes. She was, according to mythology, a wind goddess. Wind. It meant something. She'd spoken of vengeance, how I'd taken "them" from her, and how she would avenge herself on me by taking what I loved. Aello had announced the Anemoi would be avenged. Whoever or whatever the Anemoi were, they must be the ones she believed I'd taken from her.

Something else she'd said surfaced in my mind, and I recited it to Nevan, doing my best to pronounce it the way Aello had. "*Daimones. Anemoi Thuellai.* Do you know what that means?"

His brows lifted as his eyes widened a fraction. "Are you certain that's what she said?"

"Positive."

"It's ancient Greek. *Daimones* means spirits or ghosts." Nevan hesitated. "*Anemoi Thuellai* means the storm winds. In mortal mythology, the Anemoi were the wind gods and the Anemoi Theullai were the *daimones* of the storm winds."

"Wind gods?" My thoughts reeled back to a couple months ago when another villain had tried to take Nevan away from me with the help of his formerly dead wife. "The sorcerer who worked with Ceara called himself the storm-bringer because he was predominantly the essence of Notus and 'storm-bringer' was Notus's moniker. He also had Skeiron's essence in him, and Skeiron was another wind god in Greek mythology."

"Indeed."

"But in the Unseen, Notus and Skeiron were sylphs. Elemental spirits forged from the earth and the air."

"I believe you're working it all out in that lovely head of yours." He gestured with one hand. "Please continue."

"Are you humoring me? You've probably figured out the answers."

"I haven't, and I enjoy listening to my clever love sort out mysteries."

"Aw, honey, you always say the nicest things." I went back to rifling through the clues. "Skeiron attacked me with wind, making the roof of my apartment collapse on top of me. And he summoned a tornado during our battle with the sylph army. Aello summoned tornadoes twice, but not to attack me. I couldn't figure out why she bothered orchestrating a grand entrance with a twister ripping up trees or why she stepped out of a small tornado the next time I saw her."

"You have developed a theory."

I tapped my lips, concentrating on everything I'd learned from Aello. My dreams. They involved Notus and Skeiron, and in those nightmares, I'd heard Aello's voice. The former sylph kings could not have been resurrected, not after the Four Winds took care of them. What if my dream hadn't been literal? Notus and Skeiron had not returned to take revenge on me, but maybe someone else had taken up the vengeance mission on their behalf.

The truth smacked me like a wet towel to the face. "Aello must've known Skeiron and Notus. She knows I'm the Janusite and knows my full name. Skeiron knew all of that. He and Notus must be the ones Aello thinks I took from her, which I did. I tricked Skeiron into crossing the boundary, destroying him. When he and Notus got resurrected by the sorcerer, becoming a part of him, I took out the sorcerer which means I took out Skeiron and Notus too."

"Aello seeks revenge for this."

"That's not all. I thought she was trying to get rid of me with these time shifts." I twisted in his arms to face Nevan. "Now I think she wants to resurrect Skeiron and Notus. The time shifts are her attempts to alter the past so the former sylph kings will be alive again. She must've thought keeping you and me apart would do the trick, so she stopped Calder from being forged. This changed my past, but she didn't count on me being immune to the shifts."

"So the harpy tried again."

"But she'd wounded time, and it defended itself. Again, she changed my past but not me. I'm still the Janusite, and we still belong together. On her next attempt, she wiped you away but again couldn't achieve her goal."

"You restored me to the timeline and restored my memories of you."

"Aello is seriously miffed about it."

Nevan scratched his jaw. "She took Janus to prevent you from attempting to unravel her time shifts. This harpy has the power to stifle our magics. I do not know how you might enter the time stream without alerting her."

"Yeah, I haven't got that figured out either."

We lapsed into silence, each gazing out into space, searching for an answer in the air or in the recesses of our minds.

I perked up first. "I may have an idea, but you won't like it."

"Your schemes are always certain to unnerve me."

"Ha-ha. Where do harpies live?"

"I haven't a clue."

"We're going to find out." I looped my arms around his neck. "Bob is hiding out from the time shifts, but we know where he lives. He'll give us Aello's home address."

"And then what?"

"You and Max will distract Aello by assaulting her home."

Nevan snorted. "Ridiculous. Besides, Max is recovering from his injuries."

"He's all better, I can feel it."

"Wonderful. And what will you do while he and I distract Aello?"

"I'll jump into the time stream and stop her from ever acquiring dark magics."

Chapter Seventeen

As it turned out, we didn't need to make the creepy journey through the dark, green-tinged woods and across the acid river to reach Bob's lair. All I had to do was call for him. Nevan and I had poofed into the clearing at the base of the mountain that contained our home when I realized this. Throwing my head back, I hollered for the oracle.

He appeared a few seconds later looking haggard. "What is it?"

And sounding grumpy.

"You okay?" I asked.

"These time shifts are giving me a migraine that won't end." He managed a wan smile. "Other than that, I'm terrific."

"I hate to bother you, but we have an emergency. Do you know where the harpy Aello lives?"

"Harpies migrate with the winds, but they usually have a permanent nest they go back to once in a while."

"Where is Aello's nest?"

Bob rubbed his temples and grimaced, then rubbed his eyes with the heels of his hands. After a moment, his face fell and his shoulders slumped. "I'm sorry. My foresight's blocked by the time shifts. Reality keeps realigning to adjust to the changes your harpy friend is causing. If this doesn't stop soon, she could break the timeline."

"Break the timeline?" I said. "What does that mean?"

"Chaos." He raised a hand to shield his eyes from the glaring light of the sun. "Trust me, you do not want to find out what true chaos looks like. I've seen it once, longer ago than any human ever born could remember. When time breaks, the threads of reality become untethered and everything that might have been is. The strands become intertwined, overlapping and converging, often with grotesque results. Pray you never experience it."

A broken timeline? Grotesque results? A chill shimmied down my spine. It sounded like doomsday.

"How did time get broken before?" I asked.

"Same old story. An evil being bent on revenge for who-knows-what gathered enough dark magics to manipulate the time stream." Bob rubbed his eyes again. "This was eons ago, back before the elementals existed. It took all of the primordial gods to set things right."

"We better stop Aello before the problem gets that bad."

Bob flourished a hand, and a piece of parchment appeared in his palm. He offered it to me. "A map to Aello's nest. Be careful, Janusite."

I took the parchment, and he assumed the *I'm-about-to-disappear* posture.

He stopped blinking, his gaze unfocused, and intoned, "Blood for blood, life for life, the scales must be balanced. Sacrifice the past for the sake of the future."

Bob shook off whatever it was, cringed, and vanished.

The word sacrifice rang in my soul, but I had no idea what he'd meant and no time to figure it out.

"Max!" I hollered.

Nevan and I both glanced around the clearing, but the incubus did not appear.

I sucked in a deep breath and bellowed, "Max! Get your flaming red butt over here right this instant!"

My familiar materialized beside me, wobbling a little. His leg had regenerated, and the wounds from the endued shotgun shells had healed too. His pupils were dilated, though, and he gazed dreamily into empty space.

"Here I am, my mistress," he said with a slur and a clumsy attempt at a bow.

Max stumbled into me, grabbing my breasts while trying to steady himself.

I let out an annoyed sigh and batted his hands away. "What is wrong with you?"

Nevan chuckled. "He's inebriated."

"Have you been drinking?" I asked Max. "Doing drugs? High on magic or something?"

Max held up his thumb and forefinger, holding them an inch apart. "A tad of wine."

"Looks to me," I said, "like you've had more than a tad."

Nevan touched my arm. "Where did he go for healing?"

I opened my mouth to answer, but Max beat me to it. He thrust an arm into the air, wavering a bit. "The palace of Hathor, as my mistress commanded."

"Hathor?" Nevan said, his lip curling. "She is a goddess of the old order. It is said Hathor ensorcells everyone who enters her palace, essentially hypnotizing them into becoming her devotees. The details are secret, but she and her followers engage in orgies of drink and sex."

"Orgies?" I lodged my hands on my hips. "How do you know what goes on in Hathor's palace if it's a big secret? Have you been there?"

"I visited once, but I wasn't privy to the most secret rituals. Hathor found me displeasing."

"Why is that?"

He gave me a roguish grin. "I seduced her female devotees. Hathor doesn't like to share."

I eyed him with a squinty gaze. "You were ensorcelled, eh? A slave to the goddess's desires?"

"For a time, but even her magic couldn't stop me from…enjoying what other women had to offer."

"Uh-huh." I tried not to smile but succeeded only in making my lips twitch. "You really were a hound, weren't you?"

"If I'd known I would find you, I would have waited eternity without touching another female."

"I believe you. I waited all my life for you." A single word he'd spoken had gotten trapped in my brain, so I had to ask. "Is there a difference between enchantment and ensorcellment?"

"Does it matter?"

"I don't know unless you answer my question."

"As you wish." He rubbed my arms while he explained, "Enchantment is a milder form of ensorcellment. To ensorcell another being requires dark magics, which is why most elementals stay away from it and employ enchantment instead. Ensorcellment can cause undesirable side effects, mainly affecting the mind."

Max chose that moment to sway and grin like a drunken fool. "May I go back to Hathor?"

"No, you may not." I slapped his chest. "Snap out of it, Max."

"I'm afraid," Nevan said, "you'll have to wait until he comes out of the trance."

"Don't have time for that." I studied Max, weighing my options, then took hold of his face and shook it. "Time to sober up."

I tapped into my magic, summoning swirling strands of glittering blue. The strands snaked around Max's head, down his shoulders and arms, winding their way to his toes. Max's eyelids fluttered shut. My magic encased him, and I willed it to clear his mind, to free him of Hathor's ensorcellment and to sweep away any actual inebriation.

The blue tendrils dissipated with a snap and a sizzle.

I stepped back.

Max opened his eyes. He blinked swiftly, then mopped his hands over his face. Yawning, he stretched his entire body.

"Feeling better?" I asked.

"Enormously." He threw his arms out and inhaled a deep breath, expelling it in a rush. Thumping his chest, he said, "Healed and ready for duty."

I considered asking what had gone on in Hathor's palace but decided I had no need to know those details. What Nevan had said gave me all the clues I cared to have.

Max looked from me to Nevan and back again, a question in his eyes.

"This is the real Nevan," I said. "His memory has been restored."

"Ah, good." Max rubbed his hands together. "Now what?"

"Lindsey wants us," Nevan said, "to distract Aello while she attempts to enter the time stream."

"She's sticking to the plan where she goes back in time to stop Aello from acquiring dark magics."

"Indeed she is."

"You tried to talk her out of it, I'm sure."

Nevan made an exasperated noise. "Talking Lindsey out of anything is nearly impossible, as I'm sure you know."

"Hey!" I said, waving my arms between the two men. "Stop talking like I'm not here. Unless one of you has a better plan, zip it and get with the program."

Max bowed, elegantly this time but with a smirk. "Yes, mistress."

Nevan slipped his hand around mine. "I am always with your program."

"That makes one of us." I held the map to my chest. "What if I don't have enough power to stop Aello? She's been gathering more and more magic, I'd say, based on the way she keeps getting stronger while I get weaker."

"You are not weaker," Nevan said, moving to stand in front of me. "Sometimes I think you forget the prophecy Bob issued a century ago."

"I remember it."

"You've memorized the words, but you seem to forget the meaning." He grasped my shoulders, bending his head to level our gazes. "Say it, Lindsey. Say it and understand."

I flashed him a peeved look but recited the prophecy. "In the twentieth era of the mortal calendar, a girl child shall be born into an enlightened clan. She will possess the power of Janus, god of the doorways and of transitions, and like him she will face both ways, belonging to neither world but bound to everything. Boundaries fall in her presence. The veil shall open to her, she who holds the power to converge the worlds, she whose power is beyond any seen before in any realm. She is the bearer of the key and the staff, the child of the god, she is the Janusite."

"Do you recall what you inferred from the prophecy?" Nevan tightened his grip on me just enough to convey his resolve to convince me. "On the day you first manipulated time by freezing it. Do you recall?"

"Of course I do."

"Tell me."

"Ugh. I've told you before, and I don't see how—"

"Lindsey, tell me."

The intensity in his voice gave me pause, so I told him, "My family is the enlightened clan, a group of New Age believers. Facing both ways means both coming and going through the portals and moving through time. The part about boundaries means I can take elementals across the metaphysical borders in the mortal world and that I can cross the boundaries of time. I assume the veil that opens for me is the veil between realms, but I don't know what the part about converging worlds means."

"And the key and the staff?"

Despite knowing what he was doing, pushing me to accept I had the power to defeat Aello, his insistence I repeat things I'd told him several times before rankled.

Huffing, I said, "The Janus key indicates the bearer means no harm. The staff symbolizes Janus's dominion over pretty much everything—the worlds, the doorways between them, the boundaries, even time itself."

Nevan's lips ticked up at the corners. "Good, Lindsey. At last you see."

"You are so bossy." One of things I loved about him even when it annoyed me. He could be as stubborn as I was. Our mutual pigheadedness had saved us both in the past. "I get what you were trying to do, and I appreciate it."

That I could say without incurring a debt.

"Perhaps," he said, "you've overlooked the most important part of the prophecy. You wield powers beyond any seen before in any realm. Even Janus admits you have accomplished a feat he could not."

When I'd restored Nevan to the timeline. Janus had seemed shocked by that. The god had become so powerful in his own time that the other gods banded together to destroy him, fearing his powers. If I could do things he couldn't…

You are the most important being ever to be born in any realm, Bob had told me a couple months ago when I first met the oracle. *She whose power is beyond any seen before in any realm.*

Didn't that mean I had more magic than Janus himself back when he'd possessed all his powers?

A few minutes ago, Bob had pronounced the scales must be balanced and the past must be sacrificed for the sake of the future. Whose past? Mine? Maybe he'd been talking about Nevan and the way I kept bringing him back every time the past realigned to accommodate Aello's tinkering. Maybe I had to let him go to save everyone else.

No. That would mean Aello won.

I would never let her win.

Bob's prophecies could be averted. Wasn't that the point of foresight? Warn people so they could avoid catastrophe. Once, Bob had warned me Nevan would be my undoing, that he would destroy me. Well, he almost had after the sorcerer stripped his soul from his body. The Anti-Nevan, as I'd called the shell that had once been the man I loved, had tried to kill me. I'd summoned magics

I didn't know I had to bring Nevan's soul back from the void. He hadn't been my undoing. He would always be my salvation.

The prophecy had not come true. We fought together to ensure it never would.

If we could avert one prediction, we could do the same with another one. No sacrifice required.

The bullet points of the Janusite prophecy replayed in my mind, and suddenly, I understood.

"You're a genius," I told Nevan as I planted a firm kiss on his lips. "A total genius."

A wrinkle formed between his brows, above the bridge of his nose.

His adorable confusion spurred me to pepper his lips with quick little kisses. "Your bossiness paid off. I know what to do."

"Care to share?" Max asked.

"Yes." I gave Nevan one last kiss. Map in hand, I told the men, "The bearer of the key and the staff. It means I have the magic to sort of…soothe time. Show it I mean no harm. I have dominion over basically everything, so time will accept me and do as I ask. This gives me an advantage over Aello."

Nevan looked impressed, but he asked, "In what way?"

"The harpy has to jackhammer her way into the time stream and beat the past into submission to get her way. This explains the earthquakes, I think. It also explains the windstorms that accompany every single instance of her messing with time."

"Ahhhh, of course," Nevan said with appreciation. "You are one with time. She is an intruder."

"Exactly."

My husband grinned. "*You* are the genius, Lindsey."

"Couldn't have done it without you."

"If you two are planning to shag," Max said, "I'll go for a walk."

"Not having sex," I assured him. "Shouldn't you, as my familiar, be terribly impressed with what I've figured out?"

"I am impressed." Max's expression turned somber, almost regretful. "You two have a symbiotic relationship. You make each other stronger and understand each other completely. That's something most of us will never have."

"You'll find your girl someday."

He made a disgusted face. "Don't need a woman to make me happy. If Hathor couldn't convince me she's my fated mate, you can't convince me there's a bird waiting for me out there somewhere."

After more than two months with Max, I knew "bird" meant a woman.

"Fated mate?" I said. "Does your kind have those? For real?"

Max grumbled and ducked his head, kicking at the dirt. "Some say we do, but I don't believe in that bollocks."

As much as I itched to quiz him for more info, we had more important matters to discuss.

Nevan squeezed my hand. "Has your plan changed?"

"Uh-uh." I glanced from Nevan to Max and back again. "But I need both of you to make me a promise. Once you've gotten Aello's attention, you have to leave her nest before she gets there. Promise me."

"You would coerce us into incurring a debt?"

"I need to be sure you'll leave before she gets there. Aello can block your powers."

Nevan cupped my cheek in his warm hand. "I know you're afraid for us, but you do not need a magical promise. We will obey without needing a debt to enforce your request."

Max nodded. "It's true."

Of course they would. After everything that had gone down today—the worlds shifting, Max's injuries, losing Nevan, losing Janus—I'd gotten a touch paranoid.

"Forget the promise," I said. "Get the heck out of there before Aello blows in."

Nevan kissed me sweetly.

I gazed at him for a few seconds, transfixed by his swirling eyes and the love he imbued into every word, every touch, every look.

He backed up one step, squared his massive shoulders, and awaited my command.

The sylph king at my command. I always got a hot shiver when I thought about that.

I held up the map Bob had provided, studying the curving lines and strange symbols. "This doesn't make sense."

Leaning in to peer at the map, Nevan said, "If you were an elemental, it would make perfect sense. In the Unseen, maps are living things comprised of magic. Touch the paper and you'll see."

"A living thing? Is this map going to bite off my finger?"

"No, darlin', it won't."

His tone suggested I was being silly. What did he expect? Telling me a map was alive.

I clamped my lips between my teeth and touched the parchment.

A tiny green orb popped out of the parchment, hovering a hair above the page's surface. It pulsed twice.

"The starting point," Nevan said. "Follow where it leads."

"You mean we have to walk? No poofing?"

He threw an arm around my waist. "There will be poofing, love. Keep your finger on the map."

I pressed my fingertip to the parchment, and the green orb began to move.

So did we, whooshing through the deep, dark tunnel. As we moved, the little orb glided along the winding lines of the map. I assumed Nevan was somehow following those lines, following the map, though I had no idea how. I might be able to share his powers and teleport at will, but I had not passed Advanced Poofing class yet.

We touched down on top of a mountain with a three-sixty view of the neighboring peaks. Snow capped every single one of them, including the one on which we perched.

And did we ever perch.

Nevan balanced on the craggy tip of the mountain with me hugged to him. My feet dangled in empty space.

Max appeared beside us, his skin flaming, floating in midair.

"Where is it?" I asked, latching my arms around Nevan's neck. The map crinkled, partly crushed in my grip. "Where's Aello's nest?"

"There," Nevan replied, pointing straight up.

I craned my head back. *Way* back.

Above our heads floated a billowy cloud. Atop the cloud hunkered a building composed of what looked like twigs. Considering the distance between us and the cloud, I realized the twigs were actually massive trees stripped of their branches.

The harpy's nest.

"Okay," I said, folding the map and tucking it into my pocket, "it's go time. The second you guys get Aello's attention, you'll zip all of us out of here. Right?"

"All of us?" Nevan repeated. "Max and I can 'zip' ourselves. Who else are we to transport?"

"Me."

He got that adorable look of confusion again. "You will be in the time stream."

"Yeah, but I'd rather not have my physical form get ripped to shreds. I'm kinda fond of this body."

Nevan and Max both stared at me like I'd suggested we all wear pink tutus and prance around singing "tra-la-la."

"What is wrong with you two?" I demanded.

My husband answered. "Your body will not be here. You disappear when you enter the time stream. How can you not know this?"

It was my turn to stare at him dumbly. "My body goes with me? I assumed only my mind went into the time stream. When I'm in there, I feel incorporeal."

"Naturally," Max said. "You were incorporeal. We both were. Our bodies rematerialized once we exited the time stream. Why did you think you needed to have me on your person to take me with you?"

"I—" Slapping my hands on my cheeks, I groaned. "Never occurred to me I was teleporting us into the time stream. How was I supposed to know that? Nobody told me. It would've been useful to know."

Nevan peeled my hands away from my face. "You are correct. We failed to mention this, and you couldn't have known. Elementals tend to forget not everyone understands these matters as inherently as we do."

"I get that, but Janus could've told me. His mentoring sucks." Janus. Aello's prisoner. The mention of him yanked me back to the problem at hand. I took a calming breath. "Well, at least I know now. Let's get this show on the road."

Max glanced around—up, down, and sideways. "I thought we were enacting the plan here, not on a road."

"It's a figure of speech."

"Whose figure are you speaking of?" He smirked, eying me up and down. "Yours, I hope."

I lashed my arms around Nevan, suddenly aware of my feet dangling in the air, and mustered my sternest voice. "Are we ready to tick off the harpy and save the world?"

"Yes," both men said.

"Good."

I inhaled a deep breath and shut my eyes.

"Wait," Max said. "Shouldn't I go with you? What if you need a power boost?"

"I need you to stay with Nevan." I cracked one lid open. "Make sure he leaves before Aello gets here."

Nevan harrumphed. "I thought you trusted me."

"Oh, I do." I opened both eyes to meet his gaze. "But sometimes, in the thick of things, you decide protecting me is more important than your own safety. I recall a certain sword-through-the-chest incident."

"Shall I make it a promise?"

"Not necessary. But listen up. I will not pop out again right here once I'm done in the time stream. Wherever you go, I'll find you."

Max floated toward Nevan and slapped a hand on his shoulder. "Don't worry. I'll drag him away from here if he tries to stay behind."

One side of Nevan's mouth contorted in a cross between humor and annoyance. "I will flee and wait for you elsewhere."

I closed my eyes and aimed for the time stream.

The real world spiraled away from me as I soared into the ethereal home of time itself. I focused on the idea of the Janus key, willing time to understand I meant no harm and that I wanted to help it heal. The staff became my resolve to repair the damage Aello had caused and to discover the moment when she'd first absorbed dark magics. I willed time to understand my thoughts.

Please let me in, please help me. I can heal you, but only if you trust me. We are one.

The glowing river pulsed once, and I knew it had accepted me. I sensed it in my soul and in the way my powers pulsed in response.

Aello. Dark magics. The primary event that triggered the cascade of time shifts. *Take me there.*

The river shimmered and looped around to contact one moment in the past.

I dived toward it.

My body emerged in a small clearing in the woods. Disoriented by the journey through the time stream, I stood motionless for a moment, blinking repeatedly and taking slow breaths. Where was I? When was I? The surroundings gave me few clues. Trees. Whoopee, big frigging clue. At least I knew I was in the mortal world since trees in the Unseen had moss-like stuff instead of leaves or needles. I didn't know enough about trees to guess where in the world I'd ended up.

This location must have something to do with Aello. She must have acquired her first taste of dark magics here.

In the middle of nowhere? In the mortal realm?

Turning in a circle, I examined my surroundings for more clues but got nothing. Nobody in this world had enough power to jack up a harpy with dark magic. Besides, I could sense the boundaries, the ones that prevented elementals from traveling more than a mile from any portal. I sensed no boundaries nearby, which meant no natural water features within a mile in any direction. No portal. No way for Aello to get here.

I must've screwed up. Time had sent me to the wrong moment because I hadn't phrased my request correctly. What had I been thinking about in the time stream? The primary event that triggered the time shifts. The moment when something vital had changed, making it possible for Aello to devour dark power.

Maybe I hadn't screwed up. Maybe I was right where I needed to be.

Everything Aello had done became possible because of something that happened right here, right now.

A clue would've been helpful.

Reluctant to leave the spot where I'd materialized, I turned in a circle several more times, taking in as much detail as I could. Trees. Grass. Trees. Oh, there was a small bird. More trees. More grass.

"Gah!" I threw my head back to glare at the sky. "Time, what are you trying to tell me? You could be a teeny bit more specific. I'm no oracle."

A twig cracked. Leaves rustled.

I spun toward the sounds, my heart racing. On instinct, I reached for my derringer only to realize I didn't have it. I'd given the gun to Janus, and I had lost track of the weapon in the confusion following Aello's attack. *Should've brought a weapon, dummy.* Nevan's voice resounded in my mind like he was standing right beside me. *You have your weapons inside you.*

A figure traipsed out of the woods. The man halted, his surprised gaze swerving to me.

Dark-brown hair. Full lips. Striking, though completely human, hazel eyes. Muscular but not equipped with supernatural mass, and a few inches shorter than his elemental self, he may have looked less imposing. Despite his altered appearance, I would've recognized him if I'd been blindfolded. His presence tugged at something deep inside me, a connection stronger than time.

His sensual smile warmed me from my skin down to the region between my thighs. "Well, beauty, who might you be?"

That voice. That smile. I was face to face with the mortal man who would be forged and become…

Nevan.

Chapter Eighteen

UATHAL. THAT HAD BEEN HIS NAME DURING HIS MORTAL LIFE. I MUST'VE wound up on the island that would someday become known as Ireland, the land of Nevan's birth and first life, the land where he'd died and been forged. When I'd wound up was harder to determine. When I had asked Nevan how old he was, the only time I'd asked him, he had said, "Well now, I lost count after five thousand."

I'd landed somewhere in the Bronze Age.

"Are ye mute?" Tuathal inquired, sauntering closer.

Realization shivered through me. How could he speak English? This was the distant past, before the English language emerged. *Duh, Lindsey, it's magic.* Considering I could make myself invisible, auto-translating another language didn't seem so odd.

"What language are you speaking?" I asked.

He stopped ten feet from me, seeming nonplussed. "The tongue of the Parthalonians. You speak it as well, so why are ye asking me? Have ye hit your head, beauty? You seem confused."

Oh yeah, this whole situation confused the heck out of me.

Somehow, Nevan had played a vital role in the primary event. I needed to figure out what and how. What if I screwed up time worse than Aello already had? If I said the wrong thing, did the wrong thing…Then again, my very presence might have caused ripples already. Since I was one with time, I ought to sense any changes. Probably. Shutting my eyes, I let all thoughts drift away and focused on time itself. Traveling into the time stream wouldn't be necessary. I needed only to sense it, to feel if I had done any damage.

Everything felt fine. Or rather, the same as before I'd traveled back to this moment.

Time had sent me here for a reason. It must've known the answers began in this moment, which meant it must want me to intervene.

A hand touched my arm.

When I opened my eyes, Tuathal was standing inches away from me, his hand resting on my arm, concern in his eyes.

"Relax," I said. "I'm fine."

"Who are you? Why are you dressed so strangely?"

He wore a linen tunic with a hem just above the knees. A belt draped around his waist, not made of leather but of braided strands of thread or maybe animal hair. He wore sandals fashioned from a similar material with soles of leather.

I wore the outfit Max had conjured for me. Leather pants. Blouse. Boots. To an ancient Irishman, I must've looked very strange indeed.

He fingered a lock of my hair. "Soft as silk. Only wealthy women have hair as silken as yours. Are you of the nobility?"

"Not hardly." I did have the powers of a god but telling him that seemed like a bad idea. He already thought I was weird. Instead, I asked, "What were you doing right before you saw me?"

"Ahhh," he purred in that way future Nevan loved to do, "nothing before you matters."

Oh yeah, this was definitely Nevan.

Might his forging be the primary event?

I needed a straight answer from him, but I had a feeling this conversation would go much the way our very first conversation had—flirtation, evasion, and more flirtation.

"What were you doing," I repeated in a sterner tone, "right before you saw me? It's important I know."

He sighed with the same frustrated amusement as sylph Nevan. "If ye insist on knowing, I was scouting the area for enemy soldiers. The Fomorians have been conducting raids lately, and we fear they might stage an all-out assault soon."

The Fomorians. He'd told me about the enemy that had attacked his village. If the Fomorians were preparing to mount an assault, that must mean Tuathal was married to Ceara and they had a daughter, Daráine. That also made this, or a day very soon after, the day he died and became a sylph.

If time had sent me here, today must be the date of his forging.

What the hell did that have to do with Aello's vendetta? Sure, Nevan had been instrumental in taking down Skeiron, but Aello had already tried eradicating him from history. The tactic hadn't accomplished what she'd hoped. Notus was alive, but Skeiron was dead. If she wanted them both back, getting rid of Nevan clearly wouldn't do the job. The harpy also knew I could bring him back even if she annihilated him in the past.

I had no idea why I'd turned up here, in this moment.

Maybe I needed to watch events play out to understand.

Tuathal touched my cheek, skimming his fingertips down my skin, drawing me out of my thoughts with his sensual caress. "Would ye like to know anything else, beauty? I will gladly explain all the things I would love to do with you."

"Don't you have a wife?"

He compressed his lips, his jaw tightening, and retracted his hand. "I do."

"Then why are you trying to seduce me?"

"I—" Mouth open, he froze. After several seconds, he rubbed his forehead. "I have no idea. My wife and I are no longer intimate, but I should not behave this way with another woman. I never have before, but you..." He rubbed his forehead again as lines deepened across it. "I cannot explain my attraction to you. It is strong and nigh irresistible."

My throat went thick. Even in another lifetime, eons in the past from my perspective, he experienced our bond as strongly as I did. I wanted to throw my arms around him and kiss him, but I couldn't do it. He had a wife and a child. Though I knew his first marriage had not been a happy one, I also knew he would never cheat. Our bond had made him slip up for a moment. It confused him. Hell, it confused me to stand here with the human version of my husband, knowing he was married to someone else.

Tuathal stumbled backward a few steps. "I must go."

He turned to leave.

A horn blared in the distance.

Its long, low call resounded in my soul. This was it—the day Tuathal died and was reborn as Nevan. I sensed the truth, but I also remembered what he'd told me about the day the Fomorians attacked. The call had been sent out, and every able-bodied man had rallied to defend the Parthalonian village.

Tuathal stiffened. "The attack has come."

He sprinted into the woods.

I raced after him. We sped through the forest with him way ahead of me. I ran as fast as I could, but damn, he was faster. Dread coiled its icy fingers around my heart as I wondered what I would see once we arrived at the village. Had the carnage begun already? From what I knew about ancient warfare, it was brutal and gruesome, conducted with swords, spears, and bows and arrows.

Barreling out of the trees, I caught sight of the village up ahead. It occupied the center of an open plain surrounded by woods. Huts with thatched roofs comprised the village, with corrals for livestock and a larger structure that might've been a meeting hall. Along one side of the village, a small river snaked across the plain, disappearing into the trees where the landscape sloped downward.

Nevan had fallen in battle on the shores of a lake, at the base of a waterfall. He'd taken me to that same spot two months ago, though it looked much different in the twenty-first century. In that time, the ten-foot cascade emptied into a small pool, more like a big puddle. Nevan had assured me it had been bigger five thousand years earlier. The waterfall was where Notus had come to him with an offer to make him immortal. The falls and the lake must lie at the river's end or its headwaters. Which one, I had no clue.

I halted twenty feet or so past the tree line. No enemy soldiers were visible yet, but the alarm call must have signaled their approach.

Tuathal galloped toward the village.

Maybe I needed to observe this event, not participate. Less risk to the time stream.

I summoned my powers to cloak myself from view. Was I destined to watch all the men I cared about be ripped apart and reassembled? I'd witnessed Travis's forging, then Calder's, and now it seemed I must witness Nevan's forging too.

Uncertain if I could tap into Nevan's powers from this far in the past, I decided to try it anyway. I'd lost sight of Tuathal, so I willed myself to teleport to him. I popped up inside a small, thatched hut.

Tuathal crouched near the wall, murmuring words I couldn't make out to someone lying on a fur blanket. Edging closer, I peered over his shoulder.

A little girl, maybe seven or eight, lay on the blanket propped up with one arm. The graveness of her expression tugged at my heart. "I promise, Papa. I will stay here with Mama."

Movement drew my attention to the doorway as a woman entered the hut.

A chill slithered down my spine.

Ceara stomped toward her husband. "You cannot leave us, Tuathal. Your family needs you more than the village does. Protect us. Take us far away from here."

"The Fomorians have surrounded the village," he said, rising. "Soon, they will attack. There is nowhere to run, Ceara. You and Daráine will be safest here. Please do as I ask."

Ceara glared at him with a hint of the seething rage that would grow stronger after her resurrection at the sorcerer's hand. She really had hated Nevan from the start, blaming him for the fact her family forced her into an arranged marriage with him. She ought to have appreciated a good, brave man like Nevan. Instead, she loathed him for things beyond his control. After all, he'd been forced into marriage with her too, but he had made the best he could of it.

Tuathal bent to kiss his daughter's forehead. He reached for Ceara's hand.

She yanked it away. "Go, then. We do not need you."

He grabbed a sheathed sword, hooking it onto his belt, and walked out of the hut.

Into the fire, that's where he was going. Literally. He would be struck down by the enemy and reborn amid a bonfire of scalding magic. And I must bear witness to it, praying the solution to the Aello problem lay in what I would see.

Daráine sniffled.

Ceara huffed. "Crying is not permitted. You know this, but you are your father's child. Weak. Useless."

My fingers crooked into my palms, the nails scraping my skin. I wanted to smack Ceara so badly. What kind of woman belittled her daughter because she was unhappy in her marriage? The kind who would happily become the consort of an evil sorcerer. The narcissistic kind.

I wished I could spare Daráine the horrors of the battle, but at least I knew she would survive. Ceara claimed to have charged the enemy, sacrificing her own life to grant her daughter time to escape.

With one last glance at Daráine, I zipped to Tuathal.

He stood among a group of armed men arrayed in two staggered rows. They faced the woods, their weapons brandished, their expressions set in grim resolve.

The cacophony of an army's footfalls thundered ever nearer.

Within seconds, the battle commenced.

CHAPTER NINETEEN

IT WENT ON AND ON AND ON. IN THE MELEE THAT ENSUED, I LOST TRACK of Tuathal. Every time I tried to whisk myself to him, I missed the mark. He must've been moving swiftly, dashing here and there to assist his fellow warriors or to take down one of the Fomorians. Despite my invisibility, I was not immune to the effects of the battle. The close quarters meant I had little space to sidestep the fray. The clashing of swords, the shouting voices, the thudding of sandal-clad feet, the *thwack* of each arrow finding its target—all of this created a din the likes of which I had never heard in my life.

Every time one soldier attacked another, blood sprayed from the brutal wounds.

My clothes had become damp with it. Damp with the blood of men. My stomach lurched, but I somehow managed not to throw up. Helpless to do anything except watch, I zipped to the edge of the woods. I needed to keep track of Tuathal, but he was somewhere in the thick of things. Even from here, the noise of the battle seemed loud, though not as deafening as when I'd been inside it.

Everywhere, soldiers fell. The Fomorians wore crimson tunics and armor with metal helmets, but the Parthalonians had nothing to protect them.

I squeezed my eyes shut, unable to watch any more of the carnage.

Tuathal would head down or up the river at some point during the battle. How was I to find him? The melee had screwed up my ability to track his movements with my magic. But I was the Janusite. Shouldn't I be able to block out the noise and find him?

Keeping my eyes shut, I willed the din to recede—and it worked. The terrible cacophony dwindled into silence. I commanded myself to stop smelling the stench of blood on my clothes, commanded my garments to cleanse themselves. Static electricity rushed over my skin, and though I dared not open my eyes yet, I understood my clothes had become pristine again.

Tuathal. Nevan. I sensed him, waging war but alive.

I opened my eyes.

The village was burning. The fire seemed to have started near the flank of where Nevan's people had met the enemy head-on, but the blaze was spreading.

I teleported back to the hut where Nevan had left Ceara and Daráine.

Ceara shoved Daráine out the door and stalked after her, forcing the girl to walk straight toward a group of Fomorian soldiers.

"Here is the child," Ceara said. "Do with her what you wish. She is her father's daughter, not mine."

One soldier, whose helmet was bronze-ish instead of silver, stepped forward to snare Daráine's wrist. He sneered at her, then at Ceara. "Females are of great value to our tribe, the younger the better. You have done well."

"You will keep your word?" Ceara said.

"Oh yes, our king will be well pleased to have another wife to service his needs, one as young and fresh as you. The others have grown old and tired."

Ceara sidled up to the soldier, rubbing her breasts against his bare arm. "I will happily service you first, General, as thanks for sparing my life." She wrapped her arms around his bicep. "You are certain I will be the favorite queen?"

He smiled with feral hunger. "You will be everyone's favorite, lavished with all the luxuries you desire."

Was she seriously handing her daughter over to savages so she could become queen of the enemy tribe? For wealth and status, she would sell her body and soul. I shouldn't have been surprised, given that she'd done the same thing with the sorcerer, but her actions stunned me anyway.

Her own daughter.

I stared numbly at the general and Ceara as they engaged in a sloppy kiss, and the general palmed her breast through her tunic. She made a hungry little noise as if she enjoyed the prospect of becoming the Fomorians' number-one whore.

My gaze flicked to Daráine.

Wait a minute. Nevan's daughter was supposed to have survived the battle and been taken in by a family from a neighboring clan. Of course, Ceara had lied about bravely sacrificing her life to save their daughter, so she might've lied about Daráine's fate too. I could not let this sweet-faced, innocent girl who looked so much like her father suffer the fate her mother had arranged for her. No way in hell. But if I helped her, I would be altering the past. My actions might rock the timeline to its core, setting off the apocalypse Bob had feared.

"Mama," Daráine said, choking back a sob. "I do not want to go with these men. I want Papa."

"Your papa is dead," Ceara snapped, "or he soon will be. Forget about him."

Tears poured down the girl's cheeks.

Screw the timeline. No child would be enslaved to a scumbag under my watch.

I clamped a hand on Daráine's shoulder and tugged her free of the general's grasp, then I whisked us away. We materialized deep inside the woods. The Fomorians hadn't penetrated this area, and somehow, I knew they never would. This forest lay inside the boundaries of Parthalonian territory, but it held no strategic value to the enemy. I could leave Daráine here while I checked on her parents—yes, both of them—and figured out what to do with the girl. She was supposed to end up with a good family from another clan of Parthalonians.

Had I been meant to find that family for her?

The idea rippled through me almost like a shiver, accompanied by a tingling certainty of the truth of it. I had no time to consider the ramifications of this revelation, though.

I knelt before Daráine, taking hold of her shoulders, knowing she could see me as long as I was touching her. "I'm a...friend of your parents. I'm going to make sure you're safe, okay? Do you understand?"

Her lips trembled. Her amber eyes, so like Nevan's, shimmered with tears. She kept her posture solid, though, and her voice amazingly steady. "I understand."

My auto-translate seemed to work with the girl too.

She had her father's strength and his determination. I saw it in her eyes and sensed it in her soul. Despite having a wacko for a mom, this girl would become a kind and loving woman. I knew this, and I didn't even try to comprehend how I knew it.

Maybe time had whispered it in my ear.

"I need you to stay right here," I said. "I'm going to see what happened to your mother and father. You'll be safe if you stay put. Got it?"

She sniffled and nodded.

My heart hurt for her, for what she had already endured and what she must endure next. At least she would have a good home after this and a good future.

"I'll be back," I said, and rushed toward the village.

Ceara was nowhere in sight. The general was gone too.

My aim had been off. I'd targeted the spot where I had left Ceara, not for the woman herself. I couldn't explain why I needed to witness her fate, but something drove me to do it. Nevan was alive and fighting, that much I sensed. So, I concentrated on Ceara.

And materialized in the woods.

The darkness under the canopy of trees blinded me for a moment, after the brightness of the sunlit battlefield in and around the village. While I waited for my vision to adjust, my ears picked up sounds. Grunting. Gasping. Wet, rhythmic slapping. I remained invisible as I tiptoed closer to the sound. By the time I reached the spot from which the noises emanated, I could see clearly in the gloom.

And I wished I couldn't.

The Fomorian general had Ceara pinned to a tree, her tunic hiked up around her waist and one leg hitched around his hip. He thrust into her again and again, grunting each time, pounding into her while she clutched at his shoulders, a look of pure ecstasy on her face.

Voyeurism was not my thing. I'd never watched a porno movie either. Yet I could not move or speak or tear my focus away from the scene before me, despite the nausea roiling in my stomach. Shock, probably. I hadn't expected to find Nevan's wife humping someone else while he was valiantly battling the enemy. Part of me could not accept she'd been as thoroughly rotten in her mortal life as she'd been after her resurrection.

Here was the proof. She'd always been rotten to the core.

The general thrust once more, let out a long groan, and slumped against Ceara. Breathing hard, he said, "You will be a splendid concubine for the king and for the Fomorian army."

She smacked his arm. "You have not finished."

He raised his head to give her a haughty look. "Yes, I have. If you are fortunate, my seed will take root in your womb."

"Fortunate?" she hissed. "I will never bear your spawn. And you have not finished because I am not finished."

The general pushed away from her, tugging her tunic down to cover her. "Why should I care about your pleasure, concubine? You are a tool, not a lover."

Ceara glowered at him. "That was not the agreement. I am to be the king's wife, not a concubine."

He chuckled with menacing humor. "You agreed to fucking all of us. What did you expect that meant?"

"It means that I—I will be the queen but have the freedom to choose whatever lovers I desire."

The general laughed again, this time with an undeniable disdain. "We will choose when to have you, not the other way round."

Ceara's eyes went wild, her breaths mutating into feral noises.

He shook his head. "Perhaps you are too base even for us. Fomorians have higher standards for our women than the low-born Parthalonians do."

She yanked his sword out of its sheath on his belt and drove it into his gut.

The general clamped one hand around the sword's blade and the other around Ceara's throat. He pinned her to the tree again, this time with a palpable rage. Gasping for breath, he eased the sword out of his body. The sword tumbled from his grasp, splashing blood over the grass.

"You," he growled at Ceara, "will pay for that."

She spat in his face.

He gritted his teeth, summoned all the energy he had left with a visible effort that contorted his features, and crushed her throat. Her windpipe shattered with a crunching sound.

Ceara's face went slack, her body too.

The general jerked his hand away, letting her dead body crumple to the ground. He staggered backward, clutching his belly. His body hit the ground with a thud. His eyes were vacant, the life gone from him.

I gaped at the pair of vile humans who had brought on their own demises. The general had been a thug with no morals as far as I could see. Ceara had wanted to become the queenly slut of the Fomorians though not a concubine passed around like a jug of wine, and she hadn't given a fig about what happened to her daughter or her husband. Though I couldn't muster empathy for Ceara or the Fomorian general, I wished they hadn't needed to die. I wished no one had died on this day, but their fates had been sealed before I arrived, before I was even born.

Once I'd eased their eyelids shut, I rushed to Nevan—to Tuathal.

He and a Fomorian soldier stood along the banks of the river near where its waters plummeted over a cliff into the lake below. Even from here, I could tell the precipice towered high above the lake, at least fifty feet by my estimation. Tuathal and the Fomorian had gone a good distance from the village, but I heard the noises of battle not far away. The melee had spread. Tuathal and the Fomorian brandished their swords, circling each other as if measuring up the enemy. Blood and dirt covered the bodies of both men, the whites of their eyes seeming to glow compared with their darkened flesh.

Neither man could see me. I didn't want to witness this, but I knew I must.

The Fomorian lunged at Tuathal but missed when his foe veered sideways. Tuathal slashed his sword at the Fomorian, scoring a glancing blow across the man's side. A new wound opened, expelling a thin stream of blood.

A victorious look brightened Tuathal's grim features, but the victory didn't last.

The Fomorian head-butted Tuathal in the stomach, hitting him so hard the breath exploded out of Tuathal and he stumbled backward, his sword hand popping open, the weapon striking the ground. The Fomorian roared and slammed his blade straight into Tuathal's stomach.

I cried out, but no one heard me. My pulse raced. The urge to intervene had my muscles tensing in preparation.

Sneering at his foe, the Fomorian jutted his chin and thrust out his chest. He wrenched the sword from Tuathal's body and kicked him in the gut so hard he staggered backward to the cliff's edge. Tuathal clamped both hands over his wound, but blood streamed from it around his hands and between his fingers. The Fomorian raised his sword above his head, and with a victorious cry, plunged the blade into Tuathal's heart.

I squeezed my eyes shut, then forced myself to open them. I would bear witness, for Tuathal, for Nevan. I owed him that much.

The Fomorian prized his sword free of Tuathal's body and jogged off into the woods, heading for the sounds of a fracas in the distance. His footsteps faded away.

Tuathal swayed, his knees giving out, and tumbled backward over the cliff.

My heart thrashed like it wanted to climb out of my chest. I zoomed down to the base of the falls, whipping my head left and right to search for Tuathal.

His body floated in the churning foam as the waters propelled him to the shore. He lay motionless on his back, eyes shut, half on the ground and half in the water.

Soon, he would be forged. I scuffled forward a few steps, compelled by the impulse to stop this, to save the man I loved, but I couldn't. This had to happen or else the future would be altered yet again. I'd come here to fix what Aello had done, not make things worse. I could not stop what came next.

Paralyzed, I watched the life drain out of Tuathal as the rise and fall of his chest diminished until I could barely detect it. His skin had gone pale, his lips were turning blue. A phantom hand clenched around my heart. I'd seen him like this once before, on the night Skeiron ran him through with an endued sword. Back then, I'd saved Nevan. Here and now, I had no choice but to let him die.

His body lay partially in the lake with one of his arms slung out to the side, his limp hand moving up and down with the gently lapping water. Fresh blood covered his palm from when he'd clasped both hands over his gut wound. The red liquid tainted the water.

The atmosphere shifted.

I couldn't describe the sensation. It seeped inside me with an unearthly feeling of wrongness. I hadn't experienced this when Calder was forged, but I'd had Aello to worry about then.

A figure rose up out of the lake, the figure of a man clad in a golden toga. Notus had arrived.

His eyes swirled with molten shades of metal.

I didn't dare move, though my magic should've shielded me from the view of anyone, mortal or elemental.

Notus crouched beside Tuathal. In a surprisingly gentle gesture, he swept a lock of bloody hair away from Tuathal's eyes. "Mortal, hear me."

Tuathal's eyes darted behind his closed lids.

"I have come to you," Notus said, "because I witnessed your bravery today. You will be an excellent warrior in my army, but before you may join the ranks, you must be forged."

Tuathal's lids parted a sliver.

"Do not attempt to speak," Notus told him. "You are far too weak. What I offer you is this—immortality and power beyond anything your mortal mind could possibly fathom. You will be as a god, immune to the weapons of this world. You will be strong and virile, more so than in your mortal life. I offer a new life, a new world, an eternity. Will you join me?"

Blood sputtered from Tuathal's lips, but he croaked, "Yes."

Sheesh, Notus had made forging sound awesome. If I'd lain dying, I would've said yes too. The first time I had asked Nevan about his forging, he'd told me elementals didn't mention the downside or the pain involved in the transformation when they recruited new members for their tribes. The creature that forged Calder hadn't even bothered with the glossed-over spiel. I guessed the kerkopes lacked the finesse of the other elementals.

Notus hovered his hands over Tuathal and began to chant in another language. My auto-translate magic seemed incapable of deciphering the words, or maybe they weren't words at all. The chant might consist of sounds without meaning rather than phrases.

Orbs of bluish-white light ignited around the two of them, swirling and blooming outward until they encompassed me as well. Their energy sizzled on my skin. While Notus chanted on, the orbs swelled and flared into a brilliance that blinded me.

Squinting, I flung my arms up to shield my face.

The forging had begun.

Chapter Twenty

Energy whirled around us, tingling stronger and stronger every second. Tuathal howled in agony, the sound like an animal rather than a man. I squeezed my eyes shut tighter, unable to breathe or move until the blinding brilliance winked out.

I cautiously opened my eyes and lowered my arms.

Once the monkey-thing had forged Calder, both of them had vanished. Tuathal lay where he'd fallen with Notus kneeling beside him. The king of the sylphs rose and gazed down at his newborn soldier.

Tuathal lay motionless but breathing evenly, no longer a bloodied mess. No, this was not Tuathal anymore. This was Nevan.

I absorbed the sight of the body I knew so well. Massive muscles. Bronzed skin. Black hair that shimmered in the sunlight. His tunic had disappeared along with his belt, sword, and sandals. Nevan lay completely nude. I'd witnessed his rebirth, the origins of the elemental warrior who had won my heart. Despite the thrill that knowledge shivered through me, I forced myself to focus on Notus. Why hadn't he whisked them both away to the Unseen?

Another figure materialized at Notus's side.

My brain struggled to comprehend what I saw. The female elemental alongside Notus was Aello. She looked different, no longer skeletal but fleshed out with curves and those perky breasts that had seemed incongruous with the body she'd sported last time I encountered her. Her hair was white as always, her eyes dark as pitch. A sprinkle of pinkness lent the pallor of her skin a life it lacked in the future.

She slid her fingers into the hair at Notus's nape. "My love, why have you done this? We agreed to have birth children, not these unseemly forged offspring."

Unseemly? I clenched my fists. Nothing about Nevan was unseemly.

"I sensed this battle," Notus said, "and came to witness it. You know how I relish a bloody fight. I thought I might glamour myself as one of the mortals waging this battle, but then I sensed this one." He waved a finger toward Nevan. "And I…wanted to forge him."

"Forge him?" Aello said with a derisive huff. "Why? He will require much work before he will be of any use."

"I know, but he evinced a courage and strength of will I've seen in few mortals. He deserves to become one of us."

Aello glanced at Nevan, and her lip curled. "Leave him here. We will return to him in a century or so, and if he has survived, we shall teach him our ways." She clenched Notus's hair, pulling his head back just enough to make him wince. "You agree, Notus. Do you not?"

"Yes, my love, I agree." He studied Nevan's unconscious form, something akin to regret flashing over his face. He shed the emotion with a gusty breath. "Of course you are right. Only those who survive the forging and learn to care for themselves on their own are worthy of joining the sylph army."

Aello threaded her fingers through his hair and feathered her lips over his cheek. "Let us go to the palace and see to making our own blood offspring."

"You know I cannot take you to my palace. We must go to your nest, as always."

Her mouth tightened. She flexed her fingers only to curl her talons into her palms. A bead of blood oozed down one razor-sharp claw, dripping onto the ground.

Notus seemed oblivious of his lover's anger, his attention swerving to Nevan.

"As you wish," Aello said, her voice tinged with the same fury evidenced by her demeanor. "Let us leave this place."

The duo vanished.

I stared at the spot where they had been. They were leaving Nevan here alone? A newly forged elemental? He needed help to get through the transition. It involved more than surviving the actual forging. I'd seen how hard the transition was for Travis. That Nevan got through it on his own for a century amazed me and made me love him even more.

Since I'd witnessed his forging, I needed to leave. Find Daráine. Take her to a good family.

How could I leave Nevan here to suffer alone? Somehow, he'd gotten through it. I had to believe he still would.

Nevan had mentioned someone nursed him through the transition. Notus had abandoned him. Who else would come to his aid? I had to assume his vaguely remembered savior would show up.

I zoomed back to Daráine, dropping my invisibility shield.

The girl sat huddled against a tree. When Daráine spotted me, she raced over to lock her arms around my waist. "You came back."

"Of course I did." I knelt to look her in the eye. "I'm sorry, sweetie. Your parents didn't make it."

Tears sprang forth anew, trickling down her cheeks, but she nodded with a solemn understanding beyond her age.

"I'm going to take you to a family," I said, "who will take care of you and love you like you're their own child. You will be safe, I promise."

Daráine gazed into my eyes for the longest moment, her eyes large and unblinking. She stretched out one hand to touch her fingertip to the skin beneath my eye. "You are an angel?"

"Uh, no."

"You must be. You come and go like a spirit, and you saved me." She clasped her hands over her heart, looking upon me with wonder. "You are an angel."

"No, I'm Lindsey."

"The angel Lindsey."

"Um…" I stood and grasped her hand, unnerved by her rapt gaze. Never had anyone called me an angel—except for Nevan. "I'll take you to your new family. Okay?"

She nodded.

I concentrated on the concept of a good, kind family of Parthalonians who would be willing to take in an orphan. Sounded like a tall order, but hey, I was the Janusite. Why couldn't I command the universe to find me the right folks?

We zipped to a thatched hut situated amid a gently sloping landscape hemmed in by woods. A village sprawled throughout the open area. The home in front of us resided on the outer fringes of the village.

I sensed Nevan remained unconscious. Our bond, diminished when he'd been a mortal, had surged in strength until it was nearly as strong as it would be in the future.

Since I'd conveniently brought us right to the hut's door, I knocked.

The door swung inward, revealing a round-faced young woman with pink cheeks and a welcoming smile. This was Daráine's new mother. I recognized, on a level too deep to explain, this woman would care for Nevan's daughter.

"Hi," I said like an idiot while I waved my hand like one too. "This is Daráine. Her parents were killed in the battle that's going on over in the next village. She needs a new home, and I know your family will be the right one for her."

"Battle?" The woman's face blanched.

"Oh, don't worry. The Parthalonians will defeat the Fomorians before the battle ever gets this far out. You'll be safe." I glanced down at Daráine, feeling a strange tightness in my throat, and asked the woman, "Will you look after Daráine?"

The woman's mouth opened, but Daráine spoke first.

"She's an angel," Daráine said. "Lindsey is her name."

"An angel," the woman said with true awe. She seized my hand, pancaking it between hers. "I am Brónach, wife of Marcán. We will gladly care for this poor child."

"Good," I said, though her awe had me cringing inside. Why did everyone think I was an angel?

"We will love her as our own," Brónach said, squeezing my hands as burgeoning tears glistened in her eyes. "You have my word. We are honored an angel has chosen us for this sacred duty."

Honored? Sacred? Sheesh, talk about overkill. Sure, my clothes must've seemed strange to these folks, but labeling me an angel seemed like a giant leap.

Daráine hopped on her toes. "Lindsey does not always glow. I think she hides her true nature so she might walk among us."

"Of course," Brónach said like that made total sense.

Glow? What on earth were they talking about? I glanced down at myself but saw no such thing.

"She stopped glowing again," Daráine said. She fixed her amber eyes on me. "Thank you for bringing me to my new family. Will Papa be allowed to watch over me?"

No, he wouldn't. Notus forbade him from taking a peek at his daughter's life or the lives of her descendants. Telling a lie seemed like the kindest thing to do.

"I'm sure he will," I said. "Your father loves you very much."

The girl hadn't asked about her mother. I couldn't blame her.

Brónach babbled some more craziness about Lindsey the angel. My skin itched the longer she insisted on calling me an angel. I retreated as quickly as politeness allowed, saying goodbye to Daráine. The two of them retreated into the hut. As the door swung shut, Daráine waved to me.

I waved back, suddenly choked up. She wasn't my daughter, but a sharp pang stabbed into my chest at the thought of leaving her. Later, after Aello was dealt with, maybe I could take Nevan back in time to see the life his daughter had led. He deserved to know she'd been happy.

And I knew she would be.

This trip through time had shown me one thing that must have been the reason I'd come here. Aello had been Notus's lover, and though she seemed determined to call the shots in the relationship, Notus refused to accept that. He'd let her talk him into abandoning Nevan, but he had dismissed her suggestion they go to his palace. The sylph king didn't view the harpy as his equal. Notus would eventually become depraved, but in this moment, he'd held on to a scrap of humanity. He hadn't wanted to leave Nevan, but Aello commanded him to do it and he gave in.

Nevan couldn't have known Aello. He would've told me. She had known of him, though.

I should leave. My mission was done.

But Nevan needed me.

I returned to the lake where Nevan lay unconscious. Tiptoeing closer, I peered down at him searching for signs of…I didn't know what. Signs of the man I knew. Signs he was okay. His entire body was slack, and his eyes did not move behind his closed lids. How long did it take after the forging for the former human to wake up? How would he behave when he did? With no answers to guide me, I gazed out across the lake. Coldness washed through me when I noticed my own image reflected on its surface.

A soft, blue glow surrounded me.

No wonder Daráine and Brónach had mistaken me for an angelic being.

I had stopped cloaking myself when I returned to Daráine. I'd had to, or else the girl's new mother would've thought she was a little off, the way she talked to an invisible angel. I hadn't realized I was glowing. Freaking glowing.

How had that happened?

My magic shimmered blue, but it always dissipated as soon as I stopped using my powers. It never created a full-body halo.

A soft moan drew my attention down to Nevan. Eyes half closed, he raised his gaze to me.

Crap. I was supposed to be gone before he woke up. Maybe I should've blipped away the instant he saw me, but I couldn't. He gaped at me like I really was an angel, the answer to his prayers for salvation.

If I had been meant to help his daughter, maybe I'd been meant to help him too. Nevan had mentioned hazy memories of an angelic being who took care of him immediately after his transformation. He hadn't recalled what the angel looked like, only that he owed his existence and everything he had with me to the mysterious being. Whenever he called me his sweet mortal angel, he used those words because he believed I had saved him much the same way his mystery angel had saved him after his forging.

What if I was that angel?

Maybe I was giving in to a delusion that suited my desires. I wanted to stay with him, to soothe him, to care for him during this arduous transition. I loved him. The man currently gaping at me didn't know me, much less love me.

Time, if I'm not meant to stay with him, whisk me back to my present right away.

Nothing happened. I waited, growing more uneasy with every passing second and with Nevan's awed gaze trained on me. Time did not yank me out of the past and back to my present day. Delusion or not, I took that as a sign I was meant to stay, at least for a while.

I crouched beside Nevan.

He jerked. His entire body convulsed, his face wrenching with agony. An anguished cry burst out of him.

"What's wrong?" I asked. "Are you okay?"

His eyes swirled wildly, the whites stained with red. When he tried to speak, he broke into a hacking fit. His body began to tremble.

I smoothed hair from his eyes and caressed his forehead with one palm. With my other hand, I clasped one of his. The heat of his skin scorched so hot it almost burned, but I held on anyway. Christ, I'd had no idea things got this bad after the forging. No wonder Nevan and Max hadn't wanted me to see Travis right after his change.

"Shh," I murmured, rubbing my thumb in circles on the back of his hand while I kept stroking his forehead. "It's all right. You don't need to speak, just try to relax."

He sucked in a ragged breath, exhaling it gradually. His gaze stayed glued to me.

"I will not leave you," I said, "until you're through the worst of it. I promise you that."

Another convulsion seized him.

"Easy," I said. "Take it easy. I know it's hard, Nevan, but please try."

Lips parted, he furrowed his brow. He tried to speak again but managed only a croak.

"Hush," I whispered. "You need rest."

Dimly, I recognized the sounds of the battle had receded a bit but not gone away, audible behind the rush of the falls. Nevan needed a quiet, soothing place to recover. A vicious battle was not the kind of background noise that would ease his transition.

Like I had any clue about how to ease him into a new life, a new world, a new body.

I had to try.

"Close your eyes," I said, "and sleep."

A shudder racked his body, though less fiercely than the seizures had. I spread one palm over his forehead and the other over his heart, praying for some guidance on how to help him. I shut my eyes, willing his pain to lessen, knowing I didn't have the power to heal.

He sighed, his whole body relaxing.

I opened my eyes. The glittering blue of my magics streamed out of my hands and into him.

Nevan seemed…peaceful.

The noises of the battle raged on.

I transported us away from the melee, straight into the Unseen.

Chapter Twenty-One

I LOST COUNT OF THE DAYS. AFTER TAKING US INTO THE UNSEEN REALM, I'd fervently wished we could hide out in a cave somewhere far away from other elementals, somewhere lovely and peaceful. My wish had been granted. Without realizing what I'd done, I had teleported us to the perfect place for Nevan's convalescence.

What on earth was I doing? I needed to go home to my own time and find a way to defeat Aello. Nursing Nevan had not been part of the plan. How could I abandon him? Notus had forged him and run away to get it on with Aello. Nevan needed someone to care for him.

Besides, time would wait for me.

And so, I spent day after day tending to him, often simply talking to him about nothing in particular, babbling away to let him know I was here. I discovered I could conjure the things I needed, like he could—or would be able to eventually—so I conjured cloths and blankets and basic implements for making food and gathering water from the stream outside the cave. He drifted in and out of consciousness, wrenched by the occasional seizure but more often shivering. I wrapped him in blankets and laid cool cloths over his forehead. Despite his chills, he was running far too hot even for a sylph.

When I was fifteen, my mom and Ash had gotten sick while my dad was away on business. They'd had simple colds, though. I made them chicken soup from a can and got them fresh boxes of tissues. Today, I was caring for someone whose body had been ripped apart molecule by molecule and reassembled into a different kind of being. Despite having zero experience with nursing newly forged elementals, I kept trying. I fed him soups I made from conjured ingredients, dribbling the liquid into his mouth a little at a time.

Gradually, Nevan stayed awake for longer periods. After several days by my guesstimate, he began to speak, though only to say simple things like yes or no. When I asked how he felt, he told me, "Better."

That was the biggest word he used for a long while.

Every evening, I sat beside him for hours stroking his forehead and face, running my hands over his chest while my magics danced over his skin. With rapt attention, he would watch me doing this. As soon as I stopped, he would drift into a deep and peaceful sleep.

I slept when he slept, though my slumber was haunted by nightmares of tornadoes and earthquakes and everyone I loved vanishing.

One morning, I woke to find Nevan sitting up, studying me.

"Are you okay?" I asked, pushing up onto my elbows.

"I am well," he said. "The pain has greatly subsided."

"Your speech is a lot better too." I sat up and laid my palm on his forehead. "You're back to your normal temperature."

"How do you know what is normal for me? I have been…changed."

"Yeah, but I'm familiar with your kind." *And with your body*, I thought but kept it to myself. Telling him we were lovers, much less husband and wife, would damage the time stream for sure.

Or so I assumed. Time didn't confide in me.

Maybe I should've worried that I'd started to think of time as a living thing, but I didn't care about anything right now except Nevan.

He sucked in a breath, his eyes widening a touch. "You are beautiful, transcendent, a being of light and kindness."

"I can't deny I love hearing you say that, but I'm not—"

Nevan touched his fingertips to my cheek. "You are a miraculous spirit. An angel."

"No, really, I'm not." I glanced at myself and, naturally, I was glowing again. "I can see why you'd think I'm an angel, but I'm a woman, plain and simple."

"Nothing about you is plain or simple. You shimmer with heavenly light."

The sensation of his fingertips on my skin awakened parts of me that ought to stay dormant. Lust was not helpful right now.

My body disagreed.

"Are you sure you feel better?" I asked. "I mean, how much better?"

He slapped his hands on his chest, smiling. "Fully better. You have healed me with your angelic powers."

Oh jeez. I ought to nip that idea in the bud, but the way he was gazing at me with adoration, I knew he would never accept I was not an angel. Couldn't blame him. I did have powers. The glowy, glittery kind.

"Listen," I said, "since you're feeling better, I should go."

His smile crumbled. "You cannot. Please, I—"

I clapped a hand over his mouth when the P-word triggered a zing of magic between us. "Careful there. The P-word is a big no-no here in the Unseen. So is gratitude. And whatever you do, never, never, never admit to owing anyone your life."

He peeled my hand away from his mouth, smirking. "I never realized how much I would enjoy a domineering woman until you entered my life, angel."

"Call me Lindsey." What the hell, he might as well know my name. I'd probably screwed the time stream anyway by staying with him.

"Of course, angel Lindsey."

"Not angel. Lindsey. Only Lindsey, no other words before or after."

His smirk deepened. "Whatever you wish, darlin'."

My heart stuttered. He'd called me *darlin'* like he so often did in the future. He had become my Nevan.

He cupped my face in one big, warm hand. "I am appreciative of your efforts to aid in my recovery."

"Nice job with expressing gratitude without actually expressing it." I resisted the urge to turn my face into his hand and kiss it. Resisted a lot. "You're a fast learner."

"I have an excellent tutor." He rubbed his thumb over my bottom lip. "A beautiful, sensual one."

The breath caught in my throat at the husky tone of his voice. I coughed and said, "Do you remember what happened? Do you remember being human? Being forged?"

"Yes, I recall everything after I fell in combat." He withdrew his hand, grasping the nape of his neck. "However, my former life grows dimmer every day. All I can remember of it is meeting you immediately before the battle and that there was a battle. The details elude me."

"And the forging."

He grimaced. "I recall those details rather more clearly than I would like."

The Nevan I'd married remembered quite a bit about his mortal life, but maybe temporary amnesia was a common side effect of the forging.

Nevan stopped blinking, his gaze locked on mine, his eyes aflame with whorls of bronze, silver, and gold. "You came to me before the battle. That proves you are an angel."

I didn't ask how he came to that conclusion because I really didn't want to know.

"Get up," I said, hopping up and gesturing for him to do the same. "You've been lying around for days. Exercise and fresh air will do you good."

He sprang to his feet. The blanket that had covered him from the waist down slid off, puddling on the floor.

Naked Nevan. Close enough to touch.

My breaths quickened, my pulse too. I clutched my hands over my belly, desperately fighting the need to run my hands over his velvety flesh.

He tugged one of my hands free and led me out of the cave into the golden sunshine. The stream burbled softly, its water oh-so-inviting. My scalp itched. I hadn't bathed since before my time-travel adventure began.

"I must really stink," I said, not realizing until it was too late I'd spoken the words aloud.

"Stink?" Nevan said.

"You know, smell bad. I haven't bathed in days, maybe longer. Didn't want to leave you alone for more than a few minutes in case you needed me."

He waved toward the stream. "Let's bathe together."

Oh, I knew how this would go. Bathing would become fondling and fondling would escalate into thrusting and moaning. Could he have sex yet? Was his body capable of it? I didn't want to damage his recovery simply because I had a serious case of lust.

Nevan moved closer, took hold of the top button of my blouse, and unhooked it. "I will not molest you, unless you want me to. You have my word."

"And yet you're undressing me."

One side of his mouth kicked up in a half smirk. "You cannot bathe in your clothing."

"Uh-huh." I batted his hand away. "I can do this myself much faster."

He looked dubious until I poofed my clothes away. His gaze raked over my body from my toes up to my face. His tongue slipped out to moisten his lower lip when he drank in the sight of my breasts.

I leaped into the deepest part of the stream where it flared out into a small pool before narrowing again.

"Come on in," I said. "The water feels incredible."

He stared at me, his chest heaving.

I dunked my head under the water, washing away days' worth of grime. When I surfaced again, I combed my fingers through my wet hair and sighed with contentment.

Nevan jumped into the pool, catching me around the waist before I'd recovered from the mini tsunami his body had created. Pressed against his hard, hot body, I suddenly forgot all about time travel and wounds to the time stream and everything else I should've been concerned with now that he had recovered from his forging.

He seemed a lot better off than Travis was even months after his transition.

Based on the erection blossoming between our bodies, Nevan was fully capable of doing anything he wanted.

Maybe I should've stopped this, but I'd lost the will to say no.

He touched his mouth to mine in a tentative kiss. Against my lips, he whispered, "I do not know—do not remember—"

"Sex?"

"Yes." He cleared his throat and wriggled against me. "Have you and I…"

"No." Not in this time, anyway. Nevan had introduced me to the joys of making love, so it seemed appropriate I should do the same for him. I linked my hands behind his nape. "Let me show you how it's done."

I covered his mouth with my own, my heartbeat accelerating when he grasped my ass in both his hands. His erection rubbed against my belly, my nipples scraped on his chest, and the lapping of the cool water intensified every sensation. I licked at the seam of his lips until he parted them for me, then plunged my tongue deep into the heat of his mouth.

He groaned, the sound resonating in his chest, vibrating into my breasts.

Lost to the feel of him, I teased the roof of his mouth with my tongue, swirled it around his, and moaned when he responded with greedy thrusts of his own tongue. We kissed forever it seemed, entranced by the flavor of each other, unwilling to sever the intimate contact even as his cock grew harder and my sex grew wetter.

I whisked us onto the grassy bank of the stream, a cushion of greenery beneath me and Nevan above me, his body molded to mine.

He broke the kiss, gazing down at me with burning eyes. "I want ye. Don't know how to—"

"Do what feels right."

"But I need ye to like it."

I dragged my tongue up his throat to coil it around his earlobe. "I'll love it, trust me."

He regarded me for a few more seconds. Exhaling a soft growl, he slithered down my body inch by inch, his hot skin gliding over mine, the sensation delicious and arousing. His lips tickled my skin as he moved, and when he sealed his mouth around one nipple, I gasped. He suckled the peak, swirling his tongue around the areola. I clutched at his head, holding him to me, writhing beneath him while he released my nipple only to latch onto the other one and lavish it with the same attention. I bucked my hips, arching my back, my mouth falling open.

When he moved lower, his head between my legs, and his mouth closed around my taut bud, I let out a strangled cry.

"Nevan," I gasped. "Oh yes, Nevan."

He nipped and licked and sucked on my clit until I was thrashing under him, moaning and whimpering, sinking my fingers into his hair and scratching his scalp with my nails. My release detonated like a bomb, an explosion of pleasure that seized my entire body. He kept tormenting my nub until the last spasm faded away.

Breathing hard, I said, "And you claim not to remember sex. That was...wow."

Nevan lifted his head to peek at me over the hairs of my mound. "Is that all we do?"

I laughed. "No, not by a long shot. Trust your instincts."

His lips stretched into a closed-mouth smile of pure, animal hunger. "I'm very glad to hear that is not all. I relished your pleasure, but..." He glanced away. "I am feeling a powerful need to claim your body."

"Do it."

Rising to his knees, he grasped my hips and lifted them off the ground. His mouth was open, his tongue slid across his lower lip. With his gaze hooded, he stared at my groin like he was a starving man and my body was a juicy steak.

"Lindsey," he growled. "Your pink flesh glistens, so wet and delicious."

I gasped when he plunged inside me with one swift, powerful thrust. He hesitated there, buried inside my body, his chest heaving and his eyes a tempest of churning colors. God, I loved the feel of his cock filling me up, the heat and hardness of it intoxicating. Just when I started to speak, to encourage him, he withdrew partway and plowed in deep again, pulling out and thrusting in over and over at a measured pace, his every muscle taut and his expression strained with concentration and need.

I grabbed his biceps, urging him to bend toward me.

He obeyed, his gaze never wavering from mine, and I clutched his biceps while he penetrated me again and again, his hips undulating.

"Oh Nevan," I moaned, and latched my legs around him. A faint voice in the back of my mind told me I shouldn't be doing this. What if by staying with him, by having sex with him, I'd irrevocably altered the future? Our future? I shouldn't have let this happen, but I didn't give a damn about the timeline anymore. I'd become an eyewitness to his courageous but tragic death and to the forging that had shaped him into the man I loved. How could I ever have left him to suffer alone?

He wasn't suffering anymore.

Nevan slanted toward me more, his thrusts quickening and becoming more ravenous. He grunted in rhythm with every plunge of his shaft into my wet, aching flesh. I grasped his shoulders, my nails digging in, and bucked my hips into his thrusts. His face captivated me, the hunger in his expression mixing with a mild confusion and rapt adoration. No man had ever looked at me the way he did, whether he was a mortal warrior, a newly forged elemental, or the sylph king.

Magic rose inside me as my need escalated toward climax. Blue energy shimmered on my skin, only a few sparkles at first, growing into a glittering sheen that formed a second skin over my entire body. Blue sparks leaped off my skin to crackle on Nevan's.

His eyes went wide, his gaze flicking to the magic sizzling between us.

Rather than stopping or even slowing down, he accelerated the pace of his thrusts, as desperate to find release as I was, slamming into me and bouncing my body. I clung to him, and my moans escalated into whimpers and sharp cries. While my body went rigid, and my sex milked him hard, he threw his head back and bellowed. The scorching jet of his release pulsed deep inside me.

I went limp on the cushy grass bed, moaning with satisfaction. This man knew how to make love to me, even when he had no idea who I was. I silently thanked Bob for his wedding gift because I had zero ability to resist Nevan anytime, anywhere. At least the magical prophylactic ensured I wouldn't get knocked up with a dangerous hybrid pregnancy.

But I wanted children with him. I wanted it so much.

We couldn't have that.

Nevan brushed his fingertips over my cheek. "What vexes you?"

"It's complicated." I took hold of his hand, pressing it to my face. "I love being with you, Nevan."

"Why do you keep calling me that?"

Chapter Twenty-Two

I PONDERED HOW TO EXPLAIN IT BUT GAVE UP AND TOLD THE TRUTH. "It's your new name. Every elemental picks a different name after the forging. Yours is Nevan."

"How do you know this?"

"Um…Let's just say it suits you."

He smiled. "You have named me, angel Lindsey. I am grate—"

I sealed his lips shut with two fingers. "No gratitude, remember?"

"Mm." He sucked my fingers into his mouth, releasing them slowly. "I will try to remember that."

His gaze fell to my hand, the one holding his to my cheek, and his brows knit together. He raised my hand between us, studying it intently.

Blue magic sparkled along my skin and dribbled onto his.

"You have great power," he murmured. "My angel Lindsey."

Every time he called me "angel," I melted inside.

He slid his hand down to my wrist, raising my palm to his mouth. The energy on my skin crackled, and he canted his head this way and that to examine it. He lifted my hand higher and dragged his tongue from my wrist up to my palm, swirling it around the sensitive center.

I sucked in a breath.

Topaz-blue energy glittered on his tongue as he raked it up my middle finger to the tip.

"Nevan," I breathed, excitement tingling between my thighs.

He suckled my fingertip, then glided his tongue down to lap at my palm.

"Oh God," I moaned, amazed at how easily he could turn me on. I'd never thought of my palm as an erogenous zone, but whoa mama, it was.

He groaned, licking his way down to my wrist. "I want to devour you, feast on your body from head to toe, make you moan and beg for more."

"I'd beg right now, but that's another no-no in the Unseen realm."

"You brought me here, and I know you can travel in the blink of an eye." He shoved both arms under my body and hoisted me up to sit on his lap. "Take us back to the mortal world so I might feast on you for hours and hear you beg me to give you pleasure."

Helpless to resist him, I whisked us to the other side. Making love over the blood stain that marked his death sounded not the least bit sexy, so I made sure we ended up on the other side of the lake in a secluded spot shaded by tall trees.

And we enjoyed each other.

For hours, maybe longer. Time meant nothing in the bubble of our desire. My magics awakened his and mingled with the newly born powers inside him, heightening every sensation and triggering some of the most intense orgasms I'd ever known. In between rounds of mind-blowing sex, we kissed and touched, exploring each other's bodies. By the time we finally lay exhausted and thoroughly sated in each other's arms, the sun had set in the mortal realm.

Christ, how long had I been here, in this time? Nevan and Max needed me to come home, but then again, I was in the past. Did it really matter how long I stayed? I would return to the moment right after I'd left. Nevan and Max would've done as I'd instructed, leaving Aello's nest before she arrived.

Excuses, I knew this. Something about this version of Nevan, the freshly born sylph learning about his new body and new powers, entranced me. The chance to see him in this time, to understand his past in a way I never could simply from hearing him talk about it, kept me here.

I conjured the blankets from the cave, and we wrapped them around ourselves, our bodies skin to skin inside our little cocoon.

He nuzzled my cheek. "You are a revelation."

My throat went thick. He'd spoken those words to me on the night we'd first made love, the night thousands of years from now when I'd given my virginity, my heart, and my soul to him.

No more excuses. As much as I longed to stay here with him, to understand his past, I needed to go home. I'd seen him through the worst days of his transformation. He could survive on his own.

For a century?

With all these vast and incredible powers, maybe I could summon Notus and shame the jerk into taking care of Nevan. Sure, no problem. I mean, it had taken me how long to get the hang of time travel? I suddenly thought I could wave my hand and summon the sylph king, not to mention convince him to do the right thing.

Nevan had told me once Notus started out as a good king, a good man, until he let dark magics take hold of him. The same fate had destroyed Skeiron. Had Aello been the driving force behind their downfalls?

I stroked Nevan's cheek. "You don't need me anymore. The worst is over."

"You cannot leave." He pushed up on one elbow, his eyes glinting with the cold shades of fear. "Stay with me. I need you, Lindsey."

My heart hurt for him, but I forced myself to say, "I have to go. People I love are waiting for me, and they need me more than you do right now. You are strong and smart, and I know you'll be okay."

He opened his mouth as if to speak but froze. His attention swerved to the other side of the lake.

A shiver of awareness rippled through me. Someone was coming.

Notus.

I knew this, though I had no idea how. I also knew, or sensed, Aello was not with him and that he meant no harm to Nevan. Jumping up, I conjured my clothes into a pile on the ground. I didn't have the finesse to make them appear on my body. Gesturing at Nevan, I said, "Get up and put something on. Notus is coming back for you."

While I pulled my clothes on, he got up and scowled. "I would prefer to stay with you."

"I'm sorry, that's not an option." I framed his face with my hands. "No one knows you better than I do, so believe it when I say you'll be fine. One day, we will see each other again, but not for a very, very long time."

"Why must we part ways?"

"Too complicated to explain." I slapped his behind. "Cover that fine ass and prepare to meet your king."

Nevan snatched up a blanket the same color as his skin. He held it up, examining the large sheet of fabric. Frowning, he tore off a wide strip and strapped it around his hips. The cloth covered his hips and his groin but little else.

I'd witnessed the birth of his signature loincloth.

"Let's go," I said, trying really hard not to think about how much I had influenced Nevan's past while I zipped us to the other side of the lake near the falls.

We stood mere feet from the spot where he had perished.

I pulled him into my arms and whispered into his ear, "No matter what happens, I will always be here for you, somewhere, sometime. Always. But you're about to start a new life, and you need to embrace it for better or worse." I kissed him softly. "You'll do fine. I believe in you, Nevan."

Though it physically pained me to do it, I backed away into the trees, out of sight.

Nevan stared after me, his longing a palpable force.

I willed myself invisible.

A figure emerged from the water. Notus sauntered up to Nevan and said, "It is time for you to begin your new life."

Nevan barred his arms over his chest. "Why did you leave me here alone? I might have died."

The sylph king chuckled. "You are immortal. Nothing can kill you."

Bullshit. Notus had no intention of telling his new soldier about endued weapons, magically enhanced poisons, or dark spells. Though I desperately wanted to warn Nevan, I had to let this play out the way it had been meant to before I intervened. He needed to get back on the path laid out for him.

"Come with me," Notus said, stretching out an arm to indicate the lake. "The waters will ferry us into your new world."

Water was the portal to the Unseen.

Nevan glanced back at the woods, at where I hid.

"We must go," Notus said.

They leaped into the lake and vanished.

I straightened, rolling my shoulders back, and realized I was assuming the same about-to-zip-away pose that Nevan and Max always assumed. The posture felt natural. How strange that I'd accepted my powers and grown comfortable with them right when an evil witch wanted to destroy me and Janus wanted his powers back.

Janus. Max. Nevan. I had to get back to them.

Something moved in the trees to my left.

Aello, the not-skeletal version of her, strode out of the screening foliage and stopped on the spot where Nevan and Notus had stood a moment earlier. She glared down at the dried blood stain, the evidence of Nevan's demise, and tilted her head left and right. She squatted to touch the stain, lifting her fingers to her face to sniff them. Her lip curled.

"Sylphs," she snarled. "They stink of the earth even as they command the air. Newborns are the worst."

The harpy rose, muttering under her breath.

She froze, only her eyes moving.

I didn't move, didn't breathe. She couldn't see me.

"Come out and show yourself," Aello said, turning in my direction. "I can feel the air disturbance from your breaths."

From this far away? She was a wind elemental, but I'd never heard of them feeling breaths from twenty feet away. Even if I believed she could feel my exhalations, I would not uncloak myself. I should've left right then, but an inkling of something important about to happen kept me rooted in place.

Aello's gaze flitted as if she struggled to pinpoint my location. "You are the one who nursed the newborn sylph through his transition. He is stronger than any bantling should be but not strong enough to thwart my plans. You may hide yourself from my sight but know this. I will have my way, and you will never again lure my lover into doing your bidding."

Notus was her lover. Had Skeiron haunted her bed too? Maybe she'd done three-ways with the two sylphs. *Yech.* I did not need that image burned into my brain.

"I saw you," she said, "moments ago with the newborn. I know your face, and one day, I will know your name and your weaknesses. Notus was to be mine and only mine, but like any foolish male, he had to procreate. His progeny is not even his blood child." She hissed like a steam vent suddenly blown open and slapped a hand on her chest. "I was to bear his blood progeny. He swore he would wait for our child, but the siren call of a pathetic mortal lured him to this place. You called him here, I know this. Do not deny it!"

Denials wouldn't help, I knew that. Aello might have gotten more depraved and insane over the eons, but she'd clearly veered down that path even before Nevan or I came into the picture. Crouched behind a tree, I was riveted to the bizarre monologue unfolding before me.

"He would not wait!" Aello shrieked. "Our firstborn was to be the child of my womb, not a bastardized sylph forged out of a pathetic mortal. You caused it, you must have." She shook her fists in the air. "Show yourself!"

The depth of her hatred made my skin crawl. She despised me because I'd taken care of Nevan and eased his transition from mortal to elemental. In some twisted way, she thought I had stolen her chance to have Notus's firstborn offspring and that I had hypnotized the sylph king into both forging Nevan and coming back for him.

And I understood what all of this meant. I was the trigger for the primary event.

What was to come had already unfolded long before I became the Janusite. How could I have triggered Aello's time-shifting revenge plot? I hadn't traveled back in time until now, after she absorbed untold dark magics and set in motion the shifts that had damaged the time stream. This couldn't have anything to do with me.

Except I'd known almost from the start Aello harbored a seething hatred for me. Her vengeance was aimed smack at me, beginning with the first time shift. She'd altered my past repeatedly in failed attempts to get rid of me. She had erased Nevan as a means of eradicating me, though it hadn't worked. I was one with time, and she could never divorce me from the time stream.

And yet, everything she'd done had been aimed at me. How was it possible I had triggered a millennia-long quest for retribution? The truth trickled through me, raising every fine hair on my body.

Nevan had told me someone nursed him through his transition. The first time he'd seen me in the rock shop, back when he'd been glamouring to disguise his appearance, he had felt he'd known me before. From the second I'd bumped into him in the woods near the falls, I had experienced a sense of connection and belonging I'd never known in my entire life before him. We fell in love so fast, so hard. No mere coincidence had brought us together. I, the Janusite, had not accidentally bumped into him, the one and only elemental charged with finding the one and only mortal gifted with the powers of a god. We were destined to find each other, to love each other, to make each other stronger.

Fate. Immutable, undeniable. It had brought me to this moment in the distant past. By the time I was born in the twentieth century AD, I had already traveled into the past. It seemed contradictory—how could I have been here in this moment before I was born—but I understood the truth of it.

I sagged against the tree, my vision blurry as I struggled to focus but failed. Did this mean I'd never had a choice? No free will? I could not, would not, believe that. I had chosen to be with Nevan, and he had chosen to be with me. Our bond transcended time, but it existed because we chose it.

Aello howled and shook her fists at the sky.

The harpy vanished.

I dived into the time stream and sprang out in the midst of a battle.

Chapter Twenty-Three

I SQUINTED INTO THE STORM OF COMBAT RAGING AROUND ME. I hovered at the periphery of a clearing, at the edge of the battle. Powerful gusts of wind ripped grass and dirt from the earth, whirling it around the sylph soldiers clad in obsidian armor who battled an army of bare-chested soldiers with impossibly thick torsos and long, filthy hair. I had not returned to my own time. I'd intuited this the instant I emerged from the time stream. Though I had intended to go home, time must have believed I needed to witness this moment.

Time believed? Sheesh, a few hours ago I would've laughed at the idea. Now, I realized it might be true. Since I was bound to time by my powers, it served as a conduit. Unconsciously, I had known I must come to this point in history, though I didn't understand why.

Swords clashed in a deafening cacophony of metal on metal. Sparks rained down from the gnashing blades. The enemy was unfamiliar to me. They had legs as thick as tree trunks and skin the color of wet sand. Their greasy hair hung around their faces, obscuring them, but I caught glimpses of features as gnarled as a knotty pine tree.

Hands grasped my upper arms and hauled me backward. I yelped, but no one could've heard me over the din.

"Quiet," a voice hissed into my ear even as I was towed further backward into the shelter of the trees.

Those hands spun me around to confront a body sheathed in silver armor shot through with gold and bronze. Dirt and blood stained the metal and the face of the man grinning at me.

"Nevan." I grinned too, despite the brutal fight going on behind us. The fact he had blood on his face at last sank in, and my grin waned. "Are you hurt?"

"The blood is not mine." He flourished his hand the way I'd seen him do countless times, and instantly we were inside a calm, quiet bubble. He flicked his wrist. His armor and body were washed clean in a heartbeat. "I had thought to never see you again, my angel Lindsey."

"Well—"

His mouth covered mine, silencing me. I wrapped my arms around him, marveling at the way his armor fit like a true second skin, soft and hard at the same time. I'd felt his armor before, but he had never kissed me while wearing it or kissed me while in the midst of a battle. I melted like I always did for him, relishing the slick glide of his tongue over mine, responding with a matching passion. After a few seconds that seemed like a blissful eternity, we separated our lips.

Nevan swept stray hairs from my face, tucking them behind my ear. "I'm pleased to see ye, darlin', but why have ye come? This is a dangerous moment for a visit."

"Not sure why I'm here." Something important must've been about to happen, something to do with Aello, but I couldn't explain all of that to this version of Nevan. I could ask a question, though. "Have you met Notus's queen?"

He pulled his head back, tipping it to the side. "You come to me during a battle to ask me that? Notus has no queen."

"A lover, maybe?"

"I am not privy to the king's dalliances," Nevan said curtly. He backed away from me, his lips tight. "Are you interested in becoming his angel lover?"

"Absolutely not." I moved toward him, laying my hands on his breastplate. "I have no interest in your king. Only you."

His stiff posture softened a bit, as did his voice. "I am pleased to hear that."

I glanced over my shoulder at the armies doing battle. "What's going on here?"

"The gnomes have undertaken a foolish mission to defeat the sylphs." Nevan's gaze hardened into steel when he looked toward the battlefield. "They will fail."

Yes, they would. Notus remained king of the sylphs until Skeiron defeated him. Another sylph took him down, not the gnomes.

Before I undertook my mission to the past, before the first time shift, Nevan had mentioned the sylphs once fought a battle with the gnomes. The reason for their attack was a mystery. Maybe I was here to find out why. Maybe the reason related to Aello.

The ground shuddered.

I clutched at Nevan. "What was that?"

"A gnome. They strike the earth to cause a tremor and unsettle the enemy." Nevan cocked his head, listening. "I must go. The king summons me."

"Be careful."

He pulled me into his arms and ravished me with a kiss that left me breathless, my heart racing.

Then he vanished.

I knew Nevan was not the reason I'd come here. I also knew he would survive this battle and serve Notus until the king became depraved and Skeiron deposed him. After that, Nevan would serve Skeiron willingly until the new king became as depraved as Notus had been, using a bargain to turn Nevan into his slave and the seeker of the Janusite. Nevan had forsaken his duty and refused to hand me over to Skeiron even after we both knew I was the prophesied mortal gifted with a god's powers.

Cloaking myself once again, I wandered the periphery of the battle in search of whatever had drawn me here. Aello, I assumed. Where was the harpy?

The better question was why should I wait for her to show up. I had all these freaking powers at my disposal, and ever since I'd first entered the time stream, those powers had become easier and easier to tap into at will. I closed my eyes and let my mind go blank.

There.

At the instant my eyes opened, I zipped to the location I sought, to the individual I sought. The harpy squatted behind a tree, watching the combat with a look of dark glee on her face. She held her palms together, her long nails tapping against each other. Her lips peeled back from her teeth in a creepy version of a smile.

I tiptoed closer to peer past her into the clearing.

Nevan swung his sword at his opponent, their blades striking with a sharp clang of metal on metal that reverberated through the clearing despite the racket around them.

"Ohhh," Aello murmured, her voice raspy. She clacked her talons. "Strike him down, gnome. Make it painful."

She imbued the last phrase with a disturbing intensity. Her eyes burned bright red. Tendrils of roiling black magic snaked out from her talons, wending their way through the smoky, fetid air toward the gnome soldier who grappled with Nevan. The tendrils spiraled around the gnome, and his eyes began to blaze red.

He stomped his foot. The earth quivered.

Magical energy shot out into his sword. The silver blade mutated into glistening black tinged with crimson.

An eerie certainty slithered down my spine. That blade was endued. It would destroy Nevan.

The gnome rammed his huge, booted foot into Nevan's gut, knocking him off balance. While Nevan struggled to stay upright, the gnome raised his sword above his head, grasped in both his gnarly hands. The creature sliced the blade down toward Nevan's chest.

I flung my hands out. Blue energy spurted out of my palms, a jet of magic aimed straight at Nevan. It blew him sideways, out of the sword's trajectory. Nevan caught himself before he fell to the ground, sprang upright, and barreled toward the gnome. His sword plunged into the enemy soldier's chest.

It wouldn't kill the gnome, but the wound would take him out of commission for a while.

Aello flapped her head in every direction, her sharp eyes searching for me.

Not that she could see me. Her frustration increased with every whip of her head, making her eyes glow like red coals about to erupt into flames. Mouth open, breaths hissing out of her, she sprang to her feet.

"I know you are here," she hissed. "You shall not save him today."

Aello thrust her arms out.

Black energy poured forth from her talons. It boiled in the air, writhing and seeking whatever it might latch onto amid the chaos. In fact, the chaos seemed to fuel it into greater and greater power. It coiled around the gnome soldiers, transmuting them into red-eyed demons intent on a single shared goal implanted in their minds by Aello.

Destroy Nevan.

Oh, like hell she would.

I roared and flung my arms out, unleashing twin torrents of blue energy. The black and the blue collided above the heads of the warring armies.

And exploded.

Chapter Twenty-Four

THE BLAST KNOCKED ME BACKWARD ONTO MY ASS. MY EARS RANG, and the supernova flash of the explosion had rendered me temporarily blind. At least I hoped it was temporary. I lay there for a moment, immobilized by the shock of the explosion and the knowledge of what I'd done. I had intervened in the battle. What if I'd altered history?

No, time had brought me here. I'd been meant to stop Aello from destroying Nevan. He was meant to live on and find me a long, long time from this day.

As I lay there waiting for my limbs to obey me again, I wondered about this turn of events. Nevan, the version of him in this time, remembered meeting me after his forging. Why did present-day Nevan have no memory of it? He would've told me if he remembered encountering me during a battle. He had mentioned other times in his life when his memories were hazy but dismissed it as unimportant, nothing more than a side effect of living forever. Was he right? Caught in the middle of a moment present-day Nevan clearly had forgotten, I had to wonder.

My vision cleared, and my ears stopped ringing. I sat up and surveyed my surroundings.

Aello lay sprawled on her back a few feet away. Her eyes, though open, stared vacantly at the treetops above us.

I clambered to my feet, brushing off my clothes. Dirt and debris from the explosion had covered me, but I managed to get rid of the worst of it.

Aello's head rolled to the side. She locked her black gaze on me, her irises as dark as the pupils, fathomless pools of evil.

My skin crawled. I staggered backward a step.

"You," she rasped, and pushed up onto her knees. "You destroyed the entire gnome army. It is not possible!" Spittle sprayed from her lips with those words. She pounded her fists on the ground. "I will avenge myself on you if it is the last act of my existence. More power, that is what I require. Blacker magic. Darker spells. Whatever it takes to rid the universe of you."

Her hand shot up, one talon aimed at me.

I summoned my magic, cloaking myself again. Whatever I'd done had left me a touch woozy, and I did not want to tangle with Aello in this condition.

The harpy pounded her fists on the earth. Clods of dirt shot up, splatting down around her.

I rushed to the clearing.

Every last gnome was gone.

The sylphs meandered through the clearing, expressions slack, exchanging head shakes and muttered words.

Nevan stood tall and proud at the periphery of the clearing, a small smile curving his lips as if he knew a secret no one else did. He believed I had gotten rid of the gnomes. Well, I had. I hadn't meant to eradicate them, scattering them to the Four Winds. Save Nevan, that had been my only thought. Something inside me warned the gnomes hadn't wanted to assault the sylphs. Aello's hand had moved them like marionettes.

Had I eradicated the gnomes? Aello told me so, but I shouldn't believe a thing that whackjob said.

I shut my eyes and concentrated on locating the gnome army. Relief weakened my knees, but I locked them to stay upright. The gnomes had been teleported back to their home territory, unharmed. Whether Aello retained her hold on them, I couldn't tell for sure.

Eyes open again, I resumed my visual survey of the area.

Notus loitered on the other side of the clearing, his obsidian armor and every patch of exposed skin splattered with blood. He jerked his head as if sensing something, his attention directed past me.

I half turned, noticing Aello not ten feet from me. Since I was invisible again, she had no idea we stood so close to each other.

Notus marched across the clearing toward Aello.

The other sylphs, even Nevan, failed to notice their king had left the battlefield. I let my ethereal senses unfurl a bit and realized she had used dark magics to cloak herself. How could I see her? The answer hit me the second I thought the question. My Janusite powers trumped hers, at least in this time and place. Aello might have acquired dark magic, but she hadn't amassed enough to beat me yet.

Notus reached his lover, pulling her into a passionate embrace.

I sensed he was now cloaked along with her. The other sylphs seemed not to notice the couple ravaging each other with a sloppy, icky kiss that involved plenty of groping and grunting.

They broke their kiss but stayed entangled.

Notus skimmed his hands up and down Aello's arms, his gaze bound to hers, his pupils large and dark. In a hushed tone, he said, "You did this, my love, did you not? You saved my army from annihilation."

I snorted, though neither of them heard me. *She* saved the day? The harpy had wanted to annihilate Nevan even if that meant destroying the sylph army and Notus too. She'd told me once she would exact her vengeance whatever the cost, and she'd meant it.

"Yes," Aello purred in that raspy voice, "I spared you, my love. Come with me and I will ensure neither of us is ever endangered again. We will share power the likes of which you cannot imagine."

"My army needs me to command them."

"And you shall return to them forthwith." She clenched her fingers in his hair, making him wince. "Introduce me to your precious army, my love, as you promised to do long ago."

Something in her voice told me she wasn't asking.

Notus caressed her long white hair. "I promised one day to bring you into the fold. You said you understood why I cannot do so yet. My people are sylphs, you are a harpy. They will not accept you as my queen. I could introduce you as my adviser and ally."

"Adviser?" She bared her teeth, clenching his hair so hard I swore I could feel the pain. "I am your lover, the woman you vowed you wanted to bear your offspring. You dare suggest I should accept being your adviser instead of your queen?"

He shook his head, blinking several times, seeming to break free of whatever spell she'd cast over him. Notus tore her hands away from his head and took one big step backward. "You will not bear my offspring. I will procreate only via the forging. It is cleaner and simpler, my love, surely you must realize this. Children require time to raise and nurture into soldiers, but a forged being is reborn as an adult who is easily molded to suit my needs."

She flinched like he'd backhanded her across the face. "You deceived me? Swore we would have our own blood offspring when you had no intention of doing so?"

"You deceived yourself, Aello. I enjoy sharing my bed with you, but that is all. The king of the sylphs cannot take a harpy for his queen. If you wish to be introduced as my adviser—"

Aello shrieked.

The ear-splitting sound reverberated off the perimeter of the magic bubble around the three of us, though they had no clue I was within it. As Nevan had done with me earlier, Notus or Aello had ensured privacy via magical means.

Aello stomped her foot. A flush speckled her pale skin, and muscles in her neck and shoulders strained beneath her flesh. "I shall not be an adviser to you. For centuries, since you ascended the throne, I supported and bolstered you with my body, my mind, my magic. When you needed a hand during battle, I provided it. How else would you have defeated the titanium fae, the strongest fae tribe in existence?" She stomped her foot again. Clods of earth sprayed up around her sole, and the earth trembled. "I ensorcelled the gnomes so that they would gift me with their earth powers. I did this to destroy the traitor amidst your army, the one you refuse to see. He will be your undoing."

Notus went stone-still, his eyes wide.

Aello glared at him, her chest heaving with each breath, her white face now crimson. Spittle trickled down her chin. "You would not be king without me!"

While her face burned red, his coppery skin had turned faintly ashen.

He was afraid of her. An instinct told me that fact explained their entire relationship.

"You," he said, keeping his tone mild, "coerced the gnomes into attacking the sylph kingdom."

"Of course I did." She slapped a hand on his chest and dragged her talons down his skin, drawing a slender trail of blood. "To protect you."

"From what?"

Her hand shot out, one talon aimed straight at Nevan. "From him."

"Nevan is a fine soldier."

"He will be your undoing and yet you refuse to see it."

The sylph king lifted his heel, clearly intending to take a step backward, but stopped. "I might have been destroyed during the battle."

"I would have spared you." She peeled her lips back, exposing her teeth. "No longer shall I protect you."

Notus held up his hands. "Allow me to make amends, my love. I did not realize how much you desired blood offspring."

Her entire body quivered with fury. "You did not realize?"

She bellowed the words loud enough to rattle the trees in the immediate vicinity.

My ears rang in the aftermath of her outburst. That woman could holler like nobody else in the universe.

Notus stared at his wild-eyed lover with her hair whipping around her face in the breeze that seemed to emanate from her body. He took one step backward.

"I did not intend to mislead you," he said, his tone cautious. "You suggested blood children, and I neglected to inform you of my plans. That was…an unkind oversight."

"Oversight?" Her voice shrieked like an eagle's cry, only louder and far more piercing. She raised her arms, and the air around us came alive, writhing in wild currents. "You betrayed me, *my love.*"

She grated out the last two words between her locked jaws. No doubt about it, she did not consider him her love anymore.

The wind condensed into a dust devil.

Aello moved her fingers, and the dust devil inched toward Notus. "I saved your life this day. Express your appreciation to me." She twitched her fingers, and the mini tornado surged to within a few feet of Notus, who cringed but did not move. "Express it now and express it fully."

He started to speak but seemed to choke on the words. "Aello, I beg of you—"

"Do not beg." She wriggled her fingers, spurring the dust devil to spew debris at Notus and forcing him to raise his arms to protect himself. "Acknowledge the debt."

The way Notus cringed at her threats suggested to me the harpy had wielded her windy powers at him on previous occasions. An abusive girlfriend who beat her lover with tornadoes? Hell, it wouldn't be the strangest thing I'd seen. For the strong, virile king of the sylphs to be bullied by a female…I couldn't imagine what horrors she must've inflicted on him to get him so firmly under her thumb. He had tried to reassert himself, proclaiming she would never be his queen, but Aello knew she held all the power in this perverse relationship.

I ought to do something, to stop him from incurring a life debt. What, exactly? Pop my head out and inform the king I'd saved his army? I doubted he would believe me. Ah, but I did have an advantage. This was Aello of the past, before she'd absorbed immense amounts of dark magic. She seemed to command a lot of dark mojo, but nowhere near what she had in the twenty-first century. Maybe I could take her out and end the madness in this moment and in the future.

I squeezed my eyes shut and conjured an endued sword.

When I looked at the weapon, I realized I'd summoned Nevan's endued sword—his sword from the future. *Powers growing, Miss Janusite?* I didn't have total mastery of my Janusite magics, but I was getting better with it.

The invisibility cloak around me fell as I lunged toward Aello, the sword aimed at her back. The blade would pierce straight through to her heart.

Notus shoved Aello out of the way.

The sword plunged into his gut.

Chapter Twenty-Five

I STOOD FROZEN, MY HAND ON THE SWORD'S HILT AND ITS BLADE BUR-ied in his abdomen, blood oozing from the wound. A wicked zing of adrenaline electrified my veins, shortening my breaths. I could not look away from the point where the sword entered his flesh. Why had my invisibility spell failed? I sensed the answer. After sparing Nevan during the gnome battle, compounded with time travel and magically easing his transition, I had used up too much energy. I needed to rest my powers, but I didn't dare take a break.

The sword in my hand poofed away.

Aello flung out a hand, hurling me away with a gust of wind. She crouched beside Notus, assessing him with her gaze, seeming unaffected by his dire situation.

She grabbed his chin. "Acknowledge the debt, and I will see you are healed."

Blood dribbled from his mouth, but he said nothing.

"Do it," she said, "or you shall die."

He inhaled a wet, ragged breath. "I owe you my life, Aello. Thank you."

"At last you make an intelligent choice." She mashed her mouth to his. "I shall take you to a vortex where you may be healed."

They were about to leave. I had to follow them, but I needed to give my powers time to recuperate. Hell, *I* needed time to recuperate.

I tried to freeze time. The attempt made my head throb and white lights spark in my vision.

A rest, that's what I needed. Somewhere safe.

Notus and Aello disappeared.

I would find them again, but right now, I had to take refuge in a safe time and place. I sat back on my heels, my shoulders slumping. What if I couldn't do this? Save time, save the worlds, save everyone I loved.

Footsteps drew my attention to the figure approaching me from the direction of the battleground.

Nevan knelt in front of me. "Are you unwell, Lindsey?"

"Exhausted, that's all." I rubbed my neck, and a question occurred to me. "How long has it been since you saw me?"

"A few moments."

"No, how long since the first time you saw me?"

"Since my forging, three hundred twenty-eight years have elapsed."

I straightened, hands on my thighs. "That long? And you haven't forgotten me?"

"Centuries to an immortal are like hours to a human."

Why did past Nevan retain his memories of our first meeting? If my theory was right, I had always been meant to travel back in time, and everything I'd done in the past had already occurred before Nevan and I met in the twenty-first century. The Nevan of that time had no memories of meeting me in the distant past.

The headache from my failed time freeze was getting worse the more I tried to think about anything, especially the vagaries of time travel. I needed a nap. Badly. My whole body sagged, and I swayed a little.

Nevan grasped my shoulders. "You are unwell. What is wrong?"

"Magic drain." I scrubbed my hands over my face. "I need a place to rest, a safe place. A nasty piece of work is ticked at me and—"

"I know of a place." He frowned. "Have you seen Notus? No one can find the king."

"He got stabbed with an endued sword and left to find a healing vortex."

Nevan hooked a finger under my chin. "Wait here. I will inform Skeiron of what has transpired with the king, then I shall return to you. Who wounded Notus?"

I shrugged, feigning ignorance. Better not to tell him about the whole Aello thing and that I'd accidentally stabbed Notus. Way too complicated.

Nevan poofed away.

My head pulsed with pain.

He reappeared, scooped me up in his arms, and took us away. We emerged inside his underground lair. It looked a little different, but I knew it was the same place I shared with him in the future. A pallet topped with a thick padding of furs took the place of the bed I knew from my time. A plain sheet lay over the furs, thrown back like he'd just climbed out of bed. Nevan laid me down on the pallet and settled in beside me, pulling me close and tugging the sheet over us.

His armor was gone, leaving only the loincloth.

My sleepy brain lost its verbal filter, and I mumbled things I shouldn't have, things he wouldn't understand, anyway. "I don't know if I can do this, stop a crazy woman who hates me and I don't know why, not completely. God, I want a normal life. Boring, normal, safe. Oh, that sounds so good. Why do I have to save the frigging world again? Thought I could follow her into the past and keep her from getting so much dark magic, but I failed. I suck."

Nevan stroked my hair. "You are brave and clever and very, very powerful. Whatever troubles you speak of, I am certain you shall prevail."

"I used to think that. Not so sure anymore."

"Accept my word on this. You will prevail." He kissed the top of my head. "Rest, angel Lindsey. All will seem better once you are rested."

Unable to keep my eyes open any longer, I let them flutter shut. As I drifted off to sleep, a tingling sensation swept through my body, a soothing indication my powers were recovering.

It felt like I slept for days.

When I woke, I lay in Nevan's arms as before. His eyes were closed, his breathing regular and shallow. He'd fallen asleep too. Stretching as much as I could with his body cradling mine, I yawned loudly.

Nevan roused and yawned too. "How do you feel?"

"Much better. How long was I out?"

"Several hours."

I sat up and stretched some more. "Gotta get moving."

Though I felt reinvigorated in body and in powers, I suffered from a niggling doubt about my ability to defeat Aello. It seemed no matter what I did, she was two steps ahead. Maybe if I had full control of my powers...

But I didn't. Aello had abducted the one being who could teach me how to use these magics that simmered inside me.

Nevan sat up and bracketed my face with his hands. "Your doubts are plain to see on your angelic face, love. Whoever this enemy is that you must defeat, you must believe you can do it. Otherwise, you will fail."

"I know. Not as easy as it sounds to regain my self-confidence. Regenerating my powers is a piece of cake in comparison."

"While I do not understand how a slice of cake relates to your powers, I gather the phrase indicates one thing is simpler than the other."

"Yes." I ran my hands through my hair, doing my best to comb out the bed-head look with my fingers. "Maybe too much time travel has knocked me off kilter."

"Whatever it is you need to accomplish, you will succeed."

"Your confidence in me is sweet, but I have no clue how to do what needs to be done."

He thrust his hands into my hair, hauling me in for a kiss. The merging of our lips and our tongues enlivened my body, awakening parts of me that never failed to perk up whenever he touched me. As much as I would've loved to indulge in another steamy encounter with him, I really needed to move ahead with the Aello hunt.

But oh, his kiss made me long to forget everything, to drown in him.

When he pulled away, he kept his hands in my hair, his fingers massaging my scalp. "You are a miracle, Lindsey, and you have the power to succeed."

His words penetrated to the deepest parts of my soul. His belief in me gave me hope and strength, no matter which version of him spoke those words. I wanted to thank him for that so badly but knew I couldn't.

Instead, I told him, "You are the miracle, Nevan. Whenever I need a boost to keep going, you give it to me. Even in this time, when we barely know each other, you understand what I need better than I do."

Nevan skated his hands down my arms. "You were glowing while you slept."

"What?" I looked at my body but saw no such glow. "I couldn't have been."

"You were." He slid his hand down past my wrist to lace his fingers with mine. "Even while you sleep, you rejuvenate your powers."

Daráine had mentioned I glowed, and I'd seen it in my reflection in the water. I had no doubt the Nevan in my century would've mentioned it if I gave off an ethereal light while I snoozed. Only since I'd traveled back in time had my magic changed, seeming to grow from the contact with the time stream. I had no idea why that would be or what it meant.

My questions concerning Aello's motives and plans seemed more pressing. If she wanted me gone, why did she keep attacking Nevan? She tried to get gnomes to murder him, and she'd manipulated time itself in her attempts to get rid of him. My encounters with her in the past made it clear she despised me and blamed me for something. It seemed to involve her desire to have "blood offspring" with Notus, but he preferred ready-made soldiers.

Nevan had once told me elementals considered pregnancy to be unseemly and that they preferred to connive to increase their numbers via the forging. He'd also said the forging demanded a hefty price in suffering. I had witnessed that aspect. Nevan suffered for days after his transformation.

"I am glad to have seen you again," he said, lifting my hand to kiss each knuckle, "even if only for a short while. All these years, I have wondered what became of you. I have missed your light and your sweet presence."

His words set off a warmth that bloomed out through my chest, but they left me with an uneasy feeling in my gut. Nevan of the future had confessed to me he'd slept around for a long time before he became the guardian of the falls. After that, his search for the Janusite made elemental females turn their snooty little noses up at him. He had to kiss mortal woman as part of the test to determine which one might be the Janusite, and those elemental women thought his duty tainted him. Before that, he'd been a player.

And he knew nothing about me until the day we met.

Yet Nevan of this time had thought about me for over three hundred years.

I chewed the inside of my cheek for a moment. "During all this time I was away, did you…um…fool around with other women?"

His lips curved into a tender smile, and he traced a fingertip down my cheek. "In all my existence, I have been with but two women—my wife and you. Since the day I first saw you, I have wanted no one else."

Okay, that begged another question. If he'd wanted only me, why did he fool around in the future? He'd kept it up until the day Skeiron enslaved him, commanding him to search for the Janusite. It made no sense. How had Nevan forgotten me after retaining the memory of our first meeting for more than three centuries? Why would he forget?

Someone must have forced him to forget.

I considered the idea Aello might have messed with his memories, but that didn't jibe with what I knew about her. She wanted to take Nevan away from me for good, not fiddle with his recollections.

As much as I longed to linger here, ensconced in Nevan's arms, I had to track down Aello.

"Wish I could stay," I said, "but I have problems of world-shattering importance to deal with."

"I understand. Any chance I could be of assistance?"

Oh, I would've loved some backup, especially of the Nevan variety, but I wouldn't risk Aello getting her bony fingers on him or anywhere in the vicinity of him.

"You are so sweet," I said, and kissed him. "But I have to do this alone."

He nodded his understanding, though he looked bummed about it. Really bummed.

An impulse overpowered my good sense, and I kissed him again, hard. "I love you, Nevan. I always have and I always will. No matter what time or place we find ourselves in, you are the only man who will ever lay claim to a piece of my soul."

"I love you too, Lindsey. It's inexplicable but undeniable. I will wait until the end of eternity for you."

The end of eternity. I would live a finite mortal life while he would live forever. Since the moment I'd realized I loved him, I had worried what might happen to him after I died. Knowing our bond transcended time, I feared even more for his future after me. Eternity alone.

If he'd forgotten about me once, he might do it again. I prayed he would.

Never would I wish for him to suffer.

Throwing my arms around him, I hugged him so tight he choked back a gasp. "We'll see each other again, I promise."

I let go of him and zipped away, rendering myself invisible at the instant the time stream spit me out inside a gloomy cave. Nevan lived underground, but not in a cave. His home, our home, was carved out of the guts of a mountain by magic rather than by natural processes. The fae witch Ennea did her work inside a cave, but it had a homey feel thanks to the golden light of oil lamps and the scents of various potions and magical ingredients. Sometimes her laboratory smelled like a kitchen.

This place stank of damp, rotting earth and decomposing flesh with a hint of an unspecific fetid stench. *Lovely.*

As my vision adjusted to the gloom, I realized the only light came from an open fire burning on the other side of the space. A pile of wood, everything from twigs and leaves to rough-cut logs, blazed with yellowish-orange flames. The smoke spiraled up toward the ceiling and snaked out through a dark hole in the cave's roof.

In front of the fire hunched a wizened old man dressed in filthy robes. His long gray hair was too dingy to be called silver, and his scruffy beard seemed in need of grooming.

Before him stood Aello and Notus.

The sylph king stared straight ahead with bleary eyes, his jaw slack, and swayed ever so slightly.

The harpy had done more than force him into a life debt. She seemed to have enchanted him too, or more likely, ensorcelled him. Once, I'd watched Nevan enchant a girl as part of the test to determine if she had a touch of the Unseen realm in her, a prerequisite for being the Janusite, or so Skeiron had believed. That girl, Sandy, had seemed dazed. Notus behaved like he had no mind of his own.

What on earth did Aello have planned for him?

"Sorcerer," Aello said, lifting her chin, "how dare you leave me to wait outside your lair."

The old man squinted at Aello. "Why have you returned? The magic infusion I provided to you three days agone is all I can give. You know this."

His voice was reedy but clear, unlike his cloudy eyes.

"I need more," Aello said. She pointed a talon at Notus. "This one must be made to do my will."

"Control spells are dangerous." The sorcerer eyed Notus. "As is prolonged ensorcellment. If you leave him in this state, he will become mindless but not in the way you wish."

"Infuse me with more dark magic, so I might handle him myself."

The sorcerer tipped his head back, aiming a cold glare at Aello. "Infusions are not gifts, harpy. They come at a price."

"Name it."

He scratched his chin, toying with his long beard. "Bring me a fae child. Male, preferably. Only then will I consider providing another infusion."

Aello's lips peeled back in the closest approximation of a smile she seemed able to pull off. "I anticipated your request. Since last time you desired a fae girl, I knew you would ask for a male this time."

She had given this creep a little girl? What the hell had he done with the child?

The harpy waved her hand.

A boy of seven or eight appeared beside her, his hands and feet bound with rope and a gag in his mouth.

The sorcerer reached for the boy.

Aello smacked his hand away. "After the infusion."

I needed to stop this, all of it. Her infusion, whatever the hell that meant, and the payment in the form of a child.

The sorcerer gestured for Aello to kneel.

She sank to her knees, tilting her head back and opening her mouth.

He held a hand in front of her mouth, bending his fingers as if he held an invisible ball.

I summoned all the power inside me and hurled an orb of blue energy at the sorcerer. It slammed into his chest, reeling him backward. I lobbed another orb at him. He staggered backward, gurgling and clawing at his singed chest. Tendrils of glittering blue energy crawled over his skin, spreading outward from his chest into his arms and legs and up his throat. Soon, the magic engulfed him.

He stumbled into the fire.

And his body splintered.

Chapter Twenty-Six

No blood or guts spewed forth from the sorcerer. He broke apart into black-and-purple shards, and his disassembled body melted into a seething cloud of the same colors. The robes he'd worn crumpled into the flames of the burning fire, igniting and disintegrating within seconds. The dark magics his death had unleashed spread outward in a mass of roiling, screaming energy that sought a new host.

A tongue of dark magic licked at me, then recoiled.

I grabbed the fae boy and sent him home. How I did it, I had no clue. I wanted him to go back to his family, and he went. I sensed he was safe and where he belonged.

Notus remained dazed and seemingly unaware of everything unfolding around him.

Aello, still on her knees, opened her mouth wider and flung her arms out. "Take me, I welcome you into my body."

Oh hell no. This was my chance to prevent her from becoming unstoppable. I hurled orb after orb at the mass of black energy, but every one of them ricocheted and hit the wall, the ceiling, the floor. One orb nicked Notus, who gave no reaction. I kept firing off balls of blue power, funneling more and more of myself into the effort.

The dark magics flooded into Aello through her mouth.

Her body convulsed. She screamed, but the power burrowing into her muffled the sound.

Gasping for breath, I stopped throwing orbs. It was too late.

The last wisp of darkness rushed inside Aello. She dragged in a deep, rasping breath and gusted it out. A sick kind of glee overtook her features, and she let out an ear-splitting cackle. Why couldn't I stop this? No matter what I did, she won. The Janusite was supposed to be the most powerful being ever to have lived. How could I not defeat one crazy creature?

Because I had not yet embraced the full spectrum of my powers. Deep inside, I feared what might happen to me if I did. Oh, I told everyone I was cool with these powers. I'd even convinced myself of that. Here in this terrible place, confronted with another resounding failure, I at last faced up to the truth.

I was too damn scared to accept all the gifts the Four Winds had infused into me.

Aello got to her feet haltingly and turned toward Notus. She took his face in her hands. Her talons scratched his skin, drawing beads of blood. "Henceforth, you shall worship me as if I were your queen. You are correct, however, that I should not become your queen in fact. I will rule your kingdom through you. The power I have acquired will ensure this."

She sank her talons into his flesh. Crimson rivulets dribbled down his face. Black-and-purple strands of dark magics seeped out of her talons into his blood and slithered up the rivulets into his veins. He twitched and gurgled, his eyes rolling back into his head.

Aello released him. "Look at me."

Notus obeyed.

"What are you?" she asked.

"I am yours, my beloved." He smiled, slung an arm around her waist, and hauled her into his body. "We shall rule the worlds together. The dark magics we share grant us all the power we need."

Aello's gaze zeroed in on me. "You have lost your cloak, Janusite. And you have lost yet another battle with me."

I hadn't quite regained my breath from my magical exertions. Perspiration ran down my temples and into my eyes. It mutated into a cold sweat that chilled me to the core. Even if I'd had a clue what to say, my voice would've refused to work.

"Do not despair," Aello said in a sickly sweet tone, "I shall not kill your beloved sylph—not yet. He will serve Notus, and by extension me, obeying our commands without realizing his king has become a servant of the darkness. I shall enjoy deceiving the poor fool and keeping him from you." She raised one taloned finger. "The longings of his heart will pain him far more than any physical distress."

She flicked her finger.

A force like an invisible maelstrom sucked me into the time stream, propelling me forward and out into the world again.

I struck the ground face first, the breath knocked out of me, stars bursting in my vision. For the longest moment of my life, I lay there unable to move. Every bone in my body ached. Slowly, I pushed myself up onto all fours. Then, I sat back on my haunches to study my surroundings. I'd landed in a cemetery of all places, one I did not recognize. The landscape looked different too, and I knew I wasn't in Michigan anymore. Broken headstones were scattered around me. This place seemed familiar, but I couldn't quite place it. I'd returned to the present, but where in the world was I?

"Nevan!" I shouted. "Max!"

They materialized in front of me.

Nevan dropped to his knees before me and clutched my upper arms. "Why did you not come to us? What is wrong?"

"Aello clobbered me again." I shut my eyes for a moment, then met Nevan's worried gaze. "She tossed me back to the present. No, that's not right. The present-day Aello dragged me back here at the same instant the past Aello evicted me. I can feel that's what happened. I couldn't stop her, I couldn't change anything, I—"

He pulled me into his arms, my face buried against his neck. "You are exhausted, love. How much power did you employ to fight Aello?"

"Too much, twice." I raised my head. "Do you remember when we first met?"

"Of course. Slightly more than three months ago, by the waterfall."

"Nothing before that?"

"Should I recall an earlier event?"

"No, never mind." I let my forehead drop onto his shoulder. "Nothing makes sense anymore."

Nevan murmured soothing sounds and caressed my back, but even that could not expunge the guilt of my latest failure.

I curled my fingers into his chest. "Did you at least succeed in your part of the plan?"

"We ransacked Aello's nest, yes. She did not come, however, and so we left."

Another plan gone kablooey.

"Just wondering," Max said, "why are we in a cemetery? And where are we? This doesn't look like Mandan County."

"It's not," I said, raising my head again. I glanced around and suddenly realized why the landscape seemed familiar. "We're in Kentucky. This looks like the area where my parents live."

"Why would Aello dump you here?"

"Beats me." I rifled through my memories of everything I'd seen and learned during my trip into the past. "Aello put some kind of spell on Notus to make him do what she wanted. She must've ensorcelled him, and maybe that's why Notus turned into a sleaze. Aello's voodoo wrung his brain dry."

One corner of Nevan's mouth lifted. "I do adore your colorful descriptions."

I started to reply but didn't get the chance.

The earth trembled beneath us, vibrating into our bodies. The shaking escalated into rocking and rolling so fast none of us had time to react. The ground heaved upward and split apart. Headstones tumbled into the newly created chasm even as the earth continued to rumble and rock beneath us. At the instant the earthquake unleashed its final shiver and settled into an eerie calm, a shock of paranormal origins walloped me. I spluttered and twitched, struggling for breath.

Nevan held me until the effect waned.

"What was that?" he asked.

"Another time shift." I swallowed, my throat tight and dry. "A much bigger one."

Max took a step toward us and vanished.

I jerked, stunned by a realization I could not deny or explain. He was gone. Dead. Erased.

"No!" I shouted. I tried to stand, but Nevan held me fast.

"Lindsey, look." With one finger, he rotated my face toward a headstone a few feet away. "The time shift, it has…"

He trailed off, shaking his head in disbelief.

The headstone read, "Lindsey Astrid Porter, beloved daughter."

I leaned closer, staring at the date of death. I had died on the day I was born.

"That's impossible," I said. "Aello couldn't have murdered me. I'm right here."

"You are one with time," Nevan said calmly, despite the fear in his eyes. "She cannot remove you from it."

"But she took away my life." My gaze bounced here and there, a frantic search for something I prayed not to find—until I found it. "No."

The syllable came out as a gasp.

Nevan followed my line of sight, and his arms clinched me harder.

Two more headstones accompanied mine. The names on them identified the deceased as Kenneth Porter and Lucinda Porter. They'd died the same day I had.

My brother had never been born.

I scrambled to my feet, kicking Nevan in the stomach in my haste to get up. He paid no attention to the kick and sprang to his feet. We faced each other, bound by our bewilderment and fear.

Aello blinked into view right behind Nevan.

Before I could shout a warning or shove him out of the way, she rammed a sword straight through his body. Its tip protruded from his chest, blood dripping from it.

"No!" I screamed.

The harpy ripped the sword out of his body.

Nevan slumped to his knees, hands clutching his gut, blood dribbling from his lips and between his fingers.

"I have won again," Aello boasted. "Pitiful Janusite, you will never defeat me."

Roaring with an unholy rage, I ran straight at her.

She vanished.

I stumbled and fell to my knees. Scrambling around, I got in front of Nevan again.

He slumped against me and mumbled, "Endued sword."

"Shit." With one arm, I held him against me. My free hand trembled as I touched the gaping wound. *Not again, no not again.* Memories of the last time he'd been skewered by an endued sword replayed in my mind. Tears flowed down my cheeks. I cupped his face, not giving a damn that I was smearing his own blood on his cheek. "You can't leave me like this. Hold on, Nevan, please."

He tried to speak but managed only to cough up more blood.

I threw my head back and screamed, "Tris!"

Nothing.

"Triskaideka!" I bellowed. "Get out here this minute!"

A frigid certainty echoed inside me. Tris wouldn't come. He couldn't hear my call because Aello had destroyed him and Ennea too. Every ally, every friend, I'd ever had was gone. I was alone. While tears poured down my face, hot and bitter, I crushed Nevan to my chest. Sobbing, I begged for a miracle. None came.

He sucked in a wet, rattling breath. The swirling colors in his eyes went dark. His chest no longer rose and fell, and the sizzling heat of his skin cooled.

I shrieked wordlessly, mindless with a grief I'd never believed I would know. He was immortal. I'd worried about how he would feel when I died, but not...not this.

For a long, long time I stayed there with him clasped to my breast. Eventually, the tears dried up. I laid Nevan on the ground, kissed him one last time, and got to my feet, staggering slightly.

"Ah!" I screamed at the heavens. "Why do I have these powers if I can't stop a harpy from destroying the world? What good is being the Janusite?" I shook my fists in the air. "Why did you do this to me? I never wanted these powers. I can't even use them to keep an evil bitch from killing everyone I love. What's the point?"

When no one and nothing responded, I closed my eyes. Freaking out wouldn't fix anything. I needed to suck it up, get hold of myself, and think. Aello might have eradicated everyone I loved, but nothing that happened was unfixable. Whatever she could do, I could undo if only I summoned the willpower and magic to do it.

Seconds ticked by, maybe minutes, maybe longer. I concentrated on my breathing. In, out. In, out. Let my mind empty, thoughts and worries gone. In, out. In, out.

An idea hit me like a bolt of lightning. If I needed to stop a wind goddess, I should talk to the ultimate wind deities. The Four Winds.

I had no idea exactly where their temple was. Nevan had taken us there last time. These frigging powers of mine had to be good for something. They would get me there, they had to. Without conscious thought to do it, I whisked myself to the wind-swept mountaintop where the Temple of the Four Winds resided.

Chapter Twenty-Seven

THE FIRST TIME I'D VISITED THIS PLACE, WITH NEVAN AND MAX, WE had touched down on the side of the mountain and awaited permission to enter the fog-shrouded temple. Today, I popped out on the mountaintop at the base of the long series of steps that led up to the temple. A light fog surrounded the huge structure, with its Corinthian columns and massive wooden doors. The temple was composed of white stones that shined with an ethereal glow thanks to the sunlight filtering through the fog. The place seemed like a mirage or a dream, but I knew it was real. Where in the world it was located, I couldn't say. The location hardly mattered.

Steep steps embedded in the mountain stretched up the long rise to the portico where a shallower series of steps led up to the doors. The temple boasted powerful wards that prevented anyone from teleporting in its vicinity or inside its walls. So, I trudged up the steps the old-fashioned way. My legs ached by the time I reached the portico. There, I paused to catch my breath, from the hike and from the thinner air up here.

My chest ached too, though not from the altitude. Last time, Nevan had stopped several times on our journey up the mountain to literally breathe fresh air into my lungs. Today, I had to endure the journey on my own. Even with Nevan gone, I managed to tap into his air powers and refresh myself.

Did that mean he wasn't completely gone? *No wishful thinking, it's bad for you.*

With a thunderous grinding noise, the doors crept inward.

Oh yeah, I remembered the racket those doors made. My bones vibrated from it.

This was all the invitation I would receive. I rolled my shoulders back and slogged up the remaining steps and through the doors. A breeze, tepid and gentle, investigated me like phantom fingertips. My hair ruffled, and goosebumps cropped up on my skin. Yes, I recalled this too. The arduous hike up the steps was a test of my commitment to meeting the Four Winds. The breeze feeling me up was their way of determining whether I belonged here.

The breeze faded away, but no one appeared.

"Hello?" I called out. "Please, I need to talk to you. Something terrible has happened."

A female figure winked into view an arm's length in front of me.

Her white robes dragged on the polished stone floor but left her arms and head exposed. The paleness of her skin matched the white of her hair, but her eyes were a pure, glossy black and seemed to lead down into an abyss from which no mere mortal would return. A chill whispered through me, stiffening the hairs at my nape.

"Thank you," I said.

My admission of gratitude, and my previous use of the P-word, failed to cause even a whiff of a debt. This place, I sensed, had its own rules.

The wind-being canted her head, her expression curious and yet remote. The female Wind looked every bit like an avatar of power and a guardian of magical energies.

"Lindsey Astrid Porter," she said in a voice both alien and ethereal, like a mystical breeze wafting around me. "You seek our assistance. For what purpose?"

"Don't you know what's going on out there? Aello—"

"Has disrupted and contaminated the proper flow of time." The wind-being rose to hover a few inches above the floor, her robes dangling. "We are aware of this. It is your duty to repair the damage."

"I've tried, honestly I have. Nothing works." Snapshots of memory flashed in my mind. The gravestones. Max vanishing. Nevan…I sucked in a breath, tears stinging in my eyes. "I don't have the power to stop her, much less reverse what she's done."

"You are incorrect." She floated back down to the floor, her black gaze sharpening on me. "The Janusite was created for this purpose. It is your destiny."

"Aello has so much dark magic, I can't—"

"Silence!" The wind-being's voice ricocheted off the walls. She seized my chin between her thumb and forefinger, the frigidness of her flesh infecting mine. Her tone became stern, almost like a parent chastising a child. "You are the Janusite, the one being in all of eternity imbued with the essence of the god Janus, but you are much more than a vessel. You have accomplished feats Janus never achieved. Your power grows, even as you deny it. Nothing holds you back except your fears."

Hot tears trickled down my face. "I don't know how to stop Aello. I went back in time to keep her from getting all that power, but I failed. Again."

The wind-being's gaze bored into mine for a long, agonizing moment. The darkness of her eyes captured my focus, and the intensity of her gaze drilled straight down into my soul. Finally, she released my chin and said, "You work toward the wrong goal."

I flapped my arms and my head. "Then tell me what the hell I'm supposed to be doing. Please."

"We cannot. You must arrive at the proper conclusion of your own volition."

"Just what do you think I've been doing?" A single sob burst out of me, and my knees buckled. I hit the floor hard, pain arcing through my legs. "I tried. I can't do this alone. You need to stop Aello, you're the only ones who can."

The wind-being watched me, her mood unreadable, her air of remoteness becoming more pronounced. A faint breeze tousled her white hair.

My head fell forward, my shoulders caved in, and I wept.

She touched my shoulder.

I lifted my head to find her kneeling before me, her black eyes softened to a silvery gray with distinct dark pupils.

"Lindsey," she said, her voice softer too, like a warm summer breeze. "Perhaps we have asked too much of you. Pouring these powers into your mortal mind and body without a thought for how you would assimilate them, it was an oversight on our part."

My jaw went slack. Had a mystical avatar of power admitted to screwing up? Yeah, she had. Not for the first time either. Two months ago, she'd admitted she and her three windy friends had messed up when they failed to stop the sorcerer from absorbing the essences of Notus, Skeiron, and Calder.

Miraculously, I summoned my voice. "Why did you release Janus? He wants his powers back, you know."

"We are aware, and in time, you shall understand the reasons."

"Am I supposed to give him back these powers?"

"Only you may decide." The wind-being rose, her eyes turning black again. "To defeat Aello, you must answer one question. What are you willing to sacrifice to heal the time stream?"

"You mean what else. I've sacrificed everyone I love and still can't win."

"What you have lost thus far is not gone. You continue to limit your thoughts to a mortal perspective." She leaned in, her hair billowing in a wind I did not feel. "You are the Janusite."

This being expected me to understand her meaning. I didn't. My brain and body were exhausted, my powers were dwindling again, and I couldn't puzzle out any of this.

I'd worked toward the wrong goal, she had said a minute ago. *Duh.* Every plan I'd come up with had cratered, even when I managed to reverse one of her time shifts. Going back in time hadn't worked either. How could I beat the harpy when she wielded so much dark magic? Max had been erased, which meant somehow Aello had circumvented his life debt to me and rendered him no longer immune to the shifts.

So much power.

Was Janus no longer immune too? And what had Aello done with him?

I retained my powers, meaning Janus did not have them. Aello couldn't strip away my immunity to the timeline changes. Not yet. Back in the cemetery, I'd experienced an epiphany of the sucky kind, realizing the root of my problems. Now, I raised my eyes to the enigmatic being who hovered before me.

"Nothing I do works," I said, "because I'm afraid of my powers. You said as much a minute ago."

She nodded.

"If my fears are holding me back, how do I get over them?" I flattened my palms on my thighs, and my fingers bent of their own accord, scratching on my leather pants. "Aello has taken everything. I don't have the luxury of figuring out why I'm afraid. She will keep screwing with the timeline until she breaks it, won't she?"

The wind-being nodded again.

"What do I do?" I spread my hands, palms up. "Please, give me a hint."

"All that you require is inside you. Look to your natural power for the answer."

I felt my brows squish together, tightening my forehead. "I don't understand."

"Your natural power is what you have always possessed." The wind-being bent from the waist to level our gazes. "Harness your spirit and your strength of will, the only powers that will never desert you. If you require more strength, seek it from your heart, not your magic."

She straightened and began to float backward.

"Wait," I said. "May I ask one more question?"

The being stopped moving. "You may."

"Why did Nevan not remember meeting me in the past?"

"You know the answer."

I started to protest but clapped my jaw shut. Did I know? How could I? Nevan seemed to remember everything else about his past but not the time we'd spent together after his forging and, three centuries later, after the gnome battle.

My spine snapped straight as a realization zapped through me. Oh, it couldn't be.

"You understand," the wind-being said.

The weird part was, I did get it. "I'm going to ask you to make him forget, so he won't spend thousands of years longing for me but not knowing when or if he'll see me again."

She gazed at me from so nearby yet remained as remote as a distant galaxy. Her lips twitched the tiniest bit. Almost a smile? Nah, it couldn't have been.

But maybe it was.

I scrambled to my feet. "Please make sure Nevan forgets having met me in the past when I time-traveled to him. You can do that, right?"

"We can, and we will. The sylph will lose all memory of those visitations." The wind-being swept closer and leaned in low, her face inches from mine. Her eyes turned a very human shade of gray-blue. "He will forget until the present and the past become one."

Sure, whatever that meant.

"I don't suppose," I said, "you have any advice for me? About what to do next? I appreciate your advice about how to get past my fears, but I don't know how to beat Aello."

Her humanlike eyes reverted to pure black. "I have told you all I can. You must speak with the oracle." She opened her palm, revealing sprigs of a leafy green plant. "And feed him this."

Warily, I plucked the sprigs from her hand. "The oracle. You mean Bob, right?"

She vanished in a burst of wind.

Chat over. Elementals really knew nothing about politeness.

Nevan did. He was chivalrous and brave and—

I squeezed my eyes shut, determined not to cry again. Whatever lay ahead of me, I needed all my faculties and powers intact for it. I could not afford to be saddled with grief and guilt. Nevan would want me to stay strong. I would do it for him.

After one last glance around the Temple of the Four Winds, I hurried out the doors. They shut behind me with an earsplitting grinding noise. Fog enshrouded the temple as I trudged down the long, long series of steps until I'd moved outside the wards. I blinked myself into the Unseen, to the edge of the dark and slimy forest that concealed Bob's lair.

If a single one of the kerkopes attacked me this time, I'd slice the creature in half with a bolt of pure magic. No more polite Lindsey. Nobody murdered everyone I loved, murdered me, and got away with it. The wind-being had sent me here, so Bob must have some answers.

Awareness prickled my skin, lifting the hairs on my arms. I didn't need to trek through the creepy forest like I had before, I realized. I could teleport myself directly into Bob's lair because his wards were down.

Not good, not good at all.

I zipped myself into the chamber hidden within, or perhaps beneath, a gigantic boulder. I'd never quite understood the geography of this place. A semi-translucent coating of pale gold gave the dark, rock-hewn walls an otherworldly quality appropriate for the den of an oracle. A fire burned within a five-foot-wide bronze bowl perched atop legs with cat-like feet. The flames writhed and licked at the air as if they were alive, their amber color evoking Nevan's eyes.

My throat constricted, my chest too. I would get him back, somehow, some way.

What are you willing to sacrifice to heal the time stream?

The wind-being's words echoed in my brain, but I refused to answer that question. Soon I might have to, but not yet.

I squinted into the firelit gloom of the cavern, searching for a sign of the oracle. "Bob? Are you here?"

A groan drew my attention to the shadows beyond the living flames. I trotted around the bronze bowl, spotted a figure slumped against the wall, and veered toward it. Bob aimed bleary, bloodshot eyes at me as I dropped to my knees in front of him. He sat propped against the wall, his legs splayed wide. His navy-blue suit was rumpled, and his skin had turned a grayish green.

"Here," I said, thrusting the leafy sprigs the wind-being had given me at him. "You're supposed to eat this."

Bob tried to lift a hand, but it fell back down to his lap.

Holding the sprigs near his mouth, I made a train-like chugging sound. "Open up, let the choo choo in."

Despite his obvious distress, he pulled off an irritated look even as he opened his mouth.

I stuffed the sprigs in there.

He chewed hesitantly at first, then began to chomp with vigor. The sprigs sticking out of his mouth got pulled in, masticated, and swallowed within seconds. The grayish-green tone of his skin warmed into a healthier shade. His eyes ignited with green fire.

Bob sighed, his lips curving into a relaxed smile. "I needed that."

"What was that stuff?"

"Medicinal herbs." He raised his brows. "They're hard to come by. How did you get them?"

"One of the Four Winds told me to give them to you."

"Miriella," he said with a wistful tone and a smile to match. "She still cares, even though we broke up when I became an oracle."

"You had a thing with one of the Four Winds?"

"A long time ago." He pushed up with his hands, straightening his posture. "Never mind that. You want to know how to defeat Aello."

"Are you saying you know how I can do that?"

"I'm not a vending machine for answers. Stuff a little medicine in my mouth and I spit out a plan? That's not how this works."

Folding my arms over my chest, I said, "You're grumpy from your time-shift migraine. Do you have any insight or not?"

"Sure, I've got insight." He closed his eyes, and the flames behind me flared high and bright. "You cannot divest Aello of the dark magics. Only by finding a way around them can you bring an end to her reign of terror."

"The harpy has too much power."

Bob let out a frustrated sigh. "I know you're upset about Nevan, but you need to focus. The answers await if only you open your third eye to see them. You are the Janusite, Lindsey. Remember the prophecy."

"That's all you've got."

"Yes, but it's more than enough."

I bowed my head and grasped the back of my neck. More than enough? I understood Bob was not a vending machine for answers and that even an oracle had limitations, but I'd hoped for a less-fuzzy insight from him. Riddles made my head hurt.

Bob settled a hand on my shoulder. "What you've lost is not gone for good. Not this time."

Miriella had made a similar proclamation.

I dropped my hands and lifted my head. "Are you saying I can get Nevan back?"

"You can do whatever you need to do." He got to his feet, stretched, and yawned. Then, he offered me his hand and helped me up. "Look to your lineage and you will find the answer to a question you've asked since the day you opened your eyes and your mind to your destiny."

My destiny seemed to be to watch everyone I loved die. Repeatedly.

Cut the self-pity, woman. It won't get them back.

Bob took hold of my hands, his fiery green gaze locked onto me. "Here's the only piece of concrete advice I can give you. Pay one last visit to the past and you will understand Aello's true motivations."

"Any particular time in the past?"

He touched one glowing fingertip to my forehead.

Energy zapped me, firing straight into my brain.

"There," Bob said, stepping back. "That will get you where you need to go. Good luck, Lindsey."

"Isn't wishing me luck a no-no in the Unseen?"

"No, luck is not a debt. Not even a tiny one."

"Glad to hear it."

His gaze zeroed in on mine again, his eyes aflame with that preternatural green glow. "Do you remember what I said about true chaos?"

"It will happen if Aello breaks the timeline."

Bob slanted closer, and his voice grew softer, deeper, darker, infused with the weight of wisdom and certainty. "Chaos is coming."

He tapped my forehead, and I tumbled into the time stream.

Chapter Twenty-Eight

I MATERIALIZED INSIDE A CLEARING IN THE WOODS IN THE UNSEEN, based on the mossy foliage on the trees and the unnaturally azure color of the sky. My invisibility spell activated the second I touched down, shielding me from the view of the two men half a dozen feet away.

Not mere men. Sylphs. They both wore obsidian armor that glinted in shades of forest green in the sunlight. Each sylph brandished a sword, his posture battle ready. One sylph had platinum-blond hair, the other black.

Skeiron and Notus.

I hung back at the edge of the clearing, knowing I needed to observe whatever was about to go down here. This must've been the moment when Skeiron defeated Notus using the dark magics he had acquired. The dark magics Aello had invested him with.

Notus chuckled darkly. "You lack the strength to overthrow me, Skeiron. I, however, lay claim to more than enough power to smite you for this blatant attempt to usurp the throne."

Skeiron twirled his sword, aiming the point at Notus. "You, my king, have become a monster. I will end your reign this day. For the good of the kingdom."

Wow, Skeiron sounded like he meant it. Nevan had told me Skeiron used to be a decent guy and that he'd been a good king at first. The dark magics he'd absorbed to win his battle with Notus hadn't consumed him until later. I sensed the power within him, but it paled compared to the seething energies within Notus.

The king raised his sword upright, sunlight glancing off its tip. "This is your last chance to end this blasphemy."

"Blasphemy?" Skeiron sneered. "You are no god."

"Are you certain of that?" Notus spread his arms, unleashing green currents of magic that spun around him. "With power such as this, I may as well be a god."

"Never will I bow down to you."

"Do you believe you have a choice?"

Notus thrust out a hand, unfurling serpents of dark energy from his palm. The magic lashed out at Skeiron, whipping around his body and descending on him with such force his knees bent and pain contorted his features. Skeiron roared and punched his sword through the blanket of dark magic.

The energy shattered. Glistening particles rained down.

Notus thrust out his palm again.

Skeiron charged his king, plunging his sword into Notus's heart.

The king froze, his eyes wide. His sword slipped from his grasp.

"I have a choice," Skeiron growled as he ripped the sword from his king's chest.

Notus fell to his knees, gurgling, blood dribbling from his mouth. He collapsed to the ground face-first.

Despite Notus's greater magics, he had fallen. Skeiron must have acquired an endued sword. Notus had arrogantly assumed his underling could not best him, what with the boiling, vile crap Aello had funneled into him. But Skeiron, invested with dark magics he'd somehow obtained and armed with an endued weapon, had amassed just enough power to oust his king.

Skeiron snatched up Notus's sword, turning it in his hand, studying it with a strange expression.

He vanished.

I was about to leave, wondering why the hell I'd needed to witness this, when Aello appeared beside Notus.

The harpy knelt and laid a hand on his head, her eyes churning with ice blue amid the pure black of her irises. She clenched her jaw and hissed through her teeth, "He will pay for this, my love. You served me well, and no one takes away what is mine."

She hovered her palms over his body. The dark magics contained within Notus flowed out of him and into her hands. The king's flesh dissolved, and the bones disintegrated. Nothing remained except a coating of pale dust.

Aello poofed away.

I followed. Not sure how I did it, but I'd stopped trying to figure out everything. The wind-being, Miriella, had said it was my duty and my destiny to repair the damage to the time stream. Bob had told me I must take one more trip to the past so I could understand Aello's true motivations. Both of those tasks revolved around the harpy. I had to follow her.

We emerged simultaneously, the harpy and I, inside an underground space that had no exterior door, like Nevan's lair. Unlike his home, which felt comfortable and welcoming, this space seemed utilitarian. A straw mat served as a bed with only a roll of fabric as a pillow.

Skeiron hunkered in the center of the room, naked, holding a white toga in front of his body as if about to cover himself with it.

Aello tilted her head left and right, her eyes sparking with fiery red. She skimmed her gaze up and down his muscular body and ran her tongue over her bottom lip. Her hand seemed to move unconsciously to her throat, and her fingers petted her skin. She was attracted to Skeiron.

Why oh why, Bob, do I need to see this? If these two made out, I'd lose my lunch.

Not that I'd eaten lunch. When had I last consumed food of any kind? Breakfast this morning. God, I could hardly believe everything I'd experienced, including the days I'd spent with Nevan after his forging, had taken up less than one day in the present. Or the future. Whatever. In my time, the place where I belonged, it must've been afternoon in the mortal world.

Aello slunk out from behind Skeiron, circling around to his front.

Skeiron went rigid, his gaze glued to the harpy. "How have you entered my home? It is protected by powerful wards."

"None as powerful as my magics."

Or mine, you whacked-out windbag.

"What does a harpy want with me?" Notus asked.

Aello slunk closer, rested a hand on his thick bicep, and tipped her head back to flutter her eyelashes at him. "You are strong and virile, an excellent candidate to be my lover and the father of my children. You defeated Notus in spite of the potent dark magics he carried. Yes, you would make an excellent slave."

Skeiron chuckled. "Slave? Harpies are as mad as the stories claim. I am to be king of the sylphs, not the slave of an unhinged creature."

"You will change your mind."

Aello's robes disappeared, revealing her perfect body with perky breasts neither too big nor too small, a flat stomach, and a narrow waist that flared into womanly hips. Her creamy skin accentuated the dusky pink of her nipples.

Red-hot fire ignited in Skeiron's eyes, his black pupils dilating.

The harpy glided her hand up and down his arm. "You may enjoy my body for the rest of eternity, so long as you do my bidding."

"I can have your body," he said, his voice husky, "with or without your permission. A female, even one as fetching as you, lacks the power to command a king."

"You are wrong." She flung a hand up in his face. "Heed my commands."

His features went slack, his gaze blank.

She wiggled her fingers, and slender threads of dark magic snaked up his nostrils. "Henceforth, you belong to me. I had thought to kill you for taking Notus from me, but you may prove a much better instrument than he ever was. You disobeyed your king, committed treason to depose him, and acquired dark power to do it. Nothing compared to my power, but impressive nonetheless."

Maybe this was what Bob had thought I needed to see. I inched forward, tiptoeing despite knowing she couldn't see me. My human brain didn't quite believe I was invisible.

Aello placed her hand on Skeiron's face. "Eventually, I will gift you with the dark magics I gave to Notus. First, you must prove yourself to be worthy. I will observe you for a time to determine your weaknesses and make certain you are the slave I have sought. Notus thought himself above such things, and it took centuries to make him ready for the power I had to offer, but my intuition suggests you will be more amenable to serving me."

She slid both palms down his bare chest.

The toga tumbled from his hands.

Aello explored his manly parts.

Fortunately, I couldn't see those parts of him from this angle. I didn't need to watch her molest him.

"You may wonder," she said, "why I do this."

I shuffled forward half a step, not wanting to miss a word. Her true motivations, revealed at last. I knew she wanted revenge on me for taking out Skeiron, and in a way, Notus too. I hadn't killed him, but I had destroyed the sorcerer who had ingested the essences of both sylph kings.

Aello stepped back from Skeiron, who remained ensorcelled. "I had sisters. Did you know that? We ruled the skies together and chose our mates from the Anemoi, the most powerful *daimones* of the cardinal winds, who possessed powers second only to the gods themselves. I was to become the mate of Zephyrus. I would have been a supreme queen among elementals."

She began to pace in front of Skeiron, her robes materializing around her body, the long hem dragging on the stone floor.

The soon-to-be king stood as motionless as a statue, which was what she had made him into with her magic. He would not move or speak or think until she released him from whatever ensorcellment she'd woven around him.

"My sister Celaeno became jealous," Aello said. "She seduced Zephyrus and became with child by him. I was handed over to Boreas as if I were a slave to be passed from male to male. But my sister Podarge had already installed herself as Boreas's favorite bedmate. Though he would wed me, he warned me he would continue to bed my sister as well. I refused the arrangement, so Boreas married Podarge instead." Aello gritted her teeth, her shoulders bunched and her talons flicking. "I will spare you the sordid details. My other sisters became involved as well, seducing whichever Anemoi would bed them, and soon we were all fighting each other. It was a stormy period in both realms, the skies and seas whipped into a frenzy by our fury with each other."

She whirled in a circle, growling like a rabid animal.

The details of this elemental soap opera were bizarre, but I didn't get how this triggered a plot to avenge her lost lovers on me.

Aello shut her eyes, seeming to exhale out the worst of her anger. Relatively calm again, she approached Skeiron. "My sisters banded together against me. I was banished from the palace of the Harpyiai, from my home. I wandered alone for centuries until I came upon a lonely sylph who had recently ascended the throne. Notus became my lover, promising to give me the blood children I longed for. But he betrayed me."

Here it comes, a voice inside me whispered, and I leaned forward in anticipation.

"'Everyone betrays me," Aello growled, spittle spraying from her lips. "Notus forged a mortal into a sylph warrior instead of giving me a child. I imbued him with the most fearsome power imaginable. Did he employ it to elevate me? Of course not. The treacherous toad fought my ensorcellment, regaining a sliver of free will. He used the magics I granted him to subjugate his people. You will serve me better, Skeiron, shan't you?"

She trailed the tip of one talon along his jaw.

A muscle ticked there as if deep inside he fought her ensorcellment. One day he would become as warped as Notus had thanks to the nasty side effects of the voodoo Aello had woven around him.

"Yes," she purred, "you will obey me. For I will not grant you these magics until you prove yourself a loyal thrall. No more treating a lover as my equal. You are mine to command and control. To achieve the ultimate power, I require a steadfast warrior by my side." She pressed her lips to his. "I consumed the magic of a dark soothsayer, did you know? I have seen the future, one that no wise and good oracle will envision for thousands of years to come."

The harpy waved her hand.

Skeiron's toga materialized around his body.

"You shall not know of that future yet," she said, "not until the prophecy is issued. But you, my pet sylph, shall fight for me during the battle to destroy the enemy I have seen so I might appropriate her power. Once, I was to have been a queen of the Anemoi. Then, I thought to become queen of the sylphs. I no longer care to reign over the pathetic kingdom of the sylphs or that of the Anemoi. I am destined to reign over two worlds, and every being within them shall fall to their knees at my feet."

She was insane. Totally, irretrievably insane. The soothsayer's magic had given her the ability to glimpse the future, and clearly, she had foreseen the rise of the Janusite. Despite her wackadoodle obsession with revenge, she would wait thousands of years for the chance to annihilate me. She would have no choice but to wait since she seemed not to have gained the ability to screw with time until my wedding day.

Lucky me.

"Unfortunately," Aello said, "the soothsayer's magic was swiftly depleted once I ingested it. But I learned all that I needed to know."

It was clear she hadn't foreseen Skeiron's demise before she depleted her stolen magic. Aello had waited eons for Bob to issue the Janusite prophecy and for Skeiron to begin the hunt for the Janusite, all the while amassing greater and greater dark magics. Her true motivation? To avenge herself on everyone. Her sisters' betrayal had warped her mind, or maybe she'd always been warped, and Notus's betrayal had cemented that twisted outlook. Aello blamed everyone but herself for her unhappiness. Once she'd foreseen the arrival of the Janusite, of me, she'd set her sights on obtaining the power I guarded.

Suddenly, I understood. Every time she'd said "you" when speaking to me, she had meant it in the collective sense. I was not the sole object of her rage. She used me as a conduit for it. Maybe she wanted Skeiron and Notus back strictly so she could mete out her own vengeance on them, or maybe she wanted her playthings back.

My thoughts spiraled back to the moments after I'd witnessed Calder's forging. What had Aello said? *Never again shall I suffer betrayal. You took them from me, and I will have them back whatever the cost. I shall avenge what you have done before it was done.* Betrayal. That was the key to her motives. She cared little about the individual she aimed her fury at, only that she had the opportunity to spew all that hatred at someone. "You" referred to everyone who had turned on her, or in my case, possessed power she coveted.

The power to control time, drop the mystical boundaries, open the veil between realms, and converge the worlds.

Aello already controlled time without my powers. Or did she? The magics she'd consumed seemed less than reliable. I could travel through time without injuring the time stream. She did damage with every attempt. I felt the disruptions she'd caused, and the upheaval of the earth that accompanied her attempts spoke to the violence of her manipulations. With my magics, she would have the ultimate power she craved.

The bitch would never get my powers.

At last, I knew the answer to Miriella's question. What would I sacrifice to heal the time stream? To fix the damage Aello had wrought, I would give my life.

"You will forget what I have told you," Aello told Skeiron, "and remember only that you desire me above all others and wish to serve my will and mine alone."

She waved her hand in his face.

He blinked furiously and focused on her. His mouth twisted into a lustful smile. "My love, how may I serve you?"

I'd seen enough, so I returned to the present day, to the spot where Nevan lay dead. Blood stained his torso crimson, and his vacant eyes stared into nothingness.

Nevan. A weight bore down on my chest, squeezing my heart. I fell to my knees beside him, stroking my fingers through his hair, and bit down on my lip so fiercely I tasted the metallic tang of blood. Nevan's skin chilled mine.

Aello had taken too much from me. She would take no more.

I sat back on my heels and shut my eyes, replaying everything Bob and Miriella had told me. They'd wanted to help me, I sensed that much. Both had tried to advise me, each in their own way with the limitations of their positions. If oracles could provide explicit instructions for how to accomplish goals, nobody would need to make decisions on their own. I finally understood this and accepted it. To maintain free will, the powers that be—God, the Oversoul, whatever you called it—had instituted limits on what anyone gifted with foresight could see and reveal.

Bob had told me what I'd lost was not gone for good. Did that mean I could get Nevan back? And Max and my family and everyone else?

Miriella assured me nothing held me back except my fears. To let them go, I had to trust in my ability to control these powers. Nevan had always trusted me, in every way. Max believed in me too and never feared my magics. Every good elemental being who knew I was the Janusite trusted me to use the power wisely. How could I doubt myself when so many powerful beings believed in me?

No more doubt. No more fear.

I knew it wouldn't be that easy—say I was over it, and poof, I was—but I had to keep moving, keep striving for answers. One question rang like a giant bell in my mind. What on earth was I supposed to do about Aello?

I cradled my forehead in my palms, rocking in place. What else had Bob said? *Blood for blood, life for life, the scales must be balanced.* Yes, Aello would balance out the scales with her own death. The answers, Bob told me, awaited if only I could open my third eye and see them. I came from a family of New Age devotees, so I understood the concept of the third eye. It granted insight beyond what normal perception allowed. Tapping into the third eye required meditation and focus.

Which I had none of at the moment. Relax? Focus? I was sitting next to the body of the man I loved. All my friends and loved ones had been murdered.

Rein it in, Lindsey. Suck it up and do what must be done.

I looked down at Nevan, and my heart clenched. My fingers trembled as I eased his eyelids shut. I bent to touch my lips to his. "I'll fix this, I promise. We haven't come this far for one whacked-out harpy to destroy our happiness. This is not how it ends for us."

Tears threatened, but I reined it in like never before. The steel vaults in my mind, where I'd once locked up my strongest emotions, slammed shut around the anguish and the fear. I must banish all of it or I would never get through the next part.

"Not saying goodbye," I said to Nevan. "Just sending you to a safe place for a while."

I flicked my wrist Nevan-style, and his body vanished.

He lay in state inside our underground lair, but he was not gone for good.

Bob had explained that I could not divest Aello of the dark magics. I needed to find a way around them. She had circumvented Max's life debt to me, rendering him no longer immune to the time shifts, which allowed her to kill him. She'd killed Nevan too, despite our transcendent bond. If that raging nutjob could sidestep the rules, so could I.

Miriella had told me I was more than a vessel for Janus's powers and that I'd been working toward the wrong goal. I now understood she meant my attempts to undo Aello's time shifts and to prevent her from acquiring dark magics in the first place.

No more running after Aello. Ditch the wrong goal? Check.

I was created for this purpose, Miriella said. It was my destiny to repair the time stream, but I had to stop limiting my thinking to a mortal perspective. Only by embracing the full experience of being the Janusite could I see the answers. I would open my third eye to the possibilities. Expand my horizons? Check.

Nevan had always kept me centered, and I'd done the same for him. Though his heart no longer beat, he could still guide me.

I assumed the lotus position, like I'd watched my parents do so many times, and rested my hands palms up on my knees with the thumb and forefinger of each hand touching. Eyes closed, I emptied my thoughts, letting my consciousness float on a serene sea, opening up to the possibilities beyond my normal perception. Floating, floating. Sensations rushed through me, indescribable, beautiful, suffused with a purpose I could not deny. My third eye was activated. Seeing. Sensing. A wider world, a wider universe, lay open before me.

My lids flew open.

I comprehended at last, absorbing everything Bob and Miriella had told me, assimilating my new insight with their advice and my experiences. Ah yes, there it was. The right goal. To get around Aello's dark magics, I needed to do the unthinkable.

Converge the worlds.

The idea had unnerved me before. I hadn't comprehended what it actually meant. Converging the Unseen and the mortal realms did not mean the worlds would become one gruesome hodgepodge. Convergence would free up all the magics of the Unseen and pull them into the mortal world. I would have access to untold power, enough to circumvent Aello's dark magics.

Okay, awesome, I had a plan. How exactly did I enact it? My fingers drummed on my knees. Sitting here in the middle of a cemetery, in front of my own gravestone, I realized I had no clue how to converge two worlds or what chaos that might wreak in its aftermath. To unleash the Unseen would mean disrupting the veil between the worlds and dropping every boundary in the mortal realm. Elementals would have free rein.

That did not sound like a good thing.

Come on, girl, stop limiting your perspective.

Right, no limitations. I seized the sliver of doubt that had crept around my heart and stuffed it into that blasted steel vault. No more fear, no more doubts. I could—I would—do this.

Do it already, I commanded myself.

Jumping to my feet, I gazed out across the cemetery but let my vision recede until the world around me seemed like a faded photograph. And I summoned my powers.

Energy flowed into me. Blue, sparkling energy. It filled me, empowered me, gave me—

The earth heaved up beneath me.

I tumbled down the slope created by the upheaval, spinning toward a yawning chasm.

The blue sky mutated into a churning mass of purple and sapphire, clouds of pure black laced with steel gray writhed across the heavens like airborne serpents, and the trees at the periphery of the cemetery morphed into black things alive with squirming foliage composed of half green leaves and half mossy stuff.

A pair of suns burned in the sky.

I caught the edge of the chasm before I tumbled into it, dangling there with my feet swinging. The strain on my arms lanced pain through them. I scrambled to pull myself up, grunting and shouting from the effort, until I fell flat on my back on the quivering ground.

A bird swooped across the sky at the level of the treetops.

Not a bird. I squinted, struggling to see despite the tremors reverberating through me.

The pterodactyl screamed and flapped its huge wings as it soared up and out of sight.

A gushing noise issued from somewhere beyond the trees.

I scrambled to my feet and struggled to stay upright. The earth rattled like a bass drum pounded on by King Kong. More chasms split open, trees plummeted into the voids while alien voices bellowed and shrieked.

Animals? Humans? Something else?

The gushing noise swelled closer, grew louder, until I recognized the sound. *Heaven help us all.*

A tidal wave at least a hundred feet high barreled toward me. The wall of water tore trees from the earth and flung them into a maelstrom within its ever-advancing mass.

Creatures fled the woods, stampeding past me. Dinosaurs. Woolly mammoths. Saber-tooth tigers. Odd-looking horses. Cows. Emus. A blue whale was spewed out of the tidal wave. It thwacked into the ground at the other side of the cemetery, flopping in terror.

I whisked myself away with only one thought for my destination—a safe place.

My body materialized atop a craggy, windswept mountain shrouded in fog. The earth shivered here, though faintly, not with the mad chaos I'd just fled. I turned around and spied the steep white steps I'd mounted earlier. Only the last dozen or so of the steps was visible through the fog. Dread iced through my veins as I hurried up the steps, taking them two at a time, oblivious of the pain in my chest and my legs, ignoring the fact I'd become breathless from the altitude. I summoned fresh air to rejuvenate myself.

I reached the portico, my legs burning and shaking, gasping for air even as I summoned more fresh, clean air to revitalize me. The fog, though thinner here, made the giant doors seem like a monster waiting to swallow me. The thunderous grinding noise kicked up, and the doors inched apart.

Beneath my feet, the white stone of the portico floor trembled.

I sprinted into the Temple of the Four Winds.

All four of the Winds hovered midway inside the building, their stark gazes swerving to me.

"She's done it," I said, "hasn't she? Aello has broken time."

Miriella nodded solemnly.

Chapter Twenty-Nine

I WAS ABOUT TO CONVERGE THE WORLDS," I SAID, "AS A WAY TO GET around Aello's dark magics. Not sure if that would've worked, but it felt like a good plan and I've learned to trust my intuition. I can't do that now, can I? She's messed up the entire universe."

Miriella spoke, though her floaty friends watched me. "You are correct. You cannot converge the worlds until you repair the damage to the time stream."

The Four Winds all seemed shaken. For beings as powerful as they were to fear what had happened…*Bad, bad, bad.*

"How can I repair the time stream," I asked, "when everything is in chaos?"

"You must," Miriella said, her voice no longer serene and detached as it had been the other times I'd seen her. She sounded frightened. "If the damage is not repaired, everything will end."

Terrific. The end of days had come, and I was the only one who could stop it.

One of the male winds came forward, wringing his hands. "Entering the time stream amid the chaos poses a grave danger to you, but there is no alternative."

Miriella grabbed my hand, hers cool but not cold, her skin so soft I had no words to describe it. "We will gather all our powers to protect you, but only the Janusite possesses the power to save all of creation. Trust in yourself, Lindsey."

I cleared my throat. "Just to make sure I've got this straight, with time broken everything that was, is, or could have been has become a reality."

"Yes." She grasped my hand tighter. "You must exercise extreme care. With the threads of time untethered, you may encounter perversions of the world you knew, of the humans and elementals you knew. Trust no one and nothing except for yourself."

"Um, that sounds like you expect me to go back out into the chaos. I was thinking I'd jump into the time stream right here."

"No," the male wind-being said, almost shouting it. "You must locate the physical place where the break occurred and enter the time stream there. If you enter it anywhere else…"

I would die. He didn't need to finish his sentence for me to get the gist. The stark expressions and worried voices of these beings told me as much.

Miriella released my hand. "Our prayers go with you, Lindsey Astrid Porter."

"Good to know." If I needed prayers, things were even worse than I'd imagined. "I will save time, save the worlds, save everything." I shrugged, lifting my arms. "It's my destiny, right?"

Four heads nodded.

"Can I zip myself out of here? Or do I need to go outside first?"

Miriella almost smiled. "You may 'zip' from inside the temple."

"Good." I assumed the posture. "Wish me luck."

I teleported away, not really sure where I was going. I'd meant to head straight for Aello, but the turmoil consuming both worlds must've knocked me off course. I emerged alongside the falls behind where the rock shop should've been but hadn't been all day. A false night had descended on the world during the few minutes I was gone, the result of a sky overwhelmed by churning black storm clouds. A profound darkness enveloped me, rife with strange sounds. Though the trees and grass looked different, like a twisted combination of the Unseen and the mortal world, it was the creepy noises of creatures I'd never heard before that raised every hair on my body.

Everything had changed, possibly with grotesque results.

That did not make me feel better.

Aello, where was Aello?

Not here, that was for sure. I took a deep breath, exhaled it slowly, and willed my body to relax. My third eye activated. I channeled its insight into my powers, funneling glittering blue power into my body. *Aello, Aello, Aello, take me to where Aello shattered time.*

I shot through the abysmal tunnel with energies pricking at my skin, an experience I hadn't endured in a long time, not since before I discovered I was the Janusite. The broken time stream must've affected even the way teleportation worked. I tumbled head over heels through the tunnel and exploded out into the woods in the Unseen. Here, as in the mortal realm, everything had become an amalgamation of both worlds, but I sensed I was in the elemental world.

No Aello.

Gah. Chasing her through the broken timeline was like chasing a wisp of smoke. I needed to find a way to zero in on the place where she'd wrecked the worlds, the place where she had barged into the time stream and pulverized it.

A figure appeared in front of me.

I smiled. "Max!"

My heart lifted at the sight of him, until I noticed his demeanor. His eyes were wild, his hair too, and his taut muscles strained from the tension in his bunched shoulders and his fisted hands. He breathed hard, his teeth bared.

His erection stood at attention.

Max lunged for me.

I lurched backward.

He snared my arms, his fingers squeezing so tight I winced. "I haven't fed in ages. Thanks be to the Oversoul for dropping a scrumptious female in my path."

"Oh no, I am not—"

He ducked his head to sniff my neck, then raked his hot tongue up my throat and shivered with a lustful gleam in his eyes. "You taste so fucking good."

I tried to wrest free of his grasp, but he had the advantage of elemental strength. "Let me go. I do not want to have sex with you."

"Who gives a bloody damn?" He growled again, with ravenous hunger. "I must feed, and you are the meal I've been searching for."

He hauled me into his body, his stiff shaft caught between us and throbbing against my belly.

"Don't do this," I said. "Please, Max, this isn't you. It's the hunger talking, but you can fight it. You're a good man."

His laughter was harsh and dark. "I am an incubus, darling. I take what I need from whoever I can find." He bit my bottom lip. "You'll enjoy it, trust me."

I rammed my knee into his groin.

He grunted—and grinned.

"Seriously?" I said. "You think it's fun when I crush your manly parts?"

"Violence can be arousing."

Max froze with his mouth open as if he'd been about to say more. He blinked rapidly, his eyes swirling with silver and copper, and ducked his head. His body swayed a touch, just enough to make it clear something was going on inside him.

When his hands fell away from me, I shuffled backward.

He groaned miserably and lifted his head. "Lindsey?"

"Uh-huh," I said, edging backward some more. "Who are you?"

If the past and the present had become one, and if the broken time stream led to grotesque results, then I needed to be extra careful. Maybe Max looked and sounded like himself again, but how could I know he'd stay this way?

"What happened?" he asked, glancing around like he had no idea how he'd gotten here. "I remember the cemetery and..." He grimaced, peeked down at his waning erection, and grimaced again. "Oh, I remember. But it wasn't me. Was it? I would never—It felt like I was myself, but a different version of me."

He gripped the back of his head, frisking his hands up and down as if brushing away the confusion.

"Yeah, it was clearly a different you," I said, taking a cautious step toward him. "Aello has broken the time stream. Past and present are intertwined. Everything is very, very screwed up."

"That's no excuse for my behavior." He scrunched up his face. "I am so sorry, Lindsey."

"We'll chalk it up to timeline insanity."

If Max had come back from the dead, what about Nevan? I didn't have time to search for him, and if I called for him, he might show up as Nevan's evil twin. Having met an evil version of him once before, when Ceara and the sorcerer stripped his soul from his body, I had no desire to meet the Anti-Nevan again. I would find him after I healed the time stream.

"Perhaps I can help you," Max said. "I am your familiar after—"

He froze again. Something rippled through him, like a hard shiver or a jolt of magic. Whatever it was, his entire demeanor shifted.

And yeah, his dick got interested again.

Except this time, he seemed way more crazed. He breathed hard, his chest heaving, and veins stood out on his neck. He snarled and growled like an animal.

Before I could process the change, he leaped at me, whomping down inches away. "Hungry. Feed. On you."

He grabbed for me.

I slapped my hands on his chest. Blue energy surged out of me and into him, hurling him backward. He smacked down a good twenty feet away, dazed, and lifted his head to gaze at me.

He licked at the air as if sampling it. "Your magic tastes good. Ravage you. Now."

"Go hump a tree, caveman."

I zipped away.

Whirling through the tunnel, I commanded it to drop me off in the precise spot where Aello had mangled the universe. I called on all my willpower, all my magic, to issue the command.

The tunnel spit me out inside the rock shop.

Aello stood atop the sales counter, her hair billowing around her in the eerily warm and slippery wind that whipped inside the corrugated-metal building. The rows of wooden bins, each filled with different kinds of rocks, seemed to have been thrown around by an angry creature.

Yeah, like the one standing on the counter.

The harpy bellowed, throwing her hands up.

I hurled a glowing orb at her.

The orb struck her in the chest. She stumbled backward and fell off the counter.

I summoned another orb.

Aello sprang up from behind the counter, vaulted over it, and puckered her lips to blow a gale-force wind at me.

The orb snuffed out, and I flew backward straight into the wall.

Aello shrieked. "I destroyed time, and yet you exist. You retain the powers of Janus."

Her wind pinned me to the wall.

She had lost her power-dampening ability. I sensed it. Shattering the time stream had consumed too much magic, forcing her to give up at least one of her dark spells. Despite the loss, she'd held on to enough magics to remain formidable.

She sprang across the shop to me. "Give me the power."

The powers she coveted rose inside me, stronger than ever, and I understood what I must do. Destroying her was the wrong goal. I needed to stick to the new plan.

I shot out a bolt of power, enough to shatter the wind pinning me to the wall. "Sorry, Wackadoodle Dandy, I've got more important things to do."

Aello thrust her talons at my throat.

I leaped into the time stream and shut the metaphysical door behind me, sealing it with strong magics. No one else would get inside unless I allowed it. Oh yeah, I could imagine the earsplitting shriek Aello must've let out when she realized I'd locked her out.

I glanced around, chilled by the sight before me.

The river of time had splintered into countless streams. They coiled and writhed and lashed out at each other. Sparks cleaved the darkness around the rivers, crackling with enough energy to singe my skin.

How was I supposed to tame this chaos?

I didn't have time to figure that out.

A snapping, gnashing river of time energy lashed out at me.

Chapter Thirty

ICOLLARED THE STREAM AND TRIED TO TAME IT, BUT THE THING whipped and gnashed its energy like teeth. Arcs of electricity shot through my entire body, piercing me with sharp pains. How was I supposed to repair this? Angry snakes of energy lashing out every which way, every which time. The energy scorched my skin, and I had no choice but to let go of the stream.

What would I do if I'd injured myself? I would disinfect the wound and bandage it up. Great, all I had to do was figure out how to disinfect the time stream.

Bob had urged me to remember the prophecy.

Like Janus, I held dominion over doorways, transitions, boundaries, the veil between worlds, and time itself. I also wielded the power to converge the worlds.

A branch of the time stream lashed out at me, but I dodged it. More serpents of energy snarled at me, whipping their glowing streams at me. Time was pissed.

The wound needed to be repaired ASAP.

Only the Janusite had the power to fix this. *Think, Lindsey.* Two months ago, I'd used my blue magics to reinvigorate Nevan when the sorcerer had been slowly draining his soul and then I had employed the same energies to restore his soul. Just today, I'd brought Nevan back after Aello expunged him from the timeline, and later, I had revived his memories of me. Why couldn't I do the same for the time stream? Cleanse and heal it with my Janusite magics.

Repairing time wasn't quite the same thing as reinvigorating my lover, but I understood what I needed to do to make this happen even if I could not describe it. I needed to fully embrace my powers with no fear of potential consequences. After that, I would converge the worlds.

I pictured Nevan making that affectionately harried face. He would say, "Lindsey, darlin', you do come up with the most unusual ideas."

My chest ached.

Once I did this, everything would go back to the way it had been, the way it should be. Nevan would be alive. Everyone I loved would come back.

I stopped trying to dodge the serpents of energy. Let them whip me. Let them snarl and hiss at me. I gritted my teeth against another crack of time-stream energy. I closed my eyes, shutting out the chaos around me, and breathed deeply. Once. Twice. Three, four, five times until my body slackened and my mind went blank. No holding back. I threw open the gates of my mind, of my powers, and let everything pour into me.

Blue, shimmering light erupted around me, visible as ghosts behind my eyelids.

The energy kept gushing into me, warm and cool at the same time, sharp and soft, enlivening and calming. This power didn't belong to me. It *was* me. Bared to the universe, to the unknowable and unseeable source of all magical power, I absorbed all that it could give me, all that I had a right to claim. The energy bonded to me, suffused me, set my body and my soul to tingling.

When I opened my eyes, the blue magics swirled around me in a semi-transparent cloud. Beyond the encompassing cloud, the time stream curved and looped in a placid river of intersecting and diverging streams. A current of gentle warmth lapped at my skin, almost as if the time stream were thanking me.

You're welcome.

Power coursed through my veins, as natural as blood. I commanded the full potency of my magics—no fear, no reservations, no inhibitions. *I am the Janusite.* The recognition of that fact shuddered a thrill through me, because for the first time in my life, I was completely liberated. Nevan had freed my heart and soul, but today, I had unbound my full potential and embraced the power within me.

With phase one accomplished, I headed back into the world.

I surfaced in the cemetery. The three new gravestones had vanished, so at least my family and I were no longer dead.

"Lindsey."

That familiar voice made me wheel around and fling myself at the speaker. Nevan caught me, holding me up with my boots a good foot above the ground. I kissed him like I hadn't seen him in centuries, and he kissed me back with an equal passion, our lips glued together and our tongues devouring each other. I clung to him, reveling in the feel of his body, warm and alive and strong, unwilling to relinquish this moment one second sooner than necessary.

He set me down, though his hands lingered on my hips. "Is the timeline repaired? I sensed…something, and it felt like you."

"Yes, I healed the time stream." I glanced around, biting my lip. "No idea if that reversed all the shifts Aello created."

"It did," Nevan said with a certainty that stopped me.

"How can you know that?"

"Because I remember." He frisked his hands up and down my arms. "Everything. I have memories of events that did not occur in this timeline, of things Aello expunged that have not been restored, and things that cannot be but are."

Everything that could be would be. That's what true chaos meant.

"Please don't tell me," I said, "all those freaky creatures are hanging around. I repaired the damage to the time stream, so the chaos should've been undone."

"It was." Nevan grasped my upper arms and kissed my forehead. "I meant that I recall events concerning you that I had no memory of before Aello interfered with time. These events could not be, but I know they are."

"Cut out the cryptic talk and tell me what the heck you mean."

He scrubbed a hand over his mouth. "Before the first time shift, I told you about my dreams of an angel who came to me after my forging and cared for me while I adjusted. I believed those were mere dreams, but now I realize those events occurred." He smiled sweetly, cupping my face with his hands. "The angel was you, Lindsey. You stayed with me after Notus abandoned me. You cared for me. I would not have survived the transition without you by my side, without the magics that enabled you to alleviate my suffering. But it was your love that truly saved me, the warmth and sweetness of your heart."

I laid my hands over his. "Time sent me there, to witness your forging and learn about the part Aello played in your fate. She convinced Notus to leave you there. I couldn't walk away, not knowing how hard it's been for Travis—and he has lots of people who care about him and help him. You had no one. At first, I thought I was messing up the timeline by staying, but since then I've realized the truth."

"What truth is that?"

"You and I have always been meant for each other." I peeled his hands away from my face and clasped them to my heart. "I was meant to take care of you in the aftermath of your forging. That's how it always happened, even though neither of us knew it until today."

"I believe that." His lips kinked upward, and his eyes swirled with warm shades. "We made love alongside a stream in the Unseen, thousands of years ago."

"Um…yeah."

"You appeared to me again centuries later, after the gnome battle. I took you to my home, but you were far too exhausted for sex. We slept in each other's arms."

I hunched my shoulders. "Bob told me whenever I am, it's always you. And you always will be the only one I have ever had sex with in any time and in any world."

He pulled me into his arms. "Not complaining, love. I enjoyed reacquiring the memory of that day by the stream. You gave me my first sexual experience as an elemental. It seems appropriate since you are the only one I have ever loved." He winced a little. "I can't claim to have been as steadfast in my fidelity to you as you've been to me. How I could forget about you, I cannot comprehend."

"I made sure you would forget."

Nevan froze. "What?"

"When I said goodbye to you after your forging, you didn't see me again for over three hundred years. You spent all that time wondering about me, wishing you could see me."

"I don't recall telling you that."

"Not those exact words, but you did say you wondered what became of me and you missed my light and my presence."

He kissed the tip of my nose. "I said I missed your light and your *sweet* presence."

"That distinction is really important." I gazed into his eyes, determined to make him understand why I'd done this to him. "You would've spent thousands of years wondering about me, dreaming about me. Our connection transcends time, Nevan. If I'd left you with those memories of us, you would've suffered for nearly five thousand years without knowing what became of me or when you might see me again. I couldn't leave you that way."

Nevan linked his hands behind the small of my back. "What did you do?"

"I asked the Four Winds to make you forget."

He tipped his head to the side, his eyes narrowing slightly. "And they did this? Because the Janusite asked?"

"Because *I* asked. They're not as cold and remote as they seem, especially Miriella."

"Miriella? You know the name of one of the Four Winds?"

"Turns out she used to be Bob's girlfriend. Miriella said you would remember those prehistoric events when the past and the present became one. That happened a few minutes ago when Aello broke the time stream." I glanced around the cemetery. "Did everything go back to the way it was?"

"I imagine so." He whisked us to the parking lot of the rock shop. "But you'll want to see for yourself."

He knew me so well.

"Thank you, honey," I said, giving him a quick kiss.

I rushed into the shop and found Stan behind the counter. When I hugged him, he reacted like I'd shoved a gun in his mouth but quickly regained his grumpy composure. He had vague memories of something bad going down. I decided to leave him with his ignorance and hoped it gave him peace, if not bliss. We zipped to my parents' house, finding them in the midst of a game of Monopoly, unaware anything had happened. My extreme relief at seeing them alive and well clued them in to the fact something went on, and I vowed to explain everything later.

Nevan informed me of several important facts. Skeiron was dead. Notus was dead. Calder had been forged and destroyed. Travis remained a newly forged elemental struggling with his transition. Everything had gone back to the way it should have been, the way it had to be.

Aello was on the loose. Nevan hadn't needed to tell me that. I sensed her, like a storm just over the horizon.

We returned to the chasm where Janus had appeared this morning. Christ, had it only been a day? The storm clouds that had swallowed the sky earlier were gone. The sun was setting, but I had one task left to accomplish.

"Janus is Aello's hostage," I said.

Nevan nodded. "It would seem so. Unless she has destroyed him."

"She hasn't. He's alive, I can feel it."

"How?"

"I got my powers from him. It gave us a connection." When he looked an eensy bit wounded, I patted his chest and added, "Nothing like what you and I have. But I can feel he's alive and kicking."

Nevan harrumphed. "I suppose that's a good thing."

"It is." With no more time to waste, I shouted, "Max!"

He blinked into view ten feet away, wearing gray slacks and refusing to look at me.

"What's with the pants?" I asked. "Suddenly shy?"

Face pinched, Max stared at the ground with his shoulders slumped. "I had to come when you called because of the debt. You should ask for help from someone else."

"You are my familiar." I took two steps toward him, but he scuffled backward. "What is wrong with you?"

He hunched his shoulders and bowed his head. "I remember the previous timelines."

For a couple seconds, I had no idea what he meant by that. Then it hit me. He had retained his memories of the chaos after Aello broke the time stream. He remembered trying to assault me.

"Oh Max," I said, "that wasn't you."

"If I have the memory, it must've been me." He gripped his head with both hands. "I tried to—to harm you. To slake my hunger with you even though you told me you didn't want it."

Nevan stomped up beside me and hissed under his breath, "He did what?"

Slapping a hand on his chest, I gave him my sternest look. "Let me handle this. Can't you see he's beating himself up enough for the both of you?"

Nevan stepped back, though he strapped his arms over his chest and fixed his hottest glare on Max.

Well, I couldn't expect him not to be upset about this.

I inched toward Max, halting an arm's length away. "The world had descended into temporal chaos. Everything that is, was, or could be turned into reality. One version of you hadn't fed in way too long and got a little… overly frisky. That was not the real you."

He shoved his hands into his hair, rocking on his heels.

"The Max I know," I said, edging closer, "is good and kind and strong. You have fought alongside me to stop some of the worst villains in the universe. You wouldn't betray me even when the sorcerer had a hold over you. I trust you." I tugged his hands away from his head and covered them with mine. "You are my friend, Max, and I love you. No time-shifting chaos or crazy, vengeful harpies will ever change that because I know who you really are. If you can't trust yourself, then trust me."

Although I kept my focus on Max, on the top of his bowed head, I sensed Nevan had relaxed. If I could convince Max to do the same…

I threw Nevan a look that I hoped said "don't freak out about this" and then I pulled Max in for a hug. He remained stiff at first, his head down and angled away from mine. Little by little, he began to unwind that coil of tension inside himself, his body slackening. Though he did not put his arms around me, I held him until he finally grumbled out a sigh and pulled away.

With a long-suffering expression, he said, "I haven't been hugged in almost two thousand years. Naturally, it's a married woman who gives me my first cuddle in eons."

His lips twitched upward. His eyes gleamed with humor.

Thank goodness. I had my friend back.

I eyed him with mock suspicion. "How could you not have been hugged for two thousand years? You're an incubus. You've had lots and lots of sex."

"But no real intimacy." He glanced at Nevan and quickly averted his gaze, scratching behind his ear. "Must we discuss this in front of your husband?"

Nevan blustered out a sigh. "You bloody well are not discussing sex with my wife in private."

"I've never had sex with your wife, in private or in public."

"You know what I meant." Nevan clenched his fists.

I shook my head, trying not very hard to repress a smile. "Nevan, chill out. Max is teasing you." I jabbed a finger into Max's chest. "And you, stop harassing Nevan."

Despite my stern words, I was happy. Everything had gone back to the way it should've been.

But one big problem loomed ahead of us.

"We don't have time for this nonsense anyway," I said. "It's time for me to converge the worlds."

Nevan arched one brow.

Max arched both of his.

"Yes, yes," I said, holding up my hands in a staying gesture, "I know what you're both thinking, and I admit it's a stark-raving insane plan. Unless either of you has a better idea, this is what's happening. Since I can't divest Aello of her dark magics, I need to get around them."

"How does converging the worlds accomplish this?" Nevan asked.

"It's hard to explain. I feel this will work." Hooking my thumbs in the pockets of my leather pants, I thought hard about how to convince them this plan would work. "Right now, there are limitations in effect for both worlds, a kind of legal code governing the actions of elementals. Max told me about all that back when we first met." I shot Nevan a sidelong glance. "Somebody was too busy arguing with the sylph tribunal to explain the Great Bargain to me."

"Such a discussion seemed unimportant. The Great Bargain was struck long, long ago." Nevan gave me a sly smile. "If the elders who struck the Great Bargain had ever met you, my mortal love, they would have banned all debts and bargains out of sheer frustration."

"Pardon me for being polite."

His gaze swung heavenward. "Lindsey, will ye never stop saying such things?"

"We're in the mortal realm at the moment, Mr. Prickly Pants."

"You are considering merging the worlds." He moved closer to take my hands in his. "If you do this, the mortal realm will become infused with the magics of the Unseen. Debts and bargains will have real power here."

"Relax, honey, I don't plan on thanking anyone while I'm beating the crap out of Aello."

"How comforting." He bent his head to fix his intent gaze on me. "Do you have any conception of what converging the worlds will do? I have no bloody idea, but I cannot imagine it will be pleasant."

"Saving the world never is—until the saving is done." I took a breath and let it out slowly. "Listen, I know this is super-crazy dangerous. But even the Four Winds and Bob agreed this is the way to go. I have to do a lot of third-eye opening and magic gathering to get powered up. Unleashing the Unseen will give me unfettered access to all the magics I need to get around Aello's dark powers."

"I don't like this. You will be in grave danger." He nodded toward Max. "Your familiar and I are immortal and thus difficult to kill, but you are a human being. No magic is required to end your life. A rock to the head will suffice."

He was worried. I'd known he would be, and I didn't blame him. How many times had we watched each other almost die? Today, I'd seen him actually die. More than ever, I understood the risks. My knowledge of the Great Bargain made this plan even scarier, because the ancient elders of the elemental races had enacted the Bargain for a good reason. Before they instituted the rules, elementals ran wild in both realms. They rampaged through the mortal world without any limitations, taking whatever they wanted and tricking humans into making bad deals, enslaving them with the magic of debts and bargains.

Things had gotten so bad the elementals themselves realized the need for rules.

And I was about to strip away all those rules and the protections they afforded to mortals. The chaos of a broken time stream no longer seemed like the worst that could happen.

"We need lots of help," I said. "And more space. Let's blip over to the parking lot again."

Max and Nevan followed me to the gravel parking lot beside the rock shop.

"It's time to call in the cavalry," I said.

Nevan backed up, sensing what I was about to do.

I hollered as loud as I could. "Triskaideka! Ennea! Get your leprechaun asses over here and bring as many of your friends as you can. All hands on deck!"

When I glanced at Nevan, he flourished his hand in a circular gesture.

An entire garrison of sylph soldiers materialized behind him, clad in gleaming bronze armor with matching helmets, their face shields down, and tough-looking boots. Nevan had donned his armor too, though it gleamed silver with streaks of gold and bronze. The face shield of his helmet was raised so I could see his expression of grim determination.

Max had shed his slacks, now completely nude.

I gestured at his body. "Don't you want some armor or at least a shield?"

"No need." Flames burst from his skin, swathing him in fire from head to toe. "I have a different sort of armor."

He snuffed out the flames.

I wasn't convinced fire would be enough to protect him, but I had to trust his judgment on this.

"What about a weapon?" I asked him.

Max bent the fingers of one hand. A sword materialized in his grasp, its blade a shimmering crimson.

"Cool," I said. "Where are—"

Ennea and Tris appeared before I could speak their names, accompanied by a small army of their fellow leprechauns. Every one of the copper fae wielded a weapon, everything from clubs to swords. They wore no armor, only regular clothes that looked like it had come from a shopping mall. These folks had probably conjured their clothing, which meant it came from who-knew-where.

"Looks like everyone's here," I said.

"Not quite," Max said, pointing to the empty space at my left.

I opened my mouth to ask what on earth he meant but clapped it shut when Travis materialized ten feet away from me. He wore the same outfit as this morning—faded jeans and a cotton shirt that hung open, exposing his outrageously muscular chest.

Nevan's mouth crimped at one corner. "He could have the decency to button up."

"At least he wears clothing," I said. "Max is naked."

"I am well aware of that fact, but I've given up trying to convince your familiar to cover himself." Nevan aimed his sharp gaze at Travis. "Are you well enough to be here? We are about to do battle with the most powerful elemental in history."

Travis straightened and squared his shoulders. "I can do this, and I want to help."

Nevan looked to me for confirmation.

"He stays," I said. "We need all the help we can get."

"Then he needs a weapon." Nevan flicked his wrist, and a gleaming black sword appeared in Travis's hand. "That will do."

I squinted at the sword he'd conjured for Travis. "Is that Skeiron's endued sword?"

"Yes."

Travis raised and lowered the sword as if testing its weight. His lips curved into a smile of feral appreciation. "Yeah, this'll do just fine."

My husband moved to stand beside me. "May I speak to your army?"

"Don't need my permission. Most of them are your soldiers, King Nevan."

His lips twitched in an almost smile. "I thought we agreed you would call me that only when we're in bed."

"You said only when we're naked, but I couldn't resist. You are glorious in your armor."

"Our fearless leader needs a weapon." He held out both hands, palms up, and a weapon appeared in each. His left hand held my derringer in its holster, while his right held a shiny silver sword in a leather scabbard, the blade smaller than the one he usually employed in battle. "Choose one or take both."

I took both.

When I tried to clip the derringer's holster onto my waistband, I realized I needed both hands for that. I gave Nevan the sword. "Hold this for a sec." Once I'd secured the handgun, I reclaimed the sword, attached its scabbard to my waistband opposite the derringer, and whipped the sword out to flourish it in the air. "Nice. It's lighter than your usual weapon of choice."

"This one was crafted specially for you by the chief armorer of the sylph kingdom. It is endued, naturally, as is the ammunition for your little firearm." He tapped the holster on my hip. "I took the liberty of choosing the smaller ammunition."

My wonderful husband had armed me with .357 rounds and an awesome, me-size sword.

I had no choice. I had to smack a big one on his mouth. "You're the best husband ever."

"The sword is your wedding gift. I did not have an opportunity to present you with it this morning."

I turned the sword in my hand, admiring the artistry of the sylph who had created it and testing its weight to get a feel for my new weapon. "Oh honey, I love it. I would give you my wedding gift for you, but it's not appropriate for public viewing. And honestly, sexy lingerie seems pathetically inadequate compared to what you gave me."

"Any gift from you is a treasure to me. Especially if it's sexy."

Tris flapped his arms in the air. "Hey, are we gonna fight or what? Your tender moment is making me nauseous."

"Yes," I said, "we're about to fight. Nevan, make your speech."

"For everyone to understand what is at stake, they must know the truth."

About me, he meant.

I scanned my gaze over the crowd. "Do it."

My husband lifted his chin, surveying our ragtag army with a regal air. His voice boomed, echoing off the shop building. "We are about to do battle with an enemy of immense power who has a vendetta against the Janusite."

Suddenly, he had the undivided attention of every being gathered in this parking lot.

Nevan waved toward me. "My wife, Lindsey, is the Janusite."

Gasps and surprised exclamations ensued.

"Defending Lindsey," he said, "is the most important task for all of us. She is the only one who holds the power to defeat our enemy, the harpy Aello. To accomplish this feat, Lindsey must drop all the barriers between the worlds. Whatever the cost, we must prevent Aello and any minions she brings with her from leaving this location."

Max raised his hand but didn't wait for permission to speak. "What about all the elementals who will be racing over here to pillage the mortal world?"

"Leave them until after Aello is dealt with." Nevan swept his steely gaze over the crowd. "Protecting Lindsey is our primary mission. Without her, we are all doomed."

We were doomed unless I saved everyone? Jeez, no pressure there.

"Raise your hands," Nevan said, "and repeat after me."

Each of the gathered beings raised one hand—except for Max, who raised both.

"One hand," Nevan said to Max.

The incubus shrugged and smirked. "You said hands, plural."

I threw Max a chastising look.

He lowered one hand, keeping the other raised.

Satisfied, Nevan continued. "Repeat after me. I vow on my immortal existence to defend Lindsey Astrid Porter above all else until Aello is defeated."

A deafening chorus of voices repeated the statement.

Promises held no power in this world, not yet, but Nevan knew what he was doing. Nobody would dare cross the king of the sylphs who also happened to be married to the Janusite.

One mortal with the powers of a god and an army of elementals. I prayed it was enough.

Nevan grasped my hand. "It's time."

I rolled my shoulders back. "Here goes nothing."

A gust of hurricane-force wind blasted through the parking lot. Leprechauns and sylph soldiers struggled to stay on their feet as the wind spun around them, whipping up a cloud of dirt and gravel that pelted everyone in its path.

The sky turned an eerie shade of greenish black that infected the air around us. A rumbling racket, like a runaway freight train in the sky, erupted overhead.

Oh no. I knew that sound.

The blackest part of the clouds gyrated like a whirlpool, tightening into a gigantic funnel wider than the parking lot and the building combined.

And the tornado descended on us.

Chapter Thirty-One

I HAD NO TIME TO ENACT MY PLAN AND CONVERGE THE WORLDS. I HAD no time to do anything except run to get out of the path of the tornado. The winds ripped through the parking lot and the woods in a rotating mass of air that pummeled everything in its path. Trees uprooted and flew past us, raining dirt on our heads. Gravel pummeled us. A thorny bush went airborne and scraped against my arm on its way past me. Nevan kept his hand clamped around my upper arm like he thought he could anchor me to the ground, but the tempest around us had other ideas.

Yes, the storm had a mind—not of its own, but of Aello. An inhuman scream wailed behind the cacophony, evidence the harpy lurked within the tempest.

The screech of metal rending itself apart broke through the chaos.

I risked a backward glance. The roof of the shop building peeled away from the structure. The corrugated metal panels split apart, sailing through the air.

One huge chunk headed straight for me and Nevan.

He saw it too and seized me with both arms, whisking us away. We came out at the edge of the woods where giant holes scarred the earth, evidence of the uprooted trees that had taken flight. The chunk of the shop roof that had been flying toward us impacted the ground twenty feet away. Its leading edge pierced the earth even as the bulk of it crumpled from the force of the wind.

We couldn't fight a freaking tornado.

I glanced at Nevan. Maybe we could.

His gaze intersected with mine, and I knew he understood.

Nevan grasped my hand and nodded.

We faced the tornado. Our powers merged, flowing between and through us as if we had become one being. His elemental powers, his dominion over the atmosphere, joined with my Janusite magic in a mighty combination that provided all the energy we needed to do this.

Our arms raised at the same instant, and we launched a rocket of power.

It struck the twister.

The spinning mass of air and debris shattered.

Aello tumbled out of the sky amid the last wisps of the dying tornado and smacked onto the ground face-first. She didn't move, not even a little. Not so much as a finger twitched. She was not dead. Hitting the ground might've stunned her, possibly injured her, but not even an endued weapon could take her down.

Our army of allies stood shell-shocked, unable to move or do more than gape at the creature lying prone on the ground.

"Seize her!" Nevan shouted.

Max and Travis reacted first, zipping to the harpy and clamping their hands around her arms to heft her off the ground. Dazed, she swung her gaze left and right, her head lolling.

"It's time," I said to Nevan.

He grasped my meaning without further explanation. "Proceed."

Aello shrieked. The sound pierced my eardrums and lanced straight into my brain, making me wince and clap my hands over my ears.

Travis and Max took the brunt of the sonic force. They let go of Aello to shield their own ears and doubled over, their faces contorted with agony.

Creatures winked into view all around the harpy.

No, not mere creatures. I blinked swiftly, sure I must have hallucinated, but no. An army of gnomes gathered around Aello, every one of them bearing a wickedly sharp, serrated sword in one hand and a nasty, barbed club in the other. Aello had retained her hold over the gnomes after all these thousands of years.

The gnomes' weapons were endued. I felt the magic emanating from them.

Nevan and I exchanged a glance. This was it, and we both knew it.

The largest gnome, positioned in front of the small army, stamped his foot.

And the ground shuddered. Waves rippled out through the earth, knocking down anyone in its path.

Screw this. I grabbed Nevan's hand and willed time to stop. The world screeched to a halt, everything and everyone frozen in a single moment. Some of the fae hung suspended in the air, mouths agape, arms thrown out as if to break their falls.

Nevan and I alone remained unaffected by the time freeze.

"Watch her," I told Nevan, nodding toward Aello. "She's full of wicked-nasty dark magics and might be able to shake off the freeze."

"The harpy will not touch you. No one will harm you as long as I live."

A chill shivered through me. As long as he lived.

Gravestones. Nevan bleeding.

I shook off the memory and focused on my task. Power surged through me, hot and tingling, a torrent of magic so intense I gritted my teeth against the onslaught. I let every iota of it gush into me. Blue energy danced on my skin and on Nevan's, a sprinkle at first, then a downpour. When it became a torrent more powerful than Niagara Falls, more powerful than anything in the mortal world, I knew I had all that I needed.

No turning back.

I threw open the gates.

The veil between worlds disintegrated with a palpable sensation of pressure that built in a heartbeat and released with explosive force. My ears popped. I tottered but stayed upright, thanks to Nevan's solid body beside me and his hand anchoring me. He stayed grimly focused on Aello, the sword raised in his other hand.

The magic of the Unseen streamed into the mortal realm, and the indefinable essence of this world streamed into the elemental realm in a continuous, two-way flow. The worlds had converged.

When the barriers in the mortal world fell, my knees buckled. The power inside me had mushroomed, so vast and intense I could hardly breathe.

Nevan slung his arm around my waist, his attention on me for one second too long.

Aello broke free of the time freeze.

I spotted her a millisecond before she vaulted into the air headed straight for me. I released the frozen world, and everyone came alive again.

Nevan whisked me away.

When we popped out on the other side of the parking lot, beside the torn-apart shop, I punched his chest. "I have to fight her. You can't poof me away every time she makes a move."

"I will not let her harm you."

On the other side of the parking lot, Aello screamed. Her hoarse and infuriated cry echoed off the trees.

"Please, Nevan," I said, feeling the zing of a small debt about to be formed. "You have to let me do this. Trust me."

He flinched, no doubt feeling the same zing. "I will not interfere again unless you are in imminent danger of death."

"Thank you."

My gratitude sealed a debt between us, albeit a small one. To hell with magical debts. The Great Bargain had been obliterated when I brought the worlds together, but we had way more important problems.

The gnomes had sprung into action. They clashed swords with the sylphs and battered the physically smaller fae. A gnome jabbed his blade at Tris, but the leprechaun dodged it and sank his dagger into the other creature's side.

Nevan gave me a pained look. He wanted to stay here to protect me, but he also wanted to help our friends and his soldiers.

"Go," I said. "I've got this."

He raised his sword and charged into the fray.

My husband, my friends, and my allies could handle themselves, so I had to focus on my mission.

Destroy Aello.

The magic of the Unseen whirled around me, coursed through me, filled me with more power than any single being should ever have. But I owned it. The energy of two worlds converged within me.

Aello soared across the parking lot, the battlefield, toward me.

I held my ground, touching the derringer's holster with one hand while raising the sword with the other. My gun held two rounds of endued .357 ammo. Neither the sword nor the bullets would kill her unless I got around her impenetrable wall of dark magics.

The harpy whumped down inches from me, teeth gnashing, snarling like a wild beast. She thrust out her talons to nab me.

Without thinking about it, I raised a shield around my body, one so close-fitting it might as well have become part of my skin.

Aello's talons struck the barrier. Sparks flashed, firing energy down her fingers. She lurched backward half a step and snarled again.

"Give it up, windbag," I said. "You will never get my powers."

"I am owed," she said. "You do not deserve what you have been given, and I am owed this much and more."

Though I couldn't explain how, I sensed her anger was my way around her magic. Bringing the worlds together had weakened her and strengthened me. The vile magics she commanded thrived on the separation between the worlds. The convergence had diluted her power. That's why she couldn't get past my shield. Once, her dark power had been the strongest thing in either realm. Now, it paled next to the power of two worlds that simmered inside me.

Getting her royally pissed off would give me the opening I needed for the final blow.

"You remember," I said, "meeting me way back when, on the day Nevan was forged. I saw how Notus treated you. He liked screwing you, but he never intended to make you his queen. Know what? Nevan married me. I'll be his queen soon. A mere mortal will have the throne you coveted but could never get."

Aello hissed like a freaking snake and jabbed a talon at my shield. It spat energy at her, crackling it down her finger into her arm, the blue magic sparkling all the way.

She snatched her hand away and cradled it to her chest. "You shall never claim any throne. A mortal body cannot contain this much power for long."

"I'm tougher than I look." And she refused to understand, unable to accept the truth. I was not a vessel. The power belonged to me and had become a part of my essential being.

She proved my point with her next words.

"You are mortal, inherently weak in body and mind. Magic is not your destiny. Only gods and elementals have magic infused in the very essence of their being." She raised a talon but kept it clear of my shield, using motions of its razor-sharp tip to emphasize her words. "You were never meant to have this power. The Four Winds selected you at random, or perhaps they released Janus's essence and let it fall where it may. You are a worthless specimen of humanity, a pitiful creature who has no conception of what to do with real power. Your weak body will succumb to the stress of all the magics you have ingested this day, and you will die."

Her statement, meant to unnerve me, had the opposite effect. It empowered me, and words Bob had spoken resurfaced in my mind. *Look to your lineage and you will find the answer to a question you've asked since the day you opened your eyes and your mind to your destiny.*

Understanding zinged through me. Every puzzle piece clicked into position.

Janus and I were connected, not strongly, but enough we could sense things about each other. He had no interest in me as a woman, but from the start he had seemed determined to work with me, even after stating he wanted his powers back. Maybe he hadn't realized the truth at first, but I suspected he'd figured it out long before I had.

The prophecy said it all. *She is the bearer of the key and the staff, the child of the god, she is the Janusite.*

Child of the god. I'd dismissed it as a metaphor, but it was a literal statement. My lineage. I was a direct descendant of the god Janus.

Squaring my shoulders, I looked Aello straight in the eye. "You are the pathetic and weak one. How many kings have you chased and tried to ensorcell into loving you? Even under the influence of magic, Notus didn't want you. He did what you ordered him to do, but he would never make you his queen. Notus betrayed you. I bet Skeiron betrayed you too, didn't he? In fact, I'd bet no king in the whole elemental world would take you for his queen or give you the blood children you wanted. You're a nutjob, Aello. A sad, lonely old creature who can't get what she wants no matter how much power she swallows."

The harpy bared her gritted teeth, her nostrils flaring.

"Know who has the real power?" I asked, then I leaned in a touch. "Me. I am the direct descendant of the god Janus, a being so powerful the other gods destroyed him because they feared what he might do. I am the Janusite because I was born to save both worlds."

Aello's body began to tremble from the rage building inside her. I'd pushed every one of her buttons, and she was about to blow.

Black smoke wisped from her skin and her ears and churned in the spinning colors of her irises. Her body shook harder, her teeth grinding with an audible noise.

I tightened my grip on the sword and got my other hand in position to pull out the derringer if necessary. "This is my destiny, not yours."

Chapter Thirty-Two

THE BLACK SMOKE THICKENED, ROILING AROUND US BOTH, BUT IT COULD not penetrate my shield. Aello screamed like no creature I had ever heard. Even the unearthly bellows of Skeiron couldn't compare to the racket bursting out of the harpy.

I rammed my sword into the weak spot in her magics, guided by my intuition and the certainty of my purpose. The power of two worlds bore down on me, on her, and my blade pierced her magics just below her navel. I turned the blade upright, slicing open the energy that protected her.

The black smoke splintered into a million tiny, knife-like shards that rained down around us both, bouncing off my shield. The darkest magics ever conceived evacuated Aello's body and littered the ground.

I wanted to kill her so badly, but I needed one last thing from her.

Summoning the power of the worlds again, I hurled my body at hers and tackled her to the ground. I had to take care. Even without her dark magics, she had a lot of elemental energy inside her—the energy she'd been born with, the magic that belonged to her, not like the stolen power she'd amassed. She clawed at my shield but couldn't get to my skin.

All around us, the battle raged. Nevan skewered a gnome with his endued sword. The beast toppled to the ground, hitting like a car-size boulder dropped from the sky. The ground shuddered.

I rammed the tip of my sword into the soft underside of Aello's chin. "Where is Janus?"

"You will never find him." She smiled with malevolent arrogance. "You may have stripped away the dark magics, but I retain great power. If I do not return to Janus within the hour, by the mortal clock, your forefather will die."

"Bullshit."

"You may believe what you like, but the truth remains immutable."

Why was I arguing with this witch? I had more power than any being in the history of either world. If I wanted answers from the harpy, I could take them from her mind.

Keeping the sword at her throat, I flattened my other palm on her forehead. Blue energy crackled around us, glowed in my hand, and seeped into her skull. Her eyes bulged. She thrashed beneath me, but I used the strength of my shield to pin her in place.

The answer I'd sought sprang into my mind. *Janus, there you are.*

I pulled my hand away from her forehead and patted her cheek. "You are no longer necessary."

Aello shrieked in another language.

Every gnome jumped into the air and whammed back down onto the ground.

Waves, like giant swells on the sea, upraised the earth and rippled outward, each swell higher than the tallest beings in the vicinity. Fae were launched into the air by the uplift. Sylphs tumbled down the backsides of the swells.

Max and Travis rolled up and over each wave, rolling and rolling until they hit the remnants of the shop building. Three gnomes swarmed around them, their serrated swords at the ready.

Nevan landed on his back with a gnome looming over him.

The gnome raised his giant, barbed club in preparation for a killing blow.

Aello cackled.

I raised my sword, gripping it with both hands, and plunged it into Aello's chest. Blood stained her white robes, spreading outward and soaking through the fabric. She gurgled and choked, spitting blood. I ripped the blade from her chest and slashed it down toward her throat. The sword separated her head from her body.

For a frozen moment, I knelt over the dead harpy and stared into her vacant eyes. I had destroyed her. I felt the essence of Aello oozing out of her body, spiraling up toward the heavens.

A wind whipped around us. It scooped up her essence and carried it away.

The Four Winds had claimed her essence and her powers. They would lock it all away in a vault nothing and no one could breach. After their mistakes with Skeiron and Notus, the Winds would never repeat those oversights. Aello was gone, forever.

A sensation of impending doom crawled over my skin and sank its teeth into my flesh. I had thrown open the gates of both worlds, knocked down the barriers and stripped away the protection of the Great Bargain. One with both realms, I experienced the effects of the change as physical pains that stabbed into my body.

The battle in this parking lot was not the only problem. Elementals throughout the Unseen had detected the fall of the barriers and were pouring across the unprotected entryways into the mortal world, an invading horde of powerful creatures intent on storming over the now-gone boundaries to ravage my world.

A masculine cry made my attention swerve to Nevan.

The gnome had struck out with his club, but Nevan had rolled to the side just in time. With his club embedded in the dirt, the gnome abandoned it and brought out his serrated sword. He stomped his foot.

Nevan bounced off the ground. The second he hit the earth, the gnome slashed his sword downward.

I tore the derringer out of its holster, swung it up, and fired twice.

My first shot slammed into the gnome's back. He jerked, and the sword slipped out of his grasp. The second shot penetrated the back of his skull.

The gnome collapsed.

I teleported myself to Nevan, who had scrambled to his feet again. "Are you okay?"

"Yes." His gaze darted toward the shop building. "Travis and Max appear in need of assistance, though."

"Go help them."

"What will you do?"

I swallowed hard. "I have to bring the barriers back up. Elementals are going crazy with their new freedom. Anyone who's already crossed the boundaries will be destroyed, but I can't do anything about that."

"Only the worst sorts will have stampeded into the mortal world."

That made me feel a little better. I waved for him to move. "Go. Max and Travis need you."

Nevan stayed put, but his focus wavered between me and our friends. He didn't want to leave me alone, but only I could spare this world from untold carnage.

Finally, he zipped to Max and Travis.

I spread my arms wide, tilting my head back, and compelled the boundaries to re-form. They shot up like invisible walls that sprouted from the earth. Every natural body of water in the world regained its boundary protection, limiting every elemental to a one-mile radius of the water feature.

Pains lanced my body as if thousands of knives had been driven into me.

I gasped for breath, stunned by the pain. I was feeling the death of every elemental that had rampaged past the boundaries while they were down. The essences of a multitude of elemental beings were scattered to the Four Winds. I wondered briefly how that would affect the wind-beings, but they had known I would need to drop the boundaries and recreate them. I hoped they were prepared for the deluge of orphaned powers.

They could handle it. Somehow I knew this.

With the barriers up, I needed to reinstate the Great Bargain and close the veil between the worlds. I sealed the portals with a burst of magic. The fabric of both worlds shivered as the rules instituted by the Great Bargain took force once again. From here on, only mortals with a touch of the Unseen in them could cross the veil, and elementals could not travel more than one mile from any water features and the portals they concealed.

I dropped my arms and confronted the battle raging around me.

While I'd been hip-deep in magic, the noises of the battle had receded from my perception. The instant I released the supernatural energies, the melee assaulted my senses.

Max and Travis stood over the bodies of two gnomes.

Nevan was backed up to the remains of the shop building. A gnome had him pinned there with the creature's sword millimeters from his throat. Blood seeped from a wound in Nevan's side. His sword lay on the ground a few feet away.

I tried to zip to him.

A split second before I could teleport, a blade sank into the back of my shoulder. The magic of the endued sword scorched through me even as the jagged blade punched out the front of my shoulder. I cried out. The sword was yanked free of my body, and my legs crumpled. I hit the ground on my rump, slumping sideways onto the ground.

The gnome who had sneaked up behind me towered over me, my blood dripping from his sword. He hoisted the blade up over his head, preparing to plunge it into my chest.

Nevan bellowed.

Gasping for air, unable to get enough, I glanced in Nevan's direction. The grief on his face wrenched my heart and snapped me back to reality.

He zipped to my side and tackled the gnome before the beast could do me in. Nevan wrestled with the creature, struggling to get hold of the sword.

Max and Travis appeared beside me.

"Help him," I croaked, pushing up on one arm.

I sensed the gnome was about to teleport away with Nevan. The creature wanted to get him out of the way so he could return and kill me.

Max and Travis couldn't get there in time.

I flung my body at the wrestling duo.

The three of us blipped to the mile marker on US Highway 41, the edge of the boundary around the falls. A chill rushed through me, raising the hairs on my arms. This was where I had destroyed Skeiron.

My shoulder throbbed and blood ran down my arm and chest, but my wound wasn't fatal. I scrambled to my feet and fired an orb of blue energy at the gnome, since I didn't dare fire off a fatal blast that might catch Nevan too. The orb stunned the gnome enough to let Nevan get the upper hand. He snagged the sword, sprang to his knees, and raised the blade.

The gnome shook off his shock and swung his leg out to the side. He kicked it into Nevan and sent him tumbling sideways across the boundary.

"No!" I screamed.

He screamed too, in abject agony. His entire face contorted into the most horrific expression of pain I'd ever witnessed, worse than when I'd watched Skeiron being destroyed. Nevan's body shuddered with such force his back bowed up off the asphalt and his limbs convulsed. Sparks of white-hot energy tore at his flesh, rending it apart piece by piece, molecule by molecule.

I tried to grab his feet to haul him back across the boundary, but I couldn't get hold of him. The forces ripping him to shreds bit back when I touched him. Despite the protection of being the Janusite, I sensed the violent magics of the boundary would consume me too if I got caught up in them.

And I didn't give a damn.

Dimly, I realized Max and Travis had materialized behind me.

Max grabbed me around the waist and dragged me away from Nevan. I kicked and scratched at him, but he would not let go.

"I have to save him," I shouted. "Let me save him."

"No, Lindsey, it's too late." Max wrapped me in his arms, his cheek against mine. "You cannot stop the process once it's begun. If you try, you will die too. Nevan wouldn't want that."

A curtain of pure white magic enshrouded Nevan. The cloud obscured my view of him, though I knew his body was being deconstructed. Torn asunder. Destroyed.

Sobs racked my body. Tears streamed down my face, and without Max holding me up, I would've fallen into a heap on the ground. At last, I understood the truth. Nothing, not even the power of the Janusite, could stop the destruction process.

The cloud disintegrated.

Nevan was gone.

Chapter Thirty-Three

I SCREAMED SO LOUD MY THROAT BURNED AND CLOSED UP. COUGHING, sobbing, I sagged into Max. He turned me around to hold me, my face buried against his chest. Words I did not want to recall flared in my mind. *Blood for blood, life for life, the scales must be balanced. Sacrifice the past for the sake of the future.* Bob had said that. *What are you willing to sacrifice to heal the time stream?* Miriella had spoken those words. I finally understood she hadn't meant it as a choice, the way I'd taken it at the time. Powers beyond my comprehension had made the decision for me, and at last I realized why.

I had continually chosen Nevan over everything else. Maybe I could've stopped Aello sooner and avoided the chaos brought on by the time stream breaking apart. Instead of focusing on my duty as the Janusite, I had expended too much energy on bringing Nevan back every time Aello screwed with the timeline.

This was the lesson I'd needed to learn.

"It's my fault," I said, my face buried against Max's chest. "Nevan died because I wouldn't do what I was supposed to do, what I was destined to do. I put him before everything else. He died because the universe needed to teach me a lesson."

"No," Max said with fervent certainty. "That's bollocks, Lindsey. As long as I've known you, you have risked your life and the lives of everyone you love in order to protect two worlds. None of us has sacrificed as much as you have."

"Then why is he gone? It has to be my punishment."

Max took my face in his hands and forced me to look at him. "Nevan gave his life to save you. Honor that sacrifice by not blaming yourself for it."

Sacrifice. I was so sick of watching people die because of me.

I blundered backward away from Max. "This isn't over."

Max studied me for a moment until comprehension dawned on his face. "No, Lindsey."

"Yes," I snapped. "Nevan died once today. I will not let it happen again."

"If you go into the time stream again, you might damage it. You are in no condition to manipulate those sorts of magics or to manipulate time itself."

He aimed a pointed glance at my shoulder, where blood trickled from my wound.

But God, he was right. I knew it, and I hated it. Hated him for making me see it. Hated the Four Winds for putting these powers inside me.

"Think about it," Max said. "If you abuse your powers to save Nevan, you will become like Aello. She was willing to do anything to get what she wanted and ripped apart the time stream in the process. You are nothing like her, Lindsey. Don't let grief warp who you are."

My stomach hurt. My chest hurt. Something deep inside me hurt with an ache like nothing I'd ever experienced before. Max was right. If I gave in to this pain and altered the past to spare myself from the grief I had to feel, I would become exactly like Aello. She had done it to fulfill her selfish desires. Was I any different? I would risk fracturing the time stream simply to have Nevan back.

He wouldn't want that. I didn't want that.

I covered my face with my hands, silent tears streaming between my fingers. A numbness crept into me, drying up the tears, and I lowered my hands. "I have to rescue Janus. I know where he is."

"Let me do it," Max said. "You need to rest."

A wet iron blanket seemed to have dropped on top of me, so I couldn't argue with his assessment. I didn't want to go anywhere or do anything.

My gaze fell on the gnome, who lay dead with his own sword rammed through his chest.

"Travis did that," Max said. "I went for you, and he went for the gnome."

"Oh. Good." Nothing seemed anywhere close to good, but I spoke the words without really knowing or caring what I'd said.

"Tell me where Janus is," Max said, "and I will retrieve him. Travis, take Lindsey somewhere else, away from all of this."

I didn't need to speak. I simply willed Max to go to the place where Aello had hidden Janus, which turned out to be a second nest she had built in the Unseen.

Travis took my hand, about to poof us both away.

"Wait," I said. "The battle."

"You don't need to be there. Aello's gone, so is her dark magic. The fae and the sylphs can handle a passel of gnomes."

My jaw tightened. I all but growled, "No one else will die today because of me."

He studied me for a few interminable seconds, his expression unreadable. At last, he sighed and whisked us to the battlefield. The noise assaulted my ears. The metallic clashing of swords. The whumping of clubs and other blunt weapons. The grunts and shouts of warriors from three species of elementals as they attacked each other relentlessly.

"Stop!" I hollered.

Everyone froze.

Literally. I had inadvertently frozen time. Only Travis and I remained unaffected.

"Damn," Travis said in a hushed voice full of awe and a hint of fear. "You did that just by saying the word."

"I stopped time."

"Yeah, I can see that."

"Don't worry, I haven't broken the time stream. Didn't mean to freeze the world, but this'll do."

"What do you mean it'll do?" He sounded baffled, and I couldn't blame him.

"No one else is dying today," I said, gesturing toward the nearest gnome. "Not even the ones trying to kill my friends."

Travis puckered his mouth, his forehead crinkling. "You want to save the gnomes too?"

"Yes. They were ensorcelled by Aello, forced to do her bidding. It's no different from when Brennus was forced into a bad bargain with Skeiron and became his unwilling henchman." I took three steps forward, closer to the battle. "Maybe I can't bring Nevan back, but I can stop anyone else from dying because of what Aello did."

"Do what you need to do. I got your back."

He did, always. Even when he'd been jealous of Nevan, Travis had fought for me and with me, ultimately dying because he'd wanted to protect me from Ceara.

I stretched my arms out in front of me, holding my hands palms out, and released a pulse of blue energy that engulfed the battlefield.

The gnomes vanished.

Done, I lowered my hands.

"Uh," Travis began, "what'd you do with the gnomes?"

"Sent them home. I also removed the leftover effects of Aello's ensorcellment, freeing them to do what they want instead of what a dead harpy bitch wanted."

Bitterness had infected my voice, but I didn't care. I had a right to my anger and pain. After everything that had happened, I'd earned it.

The fae started clapping and cheering, but the sylph army milled around looking confused.

I called out to them, "The battle is over. Go home."

One sylph soldier stepped forward, his attention landing on me. "What of the king?"

"Go home." My throat thickened, and tears stung my eyes. I couldn't explain it to them. Not now. Not like this. Standing on a blood-spattered battlefield with my shoulder wound oozing. "Please, just go."

Maybe something in my voice clued him in, or maybe it was my expression, but the sylph nodded sharply and turned around to wave to his troops. They disappeared.

Travis laid a hand on my good shoulder. "You need a doctor, Lindsey, or at least a healing vortex."

"Not yet."

I marched straight across the parking lot to Tris and Ennea.

They were smiling and laughing, slapping their fellow fae on their backs. When they caught sight of me, Tris and Ennea fell silent, their smiles wilting.

"Did you lose anyone?" I asked.

"Nah," Tris said, "we're all good. The sylphs didn't lose nobody either."

Ennea studied me with concern in her eyes. "What is it, Lindsey? What's happened?"

"She's injured," Tris said.

"It's more than that." Ennea moved closer, searching my face. Tears burgeoned in her eyes. "Oh no, Lindsey. Tell me it's not—"

"Nevan is dead." My voice was dead too, like everything inside me. "Destroyed."

Tris was blinking furiously as if fighting back tears. "Get him to a vortex. I can power it—"

"It's too late for that. A gnome pushed him over the boundary." I sucked in a breath, or tried to, but I couldn't pull in enough oxygen. Every ragged breath only made me feel worse, made my chest tighter, made my eyes burn hotter. "I restored the boundaries. Had to do it. Elementals were flooding through the open portals and straight into the mortal world at large. I had to do it. Nevan…"

"He died protecting her," Travis said. "He died protecting all of us."

Ennea threw her arms around me, hugging me fiercely. "I'm so sorry, Lindsey."

"It ain't fair," Tris said, his voice cracking. "Nev belongs with you. He can't be gone."

Travis pulled me away from Ennea. "I know you guys loved him too, but Lindsey needs some space."

"Of course," Ennea said. She swiped at her eyes and straightened. "Anything you need, hon, you let us know. Anything."

"She needs healing," Tris said, getting hold of himself again, though his eyes glistened with a hint of moisture. "Let's get her to the vortex. I'll grab some copper from the shop." He peered over his shoulder at the roofless building with warped wall panels. "Might take me a minute to dig around and find it."

"Meet ya there," Travis said.

He grasped my good shoulder and rushed me to the vortex. I could've gotten there myself if I'd been able to think. With the battle over, the last of the adrenaline that had fueled me sluiced out of my body. I sank onto one of the stone benches that surrounded the vortex.

Travis loitered an arm's length away like a soldier guarding a queen.

I would've been a queen. If Nevan…

Ennea and Tris materialized. Tris was in the midst of wolfing down two big handfuls of raw float copper. After finishing off the lot, he dusted off his hands.

"Ready," he said.

Travis scowled at him. "Do it already."

As the vortex powered up around me, I sat there slumped on the bench, not moving, not thinking, not feeling. Though the wound healed in a matter of seconds, I barely noticed the tingling sensation of the magical energies washing through me.

Does it spin you? Sandy, a goofy blonde, had asked me that question on the day I'd met Nevan. She had thought the vortex must spin like a whirlpool. But no, it wasn't the vortex that spun. It was Nevan's eyes, those bottomless pools of swirling bronze and silver and gold.

Max and Janus turned up right as the healing energies wound down. By the look on Janus's face, I knew Max had told him about Nevan.

Janus glanced at each of my friends in turn. "May I have a moment alone with Lindsey?"

When Max looked to me for the answer, I said, "It's okay."

"Travis and I will not go far," Max said.

Both incubuses poofed away.

Ennea and Tris lingered until I waved for them to go. Once they had left, Janus sat down on the stone bench across from me. He watched me without speaking, the silence between us stretching on for a minute or more until I spoke.

"I figured it out," I said. "Why we're connected. I'm your direct descendant."

"Yes."

"Why didn't you tell me?"

He rested his elbows on his thighs, head down. "At first, I was not certain you could handle the powers you had received. My powers. After thousands of years in a kind of purgatory, I believed I was owed something." He raised his head to look at me. "I was wrong about you and about these powers. They belong to you now. You have made better use of them than I ever did, accomplished feats I would never have attempted. And you succeeded."

"I failed. Spectacularly."

"No, Lindsey, you did not. Not every battle can be won or should be won." He exhaled a long, weary breath. "You healed the time stream. You saved two worlds. In the final battle, when it counted the most, you sacrificed everything for the greater good."

"Having trouble feeling triumphant about it." Tears trickled down my cheeks. "Not sure any of this was worth it. Since I became the Janusite, I've watched people I cared about suffer and die. Today, I got to witness Calder's forging and Nevan's forging. Not experiences I ever wanted to have. I couldn't save either of them in the end. What was it all for? Why was I the special one chosen to suffer this pain? You must have loads of other descendants who would've done a better job than I have."

"You are wrong." Janus crossed the vortex to kneel in front of me. "You were not chosen at random. No one else could have borne this burden."

"Oh come on. Any of your other descendants could've done it."

He watched me, his mouth crimped and his gaze searching mine. When my skin started to itch from the intensity of his focus on me, Janus finally spoke. "I understand your pain, Lindsey. I loved a mortal once and lost her."

I couldn't speak. Had no clue what to say to that.

"She did not die," he said. "Her name was Vita. I had never loved anyone until her, but she taught me how to care for someone other than myself, showed me that even a god has much to learn about living. The other gods grew jealous of my powers and resented me for refusing to misuse my dominion over time to aid them in their petty quests. Only for Jupiter would I enter the time stream. He was—is still, I presume—a wise and good leader. The others gave in to their baser instincts far too often."

"Can you get to the point, please?"

"Of course." He rested his hands on my knees. "The other gods banded together to destroy me. I did not know it at the time, but Vita was with child. She did not know either until after I was gone. For a virtual eternity, I languished in limbo but endured visions of the woman I loved and our child. Even after she died, having lived a full and happy life, I remained connected to our lineage. To our descendants. In each generation, only one child was born."

"But I have a brother."

"The Four Winds knew the Janusite had arrived when your brother was born. After countless millennia of one child per generation, fate had given us two of you. The Winds waited until you were ready and then they gifted you with my powers."

"Why me? Why not my brother?"

"The prophecy, Lindsey. It states the Janusite will be a female."

I didn't want to be talking about this, didn't want to talk at all, but I had to ask the questions. Maybe by understanding this one thing, I would understand why I'd lost Nevan. "Bob didn't issue the prophecy until a hundred years ago. Why did the Four Winds sit around twiddling their thumbs for all those thousands of years before that?"

"No one twiddled anything. The Winds knew of the prophecy before the oracle became aware of it. They crafted the prophecy for him. You were always destined for this purpose."

"Destiny. Fabulous." I dug my nails into my thighs. "I was fated to lose the only man I've ever loved. What was the point? Making me suffer through all of this so I could watch Nevan die over and over until it stuck."

Janus pried my hands away from my thighs and closed his hands around them. "Why did you remain a virgin for so long?"

"What?" I tried to wrest my hands free, but he held fast. "Even if it was any of your business, you've got a hell of a nerve asking me now."

Tears spilled down my cheeks faster, dribbling between my lips, the saltiness mutating into a sour taste in my mouth.

"Perhaps you are correct," Janus said, "but the answer is important."

When he asks, tell him, Bob had said.

I squeezed my eyes shut, inhaling through my nostrils several times until I felt able to respond. I met Janus's gaze when I said, "Calder asked me that once. I told him I couldn't be with anyone unless it felt right. Even when I decided to sleep with Calder, I knew deep down it didn't feel quite right, but we were engaged. Then he got himself forged, and after I shot him, he disappeared. When I met Nevan—"

Janus held my hands but said nothing, though the sympathy in his eyes nearly broke me. I took several seconds to steady myself with deep breaths.

"When I met Nevan," I continued, "everything with him felt right and easy and…like it was meant to be. I fought it at first because I was afraid he'd turn out to be like Calder, but I gave myself to Nevan after four days. I'd been with Calder for six months. I've thought about it a lot since the day I found out Calder had become a monkey-thing and Nevan had to kill him. I can't deny it anymore. I never wanted anyone else, not really, because I was always meant to be with Nevan. My trip into the past proved that to me."

Janus cleared his throat and fidgeted, though he kept hold of my hands. "I had sensed you traveled into the past and experienced something profound. I was not privy to the details."

"I witnessed Nevan's forging. Turns out the angel he vaguely remembered, the one who took care of him afterward, was me. I saw him again three hundred years later. After that, I asked the Four Winds to make him forget those two times we met in the past. I didn't want Nevan to spend thousands of years pining for me, never knowing when or if we might meet again."

"That was a truly selfless act." Janus let go of my hands and moved to sit beside me on the bench. "Perhaps your story is not over yet."

"Nevan is gone forever. The last page has been written, and the book's been slammed shut."

"Perhaps. Or perhaps not." He rubbed his jaw, his gaze going distant. "I believed my story with Vita was over, but I was wrong. It will never end as long as our descendants walk the earth. We live on through them."

"Better hope my brother has kids, then. I won't be perpetuating the lineage." I stared down at my hands and suffered the disconcerting sensation they weren't mine. "I love Nevan. No one else will ever come close to him. I will never be with another man."

"I have a feeling," Janus said, "love will find you again."

"Are you an oracle all of a sudden?"

"No, I do not have prescient insight. It is my belief, or perhaps my hope for you."

We lapsed into an oddly comfortable silence. I'd known Janus for one day, the longest day of my entire life, but I felt a kinship with him that stemmed from more than having his powers or being his descendant. We had both suffered losses, endured the jealousy of other powerful beings, and survived to fight another day.

I couldn't fight anymore. This had been my last battle.

"Listen," I said. "I want to give you back your powers."

"They belong to you."

"I did what I was destined to do. I'm done." I shimmied around to face him. "This is how it's supposed to end. I finally get that. Besides, the first thing you said when you appeared in that hole in the ground was 'I want my powers back.' It's time I returned them to their rightful owner."

He hunched his shoulders, his lips twisting into an uncomfortable expression. "When I declared I wanted my powers back, I did not know you. I believed no mere mortal could harness my powers properly, and I also believed you were a foolish and frivolous creature. I was wrong about you. No one else, not even I, could have accomplished the feats you have. Not in a thousand years, much less one day."

"But—"

"It is true." Janus turned his face to me, his lips forming a small smile. "I am proud of you, Lindsey Astrid Porter."

"Thanks." It sounded lame, but I couldn't think of anything else to say.

"Do not thank me. I owe you a debt of gratitude I shall never be able to repay." He groaned, rose, and stretched. "I am alive again because you demonstrated that my powers are not tools for evil. They are tools for good. The Four Winds worried the other gods were right about me, but you proved them wrong. Thank you."

"Once you have your powers back, what will you do?"

He canted his head as if thinking hard. "I have no idea."

"You'll figure it out." I levered my body, which seemed to have morphed into solid iron, off the bench and let my shoulders sag. "How do I give you back your powers?"

"We will figure that out later." He touched my arm. "You must go home to your family. You have suffered a grievous loss only time and the support of your loved ones will heal."

Max and Travis showed up then, almost as if they'd been eavesdropping. They wouldn't do that, though. Max had likely sensed I was ready to go.

I said goodbye to Travis and Janus, and Max took me home. To my parents' house. Not to the underground lair I'd shared with Nevan. I couldn't go there yet, maybe never. To save the worlds, I'd sacrificed my past—my life with the only man I had ever loved. Whatever future lay ahead for me, I would deal with the best I could.

Alone.

Chapter Thirty-Four

I TRUDGED THROUGH THE FOOT-DEEP SNOW TOWARD A DESTINATION I knew so well, but in these conditions, I had to consult the GPS on my phone for assistance. Behind me lay the rock garden with its whimsical statuary and the shop, shuttered and vacant for the winter. In the three weeks since I had converged the worlds to stop an apocalypse, two feet of snow had fallen, shrouding the familiar landscape. I made my way down the trail to the falls in slow motion, the snow like a river of mud bogging me down with every step. I should've worn snowshoes, but I'd never been good with those.

The only sound was the crunching of my footsteps and the rushing of my breaths.

Sweat dribbled down my temples. I paused for a rest, shoving the hood of my parka off my head, inhaling the cold air and exhaling it in a cloud of condensation.

Familiar shapes stuck out of the snow.

I pushed toward them and sidestepped the drift that had covered the three stone benches. The vague outlines of the seat-shaped boulders assured me I'd found the right spot. Bending down, I brushed the snow off the nearest bench.

Further down the snow-covered path, the falls rumbled.

A sharp pang stabbed into my chest. The falls. Where I'd met Nevan.

I bit down on my bottom lip and flumped onto the stone bench. How many times had I sat here with Nevan? Before him, I'd refused to believe in the supernatural because I had allowed the taunts of other school kids to humiliate me into giving up the beliefs my family had instilled in me. Nevan showed me the truth, gently, sweetly. He'd coaxed me into believing in more than magic and other realms of reality. He had shown me a kind of love I never imagined could exist, the soul-deep kind that changed a person. And oh, he'd introduced me to sex—making love, that's what it had always been with us. However hot and fevered it might be, sex for us always began with love. Even that first time, when I'd known him for four days. I had fallen for him so fast…

My mind rewound to that night. Despite the bad guys pursuing us, we had taken one night for ourselves, one night ensconced in Nevan's underground lair protected by magical wards. He gave me pleasure, yes, but he gifted me with something far more significant.

Unbreakable, undying love.

Tears filled my eyes, blurring my vision. I sniffled, dug a tissue out of my pocket, and tore off my mittens to blow my nose and dab at my eyes. Nevan. Three weeks without him had been empty, like a yawning cavern of loneliness. Only my voice echoed back to me in the void every time I called out his name in the dark of night, certain I felt him near me.

"What are you doing here?"

I jumped at the sound of Max's voice.

My friend stood five feet in front of me, wearing only black pants. The snow around his feet and calves had already begun to melt from the inhuman heat of his body.

The tissue clutched in my fist, I gazed up at him with bleary eyes. "Hi."

He lifted one brow. "Hi? Lindsey, it's bloody freezing out here. What are you doing?"

Waiting. Praying. Dying a little more every day.

Max spanned the distance between us in two steps, wading through the snow like it was a mud puddle. He knelt in front of me, laying his hands on my knees. "You can't keep doing this. It's the dead of winter, and you could get lost or injured coming out here every day."

I hunched my shoulders. "Have to be here, just in case."

His expression softened into…not pity. Empathy. A deep and sorrowful empathy. Max understood how I felt more than anyone—except for Janus. Both of them had lost their loves a long, long time ago, and I knew the losses pained them to this day.

But the look on Max's face broke me.

A sob wrenched my body. Tears flowed down my cheeks. My eyes burned, and the salty taste of liquid pain seeped into my mouth.

Max perched on the bench's edge beside me, wrapped his arms around me, and held me until the sobs ended. Even then, he kept one arm around me.

I blew my nose, loudly, and swiped my face dry with one mitten. "Sorry."

"Don't be. You've held it all in for weeks, about time you let it out."

My gaze wandered around the snowy clearing. "I have to be here, every day. What if Nevan comes back and—"

A small, hiccuping sob cut off my words.

"Christ, Lindsey." He moved his free hand to clasp both of mine, the heat of him thawing my cold skin. "Your hands are half frozen. Put your mittens on."

I pulled my thick mittens on, but the chill would not relent. Part of it stemmed from the wintry weather. A larger part was borne out of grief.

Max squeezed me gently. "Nevan wouldn't want you to freeze to death out here waiting for him."

"Have to be here in case—"

"No, Lindsey. You need to leave this place. Go back to your family, start living again." He moved to kneel before me, his big hands around my mitten-covered ones. Even through the down-filled layers of my mittens, his radiant skin warmed mine. "You can't stay in this limbo. It's not healthy."

Yeah, I knew that. Everyone kept telling me. Stan let me bunk in the shop only because I'd sworn I wouldn't stay here for too long. We hadn't specified a length of time, though. Stan called me at the shop two or three times a week to encourage me to leave. I couldn't. I broke down in tears every time he, or anyone, suggested it. My parents several times a day. They even threatened to fly up here and drag me home with them.

I could not leave.

Bob checked in on me once or twice a week. The first time, he'd come up with an excuse to stop by, saying he really ought to remove the magical prophylactic he'd given me on the day I married Nevan and lost everything. After that, Bob didn't bother with excuses. Even Janus had checked on me periodically, despite being busy with the duties he'd regained when I returned his powers to him. The Four Winds had helped with the transfer of magics, and now the god was powerless no more. He controlled the portals, the boundaries, everything I'd had dominion over during my tenure as the Janusite.

A god had been destroyed and resurrected.

"Janus came back," I said. "He was destroyed, his essence and his powers scattered to the Four Winds. They brought him back. A frigging sorcerer resurrected Skeiron and Notus and Calder. If they could come back, Nevan might too. Skeiron and Notus were evil. Nevan's good, and he deserves to be saved, they have to see that. If those fucking wind people can't see—"

"Hush, Lindsey."

Tears streamed down my face, hot but swiftly chilled by the air. "He risked everything so many times to save worlds that don't want him. How can they leave him—" I couldn't speak the word. Dead. After all the good he'd done, selflessly and bravely, why did he have to die? "It's not fair."

"I know, I know." Max brushed his fingers over my cheeks, drying my tears. "You can't stop living because Nevan might come back someday. Go home. Let your family help you."

"But it's my fault." I sucked in a ragged breath. "If he'd never met me, he would've been safe. Nevan betrayed his king for me, protected me without a thought for the cost to himself. He fought shapeshifters and kerkopes and sorcerers and harpies for me." I covered my mouth with my hand, squeezing my eyes shut against the threatening sob. "He died *for me.*"

Max slung his arms around me and hoisted me to my feet. "I'm taking you home, Lindsey. It's time."

"Not until you let me absolve you of the life debt."

Lips scrunched, he shook his head. "You want to force me into agreeing, using your grief as the tool."

"No. I don't want to have this hanging between us anymore." I bit down on my bottom lip to stop its quivering. Didn't work. "After everything that's happened, the time has come to give up the debt. You need to face up to your past and stop letting it control you. Letting me do this will be a first step."

Max sighed and rubbed his eyes. "All right."

"Janus!" I hollered.

I'd expected the god to poof into view. Instead, he ambled out of the woods dressed in a cream-colored toga, like he'd been hanging around among the trees.

"What were you doing in there?" I asked.

Janus stopped a few feet away and scratched his cheek. "I, ah…"

Max chuckled. "The almighty god has been keeping an eye on you wherever you go."

I studied Janus, sure Max must've been exaggerating. "Is that true?"

Janus crossed his arms over his chest, averted his eyes, and let his arms drop to his sides. "Yes, it's true."

"Why have you been stalking me?"

He squished his lips into a slash and locked his arms over his chest again. "Someone needed to ensure you took no rash actions."

It took a moment for the meaning of his statement to hit me. When it finally sank in, I grinned. "You were worried about me. That's so sweet."

Janus rolled his eyes and glanced at Max. "How do you endure this child's incessant use of humiliating terms?"

"You don't like being called sweet?" Max asked. With a dismissive shrug of one shoulder, he added, "Doesn't bother me at all."

Janus scowled at Max but aimed a neutral look at me. "Why have you summoned me?"

"I need you to pull a bit of the Unseen through to this side of the falls so I can absolve Max's debt to me."

The god flourished one hand the way Nevan had always done when using his magic.

My throat constricted, but I swallowed hard and asked, "Is it done?"

Janus nodded and disappeared.

I turned to my onetime familiar. "I hereby absolve you, Max, of any and all debts and obligations to me."

The magical tether between us snapped. He was free.

"Satisfied?" Max said. "May I take you away from here now?"

"Yes and yes."

He whisked me away.

Boundaries no longer restricted him or Travis, Ennea, and Tris. One of my final acts as Janusite had been to gift them with unfettered access to the mortal world so they could visit me anytime, anywhere or travel anyplace else they wanted. After everything we'd gone through together, I trusted them without reservation. None of my friends would abuse the privilege I'd granted them.

Max and I landed in my parents' living room.

The picture window revealed a vastly different tableau from the one Max had torn me out of in Michigan. Here in Kentucky, the grass was brown and the trees leafless, but no snow had fallen. Sunshine streamed in through every window.

My parents sat on the sofa, Dad's arm around Mom. Ash occupied the recliner kitty-corner to the sofa. All their gazes veered to me and Max.

"Lindsey needs you," Max said, taking one wide step backward.

I couldn't stop it. Sobs erupted out of me, and tears blurred my vision.

"Oh sweetie," Mom said, leaping off the sofa to encompass me in a bear hug. She stroked my hair and murmured soothing sounds.

By the time the worst of it ended and I could see again, Max was gone.

No longer the Janusite, I could never enter the Unseen realm again without the help of an elemental. No longer a wife, I'd become a widow. But this world wouldn't recognize my union with a supernatural being. Most of my friends were elementals. I had become nothing. An unemployed, powerless, thirty-two-year-old human being living with her parents.

Without Nevan…

I dropped my butt onto the coffee table, my shoulders caving in. Tears trickled down my cheeks.

My brother slid forward in his chair, no more than three feet from me. "Don't cry, Zee. Nevan will come back, I know he will."

Oh God, how I prayed my ten-year-old brother was right. But I'd lost my faith in happy endings the day I had watched Nevan disintegrate.

Chapter Thirty-Five

Before I realized it, five months had gone by. I got a job. After brushing up my paralegal skills for a couple months, I landed a position at a small law firm in a nearby town. Though this kind of work had never been my passion, it paid the bills. I could've rented an apartment, but for the time being, I preferred to stay with my family rather than living alone. For the first three months, we did not talk about Nevan or the Unseen or any of the supernatural events we'd all participated in or witnessed. When spring came, I could talk about Nevan without bursting into tears or feeling like I might throw up.

Max visited me often. So did Tris and Ennea, though naturally, Tris had to act like he didn't give a hoot about anything. Whenever someone mentioned Nevan, Tris would get a funny look on his face, and I knew he gave more than a hoot. He missed Nevan. We all did.

No one more than me.

Every night, I dreamed of him. Sometimes we were doing ordinary things like holding hands and talking about the weather. Other times, I dreamed of Nevan making love to me, whispering to me in that ancient language, and I would wake up aroused and crying. Once in a while, I dreamed of the day he had died. Always, I tried to save him. And always, I failed.

Today, on this lovely May afternoon, I reclined on a beach towel with my feet outstretched, held up by my elbows braced on the towel behind me. I gazed at the waterfall in front of me, surrounded by woods. Though this waterfall featured a wide cascade no more than ten feet high, somehow it reminded me of the falls behind the rock shop. Once a week, I visited this place, always in the morning before anyone else bothered to come here. Peace and quiet, that's what I craved.

My family and friends understood this. They let me have this one potentially unhealthy habit because I'd convinced them I was not wallowing in my grief. Admiring this waterfall reminded me of Nevan, but not in a bad way. I felt closer to him here.

"Am I bothering you?"

"No, it's fine." I smiled at Max, who wore a pair of dark-green shorts in deference to the mortal realm's laws about indecent exposure, and patted the ground beside me. "Have a seat."

Yes, Max was the only one allowed to come here with me. I'd thought my parents or Ash might be offended by this, but they didn't mind at all. They understood Max and I had a special bond, a friendship with a deeper meaning. I couldn't explain what Max meant to me, except that I didn't want to think about my life without my second-best friend.

The top spot would always belong to Nevan.

Max settled on the grass beside me. "It's a lovely day."

"Uh-huh." I waved a hand. "Go on and say it."

He bent his knees to rest his arms on them. "Maybe I should stop saying it. You ignore my advice every time."

"Come on. I got a job, I hang out with my friends and family, and I haven't had a sobbing fit in months. What more do you want?"

"Stop coming here."

I shook my head. "Not an option."

He compressed his lips and hissed a breath out his nostrils. "Lindsey, it's not good for you. If you brought your family, it might be different. But you sit here for hours by yourself, daydreaming about your deceased husband. You haven't said it, but I know you're waiting for him to come back."

"Thinking about Nevan is not unhealthy."

"I know you better than that." Max twisted his torso to face me. "I wouldn't be surprised if you're thinking about going back to Michigan. To the rock shop. And the falls."

He really did know me too well. I'd thought about it ever since spring arrived and I realized the snow must've melted back home. Yeah, I supposed it wasn't a good sign that I thought of Mandan County, Michigan, as my home. That wasn't quite right, though. Nevan was my home.

"Speaking of unhealthy habits," I said, "are you still refusing to feed?"

Max turned his face away from me. "That is not the same thing."

"But it is harmful to you, way more than my fascination with waterfalls is to me."

"Your obsession with waterfalls, you mean."

I gave his thigh a light slap. "You will die if you don't have sex very soon."

His skin had developed that same faint pallor I'd noticed months ago when he had refrained from feeding. He must not have long now before he'd get sick again.

The incubus beside me threw me a mockingly suggestive glance. "Are you offering to ease my suffering?"

"Cut it out, Max. I know you are not interested in having sex with me."

He let out a pitiful sigh. "Wish I were. It might be easier."

"Sorry I can't help you." I considered his profile for a moment, then said, "Are you holding out for that special someone?"

He scoffed. "Special someone? You and Nevan might've had a spiritual connection, but an incubus is not meant for that sort of relationship. I consume sexual energy. Only a nutter would want to sign on for an eternity of that."

"I thought the women enjoyed it."

"Yes, but—" He contorted his features in frustration. "Leave it alone, Lindsey. Please."

Being me, I couldn't do that. "I know there's a girl out there for you. When you meet her, suddenly everything will make sense."

He twisted his mouth into an irritated expression. "Bollocks. There is no fated mate for me."

"You said your kind do have them, though."

"It's probably a myth." He scrubbed a hand over his eyes. "Even if it's true, I don't deserve that kind of love."

His eyes widened for a second as if he couldn't believe he'd admitted that to me.

I bumped my shoulder against his. "You deserve love, Max, and you will find it. I believe that with all my heart."

He grumbled.

"Don't be such a grump," I said. "You're a sweetie, and you will find your mate."

"I am not a sweetie."

"Yes you are." I pinched his cheeks. "Face it, Maxie, you are a sweet, sweet salamander."

He rolled his eyes. "I'm beginning to agree with Janus about your incessant need to label us with bloody ridiculous adjectives."

"Come off it," I said, bumping shoulders with him again. "You like it when I call you sweet and adorable. Even Janus has given up grumbling when I call him things like that. You badass elemental males aren't so tough after all."

"That's because you turn us all barking mad. If I develop a sudden urge to take up knitting, it will be a direct result of you telling me I'm sweet so many bloody times."

"I love you too, Max."

He tried not to smile but lost the battle.

"So," I said, "when was the last time you fed? You said the longest you went without sex was six months, and it's been that long this time."

"Bleeding hell, Lindsey." He twisted his mouth into a half scowl, but quickly ironed it out. "Since I know you won't give up asking until I answer, I suppose I have to tell you. Being with Hathor provides a much larger energy boost than any other female could give me. I can last another few months."

I started to speak, but something made me stop. A sensation shimmered inside me, like an inner tingle spiked with electricity. Every hair on my body went stiff. Goosebumps popped up all along my arms.

My gaze swerved past Max to the woods beside the waterfall.

"What is it?" Max asked, squinting in the direction where I stared.

"Not sure…"

A figure ambled out of the trees, a man, his face cloaked in shadows.

I bounded to my feet, kicking Max in the process.

The figure moseyed out of the shadows into the bright sunshine.

My hand flew to my mouth. I couldn't breathe, couldn't move, my pulse thundering in my ears and adrenaline ripping through my veins. My head grew light, my ears rang.

Nevan strolled toward us, his gaze fixed on me, his mouth curving into the most loving and beautiful smile I had ever seen.

"Bugger me," Max exclaimed, leaping to his feet.

I bolted for Nevan and hurled my body at him.

My husband caught me and spun us around and around and around. I threw my head back, laughing like a crazy person. Nevan set me down on my feet, his arms fastened around me, pressing our bodies together.

He swept hair away from my eyes. "Hello, darlin'. Did ye miss me?"

Sobs exploded out of me, this time spurred by pure joy.

He held me until I stopped crying, caressing my hair and murmuring to me. "Shh, love, it's all right. I've told you before, I will always come back to you, whatever the cost, however long it takes. Nothing will keep me from you."

"What took you so long? It's been almost six months."

"The Four Winds had to contend with a deluge of scattered powers. Elementals flooded over the boundaries once they fell. It took this long for them to sort through it all and decide what to do with me."

"I don't care why they sent you back as long as you're back for good."

He tucked an errant lock of hair behind my ear. "I am here for good, forever. The Winds know how much you have sacrificed to save the worlds. They appreciate it, and this is how they express their gratitude."

By sending him back to me.

My eyes blurred with tears, I kissed him with all the passion and devotion and longing I'd stored up inside me during these agonizing months without him. I moaned with the deepest pleasure I'd ever known, spurred by an overwhelming relief and a soul-deep satisfaction. My breasts pushed against his hard chest, but as my mind surfaced from the spell cast by our joy, I noted one important fact.

His skin did not burn with supernatural heat.

I pulled away, backing up a few steps to get the full picture of him. My mouth fell open, but I couldn't make any sounds come out of it. I gaped at him, taking in the totality of the changes.

Nevan's skin had lost its glistening bronze sheen. He sported a tan of the normal, human variety caused by moderate sun exposure. And his eyes…Once molten whirlpools of color, they had become human too, a beautiful shade of deep honey brown. His hair was black as before, and it framed his face in luxurious waves. His build had transformed from supernaturally ripped to a body stacked with muscles that would impress any mortal female but would not arouse suspicion about his origins.

The scent of him had changed too. No more thunderstorms and earth. When I'd been plastered to his new body, he had smelled of sweat and man—mortal man.

My husband had transformed into a human. A really hot human. Even his polo shirt, khaki pants, and brown loafers couldn't dim the smokin' hot appeal of my man.

I held a hand to my chest, absorbing the sight of the new Nevan one more time before I met his gaze. "Am I crazy, or are you human?"

He smiled and laughed softly. "I should've known you would figure it out quickly. My wife is intelligent and perceptive. Yes, I am human." His features tightened, and he watched me with wary eyes. "Do you mind being with a normal, puny mortal?"

Puny? Nevan? Not a chance in hell of that.

I bridged the distance between us, splaying my hands on his chest. "I love *you*, Nevan. Don't care what you look like or if you've lost all your powers. None of that defines you. The man I married is good and strong and smart, with or without supernatural mojo." I ran my hands over his chest, loving the feel of his muscles beneath his shirt. "And for the record, you could never be puny. Even as a lowly human, you are one hot guy."

"But I cannot whisk you anywhere." He looked miserable, like he expected me to dump him because he couldn't teleport anymore. His expression turned even more morose when he added, "Sex with me will not be as it was before. You may be…disappointed."

He worried I wouldn't like having sex with him when he had no powers. Was that adorable or what?

I caught his face in my hands. "It was never your powers that made the sex life-altering. It was love. Maybe you can't float us on a cloud while we do it, but trust me, we will have amazing sex."

"Ye can't know that."

"I can, and I do." I touched my lips to his, letting the contact linger for several seconds. "Was sex with me crummy because I'm not an elemental?"

"Of course not."

"Then I will love being with the new you."

Someone cleared his throat behind me.

I glanced over my shoulder at Max.

He waved toward the woods. "I should go. You two need time alone."

"Okay," I said, "but don't be a stranger."

Max nodded and vanished.

Nevan made a wistful noise. "I used to be able to do that."

"Oh honey," I said, looping my arms around his neck, "you'll get used to being a powerless mortal. It's not so bad, you know. No more worrying about boundaries, no more fighting with the tribunal, no more—"

"I can no longer protect you. What if an elemental attempts to harm you?"

"Nobody knows I used to be the Janusite."

He pulled his head back. "Used to be?"

"Yeah, I gave Janus back his powers. It's a long story that I will tell you later. The point is you should chill out, Nevan. There's a huge upside to you becoming human."

"Which is?"

"It's safe to get me knocked up."

He stared at me, not blinking, for a very long moment.

"You awake?" I said, waving a hand in his face.

"Oh yes, love, I am awake. Perhaps for the first time in my entire existence." He hugged me to his firm body. "You're right, there are significant benefits to becoming human. I can't wait to start a family with you."

"I'm excited about it too." I wound a lock of his hair around my finger. "You were a mortal once before. Do you remember what sex was like back then?"

"Vaguely." He screwed up his face. "The only woman I bedded as a mortal was my wife, Ceara. She disliked me and disliked sex. It was not a pleasurable experience."

Oh right, Ceara. The bitch who'd been resurrected by a sorcerer. She had informed Nevan that having sex with him had been horrible and that she'd wanted to murder him in his sleep, but only if she could've gotten away with it. No wonder he worried about what mortal sex would be like with me.

"You've got a new wife," I said, "one who adores you and can't get enough of your body. It will be different this time around. You're with the right woman now."

"That I am." He slid his hands up my back. "I wish I could whisk you away to your home, but alas, we will have to rely on mortal transportation."

"I have a car, but, um…" I made a sheepish face. "I'm living with my parents at the moment."

He groaned, his head drooping.

Chewing on my lip, I chewed on the problem too.

I raised one finger. "I've got it. There's a motel five miles from here."

Nevan's head sprang up, and his lips curved into the sensual smirk I knew so well. "You, my love, are a genius."

I laughed. "You're just incredibly horny and wouldn't care if I suggested we do it in the grass right here."

"A bed would be preferable. There may be creatures lurking in the grass, and I have no power to save you from them."

"Creatures?" I tried to suppress my laugh, but it snorted out of me anyway. "I assume you mean snakes and bugs."

"Yes." He swept me up in his arms. "Where is your vehicle?"

I pointed to his left. "Follow the trail."

Chapter Thirty-Six

THE MOTEL ROOM FEATURED WORN FURNITURE AND WORN BEDDING, but the proprietors kept it clean and tidy. We didn't care about the furnishings. After so long apart, with Nevan in limbo and me grieving for him, we both would've settled for the backseat of my Malibu—if my still-very-large husband could've fit in the backseat. Since he didn't, I floored the Malibu to get us to the nearest motel as fast as possible, speed limits be damned.

We stood beside the bed facing each other. Nevan had already swept the covers aside, but he'd hesitated after that, which explained why we were gazing into each other's eyes in silence instead of getting it on.

"Are you worrying," I said, "the new you will disappoint me?"

"No," he replied, settling his hands on my hips. "But I may have…ah…forgotten how to do this the mortal way."

"Relax, it's like riding a bike."

"I have never ridden a bicycle. Or driven a car. Or earned a paycheck or—"

I silenced him with one finger on his lips. "Chill out, honey. You'll adjust to the mortal way of life. It'll take time, but you will get used to it. I can teach you all about being human, you know, since I'm kind of an expert on that. Been doing it all my life."

Rather than comforting him, my statement seemed to make him miserable. "I was a sylph for longer than any civilization on earth has existed. My mortal life was a drop of water compared to the vast ocean of my immortal life. Being a sylph is essentially all I've ever known."

"Stop fretting, would you? Everything will work out, trust me." I slipped my arms around his waist, molding my body to his. "And stop thinking of this as an obstacle. You've been given a brand-new chance at life. Don't waste it."

"How do you suggest I begin this new life?"

"By making love with your wife." I stepped back and patted the bed. "Sit down and let me show you how it's done."

He gave me a dubious look. "I am the only man of any species you have ever been with. You know as little as I do about mortal sex."

"Shush." I patted the bed again. "Sit. That's an order."

A smirk tugged at his lips as he obeyed. "My, but you are fetching when you're domineering."

"Thought I was fetching when I'm vexed."

He had told me that not long after we met, when I'd gotten frustrated with his refusal to answer my questions.

Seated on the bed's edge with his feet on the floor, Nevan ran a hand up and down my thigh. "That too, darlin'. Everything about you is fetching and irresistible."

"Keep saying things like that."

He paused in running his hand along my thigh and scraped one fingernail on the denim of my jeans. "I can no longer vanish our clothes."

"Oh, that's a good thing." I moved backward out of his reach. "You're going to like the way I get my clothes off."

Nevan braced his palms on the bed behind his hips, leaning back into them. "Proceed, my sweet mortal morsel."

I pointed a finger at him. "You're a sweet mortal morsel too."

"Are ye planning to disrobe sometime this century? I don't have eternity anymore."

"Disrobing in progress."

I frisked my hands up and down my body, shimmying my hips in a sexy little dance that ensured I had Nevan's full and undivided attention. His gaze tracked the movements of my hands, and when I slipped them beneath my shirt, his tongue flicked out to moisten his lips. A soft growl resonated deep in his throat.

Pulling my hands out from under my shirt, I took hold of the top button and toyed with it. "How bad do you want to see me naked?"

"I'm beginning to feel like an incubus who hasn't fed in a century."

"Mmm, that sounds intriguing." I unhooked the top button, then the one below it, and the one below that. Nevan's hooded gaze snapped to each button in turn as I undid them. When I'd freed the last one and my blouse hung open, revealing my lacy red bra, I glided my fingers along the lapels. "Maybe I should go slower."

He dug his fingers into the bed as a breath blustered out of his nostrils. "If ye go any slower, I'll be forced to tear your clothing to shreds."

I whipped off my shirt and let it flutter down to the worn brown carpeting. "See? I was right. You love watching me undress."

"Ye aren't naked yet," he hissed through clenched teeth. "And I am not accustomed to waiting so bloody long for it."

"Guess I should take pity on you," I said, unhooking the button of my jeans, "considering you're new to the human existence and all."

"Yes, take pity on me. Immediately."

I laughed. "You are so cute when you're sexually frustrated."

Then I took pity on him. I shucked my jeans in two seconds flat, removed my bra in about three seconds, and shed my lacy red panties so fast I stumbled trying to kick them off. Nevan half rose off the bed to catch my hips and steady me, right before he sat back down and dragged me into his hard body, wedged between his thighs.

"Your turn," I purred, resting my hands on his broad, muscular shoulders. "Shall I disrobe you? Or would you rather do it yourself?"

One side of his mouth kicked up in a lopsided smirk. "I am unskilled in disrobing, since I haven't needed to do it in five thousand years. You'd best take care of the task for me, darlin', to make certain it's done right."

I grabbed his polo shirt, yanked it out of his waistband, and tore it off over his head. He lifted his arms to help me out, smiling when I tossed his shirt over my shoulder. I knelt between his legs and undid the button on his pants so fast I almost ripped it off and then jerked the zipper down, revealing a salient and salacious fact.

"You don't have any underwear on," I said, rolling my gaze up to his though my head stayed bowed. "I should've known you'd be a naughty mortal. Unless the Four Winds picked your clothes for you."

"They did, but I suspect they are not aware that most humans wear undergarments."

"Goodie for me."

I pulled his pants down, and he hoisted his hips up to let me haul them down to his ankles. My pulse accelerated the second I glimpsed his erection waving in the air between us. Removing his shoes and finally getting those pants off of him took me longer than my lust could endure, but my hands had started shaking with anticipation. At last, I had him naked.

Sitting back on my heels, I roved my gaze over his entire body. "Wow, you are no less sizzling-hot as a mere mortal. I may need to carry my derringer with me everywhere we go to keep other women from swarming over you."

He chuckled and plowed his hand into my hair, cupping my nape. "What will you do with me now?"

"You asked me that question the first time we got it on. But this time, I know exactly what I want to do with you."

I grasped his shaft in one hand and bent to close my mouth over its head. When I began to stroke and lick him, his eyes drifted shut and his head fell back. Braced with his arms, he let me do whatever I wanted with him. I feasted on him, on the flavor and feel of his cock, and relished his every response. He groaned and rocked his hips into my ministrations. His expression turned pained the longer I worked on him, and his chest heaved with each breath.

He sprang forward to grasp my head, staying my actions. Breathless, he told me, "Best stop. I have a feeling I won't be able to get in the right state again soon enough if you finish this. I need to be inside ye, love. Right away."

I relinquished his shaft. "But you taste so good."

He picked me up and tossed me onto the bed.

My body bounced, my breasts bounced, and I squeaked.

Nevan pounced on me, straddling my body on all fours. He shoved a hand between my thighs, and a delighted sort of surprise lit up his face. "Ready then, are ye?"

"For you, always." I grasped his arms. "Since it's been such a long, long time, let's skip the foreplay and get right to it."

"You know I will do anything for you."

He nudged my legs apart with one of his knees and plunged inside me.

I gasped, gripping his arms so tight my nails must've dug into his skin.

"Ahhh, Lindsey." He threw his head back as if lost in ecstasy. "This is even better than before."

"Get moving, please, before I lose my mind."

He looked down at me, poised on his straight arms. "I want ye to lose yer mind. And feel free to beg as much as ye want."

I wrapped my legs around his hips, loving the fullness of him inside me. "Please, Nevan, please make me come."

He thrust again and again, his eyes rolling back in his head like he'd never felt anything as good as this. I clung to him, lost to the bliss of making love with my husband—my very human husband who drove me wild with need for him. No need for magic. Our bodies meshed to perfection, fitting like they'd been designed for each other. We had been made for each other, for sure.

"Oh yes," I moaned as he quickened the pace, plowing into me so forcefully I bounced with each thrust. "I love you, Nevan, I love you so much."

He dropped his body onto mine, mashing me to the mattress even while his hips pumped faster and harder. I flung my arms around him and sank my teeth into his shoulder, desperate to prolong this moment but needing a release so badly I whimpered.

My body went rigid, and a climax of stunning power ripped through me.

Nevan cried out, his body rigid too as he reached his own release.

I felt him come apart inside me, and I came harder.

He went limp atop me, gasping for breath.

We lay there for a while—how long, I had no idea—enjoying the sweet pleasure generated by our unabashed lust for each other and our unbreakable bond even time could not destroy. Even death could never untie the knot that sealed our love.

Nevan rolled off of my body, lying on his side next to me. "Thank you, Lindsey."

"Thank you? For what, exactly?"

He picked up my hand and kissed the knuckles one by one. "For proving to me life as a mortal will never be less than what I had as an elemental. It is, in fact, much more."

"Sex isn't the only benefit." I flipped onto my side to face him. "No more worries about a dangerous hybrid pregnancy. We can have a baby anytime we want. If you want that."

"Of course I want children with you." He brushed his fingers through my hair. "And I would love to have a baby as soon as possible."

"Glad to hear it." I tickled his chest with my fingertips. "Because we may have just made one."

He sprang up, braced on one elbow, eyes wide. "How?"

I laughed softly. "Sometimes I forget you never lived in the age of safe sex. We didn't use a condom, and I am not on birth control pills. This means there's a chance we made a baby today."

"A chance?" His shocked expression melted into something more suggestive. He closed a hand over my breast. "We should keep trying, to make certain we're successful."

"I'm all for that."

We kept trying for three hours. Sometimes we loved each other tenderly, and sometimes we made the bed thump. By the time we checked out of the motel, the sun was sinking below the horizon and I felt sure we had made that baby we'd both wanted since the day Nevan asked me to marry him.

On the drive to my parents' house, we couldn't stop grinning at each other. Nevan had to remind me to pay attention to the road. I promised to teach him how to drive soon, and he vowed he would never get distracted while behind the wheel.

"We'll see about that," I said, winking at him. "I've got skills in distracting you."

He rested a hand on my thigh, squeezing lightly. "You have skills in everything to do with me."

"Same goes for you." Since we were waiting at a stoplight, I took the opportunity to kiss my husband. "And we have the rest of our lives to explore all the ways to drive each other crazy."

"It may take a lifetime for me to adjust to this world." He frowned. "I must find employment, correct? I have no skills in regard to that."

"Oh, you've got skills. You were king of the sylphs, which means you've got leadership down pat." I kissed his cheek. "We'll find a job that suits you. Don't worry. I have tons of experience in massaging resumes."

"As long as I have you, I believe anything is possible."

"Don't worry," said a male voice from the backseat, "everything will work out."

Nevan and I both jumped, though I yelped and he grunted. We twisted around to aim dual scowls at Bob.

He reclined across the width of the backseat, his feet propped on the armrest behind Nevan's seat and his back against the door behind my seat. The oracle had his hands linked behind his head.

I smacked his knee. "Are you trying to kill us? What if I'd been driving down the road?"

"Your car is not moving. No danger involved." He sighed and scratched his nose. "Do you want to know why I'm here, or should I go away?"

"Why are you here, Bob?"

"To give you a glimpse of your future." He swung his feet off the backseat and sat up to face us. "You've got nine months to sort out your lives."

Nevan squinted at the oracle. "Is that a threat?"

Bob shut his eyes, letting out a long sigh. "No, it's a statement of fact. Sort things out and get ready. Your lives are about to change again."

He glanced at my abdomen, and his lips formed a knowing smile.

Bob vanished.

Nevan harrumphed. "What the bloody hell was that about?"

The oracle never issued a prediction without a good reason. Nine months, he'd said. Nine months to sort out our lives.

"Oh God," I said, one hand on my belly. "I'm pregnant."

Nevan's expression blanked. "What?"

"That's what Bob meant. Right after we got engaged, he told us a way would present itself. You became a mortal, that's the way he meant." I grinned so wide I thought my jaw might dislocate. "You got me knocked up today. We're having a baby in nine months."

Nevan grinned and laughed, pulled me in for a steamy lip-lock, and showered kisses over my face and my neck and my arms. When he got to my hands, he held them to his face. "I have everything I've ever wanted."

"Me too."

"But I must find a means of earning a living."

"You will. We've got nine months to get ready."

The oracle popped in again, his head and shoulders wedged between our seats.

I jumped, again, and smacked his arm. "Quit doing that."

"Sorry, but I forgot your present." He held out a plain brown envelope big enough to hold letter-size sheets. "I conspired with the leprechauns on this. Tris and Ennea needed a little foresight to guide their magics."

Nevan plucked the envelope from Bob's hand. "Magics? Is it safe for my wife?"

"Yes." Bob winked. "And you're welcome."

He disappeared.

My husband stared at the envelope, holding it between his thumb and forefinger. He rotated it left and right while he tilted his head to study the packet.

I snatched it away from him. "You're being overly cautious, and I'm impatient."

With two fingers, I pried open the metal clasp. I tipped the envelope, letting the contents slide out onto my palm. A paperclip secured the sheaf of papers.

"What is it?" Nevan asked, leaning over to peer at the pages.

"Not sure." I removed the paperclip and flipped through the sheets. My jaw slackened. "It looks like they gave you everything a mortal man needs to blend in. Birth certificate, social security card, driver's license, college transcripts, bank accounts, even a magically manufactured life and work history." I angled the papers toward Nevan and pointed at a handwritten note as I read it aloud. "It says, 'Study hard, Nev, you're a new man with a new story.' Tris signed it himself."

"I can read, Lindsey."

"Well, you were born before the age of written language. I've never seen you read, so for all I knew, you didn't."

"That does make a Lindsey kind of sense."

I slipped the papers back inside the envelope and handed it to him. "Get to know the modern mortal version of you. His name is Nevan Liam O'Rourke. And there's a marriage license too, so I am now Lindsey O'Rourke."

"The name suits you."

A thought sprang into my mind like a firework bursting in the sky. "I've got it."

"Do I want to know what?"

I slapped the back of my hand on his chest. "Behave. I figured out what you can do to earn a living. We should buy the shop from Stan."

Nevan eyed me sideways. "How are we to afford it?"

Snatching the envelope from him, I dumped out the contents and found the page listing bank account information. Every hair on my arms and my scalp prickled and stiffened. "Holy shit. Look at the present our elemental friends gave us." I flapped the paper in his face. "They've made us well off but not so wealthy it'll raise eyebrows. We have enough money to buy the shop and a house with plenty leftover to keep us comfortable."

He gingerly took the paper I held. His brows rose. "You are correct."

"Told you."

"Are you certain you want to go back to Mandan County? Many terrible events occurred there."

"It wasn't all bad. Besides, we can make new, better memories." I kissed his cheek. "With our children. I want them to know all about you and me and the magical things we did together. But if you'd rather not buy the shop, that's okay."

Nevan grinned. "Let's do it."

We had the rest of our lives to do anything we wanted. And whatever lay beyond this world, I knew we would always be together. If time itself couldn't separate us, life after death wouldn't either. We would have a full and beautiful life on this earth with our children and grandchildren.

And we would discover the next world together.

After the Tempest

THREE MONTHS AFTER

ENJOY YOUR VACATION IN THE KEWEENAW AND THANK YOU FOR VIS-
iting our shop." I smiled brightly at the senior-citizen tourists across the
counter from me, and the expression was no longer a forced professional
smile. I loved this place and the people who patronized it. Offering the
couple the paper bag that held their purchase, I said, "And don't forget to
visit the healing vortex."

The male half of the couple took the bag. "Thanks, Lindsey. We just love
this place."

He knew my name because of the badge pinned to my shirt. Stan had
never cared about name tags, but Nevan and I had decided it made us more
approachable. Didn't take much to make anybody more approachable than
my grumpy former employer. You had to get to know him to understand he
had a softer side.

My customers wandered out the back door, heading for the vortex no
doubt.

Nevan and I had spiffed it up with an official sign to replace the simple,
hand-painted one as well as decorations on the trees and around the stone
benches. New signs with arrows on them directed visitors to the vortex and
the waterfall.

I glanced down at the postcard I'd propped up on the cash register. A
photo of Key West, Florida, adorned the front. On the backside, Stan had
scrawled a brief message letting us know he had settled into his retirement
nicely and thanking us for the generous price we'd paid for the shop and the
twenty acres on which it resided. Stan had insisted we visit him soon, and
Max offered to poof us there the elemental way. Nevan claimed he wanted
to experience airline travel, but I assured him it wasn't as glamorous as it

sounded. He relented, and next week Max would zip us to Key West for a weekend visit. My parents would take over the shop while we were away.

Yep, everybody lived in Mandan County these days.

A prickly sensation swept over me, alerting me to the presence of an elemental in the shop. Despite no longer having powers, I'd retained the ability to detect a whiff of any supernatural being who entered my vicinity and so did Nevan. Janus called it an "innate instinct." Whatever it was, my paranormal radar had just pinged.

I scanned the shop and spotted a hulking figure lumbering through the front door.

Brennus had obviously tried to glamour into a more-human form, but he hadn't gotten the hang of it yet. His coal-dark skin had lost its iridescent blue sheen, and his coal-dark eyes sported slightly lighter irises, but he had not diminished his Himalayan mountains of muscle or his birdlike mannerisms. His head twitched this way and that as he surveyed his surroundings.

Yeah, he still looked like a walking locomotive with avian instincts. He still looked supernatural.

Brennus spotted me and stalked up to the counter. "My lady."

"I'm not your lady anymore, remember?" I splayed my hands on the countertop. "Nevan is not king anymore either. You can stop calling us 'my lady' and 'your majesty.' We're just Nevan and Lindsey these days."

The shapeshifter twitched his head some more, his forehead tightening into deep lines.

"Okay, fine," I said, waving a hand in the air between us. "You can keep calling me your lady."

Brennus relaxed a bit, as much as he ever did. Considering the raven-man had spent ages serving as an assassin and a spy for Skeiron, I supposed I should cut him a little slack. Nevan was still adjusting to the mortal life, so Brennus would need time to adjust to his new life as a free being with no king to serve. The new king of the sylphs hadn't wanted a shapeshifter in his court. Janus had encouraged Bob to accept Brennus as his guardian, claiming the oracle really should have a bodyguard. Bob agreed, though it seemed like he simply wanted a bit of company.

"Did you stop in to buy a pair of agate earrings?" I asked, teasing him though I knew Brennus wouldn't get it. One day, he would grasp mortal humor—and I would keep teasing him until he did.

Brennus darted his gaze around the shop. "Beings visit this place to purchase items of value."

"Uh, yeah. It's a shop."

The shapeshifter lunged toward the nearest display, snagged an item, and thunked it onto the counter.

I tapped my fingers on the top of the float-copper bookend. "You want one bookend? Most people buy two."

He grabbed the other bookend and smacked it down beside the first. "What is the cost of these items?"

"Do you own any books?" When he only stared at me, I gave up. "Two-hundred and twenty dollars."

Brennus held his hand palm up, and money appeared there.

Realizing I did not want to know where he'd gotten it, and that he would be offended if I asked, I took the bills. Two-hundred twenty dollars exactly. I punched the transaction into the register, stuffed the receipt and the bookends into a bag, and handed it to Brennus.

He accepted the bag, stepped back, and bowed. "My lady."

The shapeshifter walked out the back door, bending over to fit through the opening.

A year ago, my life had changed because of float-copper bookends. A shoplifter stole them, and when he tried to flee, a monkey-man had murdered him. I'd met Nevan because of that, because I'd spotted the shoplifter's dead body on the trail to the falls. If not for those bookends, I might never have ended up here with Nevan, my husband, and the baby we would soon welcome into our lives. Life was so weird.

Why Brennus wanted bookends, I had no clue.

Nevan trotted up to the counter and veered behind it. Grinning, he pulled me into his arms and kissed me.

"Another successful tour?" I asked.

"Indeed. Children are not as terrible as I'd once believed."

Laughter snorted out of me. "Glad to hear it since we're having one of those in about six months."

Nevan crouched to kiss my belly, then straightened. "Our child will be like you. An angel."

Even louder laughter snorted out of me. "I think our kid will have your naughty streak and get into lots of trouble. It's your job to ride herd on our son."

Nevan stopped blinking. "Has Bob informed you of the sex?"

"I don't need an oracle to tell me that. I just know." I tousled his wavy hair. "Woman's intuition."

He grasped my hand and pressed his lips to my palm. "I've learned never to question your intuition."

"Smart man." I recalled my encounter with the shapeshifter and said, "Brennus stopped by a few minutes ago. He bought a pair of copper bookends. Do you have any idea why?"

Nevan let go of my hand. "Ah, yes. I ran into Brennus yesterday, and he expressed a desire to keep in touch with us in whatever way he could. I suggested he pop in at the shop for a visit, but then I told him he ought to purchase something so no one would mistake him for one of the rock-garden statues. I did not think he would do it."

"You were joking."

He nodded. "Brennus doesn't understand humor. I should have guessed he would take my words literally."

"You're a human being now, which means you don't understand his ways as well as you used to."

"True." Nevan glanced at the big clock on the wall behind us. "My next tour begins in ten minutes. I should go."

He kissed me again, lingering a touch longer than professionalism allowed. So what? We owned the damn place.

I flagged down our newest employee, a college student named Heidi, and left her manning the sales counter while I headed outside to check on the display racks we'd set up outside. I was browsing the bins of polished rocks when a shadow surrounded me. That sixth sense I'd hung onto told me who I would see when I turned around.

"Max," I said as I spun toward him. "I'm so glad you're here. Where have you been hiding?"

The incubus had done a better job of glamouring than Brennus had. He looked reasonably normal except for his large muscles and supernatural good looks. Even my husband couldn't help being gorgeous beyond the human norm. Poor me, surrounded by sizzling-hot men.

I might have been married and pregnant, but I could still appreciate man candy. My lust belonged exclusively to Nevan.

"Not hiding," Max said. "I've been…busy."

"Doing what?" I folded my arms over my chest. "You promised to visit regularly."

He fiddled with the rocks in a bin of Petoskey stone, seeming to scrutinize the tiny fossils within its gray matrix. He turned one shiny rock between his thumb and forefinger. "I went back to Hathor."

Max did look healthier and stronger than the last time I'd seen him. I knew how much he hated needing to visit the wacko goddess, though. She was obsessed with him.

"How did you get away from her?" I asked.

"It may sound strange," he said, rubbing his thumb over the small stone, "but you freed me from her again."

"Me? I don't have powers anymore, and I had no idea you'd gone back to Hathor."

He dumped the stone back into the bin and shoved his hands in the pockets of his jeans. "You didn't do it with magic. For two months, I struggled to break free of her enchantment but couldn't do it. Yesterday, I felt you…thinking of me. I sort of clung to that feeling, to the memory of our friendship and everything we went through together." He straightened and looked me straight in the eye. "Suddenly, I was free. I blipped the bloody hell out of there. You saved me, Lindsey. Again."

What he said sounded crazy, but over the past year, I'd learned not to dismiss crazy things. Sometimes they turned out to be true. Besides, Max would not lie to me.

"Not sure how I could do that," I said, "but I'm glad you're free."

He grunted and went back to picking through the bins.

"You know," I said, "if you found your mate you wouldn't need to go back to Hathor ever again."

Max threw his head back and groaned. "Oversoul, hear my prayer and make Lindsey Porter stop harassing me about finding a bird." He looked at me again. "I don't have a fated mate, Lindsey. Only you and Nevan are that lucky."

"Baloney." I nabbed a pretty pink stone from one of the bins and tossed it to Max. When he caught it, I said, "That's rose quartz. It's known as the love stone."

Max groaned and rolled his eyes.

I shook my head. "How can a supernatural man, an incubus no less, be such a skeptic? Rose quartz will strengthen your heart and help attract love—if you believe."

He stared at me for a moment, his mood unreadable.

"It couldn't hurt," I said.

Max tossed the stone into the air and caught it in his palm, closing his fingers around it. He studied his bent fingers. "Maybe it you believe for me, it will work."

I clasped my hand over his. "I will believe enough for the both of us. You'll find your girl, Max. I know it. And like Nevan always says, it's a mistake to doubt the intuition of Lindsey Astrid Porter."

"He's become a sage, has he?" Max smiled a little. "Never could argue with you."

"That's because I'm so bloody stubborn." I slapped his arm. "You're coming to our house for dinner tonight."

"Am I?"

"Yes, Max, you are. No more skulking in the woods alone."

He offered me the stone.

I pushed his hand away. "Keep it. That's a gift from a friend. Consider it a talisman."

Max tucked the rose quartz stone into his pocket. "Thank you, Lindsey. You are the best friend I've ever had, as a human or as an elemental."

"Aw, that's so sweet." I threw my arms around him.

When I let him go, he averted his gaze and scratched behind his ear. I'd embarrassed an incubus who preferred to walk around in the nude, only donning clothes when he entered the mortal realm.

He coughed. "I should go."

"See you tonight."

"Yes, tonight."

Max vanished.

I ambled back into the shop. Spotting a young couple just coming through the main door, I made a beeline for them. "Welcome to Rock the Keweenaw. How may I help you?"

"We heard there's some kinda vortex here," the man said.

"It's around back. Follow the signs and you'll get there." And then, without a shred of sarcasm and with a genuine smile, I said, "The vortex is amazing. The healing energies wash over you like a cool breeze, infusing your body with ancient wisdom."

These days, I meant those words I'd spoken countless times. I believed in more than the paranormal, though. I believed in life, love, and the future.

I spread an arm, gesturing toward the back door. "Let me show you the way."

ANNA DURAND IS A BESTSELLING, MULTI-AWARD-WINNING AUTHOR OF contemporary and paranormal romance. Her books have earned bestseller status on every major retailer and wonderful reviews from readers around the world. But that's the boring spiel. Here are the really cool things you want to know about Anna!

Born on Lackland Air Force Base in Texas, Anna grew up moving here, there, and everywhere thanks to her dad's job as an instructor pilot. She's lived in Texas (twice), Mississippi, California (twice), Michigan (twice), and Alaska—and now Ohio.

As for her writing, Anna has always made up stories in her head, but she didn't write them down until her teen years. Those first awful books went into the trash can a few years later, though she learned a lot from those stories. Eventually, she would pen her first romance novel, the paranormal romance *Willpower*, and she's never looked back since.

Want even more details about Anna? Get access to her extended bio when you subscribe to her newsletter and download the free bonus ebook, *Hot Scots Confidential*. You'll also get hot deleted scenes, character interviews, fun facts, and more! Plus you'll receive the short story *Tempted by a Kiss* and mutliple bonus chapters in both ebook and audiobook formats.

VISIT ANNADURAND.COM TO SIGN UP.

www.ingramcontent.com/pod-product-compliance
Lightning Source LLC
Chambersburg PA
CBHW072005180726
48291CB00001BA/9